AF517212

The yellowbacks... classics of popular fiction

The yellowjackets or yellowbacks were a great series of bestselling adventure and crime thrillers that had its origins in the mid to late 19th century following on from the 'penny dreadfuls'. They virtually began the mass market revolution of the early 20th century with a clear standard format and imprint/series livery (what would today be called branding). Hodder & Stoughton published the yellowjackets in two main series with series run dates of: 1923-1939 and later 1949-1957.

As the tagline ('where thrillers really began') on the back cover implies, the imprint and series focused on thrillers that were the bestsellers of their time. This current reissue or retro revival if you will, brings back many of these masterpieces, now classics in their own way and extends it further by including key titles from that period that were either great crime or thriller or even general commercial fiction (including sub-genres of noir, horror, gothic, romance, westerns, etc.) influences of their time. There are some perennial favourites and many rarities either lost or not easily available being revived in the current series. Writers and characters ranged from adventure heroes like Bulldog Drummond, Allan Quatermain, Richard Hannay or the Saint through thriller grandmasters Edgar Wallace and E. Phillips Oppenheim, crime and mystery maestros like Patricia Wentworth, GK Chesterton, Agatha Christie and the Detection club, to western and swashbucklers like Zane Grey, Max Brand, Captain Blood and even romance or general fiction classics like Hermina Black, Denise Robins, Marie Corelli or Stella Morton. These were books that had storytelling at their heart and always entertained.

The yellowbacks had both hardback (with varying design elements) and paperback (which built the series look) versions with the latter still carrying the imprint 'yellowjacket'. The current reissues pay tribute to both and use an amalgam of elements from both editions while retaining the complete yellow (or 'mustard-plaster') livery with the author's name in blue beveled type with a 'simulated emboss' effect and a white outer 'outline', and the book title in black. These reissues retain the distinctive size of the original mass market paperback and follow the three main category variations—the thrillers (crime, westerns, mystery, adventure) had blue lettering for the author's name, while Romance and softer general fiction had red; and other categories like humour had green.

For more detail and a full list of titles visit https://www.hachetteindia.com/home/yellowbacks

THE NIGHT-WATCHMAN
AND OTHER LONGSHOREMEN

THE NIGHT-WATCHMAN AND OTHER LONGSHOREMEN

William Wymark Jacobs (8 September 1863–1 September 1943) was an English author of short fiction and drama. He is best known for his story "The Monkey's Paw".

In 1879, Jacobs began work as a clerk in the Post Office Savings Bank. By 1885, he had his first short story published, but success came slowly. Yet Arnold Bennett in 1898 was astonished to hear that Jacobs had turned down £50 for six short stories. He was financially secure enough to be able to leave the Post Office, in 1899.

Most of his work was humorous. His favourite subject was marine life – "men who go down to the sea in ships of moderate tonnage", said *Punch*, reviewing his first collection, *Many Cargoes*, which gained popular success on publication, in 1896.

Michael Sadleir has said of Jacobs's fiction, "He wrote stories of three kinds: describing the misadventures of sailor-men ashore; celebrating the artful dodger of a slow-witted village; and tales of the macabre."

Jacobs died on 1 September 1943 at Hornsey Lane, Islington, London, at the age of 79. An obituary in *The Times* described him as "quiet, gentle and modest... not fond of large functions and crowds." Ian Hay remarked, "He invented an entirely new form of humorous narrative. Its outstanding characteristics were compression and understatement."

THE NIGHT-WATCHMAN AND OTHER LONGSHOREMEN

W. W. Jacobs

The Night-Watchman and Other Longshoremen
First published in 1932 by Hodder & Stoughton

1

The texts in these editions in most cases have been reprinted as is, with minimal editorial changes and by and large no bowdlerizing for political correctness; though in some editions, a few words and phrases considered archaic, or those considered offensive now, along with archaic punctuation may have been modified in places to make the text more accessible to today's readers. The narratives, language, beliefs, social mores and/or cultural depictions, in these volumes are a reflection of their times and must be viewed as such. They may also contain certain cultural, racial and gender prejudices and stereotypes that may be outdated or clearly wrong then and wrong today; but their removal would be tantamount to claiming these prejudices never existed. The Publisher does not endorse or support those depictions or stereotypes; and these books have been made available for a discerning audience that will read it for entertainment value and a chronicle/record of popular fiction of past times.

Cover design by Priya Singh adapted from the original classic yellowjacket by Hodder & Stoughton.

Cover illustration by Ishan Trivedi.

Series note: Some of the books in the series (unless otherwise credited) may have cover or inside illustrations from the original yellowbacks or early editions, and while full restoration has been attempted, some images may be grainy or faded due to the condition of the original material. The end notes or bonus material or blurb details may have been sourced from the public domain or free use publications such as Wikipedia and attribution is hereby made also allowing similar free use reproduction from here. Sources requiring further specific attribution may write in and further detailing and/or corrections shall be made in subsequent printings/editions.

Reprint specifications may be subject to change including but not limited to finishes, paper, colour sections.

ISBN: 978-93-5731-404-6

Hachette Book Publishing India Pvt. Ltd.
4th & 5th Floors, Corporate Centre,
Plot No. 94, Sector 44, Gurugram - 122 003, India

Typeset in Electra LT STD 10/12.5 pt by Manipal Technologies Limited, Manipal

Printed and bound in India by Manipal Technologies Limited, Manipal

This book comprises fifty-seven stories from the five volumes by W. W. Jacobs:

DEEP WATERS

SEA WHISPERS

CAPTAINS ALL

NIGHT WATCHES

SHIP'S COMPANY

Together with one other story:

LOVE-LETTERS

CONTENTS

DEEP WATERS

1

SHAREHOLDERS

A sailorman—said the night-watchman musingly—a sailorman is like a fish, he is safest when 'e is at sea. When a fish comes ashore it is in for trouble, and so is a sailorman. One poor chap I knew 'ardly ever came ashore without getting married; and when he was found out there was no less than six wimmen in the court all taking away 'is character at once. And when he spoke up about Solomon the magistrate pretty near bit 'is 'ead off.

Then look at the trouble they get in with their money! They come ashore from a long trip, smelling of it a'most, and they go from port to port like a lord. Everybody has got their eye on that money—everybody except the sailorman, that is—and afore he knows wot's 'appened, and who 'as got it, he's looking for a ship agin. When he ain't robbed of 'is money, he wastes it; and when 'e don't do either, he loses it.

I knew one chap who hid 'is money. He'd been away ten months, and, knowing 'ow easy money goes, 'e made up sixteen pounds in a nice little parcel and hid it where nobody could find it. That's wot he said, and p'r'aps 'e was right. All I know is, *he* never found it. I did the same thing myself once with a couple o' quid I ran acrost unexpected, on'y, unfortunately for me, I hid it the day afore my missus started 'er spring-cleaning.

One o' the worst men I ever knew for getting into trouble when he came ashore was old Sam Small. If he couldn't find it by 'imself, Ginger Dick and Peter Russet would help 'im look for it. Generally speaking they found it without straining their eyesight.

I remember one time they was home, arter being away pretty near a year, and when they was paid off they felt like walking gold-mines. They went about smiling all over with good-temper and 'appiness, and for the first three days they was like brothers. That didn't last, of course, and on the fourth day Sam Small, arter saying wot 'e would do to Ginger and Peter if it wasn't for the police, went off by 'imself.

His temper passed off arter a time, and 'e began to look cheerful agin. It was a lovely morning, and, having nothing to do and plenty in 'is pocket to do it with, he went along like a schoolboy with a 'arf holiday.

He went as far as Stratford on the top of a tram for a mouthful o' fresh air, and came back to his favourite coffee-shop with a fine appetite for dinner. There was a very nice gentlemanly chap sitting opposite 'im, and the way he begged Sam's pardon for splashing gravy over 'im made Sam take a liking to him at once. Nicely dressed he was, with a gold pin in 'is tie, and a fine gold watch-chain acrost his weskit; and Sam could see he 'ad been brought up well by the way he used 'is knife and fork. He kept looking at Sam in a thoughtful kind o' way, and at last he said wot a beautiful morning it was, and wot a fine day it must be in the country. In a little while they began to talk like a couple of old friends, and he told Sam all about 'is father, wot was a clergyman in the country, and Sam talked about a father of his as was living private on three 'undred a year.

"Ah, money's a useful thing," ses the man.

"It ain't everything," ses Sam. "It won't give you 'appiness. I've run through a lot in my time, so I ought to know."

"I expect you've got a bit left, though," ses the man, with a wink.

Sam laughed and smacked 'is pocket. "I've got a trifle to go on with," he ses, winking back. "I never feel comfortable without a pound or two in my pocket."

"You look as though you're just back from a v'y'ge," ses the man, looking at 'im very hard.

"I am," ses Sam, nodding. "Just back arter ten months, and I'm going to spend a bit o' money afore I sign on agin, I can tell you."

"That's wot it was given to us for," ses the man, nodding at him.

They both got up to go at the same time and walked out into the street together, and when Sam asked 'im whether he might have the pleasure of standing 'im a drink, he said he might. He talked about the different kinds of drink as they walked along till Sam, wot was looking for a high-class pub, got such a raging thirst on 'im he hardly knew wot to do with 'imself. He passed several pubs, and walked on as fast as he could to the "Three Widders."

"Do you want to go in there partikier?" ses the man, stopping at the door.

"No," ses Sam, staring.

"'Cos I know a place where they sell the best glass o' port wine in London," ses the man.

He took Sam up two or three turnings, and then led him into a quiet little pub in a back street. There was a cosy little saloon-bar with nobody in it, and arter Sam had 'ad two port wines for the look of the thing, he 'ad a pint o' six-ale because he liked it. His new pal had one too, and he 'ad just taken a pull at it and wiped his mouth, when 'e noticed a little bill pinned up at the back of the bar.

"*Lost, between—the Mint and—Tower Stairs,*" he ses, leaning forward and reading very slow, "*a gold—locket—set with—*

diamonds. Whoever will—return—the same to—Mr. Smith—Orange Villa—Barnet—will receive—thirty pounds—reward."

"'Ow much?" ses Sam, starting.

"Thirty pounds," ses the man. "Must be a good locket. Where'd you get that?" he ses, turning to the barmaid.

"Gentleman came in an hour ago," ses the gal, "and, arter he had 'ad two or three drinks with the guv'nor, he asks 'im to stick it up. 'Arf crying he was—said it 'ad belonged to his old woman wot died."

She went off to serve a customer at the other end of the bar wot was making little dents in it with his pot, and the man came back and sat down by Sam agin, and began to talk about horse-racing. At least, he tried to, but Sam couldn't talk of nothing but that locket, and wot a nice steady sailorman could do with thirty pounds.

"Well, p'r'aps you'll find it," ses the man, chaffing-like. "'Ave another pint."

Sam had one, but it only made 'im more solemn, and he got in quite a temper as 'e spoke about casuals loafing about on Tower Hill with their 'ands in their pockets, and taking gold lockets out of the mouths of hard-working sailormen.

"It mightn't be found yet," ses the man, speaking thoughtful-like. "It's wonderful how long a thing'll lay sometimes. Wot about going and 'aving a look for it?"

Sam shook his 'ead at fust, but arter turning the thing over in his mind, and 'aving another look at the bill, and copying down the name and address for luck, 'e said p'r'aps they might as well walk that way as anywhere else.

"Something seems to tell me we've got a chance," ses the man, as they stepped outside. "It's a funny feeling and I can't explain it, but it always means good luck. Last time I had it an aunt o' mine swallered 'er false teeth and left me five 'undred pounds."

"There's aunts and aunts," ses Sam, grunting. "I 'ad one once, but if she had swallered *'er* teeth she'd ha' been round to me to help 'er buy some new ones. That's the sort *she* was."

"Mind!" ses the man, patting 'im on the shoulder, "if we do find this, I don't want any of it. I've got all I want. It's all for you."

They went on like a couple o' brothers arter that, especially Sam, and when they got to the Mint they walked along slow down Tower Hill looking for the locket. It was awkward work, because, if people saw them looking about, they'd 'ave started looking too, and twice Sam nearly fell over owing to walking like a man with a stiff neck and squinting down both sides of his nose at once. When they got as far as the Stairs they came back on the other side of the road, and they 'ad turned to go back agin when a docker-looking chap stopped Sam's friend and spoke to 'im.

"I've got no change, my man," ses Sam's pal, pushing past him.

"I ain't begging, guv'nor," ses the chap, follering 'im up. "I'm trying to sell something."

"Wot is it?" ses the other, stopping.

The man looked up and down the street, and then he put his 'ead near them and whispered.

"Eh?" ses Sam's pal.

"Something I picked up," ses the man, still a-whispering.

Sam got a pinch on the arm from 'is pal that nearly made him scream, then they both stood still, staring at the docker.

"Wot is it?" ses Sam, at last.

The docker looked over his shoulder agin, and then 'e put his 'and in his trouser-pocket and just showed 'em a big, fat, gold locket with diamonds stuck all over it. Then he shoved it back in 'is pocket, while Sam's pal was giving 'im a pinch worse than wot the other was.

"It's the one," he ses, in a whisper. "Let's 'ave another look at it," he ses to the docker.

The man fished it out of his pocket agin, and held on to it tight while they looked at it.

"Where did you find it?" ses Sam.

"Found it over there, just by the Mint," ses the man, pointing.

"Wot d'ye want for it?" ses Sam's pal.

"As much as I can get," ses the man. "I don't quite know 'ow much it's worth', that's the worst of it. Wot d'ye say to twenty pounds, and chance it?"

Sam laughed—the sort of laugh a pal 'ad once give him a black eye for.

"Twenty pounds!" he ses; "twenty pounds!'Ave you gorn out of your mind, or wot! I'll give you a couple of quid for it."

"Well, it's all right, captin," ses the man, "there's no 'arm done. I'll try somebody else—or p'r'aps there'll be a big reward for it. I don't believe it was bought for a *'undred pounds.*"

He was just sheering off when Sam's pal caught 'im by the arm and asked him to let 'im have another look at it. Then he came back to Sam and led 'im a little way off, whispering to 'im that it was the chance of a lifetime.

"And if you prefer to keep it for a little while and then sell it, instead of getting the reward for it, I dare say it would be worth a hundred pounds to you," 'e ses.

"I ain't got twenty pounds," ses Sam.

"'Ow much 'ave you got?" ses his pal.

Sam felt in 'is pockets, and the docker came up and stood watching while he counted it. Altogether it was nine pounds fourteen shillings and tuppence.

"P'r'aps you've got some more at 'ome," ses his pal.

"Not a farthing," ses Sam, which was true as far as the farthing went.

"Or p'r'aps you could borrer some," ses his pal, in a soft, kind voice. "I'd lend it to you with pleasure, on'y I haven't got it with me."

Sam shook his 'ead, and at last, arter the docker 'ad said he wouldn't let it go for less than twenty, even to save 'is life, he let it go for the nine pounds odd, a silver watch-chain, two cigars wot Sam 'ad been sitting on by mistake, and a sheath-knife.

"Shove it in your pocket and don't let a soul see it," ses the man, handing over the locket. "I might as well give it away a'most. But it can't be 'elped."

He went off up the 'ill shaking his 'ead, and Sam's pal, arter watching him for a few seconds, said goodbye in a hurry and went off arter 'im to tell him to keep 'is mouth shut about it.

Sam walked back to his lodgings on air, as the saying is, and even did a little bit of a skirt-dance to a pianner-organ wot was playing. Peter and Ginger was out, and so was his landlady, a respectable woman as was minding the rest of 'is money for him, and when he asked 'er little gal, a kid of eleven, to trust 'im for some tin, she gave 'im a lecture on wasting his money instead wot took 'is breath away—all but a word or two.

He got some of 'is money from his landlady at eight o'clock, arter listening to 'er for 'arf an hour, and then he 'ad to pick it up off of the floor, and say "Thank you" for it.

He went to bed afore Ginger and Peter came in, but 'e was so excited he couldn't sleep, and long arter they was in bed he laid there and thought of all the different ways of spending a 'undred pounds. He kept taking the locket from under 'is piller and feeling it; then he felt 'e must 'ave another look at it, and arter coughing 'ard two or three times and calling out to the other two not to snore—to see if they was awake—he got out o' bed and lit the candle. Ginger and Peter was both fast asleep, with their eyes screwed up and their mouths wide open, and 'e sat on the bed and looked at the locket until he was a'most dazzled.

"'Ullo, Sam!" ses a voice. "Wot 'ave you got there?"

Sam nearly fell off the bed with surprise and temper. Then 'e hid the locket in his 'and and blew out the candle.

"Who gave it to you?" ses Ginger.

"You get off to sleep, and mind your own bisness," ses Sam, grinding 'is teeth.

He got back into bed agin and laid there listening to Ginger waking up Peter. Peter woke up disagreeable, but when Ginger told 'im that Sam 'ad stole a gold locket as big as a saucer, covered with diamonds, he altered 'is mind.

"Let's 'ave a look at it," he ses, sitting up.

"Ginger's dreaming," ses Sam, in a shaky voice. "I ain't got no locket. Wot d'you think I want a locket for?"

Ginger got out o' bed and lit the candle agin.

"Come on!" he ses, "let's 'ave a look at it. I wasn't dreaming. I've been awake all the time, watching you."

Sam shut 'is eyes and turned his back to them.

"He's gone to sleep, pore old chap," ses Ginger. "We'll have a look at it without waking 'im. You take that side, Peter! Mind you don't disturb 'im."

He put his 'and in under the bed-clo'es and felt all up and down Sam's back, very careful. Sam stood it for 'arf a minute, and then 'e sat up in bed and behaved more like a windmill than a man.

"Hold his 'ands," ses Ginger.

"Hold 'em yourself," ses Peter, dabbing 'is nose with his shirt-sleeve.

"Well, we're going to see it," ses Ginger, "if we have to make enough noise to rouse the 'ouse. Fust of all we're going to ask you perlite; then we shall get louder and louder. *Show us the locket wot you stole, Sam!*"

"Show—us—the—diamond locket!" ses Peter.

"It's my turn, Peter," ses Ginger. "One, two, three. SHOW—US—TH'—"

"Shut up," ses Sam, trembling all over. "I'll show it to you if you stop your noise."

He put his 'and under his piller, but afore he showed it to 'em he sat up in bed and made 'em a little speech. He said 'e never wanted to see their faces agin as long as he lived, and why Ginger's mother 'adn't put 'im in a pail o' cold water when 'e was born 'e couldn't understand. He said 'e didn't believe that even a mother could love a baby that looked like a cod-fish with red 'air, and as for Peter Russet, 'e believed *his* mother died of fright.

"That'll do," ses Ginger, as Sam stopped to get 'is breath. "Are you going to show us the locket, or 'ave we got to shout agin?"

Sam swallered something that nearly choked 'im, and then he opened his 'and and showed it to them. Peter told 'im to wave it so as they could see the diamonds flash, and then Ginger waved the candle to see 'ow they looked that way, and pretty near set pore Sam's whiskers on fire.

They didn't leave 'im alone till they knew as much about it as he could tell 'em, and they both of 'em told 'im that if he took a reward of thirty pounds for it, instead of selling it for a 'undred, he was a bigger fool than he looked.

"I shall turn it over in my mind," ses Sam, sucking 'is teeth. "When I want your advice I'll ask you for it."

"We wasn't thinking of you," ses Ginger; "*we was* thinking of ourselves."

"*You!*" ses Sam, with a bit of a start. "Wot's it got to do with you?"

"Our share'll be bigger, that's all," ses Ginger.

"Much bigger," ses Peter. "I couldn't dream of letting it go at thirty. It's chucking money away. Why, we might get *two* 'undred for it. Who knows?"

Sam sat on the edge of 'is bed like a man in a dream, then 'e began to make a noise like a cat with a fishbone in its throat, and then 'e stood up and let fly.

"Don't stop 'im, Peter," ses Ginger. "Let 'im go on; it'll do him good."

"He's forgot all about that penknife you picked up and went shares in," ses Peter. "I wouldn't be mean for *twenty* lockets."

"Nor me neither," ses Ginger. "But we won't let 'im be mean—for 'is own sake. We'll 'ave our rights."

"Rights!" ses Sam. "Rights! You didn't find it."

"We always go shares if we find anything," ses Ginger. "Where's your memory, Sam?"

"But I didn't find it," ses Sam.

"No, you bought it," ses Peter, "and if you don't go shares we'll split on you—see? Then you can't sell it anyway, and perhaps you won't even get the reward. We can be at Orange Villa as soon as wot you can."

"Sooner," ses Ginger, nodding. "But there's no need to do that. If 'e don't go shares I'll slip round to the police station fust thing in the morning."

"You know the way there all right," ses Sam, very bitter.

"And we don't want none o' your back-answers," ses Ginger. "Are you going shares or not?"

"Wot about the money I paid for it?" ses Sam, "and my trouble?"

Ginger and Peter sat down on the bed to talk it over, and at last, arter calling themselves a lot o' bad names for being too kind-'earted, they offered 'im five pounds each for their share in the locket.

"And that means you've got your share for next to nothing, Sam," ses Ginger.

"Some people wouldn't 'ave given you anything," ses Peter.

Sam gave way at last, and then 'e stood by making nasty remarks while Ginger wrote out a paper for them all to sign, because he said he had known Sam such a long time.

It was a'most daylight afore they got to sleep, and the fust thing Ginger did when he woke was to wake Sam up, and offer to shake 'ands with him. The noise woke Peter up, and as Sam wouldn't shake 'ands with 'im either, they both patted him on the back instead.

They made him take 'em to the little pub, arter breakfast, to read the bill about the reward. Sam didn't mind going, as it 'appened, as he 'oped to meet 'is new pal there and tell 'im his troubles, but, though they stayed there some time, 'e didn't turn up. He wasn't at the coffeeshop for dinner, neither.

Peter and Ginger was in 'igh spirits, and though Sam told 'em plain that he would sooner walk about with a couple of real pickpockets, they wouldn't leave 'im an inch.

"Anybody could steal it off of you, Sam," ses Ginger, patting 'im on the weskit to make sure the locket was still there. "It's a good job you've got us to look arter you."

"We must buy 'im a money-belt with a pocket in it," ses Peter.

Ginger nodded at 'im. "Yes," he ses, "that would be safer. And he'd better wear it next to 'is skin, with everything over it. I should feel more comfortable then."

"And wot about me?" ses Sam, turning on 'im.

"Well, we'll take it in turns," ses Ginger. "You one day, and then me, and then Peter."

Sam gave way at last, as arter all he could see it was the safest thing to do, but he 'ad so much to say about it that they got fair sick of the sound of 'is voice. They 'ad to go 'ome for 'im to put the belt on; and then at seven o'clock in the evening, arter Sam had 'ad two or three pints, they had to go 'ome agin, 'cos he was complaining of tight-lacing.

Ginger had it on next day and he went 'ome five times. The other two went with 'im in case he lost 'imself, and stood there making nasty remarks while he messed 'imself up with a penn'orth of cold cream. It was a cheap belt, and pore Ginger said that when they 'ad done with it, it would come in handy for sandpaper.

Peter didn't like it any better than the other two did, and twice they 'ad to speak to 'im about stopping in the street and trying to make 'imself more comfortable by wriggling. Sam said people misunderstood it.

Arter that they agreed to wear it outside their shirt, and even then Ginger said it scratched 'im. And every day they got more and more worried about wot was the best thing to do with the locket, and whether it would be safe to try and sell it. The idea o' walking about with a fortune in their pockets that they couldn't spend a'most drove 'em crazy.

"The longer we keep it, the safer it'll be," ses Sam, as they was walking down Houndsditch one day.

"We'll sell it when I'm sixty," ses Ginger, nasty-like.

"Then old Sam won't be 'ere to have 'is share," ses Peter.

Sam was just going to answer 'em back, when he stopped and began to smile instead. Straight in front of 'im was the gentleman he 'ad met in the coffee-shop, coming along with another man, and he just 'ad time to see that it was the docker who 'ad sold him the locket, when they both saw 'im. They turned like a flash, and, afore Sam could get 'is breath, bolted up a little alley and disappeared.

"Wot's the row?" ses Ginger, staring.

Sam didn't answer 'im. He stood there struck all of a heap.

"Do you know 'em?" ses Peter.

Sam couldn't answer 'im for a time. He was doing a bit of 'ard thinking.

"Chap I 'ad a row with the other night," he ses, at last.

He walked on very thoughtful, and the more 'e thought, the less 'e liked it. He was so pale that Ginger thought 'e was ill and advised 'im to 'ave a drop o' brandy. Peter recommended rum, so to please 'em he 'ad both. It brought 'is colour back, but not 'is cheerfulness.

He gave 'em both the slip next morning; which was easy, as Ginger was wearing the locket, and, arter fust 'aving a long ride for nothing owing to getting in the wrong train, he got to Barnet.

It was a big place; big enough to 'ave a dozen Orange Villas, but pore Sam couldn't find one. It wasn't for want of trying neither. He asked at over twenty shops, and the post office, and even went to the police-station. He must ha' walked six or seven miles looking for it, and at last, 'arf ready to drop, 'e took the train back.

He 'ad some sausages and mashed with a pint o' stout at a place in Bishopsgate, and then 'e started to walk 'ome. The only comfort he 'ad was the thought of the ten pounds Ginger and Peter 'ad paid 'im; and when he remembered that he began to cheer up and even smile. By the time he got 'ome 'e was beaming all over 'is face.

"Where've you been?" ses Ginger.

"Enjoying myself by myself," ses Sam.

"Please yourself," ses Peter, very severe, "but where'd you ha' been if we 'ad sold the locket and skipped, eh?"

"You wouldn't 'ave enjoyed yourself by yourself then," ses Ginger. "Yes, you may laugh!"

Sam didn't answer 'im, but he sat down on 'is bed and 'is shoulders shook till Ginger lost his temper and gave him a couple o' thumps on the back that pretty near broke it.

"All right," ses Sam, very firm. "Now you 'ave done for yourselves. I 'ad a'most made up my mind to go shares; now you sha'n't 'ave a ha'penny."

Ginger laughed then. "Ho!" he ses, "and 'ow are you going to prevent it?"

"We've got the locket, Sam," ses Peter, smiling and shaking 'is 'ead at 'im.

"And we'll mind it till it's sold," ses Ginger.

Sam laughed agin, short and nasty. Then he undressed 'imself very slow and got into bed. At twelve o'clock, just as

Ginger was dropping off, he began to laugh agin, and 'e only stopped when 'e heard Ginger getting out of bed to 'im.

He stayed in bed next morning, 'cos he said 'is sides was aching, but 'e laughed agin as they was going out, and when they came back he 'ad gorn.

We never know 'ow much we like anything till we lose it. A week arterwards, as Ginger was being 'elped out of a pawnshop by Peter, he said 'e would give all he 'adn't got for the locket to be near enough to Sam to hear 'im laugh agin.

2

PAYING OFF

My biggest fault, said the night-watchman gloomily, has been good nature. I've spent the best part of my life trying to do my fellow-creeturs a good turn. And what do I get for it? If all the people I've helped was to come 'ere now there wouldn't be standing room for them on this wharf. 'Arf of them would be pushed overboard—and a good place for 'em, too.

I've been like it all my life. I was good-natured enough to go to sea as a boy because a skipper took a fancy to me and wanted my 'elp, and when I got older I was good-natured enough to get married. All my life I've given 'elp and advice free, and only a day or two ago one of 'em wot I 'ad given it to came round here with her 'usband and 'er two brothers and 'er mother and two or three people from the same street, to see her give me "wot for."

Another fault o' mine has been being sharp. Most people make mistakes, and they can't bear to see anybody as don't. Over and over agin I have showed people 'ow silly they 'ave been to do certain things, and told 'em wot I should ha' done in their place, but I can't remember one that ever gave me a "thank you" for it.

There was a man 'ere 'arf an hour ago that reminded me of both of these faults. He came in *a-purpose* to remind me, and 'e brought a couple o' grinning, brass-faced monkeys with 'im to see 'im do it. I was sitting on that barrel when he came, and arter two minutes I felt as if I was sitting on red-'ot cinders. He pur-tended he 'ad come in for the sake of old times and to ask arter my 'ealth, and all the time he was doing 'is best to upset me to amuse them two pore objecks 'e 'ad brought with 'im.

Capt'in Mellun is his name, and 'e was always a foolish, soft-'eaded sort o' man, and how he 'as kept 'is job I can't think. He used to trade between this wharf and Bristol on a little schooner called the *Firefly*, and seeing wot a silly, foolish kind o' man he was, I took a little bit o' notice of 'im. Many and many a time when 'e was going to do something he'd ha' been sorry for arterwards I 'ave taken 'im round to the "Bear's Head" and stood 'im pint arter pint until he began to see reason and own up that I was in the right.

His crew was a'most as bad as wot he was, and all in one month one o' the 'ands gave a man ten shillings for a di'mond ring he saw 'im pick up, wot turned out to be worth fourpence, and another one gave five bob for a meerschaum pipe made o' chalk. When I pointed out to 'em wot fools they was they didn't like it, and a week arterwards, when the skipper gave a man in a pub 'is watch and chain and two pounds to hold, to show 'is confidence in 'im, and I told 'im exactly wot I thought of him, *'e* didn't like it.

"You're too sharp, Bill," he says, sneering like. "*My* opinion is that the pore man was run over. He told me 'e should only be away five minutes. And he 'ad got an honest face: nice open blue eyes, and a smile that done you good to look at."

"You've been swindled," I ses, "and you know it. If I'd been done like that I should never hold up my 'ead agin. Why, a child o' five would know better. You and your crew all seem to be tarred with the same brush. You ain't fit to be trusted out alone."

I believe 'e told his 'ands wot I said; anyway, two bits o' coke missed me by 'arf an inch next evening, and for some weeks not one of 'em spoke a word to me. When they see me coming they just used to stand up straight and twist their noses.

It didn't 'urt me, o' course. I took no notice of ' em. Even when one of ' em fell over the broom I was sweeping with I took no notice of 'im. I just went on with my work as if 'e wasn't there.

I suppose they 'ad been in the sulks about a month, and I was sitting 'ere one evening getting my breath arter a couple o' hours' 'ard work, when one of 'em, George Tebb by name, came off the ship and nodded to me as he passed.

"Evening, Bill," he ses.

"Evening," I ses, rather stiff.

"I wanted a word with you, Bill," he ses, in a low voice. "In fact, I might go so far as to say I want to ask you to do me a favour."

I looked at him so 'ard that he coughed and looked away.

"We might talk about it over a 'arf-pint," he ses.

"No, thank you," I ses. "I 'ad a 'arf-pint the day before yesterday, and I'm not thirsty."

He stood there fidgeting about for a bit, and then he put his 'and on my shoulder.

"Well, come to the end of the jetty," he ses. "I've got something private to say."

I got up slow-like and followed 'im. I wasn't a bit curious. Not a bit. But if a man asks for my 'elp I always give it.

"It's like this," he ses, looking round careful, "only I don't want the other chaps to hear because I don't want to be laughed at. Last week an old uncle o' mine died and left me thirty pounds. It's just a week ago, and I've already got through five of 'em, and besides that the number of chaps that want to borrow ten bob for a couple o' days would surprise you."

"I ain't so easy surprised," I ses, shaking my 'ead.

"It ain't safe with me," he ses; "and the favour I want you to do is to take care of it for me. I know it'll go if I keep it. I've got it locked up in this box. And if you keep the box I'll keep the key, and when I want a bit I'll come and see you about it."

He pulled a little box out of 'is pocket and rattled it in my ear.

"There's five-and-twenty golden goblins in there," he ses. "If you take charge of 'em they'll be all right. If you don't, I'm pretty certain I shan't 'ave one of 'em in a week or two's time."

At fust I said I wouldn't 'ave anything to do with it, but he begged so 'ard that I began to alter my mind.

"You're as honest as daylight, Bill," he ses, very earnest. "I don't know another man in the world I could trust with twenty-five quid—especially myself. Now, put it in your pocket and look arter it for me. One of the quids in it is for you, for your trouble."

He slipped the box in my coat-pocket, and then he said 'is mind was so relieved that 'e felt like 'arf a pint. I was for going to the "Bear's Head," the place I generally go to, because it is next door to the wharf, so to speak, but George wanted me to try the beer at another place he knew of.

"The wharf's all right," he ses. "There's one or two 'ands on the ship, and they won't let anybody run away with it."

From wot he said I thought the pub was quite close, but instead o' that I should think we walked pretty nearly a mile afore we got there. Nice snug place it was, and the beer was all right, although, as I told George Tebb it didn't seem to me any better than the stuff at the "Bear's Head."

He stood me two 'arf-pints and was just going to order another, when 'e found 'e 'adn't got any money left, and he wouldn't hear of me paying for it, because 'e said it was his treat.

"We'll 'ave a quid out o' the box," he ses. "I must 'ave one to go on with, anyway."

I shook my 'ead at 'im.

"Only one," he ses, "and that'll last me a fortnight. Besides, I want to give you the quid I promised you."

I gave way at last, and he put his 'and in 'is trouser-pocket for the key, and then found it wasn't there.

"I must ha' left it in my chest," he ses. "I'll 'op back and get it." And afore I could prevent 'im he 'ad waved his 'and at me and gorn.

My fust idea was to go arter 'im, but I knew I couldn't catch 'im, and if I tried to meet 'im coming back I should most likely miss 'im through the side streets. So I sat there with my pipe and waited.

I suppose I 'ad been sitting down waiting for him for about ten minutes, when a couple o' sailormen came into the bar and began to make themselves a nuisance. Big fat chaps they was, and both of 'em more than 'arf sprung. And arter calling for a pint apiece they began to take a little notice of me.

"Where d'you come from?" ses one of 'em.

"'Ome," I ses, very quiet.

"It's a good place—'ome," ses the chap, shaking his 'ead. "Can you sing 'Ome, Sweet 'Ome? You seem to 'ave got wot I might call a 'singing face.'"

"Never mind about my face," I ses, very sharp. "You mind wot you're doing with that beer. You'll 'ave it over in a minute."

The words was 'ardly out of my mouth afore 'e gave a lurch and spilt his pint all over me. From 'ead to foot I was dripping with beer, and I was in such a temper I wonder I didn't murder 'im; but afore I could move they both pulled out their pocket-'ankerchers and started to rub me down.

"That'll do," I ses at last, arter they 'ad walked round me 'arf-a-dozen times and patted me all over to see if I was dry. "You get off while you're safe."

"It was my mistake, mate," ses the chap who 'ad spilt the beer.

"You get outside," I ses. "Go on, both of you, afore I put you out."

They gave one look at me, standing there with my fists clenched, and then they went out like lambs, and I 'eard 'em trot round the corner as though they was afraid I was following. I felt a little bit damp and chilly, but beer is like seawater—you don't catch cold through it—and I sat down agin to wait for George Tebb.

He came in smiling and out o' breath in about ten minutes' time, with the key in 'is 'and, and as soon as I told 'im wot had 'appened to me with the beer he turned to the landlord and ordered me six o' rum 'ot at once.

"Drink that up," he ses, 'anding it to me; "but fust of all give me the box, so as I can pay for it."

I put my 'and in my pocket. Then I put it in the other one, and arter that I stood staring at George Tebb and shaking all over.

"Wot's the matter? Wot are you looking like that for?" he ses.

"It must ha' been them two," I ses, choking. "While they was purtending to dry me and patting me all over they must 'ave taken it out of my pocket."

"Wot are you talking about?" ses George, staring at me.

"The box 'as gorn," I ses, putting down the 'ot rum and feeling in my trouser-pocket. "The box 'as gorn, and them two must 'ave taken it."

"Gorn!" ses George. "*Gorn!* My box with twenty-five pounds in, wot I trusted you with, gorn? Wot are you talking about? It can't be—it's too crool!"

He made such a noise that the landlord, wot was waiting for 'is money, asked 'im wot he meant by it, and, arter he 'ad explained, I'm blest if the landlord didn't advise him to search me. I stood still and let George go through my pockets, and then I told 'im I 'ad done with 'im and I never wanted to see 'im agin as long as I lived.

"I dare say," ses George, "I dare say. But you'll come along with me to the wharf and see the skipper. I'm not going to lose five-and-twenty quid through your carelessness."

I marched along in front of 'im with my 'ead in the air, and when he spoke to me I didn't answer him. He went aboard the ship when we got to the wharf, and a minute or two arterwards 'e came to the side and said the skipper wanted to see me.

The airs the skipper gave 'imself was sickening. He sat down there in 'is miserable little rat-'ole of a cabin and acted as if 'e was a judge and I was a prisoner. Most of the 'ands 'ad squeezed in there too, and the things they advised George to do to me was remarkable.

"Silence!" ses the skipper. "Now, watchman, tell me exactly 'ow this thing 'appened."

"I've told you once," I ses.

"I know," ses the skipper, "but I want you to tell me agin to see if you contradict yourself. I can't understand 'ow such a clever man as you could be done so easy."

I thought I should ha' bust, but I kept my face wonderful. I just asked 'im wot the men was like that got off with 'is watch and chain and two pounds, in case they might be the same.

"That's diff'rent," he ses.

"Oh!" ses I. "'Ow?"

"I lost my own property," he ses, "but you lost George's, and 'ow a man like you, that's so much sharper and cleverer than other people, could be had so easy, I can't think. Why, a child of five would ha' known better."

"A baby in arms would ha' known better," ses the man wot 'ad bought the di'mond ring. "'Ow *could* you 'ave been so silly, Bill? At your time o' life, too!"

"That's neither 'ere nor there," ses the skipper. "The watchman has lost twenty-five quid belonging to one o' my men. The question is, wot is he going to do about it?"

"Nothing," I ses. "I didn't ask 'im to let me mind the box. He done it of 'is own free will. It's got nothing to do with me."

"Oh, hasn't it?" ses the skipper, drawing 'imself up. "I don't want to be too 'ard on you, but at the same time I can't let my man suffer. I'll make it as easy as I can, and I order you to pay 'im five shillings a week till the twenty-five pounds is cleared off."

I laughed; I couldn't 'elp it. I just stood there and laughed at 'im.

"If you don't," ses the skipper, "then I shall lay the facts of the case afore the guv'nor. Whether he'll object to you being in a pub a mile away, taking care of a box of gold while you was supposed to be taking care of the wharf, is his bisness. My bisness is to see that my man 'as 'is rights."

"'Ear, 'ear!" ses the crew.

"You please yourself, watchman," ses the skipper. "You're such a clever man that no doubt you could get a better job tomorrow. There must be 'eaps of people wanting a man like you. It's for you to decide. That's all I've got to say—five bob a week till pore George 'as got is money back, or else I put the case afore the guv'nor. *Wot* did you say?"

I said it agin, and, as 'e didn't seem to understand, I said it once more.

"Please yourself," 'e ses, when I 'ad finished. "You're an old man, and five bob a week can't be much loss to you. You've got nothing to spend it on, at your time o' life. And you've got a very soft job 'ere. Wot?"

I didn't answer 'im. I just turned round, and, arter giving a man wot stood in my way a punch in the chest, I got up on deck and on to the wharf, and said my little say all alone to myself, behind the crane.

I paid the fust five bob to George Tebb the next time the ship was up, and arter biting 'em over and over agin, and then ringing 'em on the deck 'e took the other chaps round to the "Bear's Head."

"P'r'aps it's just as well it's 'appened," he ses. "Five bob a week for nearly two years ain't to be sneezed at. It's slow, but it's sure."

I thought 'e was joking at fust, but arter working it out in the office with a bit o' pencil and paper I thought I should ha' gorn crazy. And when I complained about the time to George 'e said I could make it shorter if I liked by paying ten bob a week, but 'e thought the steady five bob a week was best for both of us.

I got to 'ate the sight of 'im. Every week regular as clockwork he used to come round to me with his 'and out, and then go and treat 'is mates to beer with my money. If the ship came up in the daytime, at six o'clock in the evening he'd be at the wharf gate waiting for me; and if it came up at night she was no sooner made fast than 'e was over the side patting my trouser-pocket and saying wot a good job it was for both of us that I was in steady employment.

Week arter week and month arter month I went on paying. I a'most forgot the taste o' beer, and if I could manage to get a screw o' baccy a week I thought myself lucky. And at last, just as I thought I couldn't stand it any longer, the end came.

I 'ad just given George 'is week's money—and 'ow I got it together that week I don't know—when one o' the chaps came up and said the skipper wanted to see me on board at once.

"Tell 'im if he wants to see me I'm to be found on the wharf," I ses, very sharp.

"He wants to see you about George's money," ses the chap. "I should go if I was you. My opinion is he wants to do you a good turn."

I 'ung fire for a bit, and then, arter sweeping up for a little while deliberate-like, I put down my broom and stepped aboard to see the skipper, wot was sitting on the cabin skylight purtending to read a newspaper.

He put it down when 'e see me, and George and the others, wot 'ad been standing in a little bunch for'ard, came aft and stood looking on.

"I wanted to see you about this money, watchman," ses the skipper, putting on 'is beastly frills agin. "O' course, we all feel that to a pore man like you it's a bit of a strain, and, as George ses, arter all you have been more foolish than wicked."

"Much more," ses George.

"I find that you 'ave now paid five bob a week for nineteen weeks," ses the skipper, "and George 'as been kind enough and generous enough to let you off the rest. There's no need for you to look bashful, George; it's a credit to you."

I could 'ardly believe my ears. George stood there grinning like a stuck fool, and two o' the chaps was on their best behaviour with their 'ands over their mouths and their eyes sticking out.

"That's all, watchman," ses the skipper; "and I 'ope it'll be a lesson to you not to neglect your dooty by going into public 'ouses and taking charge of other people's money when you ain't fit for it."

"I shan't try to do anybody else a kindness agin, if that's wot you mean," I ses, looking at 'im.

"No, you'd better not," he ses. "This partickler bit o' kindness 'as cost you four pounds fifteen, and that's a curious thing when you come to think of it. Very curious."

"Wot d'ye mean?" I ses.

"Why," he ses, grinning like a madman, "it's just wot we lost between us. I lost a watch and chain worth two pounds, and another couple o' pounds besides; Joe lost ten shillings over 'is di'mond ring; and Charlie lost five bob over a pipe. That's four pounds fifteen—just the same as you."

Them silly fools stood there choking and sobbing and patting each other on the back as though they'd never leave off, and all of a sudden I 'ad a 'orrible suspicion that I 'ad been done.

“Did you see the sovereigns in the box?” I ses, turning to the skipper.

“No,” he ses, shaking his ’ead.

“’Ow do you know they was there, then?” ses I.

“Because you took charge of ’em,” said the skipper; “and I know wot a clever, sharp chap you are. It stands to reason that you wouldn’t be esponsible for a box like that unless you saw inside of it. Why, a child o’ five wouldn’t!”

I stood there looking at ’im, but he couldn’t meet my eye. None of ’em could; and arter waiting there for a minute or two to give ’em a chance, I turned my back on ’em and went off to my dooty.

3

MADE TO MEASURE

Mr. Mott brought his niece home from the station with considerable pride. Although he had received a photograph to assist identification, he had been very dubious about accosting the pretty, well-dressed girl who had stepped from the train and gazed around with dove-like eyes in search of him. Now he was comfortably conscious of the admiring gaze of his younger fellow-townsmen.

"You'll find it a bit dull after London, I expect," he remarked, as he inserted his key in the door of a small house in a quiet street.

"I'm tired of London," said Miss Garland. "I think this is a beautiful little old town—so peaceful."

Mr. Mott looked gratified.

"I hope you'll stay a long time," he said, as he led the way into the small front room. "I'm a lonely old man."

His niece sank into an easy chair and looked about her.

"Thank you," she said slowly. "I hope I shall. I feel better already. There is so much to upset one in London."

"Noise?" queried Mr. Mott.

"And other things," said Miss Garland, with a slight shudder.

Mr. Mott sighed in sympathy with the unknown and, judging by his niece's expression, the unknowable. He rearranged the teacups, and, going to the kitchen, returned in a few minutes with a pot of tea.

"Mrs. Pett leaves at three," he said, in explanation, "to look after her children, but she comes back again at eight to look after my supper. And how is your mother?"

Miss Garland told him.

"Last letter I had from her," said Mr. Mott, stealing a glance at the girl's ring-finger, "I understood you were engaged."

His niece drew herself up.

"Certainly not," she said, with considerable vigour. "I have seen too much of married life. I prefer my freedom. Besides, I don't like men."

Mr. Mott said modestly that he didn't wonder at it, and, finding the subject uncongenial, turned the conversation on to worthier subjects. Miss Garland's taste, it seemed, lay in the direction of hospital nursing, or some other occupation beneficial to mankind at large. Simple and demure, she filled the simpler Mr. Mott with a strong sense of the shortcomings of his unworthy sex.

Within two days, under the darkling glance of Mrs. Pett, she had altered the arrangements of the house. Flowers appeared on the meal-table, knives and forks were properly cleaned, and plates no longer appeared ornamented with the mustard of a previous meal. Fresh air circulated through the house, and, passing from Mrs. Pett's left knee to the lumbar region of Mr. Mott, went on its beneficent way rejoicing.

On the fifth day of her visit, Mr. Mott sat alone in the front parlour. The window was closed, the door was closed, and Mr. Mott, sitting in an easy chair with his feet up, was aroused from a sound nap by the door opening to admit a young man who, deserted by Mrs. Pett, stood bowing awkwardly in the doorway.

"Is Miss Garland in?" he stammered.

Mr. Mott rubbed the remnants of sleep from his eyelids.

"She has gone for a walk," he said slowly.

The young man stood fingering his hat.

"My name is Hurst," he said, with slight emphasis. "Mr. Alfred Hurst."

Mr. Mott, still somewhat confused, murmured that he was glad to hear it.

"I have come from London to see Florrie," continued the intruder. "I suppose she won't be long?"

Mr. Mott thought not, and after a moment's hesitation invited Mr. Hurst to take a chair.

"I suppose she told you we are engaged?" said the latter.

"Engaged?" said the startled Mr. Mott. "Why, she told me she didn't like men."

"Playfulness," replied Mr. Hurst, with an odd look. "Ah, here she is!"

The handle of the front door turned, and a moment later the door of the room was opened and the charming head of Miss Garland appeared in the opening.

"Back again," she said brightly. "I've just been—"

She caught sight of Mr. Hurst, and the words died away on her lips. The door slammed, and the two gentlemen, exchanging glances, heard a hurried rush upstairs and the slamming of another door. Also a key was heard to turn sharply in a lock.

"She doesn't want to see you," said Mr. Mott, staring.

The young man turned pale.

"Perhaps she has gone upstairs to take her things off," he muttered, resuming his seat. "Don't—don't hurry her!"

"I wasn't going to," said Mr. Mott.

He twisted his beard uneasily, and at the end of ten minutes looked from the clock to Mr. Hurst and coughed.

"If you wouldn't mind letting her know I'm waiting," said the young man brokenly.

Mr. Mott rose, and went slowly upstairs. More slowly still, after an interval of a few minutes he came back again.

"She doesn't want to see you," he said slowly.

Mr. Hurst gasped.

"I—I must see her," he faltered.

"She won't see you," repeated Mr. Mott. "And she told me to say she was surprised at you following her down here."

Mr. Hurst uttered a faint moan, and with bent head passed into the little passage and out into the street, leaving Mr. Mott to return to the sitting-room and listen to such explanations as Miss Garland deemed advisable. Great goodness of heart in the face of persistent and unwelcome attentions appeared to be responsible for the late engagement.

"Well, it's over now," said her uncle kindly, "and no doubt he'll soon find somebody else. There are plenty of girls would jump at him, I expect."

Miss Garland shook her head.

"He said he couldn't live without me," she remarked soberly.

Mr. Mott laughed.

"In less than three months I expect he'll be congratulating himself," he said cheerfully. "Why, I was nearly cau—married, four times. It's a silly age."

His niece said "Indeed!" and, informing him in somewhat hostile tones that she was suffering from a severe headache, retired to her room.

Mr. Mott spent the evening by himself, and retiring to bed at ten-thirty was awakened by a persistent knocking at the front door at half-past one. Half awakened, he lit a candle, and, stumbling downstairs, drew back the bolt of the door, and stood gaping angrily at the pathetic features of Mr. Hurst.

"Sorry to disturb you," said the young man, "but would you mind giving this letter to Miss Garland?"

"Sorry to disturb me!" stuttered Mr. Mott. "What do you mean by it? Eh? What do you mean by it?"

"It is important," said Mr. Hurst. "I can't rest. I've eaten nothing all day."

"Glad to hear it," snapped the irritated Mr. Mott.

"If you will give her that letter, I shall feel easier," said Mr. Hurst.

"I'll give it to her in the morning," said the other, snatching it from him. "Now get off."

Mr. Hurst, still murmuring apologies, went, and Mr. Mott, also murmuring, returned to bed. The night was chilly, and it was some time before he could get to sleep again. He succeeded at last, only to be awakened an hour later by a knocking more violent than before. In a state of mind bordering upon frenzy, he dived into his trousers again and went blundering downstairs in the dark.

"Sorry to—" began Mr. Hurst.

Mr. Mott made uncouth noises at him.

"I have altered my mind," said the young man. "Would you mind letting me have that letter back again? It was too final."

"You—get—off!" said the other, trembling with cold and passion.

"I must have that letter," said Mr. Hurst doggedly. "All my future happiness may depend upon it."

Mr. Mott, afraid to trust himself with speech, dashed upstairs, and after a search for the matches found the letter, and, returning to the front door, shut it on the visitor's thanks. His niece's door opened as he passed it, and a gentle voice asked for enlightenment.

"How silly of him!" she said softly. "I hope he won't catch cold. *What* did you say?"

"I was coughing," said Mr. Mott hastily.

"You'll get cold if you're not careful," said his thoughtful niece. "That's the worst of men, they never seem to have any thought. Did he seem angry, or mournful, or what? I suppose you couldn't see his face?"

"I didn't try," said Mr. Mott crisply. "Good night."

By the morning his ill-humour had vanished, and he even became slightly facetious over the events of the night. The mood passed at the same moment that Mr. Hurst passed the window.

"Better have him in and get it over," he said irritably.

Miss Garland shuddered.

"Never!" she said firmly. "He'd be down on his knees. It would be too painful. You don't know him."

"Don't want to," said Mr. Mott.

He finished his breakfast in silence, and, after a digestive pipe, proposed a walk. The profile of Mr. Hurst, as it went forlornly past the window again, served to illustrate Miss Garland's refusal.

"I'll go out and see him," said Mr. Mott, starting up. "Are you going to be a prisoner here until this young idiot chooses to go home? It's preposterous!"

He crammed his hat on firmly and set out in pursuit of Mr. Hurst, who was walking slowly up the street, glancing over his, shoulder.

"Morning!" said Mr. Mott fiercely.

"Good morning," said the other.

"Now, look here," said Mr. Mott. "This has gone far enough, and I won't have anymore of it. Why, you ought to be ashamed of yourself, chiwying a young lady that doesn't want you. Haven't you got any pride?"

"No," said the young man." not where she is concerned."

"I don't believe you have." said the other, regarding him, "and I expect that's where the trouble is. Did she ever have reason to think you were looking after any other girls?"

"Never, I swear it," said Mr. Hurst eagerly.

"Just so," said Mr. Mott, with a satisfied nod. "That's where you made a mistake. She was too sure of you; it was too easy. No excitement. Girls like a man that other girls want; they don't want a turtle-dove in fancy trousers."

Mr. Hurst coughed.

"And they like a determined man," continued Miss Garland's uncle. "Why, in my young days, if I had been jilted, and come down to see about it, d'you think I'd have gone out of the house without seeing her? I might have been put out—by half a dozen—but I'd have taken the mantelpiece and a few other things with me. And you are bigger than I am."

"We aren't all made the same," said Mr. Hurst feebly.

"No, we're not," said Mr. Mott. "I'm not blaming you; in a way, I'm sorry for you. If you're not born with a high spirit, nothing'll give it to you."

"It might be learnt," said Mr. Hurst.

Mr. Mott laughed.

"High spirits are born, not made," he said. "The best thing you can do is to go and find another girl, and marry her before she finds you out."

Mr. Hurst shook his head.

"There's no other girl for me," he said miserably. "And everything seemed to be going so well. We've been buying things for the house for the last six months, and I've just got a good rise in my screw."

"It'll do for another girl," said Mr. Mott briskly. "Now, you get off back to town. You are worrying Florrie by staying here, and you are doing no good to anybody. Goodbye."

"I'll walk back as far as the door with you," said Mr. Hurst. "You've done me good. It's a pity I didn't meet you before."

Mr. Mott smiled.

"Remember what I've told you, and you'll do well yet," he said, patting the young man on the arm.

"I will," said Mr. Hurst, and walked on by his side, deep in thought.

"I can't ask you in," said Mr. Mott jocularly, as he reached his door, and turned the key in the lock. "Goodbye."

"Goodbye," said Mr. Hurst.

He grasped the other's outstretched hand, and with a violent jerk pulled him into the street. Then he pushed open the door, and, slipping into the passage, passed hastily into the front room, closely followed by the infuriated Mr. Mott.

"What—what—what!" stammered that gentleman.

"I'm taking your tip," said Mr. Hurst, pale but determined. "I'm going to stay here until I have seen Florrie."

"You—you're a serpent," said Mr. Mott, struggling for breath. "I—I'm surprised at you. You go out before you get hurt."

"Not without the mantelpiece," said Mr. Hurst with a distorted grin.

"A viper!" said Mr. Mott, with extreme bitterness. "If you are not out in two minutes I'll send for the police."

"Florrie wouldn't like that," said Mr. Hurst. "She's awfully particular about what people think. You just trot upstairs and tell her that a gentleman wants to see her."

He threw himself into Mr. Mott's own particular chair, and, crossing his knees, turned a deaf ear to the threats of that incensed gentleman. Not until the latter had left the room did his features reveal the timorousness of the soul within. Muffled voices sounded from upstairs, and it was evident that an argument of considerable length was in progress. It was also evident from the return of Mr. Mott alone that his niece had had the best of it.

"I've done all I could," he said, "but she declines to see you. She says she won't see you if you stay here for a month, and you couldn't do that, you know."

"Why not?" inquired Mr. Hurst.

"Why not?" repeated Mr. Mott, repressing his feelings with some difficulty. "*Food!*"

Mr. Hurst started.

"And drink," said Mr. Mott, following up his advantage. "There's no good in starving yourself for nothing, so you may as well go."

"When I've seen Florrie," said the young man firmly.

Mr. Mott slammed the door, and for the rest of the day Mr. Hurst saw him no more. At one o'clock a savoury smell passed the door on its way upstairs, and at five o'clock a middle-aged woman with an inane smile looked into the room on her way aloft with a loaded tea-tray. By supper-time he was suffering considerably from hunger and thirst.

At ten o'clock he heard the footsteps of Mr. Mott descending the stairs. The door opened an inch, and a gruff voice demanded to know whether he was going to stay there all night. Receiving a cheerful reply in the affirmative, Mr. Mott secured the front door with considerable violence, and went off to bed without another word.

He was awakened an hour or two later by the sound of something falling, and, sitting up in bed to listen, became aware of a warm and agreeable odour. It was somewhere about the hour of midnight, but a breakfast smell of eggs and bacon would not be denied.

He put on some clothes and went downstairs. A crack of light showed under the kitchen door, and, pushing it open with some force, he gazed spellbound at the spectacle before him.

"Come in," said Mr. Hurst heartily. "I've just finished."

He rocked an empty beer-bottle and patted another that was half full. Satiety was written on his face as he pushed an empty plate from him, and, leaning back in his chair, smiled lazily at Mr. Mott.

"Go on," said that gentleman hoarsely.

Mr. Hurst shook his head.

"Enough is as good as a feast," he said, reasonably. "I'll have some more tomorrow."

"Oh, will you?" said the other. "Will you?"

Mr. Hurst nodded, and, opening his coat, disclosed a bottle of beer in each breast-pocket. The other pockets, it appeared, contained food.

"And here's the money for it," he said, putting down some silver on the table. "I am determined, but honest."

With a sweep of his hand, Mr. Mott sent the money flying.

"Tomorrow morning I send for the police. Mind that!" he roared.

"I'd better have my breakfast early, then," said Mr. Hurst, tapping his pockets. "Good night. And thank you for your advice."

He sat for some time after the disappearance of his host, and then, returning to the front room, placed a chair at the end of the sofa and, with the tablecloth for a quilt, managed to secure a few hours' troubled sleep. At eight o'clock he washed at the scullery sink, and at ten o'clock Mr. Mott, with an air of great determination, came in to deliver his ultimatum.

"If you're not outside the front door in five minutes, I'm going to fetch the police," he said fiercely.

"I want to see Florrie," said the other.

"Well, you won't see her," shouted Mr. Mott.

Mr. Hurst stood feeling his chin.

"Well, would you mind taking a message for me?" he asked. "I just want you to ask her whether I am really free. Ask her whether I am free to marry again."

Mr. Mott eyed him in amazement.

"You see, I only heard from her mother," pursued Mr. Hurst, "and a friend of mine who is in a solicitor's office says that isn't good enough. I only came down here to make sure, and I think the least she can do is to tell me herself. If she won't see me, perhaps she'd put it in writing. You see, there's another lady."

"But—" said the mystified Mr. Mott. "You told me—"

"You tell her that," said the other.

Mr. Mott stood for a few seconds staring at him, and then without a word turned on his heel and went upstairs. Left to himself, Mr. Hurst walked nervously up and down the room, and, catching sight of his face in the old-fashioned glass on the mantelpiece, heightened its colour by a few pinches. The minutes seemed interminable, but at last he heard the steps of Mr. Mott on the stairs again.

"She's coming down to see you herself," he said solemnly.

Mr. Hurst nodded, and, turning to the window, tried in vain to take an interest in passing events. A light step sounded on the stairs, the door creaked, and he turned to find himself confronted by Miss Garland.

"Uncle told me—" she began coldly.

Mr. Hurst bowed.

"I am sorry to have caused you so much trouble," he said, trying to control his voice, "but you see my position, don't you?"

"No," said the girl.

"Well, I wanted to make sure," said Mr. Hurst. "It's best for all of us, isn't it? Best for you, best for me, and, of course, for my young lady."

"You never said anything about her before," said Miss Garland, her eyes darkening.

"Of course not," said Mr. Hurst. "How could I? I was engaged to you, and then she wasn't my young lady; but, of course, as soon as you broke it off—"

"Who is she?" inquired Miss Garland in a casual voice.

"You don't know her," said Mr. Hurst.

"What is she like?"

"'I can't describe her very well," said Mr. Hurst. "I can only say she's the most beautiful girl I have ever seen. I think that's what made me take to her. And she's easily pleased. She liked the things I have been buying for the house tremendously."

"Did she?" said Miss Garland, with a gasp.

"All except that pair of vases you chose," continued the veracious Mr. Hurst. "She says they are in bad taste, but she can give them to the charwoman."

"Oh!" said the girl. "Oh, indeed! Very kind of her. Isn't there anything else she doesn't like?"

Mr. Hurst stood considering.

"She doesn't like the upholstering of the best chairs," he said at last. "She thinks they are too showy, so she's going to put covers over them."

There was a long pause, during which Mr. Mott, taking his niece gently by the arm, assisted her to a chair.

"Otherwise she is quite satisfied," concluded Mr. Hurst.

Miss Garland took a deep breath, but made no reply.

"I have got to satisfy her that I am free," said the young man, after another pause. "I suppose that I can do so?"

"I—I'll think it over," said Miss Garland in a low voice. "I am not sure what is the right thing to do. I don't want to see you made miserable for life. It's nothing to me, of course, but still—"

She got up and, shaking off the proffered assistance of her uncle, went slowly and languidly up to her room. Mr. Mott followed her as far as the door, and then turned indignantly upon Mr. Hurst.

"You—you've broke her heart," he said solemnly.

"That's all right," said Mr. Hurst, with a delighted wink. "I'll mend it again."

4

SAM'S GHOST

Yes, I know, said the night-watchman thoughtfully, as he sat with a cold pipe in his mouth gazing across the river, I've 'eard it afore. People tell me they don't believe in ghosts and make a laugh of 'em, and all I say is: let them take on a night-watchman's job. Let 'em sit 'ere all alone of a night with the water lapping against the posts and the wind moaning in the corners; especially if a pal of theirs has slipped overboard, and there is little nasty bills stuck up just outside in the High Street offering a reward for the body. Twice men 'ave fallen overboard from this jetty, and I've 'ad to stand my watch here the same night, and not a farthing more for it.

One of the worst and artfullest ghosts I ever 'ad anything to do with was Sam Bullet. He was a waterman at the stairs near by 'ere; the sort o' man that 'ud get you to pay for drinks, and drink yours up by mistake arter he 'ad finished his own. The sort of man that 'ad always left his baccy-box at 'ome, but always 'ad a big pipe in 'is pocket.

He fell overboard off of a lighter one evening, and all that his mates could save was 'is cap. It was on'y two nights afore that he 'ad knocked down an old man and bit a policeman's little finger to the bone, so that, as they pointed out to the widder, p'r'aps he was taken for a wise purpose. P'r'aps he was 'appier where he was than doing six months.

"He was the sort o' chap that'll make himself 'appy *anywhere*" ses one of 'em, comforting-like.

"Not without me," ses Mrs. Bullet, sobbing, and wiping her eyes on something she used for a pocket-hankercher. "He never could bear to be away from me. Was there no last words?"

"On'y one," ses one o' the chaps, Joe Peel by name.

"As 'e fell overboard," ses the other.

Mrs. Bullet began to cry agin, and say wot a good 'usband he 'ad been. "Seventeen years come Michaelmas," she ses, "and never a cross word. Nothing was too good for me. Nothing. I 'ad only to ask to 'ave."

"Well, he's gorn now," ses Joe, "and we thought we ought to come round and tell you."

"So as you can tell the police," ses the other chap.

That was 'ow I came to hear of it fust; a policeman told me that night as I stood outside the gate 'aving a quiet pipe. *He* wasn't shedding tears; his only idea was that Sam 'ad got off too easy.

"Well, well," I ses, trying to pacify 'im, "he won't bite no more fingers; there's no policemen where he's gorn to."

He went off grumbling and telling me to be careful, and I put my pipe out and walked up and down the wharf thinking. On'y a month afore I 'ad lent Sam fifteen shillings on a gold watch and chain wot he said an uncle 'ad left 'im. I wasn't wearing it because 'e said 'is uncle wouldn't like it, but I 'ad it in my pocket, and I took it out under one of the lamps and wondered wot I ought to do.

My fust idea was to take it to Mrs. Bullet, and then, all of a sudden, the thought struck me: "*Suppose he 'adn't come by it honest?*"

I walked up and down agin, thinking. If he 'adn't, and it was found out, it would blacken his good name and break 'is pore wife's 'art. That's the way I looked at it, and for his sake and 'er sake I determined to stick to it.

I felt 'appier in my mind when I 'ad decided on that, and I went round to the "Bear's Head" and 'ad a pint. Arter that I 'ad another, and then I come back to the wharf and put the watch and chain on and went on with my work.

Every time I looked down at the chain it reminded me of Sam. I looked on to the river and thought of 'im going down on the ebb. Then I got a sort o' lonesome feeling standing on the end of the jetty all alone, and I went back to the "Bear's Head" and 'ad another pint.

They didn't find the body, and I was a'most forgetting about Sam when one evening, as I was sitting on a box waiting to get my breath back to 'ave another go at sweeping, Joe Peel, Sam's mate, came on to the wharf to see me.

He came in a mysterious sort o' way that I didn't like: looking be'ind 'im as though he was afraid of being follered, and speaking in a whisper as if 'e was afraid of being heard. He wasn't a man I liked, and I was glad that the watch and chain was stowed safe away in my trowsis-pocket.

"I've 'ad a shock, watchman," he ses.

"Oh!" I ses.

"A shock wot's shook me all up," he ses, working up a shiver. "I've seen something wot I thought people never could see, and wot I never want to see agin. *I've seen Sam!*"

I thought a bit afore I spoke. "Why, I thought he was drownded," I ses.

"So 'e is," ses Joe. "When I say I've seen 'im I mean that I 'ave seen his *ghost*!"

He began to shiver agin, all over.

"Wot was it like?" I ses, very calm.

"Like Sam," he ses, rather short.

"When was it?" I ses.

"Last night, at a quarter to twelve," he ses. "It was standing at my front door waiting for me."

"And 'ave you been shivering like that ever since?" I ses.

"Worse than that," ses Joe, looking at me very 'ard. "It's wearing off now. The ghost gave me a message for you."

I put my 'and in my trowsis-pocket and looked at 'im. Then I walked, very slow, towards the gate.

"It gave me a message for you," ses Joe, walking beside me. "'We was always pals, Joe,'" it ses, "'you and me, and I want you to pay up fifteen bob for me wot I borrowed off Bill the watchman. I can't rest until it's paid,' it ses. So here's the fifteen bob, watchman."

He put his 'and in 'is pocket and takes out fifteen bob and 'olds it out to me.

"No, no," I ses. "I can't take your money, Joe Peel. It wouldn't be right. Pore Sam is welcome to the fifteen bob—I don't want it."

"You must take it," ses Joe. "The ghost said if you didn't it would come to me agin and agin till you did, and I can't stand anymore of it."

"I can't 'elp your troubles," I ses.

"You must," ses Joe. "'Give Bill the fifteen bob,' it ses, 'and he'll give you a gold watch and chain wot I gave 'im to mind till it was paid.'"

I see his little game then. "Gold watch and chain," I ses, laughing. "You must ha' misunderstood it, Joe."

"I understood it right enough," ses Joe, getting a bit closer to me as I stepped outside the gate. "Here's your fifteen bob; are you going to give me that watch and chain?"

"Sartainly not," I ses. "I don't know wot you mean by a watch and chain. *If* I 'ad it and I gave it to anybody, I should give it to Sam's widder, not to you."

"It's nothing to do with 'er," ses Joe, very quick. "Sam was most pertikler about that."

"I expect you dreamt it all," I ses. "Where would pore Sam get a gold watch and chain from? And why should 'e go to you about it? Why didn't 'e come to me? If 'e thinks I 'ave got it let 'im come to me."

"All right, I'll go to the police-station," ses Joe.

"I'll come with you," I ses. "But 'ere's a policeman coming along. Let's go to 'im."

I moved towards 'im, but Joe hung back, and, arter using one or two words that would ha' made any ghost ashamed to know 'im, he sheered off. I 'ad a word or two with the policeman about the weather, and then I went inside and locked the gate.

My idea was that Sam 'ad told Joe about the watch and chain afore he fell overboard. Joe was a nasty customer, and I could see that I should 'ave to be a bit careful. Some men might ha' told the police about it—but I never cared much for them. They're like kids in a way, always asking questions—most of which you can't answer.

It was a little bit creepy all alone on the wharf that night. I don't deny it. Twice I thought I 'eard something coming up on tip-toe behind me. The second time I was so nervous that I began to sing to keep my spirits up, and I went on singing till three hands of the *Susan Emily*, wot was laying alongside, came up from the fo'c'sle and offered to fight me. I was thankful when daylight came.

Five nights arterwards I 'ad the shock of my life. It was the fust night for some time that there was no craft up. A dark night, and a nasty moaning sort of a wind. I 'ad just lighted the lamp at the corner of the warehouse, wot 'ad blown out, and was sitting down to rest afore putting the ladder away, when I 'appened to look along the jetty and saw a head coming up over the edge of it. In the light of the lamp I saw the dead white face of Sam Bullet's ghost making faces at me.

I just caught my breath, sharp like, and then I turned and ran for the gate like a race-horse. I 'ad left the key in the padlock, in case of anything happening, and I just gave it one turn, flung the wicket open and slammed it in the ghost's face, and tumbled out into the road.

I ran slap into the arms of a young policeman wot was passing. Nasty, short-tempered chap he was, but I don't think I was more glad to see anybody in my life. I hugged 'im till 'e nearly lost 'is breath, and then he sat me down on the kerbstone and asked me wot I meant by it.

Wot with the excitement and the running I couldn't speak at fust, and when I did he said I was trying to deceive 'im.

"There ain't no such thing as ghosts," he ses; "you've been drinking."

"It came up out o' the river and run arter me like the wind," I ses.

"Why didn't it catch you, then?" he ses, looking me up and down and all round about. "Talk sense."

He went up to the gate and peeped in, and, arter watching a moment, stepped inside and walked down the wharf, with me follering. It was my dooty; besides, I'didn't like being left all alone by myself.

Twice we walked up and down and all over the wharf. He flashed his lantern into all the dark corners, into empty barrels and boxes, and then he turned and flashed it right into my face and shook his 'ead at me.

"You've been having a bit of a lark with me," he ses, "and for two pins I'd take you. Mind, if you say a word about this to anybody, I will."

He stalked off with his 'ead in the air, and left me all alone in charge of a wharf with a ghost on it. I stayed outside in the street, of course, but every now and then I fancied I heard something moving about the other side of the gate, and once it was so distinct that I run along to the "Bear's Head" and knocked 'em up and asked them for a little brandy, for illness.

I didn't get it, of course; I didn't expect to; but I 'ad a little conversation with the landlord from 'is bedroom-winder that did me more good than the brandy would ha' done. Once or twice I thought he would 'ave fallen out, and many a man has 'ad his licence taken away for less than a quarter of wot 'e said to me that night. Arter he thought he 'ad finished and was going back to bed again, I pointed out to 'im that he 'adn't kissed me "good night," and if it 'adn't ha' been for 'is missis and two grown-up daughters and the potman I believe he'd ha' talked to me till daylight.

'Ow I got through the rest of the night I don't know. It seemed to be twenty nights instead of one, but the day came at last, and when the hands came on at six o'clock they found the gate open and me on dooty same as usual.

I slept like a tired child when I got 'ome, and arter a steak and onions for dinner I sat down and lit my pipe and tried to think wot was to be done. One thing I was quite certain about: I wasn't going to spend another night on that wharf alone.

I went out arter a bit, as far as the "Clarendon Arms," for a breath of fresh air, and I 'adjust finished a pint and was wondering whether I ought to 'ave another, when Ted Dennis came in, and my mind was made up. He 'ad been in the Army all 'is life, and, so far, he 'ad never seen anything that 'ad frightened 'im. I've seen him myself take on men twice 'is size just for the love of the thing, and, arter knocking them silly, stand 'em a pint out of 'is own pocket. When I asked 'im whether he was afraid of ghosts he laughed so 'ard that the landlord came from the other end of the bar to see wot was the matter.

I stood Ted a pint, and arter he 'ad finished it I told 'im just how things was. I didn't say anything about the watch and chain, because there was no need to, and when we came outside agin I 'ad engaged an assistant-watchman for ninepence a night.

"All you've got to do," I ses, "is to keep me company. You needn't turn up till eight o'clock of a night, and you can leave 'arf an hour afore me in the morning."

"Right-o!" ses Ted. "And if I see the ghost I'll make it wish it 'ad never been born."

It was a load off my mind, and I went 'ome and ate a tea that made my missis talk about the work'ouse, and orstritches in 'uman shape wot would eat a woman out of 'ouse and 'ome if she would let 'em.

I got to the wharf just as it was striking six, and at a quarter to seven the wicket was pushed open gentle and the ugly 'ead of Mr. Joe Peel was shoved inside.

"Hullo!" I ses. "Wot do you want?"

"I want to save your life," he ses, in a solemn voice. "You was within a inch of death last night, watchman."

"Oh!" I ses, careless-like. "'Ow do you know!"

"The ghost o' Sam Bullet told me," ses Joe. "Arter it 'ad chased you up the wharf screaming for 'elp, it came round and told me all about it."

"It seems fond of you," I ses. "I wonder why?"

"It was in a terrible temper," ses Joe, "and its face was awful to look at. 'Tell the watchman,' it ses, 'that if he don't give you the watch and chain I shall appear to 'im agin and kill 'im.'"

"All right," I ses, looking behind me to where three of the 'ands of the *Daisy* was sitting on the fo'c'sle smoking. "I've got plenty of company tonight."

"Company won't save you," ses Joe. "For the last time, are you going to give me that watch and chain, or not? Here's your fifteen bob."

"No," I ses; "even if I 'ad got it I shouldn't give it to you; and it's no use giving it to the ghost, because, being made of air, he 'asn't got anywhere to put it."

"Very good," ses Joe, giving me a black look. "I've done all I can to save you, but if you won't listen to sense, you won't.

You'll see Sam Bullet agin, and you'll not on'y lose the watch and chain but your life as well."

"All right," I ses, "and thank you kindly, but I've got an assistant, as it 'appens—a man wot wants to see a ghost."

"An assistant?" ses Joe, staring.

"An old soldier," I ses. "A man wot likes trouble and danger. His idea is to shoot the ghost and see wot 'appens."

"*Shoot!*" ses Joe. "Shoot a pore 'armless ghost. Does he want to be 'ung? Ain't it enough for a pore man to be drownded, but wot you must try and shoot 'im arterwards? Why you ought to be ashamed o' yourself. Where's your 'art?"

"It won't be shot if it don't come on my wharf," I ses. "Though I don't mind if it does when I've got somebody with me. I ain't afraid of anything living, and I don't mind ghosts when there's two of us. Besides which, the noise of the pistol 'll wake up 'arf the river."

"You take care *you* don't get woke-up," ses Joe, 'ardly able to speak for temper.

He went off stamping, and grinding 'is teeth, and at eight o'clock to the minute, Ted Dennis turned up with 'is pistol and helped me take care of the wharf. Happy as a skylark 'e was, and to see him 'iding behind a barrel with his pistol ready, waiting for the ghost, a'most made me forget the expense of it all.

It never came near us that night, and Ted was a bit disappointed next morning as he took 'is ninepence and went off. Next night was the same, and the next, and then Ted gave up hiding on the wharf for it, and sat and snoozed in the office instead.

A week went by, and then another, and still there was no sign of Sam Bullet's ghost, or Joe Peel, and every morning I 'ad to try and work up a smile as I shelled out ninepence for Ted. It nearly ruined me, and, worse than that, I couldn't explain why I was short to the missis. Fust of all she asked me *wot* I was spending it on, then she asked me *who* I was spending it on. It nearly broke up my 'ome—she did smash one kitchen-chair and a vase off the parlour mantelpiece—but I wouldn't tell 'er, and then, led away by some men on strike at Smith's wharf, Ted went on strike for a bob a night.

That was arter he 'ad been with me for three weeks, and when Saturday came, of course I was more short than ever, and people came and stood at their doors all the way down our street to listen to the missis taking my character away.

I stood it as long as I could, and then, when 'er back was turned for 'arf a moment, I slipped out. While she'd been talking I'd been thinking, and it came to me clear as daylight that there was no need for me to sacrifice myself any longer looking arter a dead man's watch and chain.

I didn't know exactly where Joe Peel lived, but I knew the part, and arter peeping into seven public-'ouses I see the man I wanted sitting by 'imself in a little bar. I walked in quiet-like, and sat down opposite 'im.

"Morning," I ses.

Joe Peel grunted.

"'Ave one with me?" I ses.

He grunted agin, but not quite so fierce, and I fetched the two pints from the counter and took a seat alongside of 'im.

"I've been looking for you," I ses.

"Oh!" he ses, looking me up and down and all over. "Well, you've found me now."

"I want to talk to you about the ghost of pore Sam Bullet," I ses.

Joe Peel put 'is mug down sudden and looked at me fierce. "Look 'ere! Don't you come and try to be funny with me," he ses. "'Cos I won't 'ave it."

"I don't want to be funny," I ses. "Wot I want to know is, are you in the same mind about that watch and chain as you was the other day?"

He didn't seem to be able to speak at fust, but arter a time 'e gives a gasp. "Wot's the game?" he ses.

"Wot I want to know is, if I give you that watch and chain for fifteen bob, will that keep the ghost from 'anging round my wharf agin?" I ses.

"Why, o' course," he ses, staring; "but you ain't been seeing it agin, 'ave you?"

"I've not, and I don't want to," I ses. "If it wants you to 'ave the watch and chain, give me the fifteen bob, and it's yours."

He looked at me for a moment as if he couldn't believe 'is eyesight, and then 'e puts his 'and into 'is trowsis-pocket and pulls out one shilling and fourpence, 'arf a clay-pipe, and a bit o' lead-pencil.

"That's all I've got with me," he ses. "I'll owe you the rest. You ought to ha' took the fifteen bob when I 'ad it."

There was no 'elp for it, and arter making 'im swear to give me the rest o' the money when e' got it, and that I shouldn't see the ghost agin, I 'anded the things over to 'im and came away. He came to the door to see me off, and if ever a man looked puzzled, 'e did. Pleased at the same time.

It was a load off of my mind. My conscience told me I'd done right, and arter sending a little boy with a note to Ted Dennis to tell 'im not to come any more, I felt 'appier than I 'ad done for a long time. When I got to the wharf that evening it seemed like a diff'rent place, and I was whistling and smiling over my work quite in my old way, when the young policeman passed.

"Hullo!" he ses. "'Ave you seen the ghost agin?"

"I 'ave not," I ses, drawing myself up. "'Ave you?"

"No," he ses. "We missed it."

"Missed it? " I ses, staring at 'im.

"Yes," he ses, nodding. "The day arter you came out screaming, and cuddling me like a frightened baby, it shipped as A.B. on the barque *Ocean King*, for Valparaiso. We missed it by a few hours. Next time you see a ghost, knock it down fust and go and cuddle the police arterwards."

5

BEDRIDDEN

July 12, 1915.—Disquieting rumours to the effect that the epidemic of Billetitis hitherto confined to the north of King's Road shows signs of spreading.

July 14.—Report that two Inns of Court men have been seen peeping over my gate.

July 16.—Informed that soldier of agreeable appearance and charming manners requests interview with me. Took a dose of Phospherine and went. Found composite photograph of French, Joffre, and Hindenburg waiting for me in the hall. Smiled (he did, I mean) and gave me the mutilated form of salute reserved for civilians. Introduced himself as Quartermaster-Sergeant Beddem, and stated that the Inns of Court O.T.C. was going under canvas next week. After which he gulped. Meantime could I take in *a* billet. Questioned as to what day the corps was going into camp said that he believed it was Monday, but was not quite sure—might possibly be Tuesday. Swallowed again and coughed a little. Accepted billet and felt completely rewarded by smile. Q.M.S. bade me goodbye, and then with the air of a man suddenly remembering something, asked me whether I could take two. Excused myself and interviewed my C.O. behind the dining-room door. Came back and accepted. Q.M.S. so overjoyed (apparently) that he fell over the scraper.

Seemed to jog his memory. He paused, and gazing in absent fashion at the topmost rose on the climber in the porch, asked whether I could take three! Added hopefully that the third was only a boy. Excused myself. Heated debate with C.O. Subject: sheets. Returned with me to explain to the Q.M.S. He smiled. C.O. accepted at once, and, returning smile, expressed regret at size and position of bedrooms available. Q.M.S. went off swinging cane jauntily.

July 17.—Billets arrived. Spoke to them about next Monday and canvas. They seemed surprised. Strange how the military authorities decline to take men into their confidence merely because they are privates. Led them upstairs. They went (for first and last time) on tiptoe.

July 18.—Saw Q.M.S. Beddem in the town. Took shelter in the "King's Arms."

Aug. 3.—Went to Cornwall.

Aug. 31.—Returned. Billets received me very hospitably.

Sept. 4.—Private Budd, electrical engineer, dissatisfied with appearance of bell-push in dining-room, altered it.

Sept. 5.—Bells out of order.

Sept. 6.—Private Merited, also an electrical engineer, helped Private Budd to repair bells.

Sept. 7.—Private Budd helped Private Merited to repair bells.

Sept. 8.—Privates Budd and Merited helped each other to repair bells.

Sept. 9.—Sent to local tradesman to put my bells in order.

Sept. 15.—Told that Q.M.S. Beddem wished to see me. Saw C.O. first. She thought he had possibly come to take some of the billets away. Q.M.S. met my approach with a smile that reminded me vaguely of picture-postcards I had seen. Awfully sorry to trouble me, but Private Montease, just back from three weeks' holiday with bronchitis, was sleeping in the wood-shed on three planks and a tin-tack. Beamed at me and waited. Went and bought another bedstead.

Sept. 16.—Private Montease and a cough entered into residence.

Sept. 17, 11.45 *p.m.*—Maid came to bedroom door with some cough lozenges which she asked me to take to the new billet. Took them. Private Montease thanked me, but said he didn't mind coughing. Said it was an heirloom; Montease cough, known in highest circles all over Scotland since time of Young Pretender.

Sept. 20.—Private Montease installed in easy chair in dining-room with touch of bronchitis, looking up trains to Bournemouth.

Sept. 21.—Private Montease in bed all day. Cook anxious to "do her bit" rubbed his chest with home-made embrocation. Believe it is same stuff she rubs chests in hall with. Smells the same, anyway.

Sept. 24.—Private Montease, complaining of slight rawness of chest, but otherwise well, returned to duty.

Oct. 5.—Cough worse again. Private Montease thinks that with care it may turn to bronchitis. Borrowed an A B C.

Oct. 6.—Private Montease relates uncanny experience. Woke up with feeling of suffocation to find an enormous black-currant and glycerine jujube wedged in his gullet. Never owned such a thing in his life. Seems to be unaware that he always sleeps with his mouth open.

Nov. 14.—Private Bowser, youngest and tallest of my billets, gazetted.

Nov. 15, 10.35 a.m.—Private Bowser in tiptop spirits said goodbye to us all.

10.45.—Told that Q.M.S. Beddem desired to see me. Capitulated. New billet, Private Early, armed to the teeth, turned up in the evening. Said that he was a Yorkshireman. Said that Yorkshire was the finest county in England, and

Yorkshireman the finest men in the world. Stood toying with his bayonet and waiting for contradiction.

Jan. 5, 1916.—Standing in the garden just after lunch was witness to startling phenomenon. Q.M.S. Beddem came towards front gate with a smile so expansive that gate after first trembling violently on its hinges swung open of its own accord. Q.M.S., with smile (sad), said he was in trouble. Very old member of the Inns of Court, Private Keen, had rejoined, and he wanted a good billet for him. Would cheerfully give up his own bed, but it wasn't long enough. Not to be outdone in hospitality by my own gate, accepted Private Keen. Q.M.S. digging hole in my path with toe of right boot, and for first and only time manifesting signs of nervousness, murmured that two lifelong friends of Private Keen's had rejoined with him. Known as the Three Inseparables. Where they were to sleep, unless I—Fled to house, and locking myself in top attic watched Q.M.S. from window. He departed with bent head and swagger cane reversed.

Jan. 6.—Private Keen arrived. Turned out to be son of an old Chief of mine. Resolved not to visit the sins of the father on the head of a child six feet two high and broad in proportion.

Feb. 6.—Private Keen came home with a temperature.

Feb. 7.—M.O. diagnosed influenza. Was afraid it would spread.

Feb. 8.—Warned the other four billets. They seemed amused. Pointed out that influenza had no terrors for men in No. 2 Company, who were doomed to weekly night-ops. under Major Carryon.

Feb. 9.—House strangely and pleasantly quiet. Went to see how Private Keen was progressing, and found the other four billets sitting in a row on his bed practising deep-breathing exercises.

Feb. 16.—Billets on night-ops. until late hour. Spoke in highest terms of Major Carryon's marching powers—also in other terms.

March 3.—Waited up until midnight for Private Merited, who had gone to Slough on his motorbike.

March 4, 1.5 *a.m.*—Awakened by series of explosions from overworked, or badly-worked, motorbike. Put head out of window and threw key to Private Merited. He seemed excited. Said he had been chased all the way from Chesham by a pink rat with yellow spots. Advised him to go to bed. Set him an example.

1.10 *a.m.* – Heard somebody in the pantry.

2.10 *a.m.* – Heard Private Merited going up stairs to bed.

2.16 *a.m.* – Heard Private Merited still going upstairs to bed.

2.20 – 3.15 *a.m.* – Heard Private Merited getting to bed.

April 3, 12.30 *a.m.* – Town hooter announced Zeppelins and excited soldier called up my billets from their beds to go and frighten them off. Pleasant to see superiority of billets over the hooter : *that* only emitted three blasts.

12.50 *a.m.* – Billets returned with exception of Private Merited, who was retained for sake of his motor-bike.

9 *a.m.* – On way to bath-room ran into Private Merited, who, looking very glum and sleepy, inquired whether I had a copy of the Exchange and Mart in the house.

10 *p.m.* – Overheard billets discussing whether it was worth while removing boots before going to bed until the Zeppelin scare was over. Joined in discussion.

May 2. – Rumours that the Inns of Court were going under canvas. Discredited them.

May 5. – Rumours grow stronger.

May 6. – Billets depressed. Begin to think perhaps there is something in rumours after all.

May 9. – All doubts removed. Tents begin to spring up with the suddenness of mushrooms in fields below Berkhamsted Place.

May 18, LIBERATION DAY. – Bade a facetious goodbye to my billets; response lacking in *bonhomie*.

May 19. – House delightfully quiet. Presented caller of unkempt appearance at back door with remains of pair of military boots, three empty shaving-stick tins, and a couple of partially bald tooth-brushes.

May 21. – In afternoon went round and looked at camp. Came home smiling, and went to favourite seat in garden to smoke. Discovered Private Early lying on it fast asleep. Went to study. Private Merited at table writing long and well-reasoned letter to his tailor. As he said he could never write properly with anybody else in the room, left him and went to bathroom. Door locked. Peevish but familiar voice, with a Scotch accent, asked me what I wanted; also complained of temperature of water.

May 22. – After comparing notes with neighbours, feel deeply grateful to Q.M.S. Beddem for sending me the six best men in the corps.

July 15. – Feel glad to have been associated, however remotely and humbly, with a corps, the names of whose members appear on the Roll of Honour of every British regiment.

6

THE CONVERT

Mr. Purnip took the arm of the new recruit and hung over him almost tenderly as they walked along; Mr. Billing, with a look of conscious virtue on his jolly face, listened with much satisfaction to his friend's compliments.

"It's such an example," said the latter. "Now we've got you the others will follow like sheep. You will be a bright lamp in the darkness."

"Wot's good enough for me *ought* to be good enough for them," said Mr. Billing modestly. "They'd better not let me catch—"

"*H'sh! H'sh!*" breathed Mr. Purnip, tilting his hat and wiping his bald, benevolent head.

"I forgot," said the other, with something like a sigh. "No more fighting; but suppose somebody hits me?"

"Turn the other cheek," replied Mr. Purnip. "They won't hit that; and when they see you standing there smiling at them—"

"After being hit?" interrupted Mr. Billing.

"After being hit," assented the other, "they'll be ashamed of themselves, and it'll hurt them more than if you struck them."

"Let's 'ope so," said the convert; "but it don't sound reasonable. I can hit a man pretty 'ard. Not that I'm bad-tempered, mind you; a bit quick, p'r'aps. And, after all, a good smack in the jaw saves any amount of argufying."

Mr. Purnip smiled, and, as they walked along, painted a glowing picture of the influence to be wielded by a first-class fighting man who refused to fight. It was a rough neighbourhood, and he recognised with sorrow that more respect was paid to a heavy fist than to a noble intellect or a loving heart.

"And you combine them all," he said, patting his companion's arm.

Mr. Billing smiled. "You ought to know best," he said modestly.

"You'll be surprised to find how easy it is," continued Mr. Purnip. "You will go from strength to strength. Old habits will disappear, and you will hardly know you have lost them. In a few months' time you will probably be wondering what you could ever have seen in beer, for example."

"I thought you said you didn't want me to give up beer?" said the other.

"We don't," said Mr. Purnip. "I mean that as you grow in stature you will simply lose the taste for it."

Mr. Billing came to a sudden full stop. "D'ye mean I shall lose my liking for a drop o' beer without being able to help myself?" he demanded in an anxious voice.

Mr. Purnip coughed.

"Of course, it doesn't happen in every case," he said hastily.

Mr. Billing's features relaxed. "Well, let's 'ope I shall be one of the fortunate ones," he said simply. "I can put up with a good deal, but when it comes to beer—"

"We shall see," said the other, smiling. "We don't want to interfere with anybody's comfort; we want to make them happier, that's all. A little more kindness between man and man; a little more consideration for each other; a little more brightness in dull lives."

He paused at the corner of the street, and, with a hearty handshake, went off. Mr. Billing, a prey to somewhat mixed emotions, continued on his way home. The little knot of earnest men and women who had settled in the district to spread light and culture had been angling for him for some time. He wondered, as he walked, what particular bait it was that had done the mischief.

"They've got me at last," he remarked, as he opened the house-door and walked into his small kitchen. "I couldn't say 'no' to Mr. Purnip."

"Wish 'em joy," said Mrs. Billing briefly. "Did you wipe your boots?"

Her husband turned without a word, and, retreating to the mat, executed a prolonged double-shuffle.

"You needn't wear it out," said the surprised Mrs. Billing.

"We've got to make people 'appier," said her husband seriously; "be kinder to 'em, and brighten up their dull lives a bit. That's wot Mr. Purnip says."

"You'll brighten 'em up all right," declared Mrs. Billing with a sniff. "I shan't forget last Tuesday week—no, not if I live to be a hundred. You'd ha' brightened up the police-station if I 'adn't got you home just in the nick of time."

Her husband, who was by this time busy under the scullery tap, made no reply. He came from it spluttering, and seizing a small towel, stood in the doorway burnishing his face and regarding his wife with a smile which Mr. Purnip himself could not have surpassed. He sat down to supper, and between bites explained in some detail the lines on which his future life was to be run. As an earnest of good faith, he consented, after a short struggle, to a slip of oilcloth for the passage; a pair of vases for the front room; and a new and somewhat expensive corn-cure for Mrs. Billing.

"And let's 'ope you go on as you've begun," said that gratified lady. "There's something in old Purnip after all. I've been worrying you for months for that oilcloth. Are you going to help me wash up? Mr. Purnip would."

Mr. Billing appeared not to hear, and, taking up his cap, strolled slowly in the direction of the "Blue Lion." It was a beautiful summer evening, and his bosom swelled as he thought of the improvements that a little brotherliness might exact in Elk Street. Engrossed in such ideas, it almost hurt him to find that, as he entered the door of the "Blue Lion," two gentlemen, forgetting all about their beer, disappeared through the other.

"Wot 'ave they run away like that for?" he demanded, looking round. "I wouldn't hurt 'em."

"Depends on wot you call hurting, Joe," said a friend.

Mr. Billing shook his head. "They've no call to be afraid of me," he said gravely. "I wouldn't hurt a fly; I've got a new 'art."

"A new wot?" inquired his friend, staring.

"A new 'art," repeated the other. "I've given up fighting and swearing, and drinking too much. I'm going to lead a new life and do all the good I can; I'm going—"

"Glory! Glory!" ejaculated a long, thin youth, and, making a dash for the door, disappeared.

"He'll know me better in time," said Mr. Billing. "Why, I wouldn't hurt a fly. I want to do good to people; not to hurt 'em. I'll have a pint," he added, turning to the bar.

"Not here you won't," said the landlord, eyeing him coldly.

"Why not?" demanded the astonished Mr. Billing.

"You've had all you ought to have already," was the reply. "And there's one thing I'll swear to—you ain't had it 'ere."

"I haven't 'ad a drop pass my lips—" began the outraged Mr. Billing.

"Yes, I know," said the other wearily, as he shifted one or two glasses and wiped the counter; "I've heard it all before, over and over again. Mind you, I've been in this business thirty years, and if I don't know when a man's had his whack, and a drop more, nobody does. You get off 'ome and ask your missis to make you a nice cup o' good strong tea, and then get up to bed and sleep it off."

"I dare say," said Mr. Billing, with cold dignity, as he paused at the door—"I dare say I may give up beer altogether."

He stood outside pondering over the unforeseen difficulties attendant upon his new career, moving a few inches to one side as Mr. Ricketts, a foe of long standing, came towards the public-house, and, halting a yard or two away, eyed him warily.

"Come along," said Mr. Billing, speaking somewhat loudly for the benefit of the men in the bar; "I shan't hurt you; my fighting days are over."

"Yes, I dessay," replied the other, edging away.

"It's all right, Bill," said a mutual friend, through the half-open door; "he's got a new 'art."

Mr. Ricketts looked perplexed. "'Art disease, d'ye mean?" he inquired hopefully. "*Can't* he fight no more?"

"A new 'art," said Mr. Billing. "It's as strong as ever it was, but it's changed—brother."

"If you call me 'brother' agin I'll give you something for yourself, and chance it," said Mr. Ricketts ferociously. "I'm a pore man, but I've got my pride."

Mr. Billing, with a smile charged with brotherly love, leaned his left cheek towards him. "Hit it," he said gently.

"Give it a smack and run, Bill," said the voice of a well-wisher inside.

"There'd be no need for 'im to run," said Mr. Billing. "I wouldn't hit 'im back for anything. I should turn the other cheek."

"Whaffor?" inquired the amazed Mr. Ricketts.

"For another swipe," said Mr. Billing radiantly.

In the fraction of a second he got the first, and reeled back staggering. The onlookers from the bar came out hastily. Mr. Ricketts, somewhat pale, stood his ground.

"You see, I don't hit you," said Mr. Billing, with a ghastly attempt at a smile.

He stood rubbing his cheek gently, and, remembering Mr. Purnip's statements, slowly, inch by inch, turned the other in the direction of his adversary. The circuit was still incomplete when Mr. Ricketts, balancing himself carefully, fetched it a smash that nearly burst it. Mr. Billing, somewhat jarred by his contact with the pavement, rose painfully and confronted him.

"I've only got two cheeks, mind," he said slowly.

Mr. Ricketts sighed. "I wish you'd got a blinking dozen," he said wistfully. "Well, so long. Be good."

He walked into the "Blue Lion" absolutely free from that sense of shame which Mr. Purnip had predicted, and, accepting a pint from an admirer, boasted noisily of his exploit. Mr. Billing, suffering both mentally and physically, walked slowly home to his astonished wife.

"P'r'aps he'll be ashamed of hisself when 'e comes to think it over," he murmured, as Mrs. Billing, rendered almost perfect by practice, administered first aid.

"I s'pect he's crying his eyes out," she said with a sniff. "Tell me if that 'urts."

Mr. Billing told her, then, suddenly remembering himself, issued an expurgated edition.

"I'm sorry for the next man that 'its you," said his wife, as she drew back and regarded her handiwork.

"Well, you needn't be," said Mr. Billing, with dignity. "It would take more than a couple o' props in the jaw to make me alter my mind when I've made it up. You ought to know that by this time. Hurry up and finish. I want you to go to the corner and fetch me a pot."

"What, ain't you going out agin?" demanded his astonished wife.

Mr. Billing shook his head. "Somebody else might want to give me one," he said resignedly, "and I've 'ad about all I want tonight."

His face was still painful next morning, but as he sat at breakfast in the small kitchen he was able to refer to Mr. Ricketts in terms which were an eloquent testimony to Mr. Purnip's teaching. Mrs. Billing, unable to contain herself, wandered off into the front room with a duster.

"Are you nearly ready to go?" she inquired, returning after a short interval.

"Five minutes," said Mr. Billing, nodding. "I'll just light my pipe and then I'm off."

"'Cos there's two or three waiting outside for you," added his wife.

Mr. Billing rose. "Ho, is there?" he said, grimly, as he removed his coat and proceeded to roll up his shirt-sleeves. "I'll learn 'em. I'll give 'em something to wait for. I'll—"

His voice died away as he saw the triumph in his wife's face, and, drawing down his sleeves again, he took up his coat and stood eyeing her in genuine perplexity.

"Tell 'em I've gorn," he said, at last.

"And what about telling lies?" demanded his wife. "What would your Mr. Purnip say to that?"

"You do as you're told," exclaimed the harassed Mr. Billing. "*I'm* not going to tell 'em; it's you."

Mrs. Billing returned to the parlour, and, with Mr. Billing lurking in the background, busied herself over a china flower-pot that stood in the window, and turned an anxious eye upon three men waiting outside. After a glance or two she went to the door.

"Did you want to see my husband?" she inquired.

The biggest of the three nodded. "Yus," he said shortly.

"I'm sorry," said Mrs. Billing, "but he 'ad to go early this morning. Was it anything partikier?"

"Gorn?" said the other in disappointed tones. "Well, you tell 'im I'll see 'im later on."

He turned away, and, followed by the other two, walked slowly up the road. Mr. Billing, after waiting till the coast was clear, went off in the other direction.

He sought counsel of his friend and mentor that afternoon, and stood beaming with pride at the praise lavished upon him. Mr. Purnip's co-workers were no less enthusiastic than their chief; and various suggestions were made to Mr. Billing as to his behaviour in the unlikely event of further attacks upon his noble person.

He tried to remember the suggestions in the harassing days that followed; baiting Joe Billing becoming popular as a pastime from which no evil results need be feared. It was creditable to his fellow-citizens that most of them refrained from violence with a man who declined to hit back, but as a butt his success was assured. The night when a gawky lad of eighteen drank up his beer, and then invited him to step outside if he didn't like it, dwelt long in his memory. And Elk Street thrilled one evening at the sight of their erstwhile champion flying up the road hotly pursued by a foeman half his size. His explanation to his indignant wife that, having turned the other cheek the night before, he was in no mood for further punishment, was received in chilling silence.

"They'll soon get tired of it," he said hopefully; "and I ain't going to be beat by a lot of chaps wot I could lick with one 'and tied behind me. They'll get to understand in time; Mr. Purnip says so. It's a pity that you don't try and do some good yourself."

Mrs. Billing received the suggestion with a sniff; but the seed was sown. She thought the matter over in private, and came to the conclusion that, if her husband wished her to participate in good works, it was not for her to deny him. Hitherto her efforts in that direction had been promptly suppressed; Mr. Billing's idea being that if a woman looked after her home and her husband properly there should be neither time nor desire for anything else. His surprise on arriving home to tea on Saturday afternoon, and finding a couple of hard-working neighbours devouring his substance, almost deprived him of speech.

"Poor things," said his wife, after the guests had gone; "they did enjoy it. It's cheered 'em up wonderful. You and Mr. Purnip are quite right. I can see that now. You can tell him that it was you what put it into my 'art."

"Me? Why, I never dreamt o' such a thing," declared the surprised Mr. Billing. "And there's other ways of doing good besides asking a pack of old women in to tea."

"I know there is," said his wife. "All in good time," she added, with a faraway look in her eyes.

Mr. Billing cleared his throat, but nothing came of it. He cleared it again.

"I couldn't let you do all the good," said his wife hastily. "It wouldn't be fair. I must help."

Mr. Billing lit his pipe noisily, and then took it out into the backyard and sat down to think over the situation. The ungenerous idea that his wife was making goodness serve her own ends was the first that occurred to him.

His suspicions increased with time. Mrs. Billing's good works seemed to be almost entirely connected with hospitality. True, she had entertained Mr. Purnip and one of the ladies from the Settlement to tea, but that only riveted his bonds more firmly. Other visitors included his sister-in-law, for whom he had a great distaste, and some of the worst-behaved children in the street.

"It's only high spirits," said Mrs. Billing; "all children are like that. And I do it to help the mothers."

"And 'cos you like children," said her husband, preserving his good humour with an effort.

There was a touch of monotony about the new life, and the good deeds that accompanied it, which, to a man of ardent temperament, was apt to pall. And Elk Street, instead of giving him the credit which was his due, preferred to ascribe the change in his behaviour to what they called being "a bit barmy on the crumpet."

He came home one evening somewhat dejected, brightening up as he stood in the passage and inhaled the ravishing odours from the kitchen. Mrs. Billing, with a trace of nervousness somewhat unaccountable in view of the excellent quality of the repast provided, poured him out a glass of beer, and passed flattering comment upon his appearance.

"Wot's the game?" he inquired.

"Game?" repeated his wife, in a trembling voice. "Nothing. 'Ow do you find that steakpudding? I thought of giving you one every Wednesday."

Mr. Billing put down his knife and fork and sat regarding her thoughtfully. Then he pushed back his chair suddenly, and, a picture of consternation and wrath, held up his hand for silence.

"W-w-wot is it?" he demanded. "A cat?"

Mrs. Billing made no reply, and her husband sprang to his feet as a long, thin wailing sounded through the house. A note of temper crept into it and strengthened it.

"*Wot is it?*" demanded Mr. Billing again.

"It's—it's Mrs. Smith's Charlie," stammered his wife.

"In—in *my* bedroom?" exclaimed her husband in incredulous accents. "Wot's it doing there?"

"I took it for the night," said his wife hurriedly. "Poor thing, what with the others being ill she's 'ad a dreadful time, and she said if I'd take Charlie for a few—for a night, she might be able to get some sleep."

Mr. Billing choked. "And wot about my sleep?" he shouted. "Chuck it outside at once. D'ye hear me?"

His words fell on empty air, his wife having already sped upstairs to pacify Master Smith by a rhythmical and monotonous thumping on the back. Also she lifted up a thin and not particularly sweet voice and sang to him. Mr. Billing, finishing his supper in indignant silence, told himself grimly that he was "beginning to have enough of it."

He spent the evening at the "Charlton Arms," and, returning late, went slowly and heavily up to bed. In the light of a shaded candle he saw a small, objectionable-looking infant fast asleep on two chairs by the side of the bed.

"*H'sh!*" said his wife in a thrilling whisper. "He's just gone off."

"D'ye mean I mustn't open my mouth in my own bedroom?" demanded the indignant man loudly.

"*H'sh!*" said his wife again.

It was too late. Master Smith, opening first one eye and then the other, finished by opening his mouth. The noise was appalling.

"*H'sh! H'sh!*" repeated Mrs. Billing as her husband began to add to the noise. "Don't wake 'im right up."

"Right up?" repeated the astonished man. "*Right up?* Why, is he doing this in 'is sleep?"

He subsided into silence, and, undressing with stealthy care, crept into bed and lay there, marvelling at his self-control. He was a sound sleeper, but six times at least he was awakened by Mrs. Billing slipping out of bed—regardless of draughts to her liege lord—and marching up and down the room with the visitor in her arms. He rose in the morning and dressed in ominous silence.

"I 'ope he didn't disturb you," said his wife anxiously.

"You've done it," replied Mr. Billing. "You've upset everything now. Since I joined the Purnip lot everybody's took advantage of me; now I'm going to get some of my own back. You wouldn't ha' dreamt of behaving like this a few weeks ago."

"Oh, Joe," said his wife entreatingly; "and everybody's been so happy!"

"Except me," retorted Joe Billing. "You come down and get my breakfast ready. If I start early I shall catch Mr. Bill Ricketts on 'is way to work. And mind, if I find that steam-orgin 'ere when I come 'ome tonight you'll hear of it."

He left the house with head erect and the light of battle in his eyes, and, meeting Mr. Ricketts at the corner, gave that justly aggrieved gentleman the surprise of his life. Elk Street thrilled to the fact that Mr. Billing had broken out again, and spoke darkly of what the evening might bring forth. Curious eyes followed his progress as he returned home from work, and a little later on the news was spread abroad that he was out and paying off old scores with an ardour that nothing could withstand.

"And wot about your change of 'art?" demanded one indignant matron, as her husband reached home five seconds ahead of Mr. Billing and hid in the scullery.

"It's changed agin," said Mr. Billing simply.

He finished the evening in the "Blue Lion," where he had one bar almost to himself, and, avoiding his wife's reproachful glance when he arrived home, procured some warm water and began to bathe his honourable scars.

"Mr. Purnip 'as been round with another gentleman," said his wife.

Mr. Billing said "Oh!"

"Very much upset they was, and 'ope you'll go and see them," she continued.

Mr. Billing said "Oh!" again; and, after thinking the matter over, called next day at the Settlement and explained his position.

"It's all right for gentlemen like you," he said civilly. "But a man like me can't call his soul 'is own—or even 'is bedroom. Everybody takes advantage of 'im. Nobody ever gives *you* a punch, and as for putting babies in your bedroom, they wouldn't dream of it."

He left amid expressions of general regret, turning a deaf ear to all suggestions about making another start, and went off exulting in his freedom.

His one trouble was Mr. Purnip, that estimable gentleman, who seemed to have a weird gift of meeting him at all sorts of times and places, never making any allusion to his desertion, but showing quite clearly by his manner that he still hoped for the return of the wanderer. It was awkward for a man of sensitive disposition, and Mr. Billing, before entering a street, got into the habit of peering round the corner first.

He pulled up suddenly one evening as he saw his tenacious friend, accompanied by a lady-member, some little distance ahead. Then he sprang forward with fists clenched as a passerby, after scowling at Mr. Purnip, leaned forward and deliberately blew a mouthful of smoke into the face of his companion.

Mr. Billing stopped again and stood gaping with astonishment. The aggressor was getting up from the pavement, while Mr. Purnip, in an absolutely correct attitude, stood waiting for him. Mr. Billing in a glow of delight edged forward, and, with a few other fortunates, stood by watching one of the best fights that had ever been seen in the district. Mr. Purnip's footwork was excellent, and the way he timed his blows made Mr. Billing's eyes moist with admiration.

It was over at last. The aggressor went limping off, and Mr. Purnip, wiping his bald head, picked up his battered and dusty hat from the roadway and brushed it on his sleeve. He turned with a start and a blush to meet the delighted gaze of Mr. Billing.

"I'm ashamed of myself," he murmured brokenly—"ashamed."

"Ashamed!" exclaimed the amazed Mr. Billing. "Why, a pro couldn't ha' done better."

"Such an awful example," moaned the other. "All my good work here thrown away."

"Don't you believe it, sir," said Mr. Billing earnestly. "As soon as this gets about you'll get more members than you want a'most. I'm coming back, for one."

Mr. Purnip turned and grasped his hand.

"I understand things now," said Mr. Billing, nodding sagely. "Turning the other cheek's all right so long as you don't do it always. If you don't let 'em know whether you are going to turn the other cheek or knock their blessed heads off, it's all right. 'Arf the trouble in the world is caused by letting people know too much."

7

HUSBANDRY

Dealing with a man, said the night-watchman thoughtfully, is as easy as a teetotaller walking along a nice wide pavement; dealing with a woman is like the same teetotaller, arter four or five whiskies, trying to get up a step that ain't there. If a man can't get 'is own way he eases 'is mind with a little nasty language, and then forgets all about it; if a woman can't get 'er own way she flies into a temper and reminds you of something you oughtn't to ha' done ten years ago. Wot a woman would do whose 'usband had never done anything wrong I can't think.

I remember a young feller telling me about a row he 'ad with 'is wife once. He 'adn't been married long and he talked as if the way she carried on was unusual. Fust of all, he said, she spoke to 'im in a cooing sort o' voice and pulled his moustache, then when he wouldn't give way she worked herself up into a temper and said things about 'is sister. Arter which she went out o' the room and banged the door so hard it blew down a vase off the fireplace. Four times she came back to tell 'im other things she 'ad thought of, and then she got so upset she 'ad to go up to bed and lay down instead of getting his tea. When that didn't do no good she refused her food, and when 'e took her up toast and tea she wouldn't look at it. Said she wanted to die. He got quite uneasy till 'e came 'ome the next night and found the best part of a loaf o' bread, a quarter o' butter, and a couple o' chops he 'ad got in for 'is supper had gorn; and then when he said 'e was glad she 'ad got 'er appetite back she turned round and said that he grudged 'er the food she ate.

And no woman ever owned up as 'ow she was wrong; and the more you try and prove it to 'em the louder they talk about something else. I know wot I'm talking about because a woman made a mistake about me once, and though she was proved to be in the wrong, and it was years ago, my missus shakes her 'ead about it to this day.

It was about eight years arter I 'ad left off going to sea and took up night-watching. A beautiful summer evening it was, and I was sitting by the gate smoking a pipe till it should be time to light up, when I noticed a woman who 'ad just passed turn back and stand staring at me. I've 'ad that sort o' thing before, and I went on smoking and looking straight in front of me. Fat, middle-aged woman she was, wot 'ad lost her good looks and found others. She stood there staring and staring, and by and by she tries a little cough.

I got up very slow then, and, arter looking all round at the evening, without seeing 'er, I was just going to step inside and shut the wicket, when she came closer.

"Bill!" she ses, in a choking sort o' voice. "*Bill!*"

I gave her a look that made her catch 'er breath, and I was just stepping through the wicket, when she laid hold of my coat and tried to hold me back.

"Do you know wot you're a-doing of?" I ses, turning on her.

"Oh, Bill, dear," she ses, "don't talk to me like that. Do you want to break my 'art? Arter all these years!"

She pulled out a dirt-coloured pocket-'ankercher and stood there dabbing her eyes with it. One eye at a time she dabbed, while she looked at me reproachful with the other. And arter eight dabs, four to each eye, she began to sob as if her 'art would break.

"Go away," I ses, very slow. "You can't stand making that noise outside my wharf. Go away and give somebody else a treat."

Afore she could say anything the potman from "The Tiger," a nasty ginger-'aired little chap that nobody liked, come by and stopped to pat her on the back.

"There, there, don't take on, mother," he ses. "Wot's he been a-doing to you?"

"You get off 'ome," I ses, losing my temper. "Wot d'ye mean trying to drag me into it? I've never seen the woman afore in my life."

"Oh, Bill!" ses the woman, sobbing louder than ever. "Oh! Oh! Oh!"

"'Ow does she know your name, then?" ses the little beast of a potman.

I didn't answer him. I might have told 'im that there's about five million Bills in England, but I didn't. I stood there with my arms folded acrost my chest, and looked at him, superior.

"Where 'ave you been all this long, long time?" she ses, between her sobs. "Why did you leave your happy 'ome and your children wot loved you?"

The potman let off a whistle that you could have 'eard acrost the river, and as for me, I thought I should ha' dropped. To have a woman standing sobbing and taking my character away like that was a'most more than I could bear.

"Did he run away from you?" ses the potman.

"Ye-ye-yes," she ses. "He went off on a v'y'ge to China over nine years ago, and that's the last I saw of 'im till tonight. A lady friend o' mine thought she reckernised 'im yesterday, and told me."

"I shouldn't cry over 'im," ses the potman, shaking his 'ead: "he ain't worth it. If I was you I should just give 'im a bang or two over the 'ead with my umberella, and then give 'im in charge."

I stepped inside the wicket—backwards—and then I slammed it in their faces, and, putting the key in my pocket, walked up the wharf I knew it was no good standing out there argufying. I felt sorry for the pore thing in a way. If she really thought I was her 'usband, and she 'ad lost me I put one or two things straight and then, for the sake of distracting my mind, I 'ad a word or two with the skipper of the *John Henry*, who was leaning against the side of his ship, smoking.

"Wot's that tapping noise?" he ses, all of a sudden. "'Ark!"

I knew wot it was. It was the handle of that umberella 'ammering on the gate. I went cold all over, and then when I thought that the potman was most likely encouraging 'er to do it I began to boil.

"Somebody at the gate," ses the skipper.

"Aye, aye," I ses. "I know all about it."

I went on talking until at last the skipper asked me whether he was wandering in 'is mind, or whether I was. The mate came up from the cabin just then, and o' course *he* 'ad to tell me there was somebody knocking at the gate.

"Ain't you going to open it?" ses the skipper, staring at me.

"Let 'em ring," I ses, off-hand.

The words was 'ardly out of my mouth afore they did ring, and if they 'ad been selling muffins they couldn't ha' kept it up harder. And all the time the umberella was doing rat-a-tat tats on the gate, while a voice—much too loud for the potman's—started calling out: "Watchman ahoy!"

"They're calling you, Bill," ses the skipper.

"I ain't deaf," I ses, very cold.

"Well, I wish I was," ses the skipper. "It's fair making my ear ache. Why the blazes don't you do your dooty, and open the gate?"

"You mind your bisness and I'll mind mine," I ses. "I know wot I'm doing. It's just some silly fools 'aving a game with me, and I'm not going to encourage 'em."

"Game with you?" ses the skipper. "Ain't they got anything better than that to play with? Look 'ere, if you don't open that gate, I will."

"It's nothing to do with you," I ses. "You look arter your ship and I'll look arter my wharf. See? If you don't like the noise, go down in the cabin and stick your 'ead in a biscuit-bag."

To my surprise he took the mate by the arm and went, and I was just thinking wot a good thing it wos to be a bit firm with people sometimes, when they came back dressed up in their coats and bowler hats and climbed on to the wharf.

"Watchman!" ses the skipper in a hoity-toity sort o' voice, "*me* and the mate is going as far as Aldgate for a breath o' fresh air. Open the gate."

I gave him a look that might ha' melted a 'art of stone, and all it done to 'im was to make 'im laugh.

"Hurry up," he ses. "It a'most seems to me that there's somebody ringing the bell, and you can let them in same time as you let us out. Is it the bell, or is it my fancy, Joe?" he ses, turning to the mate.

They marched on in front of me with their noses cocked in the air, and all the time the noise at the gate got worse and worse. So far as I could make out, there was quite a crowd outside, and I stood there with the key in the lock, trembling all over. Then I unlocked it very careful, and put my hand on the skipper's arm.

"Nip out quick," I ses in a whisper.

"I'm in no hurry," ses the skipper. "Here! Halloa, wot's up?"

It was like opening the door at a theatre, and the fust one through was that woman, shoved behind by the potman. Arter 'im came a carman, two big 'ulking brewers' draymen, a little scrap of a woman with 'er bonnet cocked over one eye, and a couple of dirty little boys.

"Wot is it?" ses the skipper, shutting the wicket behind 'em. "A beanfeast?"

"This lady wants her 'usband," ses the potman, pointing at me. "He run away from her nine years ago, and now he says he 'as never seen 'er before. He ought to be 'ung."

"Bill," ses the skipper, shaking his silly 'ead at me. "I can 'ardly believe it."

"It's all a pack o' silly lies," I ses, firing up.

"She's made a mistake."

"She made a mistake when she married you," ses the thin little woman. "If I was in 'er shoes I'd take 'old of you and tear you limb from limb."

"I don't want to hurt 'im, ma'am," ses the other woman. "I on'y want him to come 'ome to me and my five. Why, he's never seen the youngest, little Annie. She's as like 'im as two peas."

"Pore little devil," ses the carman.

"Look here!" I ses, "you clear off. All of you. 'Ow dare you come on to my wharf? If you aren't gone in two minutes I'll give you all in charge."

"Who to?" ses one of the draymen, sticking his face into mine. "You go 'ome to your wife and kids: Go on now, afore I put up my 'ands to you."

"That's the way to talk to 'im," ses the potman, nodding at 'em.

They all began to talk to me then and tell me wot I was to do, and wot they would do if I didn't. I couldn't get a word in edgeways. When I reminded the mate that when he was up in London 'e always passed himself off as a single man, 'e wouldn't listen; and when I asked the skipper whether 'is pore missus was blind, he on'y went on shouting at the top of 'is voice. It on'y showed me 'ow anxious most people are that everybody else should be good.

I thought they was never going to stop, and, if it 'adn't been for a fit of coughing, I don't believe that the scraggy little woman *could* ha' stopped. Arter one o' the draymen 'ad saved her life and spoilt 'er temper by patting 'er on the back with a hand the size of a leg o' mutton, the carman turned to me and told me to tell the truth, if it choked me.

"I have told you the truth," I ses. "She ses I'm her 'usband and I say I ain't. 'Ow's she going to prove it? Why should you believe her, and not me?"

"*She's* got a truthful face," ses the carman.

"Look here!" ses the skipper, speaking very slow, "I've got an idea wot'll settle it p'raps. You get outside," he ses, turning sharp on the two little boys.

One o' the draymen 'elped 'em to go out, and arf a minute arterwards a stone came over the gate and cut the potman's lip open. Boys will be boys.

"Now!" ses the skipper, turning to the woman and smiling with conceitedness. "Had your 'usband got any marks on 'im? Birthmark, or moles, or anything of that sort?"

"I'm sure he *is* my 'usband," ses the woman, dabbing her eyes.

"Yes, yes," ses the skipper, "but answer my question. If you can tell us any marks your 'usband had we can take Bill down into my cabin and—"

"You'll do WOT?" I ses in a loud voice.

"You speak when you're spoke to," ses the carman. "It's got nothing to do with you."

"No, he ain't got no birthmarks," ses the woman, speaking very slow—and I could see she was afraid of making a mistake and losing me—but he's got tattoo marks. He's got a mermaid tattooed on 'im."

"Where?" ses the skipper, a'most jumping.

I 'eld my breath. Five sailormen out of ten have been tattooed with mermaids, and I was one of 'em. When she spoke agin I thought I should ha' dropped.

"On 'is right arm," she ses, "unless he's 'ad it rubbed off."

"You can't rub out tattoo marks," ses the skipper.

They all stood looking at me as if they was waiting for something. I folded my arms—tight—arid stared back at 'em.

"If you ain't this lady's 'usband," ses the skipper, turning to me, "you can take off your coat and prove it."

"And if you don't we'll take it off for you," ses the carman, coming a bit closer.

Arter that things 'appened so quick, I hardly knew whether I was standing on my 'ead or my heels. Both, I think. They was all on top o' me at once, and the next thing I can remember is sitting on the ground in my shirt sleeves listening to the potman, who was making a fearful fuss because somebody 'ad bit his ear arf off. My coat was ripped up the back, and one of the draymen was holding up my arm and showing them all the mermaid, while the other struck matches so as they could see better.

"That's your 'usband right enough," he ses to the woman. "Take 'im."

"P'raps she'll carry 'im 'ome," I ses, very fierce and sarcastic.

"And we don't want none of your lip," ses the carman, who was in a bad temper because he 'ad got a fearful kick on the shin from somewhere.

I got up very slow and began to put my coat on again, and twice I 'ad to tell that silly woman that when I wanted her 'elp I'd let 'er know. Then I 'eard slow, heavy footsteps in the road outside, and, afore any of 'em could stop me, I was calling for the police.

I don't like policemen as a rule; they're too inquisitive, but when the wicket was pushed open and I saw a face with a helmet on it peeping in, I felt quite a liking for 'em.

"Wot's up?" ses the policeman, staring 'ard at my little party.

They all started telling 'im at once, and I should think if the potman showed him 'is ear once he showed it to 'im twenty times. He lost his temper and pushed it away at last, and the potman gave a 'owl that set my teeth on edge. I waited till they was all finished, and the policeman trying to get 'is hearing back, and then I spoke up in a quiet way and told 'im to clear them all off my wharf.

"They're trespassing," I ses, "all except the skipper and mate here. They belong to a little washtub that's laying alongside, and they're both as 'armless as they look."

It's wonderful wot a uniform will do. The policeman just jerked his 'ead and said "outside," and the men went out like a flock of sheep. The on'y man that said a word was the carman, who was in such a hurry that 'e knocked his bad shin against my foot as 'e went by. The thin little woman was passed out by the policeman in the middle of a speech she was making, and he was just going for the other, when the skipper stopped 'im.

"This lady is coming on my ship," he ses, puffing out 'is chest.

I looked at 'im, and then I turned to the policeman. "So long as she goes off my wharf, I don't mind where she goes," I ses. "The skipper's goings-on 'ave got nothing to do with me."

"Then she can foller him 'ome in the morning," ses the skipper. "Good night, watchman."

Him and the mate 'elped the silly old thing to the ship, and, arter I 'ad been round to the "Bear's Head" and fetched a pint for the policeman, I locked up and sat down to think things out; and the more I thought the worse they seemed. I've 'eard people say that if you have a clear conscience nothing can hurt you. They didn't know my missus.

I got up at last and walked on to the jetty, and the woman, wot was sitting on the deck of the *John Henry*, kept calling out: "Bill!" like a sick baa-lamb crying for its ma. I went back, and 'ad four pints at the "Bear's Head," but it didn't seem to do me any good and at last I went and sat down in the office to wait for morning.

It came at last, a lovely morning with a beautiful sunrise; and that woman sitting up wide awake, waiting to foller me 'ome. When I opened the gate at six o'clock she was there with the mate and the skipper, waiting, and when I left at five minutes past she was trotting along beside me.

Twice I stopped and spoke to 'er, but it was no good. Other people stopped too, and I 'ad to move on agin; and every step was bringing me nearer to my house and the missus.

I turned into our street, arter passing it three times, and the first thing I saw was my missus standing on the doorstep 'aving a few words with the lady next door. Then she 'appened to look up and see us, just as that silly woman was trying to walk arm-in-arm.

Twice I knocked her 'and away, and then, right afore my wife and the party next door, she put her arm round my waist. By the time I got to the 'ouse my legs was trembling so I could hardly stand, and when I got into the passage I 'ad to lean up against the wall for a bit.

"Keep 'er out," I ses.

"Wot do you want?" ses my missus, trembling with passion. "Wot do you think you're doing?"

"I want my 'usband—Bill," ses the woman.

My missus put her 'and to her throat and came in without a word, and the woman follered 'er. If I hadn't kept my presence o' mind and shut the door two or three more would 'ave come in too.

I went into the kitchen about ten minutes arterwards to see 'ow they was getting on. Besides which they was both calling for me.

"Now then!" ses my missus, who was leaning up against the dresser with 'er arms folded, "wot 'ave you got to say for yourself walking in as bold as brass with this hussy?"

"Bill!" ses the woman, "did you hear wot she called me?"

She spoke to me like that afore my wife, and in two minutes they was at it, hammer and tongs.

Fust of all they spoke about each other, and then my missus started speaking about me. She's got a better memory than most people, because she can remember things that never 'appened, and every time I coughed she turned on me like a tiger.

"And as for you," she ses, turning to the woman, "if you did marry 'im you should ha' made sure that he 'adn't got a wife already."

"He married me fust," ses the woman.

"When?" ses my wife. "Wot was the date?"

"Wot was the date you married 'im?" ses the other one.

They stood looking at each other like a couple o' game-cocks, and I could see as plain as a pikestaff 'ow frightened both of 'em was o' losing me.

"Look here!" I ses at last, to my missus, "talk sense. 'Ow could I be married to 'er? When I was at sea I was at sea, and when I was ashore I was with you."

"Did you use to go down to the ship to see 'im off?" ses the woman.

"No," ses my wife. "I'd something better to do."

"Neither did I," ses the woman. "P'r'aps that's where we both made a mistake."

"You get out of my 'ouse!" ses my missus, very sudden. "Go on, afore I put you out."

"Not without my Bill," ses the woman. "If you lay a finger on me I'll scream the house down."

"You brought her 'ere," ses my wife, turning to me, "now you can take 'er away?"

"I didn't bring 'er," I ses. "She follered me."

"Well, she can foller you agin," she ses. "Go on!" she ses, trembling all over. "Git out afore I start on you."

I was in such a temper that I daren't trust myself to stop. I just gave 'er one look, and then I drew myself up and went out. 'Alf the fools in our street was standing in front of the 'ouse, 'umming like bees, but I took no notice. I held my 'ead up and walked through them with that woman tailing arter me.

I was in such a state of mind that I went on like a man in a dream. If it *had* ha' been a dream I should ha' pushed 'er under an omnibus, but you can't do things like that in real life.

"Penny for your thoughts, Bill," she ses.

I didn't answer her.

"Why don't you speak to me?" she ses.

"You don't know wot you're asking for," I ses.

I was hungry and sleepy, and 'ow I was going to get through the day I couldn't think. I went into a pub and 'ad a couple o' pints o' stout and a crust o' bread and cheese for brekfuss. I don't know wot she 'ad, but when the barman tried to take for it out o' my money, I surprised 'im.

We walked about till I was ready to drop. Then we got to Victoria Park, and I 'ad no sooner got on to the grass than I laid down and went straight off to sleep. It was two o'clock when I woke, and, arter a couple o' pork-pies and a pint or two, I sat on a seat in the Park smoking, while she kep' dabbing 'er eyes agin and asking me to come 'ome.

At five o'clock I got up to go back to the wharf, and, taking no notice of 'er, I walked into the street and jumped on a bus that was passing. She jumped too, and, arter the conductor had 'elped 'er up off of 'er knees and taken her arms away from his waist, I'm blest if he didn't turn on me and ask me why I 'adn't left her at 'ome.

We got to the wharf just afore six. The *John Henry* 'ad gorn, but the skipper 'ad done all the 'arm he could afore he sailed, and, if I 'adn't kept my temper, I should ha' murdered arf a dozen of 'em.

The woman wanted to come on to the wharf, but I 'ad a word or two with one o' the foreman, who owed me arf-a-dollar, and he made that all right.

"We all 'ave our faults, Bill," he ses as 'e went out, "and I suppose she was better looking once upon a time?"

I didn't answer 'im. I shut the wicket arter 'im, quick, and turned the key, and then I went on with my work. For a long time everything was as quiet as the grave, and then there came just one little pull at the bell. Five minutes arterwards there was another.

I thought it was that woman, but I 'ad to make sure. When it came the third time I crept up to the gate.

"Hulloa!" I ses. "Who is it?"

"Me, darling," ses a voice I reckernised as the potman's. "Your missus wants to come in and sit down."

I could 'ear several people talking, and it seemed to me there was quite a crowd out there, and by and by that bell was going like mad. Then people started kicking the gate, and shouting, but I took no notice until, presently, it left off all of a sudden, and I 'eard a loud voice asking what it was all about. I suppose there was about fifty of 'em telling it at once, and then there was the sound of a fist on the gate.

"Who is it?" I ses.

"Police," ses the voice.

I opened the wicket then and looked out. A couple o' policemen was standing by the gate and arf the riff-raff of Wapping behind 'em.

"Wot's all this about?" ses one o' the policemen.

I shook my 'ead. "Ask me another," I ses.

"Your missus is causing a disturbance," he ses.

"She's not my missus," I ses, "she's a complete stranger to me."

"And causing a crowd to collect and refusing to go away," ses the other policeman.

"That's your business," I ses. "It's nothing to do with me."

They talked to each other for a moment, and then they spoke to the woman. I didn't 'ear wot she said, but I saw her shake her 'ead, and a'most direckly arterwards she was marching away between the two policemen with the crowd follering and advising 'er where to kick 'em.

I was a bit worried at fust—not about her—and then I begun to think that p'r'aps it was the best thing that could have 'appened.

I went 'ome in the morning with a load lifted off my mind; but I 'adn't been in the 'ouse two seconds afore my missus started to put it on agin. Fust of all she asked me 'ow I dared to come into the 'ouse, and then she wanted to know wot I meant by leaving her at 'ome and going out for the day with another woman.

"You told me to," I ses.

"Oh, yes," she ses, trembling with temper. "You always do wot I tell you, don't you? Always 'ave, especially when it's anything you like."

She fetched a bucket o' water and scrubbed the kitchen while I was having my brekfuss, but I kept my eye on 'er, and, the moment she 'ad finished, I did the perlite and emptied the bucket for 'er, to prevent mistakes.

I read about the case in the Sunday paper, and I'm thankful to say my name wasn't in it. All the magistrate done was to make 'er promise that she wouldn't do it again, and then he let 'er go. I should ha' felt more comfortable if he 'ad given 'er five years, but, as it turned out, it didn't matter. Her 'usband happened to read it, and, whether 'e was tired of living alone, or whether he was excited by 'earing that she 'ad got a little general shop, 'e went back to her.

The fust I knew about it was they came round to the wharf to see me. He 'ad been a fine-looking chap in 'is day, and even then 'e was enough like me for me to see 'ow she 'ad made the mistake; and all the time she was telling me 'ow it 'appened, he was looking me up and down and sniffing.

"'Ave you got a cold?" I ses at last.

"Wot's that got to do with you?" he ses. "Wot do you mean by walking out with my wife? That's wot I've come to talk about."

For a moment I thought that his bad luck 'ad turned 'is brain. "You've got it wrong," I ses, as soon as I could speak. "She walked out with me."

"'Cos she thought you was her 'usband," he ses, "but you didn't think you was me, did you?"

"'Course I didn't," I ses.

"Then 'ow dare you walk out with 'er?" he ses.

"Look 'ere!" I ses. "You get off 'ome as quick as you like. I've 'ad about enough of your family. Go on, hook it."

Afore I could put my 'ands up he 'it me hard in the mouth, and the next moment we was at it as 'ard as we could go. Nearly every time I hit 'im he wasn't there, and every time 'e hit me I wished I hadn't ha' been. When I said I had 'ad enough, 'e contradicted me and kept on, but he got tired of it at last, and, arter telling me wot he would do if I ever walked 'is wife out agin, they went off like a couple o' love-birds.

By the time I got 'ome next morning my eyes was so swelled up I could 'ardly see, and my nose wouldn't let me touch it. I was so done up I could 'ardly speak, but I managed to tell my missus about it arter I had 'ad a cup o' tea. Judging by her face anybody might ha' thought I was telling 'er something funny, and, when I ad finished, she looks up at the ceiling and ses:

"I 'ope it'll be a lesson to you," she ses.

8

FAMILY CARES

Mr. Jernshaw, who was taking the opportunity of a lull in business to weigh out pound packets of sugar, knocked his hands together and stood waiting for the order of the tall bronzed man who had just entered the shop—a well-built man of about forty—who was regarding him with blue eyes set in quizzical wrinkles.

"What, Harry!" exclaimed Mr. Jernshaw, in response to the wrinkles. "Harry Barrett!"

"That's me," said the other, extending his hand. "The rolling stone come home covered with moss."

Mr. Jernshaw, somewhat excited, shook hands, and led the way into the little parlour behind the shop.

"Fifteen years," said Mr. Barrett, sinking into a chair, "and the old place hasn't altered a bit."

"Smithson told me he had let that house in Webb Street to a Barrett," said the grocer, regarding him, "but I never thought of you. I suppose you've done well, then?"

Mr. Barrett nodded. "Can't grumble," he said modestly. "I've got enough to live on. Melbourne's all right, but I thought I'd come home for the evening of my life."

"Evening!" repeated his friend.

"Forty-three," said Mr. Barrett gravely. "I'm getting on."

"You haven't changed much," said the grocer, passing his hand through his spare grey whiskers. "Wait till you have a wife and seven youngsters. Why, boots alone—"

Mr. Barrett uttered a groan intended for sympathy. "Perhaps you could help me with the furnishing," he said slowly. "I've never had a place of my own before, and I don't know much about it."

"Anything I can do," said his friend. "Better not get much yet; you might marry, and my taste mightn't be hers."

Mr. Barrett laughed. "I'm not marrying," he said with conviction.

"Seen anything of Miss Prentice yet?" inquired Mr. Jernshaw.

"No," said the other, with a slight flush. "Why?"

"She's still single," said the grocer.

"What of it?" demanded Mr. Barrett with warmth. "What of it?"

"Nothing," said Mr. Jernshaw slowly. "Nothing; only I—"

"Well?" said the other, as he paused.

"I—there was an idea that you went to Australia to—to better your condition," murmured the grocer. "That—that you were not in a position to marry—that"

"Boy and girl nonsense," said Mr. Barrett sharply. "Why, it's fifteen years ago. I don't suppose I should know her if I saw her. Is her mother alive?"

"Rather!" said Mr. Jernshaw, with emphasis. "Louisa is something like what her mother was when you went away."

Mr. Barrett shivered.

"But you'll see for yourself," continued the other. "You'll have to go and see them. They'll wonder you haven't been before."

"Let 'em wonder," said the embarrassed Mr. Barrett. "I shall go and see all my old friends in their turn; casual-like. You might let 'em hear that I've been to see you before seeing them, and then, if they're thinking any nonsense, it'll be a hint. I'm stopping in town while the house is being decorated; next time I come down I'll call and see somebody else."

"That'll be another hint," assented Mr. Jernshaw. "Not that hints are much good to Mrs. Prentice."

"We'll see," said Mr. Barrett.

In accordance with his plan his return to his native town was heralded by a few short visits at respectable intervals. A sort of human butterfly, he streaked rapidly across one or two streets, alighted for half an hour to resume an old friendship, and then disappeared again. Having given at least half a dozen hints of this kind, he made a final return to Ramsbury and entered into occupation of his new house.

"It does you credit, Jernshaw," he said gratefully. "I should have made a rare mess of it without your help."

"It looks very nice," admitted his friend. "Too nice."

"That's all nonsense," said the owner irritably.

"All right," said Mr. Jernshaw. "I don't know the sex, then, that's all. If you think that you're going to keep a nice house like this all to yourself, you're mistaken. It's a *home;* and where there's a home a woman comes in, somehow."

Mr. Barrett grunted his disbelief.

"I give you four days," said Mr. Jernshaw.

As a matter of fact, Mrs. Prentice and her daughter came on the fifth. Mr. Barrett, who was in an easy chair, wooing slumber with a handkerchief over his head, heard their voices at the front door and the cordial invitation of his housekeeper. They entered the room as he sat hastily smoothing his rumpled hair.

"Good afternoon," he said, shaking hands.

Mrs. Prentice returned the greeting in a level voice, and, accepting a chair, gazed around the room.

"Nice weather," said Mr. Barrett.

"Very," said Mrs. Prentice.

"It's—it's quite a pleasure to see you again," said Mr. Barrett.

"We thought we should have seen you before," said Mrs. Prentice, "but I told Louisa that no doubt you were busy, and wanted to surprise her. I like the carpet; don't you, Louisa?"

Miss Prentice said she did.

"The room is nice and airy," said Mrs. Prentice, "but it's a pity you didn't come to me before deciding. I could have told you of a better house for the same money."

"I'm very well satisfied with this," said Mr. Barrett. "It's all *I* want."

"It's well enough," conceded Mrs. Prentice amiably. "And how have you been all these years?"

Mr. Barrett, with some haste, replied that his health and spirits had been excellent.

"You look well," said Mrs. Prentice. "Neither of you seems to have changed much," she added, looking from him to her daughter. "And I think you did quite well not to write. I think it was much the best."

Mr. Barrett sought for a question: a natural, artless question, that would neutralise the hideous suggestion conveyed by this remark, but it eluded him. He sat and gazed in growing fear at Mrs. Prentice.

"I—I couldn't write," he said at last, in desperation; "my wife—"

"Your *what?*" exclaimed Mrs. Prentice loudly.

"Wife," said Mr. Barrett, suddenly calm now that he had taken the plunge. "She wouldn't have liked it."

Mrs. Prentice tried to control her voice. "I never heard you were married!" she gasped. "Why isn't she here?"

"We couldn't agree," said the veracious Mr. Barrett. "She was very difficult; so I left the children with her and—"

"Chil—" said Mrs. Prentice, and paused, unable to complete the word.

"Five," said Mr. Barrett, in tones of resignation. "It was rather a wrench, parting with them, especially the baby. He got his first tooth the day I left."

The information fell on deaf ears. Mrs. Prentice, for once in her life thoroughly at a loss, sat trying to collect her scattered faculties. She had come out prepared for a hard job, but not an impossible one. All things considered, she took her defeat with admirable composure.

"I have no doubt it is much the best thing for the children to remain with their mother," she said, rising.

"Much the best," agreed Mr. Barrett.

"Whatever she is like," continued the old lady. "Are you ready, Louisa?"

Mr. Barrett followed them to the door, and then, returning to the room, watched, with glad eyes, their progress up the street.

"Wonder whether she'll keep it to herself?" he muttered.

His doubts were set at rest next day. All Ramsbury knew by then of his matrimonial complications, and seemed anxious to talk about them; complications which tended to increase until Mr. Barrett wrote out a list of his children's names and ages and learnt it off by heart.

Relieved of the attentions of the Prentice family, he walked the streets a free man; and it was counted to him for righteousness that he never said a hard word about his wife. She had her faults, he said, but they were many thousand miles away, and he preferred to forget them. And he added, with some truth, that he owed her a good deal.

For a few months he had no reason to alter his opinion. Thanks to his presence of mind, the Prentice family had no terrors for him. Heart-whole and fancy free, he led the easy life of a man of leisure, a condition of things suddenly upset by the arrival of Miss Grace Lindsay to take up a post at the elementary school. Mr. Barrett succumbed almost at once, and, after a few encounters in the street and meetings at mutual friends', went to unbosom himself to Mr. Jernshaw.

"What has she got to do with you?" demanded that gentleman.

"I—I'm rather struck with her," said Mr. Barrett.

"Struck with her?" repeated his friend sharply. "I'm surprised at you. You've no business to think of such things."

"Why not?" demanded Mr. Barrett, in tones that were sharper still.

"Why not?" repeated the other. "*Have you* forgotten your wife and children?"

Mr. Barrett, who, to do him justice, *had* forgotten, fell back in his chair and sat gazing at him, open-mouthed.

"You're in a false position—in a way," said Mr. Jernshaw sternly.

"False is no name for it," said Mr. Barrett, huskily. "What am I to do?"

"*Do?*" repeated the other, staring at him. "Nothing! Unless, perhaps, you send for your wife and children. I suppose, in any case, you would have to have the little ones if anything happened to her?"

Mr. Barrett grinned ruefully.

"Think it over," said Mr. Jernshaw.

"I will," said the other heartily.

He walked home deep in thought. He was a kindly man, and he spent some time thinking out the easiest death for Mrs. Barrett. He decided at last upon heart disease, and a fortnight later all Ramsbury knew of the letterfrom Australia conveying the mournful intelligence. It was generally agreed that the mourning and the general behaviour of the widower left nothing to be desired.

"She's at peace at last," he said, solemnly, to Jernshaw.

"I believe you killed her," said his friend.

Mr. Barrett started violently.

"I mean your leaving broke her heart," explained the other.

Mr. Barrett breathed easily again.

"It's your duty to look after the children," said Jernshaw firmly. "And I'm not the only one that thinks so."

"They are with their grandfather and grandmother," said Mr. Barrett.

Mr. Jernshaw sniffed.

"And four uncles and five aunts," added Mr. Barrett, triumphantly.

"Think how they would brighten up your house," said Mr. Jernshaw.

His friend shook his head. "It wouldn't be fair to their grandmother," he said decidedly. "Besides, Australia wants population."

He found, to his annoyance, that Mr. Jernshaw's statement that he was not alone in his views was correct. Public opinion seemed to expect the arrival of the children, and one citizen even went so far as to recommend a girl he knew, as nurse.

Ramsbury understood at last that his decision was final, and, observing his attentions to the new schoolmistress, flattered itself that it had discovered the reason. It is possible that Miss Lindsay shared their views, but if so she made no sign, and on the many occasions on which she met Mr. Barrett on her way to and from school greeted him with frank cordiality. Even when he referred to his loneliness, which he did frequently, she made no comment.

He went into half-mourning at the end of two months, and a month later bore no outward signs of his loss. Added to that his step was springy and his manner youthful. Miss Lindsay was twenty-eight, and he persuaded himself that, sexes considered, there was no disparity worth mentioning.

He was only restrained from proposing by a question of etiquette. Even a shilling book on the science failed to state the interval that should elapse between the death of one wife and the negotiations for another. It preferred instead to give minute instructions with regard to the eating of asparagus. In this dilemma he consulted Jernshaw.

"Don't know, I'm sure," said that gentleman; "besides, it doesn't matter."

"Doesn't matter?" repeated Mr. Barrett. "Why not?"

"Because I think Tillett is paying her attentions," was the reply. "He's ten years younger than you are, and a bachelor. A girl would naturally prefer him to a middle-aged widower with five children."

"In Australia," the other reminded him.

"Man for man, bachelor for bachelor," said Mr. Jernshaw, regarding him, "she might prefer you; as things are—"

"I shall ask her," said Mr. Barrett doggedly. "I was going to wait a bit longer, but if there's any chance of her wrecking her prospects for life by marrying that tailor's dummy it's my duty to risk it—for her sake. I've seen him talking to her twice myself, but I never thought he'd dream of such a thing."

Apprehension and indignation kept him awake half the night, but when he arose next morning it was with the firm resolve to put his fortune to the test that day. At four o'clock he changed his neck-tie for the third time, and at ten past sallied out in the direction of the school. He met Miss Lindsay just coming out, and, after a well-deserved compliment to the weather, turned and walked with her.

"I was hoping to meet you," he said slowly.

"Yes?" said the girl.

"I—I have been feeling rather lonely today," he continued.

"You often do," said Miss Lindsay guardedly.

"It gets worse and worse," said Mr. Barrett sadly.

"I think I know what is the matter with you," said the girl in a soft voice; "you have got nothing to do all day, and you live alone, except for your housekeeper."

Mr. Barrett assented with some eagerness, and stole a hopeful glance at her.

"You—you miss something," continued Miss Lindsay in a faltering voice.

"I do," said Mr. Barrett, with ardour.

"You miss"—the girl made an effort—"you miss the footsteps and voices of your little children."

Mr. Barrett stopped suddenly in the street, and then, with a jerk, went blindly on.

"I've never spoken of it before because it's your business, not mine," continued the girl. "I wouldn't have spoken now, but when you referred to your loneliness I thought perhaps you didn't realise the cause of it."

Mr. Barrett walked on in silent misery.

"Poor little motherless things!" said Miss Lindsay softly. "Motherless and—fatherless."

"Better for them," said Mr. Barrett, finding his voice at last.

"It almost looks like it," said Miss Lindsay with a sigh.

Mr. Barrett tried to think clearly, but the circumstances were hardly favourable. "Suppose," he said, speaking very slowly, "suppose I wanted to get married?"

Miss Lindsay started. "What again?" she said, with an air of surprise.

"How could I ask a girl to come and take over five children?"

"No woman that was worth having would let little children be sacrificed for her sake," said Miss Lindsay decidedly.

"Do you think anybody would marry me with five children?" demanded Mr. Barrett.

"She might," said the girl, edging away from him a little. "It depends on the woman.

"Would—you, for instance?" said Mr. Barrett desperately.

Miss Lindsay shrank still farther away. "I don't know; it would depend upon circumstances," she murmured.

"I will write and send for them," said Mr. Barrett significantly.

Miss Lindsay made no reply. They had arrived at her gate by this time, and, with a hurried handshake, she disappeared indoors. Mr. Barrett, somewhat troubled in mind, went home to tea.

He resolved, after a little natural hesitation, to drown the children, and reproached himself bitterly for not having disposed of them at the same time as their mother. Now he would have to go through another period of mourning and the consequent delay in pressing his suit. Moreover, he would have to allow a decent interval between his conversation with Miss Lindsay and their untimely end.

The news of the catastrophe arrived two or three days before the return of the girl from her summer holidays. She learnt it in the first half hour from her landlady, and sat in a dazed condition listening to a description of the grief-stricken father and the sympathy extended to him by his fellow-citizens. It appeared that nothing had passed his lips for two days.

"Shocking!" said Miss Lindsay briefly. "Shocking!"

An instinctive feeling that the right and proper thing to do was to nurse his grief in solitude kept Mr. Barrett out of her way for nearly a week. When she did meet him she received a limp handshake and a greeting in a voice from which all hope seemed to have departed.

"I am very sorry," she said, with a sort of measured gentleness.

Mr. Barrett, in his hushed voice, thanked her.

"I am all alone now," he said pathetically. "There is nobody now to care whether I live or die."

Miss Lindsay did not contradict him.

"How did it happen?" she inquired, after they had gone some distance in silence.

"They were out in a sailing-boat," said Mr. Barrett; "the boat capsized in a puff of wind, and they were all drowned."

"Who was in charge of them?" inquired the girl, after a decent interval.

"Boatman," replied the other.

"How did you hear?"

"I had a letter from one of my sisters-in-law, Charlotte," said Mr. Barrett. "A most affecting letter. Poor Charlotte was like a second mother to them. She'll never be the same woman again. Never!"

"I should like to see the letter," said Miss Lindsay musingly.

Mr. Barrett suppressed a start. "I should like to show it to you," he said, "but I'm afraid I have destroyed it. It made me shudder every time I looked at it."

"It's a pity," said the girl dryly. "I should have liked to see it. I've got my own idea about the matter. Are you sure she was very fond of them?"

"She lived only for them," said Mr. Barrett in a rapt voice.

"Exactly. I don't believe they are drowned at all," said Miss Lindsay suddenly. "I believe you have had all this terrible anguish for nothing. It's too cruel."

Mr. Barrett stared at her in anxious amazement.

"I see it all now," continued the girl. "Their Aunt Charlotte was devoted to them. She always had the fear that some day you would return and claim them, and to prevent that she invented the story of their death."

"Charlotte is the most truthful woman that ever breathed," said the distressed Mr. Barrett.

Miss Lindsay shook her head. "You are like all other honourable, truthful people," she said, looking at him gravely. "You can't imagine anybody else telling a falsehood. I don't believe you could tell one if you tried."

Mr. Barrett gazed about him with the despairing look of a drowning mariner.

"I'm certain I'm right," continued the girl. "I can see Charlotte exulting in her wickedness. *Why!*"

"What's the matter?" inquired Mr. Barrett, greatly worried.

"I've just thought of it," said Miss Lindsay. "She's told you that your children are drowned, and she has probably told them you are dead. A woman like that would stick at nothing to gain her ends."

"You don't know Charlotte," said Mr. Barrett feebly.

"I think I do," was the reply. "However, we'll make sure. I suppose you've got friends in Melbourne?"

"A few," said Mr. Barrett guardedly.

"Come down to the post office and cable to one of them."

Mr. Barrett hesitated. "I'll write," he said slowly. "It's an awkward thing to cable; and there's no hurry. I'll write to Tack Adams, I think."

"It's no good writing," said Miss Lindsay firmly. "You ought to know that."

"Why not?" demanded the other.

"Because, you foolish man," said the girl calmly, "before your letter got there, there would be one from Melbourne saying that he had been choked by a fishbone, or died of measles, or something of that sort."

Mr. Barrett, hardly able to believe his ears, stopped short and looked at her. The girl's eyes were moist with mirth and her lips trembling. He put out his hand and took her wrist in a strong grip.

"That's all right," he said, with a great gasp of relief. "*Phew!* At one time I thought I had lost you."

"By heart disease, or drowning?" inquired Miss Lindsay softly.

9

THE WINTER OFFENSIVE

N.B.—Having regard to the eccentricities of the Law of Libel it must be distinctly understood that the following does not refer to the distinguished officer, Lieut, Troup Horne, of the Inns of Court. Anybody trying to cause mischief between a civilian of eight stone and a soldier of seventeen by a statement to the contrary will hear from my solicitors.

Aug. 29, 1916.—We returned from the sea to find our house still our own, and the military still in undisputed possession of the remains of the grass in the fields of Berkhamsted Place. As in previous years, it was impossible to go in search of wild flowers without stumbling over sleeping members of the Inns of Court; but war is war, and we grumble as little as possible.

Sept. 28.—Unpleasant rumours to the effect that several members of the Inns of Court had attributed cases of curvature of the spine to sleeping on ground that had been insufficiently rolled. Also that they had been heard to smack their lips and speak darkly of feather beds. Respected neighbour of gloomy disposition said that if Pharaoh were still alive he could suggest an eleventh plague to him beside which frogs and flies were an afternoon's diversion.

Oct. 3.—Householders of Berkhamsted busy mending bedsteads broken by last year's billets, and buying patent taps for their beer barrels.

Oct. 15.—Informed that a representative of the Army wished to see me. Instead of my old friend Q.M.S. Beddem, who generally returns to life at this time of year, found that it was an officer of magnificent presence and two pips. A fine figure of a man, with a great resemblance to the late lamented Bismarck, minus the moustache and the three hairs on the top of the head. Asked him to be seated. He selected a chair that was all arms and legs and no hips to speak of and crushed himself into it. After which he unfastened his belt and "swelled wisibly afore my werry eyes." Said that his name was True Born and asked if it made any difference to me whether I had one officer or half a dozen men billeted on me. Said that he was the officer, and that as the rank and file were not allowed to pollute the same atmosphere, thought I should score. After a mental review of all I could remember of the *Weights and Measures Table*, accepted him. He bade a lingering farewell to the chair, and departed.

Oct. 16.—Saw Q.M.S. Beddem on the other side of the road and gave him an absolutely new thrill by crossing to meet him. Asked diffidently—as diffidently as he could, that is—how many men my house would hold. Replied eight—or ten at a pinch. He gave me a surprised and beaming smile and whipped out a huge notebook. Informed him with as much regret as I could put into a voice not always under perfect control, that I had already got an officer. Q.M.S., favouring me with a look very appropriate to the Devil's Own, turned on his heel and set off in pursuit of a lady-billetee, pulling up short on the threshold of the baby-linen shop in which she took refuge. Left him on guard with a Casabianca-like look on his face.

Nov. 1.—Lieut. True Born took up his quarters with us. Gave him my dressing-room for bedchamber. Was awakened several times in the night by what I took to be Zeppelins, flying low.

Nov. 2.—Lieut. True Born offered to bet me five pounds to twenty that the war would be over by 1922.

Nov. 3.—Offered to teach me auction bridge.

Nov. 4.—Asked me whether I could play "shove-ha'penny."

Nov. 10.—Lieut. True Born gave one of the regimental horses a riding lesson. Came home grumpy and went to bed early.

Nov. 13.—Another riding lesson. Overheard him asking one of the maids whether there was such a thing as a waterbed in the house.

Nov. 17.—Complained bitterly of horse-copers. Said that his poor mount was discovered to be suffering from saddle-soreness, broken wind, splints, weak hocks, and two bones of the neck out of place.

Dec. 9, 7 *p.m.*—One of last year's billets, Private Merited, on leave from a gunnery course, called to see me and to find out whether his old bed had improved since last year. Left his motorbike in the garage, and the smell in front of the dining-room window.

8 to 12 *p.m.*—Sat with Private Merited, listening to Lieut. True Born on the mistakes of Wellington.

12.5 *a.m.*—Rose to go to bed. Was about to turn out gas in hall when I discovered the lieutenant standing with his face to the wall playing pat-a-cake with it. Gave him three parts of a tumbler of brandy. Said he felt better and went upstairs. Arrived in his bedroom, he looked about him carefully, and then, with a superb sweep of his left arm, swept the best Chippendale looking-glass in the family off the dressing-table and dived face downwards to the floor, missing death and the corner of the chest of drawers by an inch.

12.15 *a.m.*—Rolled him on to his back and got his feet on the bed. They fell off again as soon as they were cleaner than the quilt. The lieutenant, startled by the crash, opened his eyes and climbed into bed unaided.

12.20 *a.m.*—Sent Private Merited for the M.O., Captain Geranium.

12.25 a.m.—Mixed a dose of brandy and castor oil in a tumbler. Am told it slips down like an oyster that way—bad oyster, I should think. Lieut. True Born jibbed. Reminded him that England expects that every man will take his castor oil. Reply unprintable. Apologised a moment later. Said that his mind was wandering and that he thought he was a colonel. Reassured him.

12.40 *a.m.*—Private Merited returned with the M.O. Latter nicely dressed in musical-comedy pyjamas of ravishing hue, and great-coat, with rose-tinted feet thrust into red morocco slippers. Held consultation and explained my treatment. M.O. much impressed, anxious to know whether I was a doctor. Told him "No," but that I knew all the ropes. First give patient castor oil, then diet him and call every day to make sure that he doesn't like his food. After that, if he shows signs of getting well too soon, give him a tonic... M.O. stuffy.

Dec. 10.—M.O. diagnosed attack as due to something which True Born believes to be tobacco, with which he disinfects the house, the mess-sheds, and the streets of Berkhamsted.

Dec. 11.—True Born, shorn of thirteen pipes a day out of sixteen, disparages the whole race of M.O.s.

Dec. 14.—He obtains leave to attend wedding of a great-aunt and ransacks London for a specialist who advocates strong tobacco.

Dec. 15.—He classes specialists with M.O.s. Is surprised (and apparently disappointed) that, so far, the breaking of the looking-glass has brought me no ill-luck. Feel somewhat uneasy myself until glass is repaired by local cabinetmaker.

Jan. 10, 1917.—Lieut. True Born starts to break in another horse.

Feb. 1.—Horse broken.

March 3.—Running short of tobacco, go to my billet's room and try a pipe of his. Take all the remedies except the castor oil.

April 4, 8.30 *a.m.*—Awakened by an infernal crash and discover that my poor looking-glass is in pieces again on the floor. True Born explains that its position, between the open door and the open window, was too much for it. Don't believe a word of it. Shall believe to my dying day that it burst in a frantic but hopeless attempt to tell Lieut. True Born the truth, the whole truth, and nothing but the truth.

April 6.—The lieutenant watching for some sign of misfortune to me. Says that I can't break a mirror twice without ill-luck following it. *Me!*

April 9.—Lieut. True Born comes up to me with a face full of conflicting emotions. "Your ill-luck has come at last," he says with gloomy satisfaction. "We go under canvas on the 23rd. *You are losing me!*"

10

THE SUBSTITUTE

The night-watchman had just returned to the office fire after leaving it to attend a ring at the wharf bell. He sat for sometime puffing fiercely at his pipe and breathing heavily.

"Boys!" he said at last. "That's the third time this week, and yet if I was to catch one and skin 'im alive I suppose I should get into trouble over it. Even 'is own father and mother would make a fuss, most like. Some people have boys, and other people 'ave the trouble of 'em. Our street's full of 'em, and the way they carry on would make a monkey-'ouse ashamed of itself. The man next door to me's got seven of 'em, and when I spoke to 'im friendly about it over a pint one night, he put the blame on 'is wife.

"The worst boy I ever knew used to be office-boy in this 'ere office, and I can't understand now why I wasn't 'ung for him. Undersized little chap, he was, with a face the colour o' bad pie-crust, and two little black eyes like shoe buttons. To see 'im with his little white cuffs, and a stand-up collar, and a little black bow, and a little bowler 'at, was enough to make a cat laugh. I told 'im so one day, and arter that we knew where we was. Both of us.

"By rights he ought to 'ave left the office at six-just my time for coming on. As it was, he used to stay late, purtending to work 'ard so as to get a rise. Arter all the clerks 'ad gorn 'ome he used to sit perched up on a stool yards too 'igh for him, with one eye on the ledger and the other looking through the winder at me. I remember once going off for 'arf a pint, and when I came back I found 'im with a policeman, two carmen,, and all the hands off of the *Maid Marian*, standing on the edge of the jetty, waiting for me to come up. He said that, not finding me on the wharf, 'e made sure that I must 'ave tumbled overboard, as he felt certain that I wouldn't neglect my dooty while there was breath in my body; but 'e was sorry to find 'e was mistook. He stood there talking like a little clergyman, until one of the carmen knocked his 'at over 'is eyes, and then he forgot 'imself for a bit.

"Arter that I used to wait until he 'ad gorn afore I 'ad my 'arf pint. I didn't want my good name taken away, and I had to be careful, and many's the good 'arf pint I 'ad to refuse because that little imitation monkey was sitting in the office drawing faces on 'is blotting-paper. But sometimes it don't matter 'ow careful you are, you make a mistake.

"There was a little steamer, called the *Eastern Monarch*, used to come up here in them days, once a week. Fat little tub she was, with a crew o' fattish old men, and a skipper that I didn't like. He'd been in the coasting trade all 'is life, while I've knocked about all over the world, but to hear 'im talk you'd think he knew more about things than I did.

"'Eddication, Bill,' he ses one evening, 'that's the thing! You can't argufy without it; you only talk foolish, like you are doing now.'

"'There's eddication and there's common sense,' I ses. 'Some people 'as one and some people 'as the other. Give me common sense.'

"'That's wot you want,' he ses, nodding.

"'And, o' course,' I ses, looking at 'im, 'there's some people 'asn't got either one *or* the other.'

"The office-boy came out of the office afore he could think of an answer, and the pair of 'em stood there talking to show off their cleverness, till their tongues ached. I took up my broom and went on sweeping, and they was so busy talking long words they didn't know the meaning of to each other that they was arf choked with dust afore they noticed it. When they did notice it they left off using long words, and the skipper tried to hurt my feelings with a few short ones e' knew.

"'It's no good wasting your breath on 'im,' ses the boy. 'You might as well talk to a beer-barrel.'

"He went off, dusting 'imself down with his little pocket-'ankercher, and arter the skipper 'ad told me wot he'd like to do, only he was too sorry for me to do it, 'e went back to the ship to put on a clean collar, and went off for the evening.

"He always used to go off by hisself of a evening, and I used to wonder 'ow he passed the time. Then one night I found out.

"I had just come out of the 'Bear's Head,' and stopped to look round afore going back to the wharf, when I see a couple o' people standing on the swing-bridge saying goodbye to each other. One of 'em was a man and the other wasn't.

"'Evening, cap'n,' I ses, as he came towards me, and gave a little start. 'I didn't know you 'ad brought your missis up with you this trip.'

"'Evening, Bill,' he ses, very peaceful. 'Wot a lovely evening!'

"'Bee-utiful!' I ses.

"'So fresh,' ses the skipper, sniffing in some of the air.

"'Makes you feel quite young agin,' I ses.

"He didn't say nothing to that, except to look at me out of the corner of 'is eye; and stepping on to the wharf had another look at the sky to admire it, and then went aboard his ship. If he 'ad only stood me a pint, and trusted me, things might ha' turned out different.

"Quite by chance I happened to be in the 'Bear's Head' a week arterwards, and, quite by chance, as I came out I saw the skipper saying goodbye on the bridge agin. He seemed to be put out about something, and when I said, 'Wot a lovely evening it would be if only it wasn't raining 'ard!' he said something about knocking my 'ead off.

"'And you keep your nose out o' my bisness,' he ses, very fierce.

"'Your bisness!' I ses. 'Wot bisness?'

"'There's some people as might like to know that you leave the wharf to look arter itself while you're sitting in a pub swilling gallons and gallons o' beer,' he ses, in a nasty sort o' way. 'Live and let live, that's my motter.'

"'I don't know wot you're talking about,' I ses, 'but it don't matter anyways, I've got a clear conscience; that's the main thing. I'm as open as the day, and there's nothing about me that I'd mind anybody knowing. Wot a pity it is everybody can't say the same!'

"I didn't see 'im saying goodbye the next week or the week arter that either, but the third week, arter just calling in at the 'Bear's Head,' I strolled on casual-like and got as far as the bottom of Tower Hill afore I remembered myself. Turning the corner, I a'most fell over the skipper, wot was right in the fairway, shaking 'ands with his lady-friend under the lamp-post. Both of 'em started, and I couldn't make up my mind which gave me the most unpleasant look.

"'Peep-bo!' I ses, cheerful-like.

"He stood making a gobbling noise at me, like a turkey.

"'Give me quite a start, you did,' I ses. 'I didn't dream of you being there.'

"'Get off!' he ses, spluttering. 'Get off, afore I tear you limb from limb!'Ow dare you follow me about and come spying round corners at me? Wot d'ye mean by it?'

"I stood there with my arms folded acrost my chest, as calm as a cucumber. The other party stood there watching us, and wot 'e could 'ave seen in her, I can't think. She was dressed more like a man than a woman, and it would have taken the good looks of twenty of her to 'ave made one barmaid. I stood looking at 'er like a man in a dream.

"'Well, will you know me agin?' she ses, in a nasty cracked sort of voice.

"'I could pick you out of a million,' I ses—'if I wanted to.'

"'Clear out!' ses the skipper. 'Clear out! And thank your stars there's a lady present.'

"'Don't take no notice of 'im, Cap tin Pratt,' ses the lady. 'He's beneath you. You only encourage people like that by taking notice of 'em. Goodbye.'

"She held out her 'and, and while the skipper was shaking it I began to walk back to the wharf. I 'adn't gorn far afore I heard 'im coming up behind me, and next moment 'e was walking alongside and saying things to try and make me lose my temper.

"'Ah, it's a pity your pore missis can't 'ear you!' I ses. 'I expect she thinks you are stowed away in your bunk dreaming of 'er, instead of saying things about a face as. don't belong to you.'

"'You mind your bisness,' he ses, shouting. 'And not so much about my missis! D'ye hear? Wot's it got to do with you? Who asked you to shove your oar in?'

"'You're quite mistook,' I ses, very calm. 'I'd no idea that there was anything on as shouldn't be. I was never more surprised in my life. If anybody 'ad told me, I shouldn't 'ave believed 'em. I couldn't. Knowing you, and knowing 'ow respectable you 'ave always purtended to be, and also and likewise that you ain't no chicken—'

"I thought 'e was going to 'ave a fit. He 'opped about, waving his arms and stuttering and going on in such a silly way that I didn't like to be seen with 'im. Twice he knocked my 'at off, and arter telling him wot would 'appen if 'e did it agin, I walked off and left him.

"Even then 'e wasn't satisfied, and, arter coming on to the wharf and following me up and down like a little dog, he got in front of me and told me some more things he 'ad thought of.

"'If I catch you spying on me agin,' he ses, 'you'll wish you'd never been born!'

"'You get aboard and 'ave a quiet sleep,' I ses. 'You're wandering in your mind.'

"'The lady you saw me with,' he ses, looking at me very fierce, 'is a friend o' mine that I meet sometimes for the sake of her talk.'

"'Talk!' I ses, staring at 'im. 'Talk! Wot, can't *one* woman talk enough for you? Is your missis dumb? Or wot? '

"'You don't understand,' he ses, cocking up 'is nose at me. 'She's a interleckshal woman; full of eddication and information. When my missis talks, she talks about the price o' things and says she must 'ave more money. Or else she talks about things I've done, or sometimes things I 'aven't done. It's all one to her. There's no pleasure in that sort o' talk. It don't *help* a man.'

"'I never 'eard of any talk as did,' I ses.

"'I don't suppose you did,' he ses, sneering-like. 'Now, tonight, fust of all, we talked about, the House of Lords and whether it ought to be allowed; and arter that she gave me quite a little lecture on insecks.'

"'It don't seem proper to me,' I ses. 'I 'ave spoke to my wife about 'em once or twice, but I should no more think of talking about such things to a single lady—'

"He began to jump about agin as if I'd bit 'im, and he 'ad so much to say about my 'ed and blocks of wood that I pretty near lost my temper. I should ha' lost it with some men, but 'e was a very stiff-built chap and as hard as nails.

"'Beer's your trouble,' he ses, at last. 'Fust of all you put it down, and then it climbs up and soaks wot little brains you've got. Wot you want is a kind friend to prevent you from getting it.'

"I don't know wot it was, but I 'ad a sort of sinking feeling inside as 'e spoke, and next evening, when I saw 'im walk to the end of the jetty with the office-boy and stand there talking to 'im with his 'and on his shoulder, it came on worse than ever. And I put two and two together when the guv'nor came up to me next day, and, arter talking about 'dooty ' and 'ow easy it was to get night-watchmen, mentioned in a off-'and sort of way that, if I left the wharf at all between six and six, I could stay away altogether.

"I didn't answer 'im a word. I might ha' told 'im that there was plenty of people arter me ready to give me double the money, but I knew he could never get anybody to do their dooty by the wharf like I 'ad done, so I kept quiet. It's the way I treat my missis nowadays, and it pays; in the old days I used to waste my breath answering 'er back.

"I wouldn't ha' minded so much if it 'adn't ha' been for that boy. He used to pass me, as 'e went off of a evening, with a little sly smile on 'is ugly little face, and sometimes when I was standing at the gate he'd give a sniff or two and say that he could smell beer, and he *supposed* it came from the 'Bear's Head.'

"It was about three weeks arter the guv'nor 'ad forgot 'imself, and I was standing by the gate one evening, when I saw a woman coming along carrying a big bag in her 'and. I 'adn't seen 'er afore, and when she stopped in front of me and smiled I was on my guard at once. I don't smile at other people, and I don't expect them to smile at me.

"'At last!' she ses, setting down 'er bag and giving me another smile. 'I thought I was never going to get 'ere.'

"I coughed and backed inside a little bit on to my own ground. I didn't want to 'ave that little beast of a office-boy spreading tales about me.

"'I've come up to 'ave a little fling,' she ses, smiling away harder than ever. 'My husband don't know I'm 'ere. He thinks I'm at 'ome.'

"I think I went back pretty near three yards.

"'I come up by train,' she ses, nodding.

"'Yes,' I ses, very severe, 'and wot about going back by it? '

"'Oh, I shall go back by ship,' she ses. 'Wot time do you expect the *Eastern Monarch* up?'

"'Well,' I ses, 'ardly knowing wot to make of 'er, 'she ought to be up this tide; but there's no reckoning on wot an old washtub with a engine like a sewing-machine inside 'er will do.'

"'Oh, indeed!' she ses, leaving off smiling very sudden. 'Oh, indeed! My husband might 'ave something to say about that.'

"'Your 'usband?' I ses.

"'Captin Pratt,' she ses, drawing 'erself up. 'I'm Mrs. Pratt. He left yesterday morning, and I've come up 'ere by train to give 'im a little surprise.'

"You might ha' knocked me down with a feather, and I stood there staring at her with my mouth open, trying to think.

"'Take care,' I ses at last. 'Take care as you don't give 'im too *much* of a surprise!'

"'Wot do you mean?' she ses, firing up.

"'Nothing,' I ses. 'Nothing, only I've known 'usbands in my time as didn't like being surprised—that's all. If you take my advice, you'll go straight back home agin.'

"'I'll tell 'im wot you say,' she ses, 'as soon as 'is ship comes in.'

"That's a woman all over; the moment they get into a temper they want to hurt somebody; and I made up my mind at once that, if any body was going to be 'urt, it wasn't me. And, besides, I thought it might be for the skipper's good—in the long run.

"I broke it to her as gentle as I could. I didn't tell 'er much, I just gave her a few 'ints. Just enough to make her ask for more.

"'And mind,' I ses, '*I* don't want to be brought into it. If you should 'appen to take a fancy into your 'ed to wait behind a pile of empties till the ship comes in, and then slip out and foller your 'usband and give 'im the little surprise you spoke of, it's nothing to do with me.'

"'I understand,' she ses, biting her lip. 'There's no need for 'im to know that I've been on the wharf at all.'

"I gave 'er a smile—I thought she deserved it—but she didn't smile back. She was rather a nice-looking woman in the ordinary way, but I could easy see 'ow temper spoils a woman's looks. She stood there giving little shivers and looking as if she wanted to bite somebody.

"'I'll go and hide now,' she ses.

"'Not yet,' I ses. 'You'll 'ave to wait till that little blackbeetle in the office 'as gorn.'

"'Blackbeetle?' she ses, staring.

"'Office-boy,' I ses. 'He'd better not see you at all. S'pose you go off for a bit and come back when I whistle?'

"Afore she could answer the boy came out of the office, ready to go 'ome. He gave a little bit of a start when 'e saw me talking to a lady, and then 'e nips down sudden, 'bout a couple o' yards away, and begins to do 'is bootlace up. It took 'im some time, because he 'ad to undo it fust, but 'e finished it at last, and arter a quick look at Mrs. Pratt, and one at me that I could ha' smacked his 'ed for, 'e went off whistling and showing 'is little cuffs.

"I stepped out into the road and watched 'im out o' sight. Then I told Mrs. Pratt to pick up 'er bag and foller me.

"As it 'appened there was a big pile of empties in the corner of the ware'ouse wall, just opposite the *Eastern Monarch's* berth. It might ha' been made for the job, and, arter I 'ad tucked her away behind and given 'er a box to sit on, I picked up my broom and began to make up for lost time.

"She sat there as quiet as a cat watching a mouse'ole, and I was going on with my work, stopping every now and then to look and see wheher the *Monarch* was in sight, when It 'appened to turn round and see the office-boy standing on the edge of the wharf with his back to the empties, looking down at the water. I nearly dropped my broom.

"''Ullo!' I ses, going up to 'im. 'I thought you 'ad gorn 'ome.'

"'I was going,' he ses, with a nasty oily little smile, 'and then it struck me all of a sudden 'ow lonely it was for you *all alone 'ere*, and I come back to keep you company.'

"He winked at something acrost the river as 'e spoke, and I stood there thinking my 'ardest wot was the best thing to be done. I couldn't get Mrs. Pratt away while 'e was there; besides which I felt quite sartain she wouldn't go. The only 'ope I 'ad was that he'd get tired of spying on me and go away before he found out she was 'iding on the wharf.

"I walked off in an unconcerned way—not too far—and, with one eye on 'im and the other on where Mrs. Pratt was 'iding, went on with my work. There's nothing like 'ard work when a man is worried, and I was a'most forgetting my troubles, when I looked up and saw the *Monarch* coming up the river.

"She turned to come into 'er berth, with the skipper shouting away on the bridge and making as much fuss as if 'e was berthing a liner. I helped to make 'er fast, and the skipper, arter 'e had 'ad a good look round to see who 'e could find fault with, went below to clean 'imself.

"He was up agin in about ten minutes, with a clean collar and a clean face, and a blue necktie that looked as though it 'ad got yeller measles. Good temper 'e was in, too, and arter pulling the office-boy's ear, gentle, as 'e was passing, he stopped for a moment to 'ave a word with 'im.

"'Bit late, ain't you?' he ses.

"'I've been keeping a eye on the watchman,' ses the boy. 'He works better when 'e knows there's somebody watching 'im.'

"'Look 'ere!' I ses. 'You take yourself off; I've had about enough of you. You take your little face 'ome and ask your mother to wipe its nose. Strickly speaking, you've no right to be on the wharf at all at this time.'

"'I've as much right as other people,' he ses, giving me a wicked look. 'I've got more right than some people, p'r'aps.'

"He stooped down deliberate and, picking up a bit of coke from the 'eap by the crane, pitched it over at the empties.

"'Stop that!' I ses, shouting at 'im.

"'What for?' 'e ses, shying another piece. 'Why shouldn't I?'

"''Cos I won't 'ave it,' I ses. 'D'ye hear? Stop it!'

"I rushed at 'im as he sent another piece over, and for the next two or three minutes 'e was dodging me and chucking coke at the empties, with the fool of a skipper standing by laughing, and two or three of the crew leaning over the side and cheering 'im on.

"'All right,' he ses, at last, dusting 'is hands together. 'I've finished. There's no need to make a fuss over a bit of coke.'

"'You've wasted pretty near 'arf a 'undered-weight,' I ses. 'I've a good mind to report you.'

"'Don't do that, watchman!' he ses, in a pitiful voice. 'Don't do that! 'Ere, I tell you wot I'll do. I'll pick it all up agin.'

"Afore I could move 'and or foot he 'ad shifted a couple o' cases out of 'is way and was in among the empties. I stood there dazed-like while two bits o' coke came flying back past my 'ed; then I 'eard a loud whistle, and 'e came out agin with 'is eyes rolling and 'is mouth wide open.

"'Wot's the matter?' ses the skipper, staring at 'im.

"'I—I—I'm sorry, watchman,' ses that beast of a boy, purtending 'e was 'ardly able to speak. 'I'd no idea—'

"'All right,' I ses, very quick.

"'Wot's the matter?' ses the skipper agin; and as 'e spoke it came over me like a flash wot a false persition I was in, and wot a nastytempered man 'e could be when 'e liked.

"'Why didn't you tell me you'd got a lady friend there?' ses the boy, shaking his 'ed at me. 'Why, I might 'ave hit 'er with a bit o'coke, and never forgiven myself!'

"'*Lady friend*!' ses the skipper, with a start. 'Oh, Bill, I am surprised!'

"My throat was so dry I couldn't 'ardly speak. 'It's my missis,' I ses at last.

"'Your missis?' ses the skipper. 'Wot's she 'iding behind there for?'

"'She... she's shy,' I ses, 'Always was, all 'er life. She can't bear other people. She likes to be alone with me.'

"'Oh, watchman!' ses the boy. 'I wonder where you expect to go to?'

"'Missis my grandmother!' ses the skipper, with a wink. 'I'm going to 'ave a peep.'

"'Stand back!' I ses, pushing 'im off. 'I don't spy on you, and I don't want you to come spying on me. You get off! D'ye hear me? Get off!'

"We had a bit of a struggle, till my foot slipped, and while I was waving my arms and trying to get my balance back 'e made a dash for the empties. Next moment he was roaring like a mad bull that 'ad sat down in a sorsepan of boiling water, and rushing back agin to kill me.

"I believe that if it 'adn't ha' been for a couple o' lightermen wot 'ad just come on to the jetty from their skiff, and two of his own 'ands, he'd ha' done it. Crazy with passion 'e was, and it was all the four of 'em could do to hold 'im. Every now and then he'd get a yard nearer to me, and then they'd pull 'im back a couple o' yards and beg of 'im to listen to reason and 'ear wot I 'ad to say. And as soon as I started and began to tell 'em about 'is lady friend he broke out worse than ever. People acrost the river must ha' wondered wot was 'appening. There was two lightermen, two sailormen, me and the skipper, and Mrs. Pratt all talking at once, and nobody listening but the office-boy. And in the middle of it all the wicket was pushed open and the 'ed of the lady wot all the trouble was about peeped in, and drew back agin.

"'There you are!' I ses, shouting my 'ardest. 'There she is. That's the lady I was telling you about. Now, then: put 'em face to face and clear my character. Don't let 'er escape.'

"One o' the lightermen let go o' the skipper and went arter 'er, and, just as I was giving the other three a helping 'and, 'e came back with 'er. Mrs. Pratt caught 'er breath, and as for the skipper, 'e didn't know where to look, as the saying is. I just saw the lady give 'im one quick look, and then afore I could dream of wot was coming she rushes up to me and flings 'er long, bony arms round my neck.

"'Why, William!' she ses, 'wot's the matter? Why didn't you meet me? Didn't you get my letter? Or 'ave you ceased to care for me?'

"'Let go!' I ses, struggling. 'Let go! D'ye 'ear? Wot d'ye mean by it? You've got 'old of the wrong one.'

"'Oh, William!' she ses, 'arf strangling me. ''Ow can you talk to me like that? Where's your 'art?'

"I never knew a woman so strong. I don't suppose she'd ever 'ad the chance of getting 'er arms round a man's neck afore, and she hung on to me as if she'd never let go. And all the time I was trying to explain things to them over 'er shoulder I could see they didn't believe a word I was saying. One of the lightermen said I was a 'wonder,' and the other said I was a 'fair cough-drop.' *Me!*

"She got tired of it at last, but by that time I was so done up I couldn't say a word. I just dropped on to a box and sat there getting my breath back while the skipper forgave 'is wife for 'er unjust suspicion of 'im—but told 'er not to do it again—and the office-boy was saying I'd surprised even 'im. The last I saw of the lady friend, the two lightermen was helping 'er to walk to the gate, and the two sailormen was follering 'er up behind, carrying 'er pocket-'ankercher and umberella."

11

STRIKING HARD

"You've what?" demanded Mrs. Porter, placing the hot iron carefully on its stand and turning a heated face on the head of the family.

"Struck," repeated Mr. Porter; "and the only wonder to me is we've stood it so long as we have. If I was to tell you all we've 'ad to put up with I don't suppose you'd believe me."

"Very likely," was the reply. "You can keep your fairy-tales for them that like 'em. They're no good to me."

"We stood it till flesh and blood could stand it no longer," declared her husband, "and at last we came out, shoulder to shoulder, singing. The people cheered us, and one of our leaders made 'em a speech."

"I should have liked to 'ave heard the singing," remarked his wife. "If they all sang like you it must ha' been as good as a pantermime! Do you remember the last time you went on strike?"

"This is different," said Mr. Porter, with dignity.

"All our things went, bit by bit," pursued his wife, "all the money we had put by for a rainy day, and we 'ad to begin all over again. What are we going to live on? O' course, you might earn something by singing in the street; people who like funny faces might give you something! Why not go upstairs and put your 'ead under the bed-clothes and practise a bit?"

Mr. Porter coughed. "It'll be all right," he said confidently. "Our committee knows what it's about; Bert Robinson is one of the best speakers I've ever 'eard. If we don't all get five bob a week more I'll eat my 'ead."

"It's the best thing you could do with it," snapped his wife. She took up her iron again, and turning an obstinate back to his remarks, resumed her work.

Mr. Porter lay long next morning, and, dressing with comfortable slowness, noticed with pleasure that the sun was shining. Visions of a good breakfast and a digestive pipe, followed by a walk in the fresh air, passed before his eyes as he laced his boots. Whistling cheerfully, he went briskly downstairs.

It was an October morning, but despite the invigorating chill in the air the kitchen grate was cold and dull. Herring bones and a disorderly collection of dirty cups and platters graced the table. Perplexed and angry, he looked around for his wife, and then, opening the back door, stood gaping with astonishment. The wife of his bosom, who should have had a bright fire and a good breakfast waiting for him, was sitting on a box in the sunshine, elbows on knees and puffing laboriously at a cigarette.

"*Susan*!" he exclaimed.

Mrs. Porter turned, and, puffing out her lips, blew an immense volume of smoke. "Halloa!" she said carelessly.

"Wot—wot does this mean?" demanded her husband.

Mrs. Porter smiled with conscious pride. "I made it come out of my nose just now," she replied. "At least, some of it did, and I swallowed the rest. Will it hurt me?"

"Where's my breakfast?" inquired the other hotly. "Why ain't the kitchen fire alight? Wot do you think you're doing of?"

"I'm not doing anything," said his wife, with an aggrieved air. "I'm on strike."

Mr. Porter reeled against the doorpost. "*Wot!*" he stammered. "On strike? Nonsense! You can't be."

"Oh, yes, I can," retorted Mrs. Porter, closing one eye and ministering to it hastily with the corner of her apron. "Not 'aving no Bert Robinson to do it for me, I made a little speech all to myself, and here I am."

She dropped her apron, replaced the cigarette, and, with her hands on her plump knees, eyed him steadily.

"But—but this ain't a factory," objected the dismayed man; "and, besides—*I won't 'ave it!*"

Mrs. Porter laughed—a fat, comfortable laugh, but with a touch of hardness in it.

"All right, mate," she said comfortably. "What are you out on strike for?"

"Shorter hours and more money," said Mr. Porter, glaring at her.

His wife nodded. "So am I," she said. "I wonder who gets it first?"

She smiled agreeably at the bewildered Mr. Porter, and, extracting a paper packet of cigarettes from her pocket, lit a fresh one at the stub of the first.

"That's the worst of a woman," said her husband, avoiding her eye and addressing a sanitary dustbin of severe aspect; "they do things without thinking first. That's why men are superior; before *they* do a thing they look at it all round, and upside down, and—and—make sure it can be done. Now, you get up in a temper this morning, and the first thing you do—not even waiting to get my breakfast ready first—is to go on strike. If you'd thought for two minutes you'd see as 'ow it's impossible for you to go on strike for more than a couple of hours or so."

"Why?" inquired Mrs. Porter.

"Kids," replied her husband triumphantly. "They'll be coming 'ome from school soon, won't they? And they'll be wanting their dinner, won't they?"

"That's all right," murmured the other vaguely.

"After which, when night comes," pursued Mr. Porter, "they'll 'ave to be put to bed. In the morning they'll 'ave to be got up and washed and dressed and given their breakfast and sent off to school. Then there's shopping wot must be done, and beds wot must be made."

"I'll make ours," said his wife decidedly. "For my own sake."

"And wot about the others?" inquired Mr. Porter.

"The others'll be made by the same party as washes the children, and cooks their dinner for 'em, and puts 'em to bed, and cleans the 'ouse," was the reply.

"I'm not going to have your mother 'ere," exclaimed Mr. Porter, with sudden heat. "Mind that!"

"I don't want her," said Mrs. Porter. "It's a job for a strong, healthy man, not a pore old thing with swelled legs and short in the breath."

"Strong—'ealthy—man!" repeated her husband in a dazed voice. "Strong—'eal... wot are you talking about?"

Mrs. Porter beamed on him. "You," she said sweetly.

There was a long silence, broken at last by a firework display of expletives. Mrs. Porter, still smiling, sat unmoved.

"You may smile!" raved the indignant Mr. Porter. "You may sit there smiling and smoking like a—like a man, but if you think that I'm going to get the meals ready, and soil my 'ands with making beds and washing up, you're mistook. There's some 'usbands I know as would set about you!"

Mrs. Porter rose. "Well, I can't sit here gossiping with you all day," she said, entering the house.

"Wot are you going to do?" demanded her husband, following her.

"Going to see Aunt Jane and 'ave a bit o' dinner with her," was the reply. "And after that I think I shall go to the 'pictures.'

If you 'ave bloaters for dinner be very careful with little Jemmy and the bones."

"I forbid you to leave this house!" said Mr. Porter in a thrilling voice. "If you do you won't find nothing done when you come home, and all the kids dirty and starving."

"Cheerio!" said Mrs. Porter.

Arrayed in her Sunday best, she left the house half an hour later. A glance over her shoulder revealed her husband huddled up in a chair in the dirty kitchen, gazing straight before him at the empty grate.

He made a hearty breakfast at a neighbouring coffee-shop, and, returning home, lit the fire and sat before it, smoking. The return of the four children from school, soon after midday, found him still wrestling with the difficulties of the situation. His announcement that their mother was out and that there would be no dinner was received at first in stupefied silence. Then Jemmy, opening his mouth to its widest extent, acted as conductor to an all-too-willing chorus.

The noise was unbearable, and Mr. Porter said so. Pleased with the tribute, the choir redoubled its efforts, and Mr. Porter, vociferating orders for silence, saw only too clearly the base advantage his wife had taken of his affection for his children. He took some money from his pocket and sent the leading treble out marketing, after which, with the assistance of a soprano aged eight, he washed up the breakfast things and placed one of them in the dustbin.

The entire family stood at his elbow as he cooked the dinner, and watched, with bated breath, his frantic efforts to recover a sausage which had fallen out of the frying-pan into the fire. A fourfold sigh of relief heralded its return to the pan.

"Mother always—" began the eldest boy.

Mr. Porter took his scorched fingers out of his mouth and smacked the critic's head.

The dinner was not a success. Portions of half-cooked sausages returned to the pan, and going back in the guise of cinders failed to find their rightful owners.

"Last time we had sausages," said the eight-year-old Muriel, "they melted in your mouth."

Mr. Porter glowered at her.

"Instead of in the fire," said the eldest boy, with a mournful snigger.

"If I get up to you, my lad," said the harassed Mr. Porter, "you'll know it! Pity you don't keep your sharpness for your lessons! Wot country is Africa in?"

"Why, Africa's a continent!" said the startled youth.

"Jess so," said his father; "but wot I'm asking you is: wot country is it in?"

"Asia," said the reckless one, with a side-glance at Muriel.

"And why couldn't you say so before?" demanded Mr. Porter sternly. "Now, you go to the sink and give yourself a thorough good wash. And mind you come straight home from school. There's work to be done."

He did some of it himself after the children had gone, and finished up the afternoon with a little shopping, in the course of which he twice changed his grocer and was threatened with an action for slander by his fishmonger. He returned home with his clothes bulging, although a couple of eggs in the left-hand coat pocket had done their best to accommodate themselves to his figure.

He went to bed at eleven o'clock, and at a quarter past, clad all too lightly for the job, sped rapidly downstairs to admit his wife.

"Some 'usbands would 'ave let you sleep on the doorstep all night," he said crisply.

"I know they would," returned his wife cheerfully. "That's why I married *you*. I remember the first time I let you come

'ome with me mother ses: "There ain't much of 'im, Susan,' she ses; 'still, 'arf a loaf is better than—'"

The bedroom door slammed behind the indignant Mr. Porter, and the three lumps and a depression which had once been a bed received his quivering frame again. With the sheet obstinately drawn over his head, he turned a deaf ear to his wife's panegyrics on striking and her heartfelt tribute to the end of a perfect day. Even when standing on the cold floor while she remade the bed, he maintained an attitude of unbending dignity, only relaxing when she smote him light-heartedly with the bolster. In a few ill-chosen words he expressed his opinion of her mother and her deplorable methods of bringing up her daughters.

He rose early next morning, and, after getting his own breakfast, put on his cap and went out, closing the street-door with a bang that awoke the entire family and caused the somnolent Mrs. Porter to open one eye for the purpose of winking with it. Slowly, as became a man of leisure, he strolled down to the works, and, moving from knot to knot of his colleagues, discussed the prospects of victory. Later on, with a little natural diffidence, he drew Mr. Bert Robinson apart and asked his advice upon a situation which was growing more and more difficult.

"I've got my hands pretty full as it is, you know," said Mr. Robinson hastily.

"I know you 'ave, Bert," murmured the other. "But, you see, she told me last night she's going to try and get some of the other chaps' wives to join 'er, so I thought I ought to tell you."

Mr. Robinson started. "Have you ever tried giving her a hiding?" he inquired.

Mr. Porter shook his head. "I daren't trust myself," he replied. "I might go too far, once I started."

"What about appealing to her better nature?" inquired the other.

"She ain't got one," said the unfortunate.

"Well, I'm sorry for you," said Mr. Robinson, "but I'm busy. I've got to see a labour leader this afternoon, and two reporters, and this evening there's the meeting. Try kindness first, and if that don't do, lock her up in her bedroom and keep her on bread and water."

He moved off to confer with his supporters, and Mr. Porter, after wandering aimlessly about for an hour or two, returned home at midday with a faint hope that his wife might have seen the error of her ways and provided dinner for him. He found the house empty and the beds unmade. The remains of breakfast stood on the kitchen-table, and a puddle of cold tea decorated the floor. The arrival of the children from school, hungry and eager, completed his discomfiture.

For several days he wrestled grimly with the situation, while Mrs. Porter, who had planned out her week into four days of charing, two of amusement. and Sunday in bed, looked on with smiling approval. She even offered to give him a little instruction—verbal—in scrubbing the kitchen-floor.

Mr. Porter, who was on his knees at the time, rose slowly to his full height, and, with a superb gesture, emptied the bucket, which also contained a scrubbing-brush and lump of soap, into the backyard. Then he set off down the street in quest of a staff.

He found it in the person of Maudie Stevens, aged fourteen, who lived a few doors lower down. Fresh from school the week before, she cheerfully undertook to do the housework and cooking, and to act as nursemaid in her spare time. Her father, on his part, cheerfully undertook to take care of her wages for her, the first week's, payable in advance, being banked the same evening at the "Lord Nelson."

It was another mouth to feed, but the strike-pay was coming in very well, and Mr. Porter, relieved from his unmanly tasks, walked the streets a free man. Beds were made without his interference, meals were ready (roughly) at the appointed hour, and for the first time since the strike he experienced satisfaction in finding fault with the cook. The children's content was not so great, Maudie possessing a faith in the virture of soap and water that they made no attempt to share. They were greatly relieved when their mother returned home after spending a couple of days with Aunt Jane.

"What's all this?" she demanded, as she entered the kitchen, followed by a lady-friend.

"What's all what?" inquired Mr. Porter, who was sitting at dinner with the family.

"That," said his wife, pointing at the cook-general.

Mr. Porter put down his knife and fork. "I got 'er in to help," he replied uneasily.

"Do you hear that?" demanded his wife, turning to her friend, Mrs. Gorman. "Oh, these masters!"

"Ah!" said her friend vaguely.

"A strike-breaker!" said Mrs. Porter, rolling her eyes.

"Shame!" said Mrs. Gorman, beginning to understand.

"Coming after my job, and taking the bread out of my mouth," continued Mrs. Porter fluently. "Underselling me, too, I'll be bound. That's what comes of not having pickets."

"Unskilled labour," said Mrs. Gorman, tightening her lips and shaking her head.

"Ascab!" cried Mrs. Porterwildly. "Ascab!"

"Put her out," counselled her friend.

"Put her out!" repeated Mrs. Porter, in a terrible voice. "Put her out! I'll tear her limb from limb! I'll put her in the copper and boil her!"

Her voice was so loud and her appearance so alarming that the unfortunate Maudie, emitting three piercing shrieks, rose hastily from the table and looked around for a way of escape. The road to the front-door was barred, and with a final yelp that set her employer's teeth on edge she dashed into the yard and went home *via* the back-fences. Housewives busy in their kitchens looked up in amazement at the spectacle of a pair of thin black legs descending one fence, scudding across the yard to the accompaniment of a terrified moaning, and scrambling madly over the other. At her own backdoor Maudie collapsed on the step, and, to the intense discomfort and annoyance of her father, had her first fit of hysterics.

"And the next scab that comes into my house won't get off so easy," said Mrs. Porter to her husband. "D'you understand?"

"If you 'ad some husbands—" began Mr. Porter, trembling with rage.

"Yes, I know," said his wife, nodding. "Don't cry, Jemmy," she added, taking the youngest on her knee. "Mother's only having a little game. She and dad are both on strike for more pay and less work."

Mr. Porter got up, and without going through the formality of saying goodbye to the hard-featured Mrs. Gorman put on his cap and went out. Over a couple of half-pints taken as a sedative, he realised the growing seriousness of his position.

In a dull resigned fashion he took up his household duties again, made harder now than before by the scandalous gossip of the aggrieved Mr. Stevens. The anonymous present of a much-worn apron put the finishing touch to his discomfiture; and the well-meant offer of a fair neighbour to teach him how to shake a mat without choking himself met with a reception that took her breath away.

It was a surprise to him one afternoon to find that his wife had so far unbent as to tidy up the parlour. Ornaments had been dusted and polished and the carpet swept. She had even altered the position of the furniture. The table had been pushed against the wall, and the easy chair, with its back to the window, stood stiffly confronting six or seven assorted chairs, two of which at least had been promoted from a lower sphere.

"It's for the meeting," said Muriel, peeping in.

"Meeting?" repeated her father, in a dazed voice.

"Strike-meeting," was the reply. "Mrs. Gorman and some other ladies are coming at four o'clock. Didn't mother tell you?"

Mr. Porter, staring helplessly at the row of chairs, shook his head.

"Mrs. Evans is coming," continued Muriel, in a hushed voice—"the lady what punched Mr. Brown because he kept Bobbie Evans in one day. He ain't been kept in since. I wish you—"

She stopped suddenly, and, held by her father's gaze, backed slowly out of the room. Mr. Porter, left with the chairs, stood regarding them thoughtfully. Their emptiness made an appeal that no right-minded man could ignore. He put his hand over his mouth and his eyes watered.

He spent the next half-hour in issuing invitations, and at half-past three every chair was filled by fellow-strikers. Three cans of beer, clay pipes, and a paper of shag stood on the table. Mr. Benjamin Todd, an obese, fresh-coloured gentleman of middle age, took the easy chair. Glasses and teacups were filled.

"Gentlemen," said Mr. Todd, lighting his pipe, "afore we get on to the business of this meeting I want to remind you that there is another meeting, of ladies, at four o'clock; so we've got to hurry up. O' course, if it should happen that we ain't finished—"

"Go on, Bennie!" said a delighted admirer.

"I see a female 'ead peeping in at the winder already," said a voice.

"Let 'em peep," said Mr. Todd benignly. "Then p'r'aps they'll be able to see how to run a meeting."

"There's two more 'eads," said the other. "O Lor d, I know I shan't be able to keep a straight face!"

"H'sh!" commanded Mr. Todd sternly, as the street-door was heard to open. "Be'ave yourself. As I was saying, the thing we've got to consider about this strike—"

The door opened, and six ladies, headed by Mrs. Porter, entered the room in single file and ranged themselves silently along the wall.

"Strike," proceeded Mr. Todd, who found himself gazing uneasily into the eyes of Mrs. Gorman—"strike—er—strike—"

"He said that before," said a stout lady in a loud whisper; "I'm sure he did."

"Is," continued Mr. Todd, "that we have got to keep this—this—er—"

"Strike," prompted the same voice.

Mr. Todd paused, and, wiping his mouth with a red pocket-handkerchief, sat staring straight before him.

"I move," said Mrs. Evans, her sharp features twitching with excitement, "that Mrs. Gorman takes the chair."

"'Ow can I take it when he's sitting in it?" demanded that lady.

"She's a lady that knows what she wants and how to get it," pursued Mrs. Evans, unheeding. "She understands men—"

"I've buried two 'usbands," murmured Mrs. Gorman, nodding.

"And how to manage them," continued Mrs. Evans. "I move that Mrs. Gorman takes the chair. Those in favour—"

Mr. Todd, leaning back in his chair and gripping the arms, gazed defiantly at a row of palms.

"Carried unanimously!" snapped Mrs. Evans.

Mrs. Gorman, tall and bony, advanced and stood over Mr. Todd. Strong men held their breath.

"It's my chair," she said gruffly. "I've been moved into it."

"Possession," said Mr. Todd, in as firm a voice as he could manage, "is nine points of the law. I'm here and—"

Mrs. Gorman turned, and, without the slightest warning, sat down suddenly and heavily in his lap. A hum of admiration greeted the achievement.

"Get up!" shouted the horrified Mr. Todd.

"Get up!"

Mrs. Gorman settled herself more firmly.

"Let *me* get up," said Mr. Todd, panting.

Mrs. Gorman rose, but remained in a hovering position, between which and the chair Mr. Todd, flushed and dishevelled, extricated himself in all haste. A shrill titter of laughter and a clapping of hands greeted his appearance. He turned furiously on the pallid Mr. Porter.

"What d'you mean by it?" he demanded. "Are you the master, or ain't you? A man what can't keep order in his own house ain't fit to be called a man. If my wife was carrying on like this—"

"I wish I was your wife," said Mrs. Gorman, moistening her lips.

Mr. Todd turned slowly and surveyed her.

"I don't," he said simply, and, being by this time near the door, faded gently from the room.

"Order!" cried Mrs. Gorman, thumping the arm of her chair with a large, hard-working fist. "Take your seats, ladies."

A strange thrill passed through the bodies of her companions and communicated itself to the men in the chairs. There was a moment's tense, pause, and then the end man, muttering something about "going to see what had happened to poor old Ben Todd," rose slowly and went out. His companions, with heads erect and a look of cold disdain upon their faces, followed him.

It was Mr. Porter's last meeting, but his wife had several more. They lasted, in fact, until the day, a fortnight later, when he came in with flushed face and sparkling eyes to announce that the strike was over and the men victorious.

"Six bob a week more!" he said with enthusiasm. "You see, I was right to strike, after all."

Mrs. Porter eyed him. "I am out for *four* bob a week more," she said calmly.

Her husband swallowed. "You—you don't understand'ow these things are done," he said, at last. "It takes time. We ought to re-negotiate."

"All right," said Mrs. Porter readily. "Seven shillings a week, then."

"Let's say four and have done with it." exclaimed the other hastily.

And Mrs. Porter said it.

12

DIRTY WORK

It was nearly high-water, and the night-watchman, who had stepped aboard a lighter lying alongside the wharf to smoke a pipe, sat with half-closed eyes enjoying the summer evening. The bustle of the day was over, the wharves were deserted, and hardly a craft moved on the river. Perfumed clouds of shag, hovering for a time over the lighter, floated lazily towards the Surrey shore.

"There's one thing about my job," said the night-watchman slowly, "it's done all alone by yourself. There's no foreman a-hollering at you and offering you a penny for your thoughts, and no mates to run into you from behind with a loaded truck and then ask you why you didn't look where you're going to. From six o'clock in the evening to six o'clock next morning I'm my own master."

He rammed down the tobacco with an experienced forefinger and puffed contentedly.

People like you 'ud find it lonely (he continued after a pause); I did at fust. I used to let people come and sit 'ere with me of an evening talking, but I got tired of it arter a time, and when one chap fell overboard while 'e was showing me 'ow he put his wife's mother in 'er place, I gave it up altogether. There was three foot o' mud in the dock at the time, and arter I 'ad got 'im out he fainted in my arms.

Arter that I kept myself to myself. Say wot you like, a man's best friend is 'imself. There's nobody else'll do as much for 'im, or let 'im off easier when he makes a mistake. If I felt a bit lonely I used to open the wicket in the gate and sit there watching the road, and p'r'aps pass a word or two with the policeman. Then something 'appened one night that made me take quite a dislike to it for a time.

I was sitting there with my feet outside, smoking a quiet pipe, when I 'eard a bit of a noise in the distance. Then I 'eard people running and shouts of "Stop thief!" A man came along round the corner full pelt, and, just as I got up, dashed through the wicket and ran on to the wharf. I was arter 'im like a shot and got up to 'im just in time to see him throw something into the dock. And at the same moment I 'eard the other people run past the gate.

"Wot's up?" I ses, collaring 'im.

"Nothing," he ses, breathing 'ard and struggling. "Let me go."

He was a little wisp of a man, and I shook 'im like a dog shakes a rat. I remembered my own pocket being picked, and I nearly shook the breath out of 'im.

"And now I'm going to give you in charge," I ses, pushing 'im along towards the gate.

"Wot for?" he ses, purtending to be surprised.

"Stealing," I ses.

"You've made a mistake," he ses; "you can search me if you like."

"More use to search the dock," I ses. "I see you throw it in. Now you keep quiet, else you'll get 'urt. If you get five years I shall be all the more pleased."

I don't know 'ow he did it, but 'e did. He seemed to sink away between my legs, and afore I knew wot was 'appening, I was standing upside down with all the blood rushing to my 'ead. As I rolled over he bolted through the wicket, and was off like a flash of lightning.

A couple o' minutes arterwards the people wot I 'ad 'eard run past came back agin. There was a big fat policeman with 'em—a man I 'ad seen afore on the beat—and, when they 'ad gorn on, he stopped to 'ave a word with me.

"'Ot work," he ses, taking off his 'elmet and wiping his bald 'ead with a large red handkerchief. "I've lost all my puff."

"Been running?" I ses, very perlite.

"Arter a pickpocket," he ses. "He snatched a lady's purse just as she was stepping aboard the French boat with her 'usband. Twelve pounds in it in gold, two peppermint lozenges, and a postage stamp."

He shook his 'ead, and put his 'elmet on agin.

"Holding it in her little 'and as usual," he ses. "Asking for trouble, I call it. I believe if a woman 'ad one hand off and only a finger and thumb left on the other, she'd carry 'er purse in it."

He knew a'most as much about wimmen as I do. When 'is fust wife died she said 'er only wish was that she could take 'im with her, and she made 'im promise her faithful that 'e'd never marry agin. His second wife, arter a long illness, passed away while he was playing hymns on the concertina to her, and 'er mother, arter looking at 'er very hard, went to the doctor and said she wanted an inquest.

He went on talking for a long time, but I was busy doing a bit of 'ead-work and didn't pay much attention to 'im. I was thinking o' twelve pounds, two lozenges, and a postage stamp laying in the mud at the bottom of my dock, and arter a time 'e said 'e see as 'ow I was waiting to get back to my night's rest, and went off—stamping.

I locked the wicket when he 'ad gorn away, and then I went to the edge of the dock and stood looking down at the spot where the purse 'ad been chucked in. The tide was on the ebb, but there was still a foot or two of water atop of the mud. I walked up and down, thinking.

I thought for a long time, and then I made up my mind. If I got the purse and took it to the police-station, the police would share the money out between 'em, and tell me they 'ad given it back to the lady. If I found it and put a notice in the newspaper—which would cost money—very likely a dozen or two ladies would come and see me and say it was theirs. Then if I gave it to the best-looking one and the one it belonged to turned up, there'd be trouble. My idea was to keep it—for a time—and then if the lady who lost it came to me and asked me for it I would give it to 'er.

Once I had made up my mind to do wot was right I felt quite 'appy, and arter a look up and down, I stepped round to the "Bear's Head" and 'ad a couple o' goes o' rum to keep the cold out. There was nobody in there but the landlord, and 'e started at once talking about the thief, and 'ow he 'ad run arter him in 'is shirtsleeves.

"My opinion is," he ses, "that 'e bolted on one of the wharves and 'id 'imself. He disappeared like magic. Was that little gate o' yours open?"

"I was on the wharf," I ses, very cold.

"You might ha' been on the wharf and yet not 'ave seen anybody come on," he ses, nodding.

"Wot d'ye mean?" I ses, very sharp.

"Nothing," he ses. "Nothing."

"Are you trying to take my character away?" I ses, fixing 'im with my eye.

"Lo' bless me, no!" he ses, staring at me. "It's no good to me."

He sat down in 'is chair behind the bar and went straight off to sleep with his eyes screwed up as tight as they would go. Then 'e opened his mouth and snored till the glasses shook. I suppose I've been one of the best customers he ever 'ad, and that's the way he treated me. For two pins I'd ha' knocked 'is ugly 'ead off, but arter waking him up very sudden by dropping my glass on the floor I went off back to the wharf.

I locked up agin, and 'ad another look at the dock. The water 'ad nearly gone and the mud was showing in patches. My mind went back to a sailorman wot had dropped 'is watch overboard two years before, and found it by walking about in the dock in 'is bare feet. He found it more easy because the glass broke when he trod on it.

The evening was a trifle chilly for June, but I've been used to roughing it all my life, especially when I was afloat, and I went into the office and began to take my clothes off. I took off everything but my pants, and I made sure o' them by making braces for 'em out of a bit of string. Then I turned the gas low, and, arter slipping on my boots, went outside.

It was so cold that at fust I thought I'd give up the idea. The longer I stood on the edge looking at the mud the colder it looked, but at last I turned round and went slowly down the ladder. I waited a moment at the bottom, and was just going to step off when I remembered that I 'ad got my boots on, and I 'ad to go up agin and take 'em off.

I went down very slow the next time, and anybody who 'as been down an iron ladder with thin, cold rungs, in their bare feet, will know why, and I had just dipped my left foot in, when the wharf bell rang.

I 'oped at fust that it was a runaway ring, but it kept on, and the longer it kept on, the worse it got. I went up that ladder agin and called out that I was coming, and then. I went into the office and just slipped on my coat and trousers and went to the gate.

"Wot d'you want?" I ses, opening the wicket three or four inches and looking out at a man wot was standing there.

"Are you old Bill?" he ses.

"I'm the watchman," I ses, sharp-like. "Wot d'you want?"

"Don't bite me!" he ses, purtending to draw back. "I ain't done no 'arm. I've come round about that glass you smashed at the 'Bear's Head.'"

"Glass!" I ses, 'ardly able to speak.

"Yes, glass," he ses—"thing wot yer drink out of. The landlord says it'll cost you a tanner, and 'e wants it now in case you pass away in your sleep. He couldn't come 'imself 'cos he's got nobody to mind the bar, so 'e sent me. Why! Halloa! Where's your boots? Ain't you afraid o' ketching cold?"

"You clear off," I ses, shouting at him. "D'ye 'ear me? Clear off while you're safe, and you tell the landlord that next time 'e insults me I'll smash every glass in 'is place and then sit 'im on top of 'em! Tell 'im if 'e wants a tanner out o' me to come round 'imself, and see wot he gets."

It was a silly thing to say, and I saw it arter-wards, but I was in such a temper I 'ardly knew wot I *was* saying. I slammed the wicket in 'is face and turned the key, and then I took off my clothes and went down that ladder agin.

It seemed colder than ever, and the mud when I got fairly into it was worse than I thought it could ha' been. It stuck to me like glue, and every step I took seemed colder than the one before. 'Owever, when I make up my mind to do a thing, I do it. I fixed my eyes on the place where I thought the, purse was, and every time I felt anything under my foot I reached down and picked it up—and then chucked it away as far as I could so as not to pick it up agin. Dirty job it was, too, and in five minutes I was mud up to the neck a'most. And I 'ad just got to wot I thought was the right place, and feeling about very careful, when the bell rang agin.

I thought I should ha' gorn out o' my mind. It was just a little tinkle at first, then another tinkle, but, as I stood there all in the dark and cold trying to make up my mind to take no notice of it, it began to ring like mad. I 'ad to go—I've known men climb over the gate afore now—and I didn't want to be caught in that dock.

The mud seemed stickier than ever, but I got out at last, and, arter scraping some of it off with a bit o' stick, I put on my coat and trousers and boots just as I was and went to the gate, with the bell going its 'ardest all the time.

When I opened the gate and see the landlord of the "Bear's Head" standing there I turned quite dizzy, and there was a noise in my ears like the roaring of the sea. I should think I stood there for a couple o' minutes without being able to say a word. I couldn't think of 'em.

"Don't be frightened, Bill," ses the landlord, "I'm not going to eat you."

"He looks as if he's walking in 'is sleep," ses the fat policeman, wot was standing near by. "Don't startle 'im."

"He always looks like that," ses the landlord.

I stood looking at 'im. I could speak then, but I couldn't think of any words good enough; not with a policeman standing by with a notebook in 'is pocket.

"Wot was you ringing my bell for?" I ses at last.

"Why didn't you answer it before?" ses the landlord. "D'you think I've got nothing better to do than to stand ringing your bell for three-quarters of an hour? Some people would report you."

"I know my dooty," I ses; "there's no craft up tonight, and no reason for anybody to come to my bell. If I was to open the gate every time a parcel of overgrown boys rang my bell I should 'ave enough to do."

"Well, I'll overlook it this time, seeing as you're an old man and couldn't get another sleeping-in job," he ses, looking at the policeman for him to see 'ow clever 'e was. "Wot about that tanner? That's wot I've come for."

"You be off," I ses, starting to shut the wicket. "You won't get no tanner out of me."

"All right," he ses, "I shall stand here and go on ringing the bell till you pay up, that's all."

He gave it another tug, and the policeman, instead of locking 'im up for it, stood there laughing.

I gave 'im the tanner. It was no use standing there arguing over a tanner, with a purse of twelve quid waiting for me in the dock, but I told 'im wot people thought of 'im.

"'Arf a second, watchman," ses the policeman, as I started to shut the wicket agin. "You didn't see anything of that pickpocket, did you?"

"I did not," I ses.

"'Cos this gentleman thought he might 'ave come in here," ses the policeman.

"'Ow could he 'ave come in here without me knowing it?" I ses, firing up.

"Easy," ses the landlord, "and stole your boots into the bargain."

"He might 'ave come when your back was turned," ses the policeman, "and if so, he might be 'iding there now. I wonder whether you'd mind me having a look round?"

"I tell you he ain't 'ere," I ses, very short, "but, to ease your mind, I'll 'ave a look round myself arter you've gorn."

The policeman shook his 'ead. "Well, o' course, I can't come in without your permission," he ses, with a little cough, "but I 'ave an idea that if it was your guv'nor 'ere instead of you he'd ha' been on'y too pleased to do anything 'e could to help the law. I'll beg his pardon tomorrow for asking you, in case he might object."

That settled it. That's the police all over, and that's 'ow they get their way and do as they like. I could see 'im in my mind's eye talking to the guv'nor, and letting out little things about broken glasses and such-like by accident. I drew back to let 'im pass, and I was so upset that when that little rat of a landlord follered 'im I didn't say a word.

I stood and watched them poking and prying about the wharf as if it belonged to 'em, with the light from the policeman's lantern flashing about all over the place. I was shivering with cold and temper. The mud was drying on me and I couldn't 'elp noticing the smell of it. Nobody could. And wot was worse than all was that the tide 'ad turned and was creeping over the mud in the dock.

They got tired of it at last and came back to where I was and stood there shaking their 'eads at me.

"If he was on the wharf 'e must 'ave made his escape while you was in the 'Bear's Head,'" ses the policeman.

"He *was* in my place a long time," ses the landlord.

"Well, it's no use crying over spilt milk," ses the policeman. "Funny smell about 'ere, ain't there?" he ses, sniffing, and turning to the landlord. "Wot is it?"

"I dunno," ses the landlord. "I noticed it while we was talking to 'im at the gate. It seems to foller 'im about."

"I've smelt things I like better," ses the policeman, sniffing agin. "It's just like the foreshore when somebody 'as been stirring the mud up a bit."

"If you've finished 'unting for the pickpocket I'll let you out and get on with my work," I ses, drawing myself up.

"Good night," ses the policeman, moving off.

"Good night, dear," ses the landlord. "Mind you tuck yourself up warm."

I lost my temper for a moment and afore I knew wot I was doing I 'ad got hold of him and was shoving 'im towards the gate as 'ard as I could shove. He pretty near got my coat off in the struggle, and next moment the policeman 'ad turned his lantern on me and they was both staring at me as if they couldn't believe their eyesight.

"He—he's turning black!" ses the landlord.

"He's turned black!" ses the policeman.

They both stood there looking at me with their mouths open, and then afore I knew wot he was up to, the policeman came close up to me and scratched my chest with his fingernail.

"It's mud!" he ses.

"You keep your nails to yourself," I ses. "It's nothing to do with you."

"Unless it's a case of 'tempted suicide," he ses, looking at me very 'ard.

"Ah!" ses the landlord.

"There's no mud on 'is clothes," ses the policeman, looking me over with his lantern agin. "He must 'ave gone in naked, but I should like to see 'is legs to make—All right! All right! Keep your 'air on."

"You look arter your own legs, then," I ses, very sharp, "and mind your own business."

"It is my business," he ses, turning to the landlord. "Was 'e strange in his manner at all when 'e was in your place tonight?"

"He smashed one o' my glasses," ses the landlord.

"So he did," ses the policeman. "So he did. I'd forgot that. Do you know 'im well?"

"Not more than I can 'elp," ses the landlord. "He's been in my place a good bit, but I never knew of any reason why 'e should try and do away with 'imself. If he's been disappointed in love, he ain't told me anything about it."

I suppose that couple o' fools 'ud 'ave stood there talking about me all night if I'd ha' let 'em, but I'd had about enough of it.

"Look 'ere," I ses, "you're very clever, both of you, but you needn't worry your 'eads about me. I've just been having a mud-bath, that's all."

"A *mud-bath!*" ses both of 'em, squeaking like a couple o' silly parrots.

"For rheumatics," I ses. "I 'ad it something cruel tonight, and I thought that p'r'aps the mud 'ud do it good. I read about it in the papers. There's places where you pay pounds and pounds for 'em, but, being a pore man, I 'ad to 'ave mine on the cheap."

The policeman stood there looking at me for a moment, and then 'e began to laugh till he couldn't stop 'imself.

"Love-a-duck!" he ses, at last, wiping his eyes. "I wish I'd seen it."

"Must ha' looked like a fat mermaid," ses the landlord, wagging his silly 'ead at me. "I can just see old Bill sitting in the mud a'combing his 'air and singing."

They 'ad some more talk o' that sort, just to show each other 'ow funny they was, but they went off at last, and I fastened up the gate and went into the office to clean myself up as well as I could. One comfort was they 'adn't got the least idea of wot I was arter, and I 'ad a fancy that the one as laughed last would be the one as got that twelve quid.

I was so tired that I slept nearly all day arter I 'ad got 'ome, and I 'ad no sooner got back to the wharf in the evening than I see that the landlord 'ad been busy. If there was one silly fool that asked me the best way of making mud-pies, I should think there was fifty. Little things please little minds, and the silly way some of 'em went on made me feel sorry for my sects.

By eight o'clock, 'owever, they 'ad all sheered off, and I got a broom and began to sweep up to 'elp pass the time away until low-water. On'y one craft 'ad come up that day—a ketch called the *Peewit*—and as she was berthed at the end of the jetty she wasn't in my way at all.

Her skipper came on to the wharf just afore ten. Fat, silly old man 'e was, named Fogg. Always talking about 'is 'ealth and taking medicine to do it good. He came up to me slow like, and, when 'e stopped and asked me about the rheumatics, the broom shook in my 'and.

"Look here," I ses, "if you want to be funny, go and be funny with them as likes it. I'm fair sick of it, so I give you warning."

"Funny?" he ses, staring at me with eyes like a cow. "Wot d'ye mean? There's nothing funny about rheumatics; I ought to know; I'm a martyr to it. Did you find as 'ow the mud did you any good?"

I looked at 'im—hard, but 'e stood there looking at me with his fat baby-face, and I knew he didn't mean any 'arm; so I answered 'im perlite and wished 'im good night.

"I've 'ad pretty near everything a man can have," he ses, casting anchor on a empty box, "but I think the rheumatics was about the worst of 'em all. I even tried bees for it once."

"Bees!" I ses. "*Bees!*"

"Bee-stings," he ses. "A man told me that if I could on'y persuade a few bees to sting me, that 'ud cure me. I don't know what 'e meant by persuading; they didn't *want* no persuading. I took off my coat and shirt and went and rocked one of my neighbour's beehives next door, and I thought my last hour 'ad come."

He sat on that box and shivered at the memory of it.

"Now I take Dr. Pepper's pellets instead," he ses. "I've got a box in my state-room, and if you'd like to try 'em you're welcome."

He sat there talking about the complaints he had 'ad and wot he 'ad done for them till I thought I should never have got rid of 'im. He got up at last, though, and, arter telling me to always wear flannel next to my skin, climbed aboard and went below.

I knew the hands was aboard, and arter watching 'is cabin-skylight until the light was out, I went and undressed. Then I crept back on to the jetty, and arter listening by the *Peewit* to make sure that they was all asleep, I went back and climbed down the ladder.

It was colder than ever. The cold seemed to get into my bones, but I made up my mind to 'ave that twelve quid if I died for it. I trod round and round the place where I 'ad seen that purse chucked in until I was tired, and the rubbish I picked up by mistake you wouldn't believe.

I suppose I 'ad been in there 'arf an hour, and I was standing up with my teeth clenched to keep them from chattering, when I 'appened to look round and see something like a white ball coming down the ladder. My 'art seemed to stand still for a moment, and then it began to beat as though it would burst. The white thing came down lower and lower, and then all of a sudden it stood in the mud and said, "*Ow!*"

"Who is it?" I ses. "Who are you?"

"Halloa, Bill!" it ses. "Ain't it perishing cold?"

It was the voice o' Cap'n Fogg, and if ever I wanted to kill a fellow-creetur, I wanted to then.

"'Ave you been in long, Bill?" he ses.

"About ten minutes," I ses, grinding my teeth.

"Is it doing you good?" he ses.

I didn't answer 'im.

"I was just going off to sleep," he ses, "when I felt a sort of hot pain in my left knee. O' course, I knew wot it meant at once, and instead o' taking some of the pellets I thought I'd try your remedy instead. It's a bit nippy, but I don't mind that if it does me good."

He laughed a silly sort o' laugh, and then I'm blest if e' didn't sit down in that mud and waller in it. Then he'd get up and come for'ard two or three steps and sit down agin.

"Ain't you sitting down, Bill?" he ses, arter a time.

"No," I ses, "I'm not."

"I don't think you can expect to get the full benefit unless you do," he ses, coming up close to me and sitting down agin. "It's a bit of a shock at fust, but—Halloa!"

"Wot's up?" I ses.

"Sitting on something hard," he ses. "I wish people 'ud be more careful."

He took a list to port and felt under the starboard side. Then he brought his 'and up and tried to wipe the mud off and see wot he 'ad got.

"Wot is it?" I ses with a nasty sinking sort o' feeling inside me.

"I don't know," he ses, going on wiping. "It's soft outside and 'ard inside. It— "

"Let's 'ave a look at it," I ses, holding out my 'and.

"It's nothing," he ses in a queer voice, getting up and steering for the ladder. "Bit of oyster-shell, I think."

He was up that ladder hand over fist, with me close behind 'im, and as soon as he 'ad got on to the wharf started to run to 'is ship.

"Good night, Bill," he ses, over 'is shoulder.

"Arf a moment," I ses, follering 'im.

"I must get aboard," he ses: "I believe I've got a chill," and afore I could stop 'im he 'ad jumped on and run down to 'is cabin.

I stood on the jetty for a minute or two trembling all over with cold and temper. Then I saw he 'ad got a light in 'is cabin, and I crept aboard and peeped down the skylight. And I just 'ad time to see some sovereigns on the table, when he looked up and blew out the light.

SEA WHISPERS

13

THE BRAVO

There was a chill air off the river, and the water looked cold and dark. Side-lights were already appearing, and the siren of a large steamer coming up indulged in grievous lamentations. A slight shiver altered for a moment the contour of the night-watchman's jersey. He patted it tenderly.

"There's worse things than loneliness, though," he said after a long silence, "and a man as does his dooty can always find something to do."

He got up from the bollard and, with a faint grunt, stooped and picked up his broom. A voice from the next wharf told him to take care not to overdo it.

"That's the new man next door," said the night-watchman. "He's feeling lonely and 'e wants me to answer him back—and I shan't.

"I used to feel like it myself at fust; not that I ever gave any lip to my olders and betters; but I used to feel I wanted somebody to talk to. One time I let a painter chap come and paint 'ere. He used to paint ships and things, and that lasted till one day he asked to be allowed to paint my portrait. It took 'im three evenings. He showed it to me when it was finished as if 'e was proud of it; and then 'e went straight off 'ome, packing up his things as 'e went and talking about sending for the police.

"Arter that I 'ad a dog for company. Bullterrier he was, and somebody must ha' paid a lot o' money for 'im. I had 'im a couple o' months, and then the landlord of the 'Albion' offered me a couple o' quid for 'im, and while I was trying to raise him to two pun' ten some low, dirty, sneaking thief got 'im for nothing. There's people about 'ere as would steal your whiskers off your face if they wanted 'em. And if you went to the police about it the fust thing they would ask is where you got them from.

"I 'ad another dog arter that, but 'e wasn't wot you might call a success. He bit three people in a fortnight, and then 'e bit me. The last I see of him, he was trying to swim across the river with a brick.

"A watchman is best all alone by 'imself. He can't cheat 'imself at cards, and any drink he pays for isn't money wasted. I 'ad a little lesson once about keeping myself to myself and it done me good. Though I didn't see it at the time.

"It was just such an evening as this might be. I 'ad been hard at work tidying up, and was just thinking of getting my ladder and lighting up, when the wicket was pushed open sudden and a young feller 'opped in follered by a gal. They shut it arter them very gentle and then stood there talking in w'ispers and looking round at me.

"''Ullo!' I ses. 'Wot's all this about?'

"'*Hsh!*' ses the gal. '*Hsh!*'

"'Wot d'you want?' I ses, very loud, a-purpose. 'Who asked you to come on my wharf and *hsh* me about?'

"Pretty little thing she was, about eighteen, with nice large blue eyes and brown 'air.

"'We're escaping,' she ses, coming up and catching 'old of my arm.

"'Wot 'ave you been doing?' I ses, trying to speak severe.

"'Nothing,' she ses, shaking her 'ead.

"'Wot's *he* been doing, then?' I ses.

"'Nothing that I'm ashamed of,' ses the young feller. 'I'm only walking out with my young lady, that's all.'

"'Well, you can't walk out with 'er on my wharf,' I ses, rather sharp. 'Is 'er father arter 'er, or wot?'

"He stood there looking at me like a silly fool. A rather smallish chap, dressed up to the nines, with a necktie like a rainbow in a fit. If he'd been a gal I should 'ave called 'im rather good-looking, but 'e was too pretty-pretty for a man. Twice he opened 'is mouth to speak, and only gave a silly smile instead.

"'It ain't 'er father,' he ses at last, with a funny little laugh.

"'It's the young man I used to walk out with afore I was old enough to know my own mind,' ses the gal, turning to me. 'I never reely liked 'im. He's always getting into fights; and now he says if 'e sees Charlie with me he'll knock his 'ead off and make 'im swaller it. I saw 'im behind us just now, and if your gate 'adn't been open I don't know wot would 'ave happened.'

"'But you ain't afraid of 'im?' I ses to the young man.

"'I ain't afraid of any man,' he ses, very upright. 'But I don't want my 'ead knocked off. 'Ow would you like it yourself?'

"''Ow big is he?' I ses.

"'About my size,' ses Charlie, considering.

"'Well, you needn't be afraid of a little shrimp like that,' I ses. 'Neither of you can't hurt each other enough to signify. You get off my wharf and, if he starts on you, knock 'im down. Give 'im one in the bread-basket with your left, and when 'e bends over drive with your right to 'is jaw.'

"'And s'pose 'e don't bend over?' ses Charlie.

"'He wouldn't,' ses the gal. 'Not if I know 'im. If Charlie did manage to hit 'im in the—where you said, he'd 'arf kill 'im.'

"Charlie nodded and turned pale. He could turn pale all right, but even the things I said to 'im couldn't make 'im blush. She turned red instead, and I caught one look from 'er blue eyes—when she didn't think I was looking—that fair startled me.

"'Well, I've give you good advice,' I ses, 'and if you don't take it you must leave it. If I was walking out with a gal like that I'd fight a ridgiment of soldiers for 'er; one down and t'other come up.'

"She gave me a nice look then and I began to feel a bit sorry for 'er. Gals can't 'elp their feelings, when all is said and done.

"'I'll just step outside and see if there is anybody 'anging about,' I ses; 'if not, off you go.'

"I walked to the gate, but couldn't see anybody. Then I strolled round the corner, careless-like, with my 'ands in my pockets, and the fust thing I see was a young feller walking up and down and looking all ways at once, as the saying, is. Nasty face he'd got; sharp eyes and a nose that wasn't, and big, ugly teeth.

"'Lost anything?' I ses as I passed.

"'Go an' boil your face,' he ses.

"I didn't answer 'im; I gave 'im a smile instead. Just the sort of smile kind old ladies turn round and give to little children when they pass 'em. Then I walked back slow to the wharf, and I 'ad just got one leg inside the gate when a stone came along and caught me on the other.

"Nasty smack it was, too, and if I could ha' got hold of 'im I'd ha' tore 'im limb from limb. I went round the corner to look for 'im, but o' course he 'ad disappeared, and when I got back to the wharf Charlie and the gal 'ad disappeared too.

"I got my ladder and lit the lamps. It was dark by the time I 'ad finished and 'ad a pipe in the office. I went out on the wharf again, and arter a time I began to fancy things. I thought I 'eard little rustlings and whisperings. Twice I stopped and listened and then everything was as silent as the grave. Then I 'eard a little sneeze.

"They was sitting on a box—a little box—be'ind a pile of empties in the angle of the warehouse there, holding each other's 'and. I spoke to 'em sharp at fust, but the gal was so sorry when she 'eard about my leg that I 'adn't the 'art to say much. Quite upset she was, with 'er little hanky up to 'er mouth and making funny little sobbing noises.

"'That's a nice quiet little corner,' ses Charlie, as I walked down to the gate with 'em. 'It might ha' been made for us.'

"'Only it wasn't,' I ses.

"He leaned up against me, and at fust I thought 'e was trying to hold *my* 'and. Then I felt something 'ard put into it. I s'pose I was a fool, but I remembered my own young days, and I stood there trying to think wot I could do for 'em.

"'The corner won't run away,' I ses, 'and so Icag as there's no craft alongside, or at any rate none of the hands about, I don't know why you shouldn't go there for a breath of fresh air sometimes.'

"They both thanked me at once, and I could see wot a load it was off Charlie's mind to think as 'ow 'e could go on courting in comfort and safety. The gal went off by 'erself, in case the other chap, Alf Stevens, should be 'anging about, and arter I 'ad allowed Charlie to stand me a pint in the 'Bull's Head,' he went off too.

"I didn't see anything of 'em for the next two days, but on the third evening there was a little tapping noise on the gate, and when I opened the wicket the gal put 'er little 'ead in and smiled at me.

"'Can I come in?' she ses.

"'Yes,' I ses; 'there's nothing up tonight. You can 'ave the wharf all to your two selves. Where is he? '

"'He's coming a roundabout way,' she ses. 'It's safer.'

"I didn't say nothing; arter all it was *'er* young man, but I coughed. I couldn't 'elp it. And when she patted me on the back it made me cough again. Nice little 'and she'd got, but 'arder than wot I expected. Especially the second time.

"I stood talking to 'er a little while arter she 'ad got into 'er corner. Besides the other things, I 'ad moved three or four empty barrels in front so as to make 'em quite private, and she couldn't thank me enough for it. She said it was evident I knew my way about, and she wondered 'ow many 'arts I 'ad broke afore I settled down. I told 'er of one or two, and just as she was shaking her 'ead at me and asking me whether all men was like that, or only sailormen, the wharf bell rang.

"'Oh, make 'aste,' she ses; 'it sounds as if 'e was in a hurry.'

"I trotted off and unlocked the gate and Charlie a'most fell into my arms. Pale as a ghost 'e was and shaking all over. Then I put my 'ead outside and saw Alf Stevens.

"He pulled up short as 'e see me, and we stood looking at each other; me inside and 'im outside. Then 'e steps forward, as bold as brass, to come on to the wharf.

"'Wot do you want?' I ses, blocking the way.

"'I want to come inside,' he ses, shoving 'is face close up to mine. 'I believe you've got my gal there.'

"'You run off 'ome and play,' I ses. 'I've 'ad enough o' little boys coming on to my wharf and stealing lumps o' coke. Go off an' 'ave a little game of 'opscotch all by yourself.'

"I slammed the wicket just in time, and, judging by the noise 'is fist made on it, I didn't lose anything I wanted much. He must 'ave pretty near broke 'is knuckles, and the langwidge 'e used about it was shocking. When I called out and asked 'im whether he 'ad ever been to Sunday school, it got worse.

"'You've done it now,' ses Charlie, trembling.

"'Cheer up!' I ses. 'You've got the gal and you can't expect to 'ave everything. Even if he does set about you 'e can't kill you, and if 'e does he'll be 'ung for it. I'll see as 'ow he don't escape.'

"I might 'ave saved my breath; and the gal was a'most as upset as 'e was. Alf Stevens was still outside talking to 'imself, and when I called out to ask whether he'd like a cough-lozenge they both caught 'old of me and asked me not to make 'im worse.

"'Think of poor Charlie,' says the gal.

"They was both of 'em in such a state I didn't like to leave 'em, so I found a little box for myself and sat down to keep 'em company. I told 'em some of the things wot 'ad 'appened to me while I was at sea; 'ow I'd nearly been shipwrecked three times, and 'ow on one ship we was short-'anded cos 'arf the hands was below in their bunks through fighting me. Then I made 'em feel the place on my 'ead where I'd been hit with the leg of a chair, but nothing seemed to cheer 'em up, and arter wasting about an hour of my time I got up and left 'em.

"I done a bit o' tidying up fust and then I went into the office and 'ad a look at the newspaper. By the time I'd done that it was getting late, and I was just getting up to see 'ow Charlie and Maud was getting on when I see them looking at me through the winder.

"'It's time we was going,' ses Charlie.

"'I'll come and open the gate for yer,' I ses, feeling in my pocket.

"'And wot about Alf?' ses Charlie.

"'Well, wot about 'im?' I ses.

"'Has 'e gorn?' he ses.

"'Must ha' done,' I ses. 'You'll get Alf on the brain if you ain't careful. Besides, if 'e ain't, he couldn't 'urt you much tonight. Think wot a smash he 'it that gate with 'is fist.'

"'I don't like to think of it,' he ses, with a shiver; 'it might 'ave been me.'

"'Well, I'll go and see if the coast is clear,' I ses at last.

"I crept on tiptoe to the gate and unlocked it without a sound. Then I began opening it very gentle, and I 'ad just got it open about six inches when Mister Alf rushed at it with 'is shoulder.

"He got 'arf-way in and then 'e stuck. I stood agin it like a rock, and then I began to shut it, very slow. Nine stone don't stand much chance agin fifteen, and swearing didn't 'elp 'im. He was 'arf in and 'arf out, and, arter squeedging 'im for a little while I talked to 'im about manners, I put my 'and on his chin and flung 'im into the road.

"'Now make a bolt for it,' I ses to Charlie. 'Quick! While you're safe.'

"'*Safe!*' ses Charlie. ''Ark at 'im!'

"Alf was at it agin, and the things wot 'e said 'e would do to me when 'e got 'old of me showed wot a nasty mind he'd got. I locked the gate up, and then I stood for a minute wondering wot was to be done.

"'We can't stay 'ere all night,' ses Charlie, as we walked down the wharf.

"'No, I'll see to that,' I ses.

"'If we don't go soon she'll get it from 'er father, and if we do go I shall get it from Alf Stevens,' he ses. 'If you'd on'y pulled 'im inside while you 'ad the chance and 'eld 'im we could ha' got away all right. You lost your presence o' mind.'

"'I'll lose something else in a minute,' I ses, as soon as I could speak. 'If you 'ad the pluck of a mouse you'd go out and fight 'im now.'

"'Oh, don't, Charlie,' ses the gal.

"'I won't,' he ses, 'for your sake.'

"They walked up and down arter that with their arms round each other's waists. It was all 'is arm was fit for. I walked up and down too, and while I was wondering 'ow to get rid of 'em I suddenly remembered that one o' the lightermen 'ad left 'is skiff tied up in the dock. I peeped over to make sure he 'adn't taken it away, and then I went to Charlie.

"He paid up the five bob I asked 'im for neglecting my dooty, without a murmur. I got into the boat fust, and the gal follered as if she'd been used to ladders all 'er life. Then I 'ad to go up agin 'cos Charlie wanted somebody to 'old 'is ankles while 'e came down.

"'Wot are you going to do about meeting 'er now?' I ses, as I started pulling.

"'I don't know,' he ses, 'arf crying.

"'I've got an idea,' I ses, arter thinking a bit, 'but it 'ud cost you money if it comes off.'

"'I don't mind that,' ses Charlie, sitting up as if the Bank of England belonged to 'im. 'Wot is the idea?'

"'Suppose Alf Stevens came round 'ere next Friday,' I ses, very gentle, 'and thought it was you, and it wasn't.'

"Charlie didn't answer at fust; then 'e asked me to say it all over agin.

"'Suppose it was a young feller I know dressed up like you and sitting be'ind the empties in the dark, pretending to make love to Maud,' I ses, 'and Alf comes along and sets about 'im?'

"'Who is 'e?' ses Charlie, staring.

"'He's a young feller wot's very much fancied by them as knows,' I ses. 'I see 'im boxing at 'Oxton one night, and 'e was in a class by 'imself. Wonderful, it was.'

"'Do you think 'e could beat Alf?' ses the gal, clasping her 'ands.

"'Beat 'im?' I ses. 'I tell you this chap is a *boxer*. One of the best at 'is weight I've ever seen. Alf Stevens would 'ave about as much chance with 'im as a baby would with its nurse.'

"'Sounds all right,' ses Charlie, considering. 'It's time somebody learnt 'im not to interfere where 'e ain't wanted.'

"'You be round on Friday night at seven,' I ses. 'I think I can get 'im all right. P'r'aps you'd better come by boat, in case of accidents. Bring ten bob in your pocket for Sid Groom—that's 'is name—and five for me for my trouble, and you'll find it's the best bargain you ever made in your life.'

"I put 'em ashore at the stairs, and then rowed myself back to the wharf. It was as quiet and peaceful as the grave; and though I crept up to the gate and listened, I couldn't 'ear nothing of Alf Stevens.

"I went agin in about an hour's time and looked out. At fust I thought he 'ad gorn, then I see something like a 'ead peeping round the corner.

"'Why don't you go 'ome?' I ses. 'Charlie ses he'll 'arf kill you if you ain't gorn in five minutes.'

"I thought that 'ud wake 'im up—and it did. 'Ow he could think o' such things was a puzzle to me. And 'e didn't 'ave to stop to think, neither.

I believe 'e must ha' stayed there pretty near all night. I know 'e was there at two n the morning, 'cos of 'arf a brick as took a bit out o' the gate instead of me, by mistake, but 'e wasn't there when the 'ands come on at six o'clock.

"I didn't see 'im on my way 'ome, though I was quite ready for 'im, and stopped at every corner. I 'ad something to eat and a few hours in bed, and then I went out to try and find Sid Groom.

"He was out, as usual, and if I went into one pub I went into seven or eight. A man with proper feelings can't go into a pub without 'aving something for the good of the 'ouse, and by the time I found Sid there wasn't much of Charlie's five bob left. 'Arf an hour arterwards there wasn't any; and some of it wasted on ginger-beer.

"Sid didn't like the idea of it at fust, 'cos 'e didn't like hitting a man wot wasn't a pro, but arter I 'ad talked to 'im about the ten bob and Maud's blue eyes e' gave way. He was in training at the time for a fight with a Bermondsey boy, and 'e said e' might just as well punch Alf Stevens for 'arf a quid as a punching-ball for nothing.

"'Mind,' I ses, 'we want 'im to think it's Charlie, and if you keep your back to the light and slip into 'im 'ard and quick, I don't see why 'e should know the difference.'

"'Wot's Charlie like?' he ses.

"I told 'im.

"''Ow about slipping into 'im instead of the other bloke?' he ses, spitting on the floor.

"'I don't think he'd pay you ten bob for that,' I ses, shaking my 'ead at 'im. 'You'll enjoy it all right once you start. And don't forget to put on a bowler-'at and a collar. And don't speak.'

"He said something under 'is breath wot sounded like a little bit of Alf Stevens, but I didn't take no notice, and afore I left 'im e' promised faithful to come round and give Alf the surprise of 'is life.

"I didn't see Charlie that evening, but a dirty little boy come round with a letter from 'im and I sent word back telling 'im Friday would be all right. The only thing that worried me was that Alf Stevens mightn't be there, but as I see 'im prowling about soon after the boy 'ad gorn, I 'adn't got much fear.

"Sid was the fust to turn up on Friday night. In fact, I sent 'im on in front of me. Good-looking young feller e' was, and in a bowler-'at and a clean collar 'e looked nicer than I 'ad ever seen 'im. I stood talking to 'im till the foreman 'ad gorn, and then we sat down on the jetty and waited for the others.

"They came along by boat just afore seven, and Charlie come up that ladder as if it was a mile 'igh, and asking me to give him a 'and when 'e got to the top. I interduced them in a 'urry—to stop Sid's mouth—and then I went to the gate and looked out just to make sure Alf Stevens was there.

"He was. I lit the lamps soon arterwards, all but the one near where they was going to be, and then I sat down alongside Maud, and was just going to show Sid 'ow to sit with his 'ead 'id on 'er shoulder when she got up.

"'I know 'ow to do it,' ses Sid, pushing me away. 'Just put them barrels a bit closer.'

"'Wot for?' I ses.

"''Cos I can do it better when there's nobody looking,' 'e ses.

"'Wot's the good o' doing it at all till Alf comes?' ses Charlie, fidgeting.

"Sid didn't answer 'im. He 'elped move one or two of the barrels 'imself, and then we 'eard 'im tell Maud to come and sit down.

"We stood there waiting for two or three minutes, and then Charlie, arter fidgeting about agin for a bit, put his 'ead over and asked them 'ow they was getting on.

"'You mind your own bisness,' ses Sid.

"Charlie come back to me trembling all over. 'You go and speak to 'im,' he ses at last,

"I waited a little while, and then I ses, in a off-'and way: 'Sid, I'm going to let Alf Stevens in now. Be ready.'

"'You let 'im in when I tell you, and not afore,' ses Sid, very sharp. 'We ain't 'arf done practising yet. I'm learning to be as much like Charlie to 'er as possible, so as Alf Stevens won't know the difference. And it takes time.'

"I thought Charlie would ha' fainted, and the things 'e said to me about my cleverness you wouldn't believe. If he 'ad only been as good with 'is fist, as 'is tongue he'd 'ave been all right. It might a'most ha' been my missis talking to me.

"I 'eard Big Ben strike eight, and then I 'eard a little whistle from Sid.

"'I think I know my piece now,' he ses, when I went over. 'Tell Charlie to 'ide 'imself, and then open the gate.'

"I put Charlie round the far corner and told 'im not to move and not even to put his 'ead round until they was busy, and then I walked up to the gate. I made a little noise opening the wicket, and then I stepped outside a yard or two and looked the wrong way, and a'most afore you could say 'knife' Alf Stevens bolted in and ran on to the wharf.

"''Ere!' I ses, follering 'im up, 'wot are you arter? Who told you to come on my wharf?'

"He took no more notice of me than if I was a pet lamb. He stood looking all round 'im with his 'ead bent down, and then there came the sound of two or three of the loudest kisses I ever 'eard in my life. Alf Stevens made a noise like a hyena wot wasn't laughing, and the next moment two of the barrels was rolled out o' the way and 'e stood looking at the two of 'em cuddling each other on the box.

"'Got—yer—at—last!' he ses, grinding his teeth.

"He bent over to push Sid away, but 'e 'ad got his 'ead buried in the gal's shoulder and was 'olding on to 'er as if 'e was frightened out of 'is life.

"'Stand up!' ses Alf, pulling 'im by the collar. 'Stand up and take wot's coming to you.'

"Sid got up, stooping, with his 'at over 'is eyes, and the next moment Alf was sitting on the ground wondering wot 'ad 'appened to 'im. Then 'is memory come back to 'im and 'e got up and rushed at Sid like a madman, but 'e might as well 'ave tried to 'it the moon. Sid was dancing all round 'im, punching 'im all over the place, and every now and then knocking 'im down for a change.

"I must say Alf was game. He fought as long as 'e could stand, and 'e could 'ardly walk as I 'elped 'im off the wharf. He couldn't see properly neither, 'cos he thought I was somebody quite different and asked me wot I 'ad done with my tail.

"The others came along as I stood there watching Alf 'obble away. Maud was 'anging on to Sid's arm and looking up into 'is face, and Charlie was follering up be'ind making noises like a lost kitten.

"'Didn't want to pay me the ten bob,' ses Sid to me. 'He soon altered 'is mind, though.'

"'He—he's got my young lady,' ses Charlie, arf crying, 'and ten bob too.'

"'Never mind,' I ses, patting 'im on the shoulder; 'a gal like that ain't worth troublin' about.'

"'Wot's that?' ses Sid, shoving 'is face into mine. 'Wot did you say?'

"'I mean, 'e oughtn't to trouble about any gal,' I ses, very firm. 'He ought to get a little pet dog instead. A little dog as nobody else wants.'

"Sid stood looking at me for a moment; then he put 'is arm round Maud's waist and they went off. Charlie and me stood watching them till they was out of sight, and then 'e told me wot 'e thought about Sid.

"I felt a bit sorry for 'im, but arter all bisness is bisness, and as 'e turned to go off I laid my 'and on 'is sleeve and gave a little laugh.

"'Yes?' he ses.

"'Ain't you forgot something ?' I ses.

"'Not as I knows of,' 'e ses, staring.

"'Wot about my five bob ?' I ses.

"I think 'is troubles must 'ave turned 'is brain. He gave a squeal that set my teeth on edge, and afore I could take my 'ands out o' my pockets he 'ad given me four or five bangs in the face as 'ard as 'e could hit. Then 'e turned round quick and run for all 'e was worth."

14

TAKING PAINS

Mr. Silvanus Key, changing his position in bed for the third time in five minutes, lay on his back and groaned lamentably.

"I shall never be well," he murmured faintly. "Forty-three, good-looking, with the best moustache in the town, and done for."

"Has the pain come on again?" inquired his wife softly.

"Not what you could call pain," said Mr. Key. "There's a red-hot corkscrew going through my left shoulder and a very capable monkey-wrench trying to screw my knee-joints out. The only time I get any rest is when it leaves off to spit on its hands. *O-ow! Ouch! O-o!*"

Mrs. Key rose and, standing by the side of the bed, gazed at him compassionately.

"The doctor doesn't seem to be doing you much good," she murmured.

"That'll do," said the sufferer sharply. "He is doing his best."

"So it seems," said his wife dryly. "How you can imagine that stuff out of a bottle can cure you, I can't think. It's the soul that wants treating, not the body. You want to be bathed in a stream of healing thought that would kill all those ideas of pain and—"

"*Ideas!*" shouted Mr. Key. "You wait till you get rheumatism, and neuritis, and gout, and sciatica, all mixed up together, and trying to see which can be the worst. If that blessed Circle of Healers, as you call it, was here I'd punch its head."

"Some of them are women," said his wife.

Mr. Key remarked that he supposed women possessed heads, some of them at any rate, and, licking his lips, speculated on the good to be achieved by knocking all the heads of the Circle together.

"Shake their brains up and make 'em think," he added.

His wife sighed, and bestowed upon him a look of tender and elevating love.

"You are so wilful," she murmured. "If you would only see Mr. Punshon; no foolish and nasty drugs; no clumsy interference with that wonderful combination of soul and body that we know as man. You are simply out of tune with the infinite. *I* am never ill."

"You wouldn't talk like that if you were," said Mr. Key. "You'd know better."

He lay back with closed eyes and pondered gloomily. It was his first real illness and, to an active man fond of rather more than his share of the good things of this life, extremely distasteful. He opened his eyes at a rather sharper twinge than usual and, in a few ill-chosen words, expressed his opinion that members of the medical profession were as useless as the Healers.

"And we work for love," said his wife, improving the occasion.

Mr. Key closed his eyes again, and a faint and unseemly grin passed furtively.

"Miss Olson is a healer, isn't she?" he inquired. "The pretty one. Perhaps I might—"

"She is a neophyte," said his wife coldly, "the same as myself."

"Nothing doing," murmured the graceless Mr. Key. "Still, if she wants a little practice—"

Mrs. Key implored him not to make a jest of solemn things, and spoke with some eloquence of the marvellous cures effected by Mr. Punshon. Her husband pointed out, when she had finished, that she had omitted the marvellous case of old Mr. Jackson, who, after being bedridden for over three years, was able, owing to the healer's ministrations, to spend the evenings of his life at the "Shakespeare Arms."

"It is easy to mock at things," said Mrs. Key bitterly. "Mr. Punshon would cure him of that, but the artful old man won't let him go near him."

She went out of the room, and the invalid, after turning in the bed with great care, lay gazing wistfully out of the window. There was a cheerful hum from the street below, and he thought with great bitterness of the happy people there who knew nothing of uric acid and its liking for hot joints. A visit from the doctor next day depressed him still more.

"Another week or two?" he gasped.

"You're going on beautifully," said the other, with an admiring but thoughtless pat on Mr. Key's left knee. "Sorry."

"Don't mind me," said the sufferer coldly. "Am I to go on taking that beastly physic of yours?"

The doctor nodded. "For sometime," he said, grinning. "Shut your eyes when you are taking it and tell yourself it is a vintage port. Smack your lips over it."

Mr. Key closed his eyes and groaned.

"And don't be too sorry for yourself," pursued the other. "You are not nearly so bad as some of my poor patients. Not nearly."

Mr. Key, with a faint smile, said that he could quite believe it. He also expressed his firm belief that their troubles would soon be over—one way or another.

"The last bottle," said his medical attendant, breathing hard, "was not strong enough. You are suffering from depression."

"You never see me at my best," said the other; "the moment you come into the room—"

"Goodbye," said the doctor briskly.

He went downstairs and, meeting in the hall Mrs. Key, who had just come in, announced in a loud voice that the patient was much better. A louder voice from the sick-room denied all knowledge of the fact.

For two days the patient had no reason to alter his opinion, but on the third he confided to Mrs. Key, with a happy smile, that he certainly felt much easier.

"Since when?" inquired his wife, with a mysterious expression on her face.

Mr. Key pondered. "Yesterday afternoon I got the turn, I think. It's nothing to laugh at."

"I was not laughing, I was smiling," said his wife. "With happiness," she added hastily. "But I'm not surprised. Mr. Punshon had a half-holiday yesterday afternoon."

Mr. Key gazed at her blankly.

"And instead of going out and enjoying himself stayed at home and gave you 'absent treatment.'"

"Infernal impudence!" gasped the astonished invalid. "I'll—I'll—Punshon O Lord! How many people have you told!"

"He could do you much more good if he came into contact with you," said his wife timidly.

"Fancy," murmured the other brokenly, "that ginger-bearded fraud—treating *me!* Poor Johnson pulls me round and Punshon steps in and takes the credit. I shall be the laughing stock of the town. Everybody knows what I've said about him."

"You've said things—to me—about Dr. Johnson too," said his wife.

Mr. Key lay back and regarded her for some time, deep in thought. "All right," he said at last, in a ferocious voice, "have it your own way. I'll give him a run for his money. Punshon has put his hand to the plough and he'd better finish the job. But mind, I shall take the medicine."

His wife turned upon him a face that literally shone with happiness. "It won't make much difference," she said. "Mr.

Punshon's force is much too strong for drugs to interfere with it."

She brought the healer round the following afternoon, and Mr. Key, gazing at the flabby, bearded face, with its pouched eyes and foolish mouth, waited breathlessly for developments.

"I hope it is not going to be painful," he remarked.

"We soothe," said Mr. Punshon, in a deep voice marred by adenoids.

He took a chair by the bed, and taking the patient's hands in his own, leaned forward and fixed upon him the healing glare of a pair of pale and protuberant blue eyes. Mr. Key, closing his, bit his lips to suppress a smile.

For twenty minutes the silence was unbroken except for the odd noises in Mr. Punshon's air-passages. He released the patient's hands and, folding his arms, spoke with authority.

"You feel better?"

"I do," said Mr. Key in reverent tones. "Waves of—something or other—seemed to go right through me."

Mr. Punshon smiled and, taking out a handkerchief, wiped his brow.

"You mustn't expect to be well all at once," he said, raising a warning hand. "Evil is not destroyed in five minutes. I will come in and give you further treatment tomorrow evening."

Mr. Key thanked him, and for some time after his departure lay smiling seraphically at the ceiling. Under the combined treatment of Mr. Punshon and Dr. Johnson he improved steadily, the wrath of the latter, when he heard of his collaborator, doing the invalid, according to his own account, more good than medicine.

"I've done with you," said the doctor, fuming. "It's all over the town that Punshon has cured you when I failed. What do you mean by it?"

"I'm not cured yet," said the invalid grimly. "Dear Brother Punshon has got to do a lot more for me before he has finished.

I have an idea that I am going to be one of his most difficult cases."

"All this stuff about Christian Science—" began the doctor.

"It's nothing to do with Christian Science," retorted the other. "It's a little special brand of Punshon's own. He is far too conceited to adopt anybody else's ideas. He is charged with electricity—a living magnet, that's the idea—and, in a lesser degree, he thinks he is able to magnetise his followers."

The doctor stood regarding him with a perplexed grin.

"What is the game?" he inquired bluntly.

"Game?" retorted Mr. Key loftily. "There is no 'game.' You don't understand. Magnetic healing is serious, most serious. So are the healers. If they could see a joke they wouldn't be healers. Punshon couldn't see a joke if I put it in front of his nose and burnt coloured lights round it."

"You might try," suggested the other.

"Get thee behind me, Satan," said Mr. Key severely. "Besides, I'm going to. Meantime, you had better leave Punshon a free hand. I don't want you to get the credit of his cure. You don't want it either. If you go, and I have a relapse—"

The doctor nodded. "Nobody could expect me to halve a patient with Punshon," he murmured.

"Exactly," said the other, "but you needn't put it in quite such a surgical way. It's not nice. By the way"

"Well?"

"What about one weak whisky-and-soda a day?" inquired Mr. Key, in persuasive accents.

The doctor stood for a time considering. "Better ask Punshon," he said at last, and faded slowly from the room.

A good man would have been moved by the tender gratitude displayed by Mrs. Key when she learnt that her husband had abandoned drugs entirely, in favour of spiritual treatment. The only effect on Mr. Key was to confirm him in his iniquities. His spirits rose and the hue of health returned to his cheeks. And he praised Mr. Punshon and his strange and beneficent power until that gentleman nearly fell a victim to the sin of pride.

"Walk across the room," he commanded.

Mr. Key obeyed.

"Your limbs are straight and supple," chanted the healer; "your body is strong; your soul is in command; you are healed."

"Thanks to you," breathed the admiring Mrs. Key.

"Tomorrow you can go for a walk," continued Mr. Punshon to his patient. "My work is finished."

Both husband and wife were certain as to his exact words. In fact, the excellent Mrs. Key repeated them to two or three friends the same day. And yet, just before midnight, she sat up in the small bed she occupied in the sick-room almost persuaded that she had heard a moan. Within the next minute five full-grown moans, muffled by the bedclothes, issued from the other bed.

"Aren't you well?" she inquired.

"Well?" repeated Mr. Key, bringing his head up and suppressing moan number six. "Yes, of course I am. Didn't Mr. Punshon say I was?"

In confirmation, he groaned three times and wound up with a faint shriek.

"What are you making that noise for, then?" inquired his wife, not unnaturally.

Mr. Key made no reply. It was evident by his lamentations that he wanted his breath for other purposes. His wife slipped on a dressing-gown and, lighting a candle, crossed over to him.

"What *is* the matter?" she said in alarm.

"Don't mind me," said the invalid, with a groan that made the ornaments on the mantelpiece rattle. "Go to sleep."

His wife suppressed an obvious retort and stood regarding him anxiously.

"*O-o-o-o!*" said Mr. Key. "*A-a-a-h!*" He wiped his brow with the sleeve of his pyjamas and, uttering a faint sigh, was taken suddenly with a series of noises in the throat highly reminiscent of Mr. Punshon.

"I wish I could stop that," he said fretfully. "I suppose it's Punshon's influence. Perhaps I'm too receptive. *O-oh!* My leg!"

Mrs. Key eyed him wistfully. "Which one?" she inquired.

"What the—what does that matter?" exclaimed the sufferer. "Now it's my shoulder. The *left* one," he added bitterly. "Has Jane gone to bed?"

"Long ago," replied his wife, staring.

"I can't bear it," gasped the sufferer wildly. "You'll have to tell her to get up and run for the doctor."

Mrs. Key clasped her hands. "Oh, Silvanus!" she cried reproachfully.

"I can't help it," muttered her husband. "I'd rather have Punshon, of course, but I don't like to disturb him. He could stop it. As soon as he got his blessed paw—hands—on me, it would go."

"I'll ask him to come round in the morning," said Mrs. Key.

"I can't wait," moaned the sufferer. "I'm sorry, but you'll have to ask Jane to get up and go for the doctor. It isn't far."

His wife hesitated. "If you are no better in ten minutes," she said at last, "I'll go and ask Mr. Punshon to come."

Mr. Key protested, and for fully five minutes lay silent. At the end of that time he gave a very fine representation of a soul in torment.

"Better take Jane with you," he said in a weak voice, as his wife began to dress.

"I can't leave you in the house alone," she murmured. "I'll wake her up and let her know I am going out. I shan't be long."

She hurried upstairs, and a minute or two later he heard the front door close.

"Poor thing," he murmured. "Poor thing. It is an infernal shame; but it's all for her own good."

He sat up in bed yawning, every now and then releasing a groan for the benefit of the listener upstairs. The time passed slowly, and a feeling of drowsiness almost overcame him. He hoped fervently that Punshon was as fond of sleep as he was.

He awoke with a start and sat up in bed, listening. A continuous knocking and ringing at the front door seemed to indicate that Mrs. Key had forgotten to take the key with her. It also proved that Jane could sleep as soundly at one in the morning as at seven-thirty.

With an idea that every little helped he added a few whines to the noise below, but in vain. The jangling of the bell was hideous, the knocking incessant. Then he heard, in addition, the boots of a heavy and possibly irritated man kicking the paint off his front door and voices of advice and instruction from his neighbour's bedroom window. He had just come to the conclusion that the maid had passed away in her sleep when he heard her door open and an apologetic whirlwind pass down the stairs.

Mr. Punshon entered the room in silence and, ignoring the faint smile with which the sufferer endeavoured to greet him, took a chair by the bedside and got to work with the air of a man who was going to crowd half an 'hour's work into a few minutes. Mr. Key sighed twice, and then his face resolved itself into an expression of ineffable peace.

"Magician!" he murmured.

Mr. Punshon grunted and bestowed a smile of conscious power upon the admiring Mrs. Key.

"It's wonderful," continued the sufferer. "Wonderful! I wonder what caused the relapse?"

Mr. Punshon started. "You must have been thinking wrong," he said tartly.

"I can't remember doing so," said Mr. Key in a diffident voice. "I have only been congratulating myself upon having the good sense to take your treatment. It has been a great joy to me. Great. I knew I was going to get better when I put myself into your hands. Else I shouldn't have done so."

The unconscious Mr. Punshon smiled again. "Faith helps," he admitted. "How do you feel now?"

Mr. Key looked into the red-rimmed, sleepy eyes peering into his, and hesitated.

"Almost free from pain," he said, at length. "There's just a tiny bit troubling me in the left kneecap."

The healer diverted his gaze to a knob in the bedclothes, and concentrated upon it until the veins stood out on his forehead. An unusual amount of gurgling and choking testified to his absorption.

"Did I say 'left'?" inquired Mr. Key, as the other wiped his brow. "How stupid of me! I meant 'right.'"

He brought another knob into prominence, and, patting it for Mr. Punshon's guidance, waited with calm confidence while the other swallowed a gurgle that threatened to choke him.

"I'm afraid Mr. Punshon is tired," said Mrs. Key.

"He never tires of good works," said her husband reproachfully.

Mr. Punshon smiled wanly and, suppressing a yawn, continued his ministrations.

"I feel so selfish lying here snug and warm in bed and keeping you out of yours," said Mr. Key. "But perhaps you don't care much for sleep."

"Eight hours," said Mr. Punshon somewhat shortly. "Always. Any pain in the knee now?"

Mr. Key shook his head. "It's gone," he said in a hushed voice.

Mr. Punshon leaned back with a sigh, a noisy sigh, of relief.

"Into my left shoulder," continued the invalid querulously.

Mr. Punshon got up with great suddenness and stood glowering at him. Mrs. Key, with her hands clasped, eyed them in silent dismay.

"Please don't trouble anymore," said Mr. Key gently. "I'm afraid it is a difficult case. Too difficult, perhaps. I ought not to have bothered you. I suppose Johnson would have pulled me round, in time."

He closed his eyes wearily and lay back listening in great content to an excited whispering between his wife and the healer. Then he heard the chair creak and felt a pair of clammy hands take his. For some time the stertorous breathing of Mr. Punshon was the only sound in the room. Then even that ceased, and Mr. Key, opening his eyes to ascertain the reason, discovered to his indignation that the healer had gone. Daylight was coming in at the window, and it was only too clear that his victim had taken advantage of the sleep into which Mr. Key had fallen, to escape. A clock downstairs struck five. He groaned in spirit, but soon coming to the conclusion that that was no good, gave utterance to several fleshly ones. The other bed creaked.

"Do you want anything?" inquired Mrs. Key sleepily.

"Where's Punshon?" demanded her husband in an aggrieved voice.

"Why, he left hours ago," said Mrs. Key, sitting up. "He put you into a refreshing slumber and went."

"Fetch him back," said the invalid briefly.

Mrs. Key's cry of consternation left him unmoved. Mr. Punshon had taken the case out of the doctor's hands by giving absent treatment in the first place, and, after that, had taken full charge. In a stern voice, broken by pain and marred by snufflings, Mr. Key ordered him to be fetched forthwith.

"I can't," said his wife desperately.

"Well, will you please go and ask him whether he has any objection to my consulting Dr. Johnson?"

Mrs. Key went—but only after a long argument—to return an hour later with a ferocious and demoralised-looking Mr.

Punshon who, advancing reluctantly to the foot of the bed, stood there gobbling.

"Good of you!" murmured the invalid.

Mr. Punshon took not the slightest notice.

"I do hope this pain will soon go," continued Mr. Key. "I don't want to fetch you out of your bed every night. I know you don't mind, still—"

Mr. Punshon stared at him and endeavoured—but in vain—to concentrate his mind upon healing.

"I suppose I can't have that walk you spoke of, today," said Mr. Key. "It's very disappointing. I was looking forward to it. I wanted to go round and tell people what mental healing had done for me. Some of them are so incredulous."

"You must have patience," said the healer. "Fifty years of wrong living—"

"Forty-three," murmured the invalid. "And I feel younger since you have been treating me. It almost seems as though your healthy, virile spirit has become part of myself. I feel different. A better man. I think differently. I—I breathe differently. How is Mrs. Punshon?"

"She is quite well, thank you," said the healer with some surprise.

Mr. Key half closed his eyes and a seraphic smile played around his lips. "I dream of her," he said softly.

"*Dream!* Dream of her? Dream of *my wife?*" stuttered the outraged husband in tones that nearly drowned the exclamation of the startled Mrs. Key.

Mr. Key nodded. "Ever since you started treating me," he replied. "It's very curious. I suppose your powerful mind has overcome mine and your thoughts have become my thoughts. Have any of your other patients—?"

"No, sir," interrupted the other with violence.

Mr. Key sighed. "It's very curious," he repeated. "I dreamt of her three times last night. And there's another funny thing:

since this treatment started I have had an almost irrestible craving for whisky. Do you—"

"I'm a lifelong teetotaller," said the glaring Mr. Punshon.

He stood breathing noisily for a few seconds and then, with a violent gesture, turned and walked towards the door.

"Aren't you going to give me treatment?" inquired Mr. Key in a surprised voice.

Mr. Punshon made no reply, but the slamming of the front door spoke volumes. Mr. Key turned and eyed his wife.

"He has given the case up," he said, shaking his head. "After breakfast you must send Jane round for the doctor. I can't go on like this."

He saw the doctor a few hours later, and after a lengthy explanation—with Mrs. Key holding a watching brief for the absent Mr. Punshon—requested him to treat him for the old complaint plus incipient adenoids, a nasty trick of biting his fingernails, a lamentable craving for whisky, and a few other matters.

"I am sorry you spoke so freely," said Mrs. Key after the doctor had gone. "He might talk."

"That's all right," said her husband darkly. "He never repeats anything his patients would mind."

15

HIS BROTHER'S KEEPER

I

Anthony Keller, white and dazed, came stumbling out into the small hall and closed the door of his study noiselessly behind him. Only half an hour ago he had entered the room with Henry Martle, and now Martle would never leave it again until he was carried out of it.

He took out his watch and put it back again without looking at it. He sank into a chair and, trying to still his quivering legs, strove to think. The clock behind the closed door struck nine. He had ten hours; ten hours before the woman who attended to his small house came to start the next day's work.

Ten hours! His mind refused to act. There was so much to be done, so much to be thought of. God! If only he could have the last ten minutes over again and live it differently. If Martle only had not happened to say that it was a sudden visit and that nobody knew of it.

He went into the back room, and, going to the sideboard, gulped down half a tumbler of raw whisky. It seemed to him inconceivable that the room should look the same. This pleasant room, with etchings on the walls, and his book, face downwards, just as he had left it to answer Martle's knock. He could hear the knock now, and—

The empty tumbler smashed in his hand, and he caught his breath in a sob. Somebody else was knocking. He stood for a moment quivering, and then, wiping some of the blood from his hand, kicked the pieces of glass aside and stood irresolute. The knocking came again, so loud and insistent that for one horrible moment he fancied it might arouse the thing in the next room. Then he walked to the door and opened it. A short sturdy man, greeting him noisily, stepped into the hall.

"Thought you were dead," he said breezily. "Hallo!"

"Cut myself with a broken glass," said Keller, in a constrained voice.

"Look here, that wants binding up," said his friend. "Got a clean handkerchief?"

He moved towards the door, and was about to turn the handle when Keller flung himself upon him and dragged him back. "Not there," he said thickly. "Not there."

"What the devil's the matter?" inquired the visitor, staring.

Keller's mouth worked. "Somebody in there," he muttered; "somebody in there. Come here."

He pushed him into the back room and in a dazed fashion motioned him to a chair.

"Thanks, rather not," said the other stiffly, "I just came in to smoke a pipe. I didn't know you had visitors. Anyway, I shouldn't eat them. Good night."

Keller stood staring at him. His friend stared back, then suddenly his eyes twinkled and he smiled roguishly.

"What have you got in there?" he demanded, jerking his thumb towards the study.

Keller shrank back. "Nothing," he stammered. "Nothing—no—"

"Ho, ho!" said the other. "All right. Don't worry. Mum's the word. You quiet ones are always the worst. Be good."

He gave him a playful dig in the ribs and went out chuckling. Keller, hardly breathing, watched him to the gate and, closing the door softly, bolted it and returned to the back room.

He steadied his nerves with some more whisky, and strove to steel himself to the task before him. He had got to conquer his horror and remorse, to overcome his dread of the thing in the next room, and put it where no man should ever see it. He, Anthony Keller, a quiet, ordinary citizen, had got to do this thing.

The little clock in the next room struck ten. Nine hours left. With a soft tread he went out at the back door and, unlocking the bicycle-shed, peered in. Plenty of room.

He left the door open and, returning to the house, went to the door of the study. Twice he turned the handle—and softly closed the door again. Suppose when he looked in at Martle, Martle should turn and look at him? He turned the handle suddenly and threw the door open.

Martle was quiet enough. Quiet and peaceful, and, perhaps, a little pitiful. Keller's fear passed, but envy took its place. Martle had got the best of it after all. No horror-haunted life for him; no unavailing despair and fear of the unknown. Keller, looking down at the white face and battered head, thought of the years before himself. Or would it be weeks? With a gasp he came back to the need for action, and taking Martle by the shoulders drew him, with heels dragging and scraping, to the shed.

He locked the door and put the key in his pocket. Then he drew a bucket of water from the scullery-tap and found some towels. His injured hand was still bleeding, but he regarded it with a sort of cunning satisfaction. It would account for much.

It was a long job, but it was finished at last. He sat down and thought, and then searched round and round the room for the overlooked thing which might be his undoing.

It was nearly midnight, and necessary, unless he wanted to attract the attention of any passing constable, to extinguish or lower the companionable lights. He turned them out swiftly, and, with trembling haste, passed upstairs to his room.

The thought of bed was impossible. He lowered the gas and, dropping into a chair, sat down to wait for day. Erect in the chair, his hands gripping the arms, he sat tense and listening. The quiet house was full of faint sounds, odd creakings, and stealthy rustlings. Suppose the suddenly released spirit of Martle was wandering around the house!

He rose and paced up and down the room, pausing every now and then to listen. He could have sworn that there was something fumbling blindly at the other side of the door, and once, turning sharply, thought that he saw the handle move. Sometimes sitting and sometimes walking, the hours passed until in the distance a cock smelt the dawn, and a little later the occasional note of a bird announced the approach of day.

II

In the bright light of day his courage returned, and, dismissing all else from his mind, he thought only of how to escape the consequences of his crime. Inch by inch he examined the room and the hall. Then he went into the garden, and, going round the shed, satisfied himself that no crack or hole existed that might reveal his secret. He walked the length of the garden and looked about him. The nearest house was a hundred yards away, and the bottom of the garden screened by trees. Near the angle of the fence he would dig a shallow trench and over it pile up a rockery of bricks and stones and earth. Once started he could take his time about it, and every day would make him more and more secure. There was an air of solidity and permanency about a rockery that nothing else could give.

He was back in the house when the charwoman arrived, and in a few words told her of his accident of the night before. "I cleaned up the—the mess as well as I could," he concluded.

Mrs. Howe nodded. "I'll have a go at it while you're having your breakfast," she remarked. "Good job for you, sir, that you ain't one o' them as faints at the sight of blood."

She brought coffee and bacon into the little back dining-room, and Keller, as he sat drinking his coffee and trying to eat, heard her at work in the study. He pushed away his plate at last, and filling a pipe from which all flavour had departed sat smoking and thinking.

He was interrupted by Mrs. Howe. She stood in the doorway with a question which numbed his brain, and for a time arrested speech.

"Eh?" he said at last.

"Key of the bicycle-shed," repeated the woman, staring at him. "You had a couple o' my dusters to clean your bicycle with."

Keller felt in his pockets, thinking, thinking. "H'm!" he said at last, "I'm afraid I've mislaid it. I'll look for it presently."

Mrs. Howe nodded. "You do look bad," she said, with an air of concern. "P'r'aps you hurt yourself more than what you think."

Keller forced a smile and shook his head, sinking back in his chair as she vanished, and trying to control his quivering limbs.

For a long time he sat inert, listening dully to the movements of Mrs. Howe as she bustled to and fro. He heard her washing the step at the back door, and, after that, a rasping, grating noise to which at first he paid but little heed. Then there was a faint, musical clinking as of keys knocking together. *Keys!*

He sprang from his chair like a madman, and dashed to the door. Mrs. Howe, with a bunch of odd keys tied on a string, had inserted one in the lock of the bicycle-shed, and was trying to turn it.

"Stop!" cried Keller, in a dreadful voice. "STOP!"

He snatched the keys from her, and, flinging them from him, stood mouthing dumbly at her. The fear in her eyes recalled him to his senses.

"Spoil the lock," he muttered, "spoil the lock. Sorry. I didn't mean to shout. No sleep all night. Neuralgia; 'fraid my nerves are wrong."

The woman's face relaxed and her eyes softened. "I saw you weren't yourself as soon as I saw you this morning," she exclaimed.

She went back into the house, but he thought she eyed him curiously as she passed. She resumed her work, but in a subdued fashion, and, two or three times that morning meeting his eyes, nervously turned away her own. He realised at last that he was behaving in an unusual fashion altogether. In and out of the house, and, in the garden, never far from the shed.

By lunch-time he had regained control of himself. He opened a bottle of beer, and, congratulating Mrs. Howe upon the grilling of the chops, went on to speak of her husband and the search for work which had been his only occupation since his marriage ten years before. Some of the fear went out of the woman's eyes—but not all, and it was with obvious relief that she left the room.

For some time after lunch Keller stayed in the dining-room, and that in itself was unusual. Two or three times he got up and resolved, for the sake of appearances, to take a short walk, but the shed held him. He dare not leave it unguarded. With a great effort he summoned up sufficient resolution to take him to the bottom of the garden and start his gruesome task.

He dug roughly, avoiding the shape which might have aroused comment from any chance visitor. The ground was soft and, in spite of his injured hand, he made good progress, breaking off at frequent intervals to listen, or to move aside and obtain an unobstructed view of the shed.

With a short break for tea he went on with in to his task until he was called into his simple meal at seven. The manual labour had done him good and his appearance was almost normal. To Mrs. Howe he made a casual reference to his afternoon's work and questioned where to obtain the best rock-plants.

With her departure after she had cleared away, fear descended upon him again. The house became uncanny and the shed a place of unspeakable horror. Suppose his nerve failed and he found himself unable to open it! For an hour he paced up and down in the long twilight, waiting for the dark.

It came at last, and, fighting down his fears and nausea, he drew the garden-barrow up to the shed, and took the key from his pocket. He walked to the front gate and looked up and down the silent road. Then he came back and, inserting the key in the lock, opened the door, and, in the light of an electric torch, stood looking down at what he had placed there the night before.

With his ears alert for the slightest sound, he took the inhabitant of the shed by the shoulders, and, dragging it outside, strove to lift it into the barrow. He succeeded at last, and, with the rigid body balanced precariously and the dead face looking up into his, seized the handles and slowly and silently took Martle to the place prepared for him.

He did not leave him for a long time. Not until the earth was piled high above him in a circular mound and a score or two of bricks formed the first beginnings of a rockery. Then he walked slowly up the garden, and, after attending to the shed, locked it up and went indoors.

The disposal of the body gave a certain measure of relief. He would live, with time for repentance, and, perhaps, for forgetting. He washed in the scullery, and then, fearing the shadows upstairs, drew the heavy curtains in the dining-room to shut in the light and settled himself in an easy chair. He drank until his senses were deadened; his nerves quietened, his aching limbs relaxed, and he fell into a heavy sleep.

III

He awoke at six, and, staggering to his feet, drew back the curtains and turned out the gas. Then he went upstairs, and after disarranging his bed, went to the bathroom. The cold water and a shave, together with a change of linen, did him good. He opened doors and windows, and let the clean sweet air blow through the house. The house which he must continue to inhabit because he dare not leave it. Other people might not share this taste for rockeries.

To the watchful eye of Mrs. Howe he appeared to be almost himself again. The key of the shed had turned up, and he smiled as he presented her with her "precious dusters." Then he rode off on his bicycle to order slabs of stone and plants from the nearest nurseryman.

He worked more and more leisurely as the days passed, and the rockery grew larger and more solid. Every added stone and plant seemed to increase his security. He ate well and, to his surprise, slept well; but every morning misery opened his eyes for him.

The garden was no longer a place of quiet recreation; the house, which was part of the legacy that had so delighted him only a year before, was a prison in which he must serve a lifelong sentence. He could neither let it nor sell it; other people might alter the garden—and dig. Since the fatal evening he had not looked at a newspaper for fear of reading of Martle's disappearance, and in all that time had not spoken to a friend.

Martle was very quiet. There were no shadows in the house, no furtive noises, no dim shape pattering about the garden by night. Memory was the only thing that assailed him; but it sufficed.

Then the dream came. A dream confused and grotesque, as most dreams are. He dreamt that he was standing by the rockery, in the twilight, when he thought he saw one of the stones move. Other stones followed suit. A big slab near the top came slithering down, and it was apparent that the whole pile of earth and stone was being shaken by some internal force. Something was trying to get out. Then he remembered that he was buried there, and had no business to be standing outside. He must get back. Martle had put him there, and for some reason which he was quite unable to remember he was afraid of Martle. He procured his tools and set to work. It was a long and tedious job, and made more difficult by the fact that he was not allowed to make a noise. He dug and dug, but the grave had disappeared. Then suddenly something took hold of him and held him down; down. He could neither move nor cry out.

He awoke with a scream and for a minute or two lay trembling and shaking. Thank God, it was only a dream. The room was full of sunlight, and he could hear Mrs. Howe moving about downstairs. Life was good and might yet hold something in store for him.

He lay still for ten minutes, and was about to rise when he heard Mrs. Howe running upstairs. Even before her sudden and heavy rapping on the door he scented disaster.

"Mr. Keller! Mr. Keller!"

"Well?" he said heavily.

"Your rockery!" gasped the charwoman. "Your beautiful rockery! All gone!"

"*Gone?*" shouted Keller, springing out of bed and snatching his dressing-gown from the door.

"Pulled all to pieces," said Mrs. Howe, as he opened the door. "You never see such a mess. All over the place, as if a madman had done it."

In a mechanical fashion he thrust his feet into slippers and went downstairs. He hurried down the garden, and, waving the woman back, stood looking at the ruin. Stones and earth were indeed all over the place, but the spot that mattered was untouched. He stood gazing and trembling. Who could have done it? Why was it done?

He thought of his dream and the truth burst upon him. No need for his aching back and limbs to remind him. No need to remember the sleepwalking feats of his youth. He knew the culprit now.

"Shall I go for the police?" inquired the voice of Mrs. Howe.

Keller turned a stony face upon her. "No," he said slowly. "I—I'll speak to them about it myself."

He took up the spade and began the task of reconstruction. He worked for an hour, and then went in to dress and breakfast. For the rest of the day he worked slowly and steadily, so that by evening most of the damage had been repaired. Then he went indoors to face the long night.

Sleep, man's best friend, had become his unrelenting enemy. He made himself coffee on the gas-stove and fought his drowsiness cup by cup. He read and smoked and walked about the room. Bits of his dream, that he had forgotten, came back to him and stayed with him. And ever at the back of his mind was the certainty that he was doomed.

There was only one hope left to him. He would go away for a time. Far enough away to render a visit home in his sleep impossible. And perhaps the change of scene would strengthen him and help his frayed nerves. Afterwards it might be possible to let the house for a time on condition that the garden was not interfered with. It was one risk against another.

He went down the garden as soon as it was light and completed his work. Then he went indoors to breakfast and to announce his plans for sudden departure to Mrs. Howe, his white and twitching face amply corroborating his tale of neuralgia and want of sleep.

"Things'll be all right," said the woman. "I'll ask the police to keep an eye on the house of a night. I did speak to one last night about them brutes as destroyed the rockery. If they try it again they may get a surprise."

Keller quivered but made no sign. He went upstairs and packed his bag, and two hours later was in the train on his way to Exeter, where he proposed to stay the night. After that, Cornwall, perhaps.

He secured a room at an hotel and went for a stroll to pass the time before dinner. How happy the people in the streets seemed to be, even the poorest! All free and all sure of their freedom. They could eat and sleep and enjoy the countless trivial things that make up life. Of battle and murder and sudden death they had no thought.

The light and bustle of the dining-room gave him a little comfort. After his lonely nights it was good to know that there were people all around him, that the house would be full of them whilst he slept. He felt that he was beginning a fresh existence. In future he would live amongst a crowd.

It was late when he went upstairs, but he lay awake for a few minutes. A faint sound or two reached him from downstairs, and the movements of somebody in the next room gave him a comfortable feeling of security. With a sigh of content he fell asleep.

He was awakened by a knocking; a knocking which sounded just above the head of his bed and died away almost before he had brushed the sleep from his eyes. He looked around fearfully, and then, lighting his candle, lay listening. The noise was not repeated. He had been dreaming, but he could not remember the substance of his dream. It had been unpleasant, but vague. More than unpleasant—terrifying. Somebody had been shouting at him. *Shouting!*

He fell back with a groan. The faint hopes of the night before died within him. *He* had been shouting and the strange noise came from the occupant of the next room. What had he said? And what had his neighbour heard?

He slept no more. From somewhere below he heard a clock toll the hours, and, tossing in his bed, wondered how manymore remained to him.

Day came at last and he descended to breakfast. The hour was early and only two other tables were occupied, from one of which, between mouthfuls, a bluff-looking, elderly man eyed him curiously. He caught Keller's eye at last, and spoke.

"Better?" he inquired.

Keller tried to force his quivering lips to a smile.

"Stood it as long as I could," said the other; "then I knocked. I thought perhaps you were delirious. Same words over and over again; sounded like 'Mockery' and 'Mortal,' 'Mockery' and 'Mortal.' You must have used them a hundred times."

Keller finished his coffee, and, lighting a cigarette, went and sat in the lounge. He had made his bid for freedom and failed. He looked up the times of the trains to town and rang for his bill.

IV

He was back in the silent house, upon which, in the fading light of the summer evening, a great stillness seemed to have descended. The atmosphere of horror had gone and left only a sense of abiding peace. All fear had left him, and pain and remorse had gone with it. Serene and tranquil he went into the fatal room, and, opening the window, sat by it, watching the succession of shadowy tableaux that had been his life. Some of it good and some of it bad, but most of it neither good nor bad. A very ordinary life until fate had linked it for all time with that of Martle's. He was a living man bound to a corpse with bonds that could never be severed.

It grew dark and he lit the gas and took a volume of poems from the shelves. Never before had he read with such insight and appreciation. In some odd fashion all his senses seemed to have been sharpened and refined.

He read for an hour, and then, replacing the book, went slowly upstairs. For a long time he lay in bed thinking and trying to analyse the calm and indifference which had overtaken him and, with the problem still unsolved, fell asleep.

For a time he dreamt, but of pleasant, happy things. He seemed to be filled with a greater content than he had ever known before, a content which did not leave him even when these dreams faded and he found himself back in the old one.

This time, however, it was different. He was still digging, but not in a state of frenzy and horror. He dug because something told him it was his duty to dig, and only by digging could he make reparation. And it was a matter of no surprise to him that Martle stood close by looking on. Not the Martle he had known, nor a bloody and decaying Martle, but one of grave and noble aspect. And there was a look of understanding on his face that nearly made Keller weep.

He went on digging with a sense of companionship such as he had never known before. Then suddenly, without warning, the sun blazed out of the darkness and struck him full in the face. The light was unbearable, and with a wild cry he dropped his spade and clapped his hands over his eyes. The light went, and a voice spoke to him out of the darkness.

He opened his eyes on a dim figure standing a yard or two away.

"Hope I didn't frighten you, sir," said the voice. "I called to you once or twice, and then I guessed you were doing this in your sleep."

"In my sleep," repeated Keller. "Yes."

"And a pretty mess you've made of it," said the constable, with a genial chuckle. "Lord! To think of you working at it everyday and then pulling it down every night. Shouted at you did, but you wouldn't wake."

He turned on the flashlight that had dazzled Keller, and surveyed the ruins. Keller stood by, motionless and waiting.

"Looks like an earthquake," muttered the constable. He paused, and kept the light directed upon one spot. Then he stooped down and scratched away the earth with his fingers, and tugged. He stood up suddenly and turned the light on Keller, while with the other he fumbled in his pocket. He spoke in a voice cold and official.

"Are you coming quietly?" he asked.

Keller stepped towards him with both hands outstretched.

"I am coming quietly," he said, in a low voice. "Thank God!"

16

TRUST MONEY

The night-watchman set his lips and shook his head.

"You can't learn people," he said firmly; "it ain't to be done. They all know better than wot you do, and the more iggernerant they are the more they are satisfied with themselves. I once wasted a whole morning telling my missus 'ow to make a steak-pudding, and arter it was done we 'ad to give it to the people next door. She's never forgot it, and to hear 'er talk—if you didn't know her—you'd think it was my fault. The way she twists things round would surprise anybody as wasn't married."

He gazed meditatively at a passing tug with its string of barges, and shook his head again before continuing:

"Even experience don't learn people. One chap I know used to save 'is money in a little tin money-box. He 'ad 'arf a ounce o' baccy a week and no beer. The box was so full o' sixpences he was thinking of getting another, when his wife's brother lost 'is job and didn't get another till the box was empty.

"You'd ha' thought that would 'ave learned 'im a lesson, but it didn't, and he'd pretty near got another box full when 'is wife 'ad the artfulness to break her leg and 'ad to go to the seaside for a fortnight to get well. He's saving up agin now for wot 'e calls a rainy day. He'll get it all right, and somebody else'll get the money.

"Sailormen never learn anything. If they did they wouldn't be sailormen. They're like children that never grow up. It don't matter where they go ashore with their money, they always go back aboard agin without it.

"I remember one time when old Sam Small was ashore with Peter Russet and Ginger Dick 'aving wot they called a rest; their idea of a rest being spending 'arf the day in bed and the other 'arf leaning up agin the bar of a public-'ouse telling fairy-tales to the barmaid. They was like three twins for the fust few days, and then Sam wouldn't 'ave nothing more to do with 'em owing to them telling the barmaid at the 'Turk's Head'—a very nice gal with yeller 'air and black eyes—that he 'ad got a wife and thirteen children at Melbourne.

"He walked 'ome in front of 'em as if they wasn't there, and when 'e shut the front door he seemed to 'ave the same idea. Ginger noticed it most—being just behind 'im. They 'ad words about it when they got upstairs, and Sam told 'em plain that he never wanted to see their faces agin; not even if they washed 'em.

"He purtended to be asleep while they was dressing next morning. His eyes was screwed up tight, and it didn't seem as if anything could open 'em, till Ginger said 'e thought he 'ad passed away in 'is sleep and asked Peter to get a pin and make sure. Sam woke up then, and, arter he 'ad finished speaking, Ginger and Peter said they never wanted to see *his* face agin.

"They went off by theirselves, and arter a time Sam got up and went off by 'imself. He didn't see anything of Peter or Ginger at all that day, but from wot the barmaid 'ad to say about 'is grandchildren 'e found they 'ad spent a lot o' time drinking beer and telling more lies at the 'Turk's Head.'

"He sat up in bed and spoke to 'em about it when they came in that night, but they wouldn't listen to 'im. They said that 'is troubles didn't concern them and they'd be thankful if he'd take 'em somewhere else.

"'We've done with you,' ses Ginger.

"'Forever,' ses Peter. 'And my advice to you, Sam, is to leave off afore you bursts a blood-vessel. Anybody might think the 'ouse was on fire.'

"Sam didn't speak to them at all after that and they didn't speak to 'im, but they 'ad a great deal to say about 'im to each other when 'e was in the room. It was wot Ginger called a nasty subjeck, but they never seemed to get tired of it.

"Sam 'ad made up 'is mind to leave 'em and go off on his own, and then 'e came 'ome one night so full of excitement 'e forgot all about it. He came into the room like a schoolboy and gave 'em such a nice smile they thought he 'ad lost 'is reason. Then he done a little dance all by 'imself in the middle of the room and sat down on 'is bed and laughed.

"'I've come into a forchin,' he ses to Peter as the two of 'em stood staring at 'im. 'Leastways, I shall tomorrer night.'

"Ginger coughed. But not a disagreeable cough, mind you.

"'Come into a forchin?' he ses. ''Ow?'

"Old Sam didn't seem to hear 'im. He sat on 'is bed all rosy with smiles and looking straight at the chest o' drawers as though 'e saw a pile of gold on top of it.

"'And I owe it all to you and Peter, Ginger,' he ses, bending down to undo 'is boots. 'If you 'adn't been misbe'aved, and carrying on like a couple of bald-faced monkeys purtending to be men, I shouldn't 'ave gone off on my own, and if I 'adn't ha' gone off on my own I shouldn't 'ave met 'em.'

"'Met who?' ses Ginger, who was too excited to take any notice of wot he 'ad said about monkeys.

"'Two o' the best,' ses Sam; 'two gentlemen whose on'y objeck in life is to do good to their fellow-creechers. They told me so theirselves.'

"'Did you stand 'em drinks?' ses Peter, catching Ginger's eye.

"'You've got a low mind, Peter,' ses Sam, shaking his 'ead; 'you ought to be more careful who you go about with. I've 'ad six drinks tonight, or maybe more, and I didn't pay for one of 'em. They wouldn't let me."

"'You don't always try very 'ard,' ses Peter, who was beginning to lose his temper

"'Wot 'ave they got to do with your forchin?' ses Ginger.

"'It's coming through them,' ses Sam, 'and if you and Peter was different, if you was on'y 'arf men instead of—of being wot you are, I would get forchins for you too. There's plenty more where mine's coming from.'

"'Where's that?' ses Ginger, trying to speak off-hand.

"Sam turned deaf agin, and was just going to get into bed when Ginger stopped 'im gentle-like and turning down the bed-clo'es took out a 'air-brush, an old horse-shoe, a lump o' soap, and a few other things wot 'im and Peter 'ad put there.

"'The 'orse-shoe was for luck, Sam,' he ses, with a smile. 'P'r'aps it's through that you got your forchin.'

"Sam looked at 'im as if he was looking at a dustbin with a bad smell, and then without a word he got into bed and, putting his 'ead on the piller, shut 'is eyes and went straight off to sleep. Ginger woke up the next morning dreaming that the 'ouse was on fire. The room was full o' smoke, but the moment 'e got 'is eyes open he saw that it was made by Sam, who was sitting up in bed smoking an enormous cigar with a red-and-gold band stuck on it. He purtended not to see that Ginger was looking at 'im, and the airs and graces he see fit to give 'imself with that cigar nearly made Ginger choke. Peter Russet woke up then, and arter he 'ad sniffed and sniffed as if 'e couldn't believe his nose, 'e asked Sam in a nasty voice where he 'ad pinched it from.

"'It was give to me by one o' the gentlemen I was speaking of,' ses Sam, knocking the ash off down 'is neck by mistake. 'He's got a gold case full of 'em.'

"'Gold case?' ses Ginger.

"'With diamonds on it," ses Sam. 'He said 'e would 'ave liked to give it to me, on'y it was a birthday present from 'is little boy wot died of whooping-cough.'

"Ginger scratched his 'ead, and 'e kept on scratching it till Sam said as 'ow it was vulgar, and asked 'im to go out of the room to do it.

"'But who are they?' ses Peter Russet, arter Ginger 'ad quieted down a bit.

"'Two gentlemen,' says Sam; 'two gentlemen wot knows another gentleman when they sees 'im.'

"He laid down on 'is back and blew smoke up to the ceiling, until Ginger and Peter sat down on Ginger's bed and tried to swaller their pride and ask him to tell 'em all about it. Ginger tried fust, but he 'adn't swallered enough, and when Sam sat up in bed and told 'im part of wot he thought of 'im, Peter took his side and said that if Ginger 'ad on'y been born without a mouth it 'ud be much better for 'imself and everybody else. He gave Ginger a poke in the ribs with 'is elbow to keep 'im quiet, and said that if anybody deserved to 'ave a forchin given 'im it was Sam Small.

"'One o' the best,' he ses, giving Ginger another poke with 'is elbow.

"'We all 'ave our faults, Peter,' ses Sam, with a kind smile, 'else we should all be angels.'

"'There ain't no fat angels,' ses Ginger, pushing Peter's elbow away. 'They wouldn't look nice. All the angels I've seen in pikchers 'ave got beautiful figgers.'

"Peter gave it up then, and arter telling Ginger in a whisper wot a fool 'e was, he picked up 'is trousers off of the floor and began to dress. Neither of 'em took anymore notice o' Sam, and arter laying still for a time watching 'em wash and telling Ginger that the soap wouldn't bite 'im he began talking to 'em of 'is own free will.

"He told 'em of a nice, comfortable little pub in a turning off the Mile End Road wot he 'ad found on the evening before. A little pub—clean as a new pin, and as quiet and respectable as a front-parlour. Everybody calling the landlady 'Ma' and the landlady calling most of 'em by their Christian names and asking arter their families. There was two poll parrots in cages, with not a bad word between 'em—except once when a man played the cornet outside—and a canary that almost sang its little 'art out.

"'Wot about the two gentlemen that took a fancy to you?' ses Ginger.

"Sam looked at 'im for a moment as if he was surprised at 'im speaking to 'im.

"'There was on'y one at fust,' he ses at last, very slow, 'a thin gentleman with a little black moustache, a beautiful white collar, and a silk necktie with a gold pin in it. He was drinking port wine when I went in, and arter looking me up and down, just for a moment, 'e asked me to 'ave one with 'im.'

"'Wot for?' ses Ginger.

"'He told me arterwards,' ses Sam. 'He said as 'ow I was the living image of a cousin of 'is wot 'ad lost his life at sea—saving others. He said at first he thought I was 'is ghost. There was on'y me and 'im in that bar, and the tears came into his eyes when 'e spoke of 'im.'

"'But wot about the forchin, Sam?' ses Ginger, arter waiting a bit. 'Wot's the ugly cousin got to do with it?'

"Sam sat up in bed and looked at 'im. Then 'e snapped his lips tight as if 'e was never going to open 'em agin and laid back on the piller.

"'Go on, Sam, old man,' ses Peter Russet; 'if Ginger had 'arf your looks 'e wouldn't be so bad-tempered. He's got a jealous dispersition. You was just telling us about 'ow the tears came into 'is eyes.'

"'We 'ad a long talk,' ses Sam, arter looking very 'ard at Ginger, 'and arter standing me another glass o' port wine 'e began to tell me all about 'is troubles. He 'ad got hard up through 'elping a friend, and 'e didn't know where to turn for money. He went into that little pub with fourpence ha'penny in 'is pocket and went out with five 'undred pounds.'

"''Ow?' ses Peter and Ginger, both speaking at the same time.

"'While 'e was 'aving a fit of the miserables in there and wondering wot 'e was going to do,' ses Sam, in a solemn voice, 'the door opened and a gentleman came in. A gentleman wot goes about looking for feller-creechers to do good to. That was 'ow the gentleman as was standing me port wine got 'is five hundred pounds.'

"'Did you see it?' ses Ginger, in a nasty voice.

"'I see more than that, Ginger,' ses Sam, speaking very low; 'I see enough money last night to make the three of us gentlemen for life. And Mr. Cooper—that's the gentleman wot 'as it—goes about giving it away. He gave the other gentleman, Mr. Jackson by name, five 'undred pounds for trusting 'im. He got talking to 'im and told 'im that a friend of 'is had left 'im a forchin, and as he was a rich man and didn't want it, 'e was giving it away. But on'y to people that deserved it, mind yer. And 'e said that the people 'e could trust was them as trusted others.'

"'I can't make 'ead or tail of it,' ses Ginger.

"'He took a good 'ard look at Mr. Jackson,' ses Sam, 'and then 'e put a thousand pounds into his 'and and told 'im to go for a walk with it while 'e waited for 'im in the pub. When Mr. Jackson came back he asked 'im whether *he* could trust *'im*, and Mr. Jackson, not 'aving any money, trusted 'im with 'is gold watch and chain, two rings, and a tie-pin. When 'e came back he patted 'im on the back and gave 'im five 'undred pounds. Mr. Jackson said 'e cried like a child.'

"''Cos he 'adn't gone off with the thousand pounds, d'ye mean?' ses Ginger, staring.

"'While he was telling me this,' ses Sam to Peter Russet, 'who should come in but Mr. Cooper 'imself—a short, fat gentleman with blue eyes like a innercent child's and one o' the kindest faces I ever see. It done me good to look at 'im. He was a bit stand-offish at fust, but arter a time we was all 'aving drinks together like brothers. And then Mr. Jackson took 'im a bit to one side and whispered to 'im, and I could see plain that 'e was talking about me.'

"'Cut it short,' ses Ginger, fidgeting.

"'I ain't talking to you,' ses Sam. 'Ten minutes arterwards *I* was going for a walk with a thousand pounds in my pocket in banknotes, *and* the gold cigar-case. I couldn't trust 'im when I came back as I 'ad on'y got four bob in my pocket, but tonight I'm going to meet 'im agin and trust 'im with all I've got. And Mr. Jackson told me 'e wouldn't be surprised if I got a thousand pounds. He said Mr. Cooper told 'im that he 'ad took a partikier fancy to me.'

"'I can't make 'ead or tail of it,' ses Ginger, 'but mark my words, Sam, there's a catch in it somewhere. Nobody 'ud take a fancy to you unless they was going to get something out of it.'

"Sam didn't take no notice of 'im. He got up and dressed 'imself, and when they asked 'im wot he was going to do till evening, he told 'em that was 'is business. Peter Russet and Ginger spent the day together, both of 'em wondering, if Sam did get a forchin, whether they couldn't get one the same way. At last, arter they had 'ad a few pints apiece, they made up their minds to hang about till Sam came 'ome and then follow 'im, unbeknownst, to the pub.

"*They* didn't wait for 'im in their room 'cos they thought 'e might tumble to it, and he was so late turning up that they began to think 'e wasn't coming 'ome fust arter all. Then about ha'-past six they see 'im come round the corner and go straight into the 'ouse.

"It seemed ages afore he came out agin, and when 'e did they see that he 'ad got 'is best clo'es on and a new cap. They let 'im get a good start, and then follered in a drizzling rain which made the Minories and Whitechapel full of umbrellas that kept getting in between them and Sam, especially one that nearly put Ginger's eye out. It wasn't till he 'ad turned into a quiet street off the Mile End Road that they felt sure of 'im.

"They follered, very careful, and then at last they saw 'im stop at the door of a quiet little pub at the corner of a dark little street. There wasn't a soul about, and, arter stopping a moment to pull 'is cap straight, Sam pushed open the door and stepped inside. Ginger and Peter, arter pinching each other's arms in their excitement, stood in a doorway a little way off and waited.

"'I s'pose he's drinking glasses and glasses o' port wine while we're out 'ere in the wet,' ses Ginger, arter about ten minutes.

"'Why don't they make 'aste?' ses Peter Russet. 'I believe there's a catch in it somewhere.'

"'*H'sh!*' ses Ginger, all of a sudden.

"They drew back into the doorway and just poked their 'eads out as they saw the pub door open and a man come out. He stood a moment waving his 'and to Sam, who they could see standing near the bar, and then walked off slow down the road.

"'Come on,' ses Ginger. 'Let's see where he goes.'

"They follered as quiet as they could, and then all at once they found themselves going quicker and quicker to keep up with 'im. Twice 'e went round corners, and when they got round they found 'e was ever so far in front.

"'He's been running,' ses Ginger. 'Come on! He's going off with Sam's money!'

"He started running as 'ard as he could, with Peter just be'ind, and the man in front, wot 'ad begun to run 'imself, left off—and began to walk agin.

"'Wot d'ye want?' he ses, as Ginger caught 'old of 'im, and afore Ginger could answer 'im he gave 'im a fearful bang in the face and a kick in the leg that pretty near broke it.

"Ginger gave two grunts, one for the smack in the face and the other for the kick, and then 'e sailed in at 'im like a madman, and knocked 'im all over the place. His last punch got 'im fair on the chin, and 'e went down in the gutter like a lamb that 'as been pole-axed, and hit 'is 'ead on the kerb.

"'You've killed 'im,' ses Peter, staring.

"'Good job, too,' ses Ginger, thinking of 'is pore leg. 'Gome on, let's get Sam's money back.'

"Peter looked be'ind 'im, and then, seeing there was nobody about, 'elped Ginger to empty the chap's pockets. In less than a minute they 'ad picked 'im as clean as a bone and was hurrying off, Peter 'olding a watch and chain in his 'and and Ginger stuffing things into 'is pockets and saying that it wasn't robbing to rob a thief. Especially a thief wot kicked.

"They lost their way for a bit, but Ginger didn't mind. He said the more they got lost the 'arder it would be for anybody to find 'em, but they got 'ome at last and, arter shutting the bedroom door careful, emptied out their pockets on to the bed and stood staring at each other.

"'*We've* got the forchin, Peter,' ses Ginger. 'Count it agin to make sure.'

"'Twenty-seven pounds fourteen shillings and threepence,' ses Peter, 'two watches and chains—that one is Sam's'

"'One clasp knife,' ses Ginger, 'a bit o' lead-pencil, a gold cigar-case made o' something else, and a bundle of imitation banknotes. That's wot 'e trusted Sam with, I expect, Peter.'

"'I wonder 'ow much of the twenty-seven pounds is Sam's?' ses Peter Russet.

"'I forgot that,' ses Ginger. 'He ought to pay something for that kick on the leg I got, though.'

"Peter Russet, wot 'ad seen the leg, nodded. 'I wouldn't 'ave 'ad that kick for ten pounds,' he ses, in a kind voice. 'If you 'ave to lose your leg, Ginger, I wouldn't have 'ad it for fifty.'

"Ginger 'ad another look at his leg, and then, to prevent losing it, 'e bathed it with a little cold water and put a bit o' butter on it. Arter which they went out as far as the Town of Ramsgate public-'ouse to drink each other's 'ealths.

"It took 'em a long time, both of 'em being very pleased with each other, but at last, arter the landlord 'ad been holding the door open for 'em till 'is jaws ached, they went back 'ome. They both of 'em thought it was earlier than wot it was, so they was quite surprised when they found Sam 'ad got 'ome before them and gone to bed.

"'Did—did you get the forchin, Sam?' ses Ginger, going over to the wash-stand and sousing 'is face with cold water.

"Sam gave a smile that made 'im look as if he was 'aving a fit.

"'No, Ginger,' he ses, very soft. 'I remembered your advice, old pal.'

"'Advice?' ses Ginger, staring.

"'You said as 'ow there might be a catch in it,' ses Sam, 'and knowing wot a clever 'ead-piece you've got, Ginger, I thought it over and made up my mind not to trust 'im.'

"Peter Russet made a noise that an elephant with the hiccups might ha' been proud of, and then Ginger went over and led 'im across to the wash-stand.

"'You 'old your noise,' he ses, pushing Peter's face into the water. 'You didn't lose your money arter all, then?' he ses, turning to Sam.

"'No,' ses Sam. 'At least, not that way, but arter I left the pub to come 'ome and see you and Peter, I—I 'ad a misforchin.'

"'Misforchin?' ses Ginger, staring at 'im.

"'I—I 'ad my p-pocket picked,' ses Sam, stuttering.

"Peter Russet made another noise afore Ginger could stop 'im, and then they both stood up staring at Sam.

"'A lady asked me the time,' ses Sam, shutting his eyes so as 'e couldn't see 'em, 'and while I was telling 'er one of 'er pals come up and choked me, and two others helped themselves out o' my pockets.'

"Ginger looked at Peter—just in time. Then he looked at Sam again.

"''Ow much was it?' he ses.

"'Eleven pounds and my watch and chain,' ses Sam; 'if it wasn't for seven shillings they didn't find, in another pocket, I should be starving. 'Ow long do you think a man could live on seven shillings?'

"'Me or you?' ses Ginger, considering.

"'Me,' ses pore Sam.

"'Week or ten days—with care,' ses Ginger.

"Sam thanked 'im, but not very loud, and arter saying 'e didn't care wot become of 'im and he didn't suppose 'is pals did neither, he punched 'is piller as if it was somebody e' didn't like and laid down and shut 'is eyes.

"He was up fust next morning counting 'is seven shillings over and over agin, and Peter and Ginger purtending not to notice it. They didn't see 'im agin till night-time 'cos when Peter spoke to Ginger about giving 'im his eleven pounds back, Ginger said 'e ought to be made to suffer a little for 'is foolishness fust, to be a lesson to 'im.

"'We're saving it up for 'im,' he ses. 'While we've got it he can't be spending it.'

"'Or trusting people with it,' ses Peter.

"Both of 'em felt quite kind to Sam, thinking 'ow good they was going to be to 'im, but Sam 'ardly spoke a word to 'em and was up and out next morning a'most afore they 'ad got their eyes open. Twice they came back to their room that day to see whether he 'ad turned up, and when nighttime came and 'e was still missing, Peter Russet said as 'ow he was getting uneasy about 'im.

"'Wot's 'e doing?' he ses. 'He ain't got any money to go to pubs with, and there's nowhere else for 'im to go.'

"They sat on their beds smoking and drinking some whisky they 'ad brought in with 'em, and Ginger was just helping 'imself to 'is third glass when 'e put the bottle down and sat listening.

"'Somebody coming upstairs,' he ses.

"'He's a long time about it,' ses Peter. 'He *'as* been sitting in a pub.'

"Somebody was coming up the stairs so slow it seemed as if 'e would never get to the top, and the banisters was creaking as if they would break. Then they 'eard a shuffling on the landing, and as the door opened they both jumped up and called out at the same time.

"'Lor' lumme!' ses Ginger. ''Ave you been run over, Sam?'

"Sam looked at 'im for a moment and then 'e gave a stagger and tumbled on to 'is bed.

"'Mr. Cooper!' he ses, in a faint voice.

"'Wot about 'im?' ses Ginger.

"'He done it,' ses Sam, ''im and 'is pals. I went round to the pub to see if I could find 'im, thinking 'e might 'ave been took ill the other night, and this is wot I got. He said I'd robbed *'im. Me!* He goes off with my money and then 'arf kills me. Wot for? That's wot I want to know.'

"'It's a mystery,' ses Ginger, shaking his 'ead.

"'I thought you said you didn't give 'im the money,' ses Peter.

"Sam didn't answer 'im, and arter drinking a glass o' whisky Ginger gave 'im he 'eld his 'ead in his 'ands and said 'e thought 'e was dying. When they offered to undress 'im he said 'e didn't think it was worth while, but they got 'is clo'es off arter a bit and put 'im into bed.

"'Wot did 'e do it *for*?' he ses, arter he had 'ad two more whiskies. 'D'ye think 'e's mad? His 'ead was all bandaged up.'

"Ginger shook his 'ead. 'It's a mystery,' he ses agin.

"He went acrost the room and came back with something tied up in a handkerchief and put it on Sam's bed. Sam looked at it a moment and then 'e picked it up and out tumbled eleven pounds, a watch and chain, and a imitation gold cigar-case.

"'He's fainted,' ses Peter Russet."

17

KITCHEN COMPANY

Practice makes perfect, and when Mrs. Brampton, from her seat by the window, announced the approach of the Captain, Mr. Leonard Scott kissed Miss Brampton in the small hall and made his usual dignified exit to the kitchen. To leave by the side-entrance was the best way of avoiding trouble with a man who was always looking out for it. Mr. Scott bestowed a nod upon the smiling young mistress of the kitchen, and with his hand upon the backdoor waited to hear the Captain at the front.

"One o' these days," began Clara, who loved to dwell upon the gruesome, "he'll come—"

She broke off and listened. "He's coming," she said, in a thrilling whisper. "He's coming the back way."

Mr. Scott started, hesitated, and was lost.

"Fly!" exclaimed Clara, pointing by accident to the ceiling.

The young man scowled at her, and before he had time to alter his expression found himself gazing at the burly form and inflamed visage of Captain Brampton.

"Well?" barked the latter. "What are you doing in my kitchen? Eh? What have you got to say for yourself?"

Mr. Scott coughed and tried to collect his thoughts. In the front room Mrs. Brampton and her daughter eyed each other in silent consternation. Then, in response to a peremptory bellow, Mrs. Brampton rose and made a trembling passage to the kitchen.

"What does this mean?" demanded the Captain in grating accents.

His wife stood looking helplessly from one to the other, and, instead of answering the question, passed it on.

"What does this mean, Clara?" she demanded.

"Eh?" said that astonished maiden. "What does what mean?"

"This," said the Captain sternly, with a jerk of his head towards Mr. Scott. "Did you invite him here?"

Clara started—but in a lesser degree han Mr. Scott—and looked down modestly at a hole in the hearth-rug. Mrs. Brampton and her daughter gazed at her in hushed expectation.

"I didn't, not to say, invite him," replied Clara, "but I can't help him coming here."

"*H'm!* Perhaps you didn't try," said the Captain with unexpected mildness. "How long have you known him?"

"Some time, sir," said Clara vaguely.

"Does he want to marry you?"

Clara looked at her mistress for guidance, but the latter was engaged at the moment in an eye-to-eye duel with the fermenting Mr. Scott. Over the Captain's face stole an expression of great and unusual benevolence.

"Well, well," he said slowly. "We've all been young once. He's not much to look at, but he looks clean and respectable. When do you think of getting married?"

"That's for him to say, sir," said the modest Clara.

"Well, there's no hurry," said the Captain, "no hurry. He can come round once a week for you on your evening out, but no other time, mind."

"Thank you, sir," said Clara, who was beginning to enjoy herself. "It's my evening out tonight, sir. He was going to take me to the pictures."

A stifled exclamation came from the direction where Mr. Scott was standing, which the Captain chose to interpret as an expression of gratitude. With instructions to Clara to regale her admirer with bread and cheese and one glass of beer, he shepherded his wife and daughter from the kitchen. Humming a light air, Clara began to set the table.

"What the devil did you want to say I was going to take you to the pictures for?" demanded the ungrateful Mr. Scott.

"'Cos I wanted to go," said his hostess calmly.

Mr. Scott regarded her coldly. "I will walk with you as far as the corner of this road," he said with an air of finality.

"We'll go to the best seats and I'll have a box of chocolates," said Clara. "Do you like chocolates?"

"No," said the other sternly.

"Praise be!" said the girl piously. "My other young man"

Mr. Scott coughed violently.

"All right," said the girl, "don't get excited. He's away on a job for a week or two, else I wouldn't dare to be seen with you. When the cat's away the mice will play," she added.

The young man eyed her in amazement. This was a new Clara. His lips quivered and his eyes watered. He took up his glass of beer and nodded.

"Right-o!" he agreed.

He smoked a cigarette while the girl went upstairs to dress, and a little later, watched by three pairs of eyes from the front window, sailed up the street with her arm-in-arm.

"She's too good for him," said the Captain, with decision.

"Much," assented his daughter, with a smile.

"Tailor's dummy!" soliloquised the Captain.

"Cheap tailor, too," murmured the aquies-cent Miss Brampton. "Did you notice how baggy his trousers are at the knees?"

The Captain shot a glance at her. Twenty years' experience of a wife whose only anxiety was to please him was not the best preparation for handling a daughter who, to say the least of it, had other ambitions. He began to fear that she had inherited more of his strength of character—a quality for which some of his friends found another name—than was convenient.

"He's a softy," he growled. "He ought to have a year or two at sea. That might make a man of him."

He got up and went into the garden, leaving mother and daughter to discuss the possibilities of a situation which had found them somewhat unprepared.

"It might have been worse," said Mrs. Brampton. "If your father had caught him in here—"

"He couldn't eat him," said her daughter rebelliously.

"There are worse things than being eaten," said Mrs. Brampton, with some feeling.

Miss Brampton nodded. "Taking Clara to the pictures, for instance," she remarked. "Poor Leonard!"

Her mother sniffed. "I dare say he will get over it," she said dryly. "Unless Clara's young man gets to hear of it. From what she has told me he is a very hot-tempered young man—and very strong."

"Pity father didn't find *him* in the kitchen," said the dutiful daughter.

She sat down, and in sympathetic mood tried to share the misery of the absent one at the cinema. A vision of Clara's hat, perilously near Mr. Scott's shoulder, mercifully eluded her, but, the window being open to the summer air, she was unable to help hearing the cheerful babble of laughter that heralded their return. It seemed to strike a wrong note; and the couple of noisy kisses which Clara saw fit to bestow upon the back of her hand for the Captain's benefit were registered on the wrong target.

Mrs. Brampton obtained the explanation from Clara next day, and accepted it without prejudice. Her daughter declined to accept it at all.

"You quite understand that he must not come to see you again?" she said stiffly.

"But he's got to," said the staring handmaiden. "The Captain says so. And if he plays fast-and-loose with me I'm to have him up for breach of promise. Lively for me, ain't it? When I think of Bill and his temper I get gooseflesh all over."

The ladies eyed each other in silent consternation.

"Your father *knows*," said the elder at last. "He has done this on purpose."

"Set a trap for him," said Clara, nodding. "Looks like it. And I'm the little bit o' cheese, I suppose?"

Mrs. Brampton stared at her.

"Father forgets that I am nineteen," said her daughter. "Why shouldn't I—?"

"I was only fifteen when *I* started," murmured Clara, "and not big for my age neither."

"That will do," said Mrs. Brampton.

"Yes'm," said the girl. "Still—"

"Still what?" demanded her mistress.

"I've been dragged into it," said Clara mutinously. "Nobody asked me or troubled about my feelings. I do the best I can, and that's all the thanks I get for it. Suppose I had told the Captain it was Miss Edith he was after? Where would you have been then?"

"We won't discuss it," said Mrs. Brampton with an air of feeble dignity.

She made as stately an exit as the size of the kitchen would allow, and, carefully closing the door of the sitting-room, made a few remarks on Clara's character, and more on her lack of it.

"It's no good blaming Clara," said her daughter. "It's father's doing. He wants to make Leonard look a fool first and scare him away afterwards. He'll tell all his friends about it."

"Mr. Hopkins, for one," said Mrs. Brampton, nodding sagely. "I wonder—"

"I don't," said the girl, reddening.

"Your father seems to have taken a great fancy to him," continued Mrs. Brampton. "Now, does he come here to see your father, or—"

"Or," said her daughter bitterly. "It's just like father. I suppose he will want to choose my tooth-powder for me next. But he won't get any satisfaction out of me—*or* Leonard. I'll see to that. As for Mr. Hopkins—*brrh!*"

She beamed, however, on that innocent man when her father brought him in next day to see the garden, and when the wily Captain went indoors for his pipe made no attempt to follow him. It was a pipe that was notorious for the discovery of new and unusual hiding-places, and on this occasion made no attempt to belie its reputation.

Meantime, the delighted Mr. Hopkins, under the skilful management of Miss Brampton, walked with his head in the clouds and his feet on various choice border plants.

"Hadn't you better walk on the path?" inquired the girl, who had been monopolising three-quarters of it. "It's more comfortable."

Mr. Hopkins started. "Good heavens!" he said in an alarmed voice, as he bent down to render first aid to a stock with a broken neck. "Did I do that?"

Miss Brampton nodded. "Those, too, I think," she replied, with a wave of her hand. "Don't you care for flowers?"

Mr. Hopkins, who was fearfully endeavouring to conceal the traces of his crime, made no reply. When the Captain came out they were both speechless, but he was, if anything, the redder of the two.

"These paths are very narrow, father," remarked the humane Edith.

The Captain made a noise.

"Afraid—crowding—Miss Edith," panted the offender.

The Captain made another noise. In the present company all the useful words he knew were useless.

"Did you find your pipe, father?" inquired the persevering Miss Brampton.

The Captain was understood to say "Yes." At the same time he favoured her with a glance which would have made her mother tremble. On Miss Brampton it had a bracing effect.

"Father's always mislaying his pipe," she said, with a bright laugh. "I shouldn't trouble anymore about those, if I were you, Mr. Hopkins. You can't do them any good, and you are standing on an antirrhinum."

Mr. Hopkins removed his foot hastily, and placing it carefully in the centre of the path, offered up another apology. It was received with what the Captain fondly believed to be a smile.

"Accidents will happen," he said hoarsely.

"In the best-regulated families," said Miss Brampton, with a satisfied smile.

She paid a touching tribute to the excellence of the victims after the visitor had gone, and sought for some time for an explanation of the tragedy.

"He must have been 'wool-gathering,'" she declared at length.

"What do you mean by that?" demanded her father.

"Absent-minded," said Edith. "He seemed like a man walking on air, instead of some of the best stocks in the neighbourhood. Even Clara's young man would have more sense than that."

"Clara's young man won't go into my garden," said the Captain. "The kitchen is the place for him."

He stalked out into the garden, and, digging up hopeless cases with a trowel, sought to revive the less badly injured with a water-can.

It might have been a sign of a forgiving nature, but was more likely due to an obstinate one, that he invited Mr. Hopkins back to the scene of his footwork a day or two later. Missing plants had been replaced by a consignment from the florist, and rolled paths and raked flowerbeds testified to the Captain's industry. Everything was "shipshape and Bristol fashion" as the greatly relieved visitor walked with Miss Brampton in the garden in the cool of the evening. The Captain, after satisfying himself that Mr. Hopkins was walking almost as carefully as a performer on the tightrope, had disappeared indoors.

The path was narrow, but even when Miss Brampton sent electric thrills through his being by leaning against him, Mr. Hopkins kept to it. The air was soft and the scent of the flowers delightful. Never before had his conversation been so appreciated. The low-voiced laughter of his companion was a tribute to his wit as rare as it was welcome.

"You ought to write plays," she said thoughtfully, as she planted her foot firmly on a geranium.

"You want influence to get them accepted," said Mr. Hopkins.

"I should try, if I were you, though," said the girl, nearly missing another geranium.

Mr. Hopkins purred. Miss Brampton, with downcast eyes, trod down six flowers in succession.

"Dialogue would be your strong point," mused the girl, continuing her ravages. "Crisp, and sparkling."

She took the other side as they turned at the end of the path, and in a hushed voice called his attention to some beautiful cloud effects. Mr. Hopkins, with his head at an acute angle, murmured his admiration.

"An evening to remember," he said, very softly.

He brought his gaze slowly to earth and started convulsively.

"Giddy?" inquired the girl, with much solicitude.

Mr. Hopkins shook his head and, speech failing him, pointed with a trembling finger to the prostrate victims of misdirected industry. Miss Brampton stared in her turn.

"Oh, Mr. Hopkins!" she said, in accusing tones.

"I—I haven't been near them," stammered the unfortunate.

"They must have done it themselves, then," said the girl calmly. "Perhaps they were not strong enough to stand the breeze."

Mr. Hopkins breathed heavily. "I—I really think," he began.

"Yes?" said Miss Brampton.

"I don't know what to think," concluded the other feebly.

His companion gazed wistfully at the wreckage.

"Poor father!" she said softly. "He is so fond of his garden. He seems to know every flower, but, of course, he hasn't had these long enough to know them."

Mr. Hopkins groaned and cast a fearful glance at the house.

"It's his one hobby," continued the girl. "I have heard him use worse language about cats than anything else, I think. And the doctor says excitement is so bad for him."

"I can't understand it," ventured Mr. Hopkins, with an appealing glance.

"I wonder whether father will?" said the girl. "He is coming out, I think."

Mr. Hopkins looked around panic-stricken. Then he pulled out his watch.

"Good gracious!" he murmured. "I must be going, I think. No idea so late. Appointment."

He moved hastily in the direction of the side-gate, and hardly realising the geniality of Miss Brampton's hand-clasp, disappeared. The girl stood watching until he had turned the corner and then went into the house.

"Where's Hopkins?" inquired the Captain.

"He has just gone."

"Gone!" repeated her father, "Why, I asked him to stay to supper. Did you send him off? Eh?"

His daughter shook her head. "He went off in a hurry," she murmured. "I think he had an idea that perhaps he had offend you."

"Rubbish!" grunted the Captain, eyeing her suspiciously. "What should he offend me about?"

"Knowing how fond you are of your flowers—" began Miss Brampton.

The Captain uttered a smothered cry and, springing from his chair, dashed into the garden. Cries that were anything but smothered, and words that ought to have been, brought his wife to her daughter's side. Together they watched the head of the house as, with fists raised to heaven, he danced a strange and frenzied dance down the path.

"He's wonderfully supple for his age," said the admiring daughter.

Mrs. Brampton shivered. "I don't suppose that poor young man will dare to show his face here again," she said slowly.

"If he does, there will be an accident to the rose trees," said her daughter, compressing her lips. "I've had all I can stand of Mr. Hopkins."

"And then there's Mr. Scott," said her mother plaintively. "Clara says that she thinks her young man has heard something, and if he should happen to meet them one evening—"

"It might be bad for the young man," said the girl calmly. "Leonard would have a better nose if he didn't box so much. Look at father!"

Mrs. Brampton looked.

"He—he seems to be examining the footmarks," she gasped.

"Time I changed your sensible low-heeled shoes for something more dressy," said her daughter, disappearing.

She was back before the Captain re-entered the house, and sitting cross-legged, displayed a pair of sharp-toed, high-heeled shoes of blameless aspect, which met his ardent gaze with a polished stare. He turned his back at last and stood gazing blankly out at his cherished garden.

It never occurred to him to accept defeat, and his daughter was therefore more annoyed than surprised to see Mr. Hopkins—a nervous, chastened Mr. Hopkins—back again after a few days. On this occasion, however, the Captain lingered in the garden, and from a deck-chair beneath the window watched his faltering steps.

Conscious of this scrutiny, the visitor babbled incoherences to Miss Brampton, until in self-defence she retreated to the house on the plea of a thorn in her foot.

The sound of Mr. Scott's voice in the kitchen did not add to her comfort. A glance from her window showed her that her father had taken her place with the visitor and was pointing out to him the merits of the rockery. She stole downstairs and, opening the kitchen-door, peeped in.

"I thought you were going to the cinema," she said, addressing Mr. Scott coldly.

"Can't," was the reply. "Clara's Bill is outside, and she's afraid to come."

"He's waiting for him," said Clara breathlessly. "There'll be murder done—and I shall be the cause of it."

"Cheer up," said Mr. Scott. "He'll only have a week or two in a nice comfortable hospital. You'll be able to see him on Sunday afternoons and take him grapes."

"I know who'll want the grapes," said Clara miserably. "You don't know his strength. I don't believe he knows it himself."

"Where is he?" demanded Miss Brampton.

"Outside the side-gate, miss," replied Clara. "Like a cat waiting for a mouse."

"A mouse!" ejaculated the startled Mr. Scott. "Now look here, Clara—"

"I'll go and send him away," said Miss Brampton with decision.

She slipped into the garden and, her father's back still being towards her, opened the side-gate and looked out. A bullet-headed young man, standing just outside, drew up sharply at her appearance and stood scowling at her.

"Do you want to see Clara?" she inquired.

"I'm waiting," said Mr. Bill Jones, "waiting for a toff."

Miss Brampton stood regarding him with a puzzled air. Then she had an inspiration that almost took her breath away.

"Do you mean the gentleman who is in the garden talking to father?" she inquired.

Mr. Jones's eyes glistened. He licked his lips and stood breathing hard and short. Miss Brampton, with an encouraging smile, pushed the door open.

Mr. Jones needed no further invitation. With head erect and eyes ablaze he entered the garden and, catching sight of the unconscious Mr. Hopkins, strode rapidly towards him.

"Here! What do you want?" demanded the astonished Captain.

Mr. Jones ignored him, and continuing his progress, thrust his face into that of Mr. Hopkins.

"Take my gal away, will yer?" he shouted. "Take 'er to the pictures, will yer? Take that!"

Mr. Hopkins took it and went down with a cry of anguish. Through a mist of pain he heard the voice of his assailant.

"Get up! Get up! Else I'll jump on yer."

Mr. Hopkins got up, and the appearance of Mr. Jones was so terrible that he turned and fled, with the other in hot pursuit.

"Stop!" yelled the choking Captain. "Mind the flowers! Mind the fl—"

Mr. Hopkins paid no heed; neither, to do him justice, did Mr. Jones. Firmly convinced that his life was in danger, the former performed miracles of agility, while his opponent pounded doggedly behind. A bad third, owing to his keeping to the path, the Captain followed raving in the rear.

Broken plants lay in the wake of Mr. Hopkins; churned-up earth marked the progress of Mr. Jones as he endeavoured to head him off. And at this juncture Mr. Scott appeared from the kitchen, shedding his coat.

"What the devil do you think you're doing?" he shouted.

Mr. Jones pulled up suddenly and favoured him with a menacing stare.

"Look at those flowers," cried Mr. Scott severely. "You chump-headed, mutton-headed son of a gun!"

Mr. Jones stood irresolute. He looked longingly at Mr. Hopkins taking cover behind the Captain; then with a loud roar he threw himself upon this new arrival.

Mr. Scott side-stepped neatly and smote him heavily on the chin. Mr. Jones, turning in amazement, took three more and, being by this time acclimatised, settled down to a steady mill.

"You'd better go," said the Captain harshly, to Mr. Hopkins. "This isn't a sight for you."

Mr. Hopkins went, somewhat reluctantly. He was a man of peace, but the sight of Mr. Jones's damages seemed in some way to afford him an odd feeling of satisfaction. The Captain stayed to see fair play—also the only fight with fists he had seen since he left the sea. It was with almost a sigh that he went at length to help Mr. Scott assist his adversary to his feet. The dazed Mr. Jones, with Clara's arm about his waist, was led indoors and his head placed under the scullery tap. The cooling sounds of running water and the heated comments of Mr. Jones alone broke the silence.

"Well, that's over," said Mr. Scott, tenderly dabbing his face with his handkerchief, as Miss Brampton came out. "I'm afraid Clara has jilted me, sir."

The Captain grunted and eyed him curiously.

"I was going to take her to the cinema, now I suppose I shall have to go alone. Unless—"

"Well?" barked the Captain, waiting.

"Unless Miss Brampton comes with me."

The Captain stood up and faced him, choking.

"Cinema!" he roared. "Cinema! If you want to do something to pass the evening, you can help her help me help make the garden tidy."

18

THE MODEL

I

It was getting too dark to work, and the artist, a cigarette between his lips, was sitting restfully at the open window, lazily scanning through his half-closed lids the languid life of the old Italian city below. As the objects in his studio retired farther and farther into the shadows, he arose, and taking his hat from a peg, passed slowly down the long staircase into the street. The air, which had been almost stifling during the day, was now freshening, and he passed from street to street with the aimless enjoyment of the man to whom the mere exercise of his cramped limbs is a luxury.

Standing idly at a lighted corner preparatory to turning back, his gaze fell upon a middle-aged woman of poor appearance who was passing. He started violently, and in an undecided fashion stood gazing after her retreating figure until it disappeared down a small by-street. Then, on a sudden impulse, he threw away his cigarette and started in pursuit.

At first he gained but little on her, and once or twice nearly lost her in the rapidly increasing darkness, but in the end his youth and strength told, and the woman, who had been conscious for some time that her steps were dogged, slackened her pace and walked with her hand pressed to her side, breathing distressfully. In the centre of the old stone bridge which leads from the narrow streets of the town to the open country beyond, he overtook her.

"Pardon, signora," he said softly.

The woman halted, her hand on the low stone parapet, and confronted him.

"You walk fast," he continued, smiling.

She murmured an indistinct something, and made as though to go.

"No, I have followed you some distance," said the artist, "I can't afford to lose you. Will you let me see your face! I have a reason for the request."

With a startled gesture, and not without looking right and left as though for assistance, should it be needed, she threw her head back, her pale features showing clearly in the light of an adjoining lamp.

"Beautiful!" said the artist joyfully, "beautiful!"

"Signor," said the woman with dignity, conscious of forty years and sundry wrinkles, "you mock me."

"By no means," he said anxiously; "you have the face I have sought for years. You will sit for me, will you not?"

"The signor is an artist then," said the woman, breathing more freely.

He nodded, and for the first time perceived that he had frightened her. "I was too abrupt," he said regretfully. "I saw your face and forgot all else."

The woman smiled faintly, a slight glow tinged her face and her eyes brightened. "I shall be pleased to sit, if I am any use."

"Can you come tomorrow?" asked the enthusiast.

"Yes."

"At eleven then, to this address. You will not fail me."

Smiling at his earnestness, she gave the desired assurance, and with a soft good night left him, and passed swiftly over the bridge into the darkness beyond.

For a moment the artist glanced after her as though desirous of obtaining further pledges of fidelity, and then abandoning the idea, seated himself on the parapet, and, lighting another cigarette, fell into a smoker's reverie. The river went by with a soft swish against the piles of the old bridge, the air was cool and the ghostly outlines of the old buildings on either bank, indistinct in the darkness, appeared to be nodding in sleep. All these drowsy influences combined were beginning to have a soporific effect upon the smoker, the buildings nodded more violently than ever, the river murmured more sweetly.

"He who sleeps on the parapet awakes in the stream," said a voice at his elbow in feigned solemnity.

"Ah! Rossa," said the artist, slipping to his feet, and smiling as he recognised the speaker, "I was just wishing for company home. I have news for you; at last I have been successful in my search, and my picture can be finished."

"It is time," remarked the other as he walked by his side; "and where is she who has succeeded in satisfying your exacting fancy?"

"I parted from her on the bridge," replied his friend. "Such a face, such an expression, the perfect type of bereaved maternity."

"Charming!" said Rossa dryly. "It must have been a pleasant task, the acquiring of that self-same expression."

The artist, somewhat nettled at his tone, made no reply, and they traversed the narrow ill-lighted streets almost in silence until they reached his dwelling. Then with a hearty handshake Rossa took his leave, and the other climbed the steep stairs which led to his bed to lie awake half the night, thinking of his great work and the face of his model.

II

The woman was tired and hot when she reached his studio, for the sun was nearly at its height, and its heat, imprisoned in the narrow street, was stifling to those wayfarers who could not move at leisure and take advantage of such shade as offered. She greeted the artist timidly, and gazed, not without curiosity, at the littered floor and the sketches upon the walls.

"That is what I want you for," said the artist, indicating with a nod a large unfinished canvas which stood upon an easel in the full light of the window.

His visitor crossed over, and stood looking at the roughly outlined figure of a woman upon her knees, bending over the calm, awful face of the dead Christ. She stood for some time in silence, and then as she understood what her part was to be, turned to the artist to receive his instructions.

And never had man a more devoted model.

True to time, cheerful and willing, she appeared day by day, and it required but little discernment on the part of the artist to see that her heart was in the work. Quiet and undemonstrative in manner, it was yet easy to see her devout joy at the fact that her face should have been chosen to represent that of the Virgin. Slowly but surely the work grew in strength and clearness, bit by bit the shadowy figure of the woman took life, and a weary earth-worn face now bent over the crucified Saviour.

It was while sitting at the window one morning, waiting for the appearance of his model, that the artist was surprised by a visit from his friend Rossa.

"Are you amiable to visitors this morning?" inquired the latter.

"It depends upon their criticisms," replied the artist, smiling.

"I feel at peace with all mankind at present," said Rossa.

"In that case you are welcome," said the other, "but you are the only man I allow to see it in its unfinished state."

"Always hungry for my suggestions," murmured Rossa complacently, as he advanced to the easel.

"Well?" asked the artist impatiently, after allowing plenty of time for his friend's praises.

"It is the best you have done, as good as you will ever do," said Rossa with gratifying energy. "Ah! When will you cease wasting your strength on these old-world superstitions, and use your brush on nobler themes?"

"There is none nobler," said the other gravely.

Rossa shrugged his shoulders and smiled scornfully. "Bah! You spend your strength in painting advertisements for the priests, and what do the smug-faced black-gowns do for you in return? Give you their blessing, or recommend you to wealthy patrons? Are there no noble deeds of today to bring the blood to a man's cheek and the water to his eyes, that you must go back to that hackneyed theme of eighteen centuries ago?"

"You are speaking too freely," said the artist sternly.

"Freely!" repeated Rossa. "You paint pictures to foster and encourage ideas which are against all reason, and one may not even speak of it. And the materials, bah! Do you ask for certificates of character from the women you paint as Madonnas, or do you take the first that suits?"

"To tell the truth, I have never thought of it," said the other, "but in this case the woman's face is her best certificate."

"It certainly supported her for many years," said Rossa dryly.

"What, do you know her? She told me she had never sat before," said the artist in surprise.

"Years ago I knew her well," said his friend, "but not as a model. It was in Naples. She had a large circle of acquaintances, and was commonly known as 'The Doll.' Even to an atheist there seems to be an incongruity somewhere in painting her in this character."

"Is this a jest?" asked the artist, struggling between amazement and anger.

"Ask her," said Rossa quietly. "Poor devil; I'm sorry I spoke, though. She certainly has got a sad face, and I suppose it doesn't matter to you how she got it."

The artist shook his head.

"Come," said the repentant Rossa, "don't spoil your picture and rake up this poor thing's past for nothing; perhaps I am mistaken."

His friend smiled faintly, and bidding his visitor goodbye, sat himself down in the window-seat in a brown study. A devout man, his heart was troubled. Art and religion strove within him for the mastery. He sat in perplexity until a light tap at the door announced the arrival of the model.

"It is hot, signor," said she, smiling—"scarce a breath of air in the streets, but it is cool here."

True to the minute, interested in his work, she had toiled through the heat. He looked at her coarse, work-stained hands and gentle face, and faltered.

"I told you that the picture is intended for a gift to the cathedral, did I not?" he inquired after a pause.

"Surely, signor." She smiled again. Already she saw her face and that other looking down from the cathedral wall on to the hushed crowd beneath.

"I chose your face," continued the artist, "because it seemed to me to contain all that I required for my subject; but there is one little matter of which I should have spoken before. The face that I have chosen for the Holy Mother, which is to remind the people of her divine goodness and great sorrow, must be that of a good woman. I dare not portray any other."

There was no smile on the woman's lips now, and in her face, pale one moment and flushed with shame the next, he saw that she guessed the extent of his knowledge.

"I did not think it mattered," she said at length in a low voice. "I never thought of it. There—there were two Marys, signor, and He loved both."

She looked at him humbly, with blurred eyes, but he had averted his face. He raised it at length at the sound of a door closing, and found that he was alone.

For a long time he sat motionless. At last, with the air of a man who has an unpleasant task before him, he arose and looked long and close at the nearly finished picture. Then he took it from the easel, and placing it on the floor with its face to the wall, he too went out.

III

Since the woman left the studio a year had passed. The neglected canvas still stood on the floor, its place on the easel being filled by a picture of "The Draught of Fishes." The artist, disappointed in his favourite work, had done little that was worthy since, though he was as determined as ever not to complete it. Of the woman he had seen nothing, and he had abandoned as hopeless the task of finding a substitute.

He was sitting listlessly before his easel, brush in hand, when he was interrupted by a gentle tap at the door. It opened, and a priest—an old man with white hair and brown, rugged face—entered and stood on the threshold.

"The Signor Paoli?" he inquired.

The artist rose and bowed.

"I'm afraid I intrude," said the old man. "You are busy, I see. I desired to see your pictures. Perhaps another time—"

"I am not busy," said the artist, throwing down his brush. "There are but few here. I wish there were more."

He closed the door, and stood by the old man's side as he inspected the studies on the walls and such few completed works as were left in the studio. He paused at length before the easel, and after inspecting the canvas there turned and pointed with his stick at the one which leaned against the wall.

"May I see it?" he asked.

"It is not finished," said the artist. He hesitated a moment, and then removing the canvas from the easel, crossed the room, and returning with the other, silently placed it before his visitor.

An exclamation of delight burst from the old priest's lips as he leaned on his stick and gazed on it.

"A noble work," he murmured at length, without removing his eyes. "A noble work. When will you finish it?"

"It is not to be finished," said the artist. "I discovered by accident that the woman who sat to me had led an infamous life; that the lines which I thought were caused by bereavement owed their birth to sin; that the woman who I thought mourned her dead children mourned instead her dead innocence."

"She will sin no more," said the priest gently. "Nay, I hope and believe she will mourn no more. She died last night."

"Last night?" said the startled artist. "You know of the affair, then—she told you?"

"I have known her for years," said the old man; "known her and loved her. She came to this city, and left her wickedness like a soiled garment behind her. Her father cursed her, and her mother bewailed the hour she was born; brothers and sisters forgot that she had ever been. Years ago, weary of sin, she came here, and maintained herself by hard and ill-paid toil."

"Her hands said so," muttered the artist.

"For a long time," continued the priest without noticing the interruption, "she lived alone, without the love or sympathy of a single soul; and lived a good life. But one day she saw in the streets a blind, weary old man, hustled by boys. Him she took home and nursed and fed. He told her that he had lost wife and children, wealth and sight, and had no man left to call him friend; and yet, for fear that he should not accept her bounty, she never told him that he had one child left. So that he might be fed she worked late into the night and rose with the dawn, always haunted by the fear—for her early life had left in her the seeds of death—that he might outlive her and become destitute."

He paused and looked at the artist.

"So it went on, and only I knew the story. Last night she lay dying, and the old man on his knees by her bedside kissed her hand and said that she was to him as a beloved daughter, and prayed to God for sight that he might behold her ere she died."

"It must have been a painful moment when she made herself known," said the artist.

"It might have been," answered the priest; "who knows? But she died with her poor lips sealed, though I think it was almost more than she could bear. I have seen many sad sights, may God in His mercy keep me from such another."

"Why not have told him, then?" inquired the artist after a long pause.

"There was a reason," said the old man; "she had scraped together a small sum for her father's use when she should no longer be able to work for him. It was possible, at least she thought so, that he might refuse it if he knew the donor."

The air in the room was close, and the artist opened the window. He came back to the canvas and sat for some time slowly regarding it. More slowly still he filled his brush with colour and leaned forward. Then checking himself suddenly, he looked up at the priest.

The priest smiled.

19

ARTFUL CARDS

"Gambling I don't 'old with," said the night-watchman, pursing his lips. "There's gamblers and gamblers. There's people like myself as does it now and then out of good-nature to oblige, and there's people like that squint-eyed, ginger-whiskered mate on the *Queen Mary*. If he 'ad spent as much time learning good manners as he 'as learning the three-card trick, it would ha' been better for both of us. Especially me.

"He ain't the only one. I remember teaching draughts to a man I met one evening. He was a born fool to look at, and 'e looked just the same when 'e bid me good night with seven-and-six o' mine in 'is pocket. I 'eard arterwards that he could do anything with draughts except make 'em speak.

"Most sailormen like a bit of a flutter. One chap I knew used to spend all his time ashore backing 'orses. When 'e lost, 'e lost, and when he won the bookie used to get lost. And the only time he did get his winnings he got fourteen days for the way 'e spent 'em.

"I remember one time when old Sam Small got a perfeck craze for playing cards. His idea was to make some money for 'is old age, and, instead of going out and enjoying 'imself with Ginger Dick and Peter Russet, he sat all day in the bedroom being taught by a young professional sharper 'e met in the

'Three Widders.' He even learnt 'ow to do the three-card trick—arter a fashion—and came round to show me one evening. We played for ha'pennies at fust, and I lost seven right off. Then we played for bobs, and it seemed as if I couldn't lose. I never see anybody so puzzled as Sam was, and then 'e turned round and said he'd been doing it all wrong, and asked for 'is money back. I 'ad to be firm with 'im—for his own sake.

"A man never knows 'is best friends. If he'd kept on playing cards with me it would ha' been better for both of us; instead o' that, he preferred to let strangers win 'is money. He used to take 'em to his bedroom, and one night Ginger couldn't get to bed because three or four of 'em had 'ad it for a card-table and spilt a can of beer in it.

"He could have 'ad two beds next night, 'cos to their surprise Sam didn't come 'ome. He was still missing when they went out to brekfuss next morning, and by the time arternoon came Ginger began to feel uneasy about 'im.

"'Mark my words,' he ses to Peter Russet, 'he's been and gorn and got into some trouble.'

"'Any fool could see that,' ses Peter. ''Ow much money 'ad he got on 'im? Besides the eight quid you are minding for 'im?'

"Ginger shook his 'ead. 'It's my belief he's been made away with,' he ses, jingling tha money in his trowsis-pocket. 'It all comes of 'im thinking he can play cards.'

"'P'r'aps I'd better mind 'arf of the money, in case you get robbed,' ses Peter.

"Ginger didn't hear 'im. He was too busy thinking about pore Sam. By the time twelve o'clock came, and no Sam, they felt certain that something had 'appened to 'im, and Ginger kept Peter awake 'arf the night talking to 'im about the 'appy times the three of them had 'ad together.

"'I suppose we must go out and try and eat something,' he ses next morning, shaking his 'ead.

"'I s'pose so,' ses Peter, very sorrowful; 'but it's wasting good money.'

"They went downstairs very slow, and opened the door just as Sam's friend wot taught 'im 'ow to play cards knocked on it. Sharp-faced young chap 'e was, with 'is eyes 'arf closed and a fag stuck in the corner of 'is mouth.

"''Ullo, Ginger,' he ses, nodding.

"'Wot do you want?' ses Ginger, sniffing at 'im.

"'I've got a letter for you,' he ses.

"Ginger held out his 'and for it and, arter speaking sharp to Peter Russet about good manners, stood reading it as though he couldn't believe 'is eyesight.

"'It's from Sam,' he ses, at last. 'He's lost all 'is money at cards, as I knew 'e would; and 'e wants me to send 'im five quid.'

"'Wot 'e owes,' ses the young chap.

"'He can go on owing it, then,' ses Ginger, very firm. 'If 'e wants 'is five quid let 'im come and fetch it.'

"'He can't,' ses the young chap.

"'Can't? Why not?' ses Ginger, turning on 'im.

"'He's lost other things besides money,' ses the chap. 'He played the last two hands in 'is shirt and cap, and 'e can't come 'ome in *them*. 'Ow would you like it yourself? Besides, think of the cold!'

"'Shirt and cap?' ses Ginger, staring at 'im.

"'He made 'imself a skirt out of a tater-sack this morning,' ses the young chap. 'It's a tight fit—still, it's better than nothing.'

"'All right,' ses Ginger, arter a few words on the quiet with Peter Russet, 'we'll come with you and see wot can be done. Where is he?'

"'Find out,' ses the chap. 'Why don't you give me the money same as your pal tells you to? Wot are you wasting time like this for? It's his money. He 'asn't 'ad nothing to eat since yesterday arternoon. D'you want 'im to starve?'

"Ginger led Peter away again.

"'We'll lay low and foller 'im 'ome,' he ses, in a whisper.

"'Wot about brekfuss?' ses Peter. 'I want mine something cruel.'

"'Plenty o' time,' ses Ginger. 'Think o' pore Sam; nothing to eat since yesterday arternoon.'

"He turned back to the young man, wot was doing a double-shuffle on the pavement and looking up at the chimney-pots.

"'Why don't you tell us where 'e is?' he ses, in a sharp voice.

"'Fancy,' ses the chap, lighting another fag.

"'You won't get no five pounds out o' me,' ses Ginger. 'Come along, Peter; we'll go back indoors and wait for Sam to come home. You go and tell 'im wot I said,' he ses, turning to the chap.

"'Right-o,' ses the young feller, turning away. 'So long!'

"They stood peeping out of the doorway till he 'ad turned the corner, and then they set off arter 'im. It was easy work in a way, 'cos he never looked behind 'im; but 'e seemed to be fonder o' walking than wot they was, and besides, as Peter said, no doubt he had 'ad a good brekfuss afore 'e started.

"'P'r'aps he ain't going 'ome,' ses Ginger, looking puzzled. "This is the third time he 'as been in the Minories.'

"They followed 'im into Tower Street—it was on'y the second time they 'ad been there—and then to their thankfulness he turned into a pub. They went in too—into another bar—and Ginger 'ad just ordered two pints in a whisper, and paid for 'em, when the chap finished his beer and walked out. Pore Ginger didn't even 'ave time to taste his, and the one mouthful Peter 'ad time to take went the wrong way. It was a big mouthful, and for a couple o' minutes he thought it was 'is last. Then he got 'is breath back, and, arter asking the landlord whether he thought 'e was beating carpets, went out to look for Ginger. He caught 'im up arter a time, and they went on walking till they felt ready to drop.

"'I believe 'e knows we are follering 'im,' ses Peter.

"They went on for another 'arf-hour, and then to Peter's joy they saw the chap, arter standing a long time looking at the things in a cook-shop winder, go inside.

"'He's going to 'ave his dinner,' he ses, 'and while he's 'aving it we'll go and 'ave some bread and cheese and beer.'

"'And suppose he slips out while we're away?' ses Ginger.

"'Well, we'll go one at a time,' ses Peter.

"'No, we won't,' ses Ginger. 'I ain't going to lose 'imarter all this trouble, and when we *do* find out where 'e lives I might want your help.'

"They stood outside waiting for over a hour, and then the young feller came out wiping his mouth on the back of his 'and. He stood for a moment looking up and down the street till 'is eyes fell on Ginger, wot was trying to get behind Peter, and Peter wot was trying to get behind Ginger.

"''Ullo,' he ses, coming up. 'Fancy dropping acrost you agin like this! 'Ave you been 'aving a little walk to stretch your legs?'

"'Yes; and we ain't finished yet,' ses Ginger, very fierce.

"'I'll come with you, if you like,' ses the chap. 'I ain't proud.'

"'When we want your company we'll ask you for it,' ses Peter.

"'Don't get cross,' ses the young feller, pretending to shiver. ''Cos if you do I might get frightened and *run*. Last time I was frightened by a ugly face I run three miles without stopping.'

"He lit a fag and stood there with 'is eyes 'arf closed, blowing smoke through 'is nose. Peter and Ginger stood there, waiting while 'e smoked two of 'em, and then waited outside a tobacco-shop while 'e went in to buy another packet. He got larky arter coming out, and when 'e tried to strike a match on Ginger's trowsis people 'ad to step off the pavement 'cos Ginger was using it all.

"He moved off with Peter as he saw a policeman coming along, and then to their surprise they found that the young feller was following *them*. It upset their ideas altogether, and all of a sudden Ginger stopped and turned on him.

"'Why don't you go 'ome?' he ses.

"'Wot's the good without the money?' ses the chap. 'Wot's the good of going back and telling a starving old man in a tater-sack that his pals won't help 'im?'

"'Why can't we take it to 'im?' ses Peter.

"'He wouldn't like it,' ses the chap. 'He said so. Besides, when you got there you might try and get 'im out without paying.'

"'Well, we'll give you the money now, and then come with you,' ses Ginger.

"'Why couldn't you say so afore?' ses the other. ''Ere we've been wasting the whole morning for nothing.'

"They all went into a pub and arter Ginger and Peter had 'ad a pint or two, and a crust o' bread and cheese, Ginger handed over the money and they all went out together, with the young man in the middle. Ginger's opinion of 'im went up as they walked along, and, when he led 'em into another pub a little further on, and asked 'em wot they would 'ave, he got to feel quite a liking for 'im.

"They 'ad a pint each, and, while Peter was resting 'arf-way through his, the young man thought 'e saw a spider drop into it. Ginger 'elped Peter to look for it, but they couldn't find it, and arter that they wasted a lot of time looking for the young man, but they couldn't find 'im neither.

"'If you'd kept your eye on 'im instead o' fishing round in my beei with your dirty finger, it 'ud ha' been better,' ses Peter.

"They walked 'ome, quarrelling all the way, and then they sat indoors all the evening waiting for Sam to turn up so as they could tell 'im wot they thought of 'im.

"They sat there till eleven o'clock, and then they went to bed wondering wot had 'appened to 'im; and when they got up next morning Ginger said he 'ad a feeling that they should never see 'im again.

"'He's gorn where we've all got to go,' he ses, shaking his 'ead.

"'Unless we join the Salvation Army,' ses Peter. 'There's plenty 'o time afore we get to his age.'

"'He's been made away with, that's my opinion,' ses Ginger. 'We shall never see 'imagin, anymore than we shall see that monkey-faced chap that gave us the slip yesterday.'

"They went downstairs to go out and get some brekfuss, and the very fust thing they saw was the young feller, leaning up agin the wall, smoking a fag.

"''Ullo!' he ses. 'Did you find the spider?'

"Ginger couldn't answer 'im for a minute. He stood there staring at him as if he was a ghost.

"'Wot did you run off for?' he ses, at last, growling at 'im.

"'Me?' ses the other. 'I didn't run off. But I thought that if pore old Sam 'ad to wait till you found that spider he'd never get 'is money.'

"'Is he alive?' ses Peter.

"'*Alive?*' ses the young feller. 'I on'y 'ope I shall be 'arf as lively at 'is age as wot he is. I've got another letter for you.'

"He fished it out of 'is pocket and handed it to Ginger, and then stood sucking his teeth and looking at the winder opposite while Ginger read it.

"It was a longer letter than the other. One thing was Sam called 'imself a silly fool two or three times over 'cos he 'ad gambled away the five pounds. He wanted Ginger to send 'im the other three, and said as 'ow he had 'ad awful bad luck, and never wanted to see a card agin as long as 'e lived. He told Ginger to give the other three pounds to 'is friend Sid, wot took the five pounds, and said if they followed 'im again he would never forgive 'im.

"'Fair old cough-drop, ain't he?' ses the young feller.

"'He's fell into bad 'ands,' ses Ginger, glaring at him.

"'That's right,' ses Sid, 'and we've got to get 'im out. You find the ready, and I'll do the rest.'

"Ginger read the letter agin, arter Peter 'ad done with it, and then 'e told the chap to wait while he went indoors for the money. Wot 'e really went indoors for was to tell the landlady's gal, a smart little kid of eleven, as 'ad two bilious attacks a week reg'lar to stay at 'ome and 'elp 'er mother, to foller Mr. Sid 'ome.

"'Here's the three quid,' 'e ses, coming out. 'Take it and go.'

"'And let's 'ope he won't lose that,' ses Sid. 'Are you coming to see me as far as the—I mean, as far as you can?'

"'I am not,' ses Ginger.

"'Ah, well, I don't blame you,' ses Sid. 'It's a waste of your time and mine too, ain't it? The last chap that tried to foller me 'ome seemed to think I lived in the canal. I never see a chap make 'imself so wet.'

"He gave Peter a playful little tap in the stummick, and, arter asking Ginger for a lock of his 'air to frighten the gals with, went off whistling. And he had 'ardly turned the corner afore the little gal was arter 'im.

"By the time Peter and Ginger was back from their brekfuss she was home agin, 'avingfollered the young man to his 'ouse, and seen 'im go inside. He didn't seem to 'ave any idea that 'e was being follered; and Ginger was so pleased with 'imself and 'is cleverness that Peter 'ad to remind 'im of all sorts of things he didn't want to be reminded of.

"They waited in for some time to see if Sam came 'ome, but there was no sign of 'im, and Ginger began to wonder whether he 'ad lost the three quid as well as the five.

"'We'll give 'im till eight o'clock,' he ses. 'And if he ain't 'ome by then we'll go round and fetch 'im.'

"'It's my belief they won't let 'im go,' ses Peter.

"'Or p'r'aps he's lost 'is trowsis agin,' ses Ginger. 'We'll take his other pair with us in case. And we'll get one or two to come with us to see fair play.'

"They picked up a couple o' firemen they knew that arternoon. Stiff-built chaps they was, and always ready for a bit of trouble, 'aving both 'ad Irish mothers. They 'ad a few drinks to steady themselves, and then one of 'em, Bob Mills by name, got so upset because Ginger said he thought it 'ud be better not to burn the 'ouse down, that it took three men and the landlord to get 'im outside.

"They went 'ome fust to see whether Sam 'ad turned up, and then, arter waking Bob, who 'ad gorn to sleep in Peter's bed, they set off to find 'im. It was a tall, dirty house, just off the 'Ighway, and Ginger began to think that if they got Sam out in one piece they'd be lucky. The front-door was open and a lot o' dirty-looking kids was playing on the steps.

"'It's like a bee hive,' ses Peter. "He'll take some finding.'

"'I'll find 'im,' ses Bob, spitting on his hands. 'Come along.'

"He led them up the steps and opened the fust door 'e come to as bold as brass, and popped his 'ead in.

"'Where's old Sam?' he ses, to a woman wot left off washing 'er baby to stare at 'im. 'Wot 'ave you done with 'im?'

"'*Wot?*" ses the woman.

"'We want Mr. Sam Small,' ses Ginger, putting 'is head over Bob's shoulders.

"Wot 'ave you done with 'im?' ses Bob agin.

"'Me?" ses the woman. 'Wot are you talking about? 'Ow dare you come shoving your ugly mug into a lady's room and try and take away 'er character? Wot d'ye mean by it?'

"She put the baby down on the floor very careful and took up the basin o' water. It was a small basin, but the water showed that the baby 'adn't been washed afore it wanted it, and Bob Mills was out o' that room afore you could say 'knife.'

"'He ain't there,' he ses, as the door banged be'ind 'im. 'It's a funny thing a woman can never answer a civil question without losing 'er temper. If I 'adn't kept my eye on 'er I should have 'ad that water over me.'

"'They don't use their reason,' ses Ginger, shaking his 'ead, and stopping at the next door to let 'im go in fust.

"There was nobody in that room except a little gal of ten putting 'er little brothers to bed, and the way she carried on when Bob looked in would ha' done credit to a woman of seventy. He came out gasping for breath.

"'I'll find 'im though,' he ses to Ginger. 'I'll find 'im, if I 'ave to take all the boards up. Now wot about trying upstairs?'

"There was two families in the fust room they went in, and they was both worse than each other. People came out of their rooms to listen, and the way they carried on when Ginger and 'is pals paid *them* a visit won't bear repeating. By the time they 'ad got to the second floor the whole 'ouse was roused and standing behind and offering to fight 'em.

"Bob and 'is pal went into the fust room on that floor alone, 'cos Ginger and Peter 'ad to stay outside on the landing to keep the crowd back. 'Ard work it was, too; one young woman trying to bore holes in Peter with a broom-'andle, while a dirty hand with a wedding-ring on it kept coming out of the crowd and pinching pore Ginger black and blue.

"In the middle of it there was a hullabaloo in that room that made 'em all leave off to listen. Deafening it was. People shouting and struggling and things toppling about all over the place. Then Bob and 'is mate came out carrying something that looked like a mad lion wrapped up in a blanket.

"'He was in bed, asleep,' ses Bob, panting, as a couple o' naked legs shot out and kicked anything they could find. 'Pull your end o' the blanket down, Joe.'

"'Wot's he done?' ses a woman, gaping at them.

"'Wot 'ave you done, you mean,' ses Bob, struggling. 'He's been kidnapped.'

"'And robbed,' ses Ginger, shouting with pain, as 'e got another pinch.

"'It's all right, Sam, old man,' ses Peter, pulling back the blanket to give 'im a little air. 'Now—Lor' lumme, *this ain't Sam!*'

"They all started, and Bob was so surprised that be let go of 'is end. It was the 'ead end and the langwidge the old man it belonged to used was awful. Then 'e got up very slow, and, arter feeling his 'ead and using some more langwidge about a bump 'e found there, knocked Bob down.

"In two twos they was all at it; the men fighting and the women screaming. Men Ginger hadn't seen afore seemed to turn up from nowhere to punch 'im. The four of 'em kept together as well as they could, and even when Ginger got to the bottom of the stairs 'e found the other three on top of 'im. They got outside at last, helped be'ind by the people in the 'ouse, and didn't stop for breath till they was two streets away. Bob Mills found 'is fust, and pretty near got run in for it.

"'I ought to take you by rights,' ses the policeman. 'Wot 'ave you been doing to your face? Treading on it?'

"Bob was going to answer 'im, but Ginger got his 'and over 'is mouth just in time.

"'It's all right, sir,' he ses, very perlite, 'he's on'y a little bit excited. Come on, Bob.'

"They managed to get 'im round the corner, and then e' shook 'em off and said he never wanted to see 'em again. He went off with 'is mate, and Peter and Ginger, arter being refused at three pubs because of their looks, sent a young feller in for a bottle o' whisky to take 'ome with them.

"They 'ad a drop or two when they got indoors, and then they got a bit o' rag and some cold water and began to see wot they could do to their faces.

"'And this is all through Sam,' ses Ginger, starting to grind 'is teeth and then finding they was too loose to grind.

"'It's a mystery,' ses Peter, who was sitting on Sam's bed 'olding a wet rag to his eye. 'I believe you was right, Ginger. Something seems to tell me we shall never see 'imagin.'

"Ginger said he didn't want to. His mouth was so sore 'e couldn't smoke, and arter another drop or two of whisky, e' said 'e was going to bed.

"He undressed 'imself very slow, grunting and groaning all the time, and was just getting into bed when Peter 'eld up his 'and.

"'Somebody's coming upstairs,' he ses.

"'Let 'em come,' ses Ginger, very grumpy.

"'It—it can't be Sam!' ses Peter.

"'Sounds like 'im,' ses Ginger, staring. 'It is 'im,' he ses, as they both 'eard a noise that Sam used to make when 'e thought 'e was singing.

"They stood staring at the door as it opened and Sam came into the room, looking very bright and pleased with 'imself.

"''Ullo, mates!' he ses. 'Why—wot the—Wot 'ave you been doing to yourselves?'

"He shook his 'ead, and screwed up 'is lips at 'em.

"'It's a funny thing I can't go away for a day or two without you getting into trouble,' he ses. ''Taint respectable.'

"'Ho!' ses Ginger, finding 'is voice. 'Ho, indeed. This is all the thanks we get for trying to 'elp you, is it? I s'pose you think it's more respectable to lose your trowsis at cards and play in your shirt.'

"'And a tater-sack,' ses Peter.

"'Trowsis!' ses Sam, staring at 'em, 'tater-sack? 'Ave you been drinking? Or wot?'

"Ginger looked at Peter and then 'e looked very 'ard at Sam.

"'Where—'ave—you—been?' he ses, very slow and distinct.

"'Been staying with a chap at Stratford,' ses Sam, 'elping 'imself to a drink. 'My friend Sid told me as he'd 'eard the police was arter me for gambling, so I've been staying with a pal of 'is for a, few days to let it blow over.'

"'And—and didn't you write to us?' ses Ginger, as soon as he could speak.

"'Why, wot should I want to write to you for?' ses Sam, putting down 'is glass.

"'Money,' ses Ginger, looking 'im straight in the eye.

"Sam shook his 'ead, 'I 'ad enough on me,' he ses, 'but it was just as well I left that eight quid with you, Ginger. It might 'ave gorn if I 'adn't. Wot was it you was saying about trowsis and tater-sacks, Peter? '

"'It's a joke of your friend, Sid's,' says Ginger. 'Ask him to tell it to you; you seem to tell 'im everything.'

* * *

"Him and Peter woke up at five o'clock next morning to go and look for fresh lodgings. Sam didn't wake up till eight, and then, arter reading a couple o' letters 'e found tucked under 'is chin, he went off without any brekfuss to look for Ginger and Peter, and Sid, and eight quid."

20

HANDSOME HARRY

"He's a bit of all right," said Mr. Joe Gossett, interrupting his description of the new foreman with a large wedge of bread and cheese.

His sister sniffed. "Fancy a man being called 'Handsome Harry'! *Pff!*"

"He can't help what people call him," said Mr. Gossett, "and if you was to see him you'd understand it. Five foot eleven, dark blue eyes, good teeth, and the finest short beard I ever saw in my life. All brown and gold it is. How he's escaped, I don't know."

"Escaped!" repeated his sister, in a shrewish voice.

Mr. Gossett nodded.

"Poor dear!" said Miss Gossett, quivering.

"After him like flies round a treacle-pot," continued her brother. "I've been with 'im and I ought to know."

"P'r'aps *you* was the attraction," said his mother archly.

Mr. Gossett sniffed, but not so loudly as his sister.

"I don't hold with handsome men," said Mrs. Gossett, shaking her head. "Nobody could say that I married your pore father for his good looks. His—"

"Where did I get mine from, then?" interrupted Miss Gossett.

"My side of the family," replied her mother modestly. "You was a Smithson and Joe was a Gossett."

"If the Smithsons hadn't got more good looks than what Mabel has—" began the indignant Mr. Gossett.

"What a pair we should make," said Miss Gossett, with a simper, "me and Handsome Harry! Bring him in one evening and let's have a look at him, Joe. What's his other name? If it isn't nice I shan't have him."

"His name's Cook," said her brother, "and as for you catching him, why, he'd laugh at the idea."

"Bring him in and let's have a look at him," repeated his sister, "then perhaps I'll ask Florrie Adams in one evening. I'll tell her you'll be out."

"Oh, don't tease him," said Mrs. Gossett.

"Tease him?" said the irritated Mr. Gossett, pushing his chair away and rising. "Don't make me laugh. It's a pity Mabel ain't got more sense, that's all."

"Pity you ain't a Smithson," said Miss Gossett, as he went outside for his hat. "You might have a chance then."

He closed the street door with a bang that sent a revivifying draught of fresh air through the small house, and, somewhat ruffled in spirit, set off at a smart pace down the road. The subject of Miss Adams was a sore one, the slavish admiration of some months having yielded, so far, nothing but amusement in return. A brotherly desire to give Miss Gossett some idea of the pangs of unrequited affection sent his thoughts again to the fascinations of Handsome Harry.

He turned the matter over in his mind for a day or two, and resolved at last to introduce his friend casually. If Miss Gossett were taken at a disadvantage, so much the better; he was not going to give her the chance of "window-dressing."

His trouble was wasted. The night he introduced Mr. Cook his sister had just returned from the local cinema accompanied by Miss Adams, and the first impression the visitor received was of fine clothes and languorous perfumes. In the best manner of the highest circles both girls seemed to sit aloof, with little interests of their own. Little intimate jests and giggles testified to their complete absorption.

"Good show?" inquired Mr. Gossett, in an interval.

"Pretty fair," said his sister languidly. "Leonard Firebrace was on."

"He's a darling," said Miss Adams, clasping her hands enthusiastically.

Messrs. Gossett and Cook said "*H'm!*" to each other.

"Supposed to be the handsomest man on the films," said Miss Gossett.

Mr. Cook stroked his short, well-trimmed beard and gave a finer point to the ends of his moustache. "What's he like?" he inquired in an indulgent voice.

"Like a Greek god," replied Miss Gossett, quoting from a story in her favourite periodical.

"Straight nose, well-shaped mouth, and wonderful eyes," explained Miss Adams.

"You only see men like that at the Pictures, and in dreams," said her friend with a sigh. "Think of his teeth!"

Miss Adams thought of them, and sighed in her turn. Mr. Gossett and Mr. Cook stirred restlessly. The latter even ventured on a cough; a cough more than tinged with criticism. Under the calm, straight gaze of Miss Gossett it repeated itself—with a different note—and subsided.

"I must say," remarked that lady, turning to her friend, "that I like to see good looks in a fellow. Joe!"

"Hallo!" replied her brother.

"Who is that good-looking man you were talking about the other day? One of your foremen, or something?"

Mr. Gossett gasped, and sent a wireless message with his eyebrows.

"Man you call Pretty Bertie," continued his sister, ignoring it. "No, that isn't it."

"Have you gone dotty?" inquired the embarrassed Mr. Gossett in a gruff voice.

"Or was it Lovely Charlie?" said his sister, musing. "No, I remember—Handsome Harry. That's the name. Why don't you bring him in one day and let's have a look at him?"

"Do," urged Miss Adams.

"If he's only half as good-looking as what you say he is we might fall in love with him," said Miss Gossett.

Her brother eyed her helplessly, while Mr. Cook, with an air of pained surprise, sat awaiting the inevitable explanation.

"That's him," said Mr. Gossett at last, with a jerk of the head. "Where are your eyes?"

"Him? Who?" inquired his sister.

"Handsome Harry," replied her brother. "I told you his name was Cook."

Miss Gossett threw back her head and laughed till the tears came. "Don't be so silly," she said, wiping her eyes.

"How can you?" said Miss Adams.

"It's only one of Joe's larks," said Miss Gossett, turning to the goggle-eyed Mr. Cook. "You mustn't take any notice of him. The idea of pretending you are Handsome Harry."

"As if we shouldn't have noticed it," murmured Miss Adams.

Mr. Cook turned his troubled gaze upon his friend in a mute appeal for help, but Mr. Gossett's face was as bewildered as his own.

"It's a name that some of them have given him," said Mr. Gossett at last, in a surly voice.

"How rude of them!" said his sister severely. "I shouldn't take any notice of them if I were you, Mr. Cook. But I must say I should like to see the real one."

Mr. Cook gave it up. It struck him that the explanation might lie in defective eyesight, and he recalled the story of a man who took to spectacles, and ran away from his wife a week afterwards.

A feeling of regret that so pretty a girl might have to take to glasses imparted a tenderness to his glance that was by no means wasted. Miss Gossett, lowering her eyes at first under the onslaught, ventured after a time to raise them and meet it. The gentle timidity of her glance did much to restore Mr. Cook's self-esteem. In the language of the eyes long practice had made him almost perfect, and his gaze became so ardent and so confident that Miss Gossett was moved to speech.

"What's the matter?" she demanded.

"Matter?" repeated Mr. Cook, in surprise.

"You seemed to be staring in a funny sort of way," said the girl. "You don't have fits, do you?"

"No," said Mr. Cook shortly.

"Funny look he had," said Miss Gossett, turning to the others. "I didn't like it at all. I suppose you haven't got anything in your eye, Mr. Cook? I'm a dab at taking things out."

Mr. Cook hesitated, and was lost. "I did get something in coming along," he murmured, "but I thought it was out."

He smiled with content as the ministering angel leaned over him and prised up the lid with her finger. Then he winced and drew back his head.

"Keep still," said the girl; "I'm not hurting you."

"Not much," corrected the victim. "*Ow!*"

"It's funny men can't bear a little bit of pain," observed Miss Gossett, continuing her explanations. "There! I nearly had it then."

"Perhaps it'll work itself out," suggested Mr. Cook, wincing again.

"I'll have it out if you'll only keep still," said Miss Gossett. "Anybody would think I was hurting you."

Mr. Cook drew his head back with a sudden exclamation of pain. "What have you got?" he inquired hoarsely; "a scrubbing brush?"

"Don't be silly," said the girl, as the sufferer clapped a handkerchief to his streaming eyes.

"It's out," he said, in a voice which endeavoured in vain to express surprise and gratitude. "It's out."

"I knew I could do it," said Miss Gossett. "I could have done it sooner if you hadn't flinched so much."

"My eyes are very tender," said Mr. Cook.

"That's what I thought a few minutes ago," said the girl, "but perhaps you'll grow out of it. Let's hope so."

"It's never too late to mend," observed Miss Adams oracularly.

Mr. Cook arose in dignified silence and, with a final dab at his eyes, restored his handkerchief to his pocket and announced that he must be going. At Miss Adams's suggestion, Mr. Gossett, rising with some unwillingness, offered to accompany him.

"Me and Mabel want to have a little chat," said Miss Adams, in explanation.

"All by ourselves," added Miss Gossett.

Agreeable to this strange lack of taste on the part of the ladies, the gentlemen withdrew, Mr. Cook, to whom this sort of treatment was absolutely new, walking out of the house like a man in a dream. Memories of countless conquests stirred in his brain but yielded no satisfaction.

"Very off-handish, ain't she?" he said at last.

"She learns it from Mabel," said his friend. "They're as thick as two thieves."

"I mean your sister," said Mr. Cook.

"Oh!" replied Mr. Gossett. "Her!"

"She's very nice-looking," said Mr. Cook, after a long pause.

"She seems to make people think so," said the fond brother. "How she does it, I don't know. I'm as good a judge as most men, but I can't see it."

"Well, you can take it from me," said the other impressively, "that she is about the best-looking girl I have ever seen. She's your stepsister, isn't she?"

"Stepsister?" repeated Mr. Gossett, with surprising vehemence. "No, of course she ain't. Whatever put that into your head?"

"I don't know," said Mr. Cook hurriedly. "I spoke without thinking. Of course there's a great likeness; anybody could see that."

The indignant Mr. Gossett received the assurance with a grunt, and listened in amazed silence while his friend explained to him in enraptured terms the manifold perfections of his sister.

"But you hadn't seen her till an hour ago," he protested.

"I shall have to make up for lost time," said Mr. Cook earnestly. "What about tomorrow night?"

Mr. Gossett said there was nothing about it, and declined in the most unmistakable terms to have anything to do with the affair.

"She'd only make fun of you," he said severely. "You ought to have seen her face when she was messing about with your eye."

Mr. Cook said he *had* seen it, and smacked his lips.

"And she'll do worse than that if you don't let 'er alone," continued Mr. Gossett. "Why, there was one silly fellow that used to come after her, and she led 'im such a dance that he went away and joined the Army."

"Very good place for him," said Mr. Cook approvingly. "Besides, we must have soldiers."

"When I took you round I thought you would have learnt 'er a lesson," said his friend; "instead of that you're worse than any of 'em. It makes *me* look such a fool. I expect she's talking about you now and laughing fit to kill herself."

"She's got a pretty laugh," said the other with a tender smile. "I could listen to it all day."

He heard it a night or two later, when, failing his utmost efforts to obtain an invitation from Mr. Gossett, he called without one, apparently for the purpose of telling Miss Gossett that it was a fine evening, but that a little rain would do good. After which effort he sat and watched Miss Gossett gurgling foolishly into her handkerchief.

"Don't take no notice of her," said Mrs. Gossett, somewhat disturbed.

"I like it," replied Mr. Cook simply.

"Sounds silly to me," said Mrs. Gossett, shaking her head at her daughter.

"That's why I like it," said Mr. Cook, floundering. "I like silly people."

Miss Gossett's laughter ended abruptly. "Did you come to see Joe?" she inquired with some austerity.

Mr. Cook shook his head.

"What did you come for, then?"

The visitor looked imploringly at Mrs. Gossett, but seeing no help there, turned to the daughter. "I came to tell you my eye is all right now," he said slowly. "I thought you'd like to know."

Miss Gossett gazed at him, deep in thought. "Will you be able to see your way home with it?" she said at last, in a soft voice.

The visitor became thoughtful in his turn. "Perhaps—perhaps it would be safer if somebody—somebody came with me," he murmured.

Miss Gossett nodded. "Ye-es," she said softly. "Yes, I think it would. Can you give me a couple of minutes?"

Mr. Cook, flushing with joy, said that he could, and, hardly able to believe in his good fortune, bestowed a half-wink upon Mrs. Gossett as her daughter left the room.

"Gone up to put her hat on?" he inquired in a low voice.

"P'r'aps," said the surprised Mrs. Gossett, "and p'r'aps not," she added. "If I don't expect her to do a thing, she does it, and if I expect her to do a thing she don't do it. That's Mabel."

Mr. Cook shook his head gently in sympathy. Then he prepared to rise as Miss Gossett entered the room followed by a small and extremely dirty youth in patched knickerbockers.

"This is Tommy Burrows, from next door," she said.

Mr. Cook nodded—and waited.

"By good luck, he happened to be in," continued the girl. "This is the poor gentleman, Tommy, and if you lead him safe home he will give you a shilling. You had better hold his sleeve. And mind how you cross the roads."

She stood smiling benevolently as Master Burrows, in pursuance of his instructions, took the dazed and speechless Mr. Cook by the sleeve and piloted him carefully from the room. At the street-door he paused and strove to collect his scattered faculties.

"Goodbye," said Miss Gossett brightly.

The unfortunate gasped at her, and then, obedient to a tug at his sleeve, moved slowly off. The laugh that he had so much admired was heard again, but some of its savour seemed to have departed. It was clear that he had lost the first two rounds, and, with a faint hope that Tommy's mother might have something to say to Miss Gossett on the subject, he took that hapless youth ten miles for the shilling. By the next morning he had recovered his spirits and the vitriolic scorn of Joe Gossett passed him harmlessly by. It appeared that Miss Gossett had persisted in regarding her brother as privy to the visit and chose to include him as a victim of her cleverness.

"That's all right," said Mr. Cook equably. "You shall have the laugh of her by and by."

"When?" demanded the unbeliever.

"When I marry her," was the reply.

Mr. Gossett turned and regarded his friend in amazement. "Have you gone silly or what?" he inquired huskily.

"There's nothing to go silly about," responded Mr. Cook. "I've thought all along I should be caught some time. She's got me hard and fast, and the funny thing is, I don't mind. I like it."

"But she won't have you," objected the staring Mr. Gossett. "She wouldn't look at you."

"You tell her I'm going to marry her," said Mr. Cook. "Tell her I'm going to marry her, and the sooner she makes up her mind to it the better."

Mr. Gossett took the message. The one he brought back next day lost nothing in transit.

"So there you are," he said, grinning. "She says she wouldn't have you if you were the only man in the world."

"She couldn't," said the philosophical Mr. Cook; "there'd be too many after me." He called next evening and, Miss Gossett being out, left a little bunch of flowers he had hidden beneath his coat. Mr. Gossett brought back the withered remains next day. A large and expensive box of chocolates left two days later was returned empty, but any comfort Mr. Cook might have derived from the fact vanished when he heard that it had accompanied Mr. Gossett and Miss Adams to the cinema.

"She ate the chocs with one hand while I held the other," explained Mr. Gossett. "Try Mabel with another box tonight, old man."

Mr. Cook, intent upon what he now considered would be a long, campaign, made no reply. Despite his utmost efforts he was unable to obtain speech with Miss Gossett, and a letter, sent through the post, was returned marked, "Opened by mistake." Assailed by doubts, only his looking-glass convinced him that he held a winning hand. He called again, and spent three hours of mutual boredom with Mrs. Gossett, while Miss Gossett sat upstairs in her bedroom, blaspheming.

"It's the only way to treat 'em," he said to Mr. Gossett, when that gentleman remonstrated. "Show 'em you ain't afraid of 'em and they come to heel."

"And what about my poor mother?" demanded his friend hotly. "She 'ad you all last evening, talking about the weather, and Mabel all breakfast-time talking about hairdressers' blocks and tailors' dummies. Don't you come again."

"Not till next time," said the other calmly.

As a matter of good-feeling and policy combined he decided to let a few days elapse before calling again. A slight swelling and soreness in the neck attributed to a tooth which had been troubling him for some time led to a still further delay. The distortion of face was especially trying to a man of his appearance, and, after enduring for two days the glances of his fellow-workers and the ribaldries of Mr. Gossett, he stayed away from work.

He sat at home next day with his head wrapped in a shawl. Dainties, as conceived by his landlady for an invalid, remained untouched. And he was in the depths of misery when the door opened and Mr. Gossett stepped blithely in.

"Jee-rusalem!" said that gentleman.

Mr. Cook tried to smile, and Mr. Gossett retreated a couple of paces, and placed his hand on the doorknob.

"Why don't you 'ave the tooth out?" he demanded.

"When—swelling—goes—down," croaked the invalid.

Mr. Gossett looked at him and hesitated. "Mabel wants you to come to supper," he said at last. "She sent me to ask you."

There was a long pause.

"You—told—her—'bout this," said Mr. Cook, "and she wants—to make—fun of me."

Mr. Gossett coughed.

"All right," said the other, "I'll come. I don't mind if she does laugh."

Fortunately, as Mr. Gossett observed, it was getting dark, and Mr. Cook's features attracted no attention. A little natural reluctance to enter the sitting-room gave way before a hearty push from his companion.

"It is good of you to come," said Miss Gossett, her lips trembling.

"You—asked me," said Mr. Cook, speaking slowly and painfully from one side of his mouth. "And I came—because—you thought—I wouldn't."

"Don't take no notice of her," said Mrs. Gossett. "For shame, Mabel," she added.

"I ca-can't help it," said her daughter, wiping her eyes. "He—looks so plump and well-fed."

"He looks ill," said Mrs. Gossett severely. "Have you seen a doctor?"

Mr. Cook said he didn't believe in doctors, and, turning a deaf ear to the misbehaviour of Miss Gossett, took the seat next to her at the supper-table and sat gloomily eyeing food he was unable to eat. By an effort he managed to sip a little beer, and, at Miss Gossett's earnest entreaty, ate a small quantity of rice pudding from a salt-spoon. The fact that she fed him with the first two mouthfuls atoned for much.

"Pity Florrie couldn't come to supper," said Miss Gossett, turning to her brother.

"She'll be here soon, I expect," he answered. "She 'ad an appointment, but she said she'd be sure to come if she could. There she is, I think."

Rapid steps paused at the door, followed by a knock which Mr. Gossett hastened to answer. Voices sounded in the narrow passage.

"Come in, Florrie," cried Miss Gossett. "Handsome Harry is here."

Miss Adams came in, with a broad smile revealing white teeth. Then her eyes dilated, and uttering a piercing shriek she fell back into the passage.

"Don't be silly," cried the highly gratified Miss Gossett; "he's quite harmless."

There was a smothered exclamation from Miss Adams, followed by the sound of the opening of the street-door.

"It's too bad," said Mrs. Gossett. "Mabel, I won't have it."

The voice of Miss Adams was heard outside.

"He ought to be shut up," she exclaimed in piercing tones, "or boiled," she added. "If I catch 'em, I'll never speak to you again."

"Catch what?" demanded the harassed Mr. Gossett.

The reply set the party in the parlour tingling.

"*Mumps*" she said viciously. "As if you didn't know."

The grating of Miss Gossett's chair as she pushed it back broke the silence.

"Mumps!" she wailed; "mumps! And I've been sitting next to him."

"And feeding him," added Mr. Cook gloomily. "Well! Well! Fancy—its being mumps—all the time. And at—my age too. I thought—"

He finished speaking to an empty room. The ladies were upstairs and, judging by the noise, somewhat perturbed. The voice of Mr. Gossett—from the landing—bade him begone.

He returned to work nearly three weeks later. Mr. Gossett was not there, and the voice of envy declared that five other gentlemen were also staying at home in sinful luxury with the mumps.

He went round to call the same evening, and asked for news of Joe.

"They've both got it," said Mrs. Gossett in a tired voice. "Poor Mabel! You ought to see her."

"I will," said Mr. Cook, stepping inside. "Can you send her down?"

Mrs. Gossett smiled faintly. "She wouldn't let anybody see her for a thousand pounds," she declared. "I don't think her face will ever get right again. It's like a piller."

Mr. Cook, walking to the foot of the stairs, raised his voice and called loudly upon the name of Miss Gossett. A door opened softly and a strange, cracked voice told him to go away.

"I want to see you," he answered.

"Go away," repeated the girl.

"I came to see you when I had 'em," said Mr. Cook. "Now I dare you to come down and see me. If you haven't got the pluck, say so."

"Go away—you brute!" said the voice.

"Don't be a coward," urged Mr. Cook. "Surely you ain't going to be outdone by me. I'll wait in the parlour for you. Be a sportsman."

He waited five minutes. A halting step sounded from the stairs, and a little later the door opened and a disfigured and indignant Miss Gossett entered the room and stood glowering at him.

"Poor old thing," he said tenderly.

"You gave me this," she said fiercely.

Mr. Cook shook his head. "You took it," he corrected gently. He placed his arm suddenly around her waist, and, choosing her forehead as the point of least resistance, kissed it ardently.

"It'll soon go away," he said cheerfully. "In about ten days' time we shall be the best-looking couple in the neighbourhood."

21

THE BLINDNESS OF CAPTAIN FERGUSON

I

From outside the house looked desolate enough. It stood alone where the grass of the marshes met the sand of the shore. On one side a view of marsh and cattle, dykes and gates, on the other the waters of the North Sea.

Inside, in the cosy sitting-room, the captain sat and fumed. The fire was burning low and he had mislaid his pipe, while his wife, to whom he usually looked to adjust these matters, was upstairs with the sick girl from London, who had come home in search of rest and health.

"The women are all alike," grumbled the Captain, as he rose and felt cautiously along the mantelshelf for the missing pipe, "gossiping as usual."

His fumbling hands struck against a china shepherdess and wrecked her on the fender, for blindness had come upon him late in life and his huge gnarled fists lacked the touch usually associated with those who have lost their sight. With a rueful grumble he sank back into his chair again as his wife entered the room.

"Jenny, I've smashed something," said the offender humbly. "I was looking for my pipe."

"Here's your pipe, Jem," she replied, as she thrust it into his hands. "I must leave you a little while longer. Edith is not quite so well."

"I'll come up and talk to her." said the Captain, with the air of one who possessed a sovereign remedy.

"No, you mustn't," said his wife, pushing his great form back into the chair; "she's not well enough to talk much. I'll be back soon."

The Captain, impelled by that small but resolute arm, stayed where he had fallen, and lighting his pipe fell to smoking with much enjoyment, listening to the beating of the surf and the wind, which was blowing almost a gale. The combination was so soothing that he fell asleep at length with the pipe between his teeth.

He awoke with a start and a vague confused idea that somebody had called him. Certainly a cry of some sort still rang in his ears, and placing his pipe on the table, he rose and stood with one hand on the back of his chair listening. At first only the wind and the surf, then mixed with it the faint wailing of a child. The Captain felt his way to the door and called excitedly to his wife.

"Jenny! Jenny!"

"All right, go back," called his wife quickly, from the top of the stairs. "I'm coming down now."

"I heard a cry outside," said the Captain. "The cry of a child."

"Nonsense, you've been dreaming."

"I tell you I heard it," repeated the Captain, as he threw open the house door. "Listen!"

"There!" said the Captain, holding up a warning finger. "I heard it again."

"So did I," said the wife. "It's outside."

"Get a shawl and come after me, my lass," said the Captain, taking down a coil of line made fast to the staple of the door, which he used for short wanderings. "Hallo, there! Hallo!"

He walked slowly in the darkness, listening eagerly while his wife turned her white face upwards and in broken accents thanked Heaven for her husband's blindness. Then she came downstairs, and with the agility of a girl ran by her husband.

The Captain paying out his line, and treading softly, heard her stop and cry out suddenly, and then, with an indistinct cry to him, speed back to the house.

"I've got it," she cried. "I've got it."

He turned and followed rapidly. Inside he closed the door and stood in the hall listening to the crying of a child, which now sounded through the house, and the hurried footsteps of his wife as she moved about in the room above.

"It's a baby, Jem," said his wife, coming half-way down the stairs and closely watching her husband's face as it showed in the light from the sitting-room. "Just a little child, wrapped in an old shawl and left to die. Only a few days old, by the look of it."

"Aye, aye," said the Captain very slowly. "Go upstairs, my dear. Go upstairs."

He turned and, closing the door after him, groped his way back to his chair, leaving his wife, after a moment's irresolution, to do his bidding. The fire was out and the room chill before she came down again, and the tears sprang to her tired eyes as she saw the strong, helpless man patiently awaiting her return.

"How's Edith?" he asked, without turning his head.

"She's not very well, I think," said his wife, in a low, frightened voice, "but she has just fallen asleep. I don't think I'd disturb her tonight, Jem, if I were you."

"I won't," said the Captain quietly. "I'll get to bed, too, I think. Good night."

He went slowly up the stairs and into his room, his wife following him noiselessly, and not until the door had closed behind him did she relax her watchfulness; then in a dazed condition she made her way to her daughter and fell half fainting across the bed.

In the morning, in the cool salt air and the sunshine, her flagging spirits revived and she greeted her husband in almost her usual cheery fashion as he came in from his tethered walk along the shore to breakfast.

"Edith not coming down?" he inquired, as he took his seat at the table.

"Not to breakfast," she replied, watching him.

"Best not, if she doesn't feel strong," said the Captain briskly. "I've been thinking about that child."

"Ah," said his wife, and the cup she was passing him rattled in the saucer.

"If nobody claims it," continued the Captain, "take it up to London and let old Sparling's widow have it. She'll take it if we pay her. I suppose we can't send it to the workhouse?"

"We can't keep it?" suggested his wife timidly.

"No," said the Captain, with a mirthless laugh, "we're too old to be plagued with children."

His wife said no more, but later in the morning informed him that she had written to London to make arrangements, and that Edith would not be up that day, but would come down the next.

More than a week, however, elapsed before she put in an appearance, and then very pale and trembling she came down and took her accustomed seat. To her father's great relief she came alone, yet she was but indifferent company, her thoughts being with her mother and the child who had started on their journey to London.

After this the time passed slowly and uneventfully to the dwellers in the cottage. Edith, quiet and patient, felt her life bounded by the sea and marsh, and never looked beyond. Only her mother fretted as she thought of her beautiful daughter and her wasted life. For his part the Captain seemed not to think at all, except that once when his daughter threw out a feeble suggestion of seeking employment, he drew her to his knee, and encircled her with an arm of iron.

The child was never alluded to, though many and various were the plans mother and daughter considered for its future. The child itself solved the problem; it died, and its mother, weeping bitterly over the ill-written scrawl which conveyed the news to her, prayed for death too.

If anything, she became quieter than before, despite the efforts of her father to arouse her. Sometimes it was a long walk with the blind man along the shore, at another they would put to sea in the Captain's small skiff and stay for hours on the lonely waste of waters.

Then things suddenly changed. One day, after a longer walk than usual, they were astonished as they neared the house by the unwonted sounds of a man's voice. It was a full, hearty voice, and it was evident from the animated conversation within that the stranger was feeling very much at home.

"Jem," said his wife, as he entered, "you remember George Merrick, but he's grown from a boy to a man since we saw him."

"And from apprentice to master," said the stranger, as he rose and gripped the other's hand. "All your teaching, Cap'n, all your teaching."

"You've got a ship, my lad?" inquired the Captain, as he returned the shake.

"A brand new one," replied the other. "But I've got to wait a couple of months for her and I thought I'd spend the holiday looking up my friends. I got your address from your old owners, and here I am."

"And here you'll stay till your ship's ready," said the Captain cordially. "That is if you can put up with an old blind man and his household. Lord, it's good to hear the voice of a friend in this desolate place."

"Sure I shan't be a nuisance?" asked Merrick. "You know of old how noisy I am."

"Not a bit of it, you'll liven us all up," replied the other. "It'll be a boon to me to have somebody to talk over old times with."

"Well, when you are tired of me tell me to go," laughed Merrick, and so the matter was settled.

II

With the introduction o a visitor from the outside world dullness fled from the cottage, and in a very short time George Merrick was on the happiest terms with all of them; the Captain remarking with surprise conversational powers on the part of his wife he had long since thought defunct.

All this the Captain heard, but he was a sense short. He could not see the honest admiration with which Merrick eyed the daughter while he talked to the mother, nor the subtle joy of the latter in the knowledge of it.

A sharper man might have remarked the deference in the visitor's tones when he addressed the daughter, but he did not, nor when Merrick and his daughter were from the room did it occur to him that they might be together.

It was three weeks after Merrick's arrival before his eyes were opened. The visitor had gone on an errand to the neighbouring town, and his host was sitting at the open window, smoking and listening to the clicking of his wife's needles as she knitted a mammoth sock.

"Jem," said his wife, suddenly suspending her work, "I think George Merrick wants a little talk with you this afternoon."

"He may have it," said the Captain affably.

"You—you don't seem to understand," said his wife, her voice shaking a little; "you men are all alike, I think. He wants Edith."

"*What?*" shouted the Captain.

"He spoke to me this morning," continued his wife, "and, of course, I referred him to you."

"Has he spoken to her?" inquired the Captain.

"He spoke to her last night," was the reply, "and she accepted him. I saw all along that they were taken with each other."

"And you never stopped it," said the Captain. "You let it go on."

"Of course," said his wife in surprised tones. "Why not?"

"Your memory is failing," said her husband. "Think—go back three years; go back to the night the child came."

"Jem," said his wife in a frightened whisper. "What do you mean?"

"Have you told him what you told me, or have you told him the truth?" pursued the other sternly.

His wife, breathing rapidly, made no reply.

"I have never referred to it before," said the Captain more gently. "I never would have referred to it but for this. To save my poor girl's pride—and my own—I pretended to believe the lie you told me, for I am a blind man, my dear, and harmless. When a man loses his sight he should die, for he is a moving, *dangerous* man no longer. He is a derelict, and can only hurt that which runs against him."

"It is all past and over," murmured his wife brokenly.

"So I had thought," replied the husband; "I never thought to have told my daughter's shame to another man."

"You will not," cried his wife wildly, "I will never forgive you if you do. Hasn't my darling suffered enough? We did wrong in sending such a child to that great, wicked city. And she loves him. If you tell him that, it will kill her."

"I am a proud man," said the Captain sternly, as he rose, "and no man shall enter my family under false pretences. I will tell him. If he likes to overlook it, well and good. Nobody will be happier than I shall."

"Overlook it!" repeated his wife. "To save your pride, you were content to keep your eyes shut—why do you wish to open his? Do you think he will thank you for the information?"

"Where is he?" asked the Captain.

"He is out with Edith," said his wife, crossing over and falling on her knees beside him. "Jem, don't tell him; for pity's sake let things be. Edith refused him at first; she has pride, too. She would not listen to him. But I told him before her that she loved him, and after that he would not be denied. She is a good girl—you know she is a good girl—and if you ruin her life like this, you will break my heart."

Before the Captain could reply or disengage his hands from hers, voices were heard in the hall, and Merrick entered the room and looked significantly at his hostess.

"Captain," he said in a strong voice, "I suppose Mrs. Ferguson has told you that I have asked your daughter to be my wife. I—"

"Sit down," said the Captain quietly. "Jenny, Merrick and I will settle this."

His wife rose helplessly to her feet. "Not now, Jem," she cried piteously, "not now; think first."

The Captain shook his head, and his wife, avoiding the gaze of the astonished Merrick, left the room and went upstairs to her daughter. Ten minutes later, through blinding tears, she saw Merrick quit the house and walk like a drunken man along the sands.

"He has gone," she whispered, "gone without a word."

Edith rose, pale and dry-eyed, and crosed over to the window; then flushing darkly, she bent over her mother and kissed her.

"I should not love him if he had stayed," she said.

For the rest of that day she kept her room, only going downstairs when she heard her mother's bedroom door close. Her father sat by the window, his unsmoked pipe by the sill and his hands clasped before him.

"Good night, father," she said quietly, as she crossed over to him and placed her arms about his neck. "And thank you, for—everything."

"We'll—we'll be the same as before, my girl," said the Captain, as he drew her soft cheek on to his shoulder. "It was best for you, best for him."

"You have been wonderfully good to me," said the girl in a low voice. "I thank you and love you for it."

She disengaged herself from his arms and rose, pausing at the door to bid him good night again, and passed upstairs.

* * *

An hour later, when the house was still and dark, she crept down again. It was a warm summer's night, but she shivered slightly and caught her breath when the door rattled, under the touch of her shaky fingers, as she opened it. Then she closed it behind her, and with a slight sob at the pity of it all, walked towards the sea. For a minute she paused irresolute, and a man who had walked down for a last look at the house which contained her, stepped from its shadow and stood miserably watching. Then, as he heard the grating of the boat's keel on the beach, he sprang forward eagerly, crying her name.

He was just too late; the boat floated, and the girl with a stroke of the oars sent it from the shore. Without further parley he threw off his coat and shoes, and wading in, struck out in pursuit.

"Go back," cried the girl from between her teeth. "Go back."

There was no reply, but a slight splashing in the wake of the boat spoke for itself. She bent to the oars, the noise getting fainter and fainter as she widened the distance between them.

With her face white and set, she kept on her way until, despite herself, her heart failed her, and she stopped rowing to listen. At first there was a dead silence, then she fancied she could still hear him striving to reach her.

"Go back!" she cried piteously, "go back!"

"I can't," he shouted calmly, "it's too far."

The girl sat motionless, peering through the gloom. Across the water came the sound of quick, distressed breathing, and weak, rapid strokes. With a great cry, she turned the boat's head round and pulled in the direction of the swimmer.

"Where are you?" she cried wildly; "call out."

At the faintness of the response she increased her efforts until she came alongside something which struggled manfully in the dark water, and strove to keep its white face above it. Just in time she leaned over, and, grasping it by the shoulder, drew it to the stern of the boat and held it fiercely and strongly to her breast.

"If you want to die, dear," gasped the man, as he lay a little later in the bottom of the boat, holding her hands, "pull out the plug and we'll go down together, but living or dead, you shall not go from me again."

22

WAPPING-ON-THAMES

As a residential neighbourhood Wapping is perhaps undesirable, though a considerable population contrives to exist in the narrow streets hemmed in between the dock walls and the warehouses bordering the river. For the river itself is completely hidden, except where the swing-bridges, which give entrance to the docks, afford a passing glimpse.

From a picturesque point of view Wapping was no doubt much better in the days when docks and swing-bridges were unknown; when the bow-windows of its ancient taverns projected quaintly over the river and the watermen's stairs inspired the muse of the songwriter. Then the raucous bellowings of hurrying steamers were unheard, and sailing craft thoughtfully waited for tides, while master mariners sat drinking in the bow-windows aforesaid.

The old church and the charity school, with the overgrown graveyard opposite, with its rank grass and dingy trees, are the remains of those days. The green of the churchyard is a relief to the bricks and mortar, for trees are scarce in Wapping, though there are a few others in front of the old-fashioned houses on the breezy pier-head hard by—trees which, having been coaxed to grow in that uncongenial spot, conscientiously endeavour to indicate the seasons, and make very few mistakes considering.

High Street, Wapping, the principal thoroughfare, realising, possibly, that High Streets are apt to adhere too slavishly to one pattern, appears to have determined to be original. It sternly eschews the drapers and hatters, the bootmakers and tailors of other High Streets, and confines its retail trade almost entirely to coffee-shops and taverns. The coffee-shops are as conservative as the street, and one window is much like another—herrings, rejoicing in their strength, competing for favour with bacon of guaranteed mildness and eggs of blameless exterior.

Early in the morning the night-watchmen are awakened by vans, and late at night their sleep is broken by them. For Wapping revels in vans of all shapes and all sizes, but preferably large, and has put down granite roads for their especial delectation. The vans are from all quarters of London, and their drivers from all parts of the country, but the latter are the willing victims of one dominant idea. It is the ambition of every carman—the thing for which he plots and plans, and swears and lies—to be attended to out of his turn. The more out of his turn the better, and a boy of innocent aspect and no principles, who will ably second his perjuries, is as the apple of his eye. This, and sitting in dangerous attitudes on the tail-board of the van, or doing a double-shuffle on the extreme edge of the kerb, is the van-boy's part in life. In his spare moments he watches his chief back horses, for, as a backer of horses in a blameless sense, the riverside carman has probably no equal in the world. At one time, in addition to the road, he had about two feet of pavement to manœuvre on as well, but now he has been warned off by iron posts of the most upright and rigid bearing.

Down Tower Hill, thinking no evil, comes a mildewed four-wheeler driven by an elderly cabman, who pulls up so sharply at the bottom of the hill that the horse slides a yard or two and then tries to sit down.

"Drive on, cabman!" says a shrill voice inside, as the owner of it knuckles at the glass. "What are you stopping for? It's farther on!"

"All right, lady," says the cabman. He knows that the sex requires humouring, and "clucks" the horse on exactly seventeen inches.

"Any chance o' gettin' by, sir?" he inquires with deep respect of a tall policeman.

The tall policeman eyes the traffic critically and a Pickford's van severely. Pickford's horses are pawing the pavement, while their tailboard is giving great offence to a pair of horses behind.

"Pickford!" yells the tall policeman with great suddenness.

Half a dozen voices take up the cry of "Pickford," and Pickford's representative not being forthcoming (he is at the present moment making Language, with a capital L, do for argument with the foreman), a small boy appears from the depths of the van to see what he can do.

"Put your van back a bit!" says the tall policeman austerely.

The urchin grasps the horses' heads, brings them forward a bit, thrusts them back, slipping and stumbling with their heads in the air, and having made at least a foot more space, pauses triumphantly and asks, "How's that?"

The only reply of the tall policeman, who is a man of few words, is to bawl for "Pickford" again. The cabman, in the most familiar manner, also calls for "Pickford," and a string of vehicles behind him also call on the name of "Pickford" with profane fervour. "Pickford" turns up at last in a heated condition, having signally failed with the foreman, and grasping his horses' heads, backs them violently. The commotion that ensues is tremendous, the docile and intelligent animals behind, realising that it is a case of *sauve qui peut*, going where they can.

There is now room for the procession to pass, and the cabman, having brooded over his wrongs until he is word-perfect, tells the carman his opinion of him as he goes by. It is a long opinion, quite a character-study in fact and, despite the haste of his fares, he walks his horse so that the offender shall not miss a word of it.

"Bullen's Wharf?" he inquires politely of a bystander, turning a deaf ear to his adversary's reply.

"Straight ahead," says the man addressed, "but you can't get by!"

"Ho! Carn't I?" says the cabman, with the air of a man who has just done greater things than that. "An' w'y not?"

"Cos the bridge is swung," says the other cheerfully.

The cabman swings himself off his box, and opening the door of his vehicle, breaks the news to his fares. The three ladies lean forward anxiously, and with one accord blame him for it, one lady remarking darkly that four-wheelers are all alike, and drawing offensive comparisons between the present vehicle and a hansom.

"I carn't 'elp the bridge being swung," says the cabman. "It ain't no pleasure for me standing here listening to you. Ar long 'll it be, mate?"

"I think they're almost through now," says the other. "There's just a few empty lighters going into the dock—unless the *Evening Star* is coming out," he adds thoughtfully.

Fortunately for all concerned the gallant ship mentioned does not come out. The bridge swings together again, and the cabman, gathering up his reins, rattles briskly over the stones to his destination.

If the traffic in the streets is thick, that on the river is almost as bad. Huge steamers come slowly and cautiously up, moaning plaintively with their steam-sirens whenever they see anything about to run into them. At times there appears to be no offing at all, and even penny steamers—the most expert craft on the river—give a low whistle and wonder what is going to happen next. It is usual at such moments for an old and leaky boat, laden with small boys, who prefer this mode of whiling away the dinner-hour to eating, to stop in mid-stream to recover an oar. Extraordinary feats of navigation are performed by the crew before this is accomplished, but they get it at last, and ignoring the remarks hurled at them from the various craft, settle down to work again and ram a steam collier.

Work on the wharves is in full swing, and the cranes are busy lowering goods into the gaping holds beneath. Sometimes the freight drops from the slings on to the labourers, and once a crane we knew—ordinarily a well-behaved, reliable worker—took too much aboard and plunged fifteen feet into the river below. It took the driver with it, and when his friends got him up, as a preliminary to burying him, they found, to their astonishment, that he was alive. He was never a man to make much fuss; and after he had sat on the jetty and been patted on the back, he looked round at the place the crane had left, and said that perhaps, as there didn't seem to be anything for him to do, he might have a half-holiday for once. He added, as an extra reason, that he felt a little bit shaken.

It is not until Sunday arrives that Wapping becomes quiet, and then the change is almost oppressive in its thoroughness. The streets are practically deserted in the morning, except for a few men who have got up early by force of habit rather than the promptings of virtue, and a chance cat slinking furtively along in the shadow of the warehouses, ready to dart beneath a gateway at the first sign of a dog.

23

THE INTERRUPTION

I

The last of the funeral guests had gone, and Spencer Goddard, in decent black, sat alone in his small, well-furnished study. There was a queer sense of freedom in the house since the coffin had left it; the coffin which was now hidden in its solitary grave beneath the yellow earth. The air, which for the last three days had seemed stale and contaminated, now smelt fresh and clean. He went to the open window and, looking into the fading light of the autumn day, took a deep breath.

He closed the window and, stooping down, put a match to the fire, and, dropping into his easy chair, sat listening to the cheery crackle of the wood. At the age of thirty-eight he had turned over a fresh page. Life, free and unencumbered, was before him. His dead wife's money was at last his, to spend as he pleased instead of being doled out in reluctant driblets.

He turned at a step at the door, and his face assumed the appearance of gravity and sadness it had worn for the last four days. The cook, with the same air of decorous grief, entered the room quietly and, crossing to the mantelpiece, placed upon it a photograph.

"I thought you'd like to have it, sir," she said, in a low voice, "to remind you."

Goddard thanked her, and, rising, took it in his hand and stood regarding it. He noticed with satisfaction that his hand was absolutely steady.

"It is a very good likeness—till she was taken ill," continued the woman. "I never saw anybody change so sudden."

"The nature of her disease, Hannah," said her master.

The woman nodded, and, dabbing at her eyes with her handkerchief, stood regarding him.

"Is there anything you want?" he inquired, after a time.

She shook her head. "I can't believe she's gone," she said, in a low voice. "Every now and then I have a queer feeling that she's still here—"

"It's your nerves," said her master sharply. "—and wanting to tell me something."

By a great effort Goddard refrained from looking at her.

"Nerves," he said again. "Perhaps you ought to have a little holiday. It has been a great strain upon you."

"You, too, sir," said the woman respectfully. "Waiting on her hand and foot as you have done, I can't think how you stood it. If you'd only had a nurse—"

"I preferred to do it myself, Hannah," said her master. "If I had had a nurse it would have alarmed her."

The woman assented. "And they are always peeking and prying into what doesn't concern them," she added. "Always think they know more than the doctors do."

Goddard turned a slow look upon her. The tall, angular figure was standing in an attitude of respectful attention; the cold, slaty-brown eyes were cast down, the sullen face expressionless.

"She couldn't have had a better doctor," he said, looking at the fire again. "No man could have done more for her."

"And nobody could have done more for her than you did, sir," was the reply. "There's few husbands that would have done what you did."

Goddard stiffened in his chair. "That will do, Hannah," he said curtly.

"Or done it so well," said the woman, with measured slowness.

With a strange, sinking sensation, her master paused to regain his control. Then he turned and eyed her steadily. "Thank you," he said slowly; "you mean well, but at present I cannot discuss it."

For some time after the door had closed behind her he sat in deep thought. The feeling of well-being of a few minutes before had vanished, leaving in its place an apprehension which he refused to consider, but which would not be allayed. He thought over his actions of the last few weeks, carefully, and could remember no flaw. His wife's illness, the doctor's diagnosis, his own solicitous care, were all in keeping with the ordinary. He tried to remember the woman's exact words—her manner. Something had shown him fear. What?

He could have laughed at his fears next morning. The dining-room was full of sunshine and the fragrance of coffee and bacon was in the air. Better still, a worried and commonplace Hannah. Worried over two eggs with false birth-certificates, over the vendor of which she became almost lyrical.

"The bacon is excellent," said her smiling master, "so is the coffee; but your coffee always is."

Hannah smiled in return, and, taking fresh eggs from a rosy-cheeked maid, put them before him.

A pipe, followed by a brisk walk, cheered him still further. He came home glowing with exercise and again possessed with that sense of freedom and freshness. He went into the garden—now his own—and planned alterations.

After lunch he went over the house. The windows of his wife's bedroom were open and the room neat and airy. His glance wandered from the made-up bed to the brightly-polished furniture. Then he went to the dressing-table and opened the drawers, searching each in turn. With the exception of a few odds and ends they were empty. He went out on to the landing and called for Hannah.

"Do you know whether your mistress locked up any of her things?" he inquired.

"What things?" said the woman.

"Well, her jewellery mostly."

"Oh!" Hannah smiled. "She gave it all to me," she said quietly.

Goddard checked an exclamation. His heart was beating nervously, but he spoke sternly.

"When?"

"Just before she died—of gastroenteritis," said the woman.

There was a long silence. He turned and with great care mechanically closed the drawers of the dressing-table. The tilted glass showed him the pallor of his face, and he spoke without turning round.

"That is all right, then," he said huskily. "I only wanted to know what had become of it. I thought, perhaps, Milly—"

Hannah shook her head. "Milly's all right," she said, with a strange smile. "She's as honest as we are. Is there anything more you want, sir?"

She closed the door behind her with the quietness of the well-trained servant; Goddard, steadying himself with his hand on the rail of the bed, stood looking into the future.

II

The days passed monotonously, as they pass with a man in prison. Gone was the sense of freedom and the idea of a wider life. Instead of a cell, a house with ten rooms—but Hannah, the jailer, guarding each one. Respectful and attentive, the model servant, he saw in every word a threat against his liberty—his life. In the sullen face and cold eyes he saw her knowledge of power; in her solicitude for his comfort and approval, a sardonic jest. It was the master playing at being the servant. The years of unwilling servitude were over, but she felt her way carefully with infinite zest in the game. Warped and bitter, with a cleverness which had never before had scope, she had entered into her kingdom. She took it little by little, savouring every morsel.

"I hope I've done right, sir," she said one morning. "I have given Milly notice."

Goddard looked up from his paper. "Isn't she satisfactory?" he inquired.

"Not to my thinking, sir," said the woman. "And she says she is coming to see you about it. I told her that would be no good."

"I had better see her and hear what she has to say," said her master.

"Of course, if you wish to," said Hannah; "only, after giving her notice, if she doesn't go I shall. I should be sorry to go—I've been very comfortable here—but it's either her or me."

"I should be sorry to lose you," said Goddard in a hopeless voice.

"Thank you, sir," said Hannah. "I'm sure I've tried to do my best. I've been with you some time now—and I know all your little ways. I expect I understand you better than anybody else would. I do all I can to make you comfortable."

"Very well, I leave it to you," said Goddard in a voice which strove to be brisk and commanding. "You have my permission to dismiss her."

"There's another thing I wanted to see you about," said Hannah; "my wages. I was going to ask for at rise, seeing that I'm really housekeeper here now."

"Certainly," said her master, considering, "that only seems fair. Let me see—what are you getting?"

"Thirty-six."

Goddard reflected for a moment, and then turned with a benevolent smile. "Very well," he said cordially, "I'll make it forty-two. That's ten shillings a month more."

"I was thinking of a hundred," said Hannah dryly.

The significance of the demand appalled him. "Rather a big jump," he said at last. "I really don't know that I"

"It doesn't matter," said Hannah. "I thought I was worth it—to you—that's all. You know best. Some people might think I was worth *two* hundred. That's a bigger jump, but after all a big jump is better than—"

She broke off and tittered. Goddard eyed her.

"—than a big drop," she concluded.

Her master's face set. The lips almost disappeared and something came into the pale eyes that was revolting. Still eyeing her, he rose and approached her. She stood her ground and met him eye to eye.

"You are jocular," he said at last.

"Short life and a merry one," said the woman.

"Mine or yours?"

"Both, perhaps," was the reply.

"If—if I give you a hundred," said Goddard, moistening his lips, "that ought to make your life merrier, at any rate."

Hannah nodded. "Merry and long, perhaps," she said slowly. "I'm careful, you know—very careful."

"I am sure you are," said Goddard, his face relaxing.

"Careful what I eat and drink, I mean," said the woman, eyeing him steadily.

"That is wise," he said slowly. "I am myself—that is why I am paying a good cook a large salary. But don't overdo things, Hannah; don't kill the goose that lays the golden eggs."

"I am not likely to do that," she said coldly. "Live and let live; that is my motto. Some people have different ones. But I'm careful; nobody won't catch me napping. I've left a letter with my sister, in case."

Goddard turned slowly and in a casual fashion put the flowers straight in a bowl on the table, and, wandering to the window, looked out. His face was white again and his hands trembled.

"To be opened after my death," continued Hannah. "I don't believe in doctors—not after what I've seen of them—I don't think they know enough; so if I die I shall be examined. I've given good reasons."

"And suppose," said Goddard, coming from the window, "suppose she is curious, and opens it before you die?"

"We must chance that," said Hannah, shrugging her shoulders; "but I don't think she will. I sealed it up with sealing-wax, with a mark on it."

"She might open it and say nothing about it," persisted her master.

An unwholesome grin spread slowly over Hannah's features. "I should know it soon enough," she declared boisterously, "and so would other people. Lord! There would be an upset! Chidham would have something to talk about for once. We should be in the paper—both of us."

Goddard forced a smile. "Dear me!" he said gently. "Your pen seems to be a dangerous weapon, Hannah, but I hope that the need to open it will not happen for another fifty years. You look well and strong."

The woman nodded. "I don't take up my troubles before they come," she said, with a satisfied air; "but there's no harm in trying to prevent them coming. Prevention is better than cure."

"Exactly," said her master; "and, by the way, there's no need for this little financial arrangement to be known by anybody else. I might become unpopular with my neighbours for setting a bad example. Of course, I am giving you this sum because I really think you are worth it."

"I'm sure you do," said Hannah. "I'm not sure I ain't worth more, but this'll do to go on with. I shall get a girl for less than we are paying Milly, and that'll be another little bit extra for me."

"Certainly," said Goddard, and smiled again.

"Come to think of it," said Hannah, pausing at the door, "I ain't sure I shall get anybody else; then there'll be more than ever for me. If I do the work I might as well have the money."

Her master nodded, and, left to himself, sat down to think out a position which was as intolerable as it was dangerous. At a great risk he had escaped from the dominion of one woman only to fall, bound and helpless, into the hands of another. However vague and unconvincing the suspicions of Hannah might be, they would be sufficient. Evidence could be unearthed. Cold with fear one moment, and hot with fury the next, he sought in vain for some avenue of escape. It was his brain against that of a cunning, illiterate fool; a fool whose malicious stupidity only added to his danger. And she drank. With largely increased wages she would drink more and his very life might depend upon a hiccuped boast. It was clear that she was enjoying her supremacy; later on her vanity would urge her to display it before others. He might have to obey the crack of her whip before witnesses, and that would cut off all possibility of escape.

He sat with his head in his hands. There must be a way out and he must find it. Soon. He must find it before gossip began; before the changed position of master and servant lent colour to her story when that story became known. Shaking with fury, he thought of her lean, ugly throat and the joy of choking her life out with his fingers. He started suddenly, and took a quick breath. No, not fingers—a rope.

III

Bright and cheerful outside and with his friends, in the house he was quiet and submissive. Milly had gone, and, if the service was poorer and the rooms neglected, he gave no sign. If a bell remained unanswered he made no complaint, and to studied insolence turned the other cheek of politeness. When at this tribute to her power the woman smiled, he smiled in return. A smile which, for all its disarming softness, left her vaguely uneasy.

"I'm not afraid of you," she said once, with a menacing air.

"I hope not," said Goddard in a slightly surprised voice.

"Some people might be, but I'm not," she declared. "If anything happened to me—"

"Nothing could happen to such a careful woman as you are," he said, smiling again. "You ought to live to ninety—with luck."

It was clear to him that the situation was getting on his nerves. Unremembered but terrible dreams haunted his sleep. Dreams in which some great, inevitable disaster was always pressing upon him, although he could never discover what it was. Each morning he awoke unrefreshed to face another day of torment. He could not meet the woman's eyes for fear of revealing the threat that was in his own.

Delay was dangerous and foolish. He had thought out every move in that contest of wits which was to remove the shadow of the rope from his own neck and place it about that of the woman. There was a little risk, but the stake was a big one. He had but to set the ball rolling and others would keep it on its course. It was time to act.

He came in a little jaded from his afternoon walk, and left his tea untouched. He ate but little dinner, and, sitting hunched up over the fire, told the woman that he had taken a slight chill. Her concern, he felt grimly, might have been greater if she had known the cause.

He was no better next day, and after lunch called in to consult his doctor. He left with a clean bill of health except for a slight digestive derangement, the remedy for which he took away with him in a bottle. For two days he swallowed one tablespoonful three times a day in water, without result, then he took to his bed.

"A day or two in bed won't hurt you," said the doctor. "Show me that tongue of yours again."

"But what is the matter with me, Roberts?" inquired the patient.

The doctor pondered. "Nothing to trouble about—nerves a bit wrong—digestion a little bit impaired. You'll be all right in a day or two."

Goddard nodded. So far, so good; Roberts had not outlived his usefulness. He smiled grimly after the doctor had left at the surprise he was preparing for him. A little rough on Roberts and his professional reputation, perhaps, but these things could not be avoided.

He lay back and visualised the programme. A day or two longer, getting gradually worse, then a little sickness. After that a nervous, somewhat shamefaced patient hinting at things, His food had a queer taste—he felt worse after taking it; he knew it was ridiculous, still—there was some of his beef-tea he had put aside, perhaps the doctor would like to examine it? And the medicine? Secretions, too; perhaps he would like to see those?

Propped on his elbow, he stared fixedly at the wall. There would be a trace—a faint trace—of arsenic in the secretions. There would be more than a trace in the other things. An attempt to poison him would be clearly indicated, and—his wife's symptoms had resembled his own—let Hannah get out of the web he was spinning if she could. As for the letter she had threatened him with, let her produce it; it could only recoil upon herself. Fifty letters could not save her from the doom he was preparing for her. It was her life or his, and he would show no mercy. For three days he doctored himself with sedulous care, watching himself anxiously the while. His nerve was going and he knew it. Before him was the strain of the discovery, the arrest, and the trial. The gruesome business of his wife's death. A long business. He would wait no longer, and he would open the proceedings with dramatic suddenness.

It was between nine and ten o'clock at night when he rang his bell, and it was not until he had rung four times that he heard the heavy steps of Hannah mounting the stairs.

"What d'you want?" she demanded, standing in the doorway.

"I'm very ill," he said, gasping. "Run for the doctor. Quick!"

The woman stared at him in genuine amazement. "What, at this time o' night?" she exclaimed. "Not likely."

"I'm dying!" said Goddard in a broken voice.

"Not you," she said roughly. "You'll be better in the morning."

"I'm dying," he repeated. "Go—for—the—doctor."

The woman hesitated. The rain beat in heavy squalls against the window, and the doctor's house was a mile distant on the lonely road. She glanced at the figure on the bed.

"I should catch my death o' cold," she grumbled.

She stood sullenly regarding him. He certainly looked very ill, and his death would by no means benefit her. She listened, scowling, to the wind and the rain.

"All right," she said at last, and went noisily from the room.

His face set in a mirthless smile, he heard her bustling about below. The front-door slammed violently and he was alone.

He waited for a few minutes and then, getting out of bed, put on his dressing-gown and set about his preparations. With a steady hand he added a little white powder to the remains of his beef-tea and to the contents of his bottle of medicine. He stood listening a moment at some faint sound from below, and, having satisfied himself, lit a candle and made his way to Hannah's room. For a space he stood irresolute, looking about him. Then he opened one of the drawers and, placing the broken packet of powder under a pile of clothing at the back, made his way back to bed.

He was disturbed to find that he was trembling with excitement and nervousness. He longed for tobacco, but that was impossible. To reassure himself he began to rehearse his conversation with the doctor, and again he thought over every possible complication. The scene with the woman would be terrible; he would have to be too ill to take any part in it. The less he said the better. Others would do all that was necessary.

He lay for a long time listening to the sound of the wind and the rain. Inside, the house seemed unusually quiet, and with an odd sensation he suddenly realised that it was the first time he had been alone in it since his wife's death. He remembered that she would have to be disturbed. The thought was unwelcome. He did not want her to be disturbed. Let the dead sleep.

He sat up in bed and drew his watch from beneath the pillow. Hannah ought to have been back before; in any case she could not be long now. At any moment he might hear her key in the lock. He lay down again and reminded himself that things were shaping well. He had shaped them, and some of the satisfaction of the artist was his.

The silence was oppressive. The house seemed to be listening, waiting. He looked at his watch again and wondered, with a curse, what had happened to the woman. It was clear that the doctor must be out, but that was no reason for her delay. It was close on midnight, and the atmosphere of the house seemed in some strange fashion to be brooding and hostile.

In a lull in the wind he thought he heard footsteps outside, and his face cleared as he sat up listening for the sound of the key in the door below. In another moment the woman would be in the house and the fears engendered by a disordered fancy would have flown. The sound of the steps had ceased, but he could hear no sound of entrance. Until all hope had gone, he sat listening. He was certain he had heard footsteps. Whose?

Trembling and haggard he sat waiting, assailed by a crowd of murmuring fears. One whispered that he had failed and would have to pay the penalty of failing; that he had gambled with Death and lost.

By a strong effort he fought down these fancies and, closing his eyes, tried to compose himself to rest. It was evident now that the doctor was out and that Hannah was waiting to return with him in his car. He was frightening himself for nothing. At any moment he might hear the sound of their arrival.

He heard something else, and, sitting up suddenly, tried to think what it was and what had caused it. It was a very faint sound—stealthy. Holding his breath, he waited for it to be repeated. He heard it again, the mere ghost of a sound—the whisper of a sound, but significant as most whispers are.

He wiped his brow with his sleeve and told himself firmly that it was nerves, and nothing but nerves; but, against his will, he still listened. He fancied now that the sound came from his wife's room, the other side of the landing. It increased in loudness and became more insistent, but with his eyes fixed on the door of his room he still kept himself in hand, and tried to listen instead to the wind and the rain.

For a time he heard nothing but that. Then there came a scraping, scurrying noise from his wife's room, and a sudden, terrific crash.

With a loud scream his nerve broke, and springing from the bed he sped downstairs and, flinging open the front-door, dashed into the night. The door, caught by the wind, slammed behind him.

With his hand holding the garden gate open, ready for further flight, he stood sobbing for breath. His bare feet were bruised and the rain was very cold, but he took no heed. Then he ran a little way along the road and stood for some time, hoping and listening.

He came back slowly. The wind was bitter and he was soaked to the skin. The garden was black and forbidding, and unspeakable horror might be lurking in the bushes. He went up the road again, trembling with cold. Then, in desperation, he passed through the terrors of the garden to the house, only to find the door closed. The porch gave a little protection from the icy rain, but none from the wind, and, shaking in every limb, he leaned in abject misery against the door. He pulled himself together after a time and stumbled round to the backdoor. Locked! And all the lower windows were shuttered. He made his way back to the porch, and, crouching there in hopeless misery, waited for the woman to return.

IV

He had a dim memory when he awoke of somebody questioning him, and then of being half pushed, half carried upstairs to bed. There was something wrong with his head and his chest, and he was trembling violently, and very cold. Somebody was speaking.

"You must have taken leave of your senses," said the voice of Hannah. "I thought you were dead."

He forced his eyes to open. "Doctor," he muttered, "doctor."

"Out on a bad case," said Hannah. "I waited till I was tired of waiting, and then came along. Good thing for you I did. He'll be round first thing this morning. He ought to be here now."

She bustled about, tidying up the room, his leaden eyes following her as she collected the beef-tea and other things on a tray and carried them out.

"Nice thing I did yesterday," she remarked, as she came back. "Left the missus's bedroom window open. When I opened the door this morning I found that beautiful Chippidale glass of hers had blown off the table and, smashed to pieces. Did you hear it?"

Goddard made no reply. In a confused fashion he was trying to think. Accident or not, the fall of the glass had served its purpose. Were there such things as accidents? Or was Life a puzzle—a puzzle into which every piece was made to fit? Fear and the wind... no: conscience and the wind... had saved the woman. He must get the powder back from her drawer... before she discovered it and denounced him. The medicine... he must remember not to take it...

He was very ill, seriously ill. He must have taken a chill owing to that panic flight into the garden. Why didn't the doctor come? He had come... at last... he was doing something to his chest... it was cold.

Again... the doctor... there was something he wanted to tell him... Hannah and a powder... what was it?

Later on he remembered, together with other things that he had hoped to forget. He lay watching an endless procession of memories, broken at times by a glance at the doctor, the nurse, and Hannah, who were all standing near the bed regarding him. They had been there a long time, and they were all very quiet. The last time he looked at Hannah was the first time for months that he had looked at her without loathing and hatred. Then he knew that he was dying.

24

BED CASES

The night-watchman was ill at ease, and, all ordinary positions failing to give relief, adopted several entirely out of keeping with his age and figure. A voice from the next wharf which wanted to know whether he was going on the stage, and, if so, whether he was going to wear tights, brought him at once to a more becoming position. His voice was broken with pain, but the masterly fashion in which he dealt with his tormentor's ancestors and the future behaviour of his descendants left nothing to be desired. Uncouth noises, lacking in variety, were the only retort.

"It took me sudden yesterday morning, just arter brekfuss," said the night-watchman. "The woman—if you can call 'er a woman—next, door but one 'ad given my missis best part of a tin of salmon. I wondered at the time why she gave it away—now I know. I ate it all, except one mouthful wot my missis threw in the fireplace, and in less than a couple of hours arterwards I thought my last hour 'ad come."

He clasped his hands at the waistline and rocked to and fro. Faint moans and indignant grunts attested to his suffering;

"I've been taking things for it ever since and nothing seems to do it any good," he resumed, in an interval. "Fust of all I tried a couple of pints to see wot that 'ud do; and the barman told me to go and die outside. He said wot I ought to 'ave 'ad was rum, so I 'ad a quartern. Arter that 'e *put* me outside—me being too ill to stop 'im—and an old gentleman wot was passing took me into a chemist's shop and stood treat. I don't know wot it was the chemist gave me, but a'most direckly arterwards there was a little crowd round the door peeping in, and behaving theirselves as if I was a Punch and Judy show. Some of 'em follered me 'ome, and it was all my missis could do to stop 'em coming inside and helping 'er to put me to bed."

He rose and, stifling a moan, took a few paces up and down the jetty.

"Seems to be passing off a bit for the time," he said, resuming his seat. "It sort o' comes and goes, but it comes longer than it goes. It's funny 'ow soft and kind-'earted illness makes you. Three times yesterday arternoon I called my missis upstairs to tell 'er that I couldn't pass away without letting 'er know I'd forgiven her everything. She on'y came the fust time, but that wasn't my fault. I called 'er loud enough.

"It seems to me to be the same complaint that Ginger Dick had a year or two ago—on'y worse—and he made a great deal more fuss about it, being a free-spoken man and not minding much wot he said about things he didn't like.

"It came on in a public-'ouse in the Commercial Road, and it was so sudden, and Ginger made such a funny noise, that Sam and Peter Russet thought at fust he 'ad swallered 'is pipe.

"'Wot's the matter?' ses the landlord, leaning over the bar.

"'He's swallered 'is pipe,' ses Sam.

"'You're—a—liar,' ses Ginger, groaning.

"'Wot is it, then?' ses the landlord.

"Ginger shook his 'ead. 'I don't know,' he ses in a weak voice. 'I think it's the beer.'

"'Outside,' ses the landlord. 'D'ye 'ear me? *Outside.*'

"Ginger went out with Sam propping 'im up on one side and Peter the other and the landlord shoving 'im behind. His groans was 'art-rending and the way he talked against beer made Sam and Peter blush for shame. They stood on the pavement for a little while and then they helped 'im on to a tram-car, and two minutes arterwards the conductor and five passengers helped 'im off agin.

"'Wot's to be done now?' ses Sam.

"'Shove 'im in a puddle and leave 'im,' ses Peter, very savage.

"'I can't help it—I feel as if I'd swallered fireworks,' ses Ginger.

"'Little touch o' stummick-ache,' ses Sam.

"'And they keeps going off," ses Ginger. 'Oh! Oh, my!'

"''Ave you got any pain?' ses Peter. 'That'll do! That'll do! Why can't you give a civil answer to a civil question?'

"He walked on, leaving Ginger 'anging on to Sam and talking at the top of his voice. O' course a crowd got round and told Sam wot to do, until Ginger left off being ill for a little while to attend to a chap as 'ad told Sam to stand 'im on his 'ead. If it 'adn't ha' been for a cab wot 'ad stopped to see wot the row was about Ginger would most likely 'ave been given some medicine by the doctor at the police-station, but, as it was, Sam pushed 'im into the cab and they drove off. Ginger sat on Sam's lap with one arm round 'is neck and one foot sticking out of the winder, and when Sam said they'd both be more comfortable if he sat up on the seat like a Christian, he put 'is other arm round Sam's neck and said if he 'ad anymore of 'is lip he'd choke 'im.

"It was a most uncomfortable drive—especially for Sam. When Ginger wasn't groaning he was swearing, with pain, and saying wot 'e would like to do to Sam and Peter and the cabman and landlords and a boy on a bicycle wot 'ad caught 'old of his foot as he passed and tried to pull it off. By the time they got 'ome he was raving, but he kept 'is senses, and neither Sam or the cabman could get the money for the fare out of 'is trowsis pocket, and Sam 'ad to pay it 'imself. Peter Russet came in just as Sam was trying to take Ginger's boots off without being kicked, and between 'em they got him undressed and made 'im wot they called comfortable, but wot 'e called a lot of other things.

"'He's gorn a nasty colour,' ses Sam to Peter Russet.

"'Like dirty putty,' ses Peter, nodding.

"'It's often like that—just afore the end,' ses Sam in wot 'e thought was a low voice.

"'*End!* Wot end?' ses Ginger, sitting up, with his eyes 'arf starting out of his 'ead.

"'You lay down, Ginger,' ses Sam in a kind voice; 'you lay down, and 'ope for the best. We're doing all we can for you. If you pass away it won't be our fault.'

"'*Pass away!*' ses Ginger, in a choking voice. 'I ain't going to pass away.'

"'No, no, o' course not,' ses Sam; 'still—'

"'Still wot?' ses Ginger, glaring at 'im."

"'I should stop using that bad langwidge if I was you,' ses Sam.

"'In case,' ses Peter.

"Pore Ginger looked at 'em and then he wiped the perspiration off of 'is face with the sleeve of his shirt and laid down very quiet. Even when Peter Russet sat on 'is foot by mistake he didn't say anything; but no doubt 'is thoughts was just as bad.

"He laid quite quiet for about 'arf an hour, and then, finding that 'e was still alive, he began to pick up 'is spirits a bit. Fust of all he asked Sam if 'e didn't know better than to smoke a filthy pipe, that ought to ha' been thrown away years ago, in a sick mate's bedroom; and arter that he asked Peter if 'e would mind sitting with his back towards 'im, cos he thought as 'e was better-looking that way. He went on like that till they was both tired of listening to 'im, and then all of a sudden the pain come on agin worse than ever. He couldn't describe it to 'em, cos, as soon as he started, the pain come on and he 'ad to leave off to say other things.

"'Try and bear it, Ginger,' ses Peter.

"'Think of all the pore souls wot are in worse pain than wot you are,' ses Sam.

"'And bear it in silence,' ses Peter.

"'With a brave smile on their face,' ses Sam. 'Wot are you getting out of bed for, Ginger?'

"'You'll find out as soon as I get 'old of you,' ses Ginger, 'arf crying with temper.

"Sam put 'is hands up, but afore Ginger could get up to 'im he was took bad agin and 'ad to lean up against the mantelpiece till it was over. Then 'e crawled back to bed, and, arter swallering 'ard three or four times, he fixed 'is eyes where Sam wasn't and asked him, in a perlite voice, to go and fetch 'im a doctor.

"'Why not leave it till tomorrow, Ginger?' ses Sam.

"'Cos I want 'im now,' ses Ginger, getting fierce again.

"Sam and Peter looked at each other, and then, arter saying that it was nearly nine o'clock and they was tired and they supposed most doctors 'ad gone to bed, and they didn't know where to find one, and if they did they didn't I suppose he could do Ginger any good, they put on their caps and went out grumbling.

"They walked along for some time with their 'eads down as though they expected to see a doctor sitting on the pavement waiting for them, and then Sam turned to Peter and asked 'im where they was going.

"'There's one in the Whitechapel Road,' ses Peter.

"'There must be one nearer than that,' ses Sam. 'Let's go in somewhere and ask.'

"They 'appened to be passing the 'Turk's Head' as 'e spoke, and, not wanting everybody to know their business, they went into the private bar instead of the usual, and 'ad a couple o' glasses o' bitter.

"There was on'y one other chap there, a tall young man in a black tail-coat, a bowler 'at, and a collar and necktie. He 'ad a large nose and a pair of very sharp light eyes, and he sat there as if the place belonged to 'im, stroking 'is little sandy moustache and tapping 'is boots with a cane. Sam and Peter could see at once that he never went anywhere except in private bars, and for the fust minute or two they was talking a'most in whispers. They must ha' talked a bit louder arter a bit, cos all of a sudden the gentleman emptied 'is glass and spoke to 'em.

"'What's that you want?' he ses. 'A doctor?'

"'Yes,' ses Sam, and the gentleman sat there with a smile on 'is face while Peter and Sam described Ginger's illness and repeated some of 'is remarks about it.

"'Funny you should tell me,' ses the gentleman. 'Very funny.'

"Sam looked at 'im, and waited.

"'Cos I'm a doctor myself,' ses the gentleman. 'Dr. Brown.'

"'Wot a bit o' luck!' ses Peter. 'We thought we'd got to walk no end of a way.'

"The doctor shook his 'ead.

"'I'm afraid I'm no good to you,' he ses.

"'Why not?' ses Sam, staring.

"'Too expensive,' ses the doctor. 'You see, I'm a West End man, and we're not allowed to see a patient under a pound a visit.'

"He shook his 'ead and sat smiling at them sad-like and listening to Sam, wot was sitting perched up on a stool making a noise like bronchitis, with surprise.

"'I on'y come this way for a stroll,' he ses, 'cos I like to see ships and sailormen.'

"'A—pound—a—visit?' ses Peter. 'D'ye 'ear that, Sam?'

"Sam looked at 'im, and arter a time he managed to nod.

"'P'r'aps it does seem a lot,' ses the doctor, 'but it comes cheaper in the end to have a good man.'

"'Not if the chap dies,' ses Peter.

"'My patients don't die,' ses the doctor. 'It's only cheap doctors wot loses their patients.'

"He took up 'is glass and then, finding as there was nothing in it, put it down agin. Sam gave a little cough, and arter waiting a moment asked whether 'e would do 'im the pleasure of having a drink with 'im.

"'Well, I've 'ad enough really,' ses the doctor. 'Still, I don't mind 'aving a glass of port with you.'

"Peter said he'd 'ave a port, too, afore Sam could stop 'im, and him and the doctor sat and drank Sam's 'ealth, and Peter said 'ow well he was looking and wot a fine rosy colour he'd got. Then Sam told the doctor all about Ginger's illness agin, and, in a offhand sort o' way, asked 'im wot Ginger could take for it.

"'I couldn't say without seeing 'im,' ses the doctor; 'it ain't allowed.'

"''Ow much would it be to see 'im?' ses Sam.

"'He ain't much to look at,' ses Peter, looking at him 'opeful-like.

"The doctor laughed, and then shook his 'ead at 'imself. 'Well, I don't know,' he says, 'but if you'll keep it a dead secret and not let anybody know that I said—I mean, that I'm a doctor—I don't mind seein' 'im for 'arf a dollar a visit.'

"'Ginger couldn't say anything agin that,' ses Peter.

"'Couldn't he?' ses Sam. ''Owever, he'll 'ave to put up with it. It's your turn, Peter; mine's a port.'

"'I suppose I'd better 'ave the same,' says the doctor. 'I don't believe in mixing. Tell 'im to give us the special this time. It's better.'

"Peter told 'im, and the landlord 'ad to tell 'im three times 'ow much it was afore he understood. He seemed 'arf dazed, and the noise Sam made smacking 'is lips over his wine nearly drove 'im crazy.

"The doctor got up as soon as he 'ad finished 'is glass, and they all went out into the street; Sam and Peter wondering what Ginger would say when 'e saw the doctor and what 'e would do when he 'eard the price. They went upstairs very quiet, as the doctor said he didn't want anybody to see 'im, and the fust thing they saw when they got into the room was Ginger laying face downwards on the bed with 'is arms and legs spread out, groaning.

"'Wot 'ave you been all this time for?' he ses, as soon as he 'eard them. 'You've been gone long enough to find fifty doctors!'

"'This is a good 'un, Ginger,' ses Sam, very solemn. 'One o' the best.'

"'Charges as much as twenty ordinary doctors,' ses Peter.

"'*Wot!*' ses Ginger, turning over with surprise and temper.

"The doctor smiled and, arter fust putting the chair by the side of the bed and sitting down on it, put it back very careful and sat down on the bed instead.

"'Let's have a look at your tongue,' he ses.

"Ginger put it out, and then put it in again to tell Sam that when 'e wanted to 'ear his remarks about it he'd let 'im know.

"'I've seen a worse tongue than that,' ses the doctor. 'Once.'

"'Did 'e die?' ses Ginger.

"'Never mind,' ses the doctor.

"'But I do mind,' ses Ginger, very sharp.

"'No,' ses the doctor; 'I was called in at the last moment and, arter sitting up with 'im all night, pulled 'im through.'

"'I told you wot he was, Ginger,' ses Peter Russet in a whisper that you could have 'eard downstairs.

"The doctor took 'old of Ginger's wrist; and then Sam got into trouble agin for taking upon himself to tell 'im that Ginger 'ad got a natural dark skin. The doctor took out 'is watch and they all 'eld their breath while he counted Ginger's pulse.

"'H'm!' he ses, putting the watch back. 'It's a fortunate thing you met me when you did. Now let's have a look at your chest.'

"Ginger unbuttoned 'is shirt, and the doctor, arter a good look at the ship wot was tattooed there, laid his 'ead on it amidships and listened.

"'Say ninety-nine,' he ses, 'and go on saying it.'

"'Ninety-nine,' ses Ginger, 'ninety-nine, ninety-nine, ninety—if I get up to you, Sam, you'll know it.'

"'You'd laugh yourself if you could on'y see yourself, Ginger,' ses Sam.

"'H'sh! ' ses the doctor; 'he 'asn't got much to laugh about, poor chap.'

"He moved his 'ead a bit and told Ginger to keep quiet. Then he sat up and, buttoning Ginger's shirt across 'is chest very careful, made a sign to Sam and Peter to keep quiet, and sat thinking.

"'His 'art has moved,' he ses at last; 'it's about two inches out of place.'

"'Goodbye, mates,' ses pore Ginger.

"'There's no need to say goodbye,' ses the doctor, very sharp. 'If you'll keep quite quiet and do as I tell you, you'll be all right agin, in time."

"He sat thinking agin for a bit, and then 'e sent Peter downstairs for a jug of 'ot water and a tumbler, and while it was being fetched he told Sam 'e was to be head-nurse and told 'im all he was to do.

"'You don't want to pay two or three pounds a week for a nurse, I suppose?' he ses, when Sam began to speak up for 'imself and tell 'im 'ow much he enjoyed 'is sleep.

"'I shan't be much trouble to 'im,' ses Ginger. 'I can 'elp myself.'

"'You mustn't move,' ses the doctor. 'You've got to lay quite still. Even if a fly settled on your nose you mustn't brush it off. You don't know 'ow bad you are. I want you to keep per-feck-ly still. Till tomorrow, at any rate.'

"He took the 'ot water from Peter and, arter putting a little cold to it, put 'is arm I round Ginger's neck and 'eld the tumbler to 'is lips. He 'ad four tumblers, one arter the other, except for wot went down 'is chest, and then 'e laid his 'ead back on the piller without a word.

"'That'll do 'im good,' ses the doctor, taking the 'arf-dollar wot Sam got out of Ginger's pocket. 'I'll look round agin in the morning.'

"'And wot about medicine?' ses Sam.

"'I'll bring some with me,' ses the doctor. 'Goodbye.'

"Sam and Peter went to bed early. One thing there was nothing to do, and another thing was Ginger wouldn't let 'em do it. Every time they moved 'e spoke about it and said wot it did to 'is 'art, and once, when Sam sneezed, 'e called 'im a murderer.

"It was about two o'clock in the morning when Sam woke up from a dream of a beautiful gal with yaller 'air and blue eyes wot kept calling 'im by 'is Christian name. He woke up with a smile on 'is lips and was just shutting 'is eyes to go on dreaming if 'e could, when he 'eard it again.

"'Sam! Sam! Sam! Sam!'

"'Hullo!' he ses, sitting up in bed very cross.

"'I thought you was dead,' ses Ginger. 'I've been calling you for ten minutes or more. It's made my 'eart worse.'

"'Wot d'ye want?' ses Sam.

"'I've got a nasty itching feeling between my shoulders,' ses Ginger.

"'D'you mean to say—d'you mean to say you woke me up just to tell me that?' ses Sam, 'ardly able to speak for temper.

"'I woke you up to come and rub it,' ses Ginger. 'And look sharp about it. You know I mustn't move.'

"'Hurry up, Sam,' ses Peter Russet. 'Wot are you waiting for? I want to get to sleep agin.'

"Sam got out o' bed at last and stood rubbing Ginger's back with 'is fist while Ginger kept telling 'im 'ow not to do it, and reminding 'im wot a delikit skin he 'ad got.

"He woke 'im up twice arter that. Once to give 'im a drink of water, and once to ask him 'ow old he thought the doctor was. Wot with being woke up and being afraid of being woke up, Sam 'ardly got a wink of sleep.

"Him and Peter Russet 'ad their brekfuss at a coffee-shop next mornin', and they had 'ardly got back afore the doctor come in. He seemed pleased to 'ear that the pain was better, but he told Ginger that he'd have to keep as still as he could for another day or two, and, arter putting 'is face on 'is chest agin, said that the 'art 'ad stopped moving.

"'I mean moving out of place,' he ses, as Ginger sat up making a 'orrible noise and threw 'is arms round his neck. 'Tomorrow I 'ope it will begin to move back.'

"He fished a bottle o' medicine out of 'is pocket which he said would be another bob, and, arter telling Sam to 'ave a lump o' sugar ready and pop it in quick, gave Ginger 'is fust dose. Sam popped it in all right, but unfortunately the medicine was so nasty that Ginger was quicker than wot 'e was. Anybody might ha' thought he 'ad been killed the way 'e carried on.

"'I'll look in agin this evening,' ses the doctor as he put a 'arf-dollar and a bob o' Ginger's in his pocket. 'Don't let 'im move more than can be helped and—Hullo!'

"'Wot's the matter?' ses Sam, taking 'is finger out of 'is mouth and staring at 'im.

"The doctor didn't answer 'im. He lifted up 'is eyelids instead and looked at his eyes, and then he told Ginger to open 'is mouth, and looked at 'is teeth. Then he looked at Sam agin and felt all round 'is throat.

"'Wot is it?' ses Sam, going pale.

"'It might be blood-poisoning,' ses the doctor, 'but I can't tell yet. His teeth are in a very bad state.'

""Ow shall I know if it is?" ses Sam.

"'You'll know fast enough,' ses the doctor, shaking his 'ead. "P'r'aps you'd better 'ave a quiet time at 'ome today and keep your friend company, and I'll 'ave a look at you when I come in this evening. Keep your spirits up and be as cheerful as you can—for 'is sake.'

"He left 'em all staring at each other; and then Sam sat down on 'is bed and told Peter Russet wot ought to be done to Ginger before England would be fit for decent people to live in. Peter said it was a wonder 'ow he could think of it all, and Ginger said it was because he 'ad got a nasty mind, and he told 'im wot he'd do to 'im when 'e got well agin.

"They spent most of the day quarrelling, and on'y left off to find fault with Peter when 'e came in from enjoying 'imself to see 'ow they was getting on. Sam was the worst, 'cos Ginger was afraid of'is 'art if he got too excited, but arter the doctor saw 'im in the evening 'e was as quiet as Ginger was.

"He said the poison 'ad got from Sam's finger down into 'is liver and an abscess was forming there. He showed Sam where 'is liver was—a thing he 'adn't known afore—and found out where the abscess was with 'is thumbnail. He found it twice, and was just going to find it agin when Sam pulled 'is shirt down.

"'There's no danger,' he ses, 'if you do just wot I tell you. If you keep quite quiet like your friend does, I'll 'ave you up agin in a week. If you move about or 'ave any violent shock you'll die afore you know where you are.'

"He sat talking with 'em for a little while, and, arter saying that Ginger's 'art was not going back as fast as he could wish, 'e took 'is money and went off. Peter sat looking at 'em till Sam asked 'im whether he thought they was waxworks, and then, arter punching up their pillers and tickling Ginger's toes, playful-like, 'e picked up 'is cap and went out. He spent most of 'is time out, and, when 'e did come in, all he could talk about was the drinks he'd been 'aving and 'ow glad 'e was that *his* 'art and liver was as sound as a bell.

"'I wonder you ain't sick of bed,' he ses, arter Ginger had 'ad four days of it.

"'Sick of it!' ses Ginger, choking. 'Sick of it! Why, you ugly, mutton-faced son of a—'

"'Mind your 'art, Ginger,' ses Sam.

"'I don't believe in doctoring and laying in bed,' ses Peter, picking 'is teeth with a pin. 'I believe that if you and Sam was to get up and 'ave a little dance in your shirts it 'ud do you all the good in the world. *I'd*' um to you.'

"'Mind your 'art, Ginger,' ses Sam, very quick.

"Ginger minded it, but they was both so disagreeable that Peter got up and went out agin and didn't come back until the pubs was closed. He woke 'em both up getting to bed, but when they tried to wake *'im* up arterwards they might as well 'ave tried to wake the dead. All they did was to wake each other up and then 'ave words about it.

"They wouldn't speak to Peter when 'e got up next morning, and, arter giving 'em both wot 'e called a bit of 'is mind, but wot other people would 'ave called nasty langwidge, 'e flung Ginger's trowsis into Sam's face and went off for the day.

"He didn't come back until six o'clock, but when 'e did come back 'e was a reg'lar sunbeam, smiling all over 'is face. He 'ad a look at Ginger and smiled, and then 'e went and smiled at Sam, with his 'and over 'is mouth.

"'He's drunk,' ses Sam, trying to sneer.

"'Mad *and* drunk,' ses Ginger.

"Peter didn't say anything. He went and sat down on 'is bed and covered up 'is face with his 'andkerchief and the bed shook as if there was an earthquake sitting on it.

"''Ow—'ow—'ow's the 'art, Ginger?' he ses at last.

"Ginger didn't answer 'im.

"'And Sa—Sa—Sam's pore old liver!' ses Peter, going off agin.

"He wiped 'is eyes at last, and then 'e got up and walked up and down the room fighting for 'is breath and saying 'ow it hurt 'im. And when he saw them two pore invalids laying in bed and looking at each other 'elpless, 'e sat down and laughed till 'e cried.

"'It's the d-d-doctor,' he ses at last. 'The—the landlord told me.'

"'Told you wot?' ses Ginger, grinding 'is teeth.

"'He—he ain't a doctor,' ses Peter, wiping 'is eyes; 'he's a bookmaker's clerk, and you won't see 'im agin 'cos the police are arter 'im.'

"You might have 'eard a pin drop, as the saying is, if it 'adn't ha' been for the choking noise in Sam's throat.

"'You ought to 'ave 'eard the landlord laugh when I told 'im about you and Sam,' ses Peter. 'It would ha' done you good. 'Ow much money 'as he 'ad off of you, Ginger? '

"Ginger didn't answer 'im. He got out of bed very slow, and put on 'is boots and 'is trowsis. Then 'e got up and locked the door.

"'Wot are you doing that for?' ses Sam, wot was sitting on the edge of 'is bed putting on 'is socks.

"'I'm going to give Peter something else to laugh about,' ses Ginger."

CAPTAINS ALL

25

CAPTAINS ALL

Every sailorman grumbles about the sea, said the night-watchman thoughtfully. It's human nature to grumble, and I s'pose they keep on grumbling and sticking to it because there ain't much else they can do. There's not many shore-going berths that a sailorman is fit for, and those that there are—such as a night-watchman's, for instance—wants such a good character that there's few as are equal to it.

Sometimes they get things to do ashore. I knew one man that took up butchering, and 'e did very well at it till the police took *him* up. Another man I knew gave up the sea to marry a washerwoman, and they hadn't been married six months afore she died, and back he 'ad to go to sea agin, pore chap.

A man who used to grumble awful about the sea was old Sam Small—a man I've spoke of to you before. To hear 'im go on about the sea, arter he 'ad spent four or five months' money in a fortnight, was 'artbreaking. He used to ask us wot was going to happen to 'im in his old age, and when we pointed out that he wouldn't be likely to 'ave any old age if he wasn't more careful of 'imself he used to fly into a temper and call us everything 'e could lay his tongue to.

One time when 'e was ashore with Peter Russet and Ginger Dick he seemed to 'ave got it on the brain. He started being careful of 'is money instead o' spending it, and three mornings running he bought a newspaper and read the advertisements, to see whether there was any comfortable berth for a strong, good-'arted man wot didn't like work.

He actually went arter one situation, and if it hadn't ha' been for seventy-nine other men, he said he believed he'd ha' had a good chance of getting it. As it was, all 'e got was a black eye for shoving another man, and for a day or two he was so down-'arted that 'e was no company at all for the other two.

For three or four days 'e went out by 'imself, and then, all of a sudden, Ginger Dick and Peter began to notice a great change in him. He seemed to 'ave got quite cheerful and 'appy. He answered 'em back pleasant when they spoke to 'im, and one night he lay in 'is bed whistling comic songs until Ginger and Peter Russet 'ad to get out o' bed to him. When he bought a new necktie and a smart cap and washed 'imself twice in one day they fust began to ask each other wot was up, and then they asked him.

"Up?" ses Sam; "nothing."

"He's in love," ses Peter Russet.

"You're a liar," ses Sam, without turning round.

"He'll 'ave it bad at 'is age," ses Ginger.

Sam didn't say nothing, but he kept fidgeting about as though 'e'd got something on his mind. Fust he looked out o' the winder, then he 'ummed a tune, and at last, looking at 'em very fierce, he took a toothbrush wrapped in paper out of 'is pocket and began to clean 'is teeth.

"He *is* in love," ses Ginger, as soon as he could speak.

"Or else 'e's gorn mad," ses Peter, watching 'im. "Which is it, Sam?"

Sam made believe that he couldn't answer 'im because o' the toothbrush, and arter he'd finished he 'ad such a raging toothache that 'e sat in a corner holding 'is face and looking the pictur' o' misery. They couldn't get a word out of him till they asked 'im to go out with them, and then he said 'e was going to bed. Twenty minutes arterwards, when Ginger Dick stepped back for 'is pipe, he found he 'ad gorn.

He tried the same game next night, but the other two wouldn't 'ave it, and they stayed in so long that at last 'e lost 'is temper, and, arter wondering wot Ginger's father and mother could ha' been a-thinking about, and saying that he believed Peter Russet 'ad been changed at birth for a seasick monkey, he put on 'is cap and went out. Both of 'em follered 'im sharp, but when he led 'em to a mission-hall, and actually went inside, they left 'im and went off on their own.

They talked it over that night between themselves, and next evening they went out fust and hid themselves round the corner. Ten minutes arterwards old Sam came out, walking as though 'e was going to catch a train; and smiling to think 'ow he 'ad shaken them off. At the corner of Commercial Road he stopped and bought 'imself a button-hole for 'is coat, and Ginger was so surprised that 'e pinched Peter Russet to make sure that he wasn't dreaming.

Old Sam walked straight on whistling, and every now and then looking down at 'is buttonhole, until by and by he turned down a street on the right and went into a little shop. Ginger Dick and Peter waited for 'im at the corner, but he was inside for so long that at last they got tired o' waiting and crept up and peeped through the winder.

It was a little tobacconist's shop, with newspapers and penny toys and such-like; but, as far as Ginger could see through two rows o' pipes and the *Police News*, it was empty. They stood there with their noses pressed against the glass for some time, wondering wot had 'appened to Sam, but by and by a little boy went in and then they began to 'ave an idea wot Sam's little game was.

As the shop-bell went the door of a little parlour at the back of the shop opened, and a stout and uncommon good-looking woman of about forty came out. Her 'ead pushed the *Police News* out o' the way and her 'and came groping into the winder arter a toy. Ginger 'ad a good look at 'er out o' the corner of one eye, while he pretended to be looking at a tobacco-jar with the other. As the little boy came out 'im and Peter Russet went in.

"I want a pipe, please," he ses, smiling at 'er; "a clay pipe—one o' your best."

The woman handed 'im down a box to choose from, and just then Peter, wot 'ad been staring in at the 'arf-open door at a boot wot wanted lacing up, gave a big start and ses:

"Why! Halloa!"

"Wot's the matter?" ses the woman, looking at 'im.

"I'd know that foot anywhere," ses Peter, still staring at it; and the words was hardly out of 'is mouth afore the foot 'ad moved itself away and tucked itself under its chair. "Why, that's my dear old friend Sam Small, ain't it?"

"Do you know the captin?" ses the woman, smiling at 'im.

"Cap—?" ses Peter. "*Cap*—? Oh, yes; why, he's the biggest friend I've got."

"'Ow strange!" ses the woman.

"We've been wanting to see 'im for some time," ses Ginger. "He was kind enough to lend me arf a crown the other day, and I've been wanting to pay 'im."

"Captin Small," ses the woman, pushing open the door, "here's some old friends o' yours."

Old Sam turned 'is face round and looked at 'em, and if looks could ha' killed, as the saying is, they'd ha' been dead men there and then.

"Oh, yes," he ses, in a choking voice; " 'ow are you?"

"Pretty well, thank you, *captin*," ses Ginger, grinning at 'im; "and 'ow's yourself arter all this long time?"

He held out 'is hand and Sam shook it and then shook 'ands with Peter Russet, who was grinning so 'ard that he couldn't speak.

"These are two old friends o' mine, Mrs. Finch," ses old Sam, giving 'em a warning look; "Captin Dick and Captin Russet, two o' the oldest and best friends a man ever 'ad."

"Captin Dick 'as got arf a crown for you," ses Peter Russet, still grinning.

"There now," ses Ginger, looking vexed, "if I ain't been and forgot it; I've on'y got arf a sovereign."

"I can give you change, sir," ses Mrs. Finch. "P'r'aps you'd like to sit down for five minutes?"

Ginger thanked 'er, and 'im and Peter Russet took a chair apiece in front o' the fire and began asking old Sam about 'is 'ealth, and wot he'd been doing since they saw 'im last.

"Fancy your reckernising his foot," ses Mrs. Finch, coming in with the change.

"I'd know it anywhere," ses Peter, who was watching Ginger pretending to give Sam Small the 'arf-dollar, and Sam pretending in a most lifelike manner to take it.

Ginger Dick looked round the room. It was a comfortable little place, with pictur's on the walls and antimacassars on all the chairs, and a row of pink vases on the mantelpiece. Then 'e looked at Mrs. Finch, and thought wot a nice-looking woman she was.

"This is nicer than being aboard ship with a crew o' nasty, troublesome sailormen to look arter, Captin Small," he ses.

"It's wonderful the way he manages 'em," ses Peter Russet to Mrs. Finch. "Like a lion he is."

"A roaring lion," ses Ginger, looking at Sam. "He don't know wot fear is."

Sam began to smile, and Mrs. Finch looked at 'im so pleased that Peter Russet, who 'ad been looking at 'er and the room, and thinking much the same way as Ginger, began to think that they was on the wrong tack.

"Afore 'e got stout and old," he ses, shaking his 'ead, "there wasn't a smarter skipper afloat."

"We all 'ave our day," ses Ginger, shaking his 'ead too.

"I dessay he's good for another year or two afloat yet," ses Peter Russet, considering.

"With care," ses Ginger.

Old Sam was going to say something, but 'e stopped himself just in time. "They will 'ave their joke," he ses, turning to Mrs. Finch and trying to smile. "I feel as young as ever I did."

Mrs. Finch said that anybody with arf an eye could see that, and then she looked at a kettle that was singing on the 'ob.

"I s'pose you gentlemen wouldn't care for a cup o' cocoa?" she ses, turning to them.

Ginger Dick and Peter both said that they liked it better than anything else, and arter she 'ad got out the cups and saucers and a tin o' cocoa, Ginger held the kettle and poured the water in the cups while she stirred them, and old Sam sat looking on 'elpless.

"It does seem funny to see you drinking cocoa, captin," ses Ginger, as old Sam took his cup.

"Ho!" ses Sam, firing up; "and why, if I might make so bold as to ask?"

"'Cos I've generally seen you drinking something out of a bottle," ses Ginger.

"Now, look 'ere," ses Sam, starting up and spilling some of the hot cocoa over 'is lap.

"A ginger-beer bottle," ses Peter Russet, making faces at Ginger to keep quiet.

"Yes, o' course, that's wot I meant," ses Ginger, looking surprised.

Old Sam wiped the cocoa off 'is knees without saying a word, but his weskit kept going up and down till Peter Russet felt quite sorry for 'im.

"There's nothing like it," he ses to Mrs. Finch. "It was by sticking to ginger-beer and milk and such-like that Captain Small 'ad command of a ship afore 'e was twenty-five."

"Lor'!" ses Mrs. Finch.

She smiled at old Sam till Peter got uneasy agin, and began to think p'r'aps 'e'd been praising 'im too much.

"Of course, I'm speaking of long ago now," he ses.

"Years and years afore you was born, ma'am," ses Ginger.

Old Sam was going to say something, but Mrs. Finch looked so pleased that 'e thought better of it. Some o' the cocoa 'e was drinking went the wrong way, and then Ginger patted 'im on the back and told 'im to be careful not to bring on 'is brownchitis agin. Wot with I temper and being afraid to speak for fear they should let Mrs. Finch know that 'e wasn't a captin, he could 'ardly bear 'imself, but he very near broke out when Peter Russet advised 'im to 'ave his weskit lined with red flannel. They all stayed on till closing time, and by the time they left they 'ad made theirselves so pleasant that Mrs. Finch said she'd be pleased to see them any time they liked to look in.

Sam Small waited till they 'ad turned the corner, and then he broke out so alarming that they could 'ardly do anything with 'im. Twice policemen spoke to 'im and advised 'im to go home afore they altered their minds; and he 'ad to hold 'imself in and keep quiet while Ginger and Peter Russet took 'is arms and said they were seeing him 'ome.

He started the row agin when they got indoors, and sat up in 'is bed smacking 'is lips over the things he'd like to 'ave done to them if he could. And then, arter saying 'ow he'd like to see Ginger boiled alive like a lobster, he said he knew that 'e was a noble-'arted feller who wouldn't try and cut an old pal out, and that it was a case of love at first sight on top of a tram-car.

"She's too young for you," ses Ginger; "and too good-looking besides."

"It's the nice little bisness he's fallen in love with, Ginger," ses Peter Russet. "I'll toss you who 'as it."

Ginger, who was sitting on the foot o' Sam's bed, said "no" at fust, but arter a time he pulled out arf a dollar and spun it in the air. That was the last 'e see of it, although he 'ad Sam out o' bed and all the clothes stripped off of it twice. He spent over arf an hour on his 'ands and knees looking for it, and Sam said when he was tired of playing bears p'r'aps he'd go to bed and get to sleep like a Christian.

They 'ad it all over agin next morning, and at last, as nobody would agree to keep quiet and let the others 'ave a fair chance, they made up their minds to let the best man win. Ginger Dick bought a necktie that took all the colour out o' Sam's, and Peter Russet went in for a collar so big that 'e was lost in it.

They all strolled into the widow's shop separate that night. Ginger Dick 'ad smashed his pipe and wanted another; Peter Russet wanted some tobacco; and old Sam Small walked in smiling, with a little silver brooch for 'er, that he said 'e had picked up.

It was a very nice brooch, and Mrs. Finch was so pleased with it that Ginger and Peter sat there as mad as they could be because they 'adn't thought of the same thing.

"Captin Small is very lucky at finding things," ses Ginger at last.

"He's got the name for it," ses Peter Russet.

"It's a handy 'abit," ses Ginger; "it saves spending money. Who did you give that gold, bracelet to you picked up the other night, captin?" he ses, turning to Sam.

"Gold bracelet?" ses Sam. "I didn't pick up no gold bracelet. Wot are you talking about?"

"All right, captin; no offence," ses Ginger, holding up his 'and. "I dreamt I saw one on your mantelpiece, I s'pose. P'r'aps I oughtn't to ha' said anything about it."

Old Sam looked as though he'd like to eat 'im, especially as he noticed Mrs. Finch listening and pretending not to. "Oh! That one," he ses, arter a bit o' hard thinking. "Oh! I found out who it belonged to. You wouldn't believe 'ow pleased they was at getting it back agin."

Ginger Dick coughed and began to think as 'ow old Sam was sharper than he 'ad given 'im credit for, but afore he could think of anything else to say Mrs. Finch looked at old Sam and began to talk about 'is ship, and to say 'ow much she should like to see over it.

"I wish I could take you," ses Sam, looking at the other two out o' the corner of his eye, "but my ship's over at Dunkirk, in France. I've just run over to London for a week or two to look round."

"And mine's there too," ses Peter Russet, speaking a'most afore old Sam 'ad finished; "side by side they lay in the harbour."

"Oh, dear," ses Mrs. Finch, folding her 'ands and shaking her 'ead. "I *should* like to go over a ship one arternoon. I'd quite made up my mind to it, knowing three cap tins."

She smiled and looked at Ginger, and Sam and Peter looked at 'im too, wondering whether he was going to berth his ship at Dunkirk alongside o' theirs.

"Ah, I wish I 'ad met you a fortnight ago," ses Ginger, very sad. "I gave up my ship, the *Highflyer,* then, and I'm waiting for one my owners are 'aving built for me at Newcastle. They said the *Highflyer* wasn't big enough for me. She was a nice little ship, though. I believe I've got 'er pictur' somewhere about me!"

He felt in 'is pocket and pulled out a little, crumpled-up photograph of a ship he'd been fireman aboard of some years afore, and showed it to 'er.

"That's me standing on the bridge," he ses, pointing out a little dot with the stem of his pipe.

"It's your figger," ses Mrs. Finch, straining her eyes. "I should know it anywhere."

"You've got wonderful eyes, ma'am," ses old Sam, choking with 'is pipe.

"Anybody can see that," ses Ginger. "They're the largest and the bluest I've ever seen."

Mrs. Finch told 'im not to talk nonsense, but both Sam and Peter Russet could see 'ow pleased she was.

"Truth is truth," ses Ginger. "I'm a plain man, and I speak my mind."

"Blue is my fav'rit' colour," ses old Sam, in a tender voice. "True blue."

Peter Russet began to feel out of it. "I thought brown was," he ses.

"Ho!" ses Sam, turning on 'im; "and why?"

"I 'ad my reasons," ses Peter, nodding, and shutting 'is mouth very firm.

"'I thought brown was 'is fav'rit' colour too," ses Ginger. "I don't know why. It's no use asking me; because if you did I couldn't tell you."

"Brown's a very nice colour," ses Mrs. Finch, wondering wot was the matter with old Sam.

"Blue," ses Ginger; "big blue eyes—they're the ones for me. Other people may 'ave their blacks and their browns," he ses, looking at Sam and Peter Russet, "but give me blue."

They went on like that all the evening, and every time the shop-bell went and the widow 'ad to go out to serve a customer they said in w'ispers wot they thought of each other; and once when she came back rather sudden Ginger 'ad to explain to 'er that 'e was showing Peter Russet a scratch on his knuckle.

Ginger Dick was the fust there next night, and took 'er a little chiney teapot he 'ad picked up dirt cheap because it was cracked right acrost the middle; but, as he explained that he 'ad dropped it in hurrying to see 'er, she was just as pleased. She stuck it up on the mantelpiece, and the things she said about Ginger's kindness and generosity made Peter Russet spend good money that he wanted for 'imself on a painted flower-pot next evening.

With three men all courting 'er at the same time Mrs. Finch had 'er hands full, but she took to it wonderful considering.

She was so nice and kind to 'em all that even arter a week's 'ard work none of 'em was really certain which she liked best.

They took to going in at odd times o' the day for tobacco and such-like. They used to go alone then, but they all met and did the polite to each other there of an evening, and then quarrelled all the way 'ome.

Then all of a sudden, without any warning, Ginger Dick and Peter Russet left off going there. The fust evening Sam sat expecting them every minute, and was so surprised that he couldn't take any advantage of it; but on the second, beginning by squeezing Mrs. Finch's 'and at ha'-past seven, he 'ad got best part of his arm round 'er waist by a quarter to ten. He didn't do more that night because she told him to be'ave 'imself, and threatened to scream if he didn't leave off.

He was arf-way home afore 'e thought of the reason for Ginger Dick and Peter Russet giving up, and then he went along smiling to 'imself to such an extent that people thought 'e was mad. He went off to sleep with the smile still on 'is lips, and when Peter and Ginger came in soon arter closing time and 'e woke up and asked them where they'd been, 'e was still smiling.

"I didn't 'ave the pleasure o' seeing you at Mrs. Finch's tonight," he ses.

"No," ses Ginger, very short. "We got tired of it."

"So un'ealthy sitting in that stuffy little room every evening," ses Peter.

Old Sam put his 'ead under the bedclothes and laughed till the bed shook; and every now and then he'd put his 'ead out and look at Peter and Ginger and laugh agin till he choked.

"I see 'ow it is," he ses, sitting up and wiping his eyes on the sheet." Well, we can't all win."

"Wot d'ye mean?" ses Ginger, very disagreeable.

"She wouldn't 'ave you," ses Sam, "that's wot I mean. And I don't wonder at it. I wouldn't 'ave you if I was a gal."

"You're dreaming," ses Peter Russet, sneering at 'im.

"That flower-pot o' yours'll come in handy," ses Sam, thinking 'ow he 'ad put 'is arm round the widow's waist; "and I thank you kindly for the teapot, Ginger."

"You don't mean to say as you've asked 'er to marry you?" ses Ginger, looking at Peter Russet.

"Not quite; but I'm going to," ses Sam, "and I'll bet you even arf-crowns she ses 'yes.'"

Ginger wouldn't take 'im, and no more would Peter, not even when he raised it to five shillings; and the vain way old Sam lay there boasting and talking about 'is way with the gals made 'em both feel ill.

"I wouldn't 'ave her if she asked me on 'er bended knees," ses Ginger, holding up his 'ead.

"Nor me," ses Peter. "You're welcome to 'er, Sam. When I think of the evenings I've wasted over a fat old woman I feel—"

"That'll do," ses old Sam, very sharp; "that ain't the way to speak of a lady, even if she 'as said 'no.'"

"All right, Sam," ses Ginger. "You go in and win if you think you're so precious clever."

Old Sam said that that was wot 'e was going to do, and he spent so much time next morning making 'imself look pretty that the other two could 'ardly be civil to him.

He went off a'most direckly arter breakfast, and they didn't see 'im agin till twelve o'clock that night. He 'ad brought a bottle o' whisky in with 'im, and he was so 'appy that they see plain wot had 'appened.

"She said 'yes' at two o'clock in the arter-noon," ses old Sam, smiling, arter they had 'ad a glass apiece. "I'd nearly done the trick at one o'clock, and then the shop-bell went, and I 'ad to begin all over agin. Still, it wasn't unpleasant."

"Do you mean to tell us you've asked 'er to marry you?" ses Ginger, 'olding out 'is glass to be filled agin.

"I do," ses Sam; "but I 'ope there's no ill-feeling. You never 'ad a chance, neither of you; she told me so."

Ginger Dick and Peter Russet stared at each other.

"She said she 'ad been in love with me all along," ses Sam, filling their glasses agin to cheer 'em up. "We went out arter tea and bought the engagement-ring, and then she got somebody to mind the shop and we went to the Pagoda music-'all."

"I 'ope you didn't pay much for the ring, Sam," ses Ginger, who always got very kind-'arted arter two or three glasses o' whisky. "If I'd known you was going to be in such a hurry I might ha' told you before."

"We ought to ha' done," ses Peter, shaking his 'ead.

"Told me?" ses Sam, staring at 'em. "Told me wot?"

"Why me and Peter gave it up," ses Ginger; "but, o' course, p'r'aps you don't mind."

"Mind wot?" ses Sam.

"It's wonderful 'ow quiet she kept it," ses Peter.

Old Sam stared at 'em agin, and then he asked 'em to speak in plain English wot they'd got to say, and not to go taking away the character of a woman wot wasn't there to speak up for herself.

"It's nothing agin 'er character," ses Ginger.

"It's a credit to her, looked at properly," ses Peter Russet.

"And Sam'll 'ave the pleasure of bringing of 'em up," ses Ginger.

"*Bringing of 'em up?*" ses Sam, in a trembling voice and turning pale; "bringing who up?"

"Why, 'er children," ses Ginger. "Didn't she tell you? She's got nine of 'em."

Sam pretended not to believe 'em at fust, and said they was jealous; but next day he crept down to the greengrocer's shop in the same street, where Ginger had 'appened to buy some oranges one day, and found that it was only too true. Nine children, the eldest of 'em only fifteen, was staying with diff'rent relations owing to scarlet-fever next door.

Old Sam crept back ome like a man in a dream, with a bag of oranges he didn't want, and, arter making a present of the engagement-ring to Ginger—if 'e could get it—he took the fust train to Tilbury and signed on for a v'y'ge to China.

26

THE BOATSWAIN'S MATE

Mr. George Benn, retired boatswain, sighed noisily and, with a despondent gesture, turned to the door and stood with the handle in his hand; Mrs. Waters, sitting behind the tiny bar in a tall Windsor chair, eyed him with some heat.

"My feelings'll never change," said the boatswain.

"Nor mine either," said the landlady sharply. "It's a strange thing, Mr. Benn, but you always ask me to marry you after the third mug."

"It's only to get my courage up," pleaded the boatswain. "Next time I'll do it afore I 'ave a drop; that'll prove to you I'm in earnest."

He stepped outside and closed the door before the landlady could make a selection from the many retorts that crowded to her lips. After the cool bar, with its smell of damp sawdust, the road seemed hot and dusty; but the boatswain, a prey to gloom natural to a man whose hand has been refused five times in a fortnight, walked on unheeding. His steps lagged, but his brain was active.

He walked for two miles deep in thought, and then coming to a shady bank took a seat upon an inviting piece of turf and lit his pipe. The heat and the drowsy hum of bees made him nod; his pipe hung from the corner of his mouth, and his eyes closed.

He opened them at the sound of approaching footsteps, and, feeling in his pocket for matches, gazed lazily at the intruder. He saw a tall man carrying a small bundle over his shoulder, and in the erect carriage, the keen eyes, and bronzed face had little difficulty in detecting the old soldier.

The stranger stopped as he reached the seated boatswain and eyed him pleasantly.

"Got a pipe o' baccy, mate?" he inquired.

The boatswain handed him the small metal box in which he kept that luxury.

"Lobster ain't you?" he said affably.

The tall man nodded. "Was," he replied. "Now I'm my own commander-in-chief."

"Padding it?" suggested the boatswain, taking the box from him and refilling his pipe.

The other nodded, and with the air of one disposed to conversation dropped his bundle in the ditch and took a seat beside him. "I've got plenty of time," he remarked.

Mr. Benn nodded, and for a while smoked on in silence. A dim idea which had been in his mind for some time began to clarify. He stole a glance at his companion—a man of about thirty-eight, clear eyes, with humorous wrinkles at the corners, a heavy moustache, and a cheerful expression more than tinged with recklessness.

"Ain't over and above fond o' work?" suggested the boatswain, when he had finished his inspection.

"I love it," said the other, blowing a cloud of smoke in the air, "but we can't have all we want in this world; it wouldn't be good for us."

The boatswain thought of Mrs. Waters, and sighed. Then he rattled his pocket.

"Would 'arf a quid be any good to you?" he inquired.

"Look here," began the soldier; "just because I asked you for a pipe o' baccy—"

"No offence," said the other quickly. "I mean if you earned it?"

The soldier nodded and took his pipe from his mouth. "Gardening and windows?" he hazarded, with a shrug of his shoulders.

The boatswain shook his head.

"Scrubbing, p'r'aps?" said the soldier, with a sigh of resignation. "Last house I scrubbed out I did it so thoroughly they accused me of pouching the soap. Hang 'em!"

"And you didn't?" queried the boatswain, eyeing him keenly.

The soldier rose and, knocking the ashes out of his pipe, gazed at him darkly. "I can't give it back to you," he said slowly, "because I've smoked some of it, and I can't pay you for it because I've only got twopence, and that I want for myself. So long, matey, and next time a poor devil asks you for a pipe, be civil."

"I never see such a man for taking offence in all my born days," expostulated the boatswain. "I 'ad my reasons for that remark, mate. Good reasons they was."

The soldier grunted and, stooping, picked up his bundle.

"I spoke of arf a sovereign just now," continued the boatswain impressively, "and when I tell you that I offer it to you to do a bit o' burgling, you'll see 'ow necessary it is for me to be certain of your honesty."

"*Burgling?*" gasped the astonished soldier. "*Honesty?* 'Struth; are you drunk or am I?"

"Meaning," said the boatswain, waving the imputation away with his hand, "for you to pretend to be a burglar."

"We're *both* drunk, that's what it is," said the other resignedly.

The boatswain fidgeted. "If you don't agree, mum's the word and no 'arm done," he said, holding out his hand.

"Mum's the word," said the soldier, taking it. "My name's Ned Travers, and, barring cells for a spree now and again, there's nothing against it. Mind that."

"Might 'appen to anybody," said Mr. Benn soothingly. "You fill your pipe and don't go chucking good tobacco away agin."

Mr. Travers took the offered box and, with economy born of adversity, stooped and filled up first with the plug he had thrown away. Then he resumed his seat and, leaning back luxuriously, bade the other "fire away."

"I ain't got it all ship-shape and proper yet," said Mr. Benn slowly, "but it's in my mind's eye. It's been there off and on like for some time."

He lit his pipe again and gazed fixedly at the opposite hedge. "Two miles from here, where I live," he said, after several vigorous puffs, "there's a little public-'ouse called the 'Beehive,' kept by a lady wot I've got my eye on."

The soldier sat up.

"She won't 'ave me," said the boatswain, with an air of mild surprise.

The soldier leaned back again.

"She's a lone widder," continued Mr. Benn, shaking his head, "and the 'Beehive' is in a lonely place. It's right through the village, and the nearest house is arf a mile off."

"Silly place for a pub," commented Mr. Travers.

"I've been telling her 'ow unsafe it is," said the boatswain. "I've been telling her that she wants a man to protect her, and she only laughs at me. She don't believe it; d'ye see? Likewise I'm a small man—small, but stiff. She likes tall men."

"Most women do," said Mr. Travers, sitting upright and instinctively twisting his moustache. "When I was in the ranks—"

"My idea is," continued the boatswain, slightly raising his voice, "to kill two birds with one stone—prove to her that she does want being protected, and that I'm the man to protect her. D'ye take my meaning, mate?"

The soldier reached out a hand and felt the other's biceps. "Like a lump o' wood," he said approvingly.

"My opinion is," said the boatswain, with a faint smirk, "that she loves me without knowing it."

"They often do," said Mr. Travers, with a grave shake of his head.

"Consequently I don't want 'er to be disappointed," said the other.

"It does you credit," remarked Mr. Travers.

"I've got a good head," said Mr. Benn, "else I shouldn't 'ave got my rating as boatswain as soon as I did; and I've been turning it over in my mind, over and over agin, till my brain-pan fair aches with it. Now, if you do what I want you to tonight and it comes off all right, damme, I'll make it a quid."

"Go on, Vanderbilt," said Mr. Travers; "I'm listening."

The boatswain gazed at him fixedly. "You meet me 'ere in this spot at eleven o'clock tonight," he said solemnly, "and I'll take you to her 'ouse and put you through a little winder I knows of. You goes upstairs and alarms her, and she screams for help. I'm watching the house, faithful-like, and hears 'er scream. I dashes in at the winder, knocks you down, and rescues her. D'ye see?"

"I hear," corrected Mr. Travers coldly.

"She clings to me," continued the boatswain, with a rapt expression of face, "in her gratitoode, and, proud of my strength and pluck, she marries me."

"An' I get a five years' honeymoon," said the soldier.

The boatswain shook his head and patted the other's shoulder. "In the excitement of the moment you spring up and escape," he said, with a kindly smile. "I've thought it all out. You can run much faster than I can; anyways, you *will*. The nearest 'ouse is arf a mile off, as I said, and her servant is staying till tomorrow at 'er mother's, ten miles away."

Mr. Travers rose to his feet and stretched himself. "Time I was toddling," he said, with a yawn. "Thanks for amusing me, mate."

"You won't do it?" said the boatswain, eyeing him with much concern.

"I'm hanged if I do," said the soldier emphatically. "Accidents will happen, and then where should I be?"

"If they did," said the boatswain, "I'd own up and clear you."

"You might," said Mr. Travers, "and then again you mightn't. So long, mate."

"I—I'll make it two quid," said the boatswain, trembling with eagerness. "I've took a fancy to you; you're just the man for the job."

The soldier, adjusting his bundle, glanced at him over his shoulder. "Thankee," he said, with mock gratitude.

"Look 'ere," said the boatswain, springing up and catching him by the sleeve; "I'll give it to you in writing. Come, you ain't faint-hearted? Why, a bluejacket 'ud do it for the fun o' the thing. If I give it to you in writing, and there should be an accident, it's worse for me than it is for you, ain't it?"

Mr. Travers hesitated and, pushing his cap back, scratched his head.

"I gives you the two quid afore you go into the house," continued the boatswain, hastily following up the impression he had made. "I'd give 'em to you now if I'd got 'em with me. That's *my* confidence in *you;* I likes the look of you. Soldier or sailor, when there is a man's work to be done, give 'em to me afore anybody."

The soldier seated himself again and let his bundle fall to the ground. "Go on," he said slowly. "Write it out fair and square and sign it, and I'm your man."

The boatswain clapped him on the shoulder and produced a bundle of papers from his pocket. "There's letters there with my name and address on 'em," he said. "It's all fair, square, and above-board. When you've cast your eyes over them I'll give you the writing."

Mr. Travers took them and, relighting his pipe, smoked in silence, with various side glances at his companion as that enthusiast sucked his pencil and sat twisting in the agonies of composition. The document finished—after several failures had been retrieved and burnt by the careful Mr. Travers—the boatswain heaved a sigh of relief, and handing it over to him, leaned back with a complacent air while he read it.

"Seems all right," said the soldier, folding it up and putting it in his waistcoat-pocket. "I'll be here at eleven tonight."

"Eleven it is," said the boatswain briskly, "and, between pals—here's arf a dollar to go on with."

He patted him on the shoulder again, and with a caution to keep out of sight as much as possible till night, walked slowly home. His step was light, but he carried a face in which care and exultation were strangely mingled.

By ten o'clock that night care was in the ascendant, and by eleven, when he discerned the red glow of Mr. Travers's pipe set as a beacon against a dark background of hedge, the boatswain was ready to curse his inventive powers. Mr. Travers greeted him cheerily and, honestly attributing the fact to good food and a couple of pints of beer he had had since the boatswain left him, said that he was ready for anything.

Mr. Benn grunted and led the way in silence. There was no moon, but the night was clear, and Mr. Travers, after one or two light-hearted attempts at conversation, abandoned the effort and fell to whistling softly instead.

Except for one lighted window the village slept in darkness, but the boatswain, who had been walking with the stealth of a Red Indian on the warpath, breathed more freely after they had left it behind. A renewal of his antics a little farther on apprised Mr. Travers that they were approaching their destination, and a minute or two later they came to a small inn standing just off the road. "All shut up and Mrs. Waters abed, bless her," whispered the boatswain, after walking carefully round the house. "How do you feel?"

"I'm all right," said Mr. Travers. "I feel as if I'd been burgling all my life. How do you feel?"

"Narvous," said Mr. Benn, pausing under a small window at the rear of the house. "This is the one."

Mr. Travers stepped back a few paces and gazed up at the house. All was still. For a few moments he stood listening and then rejoined the boatswain.

"Goodbye, mate," he said, hoisting himself on to the sill. "Death or victory."

The boatswain whispered and thrust a couple of sovereigns into his hand. "Take your time; there's no hurry," he muttered. "I want to pull myself together. Frighten 'er enough, but not too much. When she screams I'll come in."

Mr. Travers slipped inside and then thrust his head out of the window. "Won't she think it funny you should be so handy?" he inquired.

"No; it's my faithful 'art," said the boatswain, "keeping watch over her every night—that's the ticket. She won't know no better."

Mr. Travers grinned, and removing his boots passed them out to the other. "We don't want her to hear me till I'm upstairs," he whispered.

"Put 'em outside, handy for me to pick up."

The boatswain obeyed, and Mr. Travers—who was by no means a good hand at darning socks—shivered as he trod lightly over a stone floor. Then, following the instructions of Mr. Benn, he made his way to the stairs and mounted noiselessly.

But for a slight stumble half-way up his progress was very creditable for an amateur. He paused and listened and, all being silent, made his way to the landing and stopped outside a door. Despite himself his heart was beating faster than usual.

He pushed the door open slowly and started as it creaked. Nothing happening, he pushed again, and standing just inside saw, by a small ewer silhouetted against the casement, that he was in a bedroom. He listened for the sound of breathing, but in vain.

"Quiet sleeper," he reflected; "or perhaps it is an empty room. Now, I wonder whether—"

The sound of an opening door made him start violently, and he stood still, scarcely breathing, with his ears on the alert. A light shone on the landing, and peeping round the door he saw a woman coming along the corridor—a younger and better-looking woman than he had expected to see. In one hand she held aloft a candle, in the other she bore a double-barrelled gun. Mr. Travers withdrew into the room and, as the light came nearer, slipped into a big cupboard by the side of the fireplace and, standing bolt upright, waited. The light came into the room.

"Must have been my fancy," said a pleasant voice.

"Bless her," smiled Mr. Travers.

His trained ear recognised the sound of cocking triggers. The next moment a heavy body bumped against the door of the cupboard and the key turned in the lock.

"Got you!" said the voice triumphantly. "Keep still; if you try and break out I shall shoot you."

"All right," said Mr. Travers hastily; "I won't move."

"Better not," said the voice. "Mind, I've got a gun pointing straight at you."

"Point it downwards, there's a good girl," said Mr. Travers earnestly; "and take your finger off the trigger. If anything happened to me you'd never forgive yourself."

"It's all right so long as you don't move," said the voice; "and I'm not a girl," it added sternly.

"Yes, you are," said the prisoner. "I saw you. I thought it was an angel at first. I saw your little bare feet and—"

A faint scream interrupted him.

"You'll catch cold," urged Mr. Travers.

"Don't you trouble about me," said the voice tartly.

"I won't give any trouble," said Mr. Travers, who began to think it was time for the boatswain to appear on the scene. "Why don't you call for help? I'll go like a lamb."

"I don't want your advice," was the reply. "I know what to do. Now, don't you try and break out. I'm going to fire one barrel out of the window, but I've got the other one for you if you move."

"My dear *girl*," protested the horrified Mr. Travers, "you'll alarm the neighbourhood."

"Just what I want to do," said the voice, "Keep still, mind."

Mr. Travers hesitated. The game was up, and it was clear that in any case the stratagem of the ingenious Mr. Benn would have to be disclosed.

"Stop!" he said earnestly. "Don't do anything rash. I'm not a burglar; I'm doing this for a friend of yours—Mr. Benn."

"*What?*" said an amazed voice.

"True as I stand here," asseverated Mr. Travers. "Here, here's my instructions. I'll put 'em under the door, and if you go to the back window you'll see him in the garden waiting."

He rustled the paper under the door, and it was at once snatched from his fingers. He regained an upright position and stood listening to the startled and indignant exclamations of his jailer as she read the boatswain's permit:

> *This is to give notice that I, George Benn, being of sound mind and body, have told Ned Travers to pretend to be a burglar at Mrs. Waters's. He ain't a burglar, and I shall be outside all the time. It's all above-board and ship-shape.*
>
> *(Signed) George Benn.*

"Sound mind—above-board—ship-shape," repeated a dazed voice. "*Where is he?*"

"Out at the back," replied Mr. Travers. "If you go to the window you can see him. Now, do put something round your shoulders, there's a good girl."

There was no reply, but a board creaked. He waited for what seemed a long time, and then the board creaked again.

"Did you see him?" he inquired.

"I did," was the sharp reply. "You both ought to be ashamed of yourselves. You ought to be punished."

"There *is* a clothes-peg sticking into the back of my head," remarked Mr. Travers. "What are you going to do?"

There was no reply.

"What are you going to do?" repeated Mr. Travers, somewhat uneasily. "You look too nice to do anything hard; leastways, so far as I can judge through this crack."

There was a smothered exclamation, and then sounds of somebody moving hastily about the room and the swish of clothing hastily donned.

"You ought to have done it before," commented the thoughtful Mr. Travers. "It's enough to give you your death of cold."

"Mind your business," said the voice sharply. "Now, if I let you out, will you promise to do exactly as I tell you?"

"Honour bright," said Mr. Travers fervently.

"I'm going to give Mr. Benn a lesson he won't forget," proceeded the other grimly. "I'm going to fire off this gun, and then run down and tell him I've killed you."

"*Eh?*" said the amazed Mr. Travers. "Oh, lord!"

"*H'sh!* Stop that laughing," commanded the voice. "He'll hear you. Be *quiet*!"

The key turned in the lock, and Mr. Travers, stepping forth, clapped his hand over his mouth and endeavoured to obey.

Mrs. Waters, stepping back with the gun ready, scrutinised him closely.

"Come on to the landing," said Mr. Travers eagerly. "We don't want anybody else to hear. Fire into this."

He snatched a patchwork rug from the floor and stuck it up against the balusters.

"You stay here," said Mrs. Waters.

He nodded.

She pointed the gun at the hearth-rug, the walls shook with the explosion, and, with a shriek that set Mr. Travers's teeth on edge, she rushed downstairs and, drawing back the bolts of the back door, tottered outside and into the arms of the agitated boatswain.

"Oh! Oh! Oh!" she cried.

"What—what's the matter?" gasped the boatswain.

The widow struggled in his arms. "A burglar," she said in a tense whisper. "But it's all right; I've killed him."

"Kill—" stuttered the other. "Kill—*Killed him?*"

Mrs. Waters nodded and released herself.

"First shot," she said, with a satisfied air.

The boatswain wrung his hands. "Good heavens!" he said, moving slowly towards the door. "Poor fellow!"

"Come back," said the widow, tugging at his coat.

"I was—was going to see—whether I could do anything for 'im," quavered the boatswain. "Poor fellow!"

"You stay where you are," commanded Mrs. Waters. "I don't want any witnesses. I don't want this house to have a bad name. I'm going to keep it quiet."

"Quiet?" said the shaking boatswain. "How?"

"First thing to do," said the widow, thoughtfully, "is to get rid of the body. I'll bury him in the garden, I think. There's a very good bit of ground behind those potatoes. You'll find the spade in the tool-house."

The horrified Mr. Benn stood stock-still regarding her.

"While you'redigging the grave," continued Mrs. Waters calmly, "I'll go in and clean up the mess."

The boatswain reeled and then fumbled with trembling fingers at his collar.

Like a man in a dream he stood watching as she ran to the tool-house and returned with a spade and pick; like a man in a dream he followed her on to the garden.

"Be careful," she said sharply; "you're treading down my potatoes."

The boatswain stopped dead and stared at her. Apparently unconscious of his gaze, she began to pace out the measurements and then, placing the tools in his hands, urged him to lose no time.

"I'll bring him down when you're gone," she said, looking towards the house.

The boatswain wiped his damp brow with the back of his hand. "How are you going to get it downstairs?" he breathed.

"Drag it," said Mrs. Waters briefly.

"Suppose he isn't dead?" said the boatswain, with a gleam of hope.

"Fiddlesticks!" said Mrs. Waters. "Do you think I don't know? Now, don't waste time talking; and mind you dig it deep. I'll put a few cabbages on top afterwards—I've got more than I want."

She re-entered the house and ran lightly upstairs. The candle was still alight and the gun was leaning against the bed-post; but the visitor had disappeared. Conscious of an odd feeling of disappointment, she looked round the empty room.

"Come and look at him," entreated a voice, and she turned and beheld the amused countenance of her late prisoner at the door.

"I've been watching from the back window," he said, nodding. "You're a wonder; that's what you are. Come and look at him."

Mrs. Waters followed, and leaning out of the window watched with simple pleasure the efforts of the amateur sexton. Mr. Benn was digging like one possessed, only pausing at intervals to straighten his back and to cast a fearsome glance around him. The only thing that marred her pleasure was the behaviour of Mr. Travers, who was struggling for a place with all the fervour of a citizen at the Lord Mayor's show.

"Get back," she said, in a fierce whisper. "He'll see you."

Mr. Travers with obvious reluctance obeyed, just as the victim looked up.

"Is that you, Mrs. Waters?" inquired the boatswain fearfully.

"Yes, of course it is," snapped the widow. "Who else should it be, do you think? Go on! What are you stopping for?"

Mr. Benn's breathing as he bent to his task again was distinctly audible. The head of Mr. Travers ranged itself once more alongside the widow's. For a long time they gazed in silence.

"Won't you come down here, Mrs. Waters?" called the boatswain, looking up so suddenly that Mr. Travers's head bumped painfully against the side of the window. "It's a bit creepy, all alone."

"I'm all right," said Mrs. Waters.

"I keep fancying there's something dodging behind them currant bushes," pursued the unfortunate Mr. Benn hoarsely. "How you can stay there alone I can't think. I thought I saw something looking over your shoulder just now. Fancy if it came creeping up behind and caught hold of you!"

The widow gave a sudden faint scream.

"If you do that again—" she said, turning fiercely on Mr. Travers.

"He put it into my head," said the culprit humbly; "I should never have thought of such a thing by myself. I'm one of the quietest and best-behaved—"

"Make haste, Mr. Benn," said the widow, turning to the window again; "I've got a lot to do when you've finished."

The boatswain groaned and fell to digging again, and Mrs. Waters, after watching a little while longer, gave Mr. Travers some pointed instructions about the window and went down to the garden again.

"That will do, I think," she said, stepping into the hole and regarding it critically. "Now you'd better go straight off home, and, mind, not a word to a soul about this."

She put her hand on his shoulder, and noticing with pleasure that he shuddered at her touch led the way to the gate. The boatswain paused for a moment, as though about to speak, and then, apparently thinking better of it, bade her goodbye in a hoarse voice and walked feebly up the road. Mrs. Waters stood watching until his steps died away in the distance, and then, returning to the garden, took up the spade and stood regarding with some dismay the mountainous result of his industry. Mr. Travers, who was standing just inside the back door, joined her.

"Let me," he said gallantly.

The day was breaking as he finished his task. The clean, sweet air and the exercise had given him an appetite to which the smell of cooking bacon and hot coffee that proceeded from the house had set a sharper edge. He took his coat from a bush and put it on. Mrs. Waters appeared at the door.

"You had better come in and have some breakfast before you go," she said brusquely; "there's no more sleep for me now."

Mr. Travers obeyed with alacrity, and after a satisfying wash in the scullery came into the big kitchen with his face shining and took a seat at the table. The cloth was neatly laid, and Mrs. Waters, fresh and cool, with a smile upon her pleasant face, sat behind the tray. She looked at her guest curiously: Mr. Travers's spirits being somewhat higher than the state of his wardrobe appeared to justify.

"Why don't you get some settled work?" she inquired, with gentle severity, as he imparted snatches of his history between bites.

"Easier said than done," said Mr. Travers serenely. "But don't you run away with the idea that I'm a beggar, because I'm not. I pay my way, such as it is. And, by the by, I s'pose I haven't earned that two pounds Benn gave me?"

His face lengthened, and he felt uneasily in his pocket.

"I'll give them to him when I'm tired of the joke," said the widow, holding out her hand and watching him closely.

Mr. Travers passed the coins over to her. "Soft hand you've got," he said musingly. "I don't wonder Benn was desperate. I dare say I should have done the same in his place."

Mrs. Waters bit her lip and looked out at the window; Mr. Travers resumed his breakfast.

"There's only one job that I'm really fit for, now that I'm too old for the Army," he said confidentially, as, breakfast finished, he stood at the door ready to depart.

"Playing at burglars?" hazarded Mrs. Waters.

"Landlord of a little country public-house," said Mr. Travers simply.

Mrs. Waters fell back and regarded him with open-eyed amazement.

"Good morning," she said as soon as she could trust her voice.

"Goodbye," said Mr. Travers reluctantly. "I should like to hear how old Benn takes this joke, though."

Mrs. Waters retreated into the house and stood regarding him. "If you're passing this way again and like to look in—I'll tell you," she said after a long pause. "Goodbye."

"I'll look in in a week's time," said Mr. Travers.

He took the proffered hand and shook it warmly. "It would be the best joke of all," he said, turning away.

"What would?"

The soldier confronted her again.

"For old Benn to come round here one evening and find me landlord. Think it over."

Mrs. Waters met his gaze soberly. "I'll think it over when you have gone," she said softly. "Now go."

27

THE NEST EGG

Artfulness, said the night-watchman, smoking placidly, is a gift, but it don't always pay. I've met some artful ones in my time—plenty of 'em; but I can't truthfully say as 'ow any of them was the better for meeting me.

He rose slowly from the packing-case on which he had been sitting and, stamping down the point of a rusty nail with his heel, resumed his seat, remarking that he had endured it for some time under the impression that it was only a splinter.

I've surprised more than one in my time, he continued slowly. When I met one of these 'ere artful ones I used fust of all to pretend to be more stupid than wot I really am.

He stopped and stared fixedly.

More stupid than I looked, he said.

He stopped again.

More stupid than wot they thought I looked, he said, speaking with marked deliberation. And I'd let 'em go on and on until I thought I had 'ad about enough, and then turn round on 'em. Nobody ever got the better o' me except my wife, and that was only before we was married. Two nights arterwards she found a fish-hook in my trouser-pocket, and arter that I could ha' left untold gold there—if I'd ha' had it. It spoilt wot some people call the honeymoon, but it paid in the long run.

One o' the worst things a man can do is to take up artfulness all of a sudden. I never knew it to answer yet, and I can tell you of a case that'll prove my words true.

It's some years ago now, and the chap it 'appened to was a young man, a shipmate o' mine, named Charlie Tagg. Very steady young chap he was, too steady for most of 'em. That's 'ow it was me and 'im got to be such pals.

He'd been saving up for years to get married, and all the advice we could give 'im didn't 'ave any effect. He saved up nearly every penny of 'is money and gave it to his gal to keep for 'im, and the time I'm speaking of she'd got seventy-two pounds of 'is and seventeen-and-six of 'er own to set up housekeeping with.

Then a thing happened that I've known to 'appen to sailormen afore. At Sydney 'e got silly on another gal, and started walking out with her, and afore he knew wot he was about he'd promised to marry 'er too.

Sydney and London being a long way from each other was in 'is favour, but the thing that troubled 'im was 'ow to get that seventy-two pounds out of Emma Cook, 'is London gal, so as he could marry the other with it. It worried 'im all the way home, and by the time we got into the London river 'is head was all in a maze with it. Emma Cook 'ad got it all saved up in the bank, to take a little shop with when they got spliced, and 'ow to get it he could not think.

He went straight off to Poplar, where she lived, as soon as the ship was berthed. He walked all the way so as to 'ave more time for thinking, but wot with bumping into two old gentlemen with bad tempers, and being nearly run over by a cabman with a white 'orse and red whiskers, he got to the house without 'aving thought of anything.

They was just finishing their tea as 'e got there, and they all seemed so pleased to see 'im that it made it worse than ever for 'im. Mrs. Cook, who 'ad pretty near finished, gave 'im her own cup to drink out of, and said that she 'ad dreamt of 'im the night afore last, and old Cook said that he 'ad got so good-looking 'e shouldn't 'ave known him.

"I should 'ave passed 'im in the street," he ses. "I never see such an alteration."

"They'll be a nice-looking couple," ses his wife, looking at a young chap, named George Smith, that 'ad been sitting next to Emma.

Charlie Tagg filled 'is mouth with bread and butter, and wondered 'ow he was to begin. He squeezed Emma's 'and just for the sake of keeping up appearances, and all the time 'e was thinking of the other gal waiting for 'im thousands o' miles away.

"You've come 'ome just in the nick o' time," ses old Cook; "if you'd done it o' purpose you couldn't 'ave arranged it better."

"Somebody's birthday?" ses Charlie, trying to smile.

Old Cook shook his 'ead. "Though mine is next Wednesday," he ses, "and thank you for thinking of it. No; you're just in time for the biggest bargain in the chandlery line that anybody ever 'ad a chance of. If you 'adn't ha' come back we should have 'ad to ha' done it without you."

"Eighty pounds," ses Mrs. Cook, smiling at Charlie. "With the money Emma's got saved and your wages this trip you'll 'ave plenty. You must come round arter tea and 'ave a look at it."

"Little place not arf a mile from 'ere," ses old Cook. "Properly worked up, the way Emma'll do it, it'll be a little fortune. I wish I'd had a chance like it in my young time."

He sat shaking his 'ead to think wot he'd lost, and Charlie Tagg sat staring at 'im and wondering wot he was to do.

"My idea is for Charlie to go for a few more v'y'ges arter they're married while Emma works up the business," ses Mrs. Cook; "she'll be all right with young Bill and Sarah Ann to 'elp her and keep 'er company while he's away."

"We'll see as she ain't lonely," ses George Smith, turning to Charlie.

Charlie Tagg gave a bit of a cough and said it wanted considering. He said it was no good doing things in a 'urry and then repenting of 'em all the rest of your life. And 'e said he'd been given to understand that chandlery wasn't wot it 'ad been, and some of the cleverest people 'e knew thought that it would be worse before it was better. By the time he'd finished they was all looking at 'im as though they couldn't believe their ears.

"You just step round and 'ave a look at the place," ses old Cook; "if that don't make you alter your tune, call me a sinner."

Charlie Tagg felt as though 'e could ha' called 'im a lot o' worse things than that, but he took up 'is hat and Mrs. Cook and Emma got their bonnets on and they went round.

"I don't think much of it for eighty pounds," ses Charlie, beginning his artfulness as they came near a big shop, with plate-glass and a double front.

"Eh?" ses old Cook, staring at 'im. "Why, that ain't the place. Why, you wouldn't get that for eight 'undred."

"Well, I don't think much of it," ses Charlie; "if it's worse than that I can't look at it—I can't, indeed."

"You ain't been drinking, Charlie?" ses old Cook, in a puzzled voice.

"Certainly not," ses Charlie.

He was pleased to see 'ow anxious they all looked, and when they did come to the shop 'e set up a laugh that old Cook said chilled the marrer in 'is bones. He stood looking in a 'elpless sort o' way at his wife and Emma, and then at last he ses: "There it is; and a fair 'bargain at the price."

"I s'pose *you* ain't been drinking?" ses Charlie.

"Wot's the matter with it?" ses Mrs. Cook, flaring up.

"Come inside and look at it," ses Emma, taking 'old of his arm.

"Not me," ses Charlie, hanging back. "Why, I wouldn't take it at a gift."

He stood there on the kerbstone, and for all they could do 'e wouldn't budge. He said it was a bad road and a little shop, and 'ad got a look about it he didn't like. They walked back 'ome like a funeral procession, and Emma 'ad to keep saying "*H'sh!*" In w'ispers to 'er mother all the way.

"I don't know wot Charlie does want, I'm sure," ses Mrs. Cook, taking off 'er bonnet as soon as she got indoors, and pitching it on the chair he was just going to set down on.

"It's so awk'ard," ses old Cook, rubbing his 'ead. "Fact is, Charlie, we pretty near gave 'em to understand as we'd buy it."

"It's as good as settled," ses Mrs. Cook, trembling all over with temper.

"They won't settle till they get the money," ses Charlie. "You may make your mind easy about that."

"Emma's drawn it all out of the bank ready," ses old Cook, eager like.

Charlie felt 'ot and cold all over. "I'd better take care of it," he ses, in a trembling voice. "You might be robbed."

"So might you be," ses Mrs. Cook. "Don't you worry; it's in a safe place."

"Sailormen are always being robbed," ses George Smith, who 'ad been helping young Bill with 'is sums while they 'ad gone to look at the shop. "There's more sailormen robbed than all the rest put together."

"They won't rob Charlie," ses Mrs. Cook, pressing 'er lips together. "I'll take care o' that."

Charlie tried to laugh, but 'e made such a queer noise that young Bill made a large blot on 'is exercise-book, and old Cook, wot was lighting his pipe, burnt 'is fingers through not looking wot 'e was doing.

"You see," ses Charlie, "if I was robbed, which ain't at all likely, it 'ud only be me losing my own money; but if you was robbed of it you'd never forgive yourselves."

"I dessay I should get over it," ses Mrs. Cook, sniffing. "I'd 'ave a try, at all events."

Charlie started to laugh agin, and old Cook, who had struck another match, blew it out and waited till he'd finished.

"The whole truth is," ses Charlie, looking round, "I've got something better to do with the money. I've got a chance offered me that'll make me able to double it afore you know where you are."

"Not afore I know where I am," ses Mrs. Cook, with a laugh that was worse than Charlie's.

"The chance of a lifetime," ses Charlie, trying to keep 'is temper. "I can't tell you wot it is, because I've promised to keep it secret for a time. You'll be surprised when I do tell you."

"If I wait till then till I'm surprised," ses Mrs. Cook, "I shall 'ave to wait a long time. My advice to you is to take that shop and ha' done with it."

Charlie sat there arguing all the evening, but it was no good, and the idea o' them people sitting there and refusing to let 'im have his own money pretty near sent 'im crazy. It was all 'e could do to kiss Emma good night, and 'e couldn't have helped slamming the front door if he'd been paid for it. The only comfort he 'ad got left was the Sydney gal's photygraph, and he took that out and looked at it under nearly every lamp-post he passed.

He went round the next night and 'ad another try to get 'is money, but it was no use; and all the good he done was to make Mrs. Cook in such a temper that she 'ad to go to bed before he 'ad arf finished. It was no good talking to old Cook and Emma, because they daren't do anything without 'er, and it was no good calling things up the stairs to her because she didn't answer. Three nights running Mrs. Cook went off to bed afore eight o'clock, for fear she should say something to 'im as she'd be sorry for arterwards; and for three nights Charlie made 'imself so disagreeable that Emma told 'im plain the sooner 'e went back to sea agin the better she should like it. The only one who seemed to enjoy it was George Smith, and 'e used to bring bits out o' newspapers and read to 'em, showing 'ow silly people was done out of their money.

On the fourth night Charlie dropped it and made 'imself so amiable that Mrs. Cook stayed up and made 'im a Welsh rare-bit for 'is supper, and made 'im drink two glasses o' beer instead o' one, while old Cook sat and drank three glasses o' water just out o' temper, and to show that 'e didn't mind. When she started on the chandler's shop agin Charlie said he'd think it over, and when 'e went away Mrs. Cook called 'im her sailor-boy and wished 'im pleasant dreams.

But Charlie Tagg 'ad got better things to do than to dream, and 'e sat up in bed arf the night thinking out a new plan he'd thought of to get that money. When 'e did fall asleep at last 'e dreamt of taking a little farm in Australia and riding about on 'orseback with the Sydney gal watching his men at work.

In the morning he went and hunted up a shipmate of 'is, a young feller named Jack Bates. Jack was one o' these 'ere chaps, nobody's enemy but their own, as the saying is; a good-'arted, free-'anded chap as you could wish to see. Everybody liked 'im, and the ship's cat loved 'im. He'd ha' sold the shirt off 'is back to oblige a pal, and three times in one week he got 'is face scratched for trying to prevent 'usbands knocking their wives about.

Charlie Tagg went to 'im because he was the only man 'e could trust, and for over arf an hour he was telling Jack Bates all 'is troubles, and at last, as a great favour, he let 'im see the Sydney gal's photygraph, and told him that all that pore gal's future 'appiness depended upon 'im.

"I'll step round tonight and rob 'em of that seventy-two pounds," ses Jack; "it's your money, and you've a right to it."

Charlie shook his 'ead. "That wouldn't do," he ses; "besides, I don't know where they keep it. No; I've got a better plan that

that. Come round to the 'Crooked Billet,' so as we can talk it over in peace and quiet."

He stood Jack three or four arf-pints afore 'e told 'im his plan, and Jack was so pleased with it that he wanted to start at once, but Charlie persuaded 'im to wait.

"And don't you spare me, mind, out o' friendship," ses Charlie, "because the blacker you paint me the better I shall like it."

"You trust me, mate," ses Jack Bates; "if I don't get that seventy-two pounds for you, you may call me a Dutchman. Why, it's fair robbery, I call it, sticking to your money like that."

They spent the rest o' the day together, and when evening came Charlie went off to the Cooks'. Emma 'ad arf expected they was going to a theayter that night, but Charlie said he wasn't feeling the thing, and he sat there so quiet and miserable they didn't know wot to make of 'im.

"'Ave you got any trouble on your mind, Charlie," ses Mrs. Cook, "or is it the toothache?"

"It ain't the toothache," ses Charlie.

He sat there pulling a long face and staring at the floor, but all Mrs. Cook and Emma could do 'e wouldn't tell them wot was the matter with 'im. He said 'e didn't want to worry other people with 'is troubles; let everybody bear their own, that was 'is motto. Even when George Smith offered to go to the theayter with Emma instead of 'im he didn't fire up, and, if it 'adn't ha' been for Mrs. Cook, George wouldn't ha' been sorry that 'e spoke.

"Theayters ain't for me," ses Charlie, with a groan. "I'm more likely to go to jail, so far as I can see, than a theayter."

Mrs. Cook and Emma both screamed and Sarah Ann did 'er first highstericks, and very well, too, considering that she 'ad only just turned fifteen.

"Jail!" ses old Cook, as soon as they 'ad quieted Sarah Ann with a bowl o' cold water that young Bill 'ad the presence o' mind to go and fetch. "Jail! What for?"

"You wouldn't believe if I was to tell you," ses Charlie, getting up to go, "and besides, I don't want any of you to think as 'ow I am worse than wot I am."

He shook his 'ead at them sorrowful-like, and afore they could stop 'im he 'ad gone. Old Cook shouted arter 'im, but it was no use, and the others was running into the scullery to fill the bowl agin for Emma.

Mrs. Cook went round to 'is lodgings next morning, but found that 'e was out. They began to fancy all sorts o' things then, but Charlie turned up agin that evening more miserable than ever.

"I went round to see you this morning," ses Mrs. Cook, "but you wasn't at 'ome."

"I never am, 'ardly," ses Charlie. "I can't be—it ain't safe."

"Why not?" ses Mrs. Cook, fidgeting.

"If I was to tell you, you'd lose your good opinion of me," ses Charlie.

"It wouldn't be much to lose," ses Mrs. Cook, firing up.

Charlie didn't answer 'er. When he did speak he spoke to the old man, and he was so down-'arted that 'e gave 'im the chills a'most. He 'ardly took any notice of Emma, and when Mrs. Cook spoke about the shop agin, said that chandlers' shops was for happy people, not for 'im.

By the time they sat down to supper they was nearly all as miserable as Charlie 'imself. From words he let drop they all seemed to 'ave the idea that the police was arter 'im, and Mrs. Cook was just asking 'im for wot she called the third and last time, but wot was more likely the hundred and third, wot he'd done, when there was a knock at the front door, so loud and so sudden that old Cook and young Bill both cut their mouths at the same moment.

"Anybody 'ere o' the name of Emma Cook?" ses a man's voice, when young Bill opened the door.

"She's inside," ses the boy, and the next moment Jack Bates followed 'im into the room, and then fell back with a start as 'e saw Charlie Tagg.

"Ho, 'ere you are, are you?" he ses, looking at 'im very black.

"Wot's the matter?" ses Mrs. Cook, very sharp.

"I didn't expect to 'ave the pleasure o' seeing you 'ere, my lad," ses Jack, still staring at Charlie, and twisting 'is face up into awful scowls. "Which is Emma Cook?"

"Miss Cook is my name," ses Emma, very sharp. "Wot d'ye want?"

"Very good," ses Jack Bates, looking at Charlie agin; "then p'r'aps you'll do me the kindness of telling that lie o' yours agin afore this young lady.

"It's the truth," ses Charlie, looking down at 'is plate.

"If somebody don't tell me wot all this is about in two minutes, I shall do something desprit," ses Mrs. Cook, getting up.

"This 'ere—er—man," ses Jack Bates, pointing at Charlie, "owes me seventy-five pounds and won't pay. When I ask 'im for it he ses a party he's keeping company with, by the name of Emma Cook, 'as got it, and he can't get it."

"So she has," ses Charlie, without looking up.

"Wot does 'e owe you the money for?" ses Mrs. Cook.

" 'Cos I lent it to 'im," ses Jack.

"Lent it? What for?" ses Mrs. Cook.

" 'Cos I was a fool, I s'pose," ses Jack Bates; "a good-natured fool. Anyway, I'm sick and tired of asking for it, and if I don't get it tonight I'm going to see the police about it."

He sat down on a chair with 'is hat cocked over one eye, and they all sat staring at 'im as though they didn't know wot to say next.

"So this is wot you meant when you said you'd got the chance of a lifetime, is it?" ses Mrs. Cook to Charlie. "This is wot you wanted it for, is it? Wot did you borrow all that money for?"

"Spend," ses Charlie, in a sulky voice.

"Spend!" ses Mrs. Cook, with a scream; "wot in?"

"Drink and cards mostly," ses Jack Bates, remembering wot Charlie 'ad told 'im about blackening 'is character.

You might ha' heard a pin drop a'most, and Charlie sat there without saying a word.

"Charlie's been led away," ses Mrs. Cook, looking 'ard at Jack Bates. "I s'pose you lent 'im the money to win it back from 'im at cards, didn't you?"

"And gave 'im too much licker fust," ses old Cook. "I've 'eard of your kind. If Charlie takes my advice 'e won't pay you a farthing. I should let you do your worst if I was 'im; that's wot I should do. You've got a low face; a nasty, ugly, low face."

"One o' the worst I ever see," ses Mrs. Cook. "It looks as though it might ha' been cut out o' the *Police News*."

"'Owever could you ha' trusted a man with a face like that, Charlie?" ses old Cook. "Come away from 'im, Bill; I don't like such a chap in the room."

Jack Bates began to feel very awk'ard. They was all glaring at 'im as though they could eat 'im, and he wasn't used to such treatment. And, as a matter o' fact, he'd got a very good-'arted face.

"You go out o' that door," ses old Cook, pointing to it. "Go and do your worst. You won't get any money 'ere."

"Stop a minute," ses Emma, and afore they could stop 'er she ran upstairs. Mrs. Cook went arter 'er and 'igh words was heard up in the bedroom, but by and by Emma came down holding her head very 'igh and looking at Jack Bates as though he was dirt.

"How am I to know Charlie owes you this money?" she ses.

Jack Bates turned very red, and arter fumbling in 'is pockets took out about a dozen dirty bits o' paper, which Charlie 'ad given 'im for I O U's. Emma read 'em all, and then she threw a little parcel on the table.

"There's your money," she ses; "take it and go."

Mrs. Cook and 'er father began to call out, but it was no good.

"There's seventy-two pounds there," ses Emma, who was very pale, "and 'ere's a ring you can have to 'elp make up the rest." And she drew Charlie's ring off and throwed it on the table. "I've done with 'im for good," she ses, with a look at 'er mother.

Jack Bates took up the money and the ring, and stood there looking at 'er and trying to think wot to say. He'd always been uncommon partial to the sex, and it did seem 'ard to stand there and take all that on account of Charlie Tagg.

"I only wanted my own," he ses at last, shuffling about the floor.

"Well, you've got it," ses Mrs. Cook, "and now you can go."

"You're p'isoning the air of my front parlour," ses old Cook, opening the winder a little at the top.

"P'r'aps I ain't so bad as you think I am," ses Jack Bates, still looking at Emma, and with that 'e walked over to Charlie and dumped down the money on the table in front of 'im. "Take it," he ses, "and don't borrow anymore. I make you a free gift of it. P'r'aps my 'art ain't as black as my face," he ses, turning to Mrs. Cook.

They was all so surprised at fust that they couldn't speak, but old Cook smiled at 'im and put the winder up agin. And Charlie Tagg sat there arf mad with temper, looking as though 'e could eat Jack Bates without any salt, as the saying is.

"I—I can't take it," he ses at last, with a stammer.

"Can't take it? Why not?" ses old Cook, staring. "This gentleman 'as given it to you."

"A free gift," ses Mrs. Cook, smiling at Jack very sweet.

"I can't take it," ses Charlie, winking at Jack to take the money up and give it to 'im outside on the quiet, as arranged. "I 'ave my pride."

"So 'ave I," ses Jack. "Are you going to take it?"

Charlie gave 'im another look. "No," he ses, "I can't take a favour. I borrowed the money and I'll pay it back."

"Very good," ses Jack, taking it up. "It's my money, ain't it?"

"Yes," ses Charlie, taking no notice of Mrs. Cook and 'er husband, wot was both talking to 'im at once, and trying to persuade 'im to alter his mind.

"Then I give it to Miss Emma Cook," ses Jack Bates, putting it into her hands. "Good night everybody and good luck."

He slammed the front door behind 'im and they 'eard 'im go off down theroad as if 'e was going for fire-engines. Charlie sat there for a moment struck all of a heap, and then 'e jumped up and dashed arter 'im. He just saw 'im disappearing round a corner, and he didn't see 'im agin for a couple o' year afterwards, by which time the Sydney gal had 'ad three or four young men arter 'im, and Emma, who 'ad changed her name to Smith, was doing one of the best businesses in the chandlery line in Poplar.

28

THE CONSTABLE'S MOVE

Mr. Bob Grummit sat in the kitchen with his corduroy-clad legs stretched on the fender. His wife's half-eaten dinner was getting cold on the table; Mr. Grummit, who was badly in need of cheering up, emptied his half-empty glass of beer and wiped his lips with the back of his hand.

"Come away, I tell you," he called. "D'ye hear? Come away. You'll be locked up if you don't."

He gave a little laugh at the sarcasm, and sticking his short pipe in his mouth lurched slowly to the front-room door and scowled at his wife as she lurked at the back of the window watching intently the furniture which was being carried in next door.

"Come away or else you'll be locked up," repeated Mr. Grummit. "You mustn't look at policemen's furniture; it's agin the law."

Mrs. Grummit made no reply, but, throwing appearances to the winds, stepped to the window until her nose touched, as a walnut sideboard with bevelled glass back was tenderly borne inside under the personal supervision of Police-Constable Evans.

"They'll be 'aving a pianner next," said the indignant Mr. Grummit, peering from the depths of the room.

"They've got one," responded his wife; "there's the end of it stickin' up in the van."

Mr. Grummit advanced and regarded the end fixedly. "Did you throw all them tin cans and things into their yard wot I told you to?" he demanded.

"He picked up three of 'em while I was upstairs," replied his wife. "I 'eard 'im tell her that they'd come in handy for paint and things."

"That's 'ow coppers get on and buy pianners," said the incensed Mr. Grummit, "sneaking other people's property. I didn't tell you to throw good 'uns over, did I? Wot d'ye mean by it?"

Mrs. Grummit made no reply, but watched with bated breath the triumphal entrance of the piano. The carman set it tenderly on the narrow footpath, while P.G. Evans, stooping low, examined it at all points, and Mrs. Evans, raising the lid, struck a few careless chords.

"Showing off," explained Mrs. Grummit, with a half turn; "and she's got fingers like carrots."

"It's a disgrace to Mulberry Gardens to 'ave a copper come and live in it," said the indignant Grummit; "and to come and live next door to *me*!—That's what I can't get over. To come and live next door to a man wot has been fined twice, and both times wrong. Why, for two pins I'd go in and smash 'is planner first and 'im after it. He won't live 'ere long, you take my word for it."

"Why not?" inquired his wife.

"Why?" repeated Mr. Grummit. "Why? Why, becos I'll make the place too 'ot to hold him. Ain't there enough houses in Tunwich without 'im a-coming and living next door to me?"

For a whole week the brain concealed in Mr. Grummit's bullet-shaped head worked in vain, and his temper got correspondingly bad. The day after the Evanses' arrival he had found his yard littered with tins which he recognised as old acquaintances, and since that time they had travelled backwards and forwards with monotonous regularity. They sometimes made as many as three journeys a day, and on one occasion the heavens opened to drop a battered tin bucket on the back of Mr. Grummit as he was tying his bootlace. Five minutes later he spoke of the outrage to Mr. Evans, who had come out to admire the sunset.

"I heard something fall," said the constable, eyeing the pail curiously.

"You threw it," said Mr. Grummit, breathing furiously.

"Me? Nonsense," said the other easily. "I was having tea in the parlour with my wife and my mother-in-law, and my brother Joe and his young lady."

"Anymore of 'em?" demanded the hapless Mr. Grummit, aghast at this list of witnesses for an alibi.

"It ain't a bad pail, if you look at it properly," said the constable. "I should keep it if I was you; unless the owner offers a reward for it. It'll hold enough water for your wants."

Mr. Grummit flung indoors and, after wasting sometime concocting impossible measures of retaliation with his sympathetic partner, went off to discuss affairs with his intimates at the "Bricklayers' Arms." The company, although unanimously agreeing that Mr. Evans ought to be boiled, were miserably deficient in ideas as to the means by which such a desirable end was to be attained.

"Make 'im a laughing-stock, that's the best thing," said an elderly labourer. "The police don't like being laughed at."

"'Ow?" demanded Mr. Grummit, with some asperity.

"There's plenty o' ways," said the old man.

"I should find 'em out fast enough if I 'ad a bucket dropped on my back, I know."

Mr. Grummit made a retort the feebleness of which was somewhat balanced by its ferocity, and subsided into glum silence. His back still ached, but, despite that aid to intellectual effort, the only means he could imagine of making the constable look foolish contained an almost certain risk of hard labour for himself.

He pondered the question for a week, and meanwhile the tins—to the secret disappointment of Mr. Evans—remained untouched in his yard. For the whole of the time he went about looking, as Mrs. Grummit expressed it, as though his dinner had disagreed with him.

"I've been talking to old Bill Smith," he said suddenly, as he came in one night.

Mrs. Grummit looked up, and noticed with wifely pleasure that he was looking almost cheerful.

"He's given me a tip," said Mr. Grummit, with a faint smile; "a copper mustn't come into a free-born Englishman's 'ouse unless he's invited."

"Wot of it?" inquired his wife. "You wasn't thinking of asking him in, was you?"

Mr. Grummit regarded her almost playfully.

"If a copper comes in without being told to," he continued, "he gets into trouble for it. Now d'ye see?"

"But he won't come," said the puzzled Mrs. Grummit.

Mr. Grummit winked. "Yes 'e will, if you scream loud enough," he retorted. "Where's the copper-stick?"

"Have you gone mad?" demanded his wife, "or do you think I 'ave?"

"You go up into the bedroom," said Mr. Grummit, emphasising his remarks with his forefinger, "and I'll come up and beat the bed black and blue with the copper-stick while you scream for mercy and cal out 'Help!' 'Murder!' and things like that. Don't call out 'Police!' cos Bill ain't sure about that part. Ten chances to one Evans will come bursting in to save your life—I'll leave the door on the latch—and there you are. He's sure to get into trouble for it. Bill said so. He's made a study o' that sort o' thing."

Mrs. Grummit pondered this simple plan so long that her husband began to lose patience. At last, against her better sense, she rose and fetched the weapon in question.

"And you be careful what you're hitting," she said, as they went upstairs to bed. "We'd better have 'igh words first, I s'pose?"

"You pitch into me with your tongue, like you used to afore I broke you of it," said Mr. Grummit amiably.

Mrs. Grummit, first listening to make sure that the constable and his wife were in the bedroom the other side of the flimsy wall, complied, and in a voice that rose gradually to a piercing falsetto told Mr. Grummit things that had been rankling in her mind for several months. She raked up misdemeanours that he had long since forgotten, and, not content with that, had a fling at the entire Grummit family, beginning with her mother-in-law and ending with Mr. Grummit's youngest sister. The hand that held the copper-stick itched.

"Anymore to say?" demanded Mr. Grummit, advancing upon her.

Mrs. Grummit emitted a genuine shriek, and Mr. Grummit, suddenly remembering himself, stopped short and attacked the bed with extraordinary fury. The room resounded with the blows, and the efforts of Mrs. Grummit were a revelation even to her husband.

"I can hear 'im moving," whispered Mr. Grummit, pausing to take breath.

"*Mur—der!*" wailed his wife. "*Help! Help!*"

Mr. Grummit, changing the stick into his left hand, renewed the attack; Mrs. Grummit, whose voice was becoming exhausted, sought a temporary relief in moans.

"Is—he—deaf?" panted the wife-beater, "or wot?"

He knocked over a chair, and Mrs. Grummit contrived another frenzied scream. A loud knocking sounded on the wall.

"*Hel—lp!*" moaned Mrs. Grummit.

"Halloa, there!" came the voice of the constable. "Why don't you keep that baby quiet? We can't get a wink of sleep."

Mr. Grummit dropped the stick on the bed and turned a dazed face to his wife.

"He—he's afraid—to come in," he gasped. "Keep it up, old gal."

He took up the stick again and Mrs. Grummit did her best, but the heart had gone out of the thing, and he was about to give up the task as hopeless when the door below was heard to open with a bang.

"Here he is," cried the jubilant Grummit. "Now!"

His wife responded, and at the same moment the bedroom door was flung open, and her brother, who had been hastily fetched by the neighbours on the other side, burst into the room, and with one hearty blow sent Mr. Grummit sprawling.

"Hit my sister, will you!" he roared, as the astounded Mr. Grummit rose. "Take that!"

Mr. Grummit took it, and several other favours, while his wife, tugging at her brother, endeavoured to explain. It was not, however, until Mr. Grummit claimed the usual sanctuary of the defeated by refusing to rise that she could make herself heard.

"Joke?" repeated her brother incredulously. "Joke?"

Mrs. Grummit in a husky voice explained. Her brother passed from incredulity to amazement and from amazement to mirth. He sat down gurgling, and the indignant face of the injured Grummit only added to his distress.

"Best joke I ever heard in my life," he said, wiping his eyes. "Don't look at me like that, Bob; I can't bear it."

"Get off 'ome," responded Mr. Grummit, glowering at him.

"There's a crowd outside, and half the doors in the place open," said the other. "Well, it's a good job there's no harm done. So long."

He passed, beaming, down the stairs, and Mr. Grummit, drawing near the window, heard him explaining in a broken voice to the neighbours outside. Strong men patted him on the back and urged him gruffly to say what he had to say and laugh afterwards. Mr. Grummit turned from the window, and in a slow and stately fashion prepared to retire for the night. Even the sudden and startling disappearance of Mrs. Grummit as she got into bed failed to move him.

"The bed's broke, Bob," she said faintly.

"Beds won't last forever," he said shortly; "sleep on the floor."

Mrs. Grummit clambered out, and after some trouble secured the bedclothes and made up a bed in a corner of the room. In a short time she was fast asleep; but her husband, broad awake, spent the night in devising further impracticable schemes for the discomfiture of the foe next door.

He saw Mr. Evans next morning as he passed on his way to work. The constable was at the door smoking in his shirt-sleeves, and Mr. Grummit felt instinctively that he was waiting there to see him pass.

"I heard you last night," said the constable playfully. "My word! Good gracious!"

"Wot's the matter with you!" demanded Mr. Grummit, stopping short.

The constable stared at him. "She has been knocking you about," he gasped. "Why, it must ha' been *you* screaming, then! I thought it sounded loud. Why don't you go and get a summons and have her locked up? I should be pleased to take her."

Mr. Grummit faced him, quivering with passion. "Wot would it cost if I set about you?" he demanded huskily.

"Two months," said Mr. Evans, smiling serenely; "p'r'aps three."

Mr. Grummit hesitated and his fists clenched nervously. The constable, lounging against his doorpost, surveyed him with a dispassionate smile. "That would be besides what you'd get from me," he said softly.

"Come out in the road," said Mr. Grummit, with sudden violence.

"It's agin the rules," said Mr. Evans; "sorry I can't. Why not go and ask your wife's brother to oblige you?"

He went in laughing and closed the door, and Mr. Grummit, after a frenzied outburst, proceeded on his way, returning the smiles of such acquaintances as he passed with an icy stare or a strongly-worded offer to make them laugh the other side of their face. The rest of the day he spent in working so hard that he had no time to reply to the anxious inquiries of his fellow-workmen.

He came home at night glum and silent, the hardship of not being able to give Mr. Evans his deserts without incurring hard labour having weighed on his spirits all day. To avoid the annoyance of the piano next door, which was slowly and reluctantly yielding up "The Last Rose of Summer" note by note, he went out at the back, and the first thing he saw was Mr. Evans mending his path with tins and other bric-à-brac.

"Nothing like it," said the constable, looking up. "Your missus gave 'em to us this morning. A little gravel on top, and there you are.'"

He turned whistling to his work again, and the other, after endeavouring in vain to frame a suitable reply, took a seat on an inverted washtub and lit his pipe. His one hope was that Constable Evans was going to try and cultivate a garden.

The hope was realised a few days later, and Mr. Grummit at the back window sat gloating over a dozen fine geraniums, some lobelias and calceolarias, which decorated the constable's plot of ground. He could not sleep for thinking of them.

He rose early the next morning, and, after remarking to Mrs. Grummit that Mr. Evans's flowers looked as though they wanted rain, went off to his work. The cloud which had been on his spirits for some time had lifted, and he whistled as he walked. The sight of flowers in front windows added to his good humour.

He was still in good spirits when he left off work that afternoon, but some slight hesitation about returning home sent him to the "Bricklayers' Arms" instead. He stayed there until closing time, and then, being still disinclined for home, paid a visit to Bill Smith, who lived the other side of Tunwich. By the time he started for home it was nearly midnight.

The outskirts of the town were deserted and the houses in darkness. The clock of Tunwich church struck twelve, and the last stroke was just dying away as he turned a corner and ran almost into the arms of the man he had been trying to avoid.

"Halloa!" said Constable Evans sharply. "Here, I want a word with you."

Mr. Grummit quailed. "With me, sir?" he said, with involuntary respect.

"What have you been doing to my flowers?" demanded the other hotly.

"Flowers?" repeated Mr. Grummit, as though the word were new to him. "Flowers? What flowers?"

"You know well enough," retorted the constable. "You got over my fence last night and smashed all my flowers down."

"You be careful wot you're saying," urged Mr. Grummit. "Why, I love flowers. You don't mean to tell me that all them beautiful flowers wot you put in so careful 'as been spoiled?"

"You know all about it," said the constable, choking. "I shall take out a summons against you for it."

"Ho!" said Mr. Grummit. "And wot time do you say it was when I done it?"

"Never you mind the time," said the other.

"Cos it's important," said Mr. Grummit. "My wife's brother—the one you're so fond of—slept in my 'ouse last night. He was ill arf the night, pore chap; but, come to think of it, it'll make 'im a good witness for my innocence."

"If I wasn't a policeman," said Mr. Evans, speaking with great deliberation, "I'd take hold o' you, Bob Grummit, and I'd give you the biggest hiding you've ever had in your life."

"If you wasn't a policeman," said Mr. Grummit yearningly, "I'd arf murder you."

The two men eyed each other wistfully, loath to part.

"If I gave you what you deserve I should get into trouble," said the constable.

"If I gave you a quarter of wot you ought to 'ave I should go to quod," sighed Mr. Grummit.

"I wouldn't put you there," said the constable earnestly; "I swear I wouldn't."

"Everything's beautiful and quiet," said Mr. Grummit, trembling with eagerness, "and I wouldn't say a word to a soul. I'll take my solemn davit I wouldn't."

"When I think o' my garden—" began the constable. With a sudden movement he knocked off Mr. Grummit's cap, and then, seizing him by the coat, began to hustle him along the road. In the twinkling of an eye they had closed.

Tunwich church chimed the half-hour as they finished, and Mr. Grummit, forgetting his own injuries, stood smiling at the wreck before him. The constable's helmet had been smashed and trodden on; his uniform was torn and covered with blood and dirt, and his good looks marred for a fortnight at least. He stooped with a groan, and, recovering his helmet, tried mechanically to punch it into shape. He stuck the battered relic on his head, and Mr. Grummit fell back awed, despite himself.

"It was a fair fight," he stammered.

The constable waved him away. "Get out o' my sight before I change my mind," he said fiercely; "and mind, if you say a word about this it'll be the worse for you."

"Do you think I've gone mad?" said the other. He took another look at his victim and, turning away, danced fantastically along the road home. The constable, making his way to a gas-lamp, began to inspect damages.

They were worse even than he had thought, and, leaning against the lamp-post, he sought in vain for an explanation that, in the absence of a prisoner, would satisfy the inspector. A button which was hanging by a thread fell tinkling on to the footpath, and he had just picked it up and placed it in his pocket when a faint distant outcry broke upon his ear.

He turned and walked as rapidly as his condition would permit in the direction of the noise. It became louder and more imperative, and cries of "Police!" became distinctly audible. He quickened into a run, and turning a corner beheld a little knot of people standing at the gate of a large house. Other people only partially clad were hastening towards them. The constable arrived out of breath.

"Better late than never," said the owner of the house sarcastically.

Mr. Evans, breathing painfully, supported himself with his hand on the fence.

"They went that way, but I suppose you didn't see them," continued the householder. "Halloa!" he added, as somebody opened the hall door and the constable's damaged condition became visible in the gas-light. "Are you hurt?"

"Yes," said Mr. Evans, who was trying hard to think clearly. To gain time he blew a loud call on his whistle.

"The rascals!" continued the other. "I think I should know the big chap with a beard again, but the others were too quick for me."

Mr. Evans blew his whistle again—thoughtfully. The opportunity seemed too good to lose.

"Did they get anything?" he inquired.

"Not a thing," said the owner triumphantly. "I was disturbed just in time."

The constable gave a slight gulp. "I saw the three running by the side of the road," he said slowly. "Their behaviour seemed suspicious, so I collared the big one, but they set on me like wild cats. They had me down three times; the last time I laid my head open against the kerb, and when I came to my senses again they had gone."

He took off his battered helmet with a flourish and, amid a murmur of sympathy, displayed a nasty cut on his head. A sergeant and a constable, both running, appeared round the corner and made towards them.

"Get back to the station and make your report," said the former, as Constable Evans, in a somewhat defiant voice, repeated his story. "You've done your best; I can see that."

Mr. Evans, enacting to perfection the part of a wounded hero, limped painfully off, praying devoutly as he went that the criminals might make good their escape. If not, he reflected that by the rules of the Service the word of a policeman was at least equal to that of three burglars.

He repeated his story at the station, and, after having his head dressed, was sent home and advised to keep himself quiet for a day or two. He was off duty for four days, and the *Tunwich Gazette* having devoted a column to the affair, headed "A Gallant Constable," modestly secluded himself from the public gaze for the whole of that time.

To Mr. Grummit, who had read the article in question until he could have repeated it backwards, this modesty was particularly trying. The constable's yard was deserted and the front door ever closed. Once Mr. Grummit even went so far as to tap with his nails on the front parlour window, but the only response was the sudden lowering of the blind. It was not until a week afterwards that his eyes were gladdened by a sight of the constable sitting in his yard; and fearing that even then he might escape him, he ran out on tip-toe and put his head over the fence before the latter was aware of his presence.

"Wot about that 'ere burglary?" he demanded in truculent tones.

"Good evening, Grummit," said the constable, with a patronising air.

"Wot about that burglary?" repeated Mr. Grummit with a scowl. "I don't believe you ever saw a burglar."

Mr. Evans rose and stretched himself gracefully. "You'd better run indoors, my good man," he said slowly.

"Telling all them lies about burglars," continued the indignant Mr. Grummit, producing his newspaper and waving it. "Why, *I* gave you that black eye, *I* smashed your 'elmet, *I* cut your silly 'ead open, *I*— "

"You've been drinking," said the other severely.

"You mean to say I didn't?" demanded Mr. Grummit ferociously.

Mr. Evans came closer and eyed him steadily. "I don't know what you're talking about," he said calmly.

Mr. Grummit, about to speak, stopped appalled at such hardihood.

"Of course, if you mean to say that you were one o' them burglars," continued the constable, "why, say it and I'll take you with pleasure. Come to think of it, I did seem to remember one o' their voices."

Mr. Grummit, with his eyes fixed on the other's, backed a couple of yards and breathed heavily.

"About your height, too, he was," mused the constable. "I hope for your sake you haven't been saying to anybody else what you said to me just now."

Mr. Grummit shook his head. "Not a word," he faltered.

"That's all right, then," said Mr. Evans. "I shouldn't like to be hard on a neighbour; not that we shall be neighbours much longer."

Mr. Grummit, feeling that a reply was expected of him, gave utterance to a feeble "Oh!"

"No," said Mr. Evans, looking round disparagingly. "It ain't good enough for us now; I was promoted to sergeant this morning. A sergeant can't live in a common place like this."

Mr. Grummit, a prey to a sickening fear, drew near the fence again. "A—a sergeant?" he stammered.

Mr. Evans smiled and gazed carefully at a distant cloud. "For my bravery with them burglars the other night, Grummit," he said modestly. "I might have waited years if it hadn't been for them."

He nodded to the frantic Grummit and turned away; Mr. Grummit, without any adieu at all, turned and crept back to the house.

29

BOB'S REDEMPTION

Gratitoode! said the night-watchman, with a hard laugh. *Hmf!* Don't talk to me about gratitoode; I've seen too much of it. If people wot I've helped in my time 'ad only done arf their dooty—arf, mind you—I should be riding in my carriage.

Forgetful of the limitations of soap-boxes, he attempted to illustrate his remark by lolling, and nearly went over backwards. Recovering himself by an effort, he gazed sternly across the river and smoked fiercely. It was evident that he was brooding over an ill-used past.

'Arry Thomson was one of them, he said at last. For over six months I wrote all 'is love-letters for him, 'e being an iggernerant sort of man and only being able to do the kisses at the end, which he always insisted on doing 'imself: being jealous. Only three weeks arter he was married 'e come up to where I was standing one day and set about me without saying a word. I was a single man at the time and I didn't understand it. My idea was that he 'ad gone mad and, being pretty artful and always 'aving a horror of mad people, I let 'im chase me into a police-station. Leastways, I would ha let 'im, but he didn't come, and I all but got fourteen days for being drunk and disorderly.

Then there was Bill Clark. He 'ad been keeping comp'ny with a gal and got tired of it, and to oblige 'im I went to her and told 'er he was a married man with five children. Bill was as pleased as Punch at fust, but as soon as she took up with another chap he came round to me and said as I'd ruined his life. We 'ad words about it—naturally—and I did ruin it then to the extent of a couple o' ribs. I went to see 'im in the horsepittle—a place I've always been fond of—and the langwidge he used to me was so bad that they sent for the Sister to 'ear it.

That's on'y two out of dozens I could name. Arf the unpleasantnesses in my life 'ave come out of doing kindnesses to people, and all the gratitoode I've 'ad for it I could put in a pint-pot with a pint o' beer already in it.

The only case o' real gratitoode I ever heard of 'appened to a shipmate o' mine—a young chap named Bob Evans. Coming home from Auckland in a barque called the *Dragon Fly* he fell overboard, and another chap named George Crofts, one o' the best swimmers I ever knew, went overboard arter 'im and saved his life.

We was hardly moving at the time, and the sea was like a duck pond, but to 'ear Bob Evans talk you'd ha' thought that George Crofts was the bravest-'arted chap that ever lived. He 'adn't liked him afore, same as the rest of us, George being a sly, mean sort o' chap; but arter George 'ad saved his life 'e couldn't praise 'im enough. He said that so long as he 'ad a crust George should share it, and wotever George asked 'im he should have.

The unfortnit part of it was that George took 'im at his word, and all the rest of the v'y'ge he acted as though Bob belonged to 'im, and by the time we got into the London river Bob couldn't call his soul 'is own. He used to take a room when he was ashore and live very steady, as 'e was saving up to get married, and as soon as he found that out George invited 'imself to stay with him.

"It won't cost you a bit more," he ses, "not if you work it properly."

Bob didn't work it properly, but George having saved his life, and never letting 'im forget it, he didn't like to tell him so. He thought he'd let 'im see gradual that he'd got to be careful because of 'is gal, and the fust evening they was ashore 'e took 'im along with 'im to see her.

Gerty Mitchell—that was the gal's name—'adn't heard of Bob's accident, and when she did she gave a little scream, and putting 'er arms round his neck, began to kiss 'im right in front of George and her mother.

"You ought to give him one too," ses Mrs. Mitchell, pointing to George.

George wiped 'is mouth on the back of his 'and, but Gerty pretended not to 'ear.

"Fancy if you'd been drownded!" she ses, hugging Bob agin.

"He was pretty near," ses George, shaking his 'ead. "I'm a pore swimmer, but I made up my mind either to save 'im or else go down to a watery grave myself."

He wiped his mouth on the back of his 'and agin, but all the notice Gerty took of it was to send her young brother Ted out for some beer. Then they all 'ad supper together, and Mrs. Mitchell drank good luck to George in a glass o' beer, and said she 'oped that 'er own boy would grow up like him. "Let 'im grow up a good and brave man, that's all I ask," she ses. "I don't care about 'is looks."

"He might have both," ses George sharp-like. "Why not?"

Mrs. Mitchell said she supposed he might, and then she cuffed young Ted's ears for making a noise while 'e was eating, and then cuffed 'im agin for saying that he'd finished 'is supper five minutes ago.

George and Bob walked 'ome together, and all the way there George said wot a pretty gal Gerty was and 'ow lucky it was for Bob that he 'adn't been drownded. He went round to tea with 'im the next day to Mrs. Mitchell's, and arter tea, when

Bob and Gerty said they was going out to spend the evening together, got 'imself asked too.

They took a tram-car and went to a music-hall, and Bob paid for the three of 'em. George never seemed to think of putting his 'and in his pocket, and even arter the music-hall, when they all went into a shop and 'ad stewed eels, he let Bob pay.

As I said afore, Bob Evans was chock-full of gratefulness, and it seemed only fair that he shouldn't grumble at spending a little over the man wot 'ad risked 'is life to save his; but wot with keeping George at his room, and paying for 'im every time they went out, he was spending a lot more money than 'e could afford.

"You're on'y young once, Bob," George said to him when 'e made a remark one arter-noon as to the fast way his money was going, "and if it hadn't ha' been for me you'd never 'ave lived to grow old."

Wot with spending the money and always 'aving George with them when they went out, it wasn't long afore Bob and Gerty 'ad a quarrel. "I don't like a pore-spirited man," she ses. "Two's company and three's none, and besides, why can't he pay for 'imself? He's big enough. Why should you spend your money on 'im? He never pays a farthing."

Bob explained that he couldn't say anything because 'e owed his life to George, but 'e might as well 'ave talked to a lamp-post. The more he argued the more angry Gerty got, and at last she ses: "Two's company and three's none, and if you and me can't go out without George Crofts, then me and 'im 'll go out without you."

She was as good as her word too, and the next night, while Bob 'ad gone out to get some 'bacca, she went off alone with George. It was ten o'clock afore they came back agin, and Gerty's eyes were all shining and 'er cheeks as pink as roses. She shut 'er mother up like a concertina the moment she began to find fault with 'er, and at supper she sat next to George and laughed at everything 'e said.

George and Bob walked all the way 'ome arter supper without saying a word but arter they got to their room George took a side-look at Bob, and then he ses, sudden-like: "Look 'ere! I saved your life, didn't I?"

"You did," ses Bob, "and I thank you for it."

"I saved your life," ses George agin, very solemn. "If it hadn't ha' been for me you couldn't ha' married *anybody*."

"That's true," ses Bob.

"Me and Gerty 'ave been having a talk," ses George, bending down to undo his boots. "We've been getting on very well together; you can't 'elp your feelings, and the long and the short of it is, the pore gal has fallen in love with me."

Bob didn't say a word.

"If you look at it this way it's fair enough," ses George. "I gave you your life and you give me your gal. We're quits now. You don't owe me anything and I don't owe you anything. That's the way Gerty puts it, and she told me to tell you so."

"If—if she don't want me I'm agreeable," ses Bob in a choking voice. "We'll call it quits, and next time I tumble overboard I 'ope you won't be handy."

He took Gerty's photygraph out of 'is box and handed it to George. "You've got more right to it now than wot I 'ave," he ses. "I shan't go round there anymore; I shall look out for a ship tomorrow."

George Crofts said that perhaps it was the best thing he could do, and 'e asked 'im in a off-hand sort o' way 'ow long the room was paid up for.

Mrs. Mitchell 'ad a few words to say about it next day, but Gerty told 'er to save 'er breath for walking upstairs. The on'y thing that George didn't like when they went out was that young Ted was with them, but Gerty said she preferred it till she knew 'im better; and she 'ad so much to say about his noble behaviour in saving life that George gave way. They went out looking at the shops, George thinking that that was the cheapest way of spending an evening, and they were as happy as possible till Gerty saw a brooch she liked so much in a window that he couldn't get 'er away.

"It *is* a beauty," she ses. "I don't know when I've seen a brooch I liked better. Look here! Let's all guess the price and then go in and see who's right."

They 'ad their guesses, and then they went in and asked, and as soon as Gerty found that it was only three-and-sixpence she began to feel in her pocket for 'er purse, just like your wife does when you go out with 'er, knowing all the time that it's on the mantelpiece with twopence-ha'penny and a cough lozenge in it.

"I must ha' left it at 'ome," she ses, looking at George.

"Just wot I've done," ses George, arter patting 'is pockets.

Gerty bit 'er lips and, for a minute or two, be civil to George she could not. Then she gave a little smile and took 'is arm agin, and they walked on talking and laughing till she turned round of a sudden and asked a big chap as was passing wot 'e was shoving 'er for.

"Shoving you?"ses he. "Wot do you think I want to shove *you* for?"

"Don't you talk to me," ses Gerty, firing up. "George, make 'im beg my pardon."

"You ought to be more careful," ses George, in a gentle sort o' way.

"Make 'im beg my pardon," ses Gerty, stamping 'er foot; "if he don't, knock 'im down."

"Yes, knock 'im down," ses the big man, taking hold o' George's cap and rumpling his hair.

Pore George, who was never much good with his fists, hit 'im in the chest, and the next moment he was on 'is back in the middle o' the road wondering wot had 'appened to 'im. By the time 'e got up the other man was arf a mile away; and young Ted stepped up and wiped 'im down with a pocket-'andkerchief while Gerty explained to 'im 'ow she saw 'im slip on a piece o' banana peel.

"It's 'ard lines," she ses; "but never mind, you frightened 'im away, and I don't wonder at it. You do look terrible when you're angry, George; I didn't know you."

She praised 'im all the way 'ome, and if it 'adn't been for his mouth and nose George would 'ave enjoyed it more than 'e did. She told 'er mother how 'e had flown at a big man wot, 'ad insulted her, and Mrs. Mitchell shook her 'ead at 'im and said his bold spirit would lead 'im into trouble afore he 'ad done.

They didn't seem to be able to make enough of 'im, and next day when he went round Gerty was so upset at the sight of 'is bruises that he thought she was going to cry. When he had 'ad his tea she gave 'im a cigar she had bought for 'im herself, and when he 'ad finished smoking it she smiled at him, and said that she was going to take 'im out for a pleasant evening to try and make up to 'im for wot he 'ad suffered for 'er.

"We're all going to stand treat to each other," she ses. "Bob always would insist on paying foreverything, but I like to feel a bit independent. Give and take—that's the way I like to do things."

"There's nothing like being independent," ses George. "Bob ought to ha' known that."

"I'm sure it's the best plan," ses Gerty. "Now, get your 'at on. We're going to a theayter, and Ted shall pay the bus fares."

George wanted to ask about the theayter, but 'e didn't like to, and arter Gerty was dressed they went out and Ted paid the bus fares like a man.

"Here you are," ses Gerty, as the bus stopped outside the theayter. "Hurry up and get the tickets, George; ask for three upper circles."

She bustled George up to the pay place, and as soon as she 'ad picked out the seats she grabbed 'old of the tickets and told George to make haste.

"Twelve shillings it is," ses the man, as George put down arf a crown.

"Twelve?" ses George, beginning to stammer. "Twelve? Twelve? Twel—?"

"Twelve shillings," ses the man; "three upper circles you've 'ad."

George was going to fetch Gerty back and 'ave cheaper seats, but she 'ad gone inside with young Ted, and at last, arter making an awful fuss, he paid the rest o' the money and rushed in arter her, arf crazy at the idea o' spending so much money.

"Make 'aste," ses Gerty, afore he could say anything; "the band 'as just begun."

She started running upstairs, and she was so excited that, when they got their seats and George started complaining about the price, she didn't pay any attention to wot he was saying, but kept pointing out ladies' dresses to 'im in w'ispers and wondering wot they 'ad paid for them. George gave it up at last, and then he sat wondering whether he 'ad done right arter all in taking Bob's gal away from him.

Gerty enjoyed it very much, but when the curtain came down after the first act she leaned back in her chair and looked up at George and said she felt faint and thought she'd like to 'ave an ice-cream. "And you 'ave one too, dear," she ses, when young Ted 'ad got up and beckoned to the gal, "and Ted 'ud like one too, I'm sure."

She put her 'ead on George's shoulder and looked up at 'im. Then she put her 'and on his and stroked it, and George, reckoning that arter all ice-creams were on'y a ha'penny or at the most a penny each, altered 'is mind about not spending anymore money, and ordered three.

The way he carried on when the gal said they was three shillings was alarming. At fust 'e thought she was 'aving a joke with 'im, and it took another gal and the fireman and an old gentleman wot was sitting behind 'im to persuade 'im different. He was so upset that 'e couldn't eat his arter paying for it, and Ted and Gerty had to finish it for 'im.

"They're expensive, but they're worth the money," ses Gerty. "You are good to me, George. I could go on eating 'em all night, but you mustn't fling your money away like this always."

"I'll see to that," ses George, very bitter. "I thought we was going to stand treat to each other? That was the idea, I understood."

"So we are," ses Gerty. "Ted stood the bus fares, didn't he?"

"He did," ses George, "wot there was of 'em; but wot about you?"

"*Me?*" ses Gerty, drawing her 'ead back and staring at 'im. "Why, 'ave you forgot that cigar already, George?"

George opened 'is mouth, but 'e couldn't speak a word. He sat looking at 'er and making a gasping noise in 'is throat, and fortunately just as 'e got 'is voice back the curtain went up agin, and everybody said, "*H'sh!*"

He couldn't enjoy the play at all, 'e was so upset, and he began to see more than ever 'ow wrong he 'ad been in taking Bob's gal away from 'im. He walked downstairs into the street like a man in a dream, with Gerty sticking to 'is arm and young Ted treading on 'is heels behind.

"Now you mustn't waste anymore money, George," ses Gerty, when they got outside. "We'll walk 'ome."

George 'ad got arf a mind to say something about a bus, but he remembered in time that very likely young Ted hadn't got anymore money. Then Gerty said she knew a short cut, and she took them, walking along little, dark, narrow streets and places, until at last, just as George thought they must be pretty near 'ome, she began to dab her eyes with 'er pocket-'andkerchief and say she'd lost 'er way.

"You two go 'ome and leave me," she ses, arf crying. "I can't walk another step."

"Where are we?" ses George, looking round.

"I don't know," ses Gerty. "I couldn't tell you if you paid me. I must 'ave taken a wrong turning. Oh, hurrah! Here's a cab!"

Afore George could stop 'er she held up 'er umbrella, and a 'ansom cab, with bells on its horse, crossed the road and pulled up in front of 'em. Ted nipped in first and Gerty followed 'im.

"Tell 'im the address, dear, and make 'aste and get in," ses Gerty.

George told the cabman, and then he got in and sat partly on Ted's knee, partly on Gerty's umbrella, and mostly on nothing.

"You *are* good to me, George," ses Gerty, touching the back of 'is neck with the brim of her hat. "It ain't often I get a ride in a cab. All the time I was keeping company with Bob we never 'ad one once. I only wish I'd got the money to pay for it."

George, who was going to ask a question, stopped 'imself, and then he kept striking matches and trying to read all about cab fares on a bill in front of 'im.

"'Ow are we to know 'ow many miles it is?" he ses at last.

"I don't know," ses Gerty; "leave it to the cabman. It's his bisness, ain't it? And if 'e don't know he must suffer for it."

There was hardly a soul in Gerty's road when they got there, but afore George 'ad settled with the cabman there was a policeman moving the crowd on and arf the winders in the road up. By the time George had paid 'im, and the cabman 'ad told him wot 'e looked like, Gerty and Ted 'ad disappeared indoors, all the lights was out, and, in a state o' mind that won't bear thinking of, George walked 'ome to his lodging.

Bob was asleep when he got there, but 'e woke 'im up and told 'im about it, and then arter a time he said that he thought Bob ought to pay arf because he 'ad saved 'is life.

"Cert'nly not," ses Bob. "We're quits now; that was the arrangement. I only wish it was me spending the money on her; I shouldn't grumble."

George didn't get a wink o' sleep all night for thinking of the money he 'ad spent, and next day when he went round he 'ad almost made up 'is mind to tell Bob that if 'e liked to pay up the money he could 'ave Gerty back; but she looked so pretty, and praised 'im up so much for 'is generosity, that he began to think better of it. One thing 'e was determined on, and that was never to spend money like that agin for fifty Gertys.

There was a very sensible man there that evening that George liked very much. His name was Uncle Joe, and when Gerty was praising George to 'is face for the money he 'ad been spending, Uncle Joe, instead o' looking pleased, shook his 'ead over it.

"Young people will be young people, I know," he ses, "but still I don't approve of extravagance. Bob Evans would never 'ave spent all that money over you."

"Bob Evans ain't everybody," ses Mrs. Mitchell, standing up for Gerty.

"He was steady, anyway," ses Uncle Joe. "Besides, Gerty ought not to ha' let Mr. Crofts spend his money like that. She could ha' prevented it if she'd ha' put 'er foot down and insisted on it."

He was so solemn about it that everybody began to feel a bit upset, and Gerty borrowed Ted's pocket-'andkerchief, and then wiped 'er eyes on the cuff of her dress instead.

"Well, well," ses Uncle Joe; "I didn't mean to be 'ard, but don't do it no more. You are young people, and can't afford it."

"We must 'ave a little pleasure sometimes," ses Gerty.

"Yes, I know," ses Uncle Joe; "but there's moderation in everything. Look 'ere, it's time somebody paid for Mr. Crofts. Tomorrow's Saturday, and, if you like, I'll take you all to the Crystal Palace."

Gerty jumped up off of 'er chair and kissed 'im, while Mrs. Mitchell said she knew 'is bark was worse than 'is bite, and asked 'im who was wasting his money now?

"You meet me at London Bridge Station at two o'clock," ses Uncle Joe, getting up to go. "It ain't extravagance for a man as can afford it."

He shook 'ands with George Crofts and went, and arter George 'ad stayed long enough to hear a lot o' things about Uncle Joe which made 'im think they'd get on very well together, he went off too.

They all turned up very early the next arter-noon, and Gerty was dressed so nice that George couldn't take his eyes off of her. Besides her there was Mrs. Mitchell and Ted and a friend of 'is named Charlie Smith.

They waited some time, but Uncle Joe didn't turn up, and they all got looking at the clock and talking about it, and 'oping he wouldn't make 'em miss the train.

"Here he comes!" ses Ted at last.

Uncle Joe came rushing in, puffing and blowing as though he'd bust. "Take 'em on by this train, will you?" he ses, catching 'old o' George by the arm. "I've just been stopped by a bit o' business I must do, and I'll come on by the next, or as soon arter as I can."

He rushed off again, puffing and blowing his 'ardest, in such a hurry that he forgot to give George the money for the tickets. However, George borrowed a pencil of Mrs. Mitchell in the train, and put down on paper 'ow much they cost, and Mrs. Mitchell said if George didn't like to remind 'im she would.

They left young Ted and Charlie to stay near the station when they got to the Palace, Uncle Joe 'aving forgotten to say where he'd meet 'em, but train arter train came in without 'im, and at last the two boys gave it up.

"We're sure to run across 'im sooner or later," ses Gerty. "Let's 'ave something to eat; I'm so hungry."

George said something about buns and milk, but Gerty took 'im up sharp. "Buns and milk?" she ses. "Why, uncle would never forgive us if we spoilt his treat like that."

She walked into a refreshment place and they 'ad cold meat and bread and pickles and beer and tarts and cheese, till even young Ted said he'd 'ad enough, but still they couldn't see any signs of Uncle Joe. They went on to the roundabouts to look for 'im, and then into all sorts o' shows at sixpence a head, but still there was no signs of 'im, and George 'ad to start on a fresh bit o' paper to put down wot he'd spent.

"I suppose he must ha' been detained on; important business," ses Gerty at last.

"Unless it's one of 'is jokes," ses Mrs. Mitchell, shaking her 'ead. "You know wot your uncle is, Gerty."

"There now, I never thought o' that," ses Gerty, with a start; "p'r'aps it is."

"*Joke?*" ses George, choking and staring from one to the other.

"I was wondering where he'd get the money from," ses Mrs. Mitchell to Gerty. "I see it all now; I never see such a man for a bit o' fun in all my born days. And the solemn way he went on last night, too. Why, he must ha' been laughing in 'is sleeve all the time. It's as good as a play."

"Look here!" ses George, 'ardly able to speak; "do you mean to tell me he never *meant* to come?"

"I'm afraid not," ses Mrs. Mitchell, "knowing wot he is. But don't you worry; I'll give him a bit o' my mind when I see 'im."

George Crofts felt as though he'd burst, and then 'e got his breath, and the things 'e said about Uncle Joe was so awful that Mrs. Mitchell told the boys to go away.

"How dare you talk of my uncle like that?" ses Gerty, firing up.

"You forget yourself, George," ses Mrs. Mitchell. "You'll like 'im when you get to know 'im better."

"Don't you call me George," ses George Crofts, turning on 'er. "I've been done, that's wot I've been. I 'ad fourteen pounds when I was paid off, and it's melting like butter."

"Well, we've enjoyed ourselves," ses Gerty, "and that's what money was given us for. I'm sure those two boys 'ave had a splendid time, thanks to you. Don't go and spoil all by a little bit o' temper."

"Temper!" ses George, turning on her. "I've done with you; I wouldn't marry you if you was the on'y gal in the world. I wouldn't marry you if you paid me."

"Oh, indeed!" ses Gerty; "but if you think you can get out of it like that you're mistaken. I've lost my young man through you, and I'm not going to lose you too. I'll send my two big cousins round to see you tomorrow."

"They won't put up with no nonsense, I can tell you," ses Mrs. Mitchell.

She called the boys to her, and then she and Gerty, arter holding their 'eads very high and staring at George, went off and left 'im alone. He went straight off 'ome, counting 'is money all the way and trying to make it more, and arter telling Bob 'ow he'd been treated, and trying hard to get 'im to go shares in his losses, packed up his things and cleared out, all boiling over with temper.

Bob was so dazed he couldn't make head or tail out of it, but 'e went round to see Gerty the first thing next morning, and she explained things to him.

"I don't know when I've enjoyed myself so much," she ses, wiping her eyes, "but I've had enough gadding about for once, and if you come round this evening we'll have a nice quiet time together looking at the furniture shops."

30

OVER THE SIDE

Of all classes of men, those who follow the sea are probably the most prone to superstition. Afloat upon the black waste of waters, at the mercy of wind and sea, with vast depths and strange creatures below them, a belief in the supernatural is easier than ashore, under the cheerful gas-lamps. Strange stories of the sea are plentiful, and an incident which happened within my own experience has made me somewhat chary of dubbing a man fool or coward because he has encountered something he cannot explain. There are stories of the supernatural with prosaic sequels; there are others to which the sequel has never been published.

I was fifteen years old at the time, and as my (father, who had a strong objection to the sea, would not apprentice me to it, I shipped before the mast on a sturdy little brig called the *Endeavour*, bound for Riga. She was a small craft, but the skipper was as fine a seaman as one could wish for, and in fine weather an easy man to sail under. Most boys have a rough time of it when they first go to sea, but with a strong sense of what was good for me, I had attached myself to a brawny, good-natured infant, named Bill Smith, and it was soon understood that whoever hit me struck Bill by proxy. Not that the crew were particularly brutal, but a sound cuffing occasionally is held by most seamen to be beneficial to a lad's health and morals. The only really spiteful fellow among them was a man named Jem Dadd. He was a morose, sallow-looking man of about forty, with a strong taste for the supernatural, and a stronger taste still for frightening his fellows with it. I have seen Bill almost afraid to go on deck of a night for his trick at the wheel, after a few of his reminiscences. Rats were a favourite topic with him, and he would never allow one to be killed if he could help it, for he claimed for them that they were the souls of drowned sailors, hence their love of ships and their habit of leaving them when they became unseaworthy. He was a firm believer in the transmigration of souls, some idea of which he had, no doubt, picked up in Eastern ports, and gave his shivering auditors to understand that his arrangements for his own immediate future were already perfected.

We were six or seven days out when a strange thing happened. Dadd had the second watch one night, and Bill was to relieve him. They were not very strict aboard the brig in fair weather, and when a man's time was up he just made the wheel fast, and, running for'ard, shouted down the fo'c's'le. On this night I happened to awake suddenly, in time to see Bill slip out of his bunk and stand by me, rubbing his red eyelids with his knuckles.

"Dadd's giving me a long time," he whispered, seeing that I was awake; "it's a whole hour after his time."

He pattered up on deck, and I was just turning over, thankful that I was too young to have a watch to keep, when he came softly down again and, taking me by the shoulders, shook me roughly.

"Jack," he whispered. "Jack."

I raised myself on my elbows, and, in the light of the smoking lamp, saw that he was shaking all over.

"Come on deck," he said thickly.

I put on my clothes and followed him quietly to the sweet, cool air above. It was a beautiful clear night, but, from his manner, I looked nervously around for some cause of alarm. I saw nothing. The deck was deserted, except for the solitary figure at the wheel.

"Look at him," whispered Bill, bending a contorted face to mine.

I walked aft a few steps, and Bill followed slowly. Then I saw that Jem Dadd was leaning forward clumsily on the wheel, with his hands clenched on the spokes.

"He's asleep," said I, stopping short.

Bill breathed hard. "He's in a queer sleep."

"Kind o' trance more like. Go closer."

I took fast hold of Bill's sleeve and we both went. The light of the stars was sufficient to show that Dadd's face was very white, and that his dim, black eyes were wide open, and staring in a very strange and dreadful manner straight before him.

"Dadd," said I softly, "Dadd!"

There was no reply, and, with a view of arousing him, I tapped one sinewy hand as it gripped the wheel, and even tried to loosen it.

He remained immovable, and, suddenly with a great cry, my courage deserted me and Bill and I fairly bolted down into the cabin and woke the skipper.

Then we saw how it was with Jem, and two strong seamen forcibly loosened the grip of those rigid fingers, and, laying him on the deck, covered him with a piece of canvas. The rest of the night two men stayed at the wheel, and, gazing fearfully at the outline of the canvas, longed for dawn.

It came at last and, breakfast over, the body was sewn up in canvas, and the skipper held a short service compiled from a Bible which belonged to the mate, and what he remembered of the Burial Service proper. Then the corpse went overboard with a splash, and the men, after standing awkwardly together for a few minutes, slowly dispersed to their duties.

For the rest of that day we were all very quiet and restrained; pity for the dead man being mingled with a dread of taking the wheel when night came.

"The wheel's haunted," said the cook solemnly; "mark my words, there's more of you will be took the same way Dadd was."

The cook, like myself, had no watch to keep.

The men bore up pretty well until night came on again, and then they unanimously resolved to have a double watch. The cook, sorely against his will, was impressed into the service, and I, glad to oblige my patron, agreed to stay up with Bill.

Some of the pleasure had vanished by the time night came, and I seemed only just to have closed my eyes when Bill came, and, with a rough shake or two, informed me that the time had come. Any hope that I might have had of escaping the ordeal was at once dispelled by his expectant demeanour, and the helpful way in which he assisted me with my clothes, and, yawning terribly, I followed him on deck.

The night was not so clear as the preceding one, and the air was chilly, with a little moisture in it. I buttoned up my jacket, and thrust my hands in my pockets.

"Everything quiet?" asked Bill as he stepped up and took the wheel.

"Aye, aye," said Roberts, "quiet as the grave, and, followed by his willing mate, he went below.

I sat on the deck by Bill's side as, with a light touch on the wheel, he kept the brig to her course. It was weary work sitting there, doing nothing, and thinking of the warm berth below, and I believe that I should have fallen asleep, but that my watchful companion stirred me with his foot whenever he saw me nodding.

I suppose I must have sat there, shivering and yawning, for about an hour, when, tired of inactivity, I got up and went and leaned over the side of the vessel. The sound of the water gurgling and lapping by was so soothing that I began to doze.

I was recalled to my senses by a smothered cry from Bill, and, running to him, I found him staring to port in a very intense and uncomfortable fashion. At my approach he took one hand from the wheel, and gripped my arm so tightly that I was like to have screamed with the pain of it.

"Jack," said he in a shaky voice, "while you was away something popped its head up and looked over the ship's side."

"You've been dreaming," said I, in a voice that was a very fair imitation of Bill's own.

"Dreaming," repeated Bill, "dreaming! Ah, *look there!*"

He pointed with outstretched finger, and my heart seemed to stop beating as I saw a man's head appear above the side. For a brief space it peered at us in silence, and then a dark figure sprang like a cat on to the deck, and stood crouching a short distance away.

A mist came before my eyes, and my tongue failed me, but Bill let off a roar, such as I have never heard before or since. It was answered from below, both aft and for'ard, and the men came running up on deck just as they left their beds.

"What's up?" shouted the skipper, glancing aloft.

For answer, Bill pointed to the intruder, and the men, who had just caught sight of him, came up and formed a compact knot by the wheel.

"Come over the side, it did," panted Bill "come over like a ghost out of the sea."

The skipper took one of the small lamps from the binnacle, and, holding it aloft, walked boldly up to the cause of alarm. In the little patch of light we saw a ghastly black-bearded man, dripping with water, regarding us with unwinking eyes, which glowed red in the light of the lamp.

"Where did you come from?" asked the skipper.

The figure shook its head.

"Where did you come from?" he repeated, walking up, and laying his hand on the other's shoulder.

Then the intruder spoke, but in a strange fashion and in strange words. We leaned forward to listen, but even when he repeated them, we could make nothing of them.

"He's a furriner," said Roberts.

"Blest if I've ever 'eard the lingo afore," said Bill. "Does anybody rekernize it?"

Nobody did, and the skipper, after another attempt, gave it up, and falling back upon the universal language of signs, pointed first to the man and then to the sea. The other understood him, and, in a heavy, slovenly fashion, portrayed a man drifting in an open boat, and clutching and clambering up the side of a passing ship. As his meaning dawned upon us, we rushed to the stern, and, leaning over, peered into the gloom, but the night was dark, and we saw nothing.

"Well," said the skipper, turning to Bill, with a mighty yawn, "take him below, and give him some grub, and the next time a gentleman calls on you, don't make such a confounded row about it."

He went below, followed by the mate, and after some slight hesitation, Roberts stepped up to the intruder, and signed to him to follow. He came stolidly enough, leaving a trail of water on the deck, and, after changing into the dry things we gave him, fell to, but without much appearance of hunger, upon some salt beef and biscuit, regarding us between bites with black, lacklustre eyes.

"He seems as though he's a-walking in his sleep," said the cook.

"He ain't very hungry," said one of the men; "he seems to mumble his food."

"Hungry!" repeated Bill, who had just left the wheel. "Course he ain't famished. He had his tea last night."

The man stared at him in bewilderment.

"Don't you see?" said Bill, still in a hoarse whisper; "ain't you ever seen them eyes afore? Don't you know what he used to say about dying? It's Jem Dadd come back to us. Jem Dadd got another man's body, as he always said he would."

"Rot!" said Roberts, trying to speak bravely, but he got up, and, with the others, huddled together at the end of the fo'c's'le and stared in a bewildered fashion at the sodden face and short squat figure of our visitor. For his part, having finished his meal, he pushed his plate from him, and, leaning back on the locker, looked at the empty bunks.

Roberts caught his eye, and, with a nod and a wave of his hand, indicated the bunks. The fellow rose from the locker and, amid a breathless silence, climbed into one of them—Jem Dadd's!

He slept in the dead sailor's bed that night, the only man in the fo'c's'le who did sleep properly, and turned out heavily and lumpishly in the morning for breakfast.

The skipper had him on deck after the meal, but could make nothing of him. To all his questions he replied in the strange tongue of the night before, and, though our fellows had been to many ports, and knew a word or two of several languages, none of them recognised it. The skipper gave it up at last, and, left to himself, he stared about him for some time, regardless of our interest in his movements, and then, leaning heavily against the side of the ship, stayed there so long that we thought he must have fallen asleep.

"He's half dead *now*!" whispered Roberts.

"Hush!" said Bill, "mebbe he's been in the water a week or two, and can't quite make it out. See how he's looking at it now."

He stayed on deck all day in the sun, but, as night came on, returned to the warmth of the fo'c's'le. The food we gave him remained untouched, and he took little or no notice of us, though I fancied that he saw the fear we had of him. He slept again in the dead man's bunk, and when morning came still lay there.

Until dinnertime nobody interfered with him, and then Roberts, pushed forward by the others, approached him with some food. He motioned it away with a dirty, bloated hand, and, making signs for water, drank it eagerly.

For two days he stayed there quietly, the black eyes always open, the stubby fingers always on the move. On the third morning Bill, who had conquered his fear sufficiently to give him water occasionally, called softly to us.

"Come and look at him," said he. "What's the matter with him?"

"He's dying!" said the cook, with a shudder.

"He can't be going to die *yet*!" said Bill blankly.

As he spoke the man's eyes seemed to get softer and more life-like, and he looked at us piteously and helplessly. From face to face he gazed in mute inquiry, and then, striking his chest feebly with his fist, uttered two words.

We looked at each other blankly, and he repeated them eagerly, and again touched chest.

"It's his name," said the cook, and we all repeated them.

He smiled in an exhausted fashion, and then, rallying his energies, held up a forefinger; as we stared at this new riddle, he lowered it, and held up all four fingers, doubled.

"Come away," quavered the cook; "he's putting a spell on us."

We drew back at that, and back farther still, as he repeated the motions. Then Bill's face cleared suddenly, and he stepped towards him.

"He means his wife and younkers!" he shouted eagerly. "This ain't no Jem Dadd!"

It was good then to see how our fellows drew round the dying sailor, and strove to cheer him. Bill, to show he understood the finger business, nodded cheerily, and held his hand at four different heights from the floor. The last was very low, so low that the man set his lips together, and strove to turn his heavy head from us.

"Poor devil!" said Bill, "he wants us to tell his wife and children what's become of him. He must ha' been dying when he come aboard. What was his name, again?"

But the name was not easy to English lips and we had already forgotten it.

"Ask him again," said the cook, "and write it down. Who's got a pen?"

He went to look for one as Bill turned to the sailor to get him to repeat it. Then he turned round again, and eyed us blankly, for, by this time, the owner had himself forgotten it.

31

FOUR PIGEON

The old man took up his mug and shifted along the bench until he was in the shade of the elms that stood before the "Cauliflower." The action also had the advantage of bringing him opposite the two strangers who were refreshing themselves after the toils of a long walk in the sun.

"My hearing ain't wot it used to be," he said tremulously. "When you asked me to have a mug o' ale just now I 'ardly heard you; and if you was to ask me to 'ave another I mightn't hear you at all."

One of the men nodded.

"Not over there," piped the old man. "That's why I come over here," he added after a pause. It 'ud be rude like to take no notice; if you was to ask me."

He looked round as the landlord approached, and pushed his mug gently in his direction. The landlord, obeying a nod from the second stranger, filled it.

"It puts life into me," said the old man, raising it to his lips and bowing. "It makes me talk."

"Time we were moving, Jack," said the first traveller hastily. The second, assenting to this as an abstract proposition, expressed, however, a determination to finish his pipe first.

I heard you saying something about shooting, continued the old man, and that reminds me of some shooting we 'ad here once in Claybury. We've always 'ad a lot 'o game in these parts, and if it wasn't for a low, poaching fellow named Bob Pretty—Claybury's disgrace I call 'im—we'd 'ave a lot more.

It happened in this way. Squire Rockett was going abroad to foreign parts for a year, and he let the Hall to a gentleman from London named Sutton. A real gentleman 'e was, open-'anded and free, and just about October he 'ad a lot of 'is friends come down from London to 'elp 'im kill the pheasants.

The first day they frightened more than they killed, but they enjoyed theirselves all right until one gentleman, who 'adn't shot a single thing all day, shot pore Bill Chambers, wot was beating with about a dozen more.

Bill got most of it in the shoulder and a little in the cheek, but the row he see fit to make you'd ha' thought he'd been killed. He laid on the ground groaning with 'is eyes shut, and everybody thought 'e was dying till Henery Walker stooped down and asked 'im whether 'e was hurt.

It took four men to carry Bill 'ome, and he was that particular you wouldn't believe. They 'ad to talk in whispers, and when Peter Gubbins forgot 'imself and began to whistle he asked him where his 'art was. When they walked fast he said they jolted 'im, and when they walked slow 'e asked 'em whether they'd gone to sleep or wot.

Bill was in bed for nearly a week, but the gentleman was very nice about it and said that it was his fault. He was a very pleasant-spoken gentleman, and, arter sending Dr. Green to him and saying he'd pay the bill, 'e gave Bill Chambers ten pounds to make up for 'is sufferings.

Bill 'ad intended to lay up for another week, and the doctor, wot 'ad been calling twice a day, said he wouldn't be responsible for 'is life if he didn't but the ten pounds was too much for 'im, and one evening, just a week arter the accident, he turned up at this "Cauliflower" public-'ouse and began to spend 'is money.

His face was bandaged up, and when'e come in he walked feeble-like and hardly spoke above a w'isper. Smith, the landlord, got 'im a easy chair, and a couple of pillers out o' the parlour, and Bill sat there like a king, telling us all about his sufferings and wot it felt like to be shot.

I always have said wot a good thing beer is, and it done Bill more good than doctor's medicine. When he came in he could 'ardly crawl, and at nine o'clock 'e was out of that easy chair and dancing on the table as well as possible. He smashed three mugs and upset about two pints o' beer, but he just put his 'and in his pocket and paid for 'em without a word.

"There's plenty more where that came from," he ses, pulling out a handful o' money.

Peter Gubbins looked at it, 'ardly able to speak. "It's worth while being shot to 'ave all that money," he ses at last.

"Don't you worry yourself, Peter," ses Bob Pretty; "there's plenty more of you as'll be shot afore them gentlemen at the Hall 'as finished. Bill's the fust, but 'e won't be the last—not by a long chalk."

"They're more careful now," ses Dicky Weed, the tailor.

"All right; 'ave it your own way," ses Bob, nasty-like. "I don't know much about shooting, being on'y a pore labourin' man. All I know is I shouldn't like to go beating for them. I'm too fond o' my wife and family."

"There won't be no more shot," ses Sam Jones, off-hand like.

"We're too careful," ses Peter Gubbins.

"Bob Pretty don't know everything," ses Dicky Weed.

"I'll bet you what you like there'll be some more of you shot," ses Bob Pretty, in a temper. "Now, then."

"'Ow much'll you bet, Bob," ses Sam Jones, with a wink at the others.

"I can see you winking, Sam Jones," ses Bob Pretty, "but I'll do more than bet—the last bet I won is still owing to me. Now, look 'ere, I'll back my opinion: I'll pay you sixpence a week all the time you're beating if you promise to give me arf of wot you get if you're shot. I can't say fairer than that."

"Will you give me sixpence a week, too?" ses Henery Walker, jumping up.

"I will," ses Bob; "and anybody else that likes. And wot's more, I'll pay in advance. Fust sixpences now."

Claybury men 'ave never been backward when there's been money to be made easy, and they all wanted to join Bob Pretty's club, as he called it. But fust of all 'e asked for a pen and ink, and then he got Smith, the landlord, being a scholard, to write out a paper for them to sign. Henery Walker was the fust to write 'is name, and then Sam Jones, Peter Gubbins, Ralph Thomson, Jem Hall, and Walter Bell wrote theirs. Bob stopped 'em then, and said six 'ud be enough to go on with; and then 'e paid up the sixpences and wished 'em luck.

O' course they was glad of the money but wot they liked a'most as well as the sixpences was the idea o' getting the better o' Bob Pretty. As I said afore, he was a poacher, and that artful that up to that time nobody 'ad ever got the better of 'im.

They made so much fun of 'im the next night that Bob turned sulky and went off 'ome, and for two or three nights he 'ardly showed his face; and the next shoot they 'ad he went off to Wickham and nobody saw 'im all day.

That very day Henery Walker was shot. Several gentlemen fired at a rabbit that was started, and the next thing they knew Henery Walker was lying on the ground calling out that 'is leg 'ad been shot off.

He made more fuss than Bill Chambers a'most—'specially when they dropped 'im off a hurdle carrying him 'ome—and the things he said to Dr. Green for rubbing his 'ands as he came into the bedroom was disgraceful.

The fust Bob Pretty 'eard of it was up at the "Cauliflower" at eight o'clock that evening, and he set down 'is beer and set off to see Henery as fast as 'is legs could carry 'im. Henery was asleep when 'e got there, and, do all he could, Bob Pretty couldn't wake 'im till he sat down gentle on 'is bad leg.

"It'son'y me, old pal," he ses, smiling at 'im as Henery woke and screamed at 'im to get up.

Henery Walker was going to say something bad, but 'e thought better of it, and he lay there arf busting with rage, and watching Bob out of the corner of one eye.

"I quite forgot you was on my club till Smith reminded me of it," ses Bob. "Don't you take a farthing less than ten pounds, Henery."

Henery Walker shut his eyes again. "I forgot to tell you I made up my mind this morning not to belong to your club anymore, Bob," he ses.

"Why didn't you come and tell me, Henery, instead of leaving it till it was too late?" ses Bob, shaking 'is head at 'im.

"I shall want all that money," ses Henery in a weak voice. "I might 'ave to have a wooden leg, Bob."

"Don't meet troubles arf way, Henery," ses Bob in a kind voice. "I've no doubt Mr. Sutton'll throw in a wooden leg if you want it, and look here: if he does, I won't trouble you for my arf of it."

He said good night to Henery and went off, and when Mrs. Walker went up to see 'ow Henery was getting on he was carrying on that alarming that she couldn't do nothing with 'im.

He was laid up for over a week, though it's my opinion he wasn't much hurt, and the trouble was that nobody knew which gentleman 'ad shot 'im. Mr. Sutton talked it over with them, and at last, arter a good deal 'o trouble, and Henery pulling up 'is trousers and showing them 'is leg till they was fair sick of the sight of it, they paid 'im ten pounds, the same as they 'ad Bill.

It took Bob Pretty two days to get his arf, but he kept very quiet about it, not wishing to make a fuss in the village for fear Mr. Sutton should get to hear of the club. At last he told Henery Walker that 'e was going to Wickham to see 'is lawyer about it, and arter Smith the landlord 'ad read the paper to Henery and explained 'ow he'd very likely 'ave to pay more than the whole ten pounds then, 'e gave Bob his arf and said he never wanted to see 'im again as long as he lived.

Bob stood treat up at the "Cauliflower" that night, and complained of 'ow bad he'd been treated. The tears stood in 'is eyes a'most, and at last 'e said that if 'e thought there was going to be anymore fuss of that kind he'd wind up the club.

"It's the best thing you can do," ses Sam Jones; "I'm not going to belong to it any longer, so I give you notice. If so be as I get shot I want the money for myself."

"Me, too," ses Peter Gubbins; "it 'ud fair break my 'art to give Bob Pretty five pounds. Why, I'd sooner give it to my wife."

All the other chaps said the same thing, but Bob pointed out to them that they 'ad taken their sixpences on'y the night afore, and they must stay in for the week. He said that was the law. Some of 'em talked about giving 'im 'is sixpences back, but Bob said if they did they must pay up all the sixpences they had 'ad for three weeks. The end of it was they said they'd stay in for that week and not a moment longer.

The next day Sam Jones and Peter Gubbins altered their minds. Sam found a couple o' shillings that his wife 'ad hidden in her Sunday bonnet, and Peter Gubbins opened 'is boy's money-box to see 'ow much there was in it. They came up to the "Cauliflower" to pay Bob their eighteenpences, but he wasn't there, and when they went to his 'ouse Mrs. Pretty said as 'ow he'd gone off to Wickham and wouldn't be back till Saturday. So they 'ad to spend the money on beer instead.

That was on Tuesday, and things went on all right till Friday, when Mr. Sutton 'ad another shoot. The birds was getting scarce and the gentlemen that anxious to shoot them there was no 'olding them. Once or twice the keepers spoke to 'em about carefulness, and said wot large families they'd got, but it wasn't much good. They went on blazing away, and just at the corner of the wood Sam Jones and Peter Gubbins was both hit; Sam in the leg and Peter in the arm.

The noise that was made was awful; everybody shouting that they 'adn't done it, and all speaking at once, and Mr. Sutton was dancing about a'most beside 'imself with rage. Pore Sam and Peter was 'elped along by the others; Sam being carried and Peter led, and both of 'em with the idea of getting all they could out of it, making such 'orrible noises that Mr. Sutton couldn't hear 'imself calling his friends names.

"There seems to be wounded men calling out all over the place," he ses, stamping his foot.

"I think there *is* another one over there, sir," ses one o' the keepers, pointing.

Sam Jones and Peter Gubbins both left off to listen, and then they all heard it distinctly. A dreadful noise it was, and when Mr. Sutton and one or two more follered it up they found poor Walter Bell lying on 'is face in a bramble.

"Wot's the matter?" ses Mr. Sutton, shouting at 'im. "Wot are you making that noise for?"

"I've been shot from behind," ses Walter. "I'd got something in my boot, and I was just stooping down to fasten it up agin when I got it."

"But there oughtn't to be anybody *here*," ses Mr. Sutton to one of the keepers.

"They get all over the place, sir," ses the keeper, scratching his 'ead. "I fancied I 'eard a gun go off here a minute or two arter the others was shot."

"I believe he's done it' imself," says Mr. Sutton, dancing with rage.

"I don't see 'ow he could, sir," ses the keeper, touching his cap and looking at Walter, as was still lying with 'is face on 'is arms.

They carried Walter 'ome that way on a hurdle, and Dr. Green spent all the rest o' that day picking shots out o' them three men and telling 'em to keep still. He 'ad to do Sam Jones by candlelight, with Mrs. Jones 'olding the candle with one hand and crying with the other. Twice the doctor told her to keep steady, and poor Sam 'ad only just passed the remark, "How 'ot it was for October," when they discovered that the bed was on fire.

Sam didn't give no trouble. He got off of the bed by 'imself, and, when it was all over and the fire put out, the doctor found him sitting on the stairs with the leg of a broken chair in 'is hand calling for 'is wife.

Of course, there was a terrible to-do about it in Claybury, and up at the Hall, too. All of the gentlemen said as 'ow they hadn't done it, and Mr. Sutton was arf crazy with rage. He said that they 'ad made 'im the laughing stock of the neighbourhood, and that they oughtn't to shoot with anything but pop-guns. They got to such high words over it that two of the gentlemen went off 'ome that very night.

There was a lot of talk up at the "Cauliflower," too, and more than one pointed out 'ow lucky Bob Pretty was in getting four men out of the six in his club. As I said afore, Bob was away at the time, but he came back the next night and we 'ad the biggest row here you could wish for to see.

Henery Walker began it. "I s'pose you've 'eard the dreadful news, Bob Pretty?" he ses, looking at 'im.

"I 'ave," ses Bob; "and my 'art bled for 'em. I told you wot those gentlemen was like, didn't I? But none of you would believe me. Now you can see as I was right."

"It's very strange," ses Henery Walker, looking round; "it's very strange that all of us wot's been shot belonged to Bob Pretty's precious club."

“It’s my luck, Henery,” ses Bob. “I always was lucky from a child.”

“And I s’pose you think you’re goin to ’ave arf of the money they get?” ses Henery Walker.

“Don’t talk about money while them pore chaps is suffering,” ses Bob. “I’m surprised at you, Henery.”

“You won’t ’ave a farthing of it,” ses Henery Walker, shaking ’is fist at him; “and wot’s more, Bob Pretty, I’m going to ’ave my five pounds back.”

“Don’t you believe it, Henery,” ses Bob, smiling at ’im.

“I’m going to ’ave my five pounds back,” ses Henery, *“and you know why.* I know wot your club was for now, and we was all a pack o’ silly fools not to see it afore.”

“Speak for yourself, Henery,” ses Jem Hall, who thought Henery was looking at ’im.

“I’ve been putting two and two together,” ses Henery, looking round, “and it’s as plain as the nose on your face. Bob Pretty hid up in the wood and shot us all himself!”

For a moment you might ’ave heard a pin drop, and then there was such a noise nobody could hear theirselves speak. Everybody was shouting his ’ardest, and the on’y quiet one there was Bob Pretty ’imself.

“Poor Henery; he’s gorn crazy,” he ses, shaking his ’ead.

“You’re a murderer,” ses Ralph Thomson, shaking ’is fist at him.

“Henery Walker’s gorn crazy,” ses Bob agin. “Why, I ain’t been near the place. There’s a dozen men’ll swear that I was at Wickham each time these misfortunate accidents ’appened.”

“Men like you, they’d swear anything for a pot o’ beer,” ses Henery. “But I’m not going to waste time talking to you, Bob Pretty. I’m going straight off to tell Mr. Sutton.”

“I shouldn’t do that if I was you, Henery,” ses Bob.

“I dessay,” ses Henery Walker; “but then you see I am.”

"I thought you'd gorn mad, Henery," ses Bob, taking a drink o' beer that somebody 'ad left on the table by mistake, "and now I'm sure of it. Why, if you tell Mr. Sutton that it wasn't his friends that shot them pore fellers, he won't pay them anything. 'Taint likely 'e would, is it?"

Henery Walker, wot 'ad been standing up looking fierce at 'im, sat down agin, struck all of a heap.

"And he might want your ten pounds back, Henery," said Bob in a soft voice. "And seeing as 'ow you was kind enough to give five to me, and spent most of the other, it 'ud come 'ard on you, wouldn't it? Always think afore you speak, Henery. I always do."

Henery Walker got up and tried to speak, but 'e couldn't, and he didn't get 'is breath back till Bob said it was plain to see that he 'adn't got a word to say for 'imself. Then he shook 'is fist at Bob and called 'im a low, thieving, poaching murderer.

"You're not yourself, Henery," ses Bob. "When you come round you'll be sorry for trying to take away the character of a pore labourin' man with a ailing wife and a large family. But if you take my advice you won't say anything more about your wicked ideas; if you do, these pore fellers won't get a farthing. And you'd better keep quiet about the club, mates, for their sakes. Other people might get the same crazy ideas in their silly 'eads as Henery. Keepers especially."

That was on'y common sense; but, as John Biggs said, it did seem 'ard to think as 'ow Bob Pretty should be allowed to get off scot-free, and with Henery Walker's five pounds too. "There's one thing," he ses to Bob; "you won't 'ave any of these other pore chaps' money; and, if they're men, they ought to make it up to Henery Walker for the money he 'as saved 'em by finding you out."

"They've got to pay me fust," ses Bob. "I'm a pore man, but I'll stick up for my rights. As for me shooting 'em, they'd ha' been 'urt a good deal more if I'd done it—especially Mr. Henery Walker. Why, they're hardly 'urt at all."

"Don't answer 'im, Henery," ses John Biggs. "You save your breath to go and tell Sam Jones and the others about it. It'll cheer 'em up."

"And tell 'em about my arf, in case they get too cheerful and go overdoing it," ses Bob Pretty, stopping at the door. "Good night, all."

Nobody answered 'im; and arter waiting a little bit Henery Walker set off to see Sam Jones and the others. John Biggs was quite right about its making 'em cheerful, but they see as plain as Bob 'imself that it 'ad got to be kept quiet. "Till we've spent the money, at any rate," ses Walter Bell; "then p'r'aps Mr. Sutton might get Bob locked up for it."

Mr. Sutton went down to see 'em all a day or two arterwards. The shooting-party was broken up and gone 'ome, but they left some money behind 'em. Ten pounds each they was to 'ave, same as the others, but Mr. Sutton said that he 'ad heard 'ow the other money was wasted at the "Cauliflower," and 'e was going to give it out to 'em ten shillings a week until the money was gorn. He 'ad to say it over and over agin afore they understood 'im, and Walter Bell 'ad to stuff the bedclo'es in 'is mouth to keep civil.

Peter Gubbins, with 'is arm tied up in a sling, was the fust one to turn up at the "Cauliflower," and he was that down'arted about it we couldn't do nothing with 'im. He 'ad expected to be able to pull out ten golden sovereigns, and the dis-app'intment was too much for 'im.

"I wonder 'ow they heard about it," ses Dicky Weed.

"I can tell you," ses Bob Pretty, wot 'ad been sitting up in a corner by himself, nodding and smiling at Peter, wot wouldn't look at 'im. "A friend 'o mine at Wickham wrote to him about it. He was so disgusted at the way Bill Chambers and Henery Walker come up 'ere wasting their 'ard-earned money, that he sent 'im a letter, signed 'A Friend of the Working Man,' telling 'im about it and advising 'im what to do."

"A friend o' yours?" ses John Biggs, staring at'im. "What for?"

"I don't know," ses Bob; "he's a wunnerful good scholard, and he likes writin' letters. He's going to write another tomorrer, unless I go over and stop 'im."

"Another?" ses Peter, who 'ad been tellin' everybody that e' wouldn't speak to 'im agin as long as he lived. "Wot about?"

"About the idea that I shot you all," ses Bob. "I want my character cleared. O' course, they can't prove anything against me—I've got my witnesses. But, taking one thing with another, I see now that it does look suspicious, and I don't suppose any of you'll get anymore of your money. Mr. Sutton is so sick o' being laughed at, he'll jump at anything."

"You dursn't do it, Bob," ses Peter, all of a tremble.

"It ain't me, Peter, old pal," ses Bob, "it's my friend. But I don't mind stopping 'im for the sake of old times if I get my arf. He'd listen to me, I feel sure."

At fust Peter said he wouldn't get a farthing out of 'im if his friend wrote letters till Doomsday; but by and by he thought better of it, and asked Bob to stay there while he went down to see Sam and Walter about it. When 'e came back he'd got the fust week's money for Bob Pretty; but he said he left Walter Bell carrying on like a madman, and, as for Sam Jones, he was that upset 'e didn't believe he'd last out the night.

32

THE TEMPTATION OF SAMUEL BURGE

Mr. Higgs, jeweller, sat in the small parlour behind his shop, gazing hungrily at a supper-table which had been laid some time before. It was a quarter to ten by the small brass clock on the mantelpiece, and the jeweller rubbing his hands over the fire tried in vain to remember what etiquette had to say about starting a meal before the arrival of an expected guest.

"He must be coming by the last train after all, sir," said the housekeeper, entering the room and glancing at the clock. "I suppose these London gentlemen keep such late hours they don't understand us country folk wanting to get to bed in decent time. You must be wanting your supper, sir."

Mr. Higgs sighed. "I shall be glad of my supper," he said slowly, "but I dare say our friend is hungrier still. Travelling is hungry work."

"Perhaps he is thinking over his words for the seventh day," said the housekeeper solemnly. "Forgetting hunger and thirst and all our poor earthly feelings in the blessedness of his work."

"Perhaps so," assented the other, whose own earthly feelings were particularly strong just at that moment.

"Brother Simpson used to forget all about meal-times when he stayed here," said the housekeeper, clasping her hands. "He used to sit by the window with his eyes half closed and shake his head at the smell from the kitchen and call it fleshpots of Egypt. He said that if it wasn't for keeping up his strength for the work, luscious bread and fair water was all he wanted. I expect Brother Burge will be a similar sort of man."

"Brother Clark wrote and told me that he only lives for his work," said the jeweller, with another glance at the clock. "The chapel at Clerkenwell is crowded to hear him. It's a blessed favour and privilege to have such a selected instrument staying in the house. I'm curious to see him; from what Brother Clark said I rather fancy that he was a little bit wild in his younger days."

"Hallelujah!" exclaimed the housekeeper with fervour. "I mean, to think as he's seen the error of his ways," she added sharply, as her master looked up.

"There he is," said the latter, as the bell rang.

The housekeeper went to the side-door, and drawing back the bolt admitted the gentleman whose preaching had done so much for the small but select sect known as the Seventh Day Primitive Apostles. She came back into the room followed by a tall stout man, whose upper lip and short stubby beard streaked with grey seemed a poor match for the beady eyes which lurked behind a pair of clumsy spectacles.

"Brother Samuel Burge?" inquired the jeweller, rising.

The visitor nodded, and regarding him with a smile charged with fraternal love, took his hand in a huge grip and shook it fervently.

"I am glad to see you, Brother Higgs," he said, regarding him fondly. "Oh, 'ow my eyes have yearned to be set upon you! Oh, 'ow my ears 'ave longed to hearken unto the words of your voice!"

He breathed thickly, and taking a seat sat with his hands upon his knees, looking at a fine piece of cold beef which the housekeeper had just placed upon the table.

"Is Brother Clark well?" inquired the jeweller, placing a chair for him at the table and taking up his carving-knife.

"Dear Brother Clark is in excellent 'ealth, I thank you," said the other, taking the proffered chair. "Oh! What a man he is; what a instrument for good. Always stretching out them blessed hands of 'is to make one of the fallen a Seventh Day Primitive."

"And success attends his efforts?" said the jeweller.

"Success, Brother!" repeated Mr. Burge, eating rapidly and gesticulating with his knife. "Success ain't no name for it. Why, since this day last week he has saved three pickpockets, two Salvationists, one bigamist and a Roman Catholic."

Brother Higgs murmured his admiration. "You are also a power for good," he said wistfully. "Brother Clark tells me in his letter that your exhortations have been abundantly blessed."

Mr. Burge shook his head. "A lot of it falls by the wayside," he said modestly, "but some of it is an eye-opener to them as don't entirely shut their ears. Only the day before yesterday I 'ad two jemmies and a dark lantern sent me with a letter saying as 'ow the owner had no further use for 'em."

The jeweller's eyes glistened with admiration not quite untinged with envy. "Have you expounded the Word for long?" he inquired.

"Six months," replied the other. "It come to me quite natural—I was on the penitent bench on the Saturday, and the Wednesday afterwards I preached as good a sermon as ever I've preached in my life. Brother Clark said it took 'is breath away."

"Andhe's a judge, too," said the admiring jeweller.

"Now," continued Brother Burge, helping himself plentifully to pickled walnuts. "Now there ain't standing room in our Bethel when I'm expounding. People come to hear me from all parts—old and young—rich and poor—and the Apostles that don't come early 'ave to stand outside and catch the crumbs I throw 'em through the winders."

"It is enough," sighed Brother Higgs, whose own audience was frequently content to be on the wrong side of the window, "it is enough to make a man vain."

"I struggle against it, Brother," said Mr. Burge, passing his cup up for some more tea. "I fight against it hard, but once the Evil One was almost too much for me; and in spite of myself, and knowing besides that it was a plot of 'is, I nearly felt uplifted."

Brother Higgs, passing him some more beef, pressed for details.

"He sent me two policemen," replied the other, scowling darkly at the meanness of the trick. "One I might 'ave stood, but two come to being pretty near too much for me. They sat under me while I gave 'em the Word 'ot and strong, and the feeling I had standing up there and telling policemen what they ought to do I shall never forget."

"But why should policemen make you proud?" asked the puzzled listener.

Mr. Burge looked puzzled in his turn. "Why, hasn't Brother Clark told you about me?" he inquired.

Mr. Higgs shook his head. "He sort of—suggested that—that you had been a little bit wild before you came to us," he murmured apologetically.

"A—little—bit—wild?" repeated Brother Burge, in horrified accents. "Me?—A little bit *wild?*"

"No doubt he exaggerated a little," said the jeweller hurriedly. "Being such a good man himself, no doubt things would seem wild to him that wouldn't to us—to me, I mean."

"A little bit wild," said his visitor again. "Sam Burge, the Converted Burglar, a little bit *wild*. Well, well!"

"Converted *what*?" shouted the jeweller, half rising from his chair.

"Burglar," said the other shortly. "Why, I should think I know more about the inside o' gaols than anybody in England; I've pretty near killed three policemen, besides breaking a gent's leg and throwing a footman out of window, and then Brother Clark goes and says I've been a little bit wild. I wonder what he would 'ave?"

"But you—you've quite reformed now?" said the jeweller, resuming his seat and making a great effort to hide his consternation.

"I 'ope so," said Mr. Burge, with alarming humility; "but it's an uncertain world, and far be it from me to boast. That's why I've come here."

Mr. Higgs, only half comprehending, sat back gasping.

"If I can stand this," pursued Brother Burge, gesticulating wildly in the direction of the shop, "if I can stand being here with all these 'ere pretty little things to be 'ad for the trouble of picking of 'em up, I can stand anything. Tempt me, I says to Brother Clark. Put me in the way o' temptation, I says. Let me see whether the Evil One or me is the strongest; let me 'ave a good old up and down with the Powers o' Darkness, and see who wins."

Mr. Higgs, gripping the edge of the table with both hands, gazed at this new Michael in speechless consternation.

"I think I see his face now," said Brother Burge, with tender enthusiasm. "All in a glow it was, and he patted me on the shoulder and says, 'I'll send you on a week's mission to Duncombe,' he says, and 'you shall stop with Brother Higgs who 'as a shop full o' cunning wrought vanities in silver and gold.'"

"But suppose," said the jeweller, finding his voice by a great effort, "suppose victory is not given unto you."

"It won't make any difference," replied his visitor. "Brother Clark promised that it shouldn't. ' If you fall, Brother,' he says, 'we'll help you up again. When you are tired of sin come back to us—there's always a welcome.'"

"But—" began the dismayed jeweller.

"We can only do our best," said Brother Burge, "the rest we must leave. I 'ave girded my loins for the fray, and taken much spiritual sustenance on the way down from this little hymn-book."

Mr. Higgs paid no heed. He sat marvelling over the fatuousness of Brother Clark and trying to think of ways and means out of the dilemma into which that gentleman's perverted enthusiasm had placed him. He wondered whether it would be possible to induce Brother Burge to sleep elsewhere by offering to bear his hotel expenses, and at last, after some hesitation, broached the subject.

"What!" exclaimed the other, pushing his plate from him and regarding him with great severity. "Go and sleep at a hotel? After Brother Clark has been and took all this trouble? Why, I wouldn't think of doing such a thing."

"Brother Clark has no right to expose you to such a temptation," said Mr. Higgs with great warmth.

"I wonder what he'd say if he 'eard you," remarked Mr. Burge sternly. "After his going and making all these arrangements, for you to try and go and upset 'em. To ask me to shun the fight like a coward; to ask *me* to go and hide in the rear-ranks in a hotel with everything locked up, or a Coffee Pallis with nothing to steal."

"I should sleep far more comfortably if I knew that you were not undergoing this tremendous strain," said the unhappy Mr. Higgs, "and besides that, if you did give way, it would be a serious business for me—that's what I want you to look at. I am afraid that if—if unhappily you did fall, I couldn't prevent you."

"I'm sure you couldn't," said the other cordially. "That's the beauty of it; that's where the Evil One's whispers get louder and louder. Why, I could choke you between my finger and thumb. If unfortunately our fallen nature should be too strong for me, don't interfere whatever you do. I mightn't be myself."

Mr. Higgs rose and faced him gasping. "Not even—call for—the police—I suppose," he jerked out.

"That would be interfering," said Brother Burge coldly.

The jeweller tried to think. It was past eleven. The housekeeper had gone to spend the night with an ailing sister, and a furtive glance at Brother Burge's small shifty eyes and fat unwholesome face was sufficient to deter him from leaving him alone with his property, while he went to ask the police to give an eye to his house for the night. Besides, it was more than probable that Mr. Burge would decline to allow such a proceeding. With a growing sense of his peril he resolved to try flattery.

"It was a great thing for the Brethren to secure a man like you," he said.

"I never thought they'd ha' done it," said Mr. Burge frankly. "I've 'ad all sorts trying to convert me; crying over me and praying over me. I remember the first dear good man that called me a lorst lamb. He didn't say anything else for a month."

"So upset," hazarded the jeweller.

"I broke his jor, pore feller," said Brother Burge, a sad but withal indulgent smile lighting up his face at the vagaries of his former career. "What time do you go to bed, Brother?"

"Any time," said the other reluctantly. "I suppose you are tired with your journey?"

Mr. Burge assented, and rising from his chair yawned loudly and stretched himself. In the small room with his huge arms raised he looked colossal.

"I suppose," said the jeweller, still seeking to reassure himself, "I suppose dear Brother Clark felt pretty certain of you, else he wouldn't have sent you here?"

"Brother Clark said 'What is a jeweller's shop compared with a 'uman soul, a priceless 'uman soul?'" replied Mr. Burge. "What is a few gew-gaws to decorate them that perish, and make them vain, when you come to consider the opportunity of such a trial, and the good it'll do and the draw it'll be—if I do win—and testify to the congregation to that effect? Why, there's sermons for a lifetime in it."

"So there is," said the jeweller, trying to look cheerful. "You've got a good face, Brother Burge, and you'll do a lot of good by your preaching. There is honesty written in every feature."

Mr. Burge turned and surveyed himself in the small pier-glass. "Yes," he said, somewhat discontentedly, "I don't look enough like a burglar to suit some of 'em."

"Some people are hard to please," said the other warmly

Mr. Burge started and eyed him thoughtfully, and then as Mr. Higgs after some hesitation walked into the shop to turn the gas out, stood in the doorway watching him. A smothered sigh as he glanced round the shop bore witness to the state of his feelings.

The jeweller hesitated again in the parlour, and then handing Brother Burge his candle turned out the gas, and led the way slowly upstairs to the room which had been prepared for the honoured visitor. He shook hands at the door and bade him an effusive good night, his voice trembling despite himself as he expressed a hope that Mr. Burge would sleep well. He added casually that hehimself was a very light sleeper.

Tonight sleep of any kind was impossible. He had given up the front room to his guest, and his own window looked out on an overgrown garden. He sat trying to read, with his ears alert for the slightest sound. Brother Burge seemed to be a long time undressing. For half an hour after he had retired he could hear him moving restlessly about his room.

Twelve o'clock struck from the tower of the parish church, and was followed almost directly by the tall clock standing in the hall downstairs. Scarcely had the sounds died away than a low oaning from the next room caused the affrighted jeweller to start from his chair and place his ear against the wall. Two or three hollow groans came through the plaster, followed by ejaculations which showed clearly that Brother Burge was at that moment engaged in a terrific combat with the Powers of Darkness to decide whether he should, or should not, rifle his host's shop. His hands clenched and his ear pressed close to the wall, the jeweller listened to a monologue which increased in interest with every word.

"I tell you I won't," said the voice in the next room with a groan, "I *won't*. Get thee behind me—Get thee—No, and don't shove me over to the door; if you can't get behind me without doing that, stay where you are. Yes, I know it's a fortune as well as what you do; but it ain't *mine*."

The listener caught his breath painfully.

"Diamond rings," continued Brother Burge in a suffocating voice. "Stop it, I tell you. No, I won't just go and look at 'em."

A series of groans which the jeweller noticed to his horror got weaker and weaker testified to the greatness of the temptation. He heard Brother Burge rise, and then a succession of panting snarls seemed to indicate a fierce bodily encounter.

"I don't—want to look at 'em," said Brother Burge in an exhausted voice. "What's—the good of—*looking* at 'em? It's like you, you know diamonds are my weakness. What does it matter if he is asleep? What's my knife got to do with you?"

Brother Higgs reeled back and a mist passed before his eyes. He came to himself at the sound of a door opening, and impelled with a vague idea of defending his property, snatched up his candle and looked out on to the landing.

The light fell on Brother Burge, fully dressed and holding his boots in his hand. For a moment they gazed at each other in silence; then the jeweller found his voice.

"I thought you were ill, Brother," he faltered.

An ugly scowl lit up the other's features. "Don't you tell me any of your lies," he said fiercely. "You're watching me; that's what you're doing. Spying on me."

"I thought that you were being tempted," confessed the trembling Mr. Higgs.

An expression of satisfaction which he strove to suppress appeared on Mr. Burge's face.

"So I was," he said sternly. "So I was; but that's my business. I don't want your assistance; I can fight my own battles. You go to bed—I'm going to tell the congregation I won the fight single-'anded."

"So you have, Brother," said the other eagerly; "but it's doing me good to see it. It's a lesson to me; a lesson to all of us the way you wrestled."

"I thought you was asleep," growled Brother Burge, turning back to his room and speaking over his shoulder. "You get back to bed; the fight ain't half over yet. Get back to bed and keep quiet."

The door closed behind him, and Mr. Higgs, still trembling, regained his room and looked in agony at the clock. It was only half-past twelve and the sun did not rise until six. He sat and shivered until a second instalment of groans in the next room brought him in desperation to his feet.

Brother Burge was in the toils again, and the jeweller despite his fears could not help realising what a sensation the story of his temptation would create. Brother Burge was now going round and round his room like an animal in a cage, and sounds as of a soul wrought almost beyond endurance smote upon the listener's quivering ear. Then there was a long silence more alarming even than the noise of the conflict. Had Brother Burge won? And was he now sleeping the sleep of the righteous, or—? Mr. Higgs shivered and put his ear to the wall. Then he heard his guest move stealthily across the floor; the boards creaked and the handle of the door turned.

Mr. Higgs started, and with a sudden flash of courage born of anger and desperation seized a small brass poker from the fireplace, and taking the candle in his other hand went out on to the landing again. Brother Burge was closing his door softly, and his face when he turned it upon the jeweller was terrible in its wrath. His small eyes snapped with fury, and his huge hands opened and shut convulsively.

"What, agin!" he said in a low growl. "After all I told you!"

Mr. Higgs backed slowly as he advanced.

"No noise," said Mr. Burge in a dreadful whisper. "One scream and I'll—*What were you going to do with that poker?*"

He took a stealthy step forward.

"I—I," began the jeweller. His voice failed him. "Burglars," he mouthed, "downstairs."

"*What?*" said the other, pausing.

Mr. Higgs threw truth to the winds. "I heard them in the shop," he said, recovering, "that's why I took up the poker. Can't you hear them?"

Mr. Burge listened for the fraction of a second. "Nonsense," he said huskily.

"I heard them talking," said the other recklessly. "Let's go down and call the police."

"Call 'em from the winder," said Brother Burge, backing with some haste, "they might 'ave pistols or something, and they're ugly customers when they're disturbed."

He stood with strained face listening.

"Here they come," whispered the jeweller with a sudden movement of alarm.

Brother Burge turned, and bolting into his room clapped the door to and locked it. The jeweller stood dumbfounded on the landing; then he heard the window go up and the voice of Brother Burge, much strengthened by the religious exercises of the past six months, bellowing lustily for the police.

For a few seconds Mr. Higgs stood listening and wondering what explanation he should give. Still thinking, he ran downstairs and, throwing open the pantry window, unlocked the door leading into the shop and scattered a few of his cherished possessions about the floor. By the time he had done this, people were already beating upon the street door and exchanging hurried remarks with Mr. Burge at the window above. The jeweller shot back the bolts, and half a dozen neighbours, headed by the butcher opposite, clad in his nightgown and armed with a cleaver, burst into the passage. A constable came running up just as the pallid face of Brother Burge peered over the balusters. The constable went upstairs three at a time, and twisting his hand in the ex-burglar's neck-cloth bore him backwards.

"I've got one," he shouted. "Come up and hold him while I look round."

The butcher was beside him in a moment; Brother Burge, struggling wildly, called loudly upon the name of Brother Higgs.

"That's all right, constable." said the latter, "that's a friend of mine."

"Friend o' yours, sir?" said the disappointed officer, still holding him.

The jeweller nodded. "Mr. Samuel Burge the Converted Burglar," he said mechanically.

"Conver—" gasped the astonished constable. "Converted burglar? *Here*!"

"He is a preacher now," added Mr. Higgs.

"Preacher?" retorted the constable. "Why, it's as plain as a pikestaff. Confederates: his part was to go down and let 'em in."

Mr. Burge raised a piteous outcry. "I hope you may be forgiven for them words," he cried piously.

"What time did you go up to bed?" pursued the constable.

"About half-past eleven," replied Mr. Higgs.

The other grunted with satisfaction. "And he's fully dressed, with his boots off," he remarked. "Did you hear him go out of his room at all?"

"He did go out," said the jeweller truthfully, "but—"

"I thought so," said the constable, turning to his prisoner with affectionate solicitude. "Now you come along o' me. Come quietly, because it'll be the best for you in the end."

"You won't get your skull split open then," added the butcher, toying with his cleaver.

The jeweller hesitated. He had no desire to be left alone with Mr. Burge again; and a sense of humour, which many years' association with the Primitive Apostles had not quite eradicated, strove for hearing.

"Think of the sermon it'll make," he said encouragingly to the frantic Mr. Burge, "think of the congregation!"

Brother Burge replied in language which he had not used in public since he had joined the Apostles. The butcher and another man stood guard over him while the constable searched the premises and made all secure again. Then with a final appeal to Mr. Higgs, who was keeping in the background, he was piloted to the police station by the energetic constable and five zealous assistants.

A diffidence, natural in the circumstances, prevented him from narrating the story of his temptation to the magistrates next morning, and Mr. Higgs was equally reticent. He was put back while the police communicated with London, and in the meantime Brother Clark and a band of Apostles flocked down to his support.

On his second appearance before the magistrates he was confronted with his past; and his past, to the great astonishment of the Brethren, being free from all blemish with the solitary exception of fourteen days for stealing milk-cans, he was discharged with a caution. The disillusioned Primitive Apostles also gave him his freedom.

33

THE MADNESS OF MR. LISTER

Old Jem Lister, of the *Susannah*, was possessed of two devils—the love of strong drink and avarice—and the only thing the twain had in common was to get a drink without paying for it. When Mr. Lister paid for a drink, the demon of avarice masquerading as conscience preached a teetotal lecture, and when he showed signs of profiting by it, the demon of drink would send him hanging round public-house doors cadging for drinks in a way which his shipmates regarded as a slur upon the entire ship's company. Many a healthy thirst reared on salt beef and tickled with strong tobacco had been spoiled by the sight of Mr. Lister standing by the entrance, with a propitiatory smile, waiting to be invited in to share it, and on one occasion they had even seen him (him, Jem Lister, A.B.) holding a horse's head, with ulterior motives.

It was pointed out to Mr. Lister at last that his conduct was reflecting discredit upon men who were fully able to look after themselves in that direction, without having any additional burden thrust upon them. Bill Henshaw was the spokesman, and on the score of violence (miscalled firmness) his remarks left little to be desired. On the score of profanity, Bill might recall with pride that in the opinion of his fellows he had left nothing unsaid.

"You ought to ha' been a member o' Parliament, Bill," said Harry Lea, when he had finished.

"It wants money," said Henshaw, shaking his head.

Mr. Lister laughed, a senile laugh, but not lacking in venom.

"That's what we've got to say," said Henshaw, turning upon him suddenly. "If there's anything I hate in this world, it's a drinking miser. You know our opinion, and the best thing you can do is to turn over a new leaf now."

"Take us all into the 'Goat and Compasses,'" urged Lea; "bring out some o' those sovrins you've been hoarding."

Mr. Lister gazed at him with frigid scorn, and finding that the conversation still seemed to centre round his unworthy person, went up on deck and sat glowering over the insults which had been heaped upon him. His futile wrath when Bill dogged his footsteps ashore next day and revealed his character to a bibulous individual whom he had almost persuaded to be a Christian—from his point of view—bordered upon the maudlin, and he wandered back to the ship, wild-eyed and dry of throat.

For the next two months it was safe to say that every drink he had he paid for. His eyes got brighter and his complexion clearer, nor was he as pleased as one of the other sex might have been when the self-satisfied Henshaw pointed out these improvements to his companions, and claimed entire responsibility for them. It is probable that Mr. Lister, under these circumstances, might in time have lived down his taste for strong drink, but that at just that time they shipped a new cook.

He was a big, cadaverous young fellow, who looked too closely after his own interests to be much of a favourite with the other men forward. On the score of thrift, it was soon discovered that he and Mr. Lister had much in common, and the latter, pleased to find a congenial spirit, was disposed to make the most of him, and spent, despite the heat, much of his spare time in the galley.

"You keep to it," said the greybeard impressively; "money was made to be took care of; if you don't spend your money you've always got it. I've always been a saving man—what's the result?"

The cook, waiting some time in patience to be told, gently inquired what it was.

"'Ere am I," said Mr. Lister, good-naturedly helping him to cut a cabbage, "at the age of sixty-two with a bank-book down below in my chest, with one hundered an' ninety pounds odd in it."

"One 'undered and ninety pounds!" repeated the cook, with awe.

"To say nothing of other things," continued Mr. Lister, with joyful appreciation of the effect he was producing. "Altogether I've got a little over four 'undered pounds."

The cook gasped, and with gentle firmness took the cabbage from him as being unfit work for a man of such wealth.

"It's very nice," he said slowly. "It's very nice. You'll be able to live on it in your old age.

Mr. Lister shook his head mournfully, and his eyes became humid.

"There's no old age for me," he said sadly; "but you needn't tell them," and he jerked his thumb towards the forecastle.

"No, no," said the cook.

"I've never been one to talk over my affairs," said Mr. Lister in a low voice. "I've never yet took fancy enough to anybody so to do. No, my lad, I'm saving up for somebody else."

"What are you going to live on when you're past work then?" demanded the other.

Mr. Lister took him gently by the sleeve, and his voice sank with the solemnity of his subject: "I'm not going to have no old age," he said resignedly.

"Not going to live!" repeated the cook, gazing unsteadily at a knife by his side. "How do you know?"

"I went to a orsepittle in London," said Mr. Lister. "I've been to two or three altogether, while the money I've spent on doctors is more than I like to think of, and they're all surprised to think that I've lived so long. I'm so chock-full o' complaints, that they tell me I can't live more than two years, and I might go off at any moment."

"Well, you've got money," said the cook, "why don't you knock off work now and spend the evenin' of your life ashore? Why should you save up for your relations?"

"I've got no relations," said Mr. Lister; "I'm all alone. I s'pose I shall leave my money to some nice young feller, and I hope it'll do 'im good."

With the dazzling thoughts which flashed through the cook's brain the cabbage dropped violently into the saucepan, and a shower of cooling drops fell on both men.

"I s'pose you take medicine?" he said at length.

"A little rum," said Mr. Lister faintly; "the doctors tell me that it is the only thing that keeps me up—o' course, the chaps down there"—he indicated the forecastle again with a jerk of his head—"accuse me o' taking too much."

"What do you take any notice of 'em for?" inquired the other indignantly.

"I s'pose it is foolish," admitted Mr. Lister; "but I don't like being misunderstood. I keep my troubles to myself as a rule, cook. I don't know what's made me talk to you like this. I 'eard the other day you was keeping company with a young woman."

"Well, I won't say as I ain't," replied the other, busying himself over the fire.

"An' the best thing, too, my lad," said the old man warmly. "It keeps you stiddy, keeps you out of public-'ouses; not as they ain't good in moderation—I 'ope you'll be 'appy."

The cook thanked him, and noticed that Mr. Lister was fidgeting with a piece of paper.

"A little something I wrote the other day," said the old man, catching his eye. "If I let you see it, will you promise not to tell a soul about it, and not to give me no thanks?"

The wondering cook promised, and, the old man being somewhat emphatic on the subject, backed his promise with a home-made affidavit of singular power and profanity.

"Here it is, then," said Mr. Lister.

The cook took the paper, and as he read the letters danced before him. He blinked his eyes and started again, slowly. In plain black and white, and nondescript-coloured fingermarks, Mr. Lister, after a general statement as to his bodily and mental health, left the whole of his estate to the cook. The will was properly dated and witnessed, and the cook's voice shook with excitement and emotion as he offered to hand it back.

"I don't know what I've done for you to do this," he said.

Mr. Lister waved it away again. "Keep it," he said simply; "while you've got it on you, you'll know it's safe."

From this moment a friendship sprang up between the two men which puzzled the remainder of the crew not a little. The attitude of the cook was as that of a son to a father: the benignancy of Mr. Lister beautiful to behold. It was noticed, too, that he had abandoned the reprehensible practice of hanging round tavern doors in favour of going inside and drinking the cook's health.

For about six months the cook, although always in somewhat straitened circumstances, was well content with the tacit bargain, and then, bit by bit, the character of Mr. Lister was revealed to him. It was not a nice character, but subtle; and when he made the startling discovery that a will could be rendered invalid by the simple process of making another one the next day, he became as a man possessed. When he ascertained that Mr. Lister when at home had free quarters at the house of a married niece, he used to sit about alone, and try and think of ways and means of securing capital sunk in a concern which seemed to show no signs of being wound up.

"I've got a touch of the 'art again, lad," said the elderly invalid, as they sat alone in the forecastle one night at Seacole.

"You move about too much," said the cook. "Why not turn in and rest?"

Mr. Lister, who had not expected this, fidgeted. "I think I'll go ashore a bit and try the air," he said suggestively. "I'll just go as far as the 'Black Horse ' and back. You won't have me long now, my lad."

"No, I know," said the cook; "that's what's worrying me a bit."

"Don't worry about me," said the old man, pausing with his hand on the other's shoulder; "I'm not worth it. Don't look so glum, lad."

"I've got something on my mind, Jem," said the cook, staring straight in front of him.

"What is it?" inquired Mr. Lister.

"You know what you told me about those pains in your inside?" said the cook, without looking at him.

Jem groaned and felt his side.

"And what you said about its being a relief to die," continued the other, "only you was afraid to commit suicide?"

"Well?" said Mr. Lister.

"It used to worry me," continued the cook earnestly. "I used to say to myself, 'Poor old Jem,' I ses, 'why should 'e suffer like this when he wants to die? It seemed 'ard.'"

"It is 'ard," said Mr. Lister, "but what about it?"

The other made no reply, but looking at him for the first time, surveyed him with a troubled expression.

"What about it?" repeated Mr. Lister with some emphasis.

"You did say you wanted to die, didn't you?" said the cook. "Now suppose—suppose—"

"Suppose what?" inquired the old man sharply. "Why don't you say what you're agoing to say?"

"Suppose," said the cook, "suppose someone what liked you, Jem—what liked you, mind—'eard you say this over and over again, an' see you sufferin' and 'eard you groanin' and not able to do nothin' for you except lend you a few shillings here and there for medicine, or stand you a few glasses o' rum; suppose they knew a chap in a chemist's shop?"

"Suppose they did?" said the other, turning pale.

"A chap what knows all about p'isons," continued the cook, "p'isons what a man can take without knowing it in 'is grub. Would it be wrong, do you think, if that friend I was speaking about put it in your food to put you out of your misery?"

"*Wrong?*" said Mr. Lister with glassy eyes. "*Wrong!* Look 'ere, cook—"

"I don't mean anything to give him pain," said the other, waving his hand; "you ain't felt no pain lately, 'ave you, Jem?"

"Do you mean to say—" shouted Mr. Lister.

"I don't mean to say anything," said the cook. "Answer my question. You ain't felt no pain lately, 'ave you?"

"Have—you—been—putting—p'ison—in—my— witties?" demanded Mr. Lister in trembling accents.

"If I 'ad, Jem, supposin' that I 'ad," said the cook, in accents of reproachful surprise, "do you mean to say that you'd mind?"

"*Mind?*" said Mr. Lister with fervour. "MIND! I'd 'ave you 'ung!"

"But you said you wanted to die," said the surprised cook.

Mr. Lister swore at him with startling vigour. "I'll 'ave you 'ung," he repeated wildly.

"Me," said the cook artlessly. "What for?"

"For giving me p'ison," said Mr. Lister frantically. "Do you think you can deceive me by your roundabouts? Do you think I can't see through you?"

The other with a sphinx-like smile sat unmoved. "Prove it," he said darkly. "But supposin' if anybody '*ad* been givin' you p'ison, would you like to take something to prevent its acting?"

"I'd take gallons of it," said Mr. Lister feverishly.

The other sat pondering, while the old man watched him anxiously. "It's a pity you don't know your own mind, Jem," he said at length; "still, you know your own business best. But it's very expensive stuff."

"How much?" inquired the other.

"Well, they won't sell more than two shillings-worth at a time," said the cook, trying to speak carelessly, "but if you like to let me 'ave the money, I'll go ashore to the chemist's and get the first lot now."

Mr. Lister's face was a study in emotions, which the other tried in vain to decipher. Then he slowly extracted the amount from his trousers-pocket, and handed it over without a word.

"I'll go at once," said the cook, with a little feeling, "and I'll never take a man at his word again, Jem."

He ran blithely up on deck, and stepping ashore, spat on the coins for luck and dropped them in his pocket. Down below, Mr. Lister, with his chin in his hand, sat in a state of mind pretty evenly divided between rage and fear.

The cook, who was in no mood for company, missed the rest of the crew by two public-houses, and having purchased a baby's teething powder and removed the label, had a congratulatory drink or two before going on board again. A chatter of voices from the forecastle warned him that the crew had returned, but the tongues ceased abruptly as he descended, and three pairs of eyes surveyed him in grim silence.

"What's up?" he demanded.

"Wot 'ave you been doin' to poor old Jem?" demanded Henshaw sternly.

"Nothin'," said the other shortly.

"You ain't been p'isoning him?" demanded Henshaw.

"Certainly not," said the cook emphatically.

"He ses you told 'im you p'isoned 'im," said Henshaw solemnly, "and 'e give you two shillings to get something to cure 'im. It's too late now."

"*What?*" stammered the bewildered cook.

He looked round anxiously at the men. They were all very grave, and the silence became oppressive.

"Where is he?" he demanded.

Henshaw and the others exchanged glances.

"He's gone mad," said he slowly.

"Mad?" repeated the horrified cook, and, seeing the aversion of the crew, in a broken voice he narrated the way in which he had been victimised.

"Well, you've done it now," said Henshaw when he had finished. "He's gone; right orf 'is'ed."

"Where is he?" inquired the cook.

"Where you can't follow him," said the other slowly.

"Heaven?" hazarded the unfortunate.

"No; skipper's bunk," said Lea.

"Oh, can't I foller 'im?" said the cook, starting up. "I'll soon 'ave 'im out o' that."

"Better leave 'im alone," said Henshaw, "He was that wild we couldn't do nothing with 'im, singing an' larfin' and crying all together—I certainly thought he was p'isoned."

"I'll swear I ain't touched him," said the cook.

"Well, you've upset his reason," said Henshaw; "there'll be an awful row when the skipper comes aboard and finds 'im in 'is bed."

"Well, come an' 'elp me to get 'im out," said the cook.

"Iain't going to be mixed up in it," said Henshaw, shaking his head.

"Don't you, Bill," said the other two.

"Wot the skipper'll say I don't know," said Henshaw; "anyway, it'll be said to you, not us."

"I'll go and get 'im out if 'e was five madmen," said the cook, compressing his lips.

"You'll have to carry 'im out, then," said Henshaw. "I don't wish you no 'arm, cook, and perhaps it would be as well to get 'im out afore the skipper or mate comes aboard. If it was me, I know what I should do."

"What?" inquired the cook breathlessly.

"Draw a sack over his head," said Henshaw impressively; "he'll scream like blazes as soon as you touch him, and rouse the folks ashore if you don't. Besides that, if you draw it well down it'll keep his arms fast."

The cook thanked him fervently, and routing out a sack, rushed hastily on deck, his departure being the signal for Mr. Henshaw and his friends to make preparations for retiring for the night so hastily as almost to savour of panic.

The cook, after a hasty glance ashore, went softly below with the sack over his arm and felt his way in the darkness to the skipper's bunk. The sound of deep and regular breathing reassured him, and without undue haste he opened the mouth of the sack and gently raised the sleeper's head.

"Eh? Wha—" began a sleepy voice.

The next moment the cook had bagged him, and gripping him tightly round the middle, turned a deaf ear to the smothered cries of his victim as he strove to lift him out of the bunk. In the exciting time which followed, he had more than one reason for thinking that he had caught a centipede.

"Now, you keep still," he cried breathlessly. "I'm not going to hurt you."

He got his burden out of bed at last, and staggered to the foot of the companion-ladder with it. Then there was a halt, two legs sticking obstinately across the narrow way and refusing to be moved, while a furious humming proceeded from the other end of the sack.

Four times did the exhausted cook get his shoulder under his burden and try and push it up the ladder, and four times did it wriggle and fight its way down again. Half crazy with fear and rage, he essayed it for the fifth time, and had got it half-way up when there was a sudden exclamation of surprise from above, and the voice of the mate sharply demanding an explanation.

"What the blazes are you up to?" he cried.

"It's all right, sir," said the panting cook; "old Jem's had a drop too much and got down aft, and I'm getting 'im for'ard again."

"Jem?" said the astonished mate. "Why, he's sitting up here on the fore-hatch. He came aboard with me."

"Sitting," began the horrified cook; "sit—oh, lor!"

He stood with his writhing burden wedged between his body and the ladder, and looked up despairingly at the mate.

"I'm afraid I've made a mistake," he said in a trembling voice.

The mate struck a match and looked down.

"Take that sack off," he ordered sternly.

The cook placed his burden upon its feet, and running up the ladder stood by the mate shivering. The latter struck another match, and the twain watched in breathless silence the writhings of the strange creature below as the covering worked slowly upwards. In the fourth match it got free, and revealed the empurpled visage of the master of the *Susannah*.

For the fraction of a second the cook gazed at him in speechless horror, and then, with a hopeless cry, sprang ashore and ran for it, hotly pursued by his enraged victim. At the time of sailing he was still absent, and the skipper, loath to part two such friends, sent Mr. James Lister, at the urgent request of the anxious crew, to look for him.

34

THE WHITE CAT

The traveller stood looking from the tap-room window of the "Cauliflower" at the falling rain. The village street below was empty, and everything was quiet with the exception of the garrulous old man smoking with much enjoyment on the settle behind him.

It'll do a power o' good, said the ancient, craning his neck round the edge of the settle and turning a bleared eye on the window. I ain't like some folk; I never did mind a drop o' rain.

The traveller grunted and, returning to the settle opposite the old man, fell to lazily stroking a cat which had strolled in, attracted by the warmth of the small fire which smouldered in the grate.

He's a good mouser, said the old man, but I expect that Smith the landlord would sell 'im to anybody for arf a crown; but we 'ad a cat in Claybury once that you couldn't ha' bought for a hundred golden sovereigns.

The traveller continued to caress the cat.

A white cat, with one yaller eye and one blue one, continued the old man. It sounds queer, but it's as true as I sit 'ere wishing that I 'ad another mug o' ale as good as the last you gave me.

The traveller, with a start that upset the cat's nerves, finished his own mug, and then ordered both to be refilled. He stirred the fire into a blaze, and, lighting his pipe and putting one foot on to the hob, prepared to listen.

It used to belong to old man Clark, young Joe Clark's uncle, said the ancient, smacking his lips delicately over the ale and extending a tremulous claw to the tobacco-pouch pushed towards him; and he was never tired of showing it off to people. He used to call it 'is blue-eyed darling, and the fuss 'e made o' that cat was sinful.

Young Joe Clark couldn't bear it, but being down in 'is uncle's will for five cottages and a bit o' land bringing in about forty pounds a year, he 'ad to 'ide his feelings and pretend as he loved it. He used to take it little drops o' cream and tit-bits o' meat, and old Clark was so pleased that 'e promised 'im that he should 'ave the cat along with all the other property when 'e was dead.

Young Joe said he couldn't thank 'im enough, and the old man, who 'ad been ailing a long time, made 'im come up every day to teach 'im 'ow to take care of it arter he was gone. He taught Joe 'ow to cook its meat and then chop it up fine; 'ow it liked a clean saucer every time for its milk; and 'ow he wasn't to make a noise when it was asleep.

"Take care your children don't worry it, Joe," he ses one day, very sharp. "One o' your boys was pulling its tail this morning, and I want you to clump his 'ead for 'im."

"Which one was it?" ses Joe.

"The slobbery-ndsed one," ses old Clark.

"I'll give 'im a clout as soon as I get 'ome," ses Joe, who was very fond of 'is children.

"Go and fetch 'im and do it 'ere," ses the old man; "that'll teach 'im to love animals."

Joe went off 'ome to fetch the boy, and arter his mother 'ad washed his face, and wiped his nose, an' put a clean pinneyfore on 'im, he took 'im to 'is uncle's and clouted his 'ead for 'im. Arter that Joe and 'is wife 'ad words all night long, and next morning old Clark, coming in from the garden, was just in time to see 'im kick the cat right acrost the kitchen.

He could 'ardly speak for a minute, and when 'e could, Joe see plain wot a fool he'd been. Fust of all 'e called Joe every name he could think of—which took 'im a long time—and then he ordered 'im out of 'is house.

"You shall 'ave my money when your betters have done with it," he ses, "and not afore. That's all you've done for yourself."

Joe Clark didn't know wot he meant at the time, but when old Clark died three months arterwards 'e found out. His uncle 'ad made a new will and left everything to old George Barstow for as long as the cat lived, providing that he took care of it. When the cat was dead the property was to go to Joe.

The cat was only two years old at the time, and George Barstow, who was arf crazy with joy, said it shouldn't be 'is fault if it didn't live another twenty years.

The funny thing was the quiet way Joe Clark took it. He didn't seem to be at all cut up about it, and when Henery Walker said it was a shame, 'e said he didn't mind, and that George Barstow was a old man, and he was quite welcome to 'ave the property as long as the cat lived.

"It must come to me by the time I'm an old man," he ses, "and that's all I care about."

Henery Walker went off, and as 'e passed the cottage where old Clark used to live, and which George Barstow 'ad moved into, 'e spoke to the old man over the palings and told 'im wot Joe Clark 'ad said. George Barstow only grunted and went on stooping and prying over 'is front garden.

"Bin and lost something?" ses Henery Walker, watching 'im.

"No; I'm finding," ses George Barstow, very fierce, and picking up something. "That's the fifth bit o' powdered liver I've found in my garden this morning."

Henery Walker went off whistling, and the opinion he'd 'ad o' Joe Clark began to improve. He spoke to Joe about it that arternoon, and Joe said that if 'e ever accused 'im o' such a thing agin he'd knock 'is 'ead off. He said that he 'oped the cat 'ud live to be a hundred, and that 'e'd no more think of giving it pisoned meat than Henery Walker would of paying for 'is drink so long as 'e could get anybody else to do it for 'im.

They 'ad bets up at this 'ere "Cauliflower" I public-'ouse that evening as to 'ow long that cat 'ud live. Nobody gave it more than a month, and Bill Chambers sat and thought o' so many ways o' killing it on the sly that it was wunnerful to hear 'im.

George Barstow took fright when he 'eard of them, and the care 'e took o' that cat was beautiful for to behold. Arf its time it was shut up in the back bedroom, and the other arf George Barstow was fussing arter it till that cat got to hate 'im like pison. Instead o' giving up work as he'd thought to do, 'e told Henery Walker that 'e'd never worked so 'ard in his life.

"Wot about fresh air and exercise for it?" ses Henery.

"Wot about Joe Clark?" ses George Barstow. "I'm tied 'and and foot. I dursent leave the house for a moment. I ain't been to the 'Cauliflower' since I've 'ad it, and three times I got out o' bed last night to see if it was safe."

"Mark my words," ses Henery Walker; "if that cat don't 'ave exercise, you'll lose it."

"I shall lose it if it does 'ave exercise," ses George Barstow, "that I know."

He sat down thinking, arter Henery Walker 'ad gone, and then he 'ad a little collar and chain made for it, and took it out for a walk. Pretty nearly every dog in Claybury went with 'em, and the cat was in such a state o' mind afore they got 'ome he couldn't do anything with it. It 'ad a fit as soon as they got indoors, and George Barstow, who 'ad read about children's fits in the almanac, gave it a warm bath. It brought it round immediate, and then it began to tear round the room and up and downstairs till George Barstow was afraid to go near it.

It was so bad that evening, sneezing, that George Barstow sent for Bill Chambers, who'd got a good name for doctoring animals, and asked 'im to give it something. Bill said he'd got some powders at 'ome that would cure it at once, and he went straight off and fetched 'em and mixed one up with a bit o' butter.

"That's the way to give a cat medicine," he ses; "smear it with the butter and then it'll lick it off, powder and all."

He was just going to rub it on the cat when George Barstow caught 'old of 'is arm and stopped 'im.

"How do I know it ain't pison?" he ses. I "You're a friend o' Joe Clark's, and for all I know he may ha' paid you to pison it."

"I wouldn't do such a thing," ses Bill. "You ought to know me better than that."

"All right," ses George Barstow; "you eat it then, and I'll give you two shillings instead o' one. You can easy mix some more."

"Not me," ses Bill Chambers, making a face.

"Well, three shillings, then," ses George Barstow, getting more and more suspicious like; "four shillings—five shillings."

Bill Chambers shook his 'ead, and George Barstow, more and more certain that he 'ad caught 'im trying to kill 'is cat and that 'e wouldn't eat the stuff, rose 'im up to ten shillings.

Bill looked at the butter and then 'e looked at the ten shillings on the table, and at last he shut 'is eyes and gulped it down and put the money in 'is pocket.

"You see, I 'ave to be careful, Bill," ses George Barstow, rather upset.

Bill Chambers didn't answer 'im. He sat there as white as a sheet, and making such extraordinary faces that George was arf afraid of 'im.

"Anything wrong, Bill?" he ses at last.

Bill sat staring at 'im, and then all of a sudden he clapped 'is 'andkerchief to 'is mouth and, getting up from his chair, opened the door and rushed out. George Barstow thought at fust that he 'ad eaten pison for the sake o' the ten shillings, but when 'e remembered that Bill Chambers 'ad got the most delikit stummick in Clay bury he altered 'is mind.

The cat was better next morning, but George Barstow had 'ad such a fright about it 'e wouldn't let it go out of 'is sight, and Joe Clark began to think that 'e would 'ave to wait longer for that property than 'e had thought, arter all. To 'ear 'im talk anybody'd ha' thought that 'e loved that cat. We didn't pay much attention to it up at the "Cauliflower" 'ere, except maybe to wink at 'im—a thing he couldn't abear—but at 'ome, o' course, his young 'uns thought as everything he said was Gospel; and one day, coming 'ome from work, as he was passing George Barstow's he was paid out for his deceitfulness.

"I've wronged you, Joe Clark," ses George Barstow, coming to the door, "and I'm sorry for it."

"Oh!" ses Joe, staring.

"Give that to your little Jimmy," ses George Barstow, giving 'im a shilling. "I've give 'im one, but I thought arterwards it wasn't enough."

"What for?" ses Joe, staring at 'im agin.

"For bringing mycat 'ome," ses George Barstow. "'Ow it got out I can't think, but I lost it for three hours, and I'd about given it up when your little Jimmy brought it to me in 'is arms. He's a fine little chap and 'e does you credit."

Joe Clark tried to speak, but he couldn't get a word out, and Henery Walker, wot 'ad just come up and 'eard wot passed, took hold of 'is arm and helped 'im home. He walked like a man in a dream, but arf-way he stopped and cut a stick from the hedge to take 'ome to little Jimmy. He said the boy 'ad been asking him for a stick for some time, but up till then 'e'd always forgotten it.

At the end o' the fust year that cat was still alive, to everybody's surprise; but George Barstow took such care of it 'e never let it out of 'is sight. Every time 'e went out he took it with 'im in a hamper, and, to prevent its being pisoned, he paid Isaac Sawyer, who 'ad the biggest family in Claybury, sixpence a week to let one of 'is boys taste its milk before it had it.

The second year it was ill twice, but the horse-doctor that George Barstow got for it said that it was as 'ard as nails, and with care it might live to be twenty. He said that it wanted more fresh air and exercise; but when he 'eard 'ow George Barstow come by it he said that p'r'aps it would live longer indoors arter all.

At last one day, when George Barstow 'ad been living on the fat o' the land for nearly three years, that cat got out agin. George 'ad raised the front-room winder two or three inches to throw something outside, and, afore he knew wot was 'appening, the cat was outside and going up the road about twenty miles an hour.

George Barstow went arter it, but he might as well ha' tried to catch the wind. The cat was arf wild with joy at getting out agin, and he couldn't get within arf a mile of it.

He stayed out all day without food or drink, follering it about until it came on dark, and then, o' course, he lost sight of it, and, hoping against 'ope that it would come home for its food, he went 'ome and waited for it. He sat up all night dozing in a chair in the front room with the door left open, but it was all of no use; and arter thinking for a long time wot was best to do, he went out and told some o' the folks it was lost and offered a reward of five pounds for it.

You never saw such a hunt then in all your life. Nearly every man, woman, and child in Claybury left their work or school and went to try and earn that five pounds. By the arternoon George Barstow made it ten pounds provided the cat was brought 'ome safe and sound, and people as was too old to walk stood at their cottage doors to snap it up as it came by.

Joe Clark was hunting for it 'igh and low, and so was 'is wife and the boys. In fact, I b'lieve that everybody in Claybury excepting the parson and Bob Pretty was trying to get that ten pounds.

O' course, we could understand the parson—'is pride wouldn't let 'im; but a low, poaching, thieving rascal like Bob Pretty turning up 'is nose at ten pounds was more than we could make out. Even on the second day, when George Barstow made it ten pounds down and a shilling a week for a year besides, he didn't offer to stir; all he did was to try and make fun o' them as *was* looking for it.

"Have you looked everywhere you can think of for it, Bill?" he ses to Bill Chambers.

"Yes, I 'ave," ses Bill.

"Well, then, you want to look everywhere else," ses Bob Pretty. "I know where I should look if I wanted to find it."

"Why don't you find it, then?" ses Bill.

"'Cos I don't want to make mischief," ses Bob Pretty. "I don't want to be unneigh-bourly to Joe Clark by interfering at all."

"Not for all that money?" ses Bill.

"Not for fifty pounds," ses Bob Pretty; "you ought to know me better than that, Bill Chambers."

"It's my belief that you know more about where that cat is than you ought to," ses Joe Gubbins.

"You go on looking for it, Joe," ses Bob Pretty, grinning; "it's good exercise for you, and you've only lost two days' work."

"I'll give you arf a crown if you let me search your 'ouse, Bob," ses Bill Chambers, looking at 'im very 'ard.

"I couldn't do' it at the price, Bill," ses Bob Pretty, shaking his 'ead. "I'm a pore man, but I'm very partikier who I 'ave come into my 'ouse."

O' course, everybody left off looking at once when they heard about Bob—not that they believed that he'd be such a fool as to keep the cat in his 'ouse; and that evening, as soon as it was dark, Joe Clark went round to see 'im.

"Don't tell me as that cat's found, Joe," ses Bob Pretty, as Joe opened the door.

"Not as I've 'eard of," said Joe, stepping inside. "I wanted to speak to you about it; the sooner it's found the better I shall be pleased."

"It does you credit, Joe Clark," ses Bob Pretty.

"It's my belief that it's dead," ses Joe, looking at 'im very 'ard; "but I want to make sure afore taking over the property."

Bob Pretty looked at 'im and then he gave a little cough. "Oh, you want it to be found dead," he ses. "Now, I wonder whether that cat's worth most dead or alive?"

Joe Clark coughed then. "Dead, I should think," he ses at last.

"George Barstow's just 'ad bills printed offering fifteen pounds for it," ses Bob Pretty.

"I'll give that or more when I come into the property," ses Joe Clark.

"There's nothing like ready-money, though, is there?" ses Bob.

"I'll promise it to you in writing, Bob," ses Joe, trembling.

"There's some things that don't look well in writing, Joe," says Bob Pretty, considering; "besides, why should you promise it to *me?*"

"O' course, I meant if you found it," ses Joe.

"Well, I'll do my best, Joe," ses Bob Pretty; "and none of us can do no more than that, can they?"

They sat talking and argufying over it for over an hour, and twice Bob Pretty got up and said 'e was going to see whether George Barstow wouldn't offer more. By the time they parted they was as thick as thieves, and next morning Bob Pretty was wearing Joe Clark's watch and chain, and Mrs. Pretty was up at Joe's 'ouse to see whether there was any of 'is furniture as she 'ad a fancy for.

She didn't seem to be able to make up 'er mind at fust between a chest o' drawers that 'ad belonged to Joe's mother and a grandfather clock. She walked from one to the other for about ten minutes, and then Bob, who 'ad come in to 'elp her, told 'er to 'ave both.

"You're quite welcome," he ses; "ain't she, Joe?"

Joe Clark said "Yes," and arter he 'ad helped them carry 'em 'ome the Prettys went back and took the best bedstead to pieces, cos Bob said as it was easier to carry that way. Mrs. Clark 'ad to go and sit down at the bottom o' the garden with the neck of 'er dress undone to give herself air, but when she saw the little Prettys each walking 'ome with one of 'er best chairs on their 'eads she got up and walked up and down like a mad thing.

"I'm sure I don't know where we are to put it all," ses Bob Pretty to Joe Gubbins, wot was looking on with other folks, "but Joe Clark is that generous he won't 'ear of our leaving anything."

"Has 'e gorn mad?" ses Bill Chambers, I staring at 'im.

"Not as I knows on," ses Bob Pretty. "It's 'is good-'artedness, that's all. He feels sure that that cat's dead, and that he'll 'ave George Barstow's cottage and furniture. I told 'im he'd better wait till he'd made sure, but 'e wouldn't."

Before they'd finished the Prettys 'ad picked that 'ouse as clean as a bone, and Joe Clark 'ad to go and get clean straw for his wife and children to sleep on; not that Mrs. Clark 'ad any sleep that night, nor Joe neither.

Henery Walker was the fust to see what it really meant, and he went rushing off as fast as 'e could run to tell George Barstow. George couldn't believe 'im at fust, but when 'e did he swore that if a 'air of that cat's head was harmed 'e'd 'ave the law o' Bob Pretty, and arter Henery Walker 'ad gone 'e walked round to tell 'im so.

"You're not yourself, George Barstow, else you wouldn't try and take away my character like that," ses Bob Pretty.

"Wot did Joe Clark give you all them things for?" ses George, pointing to the furniture.

"Took a fancy to me, I s'pose," ses Bob. "People do sometimes. There's something about me at times that makes 'em like me."

"He gave 'em to you to kill my cat," ses George Barstow. "It's plain enough for anybody to see."

Bob Pretty smiled. "I expect it'll turn up safe and sound one o' these days," he ses, "and then you'll come round and beg my pardon. P'r'aps—"

"P'r'aps wot?" ses George Barstow, arter waiting a bit.

"P'r'aps somebody 'as got it and is keeping it till you've drawed the fifteen pounds out o' the bank," ses Bob, looking at 'im very hard.

"I've taken it out o' the bank," ses George, starting; "if that cat's alive, Bob, and you've got it, there's the fifteen pounds the moment you 'and it over."

"Wot d'ye mean—me got it?" ses Bob Pretty. "You be careful o' my character."

"I mean if you know where it is," ses George Barstow, trembling all over.

"I don't say I couldn't find it, if that's wot you mean," ses Bob. "I can gin'rally find things when I want to."

"You find me that cat, alive and well, and the money's yours, Bob," ses George, 'ardly able to speak, now that 'e fancied the cat was still alive.

Bob Pretty shook his 'ead. "No; that won't do," he ses. "S'pose I did 'ave the luck to find that pore animal, you'd say I'd had it all the time and refuse to pay."

"I swear I wouldn't, Bob," ses George Barstow, jumping up.

"Best thing you can do if you want me to try and find that cat," says Bob Pretty, "is to give me the fifteen pounds now, and I'll go and look for it at once. I can't trust you, George Barstow."

"And I can't trust you," ses George Barstow.

"Very good," ses Bob, getting up; "there's no 'arm done. P'r'aps Joe Clark'll find the cat is dead and p'r'aps you'll find it's alive. It's all one to me."

George Barstow walked off 'ome, but he was in such a state o' mind 'e didn't know wot to do. Bob Pretty turning up 'is nose at fifteen pounds like that made 'im think that Joe Clark 'ad promised to pay 'im more if the cat was dead; and at last, arter worrying about it for a couple o' hours, 'e came up to this 'ere "Cauliflower" and offered Bob the fifteen pounds.

"Wot's this for?" ses Bob.

"For finding my cat," ses George.

"Look here," ses Bob, handing it back, "I've 'ad enough o' your insults; I don't know where your cat is."

"I mean for trying to find it, Bob," ses George Barstow.

"Oh, well, I don't mind that," ses Bob, taking it. "I'm a 'ard-working man, and I've got to be paid for my time; it's on'y fair to my wife and children. I'll start now."

He finished up 'is beer, and while the other chaps was telling George Barstow wot a fool he was Joe Clark slipped out arter Bob Pretty and began to call 'im all the names he could think of.

"Don't you worry," ses Bob; "the cat ain't found yet."

"Is it dead?" ses Joe Clark, 'ardly able to speak.

"'Ow should I know?" ses Bob; "that's wot I've got to try and find out. That's wot you gave me your furniture for, and wot George Barstow gave me the fifteen pounds for, ain't it? Now, don't you stop me now, 'cos I'm goin' to begin looking."

He started looking there and then, and for the next two or three days George Barstow and Joe Clark see 'im walking up and down with his 'ands in 'is pockets looking over garden fences and calling "Puss." He asked everybody 'e see whether they 'ad seen a white cat with one blue eye and one yaller one, and every time 'e came into the "Cauliflower" he put his 'ead over the bar and called "Puss," 'cos, as 'e said, it was as likely to be there as anywhere else.

It was about a week arter the cat 'ad disappeared that George Barstow was standing at 'is door talking to Joe Clark, who was saying the cat must be dead and 'e wanted 'is property, when he sees a man coming up the road carrying a basket stop and speak to Bill Chambers. Just as 'e got near them an awful "miaow" come from the basket and George Barstow and Joe Clark started as if they'd been shot.

"He's found it!" shouts Bill Chambers, pointing to the man.

"It's been living with me over at Ling for a week pretty nearly," ses the man. "I tried to drive it away several times, not knowing that there was fifteen pounds offered for it."

George Barstow tried to take 'old of the basket.

"I want that fifteen pounds fust," ses the man.

"That's on'y right and fair, George," ses Bob Pretty, who 'ad just come up. "You've got all the luck, mate. We've been hunting 'igh and low for that cat for a week."

Then George Barstow tried to explain to the man and call Bob Pretty names at the same time; but it was all no good. The man said it 'ad nothing to do with 'im wot he 'ad paid to Bob Pretty; and at last they fetched Policeman White over from Cudford, and George Barstow signed a paper to pay five shillings a week till the reward was paid.

George Barstow 'ad the cat for five years arter that, but he never let it get away agin. They got to like each other in time and died within a fortnight of each other, so that Joe Clark got 'is property arter all.

NIGHT WATCHES

35

BACK TO BACK

Mrs. Scutts, concealed behind the curtain, gazed at the cab in uneasy amazement. The cabman clambered down from the box and, opening the door, stood by with his hands extended ready for any help that might be needed. A stranger was the first to alight, and, with his back towards Mrs. Scutts, seemed to be struggling with something in the cab. He placed a dangling hand about his neck and, staggering under the weight, reeled backwards supporting Mr. Scutts, whose other arm was round the neck of a third man. In a flash Mrs. Scutts was at the door.

"Oh, Bill!" she gasped. "And by daylight, too!"

Mr. Scutts raised his head sharply and his lips parted; then his head sank again, and he became a dead weight in the grasp of his assistants.

"He's all right," said one of them, turning to Mrs. Scutts.

A deep groan from Mr. Scutts confirmed the statement.

"What is it?" inquired his wife anxiously.

"Just a little bit of a railway accident," said one of the strangers. "Train ran into some empty trucks. Nobody hurt—seriously," he added, in response to a terrible and annoyed groan from Mr. Scutts.

With his feet dragging helplessly, Mr. Scutts was conveyed over his own doorstep and placed on the sofa.

"All the others went off home on their own legs," said one of the strangers reproachfully. He said he couldn't walk, and he wouldn't go to a hospital."

"Wanted to die at home," declared the sufferer. "I ain't going to be cut about at no 'ospitals."

The two strangers stood by watching him; then they looked at each other.

"I don't want—no—'ospitals," gasped Mr. Scutts. "I'm going to have my own doctor."

"Of course the company will pay the doctor's bill," said one of the strangers to Mrs. Scutts; "or they'll send their own doctor. I expect he'll be all right tomorrow."

"I 'ope so," said Mr. Scutts, "but I don't think it. Thank you for bringing of me 'ome."

He closed his eyes languidly, and kept them closed until the men had departed.

"Can't you walk, Bill?" inquired the tearful Mrs. Scutts.

Her husband shook his head. "You go and fetch the doctor," he said slowly. "That new one round the corner."

"He looks such a boy," objected Mrs. Scutts.

"You go and fetch 'im," said Mr. Scutts, raising his voice. "D'ye hear!"

"But—" began his wife.

"If I get up to you, my gal," said the forgetful Mr. Scutts, "you'll know it."

"Why, I thought—" said his wife in surprise.

Mr. Scutts raised himself on the sofa and shook his fist at her. Then, as a tribute to appearances, he sank back and groaned again. Mrs. Scutts, looking somewhat relieved, took her bonnet from a nail and departed.

The examination was long and tedious, but Mr. Scutts, beyond remarking that he felt chilly, made no complaint. He endeavoured, but in vain, to perform the tests suggested, and even did his best to stand, supported by his medical attendant.

Self-preservation is the law of Nature, and when Mr. Scutts's legs and back gave way he saw to it that the doctor was underneath.

"We'll have to get you up to bed," said the latter, rising slowly and dusting himself.

Mr. Scutts, who was lying full length on the floor, acquiesced, and sent his wife for some neighbours. One of them was a professional furniture-remover, and, half-way up the narrow stairs, the unfortunate had to remind him that he was dealing with a British working man, and not a piano. Four pairs of hands deposited Mr. Scutts with mathematical precision in the centre of the bed and then proceeded to tuck him in, while Mrs. Scutts drew the sheet in a straight line under his chin.

"Don't *look* much the matter with 'im," said one of the assistants.

"You can't tell with a face like that," said the furniture-remover. "It's wot you might call a 'appy face. Why, he was 'arf smiling as we carried 'im up the stairs."

"You're a liar," said Mr. Scutts, opening his eyes.

"All right, mate," said the furniture-remover; "all right. There's no call to get annoyed about it. Good old English pluck, I call it. Where d'you feel the pain?"

"All over," said Mr. Scutts briefly.

His neighbours regarded him with sympathetic eyes, and then, led by the furniture-remover, filed out of the room on tip-toe. The doctor, with a few parting instructions, also took his departure.

"If you're not better by the morning," he said, pausing at the door, "you must send for your club doctor."

Mr. Scutts, in a feeble voice, thanked him, and lay with a twisted smile on his face listening to his wife's vivid narrative to the little crowd which had collected at the front door. She came back, followed by the next-door neighbour, Mr. James Flynn, whose offers of assistance ranged from carrying Mr.

Scutts out pick-a-back when he wanted to take the air, to filling his pipe for him and fetching his beer.

"But I dare say you'll be up and about in a couple o' days," he concluded. "You wouldn't look so well if you'd got anything serious the matter; rosy, fat cheeks and—"

"That'll do," said the indignant invalid. "It's my back that's hurt, not my face."

"I know," said Mr. Flynn, nodding sagely; "but if it was hurt bad your face would be as white as that sheet—whiter."

"The doctor said as he was to be kep' quiet," remarked Mrs. Scutts sharply.

"Right-o," said Mr. Flynn. "Ta-ta, old pal. Keep your pecker up, and if you want your back rubbed with turps, or anything of that sort, just knock on the wall."

He went, before Mr. Scutts could think of a reply suitable for an invalid and, at the same time, bristling with virility. A sinful and foolish desire to leap out of bed and help Mr. Flynn downstairs made him more rubicund than ever.

He sent for the club doctor next morning, and, pending his arrival, partook of a basin of arrow-root and drank a little beef-tea. A bottle of castor-oil and an empty pill-box on the table by the bedside added a little local colour to the scene.

"Any pain?" inquired the doctor, after an examination in which bony and very cold fingers had played a prominent part.

"Not much pain," said Mr. Scutts. "Don't seem to have no strength in my back."

"Ah!" said the doctor.

"I tried to get up this morning to go to my work," said Mr. Scutts, "but I can't stand—I couldn't get out of bed."

"Fearfully upset, he was, pore dear," testified Mrs. Scutts. "He can't bear losing a day. I s'pose—I s'pose the railway company will 'ave to do something if it's serious, won't they, sir?"

"Nothing to do with me," said the doctor. "I'll put him on the club for a few days; I expect he will be all right soon. He's got a healthy colour—a very healthy colour."

Mr. Scutts waited until he had left the house and then made a few remarks on the colour question that for impurity of English and strength of diction have probably never been surpassed.

A second visitor that day came after dinner—a tall man in a frock-coat, bearing in his hand a silk hat, which, after a careful survey of the room, he hung on a knob of the bedpost.

"Mr. Scutts?" he inquired, bowing.

"That's me," said Mr. Scutts, in a feeble voice.

"I've called from the railway company," said the stranger. "We have seen now all those who left their names and addresses on Monday afternoon, and I am glad to say that nobody was really hurt. Nobody."

Mr. Scutts, in a faint voice, said he was glad to hear it.

"Been a wonder if they had," said the other cheerfully. "Why, even the paint wasn't knocked off the engine. The most serious damage appears to be two top-hats crushed and an umbrella broken."

He leaned over the bed-rail and laughed joyously. Mr. Scutts, through half-closed eyes, gazed at him in silent reproach.

"I don't say that one or two people didn't receive a little bit of a shock to their nerves," said the visitor thoughtfully. "One lady even stayed in bed next day. However, I made it all right with them. The company is very generous, and although of course there is no legal obligation, they made several of them a present of a few pounds so that they could go away for a little change, or anything of that sort, to quiet their nevres."

Mr. Scutts, who had been listening with closed eyes, opened them languidly and said, "Oh."

"I gave one gentleman twenty pounds!" said the visitor, jingling some coins in his trouser-pocket. "I never saw a man so pleased and grateful in my life. When he signed the receipt for it—I always get them to sign a receipt, so that the company can see that I haven't kept the money for myself—he nearly wept for joy."

"I should think he would," said Mr. Scutts, slowly—"if he wasn't hurt."

"You're the last on my list," said the other hastily. He produced a slip of paper from his pocketbook and placed it on the small table, with a fountain pen. Then, with a smile that was both tender and playful, he plunged his hand in his pocket and poured a stream of gold on the table.

"What do you say to thirty pounds?" he said, in a hushed voice. "Thirty golden goblins?"

"What for?" inquired Mr. Scutts, with a notable lack of interest.

"For—well, to go away for a day or two," said the visitor. "I find you in bed; it may be a cold or a bilious attack; or perhaps you had a little upset of the nerves when the trains kissed each other."

"I'm in bed—because—I can't walk—or stand," said Mr. Scutts, speaking very distinctly. "I'm on my club, and if as 'ow I get well in a day or two, there's no reason why the company should give me any money. I'm pore, but I'm honest."

"Take my advice as a friend," said the other; "take the money while you can get it."

He nodded significantly at Mr. Scutts and closed one eye. Mr. Scutts closed both of his.

"I 'ad my back hurt in the collision," he said, after a long pause. "I 'ad to be helped 'ome. So far it seems to get worse, but I 'ope for the best."

"Dear me," said the visitor; "how sad! I suppose it has been coming on for a long time. Most of these back cases do. At least all the doctors say so."

"It was done in the collision," said Mr. Scutts, mildly but firmly. "I was as right as rain before then."

The visitor shook his head and smiled. "Ah! You would have great difficulty in proving that," he said softly; "in fact, speaking as man to man, I don't mind telling you it would be impossible.

I'm afraid I'm exceeding my duty, but, as you're the last on my list, suppose—suppose we say forty pounds. Forty! A small fortune."

He added some more gold to the pile on the table, and gently tapped Mr. Scutts's arm with the end of the pen.

"Good afternoon," said the invalid.

The visitor, justly concerned at his lack of intelligence, took a seat on the edge of the bed and spoke to him as a friend and a brother, but in vain. Mr. Scutts reminded him at last that it was medicine-time, after which, pain and weakness permitting, he was going to try to get a little sleep.

"Forty pounds!" he said to his wife, after the official had departed. "Why didn't 'e offer me a bag o' sweets?"

"It's a lot o' money," said Mrs. Scutts wistfully.

"So's a thousand," said her husband. "I ain't going to 'ave my back broke for nothing, I can tell you. Now, you keep that mouth o' yours shut, and if I get it, you shall 'ave a new pair o' boots."

"A thousand!" exclaimed the startled Mrs. Scutts. "Have you took leave of your senses, or what?"

"I read a case in the paper where a man got it," said Mr. Scutts. "He 'ad his back 'urt too, pore chap. How would you like to lay on your back all your life for a thousand pounds?"

"Will you 'ave to lay abed all your life?" inquired his wife, staring.

"Wait till I get the money," said Mr. Scutts; "then I might be able to tell you better."

He gazed wistfully at the window. It was late October, but the sun shone and the air was clear. The sound of traffic and cheerful voices ascended from the little street. To Mr. Scutts it all seemed to be a part of a distant past.

"If that chap comes round tomorrow and offers me five hundred," he said slowly. "I don't know as I won't take it. I'm sick of this mouldy bed."

He waited expectantly next day, but nothing happened, and after a week of bed he began to realise that the job might be a long one. The monotony, to a man of his active habits, became almost intolerable, and the narrated adventures of Mr. James Flynn, his only caller, filled him with an uncontrollable longing to be up and doing.

The fine weather went, and Mr. Scutts, in his tumbled bed, lay watching the rain beating softly on the window-panes. Then one morning he awoke to the darkness of a London fog.

"It gets worse and worse," said Mrs. Scutts, as she returned home in the afternoon with a relish for his tea. "Can't see your 'and before your face."

Mr. Scutts looked thoughtful. He ate his tea in silence, and after he had finished lit his pipe and sat up in bed smoking.

"Penny for your thoughts," said his wife.

"I'm going out," said Mr. Scutts, in a voice that defied opposition. "I'm going to 'ave a walk, and when I'm far enough away I'm going to 'ave one or two drinks. I believe this fog is sent a-purpose to save my life."

Mrs. Scutts remonstrated, but in vain, and at half-past six the invalid, with his cap over his eyes and a large scarf tied round the lower part of his face, listened for a moment at his front door and then disappeared in the fog.

Left to herself, Mrs. Scutts returned to the bedroom and, poking the tiny fire into a blaze, sat and pondered over the wilfulness of men.

She was awakened from a doze by a knocking at the street-door. It was just eight o'clock, and inwardly congratulating her husband on his return to common sense and home, she went down and opened it. Two tall men in silk hats entered the room.

"Mrs. Scutts?" said one of them.

Mrs. Scutts, in a dazed fashion, nodded.

"We have come to see your husband," said the intruder. "I am a doctor."

The panic-stricken Mrs. Scutts tried in vain to think.

"He—he's asleep," she said, at last.

"Doesn't matter," said the doctor.

"Not a bit," said his companion.

"You—you can't see him," protested Mrs. Scutts. "He ain't to be seen."

"He'd be sorry to miss me," said the doctor, eyeing her keenly as she stood on guard by the inner door. "I suppose he's at home?"

"Of course," said Mrs. Scutts, stammering and flushing. "Why, the pore man can't stir from his bed."

"Well, I'll just peep in at the door, then," said the doctor. "I won't wake him. You can't object to that. If you do—"

Mrs. Scutts's head began to swim. "I'll go up and see whether he's awake," she said.

She closed the door on them and stood with her hand to her throat, thinking. Then, instead of going upstairs, she passed into the yard and, stepping over the fence, opened Mr. Flynn's back door.

"Halloa!" said that gentleman, who was standing in the scullery removing mud from his boots. "What's up?"

In a frenzied gabble Mrs. Scutts told him. "You must be 'im," she said, clutching him by the coat and dragging him towards the door. "They've never seen 'im, and they won't know the difference."

"But—" exclaimed the astonished James.

"Quick!" she said sharply. "Go into the back room and undress, then nip into his room and get into bed. And mind, be fast asleep all the time."

Still holding the bewildered Mr. Flynn by the coat, she led him into the house and waved him upstairs, and stood below listening until a slight creaking of the bed announced that he had obeyed orders. Then she entered the parlour.

"He's fast asleep," she said softly; "and mind, I won't 'ave him disturbed. It's the first real sleep he's 'ad for nearly a week. If you promise not to wake 'im you may just have a peep."

"We won't disturb him," said the doctor, and, followed by his companion, noiselessly ascended the stairs and peeped into the room. Mr. Flynn was fast asleep, and not a muscle moved as the two men approached the bed on tip-toe and stood looking at him. The doctor turned after a minute and led the way out of the room.

"We'll call again," he said softly.

"Yes, sir," said Mrs. Scutts. "When?"

The doctor and his companion exchanged glances. "I'm very busy just at present," he said slowly. "We'll look in some time and take our chance of catching him awake."

Mrs. Scutts bowed them out, and in some perplexity returned to Mr. Flynn. "I don't like the look of 'em," she said, shaking her head. "You'd better stay in bed till Bill comes 'ome in case they come back."

Right-o," said the obliging Mr. Flynn. "Just step in and tell my landlady I'm 'aving a chat with Bill."

He lit his pipe and sat up in bed smoking until a knock at the front door at half-past eleven sent him off to sleep again. Mrs. Scutts, who was sitting downstairs, opened it and admitted her husband.

"All serene?" he inquired. "What are you looking like that for? What's up?"

He sat quivering with alarm and rage as she told him, and then, mounting the stairs with a heavy tread, stood gazing in helpless fury at the slumbering form of Mr. James Flynn.

"Get out o' my bed," he said at last, in a choking voice.

"What, Bill!" said Mr. Flynn, opening his eyes.

"Get out o' my bed," repeated the other. "You've made a nice mess of it between you. It's a fine thing if a man can't go out for 'arf a pint without coming home and finding all the riff-raff of the neighbourhood in 'is bed."

"'Ow's the pore back, Bill?" inquired Mr. Flynn, with tenderness.

Mr. Scutts gurgled at him. "Outside!" he said as soon as he could get his breath.

"Bill," said the voice of Mrs. Scutts, outside the door.

"Halloa," growled her husband.

"He mustn't go," said Mrs. Scutts. "Those gentlemen are coming again, and they think he is you."

"WHAT!" roared the infuriated Mr. Scutts.

"Don't you see? It's me what's got the pore back now, Bill," said Mr. Flynn. "You can't pass yourself off as me, Bill; you ain't good-looking enough."

Mr. Scutts, past speech, raised his clenched fists to the ceiling.

"He'll 'ave to stay in your bed," continued the voice of Mrs. Scutts. "He's got a good 'art, and I know he'll do it; won't you, Jim?"

Mr. Flynn pondered. "Tell my landlady in the morning that I've took your back room," he said. "What a fortunit thing it is I'm out o' work. What are you walking up and down like that for, Bill? Back coming on agin?"

"Then o' course," pursued the voice of Mrs. Scutts, in meditative accents, "there's the club doctor and the other gentleman that knows Bill. They might come at any moment. There's got to be two Bills in bed, so that if one party comes one Bill can nip into the back room, and if the other Bill—party, I mean—comes, the other Bill—you know what I mean!"

Mr. Scutts swore himself faint.

"That's how it is, mate," said Mr. Flynn. "It's no good standing there saying your little piece of poetry to yourself. Take off your clo'es and get to bed like a little man. Now! Now! Naughty! Naughty!"

"P'r'aps I oughtn't to 'ave let 'em up, Bill," said his wife; "but I was afraid they'd smell a rat if I didn't. Besides, I was took by surprise."

"You get off to bed," said Mr. Scutts. "Get off to bed while you're safe."

"And get a good night's rest," added the thoughtful Mr. Flynn. "If Bill's back is took bad in the night I'll look after it."

Mr. Scutts turned a threatening face on him. 'For two pins—" he began.

"For two pins I'll go back 'ome and stay there," said Mr. Flynn.

He put one muscular leg out of bed, and then, at the earnest request of Mr. Scutts, put it back again. In a few simple, manly words the latter apologised, by putting all the blame on Mrs. Scutts, and removing his clothes, got into bed.

Wrapped in bedclothes, they passed the following day listening for knocks at the door and playing cards. By evening both men were weary, and Mr. Scutts made a few pointed remarks concerning dodging doctors and deceitful visitors to which Mr. Flynn listened in silent approval.

"They mightn't come for a week," he said dismally. "It's all right for you, but where do I come in? Halves?"

Mr. Scutts had a rush of blood to the head.

"You leave it to me, mate," he said, controlling himself by an effort. "If I get ten quid, say, you shall have 'arf."

"And suppose you get more?" demanded the other.

"We'll see," said Mr. Scutts vaguely.

Mr. Flynn returned to the charge next day, but got no satisfaction. Mr. Scutts preferred to talk instead of the free board and lodging his friend was getting. On the subject of such pay for such work he was almost eloquent.

"I'll bide my time," said Mr. Flynn darkly. "Treat me fair and I'll treat you fair."

His imprisonment came to an end on the fourth day. There was a knock at the door, and the sound of men's voices, followed by the hurried appearance of Mrs. Scutts.

"It's *Jim's* lot," she said, in a hurried whisper. "I've just come up to get the room ready."

Mr. Scutts took his friend by the hand, and after warmly urging him not to forget the expert instructions he had received concerning his back, slipped into the back room, and, a prey to forebodings, awaited the result.

"Well, he looks better," said the doctor, regarding Mr. Flynn.

"Much better," said his companion.

Mrs. Scutts shook her head. "His pore back don't seem no better, sir," she said in a low voice. "Can't you do something for it?"

"Let me have a look at it," said the doctor. "Undo your shirt."

Mr. Flynn, with slow fingers, fumbled with the button at his neck and looked hard at Mrs. Scutts.

"She can't bear to see me suffer," he said, in a feeble voice, as she left the room.

He bore the examination with the fortitude of an early Christian martyr. In response to inquiries he said he felt as though the mainspring of his back had gone.

"How long since you walked?" inquired the doctor.

"Not since the accident," said Mr. Flynn firmly.

"Try now," said the doctor.

Mr. Flynn smiled at him reproachfully.

"You can't walk because you think you can't," said the doctor; "that is all. You'll have to be encouraged the same way that a child is. I should like to cure you, and I think I can."

He took a small canvas bag from the other man and opened it. "Forty pounds," he said. "Would you like to count it?"

Mr. Flynn's eyes shone.

"It is all yours," said the doctor, "if you can walk across the room and take it from that gentleman's hand."

"Honour bright?" asked Mr. Flynn, in tremulous tones, as the other man held up the bag and gave him an encouraging smile.

"Honour bright," said the doctor.

With a spring that nearly broke the bed, Mr. Flynn quitted it and snatched the bag, and at the same moment, Mrs. Scutts, impelled by a maddened arm, burst into the room.

"Your back!" she moaned. "It'll kill you. Get back to bed."

"I'm cured, lovey," said Mr. Flynn simply.

"His back is as strong as ever," said the doctor, giving it a thump.

Mr. Flynn, who had taken his clothes from a chair and was hastily dressing himself, assented.

"But if you'll wait 'arf a tick I'll walk as far as the corner with you," he said quickly. "I'd like to make sure it's all right."

He paused at the foot of the stairs and, glancing up at the pallid and murderous face of Mr. Scutts, which protruded from the back bedroom, smiled at him rapturously. Then, with a lordly air, he tossed him five pieces of gold.

36

KEEPING WATCH

"Human natur'!" said the night-watchman, gazing fixedly at a pretty girl in a passing waterman's skiff. "Human natur'!"

He sighed, and, striking a match, applied it to his pipe and sat smoking thoughtfully.

"The young fellow is pretending that his arm is at the back of her by accident," he continued; "and she's pretending not to know that it's there. When he's allowed to put it round 'er waist whenever he wishes, he won't want to do it. She's artful enough to know that, and that's why they are all so standoffish until the thing is settled. She'll move forward 'arf an inch presently, and 'arf a minute arterwards she'll lean back agin without thinking. She's a nice-looking gal, and what she can see in a tailor's dummy like that, I can't think."

He leaned back on his box and, folding his arms, emitted a cloud of smoke.

"Human natur's a funny thing. I've seen a lot of it in my time, and if I was to 'ave my life all over agin I expect I should be just as silly as them two in the skiff. I've known the time when I would spend money as free over a gal as I would over myself. I on'y wish I'd got all the money now that I've spent on peppermint lozenges.

"That gal in the boat reminds me o' one I used to know a few years ago. Just the same innercent baby look—a look as if butter wouldn't melt in 'er mouth—and a artful disposition that made me sorry for 'er sects.

"She used to come up to this wharf once a week in a schooner called the *Belle*. Her father, Cap'n Butt, was a widow-man, and 'e used to bring her with 'im, partly for company and partly because 'e could keep'is eye on her. Nasty eye it was, too, when he 'appened to be out o'temper.

"I'd often took a bit o' notice o' the gal; just giving 'er a kind smile now and then as she sat on deck, and sometimes—when 'er father wasn't looking—she'd smile back. Once, when 'e was down below, she laughed right out. She was afraid of 'im, and by and by I noticed that she daren't even get off the ship and walk up and down the wharf without asking 'im. When she went out 'e was with 'er, and, from one or two nasty little snacks I 'appened to overhear when the skipper thought I was too far away, I began to see that something was up.

"It all came out one evening, and it only came out because the skipper wanted my help. I was standing leaning on my broom to get my breath back arter a bit o' sweeping, when he came up to me, and I knew at once, by the nice way 'e spoke, that he wanted me to do something for 'im.

"'Come and 'ave a pint, Bill,' he ses.

"I put my broom agin the wall, and we walked round to the 'Bull's Head' like a couple o' brothers. We 'ad two pints apiece, and then he put his and on my shoulder and talked as man to man.

"'I'm in a little bit o' difficulty about that gal o' mine,' he ses, passing me his baccy-box. 'Six months ago she dropped a letter out of 'er pocket, and I'm blest if it wasn't from a young man. A young *man*!'

"'You surprise me,' I ses, meaning to be sarcastic.

"'I surprised her,' he ses, looking very fierce. 'I went to 'er box and I found a pile of 'em—a pile of 'em—tied up with a piece o' pink ribbon. And a photygraph of my lord. And of all the narrer-chested, weak-eyed, slack-baked, spindly-legged sons of a gun you ever saw in your life, he is the worst. If I on'y get my 'ands on him I'll choke 'im with his own feet.'

"He washed 'is mouth out with a drop o' beer and stood scowling at the floor.

"'Arter I've choked 'im I'll twist his neck,' he ses. 'If he 'ad on'y put his address on 'is letters, I'd go round and do it now. And my daughter, my only daughter, won't tell me where he lives.'

"'She ought to know better,' I ses.

"He took hold o' my 'and and shook it. 'You've got more sense than one 'ud think to look at you, Bill,' he ses, not thinking wot he was saying. 'You see wot a mess I'm in.'

"Yes,' I ses.

"'I'm a nurse, that's wot I am,' he ses, very savage. 'Just a nursemaid. I can't move 'and or foot without that gal. 'Ow'd you like it, yourself, Bill?"

"'It must be very orkard for you,' I ses. 'Very orkard indeed.'

"'Orkard!' he ses; 'it's no name for it, Bill. I might as well be a Sunday-school teacher and ha' done with it. I never 'ad such a dull time in all my life. Never. And the worst of it is, it's spiling my temper. And all because o' that narrer-eyed, red-chested—you know wot I mean!"

"He took another mouthful o' beer, and then he took 'old of my arm. 'Bill,' he ses, very earnest, 'I want you to do me a favour.'

"'Go ahead,' I ses.

"'I've got to meet a pal at Charing Cross at ha'-past seven,' he ses; 'and we're going to make a night of it. I've left Winnie in charge o' the cook, and I've told 'im plain that, if she ain't there when I come back, I'll skin 'im alive. Now, I want you to watch 'er, too. Keep the gate locked, and don't let anybody in you don't know. Especially that monkey-faced imitation of a man. Here 'e is. That's his likeness.'

"He pulled a photygraph out of 'is coat-pocket and 'anded it to me.

"'That's 'im,' he ses. 'Fancy a gal getting love-letters from a thing like that. And she was on'y twenty last birthday. Keep your eye on 'er, Bill, and don't let 'er out of your sight. You're worth two o' the cook.'

"He finished 'is beer, and, cuddling my arm, stepped back to the wharf. Miss Butt was sitting on the cabin skylight reading a book, and old Joe, the cook, was standing near 'er pretending to swab the decks with a mop.

"'I've got to go out for a little while—on business,' ses the skipper. 'I don't s'pose I shall be long, and, while I'm away, Bill and the cook will look arter you.'

"Miss Butt wrinkled up 'er shoulders.

"'The gate'll be locked, and you're not to leave the wharf. D'ye 'ear?'

"The gal wriggled 'er shoulders agin and went on reading, but she gave the cook a look out of 'er innercent baby eyes that nearly made 'im drop the mop.

"'Them's my orders,' ses the skipper, swelling his chest and looking round, 'to everybody. You know wot'll 'appen to you, Joe, if things ain't right when I come back. Come along, Bill, and lock the gate arter me. An' mind, for your own sake, don't let anything 'appen to that gal while I'm away.'

"'Wot time'll you be back?' I ses, as 'e stepped through the wicket.

"'Not afore twelve, and p'r'aps a good bit later,' he ses, smiling all over with 'appiness. 'But young slab-chest don't know I'm out, and Winnie thinks I'm just going out for 'arf an hour, so it'll be all right. So long.'

"I watched 'im up the road, and I must say I began to wish I 'adn't taken the job on. Arter all, I 'ad on'y had two pints and a bit o' flattery, and I knew wot 'ud 'appen if anything went wrong. Built like a bull he was, and fond o' using his strength. I locked the wicket careful, and, putting the key in my pocket, began to walk up and down the wharf.

"For about ten minutes the gal went on reading and didn't look up once. Then, as I passed, she gave me a nice smile and shook 'er little fist at the cook, wot 'ad got 'is back towards 'er. I smiled back, o' course, and by and by she put her book down and climbed on to the side o' the ship and held out her 'and for me to 'elp her ashore.

"'I'm so tired of the ship,' she ses, in a soft voice; 'it's like a prison. Don't you get tired of the wharf?'

"'Sometimes,' I ses; 'but it's my dooty.'

"'Yes,' she ses. 'Yes, of course. But you're a big, strong man, and you can put up with things better.'

"She gave a little sigh, and we walked up and down for a time without saying anything.

"'And it's all father's foolishness,' she ses, at last; 'that's wot makes it so tiresome. I can't help a pack of silly young men writing to me, can I?'

"'No, I s'pose not,' I ses.

"'Thank you,' she ses, putting 'er little 'and on my arm. 'I knew that you were sensible, I've often watched you when I've been sitting alone on the schooner, longing for somebody to speak to. And I'm a good judge of character. I can read you like a book.'

"She turned and looked up at me. Beautiful blue eyes she'd got, with long, curling lashes, and teeth like pearls.

"'Father is so silly,' she ses, shaking her 'ead and looking down; 'and it's so unreasonable, because, as a matter of fact, I don't like young men. Oh, I beg your pardon, I didn't mean that. I didn't mean to be rude.'

"'Rude?' I ses, staring at her.

"'Of course it was a rude thing for me to say,' she ses, smiling; 'because you are still a young man yourself.'

"I shook my 'ead. 'Youngish,' I ses.

"'Young!' she ses, stamping 'er little foot.

"She gave me another look, and this time 'er blue eyes seemed large and solemn. She walked along like one in a dream, and twice she tripped over the planks and would 'ave fallen if I hadn't caught 'er round the waist.

"'Thank you,' she ses. 'I'm very clumsy. How strong your arm is!'

"We walked up and down agin, and every time we went near the edge of the jetty she 'eld on to my arm for fear of stumbling agin. And there was that silly cook standing about on the schooner on tiptoe and twisting his silly old neck till I wonder it didn't twist off.

"'Wot a beautiful evening it is!' she ses, at last, in a low voice. 'I 'ope fatherisn't coming back early. Do you know wot time he is coming home?'

"'About twelve,' I ses; 'but don't tell 'im I told you so.'

"'O' course not,' she ses, squeezing my arm. 'Poor father! I hope he is enjoying himself as much as I am.'

"We walked down to the jetty agin arter that, and sat side by side looking acrost the river. And she began to talk about Life, and wot a strange thing it was; and 'ow the river would go on flowing down to the sea thousands and thousands o' years arter we was both dead and forgotten. If it hadn't ha' been for her little 'ead leaning agin my shoulder I should have 'ad the creeps.

"'Let's go down into the cabin,' she ses, at last, with a little shiver; 'it makes me melancholy sitting here and thinking of the "might-have-beens."'

"I got up first and 'elped her up, and, arter both staring hard at the cook, wot didn't seem to know 'is place, we went down into the cabin. It was a comfortable little place, and arter she 'ad poured me out a glass of 'er father's whisky, and filled my pipe for me, I wouldn't ha' changed places with a king. Even when the pipe wouldn't draw I didn't mind.

"'May I write a letter?' she ses, at last.

"'Sartainly,' I ses.

"She got out her pen and ink and paper, and wrote. 'I shan't be long,' she ses, looking up and nibbling 'er pen. 'It's a letter to my dressmaker; she promised my dress by six o'clock this afternoon, and I am just writing to tell her that if I don't have it by ten in the morning she can keep it.'

"'Quite right,' I ses; 'it's the on'y way to get things done.'

"'It's *my* way,' she ses, sticking the letter in an envelope and licking it down. 'Nice name, isn't it?'

"She passed it over to me, and I read the name and address: 'Miss Minnie Miller, 17, John Street, Mile End Road.'

"'That'll wake her up,' she ses, smiling. 'Will you ask Joe to take it for me?'

"'He—he's on guard,' I ses, smiling back at 'er and shaking my 'ead.

"'I know,' she ses, in a low voice. 'But I don't want any guard—only you. I don't like guards that peep down skylights.'

"I looked up just in time to see Joe's 'ead disappear. Then I nipped up, and arter I 'ad told 'im part of wot I thought about 'im I gave 'im the letter and told 'im to sheer off.

"'The skipper told me to stay 'ere,' he ses, looking obstinate.

"'You do as you're told,' I ses. 'I'm in charge, and I take full responsibility. I shall lock the gate arter you. Wot are you worrying about?

"'And here's a shilling, Joe, for a bus fare,' ses the gal, smiling. 'You can keep the change.'

"Joe took off 'is cap and scratched 'is silly bald 'ead.

"'Come on,' I ses; 'it's a letter to a dressmaker. A letter that must go tonight.'

"'Else it's no use,' ses the gal. 'You don't know 'ow important it is.'

"'All right,' ses Joe. ''Ave it your own way. So long as you don't tell the skipper, I don't mind. If anything 'appens you'll catch it too, Bill.'

"He climbed ashore, and I follered 'im to the gate and unlocked it. He was screwing up 'is eye ready for a wink, but I give 'im such a look that he thought better of it, and, arter rubbing his eye with 'is finger as though he 'ad got a bit o' dust in it, he went off.

"I locked the gate and went back to the cabin, and for some time we sat talking about fathers and the foolish ideas they got into their 'eads, and things o' that sort. So far as I remember, I 'ad two more goes o' whisky and one o' the skipper's cigars, and I was just thinking wot a beautiful thing it was to be alive and 'ealthy and in good spirits, talking to a nice gal that understood wot you said a'most afore you said it, when I 'eard three blows on a whistle.

"'Wot's that?' I ses, starting up. 'Police whistle?'

"'I don't think so,' ses Miss Butt, putting her 'and on my shoulder. 'Sit down and stay where you are. I don't want *you* to get hurt, if it is. Let somebody I don't like go.'

"I sat down agin and listened, but there was no more whistling.

"'Boy in the street, I expect,' ses the gal, going into the state-room. 'Oh, I've got something to show you. Wait a minute.'

"I 'eard her moving about, and then she comes back into the cabin.

"'I can't find the key of my box,' she ses, 'and it's in there. I wonder whether you've got a key that would open it. It's a padlock.'

"I put my 'and in my pocket and pulled out my keys. 'Shall I come and try?' I ses.

"'No, thank you,' she ses, taking the keys. 'This looks about the size. What key is it?'

"'It's the key of the gate,' I ses, 'but I don't suppose it'll fit.'

"She went back into the state-room agin, and I 'eard her fumbling at a lock. Then she came back into the cabin, breathing rather hard, and stood thinking.

"'I've just remembered,' she ses, pinching her chin. 'Yes!'

"She stepped to the door and went up the companion-ladder, and the next moment I 'eard a sliding noise and a key turn in a lock. I jumped to the foot of the ladder and, 'ardly able to believe my senses, saw that the hatch was closed. When I found that it was locked too, you might ha' knocked me down with a feather.

"I went down to the cabin agin, and, standing on the locker, pushed the skylight up with my 'ead and tried to look out. I couldn't see the gate, but I 'eard voices and footsteps, and a little while arterwards I see that gal coming along the wharf arm in arm with the young man she 'ad told me she didn't like, and dancing for joy. They climbed on to the schooner, and then they both stooped down with their hands on their knees and looked at me.

"'Wot is it?' ses the young man, grinning.

"'It's a watchman,' ses the gal. 'It's here to take charge of the wharf, you know, and see that nobody comes on.'

"'We ought to ha' brought some buns for it,' ses the young man; 'look at it opening its mouth.'

"They both laughed fit to kill themselves, but I didn't move a muscle.

"'You open the companion,' I ses, 'or it'll be the worse for you. D'ye hear? Open it!'

"'Oh, Alfred,' ses the gal, 'he's losing 'is temper. Wotever shall we do?'

"'I don't want no more nonsense,' I ses, trying to fix 'er with my eye. 'If you don't let me out it'll be the worse for you.'

"'Don't you talk to my young lady like that,' ses the young man.

"'Your young lady?' I ses. 'H'mm! You should ha' seen 'er 'arf an hour ago.'

"The gal looked at me steady for a moment.

"'He put 'is nasty fat arm round my waist, Alfred,' she ses.

"'*Wot!*' ses the young man, squeaking. 'WOT!'

"He snatched up the mop wot that nasty, untidy cook 'ad left leaning agin the side, and afore I 'ad any idea of wot 'e was up to he shoved the beastly thing straight in my face.

"'Next time,' he ses, 'I'll tear you limb from limb!'

"I couldn't speak for a time, and when I could 'e stopped me with the mop agin. It was like a chained lion being tormented by a monkey. I stepped down on to the cabin floor, and then I told 'em both wot I thought of 'em.

"'Come along, Alfred,' ses the gal, 'else the cook'll be back before we start.'

"'He's all right,' ses the young man. 'Minnie's looking arter him. When I left he'd got 'arf a bottle of whisky in front of 'im.'

"'Still, we may as well go,' ses Miss Butt. 'It seems a shame to keep the cab waiting.'

"'All right,' he ses. 'I just want to give this old chump one more lick with the mop and then we'll go.'

"He peeped down the skylight and waited, but I kept quite quiet with my back towards 'im.

"'Come along,' ses Miss Butt.

"'I'm coming,' he ses. 'Hi! You down there! When the cap'n comes back tell 'im that I'm taking Miss Butt to an aunt o' mine in the country. And tell 'im that in a week or two he'll 'ave the largest and nicest piece of wedding cake he 'as ever 'ad in his life. So long!'

"'Goodbye, watchman,' ses the gal.

"They moved off without another word—from them, I mean. I heard the wicket slam, and then I 'eard a cab drive off over the stones. I couldn't believe it at first. I couldn't believe a gal with such beautiful blue eyes could be so hard-'earted, and for a long time I stood listening and hoping to 'ear the cab come back. Then I stepped up to the companion and tried to shift it with my shoulders.

"I went back to the cabin at last, and arter lighting the lamp I 'ad another sup o' the skipper's whisky to clear my 'ead, and sat down to try and think wot tale I was to tell 'im. I sat for pretty near three hours without thinking of one, and then I 'eard the crew come on to the wharf.

"They was a bit startled when they saw my 'ead at the skylight, and then they all started at the same time asking me wot I was doing. I told 'em to let me out fust and then I'd tell 'em, and one of 'em 'ad just stepped round to the companion when the skipper come on to the wharf and stepped aboard. He stooped down and peeped at me through the skylight as though he couldn't believe 'is eyesight, and then, arter sending the hands for'ard and telling 'em to stay there, *wotever 'appened*, he unlocked the companion and came down."

37

THE UNDERSTUDY

"Dogs on board ship is a nuisance," said the night-watchman, gazing fiercely at the vociferous mongrel that had chased him from the deck of the *Henry William*; "the skipper asks me to keep an eye on the ship, and then leaves a thing like that down in the cabin."

He leaned against a pile of empty casks to recover his breath, shook his fist at the dog, and said, slowly,—

Some people can't make too much of 'em. They talk about a dog's honest eyes and his faithful 'art. I 'ad a dog once, and I never saw his eyes look so honest as they did one day when 'e was sitting on a pound o' beefsteak we was 'unting high and low for.

I've known dogs to cause a lot of trouble in my time. A man as used to live in my street told me he 'ad been in jail three times because dogs follered him 'ome and wouldn't go away when he told 'em to. He said that some men would ha' kicked 'em out into the street, but he thought their little lives was far too valuable to risk in that way.

Some people used to wink when 'e talked like that, but I didn't: I remembered a dog that took a fancy to old Sam Small and Ginger Dick and Peter Russet once in just the same way.

It was one night in a little public-'ouse down Commercial Road way. They 'ad on'y been ashore a week, and, 'aving been turned out of a music-'all the night afore because a man Ginger Dick had punched in the jaw wouldn't behave 'imself, they said they'd spend the rest o' their money on beer instead. There was just the three of 'em sitting by themselves in a cosy little bar, when the door was pushed open and a big black dog came in.

He came straight up to Sam and licked his 'and. Sam was eating a arrowroot biscuit with a bit o' cheese on it at the time. He wasn't wot you'd call a partickler sort o' man, but, seeing as 'ow the dog was so careless that 'e licked the biscuit a'most as much as he did his 'and, he gave it to 'im. The dog took it in one gulp, and then he jumped up on Sam's lap and wagged his tail in 'is face for joy and thankfulness.

"He's took a fancy to you, Sam," ses Ginger.

Sam pushed the dog off on to the floor and wiped his face.

"He's a good dog, by the look of 'im," ses Peter Russet, who was country-bred.

He bought a sausage-roll, and him and the dog ate it between 'em. Then Ginger Dick bought one and gave it to 'im, and by the time it was finished the dog didn't seem to know which one of 'em he loved the most.

"Wonder who he belongs to?" ses Ginger. "Is there any name on the collar, Peter?"

Peter shook his 'ead. "It's a good collar, though," he ses. "I wonder whether he's been and lost 'imself?"

Old Sam, wot was always on the lookout for money, put his beer down and wiped 'is mouth. "There might be a reward out for 'im," he ses. "I think I'll take care of 'im for a day or two, in case."

"We'll all take care of 'im," ses Ginger; "and if there's a reward we'll go shares. Mind that!"

"I found 'im," ses Sam, very disagreeable. "He came up to me as if he'd known me all 'is life."

"No," ses Ginger. "Don't you flatter yourself. He came up to you because he didn't know you, Sam."

"If he 'ad, he'd ha' *bit* your 'and," ses Peter Russet.

"Instead o' washing it," ses Ginger.

"Go on!" ses Sam, 'olding his breath with passion. "Go on!"

Peter opened 'is mouth, but just then another man came into the bar, and, arter ordering 'is drink, turned round and patted the dog's 'ead.

"That's a good dog; 'ow old is he?" he ses to Ginger.

"Two years last April," ses Ginger, without moving an eyelid.

"*Fifth* of April," ses old Sam, very quick and fierce.

"At two o'clock in the morning," ses Peter.

The man took up 'is beer and looked at 'em; then 'e took a drink and looked at 'em again. Arter which he 'ad another look at the dog.

"I could see 'e was very valuable," he ses. "I see that the moment I set eyes on 'im. Mind you don't get 'im stole."

He finished up 'is beer and went out; and he 'ad 'ardly gone afore Ginger took a piece o' thick string out of 'is pocket and fastened it to the dog's collar.

"Make yourself at 'ome, Ginger," ses Sam, very nasty.

"I'm going to," ses Ginger. "That chap knows something about dogs, and, if we can't get a reward for 'im, p'r'aps we can sell 'im."

They 'ad another arf-pint each, and then, Ginger taking 'old of the string, they went out into the street.

"Nine o'clock," ses Peter. "It's no good going 'ome yet, Ginger."

"We can 'ave a glass or two on the way," ses Ginger; "but I shan't feel comfortable in my mind till we've got the dog safe 'ome. P'r'aps the people wot 'ave lost it are looking for it now."

They 'ad another drink farther on, and a man in the bar took such a fancy to the dog that 'e offered Ginger five shillings for it and drinks round.

"That shows 'ow valuable it is," ses Peter Russet when they got outside. "Hold that string tight, Ginger. Wot's the matter?"

"He won't come," ses Ginger, tugging at the string. "Come on, old chap! Good dog! Come on!"

He stood there pulling at the dog, wot was sitting down and being dragged along on its stummick. He didn't know its name, but 'e called it a few things that seemed to ease 'is mind, and then he 'anded over the string to Sam, wot 'ad been asking for it, and told 'im to see wot *he* could do.

"We shall 'ave a crowd round us in a minute," ses Peter. "Mind you don't bust a blood-vessel, Sam."

"And be locked up for stealing it, p'r'aps," ses Ginger. "Better let it go, Sam."

"Wot, arter refusing five bob for it?" ses Sam. "Talk sense, Ginger, and give it a shove be'ind."

Ginger gave it a shove, but it was no good. There was three or four people coming along the road, and Sam made up his mind in an instant and 'eld up 'is 'and to a cab that was passing.

It took the three of 'em to get the dog into the cab, and as soon as it was in the cabman told 'em to take it out again. They argufied with 'im till their tongues ached, and at last, arter paying 'im four shillings and sixpence afore they started, he climbed up on the box and drove off.

The door was open when they got to their lodgings, but they 'ad to be careful because o' the landlady. It took the three of 'em to pull and push that dog upstairs, and Ginger took a dislike to dogs that 'e never really got over. They got 'im in the bedroom at last, and, arter they 'ad given 'im a drink o' water out o' the wash-hand basin, Ginger and Peter started to find fault with Sam Small.

"I know wot I'm about," ses Sam; "but, o' course, if you don't want your share, say so. Wot?"

"Talk sense!" ses Ginger. "We paid our share o' the cab, didn't we? And more fools us."

"There won't be no share," ses Peter Russet; "but if there is, we're going to 'ave it."

They undressed themselves and got into bed, and Ginger 'adn't been in his five minutes afore the dog started to get in with 'im. When Ginger pushed 'im off 'e seemed to think he was having a game with 'im, and, arter pretending to bite 'im in play, he took the end of the counterpane in 'is mouth and tried to drag it off.

"Why don't you get to sleep, Ginger?" ses Sam, who was just dropping off. "'Ave a game with 'im in the morning."

Ginger gave the dog a punch in the chest, and, arter saying a few o' the things he'd like to do to Sam Small, he cuddled down in 'is bed and they all went off to sleep. All but the dog, that is. He seemed uneasy in 'is mind, and if 'e woke 'em up once by standing on his 'ind-legs and putting his fore-paws on their chest to see if they was still alive, he did arf-a-dozen times.

He dropped off to sleep at last, scratching 'imself, but about three o'clock in the morning Ginger woke up with a 'orrible start and sat up in bed shivering. Sam and Peter woke up too, and, raising themselves in bed, looked at the dog, wot was sitting on its tail, with its 'ead back, moaning fit to break its 'art.

"Wot's the matter?" ses old Sam, in a shaky voice. "Stop it! Stop it, d'ye hear!"

"P'r'aps it's dying," ses Ginger, as the dog let off a 'owl like a steamer coming up the river. "Stop it, you brute!"

"He'll wake the 'ouse up in a minute," ses Peter. "Take 'im downstairs and kick 'im into the street, Sam."

"Take 'im yourself," ses Sam. "*Hsh!* Somebody's coming upstairs. Poor old doggie. Come along, then. Come along."

The dog left off his 'owling, and went over and licked 'im just as the landlady and one or two more came to the door and called out to know wot they meant by it.

"It's all right, missis," ses Sam. "It's on'y pore Ginger. You keep quiet," he ses in a whisper, turning to Ginger.

"Wot's he making that row about?" ses the landlady. "He made my blood run cold."

"He's got a touch o' toothache," ses Sam. "Never mind, Ginger," 'e ses in a hurry, as the dog let off another 'owl; "try and bear it."

"He's a coward, that's wot 'e is," ses the landlady, very fierce. "Why, a child o' five wouldn't make such a fuss."

"Sounds more like a dog than a 'uman being," ses another voice. "You come outside, Ginger, and I'll give you something to cry for."

They waited a minute or two, and then, everything being quiet, they went back to bed, while old Sam talked to Ginger about wot 'e called 'is "presence o' mind," and Ginger talked to 'im about wot he'd do to 'im if 'e wasn't a fat old man with one foot in the grave.

They was all in a better temper when they woke up in the morning, and while Sam was washing they talked about wot they was to do with the dog.

"We can't lead 'im about all day," ses Ginger; "and if we let 'im off the string he'll go off 'ome."

"He don't know where his 'ome is," ses Sam, very severe; "but he might run away, and then the pore thing might be starved or else ill-treated, I 'ave 'eard o' boys tying tin cans to their tails."

"I've done it myself," ses Ginger, nodding.

"Consequently it's our dooty to look arter 'im," ses Sam.

"I'll go down to the front door," ses Peter, "and when I whistle, bring him down."

Ginger stuck his 'ead out o' the window, and by and by, when Peter whistled, him and Sam took the dog downstairs and out into the street.

"So far so good," ses Sam; "now, wot about brekfuss?"

They 'ad their brekfuss in their usual coffee-shop, and the dog took bits from all of them. Unfortunately, 'e wasn't used to haddick bones, and arter two of the customers 'ad gorn out and two more 'ad complained to the landlord, they 'ad to leave their brekfusses and take 'im outside for a breath o' fresh air.

"Now, wot are we going to do?" ses Ginger. "I'm beginning to be sick of the sight of 'im. 'Ave we got to lead 'im about all day on a bit o' string?"

"Let's take 'im round the corner and lose 'im," ses Peter Russet.

"You give me 'old o' that string," ses Sam. "If you don't want shares, that's all right. If I'm going to look arter 'im I'll 'ave it all."

That made Ginger and Peter look at each other. Direckly Sam began to talk about money they began to think they might be losing something.

"And wot about 'aving 'im in our bedroom and keeping us awake all night?" ses Peter.

"And putting it on to me with the toothache," ses Ginger. "No; you can look arter 'im, Sam, while me and Peter goes off and enjoys ourselves; and if you get anything we go shares, mind."

"All right," ses Sam, turning away with the dog.

"And suppose Sam gets a reward or sells it, and then tells us that it ran away and 'e lost it?" ses Peter.

"O' course; I never thought o' that," ses Ginger. "You've got your 'ead on straight, Peter."

"I see 'im smile, that's why," ses Peter Russet.

"You're a liar," ses Sam.

"We'll stick together," ses Ginger. "Leastways, one of us'll keep with you, Sam."

They settled it that way at last, and while Ginger went for a walk down round about where they 'ad found the dog, Sam

Small and Peter waited for him in a little public-'ouse down Limehouse way. Their idea was that there would be bills up, and when Ginger came back and said there wasn't, they 'ad a lot to say about people wot wasn't fit to 'ave dogs because they didn't love 'em.

They 'ad a miserable day. When the dog got sick o' sitting in a pub 'e made such a noise they 'ad to take 'im out; and when 'e got tired o' walking about he sat down on the pavement and they 'ad to drag 'im along to the nearest pub agin. At five o'clock in the arternoon Ginger Dick was talking about twopenn'orth o' rat poison.

"Wot are we to do with 'im till twelve o'clock tonight?" ses Peter.

"And s'pose we can't smuggle 'im into the 'ouse agin?" ses Ginger. "Or suppose he makes that noise agin in the night?"

They 'ad a pint each to 'elp them to think wot was to be done. And, arter a lot o' talking and quarrelling, they did wot a lot of other people 'ave done when they got into trouble: they came to me.

I 'ad on'y been on dooty about arf an hour when the three of 'em turned up at the wharf with the dog, and, arter saying 'ow well I looked and that I seemed to get younger every time they saw me, they asked me to take charge of the dog for 'em.

"It'll be company for you," ses old Sam. "It must be very lonely 'ere of a night. I've often thought of it."

"And of a daytime you could take it 'ome and tie it up in your backyard," ses Ginger.

I wouldn't 'ave anything to do with it at fust, but at last I gave way. They offered me four-pence a day for its keep, and, as I didn't want to run any risk, I made 'em give me a couple o' bob to go on with.

They went off as though they'd left a load o' care be'ind 'em, and arter tying the dog up to a crane I went on with my work.

They 'adn't told me wot the game was, but, from one or two things they'd let drop, I'd got a pretty good idea.

The dog 'owled a bit at fust, but he quieted down arter a bit. He was a nice-looking animal, but one dog is much the same as another to me, and if I 'ad one ten years I don't suppose I could pick it out from two or three others.

I took it off 'ome with me when I left at six o'clock next morning, and tied it up in my yard. My missis 'ad words about it, o' course—that's wot people get married for—but when she found it woke me up three times she quieted down and said wot a nice coat it 'ad got.

The three of 'em came round next evening to see it, and they was so afraid of its being lost that when they stood me a pint at the "Bull's Head" we'ad to take it with us. Ginger was going to buy a sausage-roll for it, but, arter Sam 'ad pointed out that they was paying me four-pence a day for its keep, he didn't. And Sam 'ad the cheek to tell me that it liked a nice bit o' fried steak as well as anything.

A lot o' people admired that dog. I remember, on the fourth night I think it was, the barge *Dauntless* came alongside, and arter she was made fast the skipper came ashore and took a little notice of it.

"Where did you get 'im?" he ses.

I told 'im 'ow it was, and he stood there for some time patting the dog on the 'ead and whistling under 'is breath.

"It's much the same size as my dog," he ses; "that's a black retriever, too."

I ses "Oh!"

"I'm afraid I shall 'ave to get rid of it," he ses. "It's on the barge now. My missis won't 'ave it in the 'ouse anymore cos it bit the baby. And o' course it was no good p'inting out to 'er that it was its fust bite. Even the law allows one bite, but it's no good talking about the law to wimmen."

"Except when it's on their side," I ses.

He patted the dog's 'ead agin and whistled, and a big black dog came up out of the cabin and sprang ashore. It went up and put its nose to Sam's dog, and they both growled like thunderstorms.

"Might be brothers," ses the skipper, "on'y your dog's got a better 'ead and a better coat. It's a good dog."

"They're all alike to me," I ses. "I couldn't tell 'em apart, not if you paid me'."

The skipper stood there a moment, and then he ses: "I wish you'd let me see 'ow my dog looks in your dog's collar," he ses.

"Whaffor?" I ses.

"On'y fancy," he ses. "Oh, Bill!"

"Yes," I ses.

"It ain't Christmas," he ses, taking my arm and walking up and down a bit, "but it will be soon, and then I mightn't see you. You've done me one or two good turns, and I should like to make you a Christmas-box of three arf-dollars."

I let 'im give 'em to me, and then, just to please 'im, I let 'im try the collar on 'is dog, while I swept up a bit.

"It looked beautiful on 'im," he ses, when I'd finished; but I've put it back agin. Come on, Bruno. Good-night, Bill."

He got 'is dog on the barge agin arter a bit o' trouble, and arter making sure that my dog 'ad got its own collar on I went on with my work.

The dog didn't seem to be quite 'imself next day, and he was so fierce in the yard that my missis was afraid to go near 'im. I was going to ask the skipper about it, as 'e seemed to know more about dogs than I did, but when I got to the wharf the barge had sailed.

It was just getting dark when there came a ring at the gate-bell, and afore I could answer it arf-a-dozen more, as fast as the bell could go. And when I opened the wicket Sam Small and Ginger and Peter Russet all tried to get in at once.

"Where's the dog?" ses Sam.

"Tied up," I ses. "Wot's the matter? 'Ave you all gorn mad?"

They didn't answer me. They ran on to the jetty, and afore I could turn round a'most they 'ad got the dog loose and was dragging it towards me, smiling all over their faces.

"Reward," ses Ginger, as I caught 'old of 'im by the coat. "Five pounds—landlord of a pub—at Bow—come on, Sam!"

"Why don't you keep your mouth shut, Ginger?" ses Sam.

"Five pounds!" I ses. "Five pounds! Hurrah!"

"Wot are you hurraying about?" ses Sam, very short.

"Why," I ses, "I s'pose—Here, arf a moment!"

"Can't stop," ses Sam, going arter the others.

I watched 'em up the road, and then I locked the gate and walked up and down the wharf thinking what a funny thing money is, and 'ow it alters people's natures. And arter all, I thought that three arf-dollars earned honest was better than a reward for hiding another man's dog.

I finished tidying up, and at nine o'clock I went into the office for a quiet smoke. I couldn't 'elp wondering 'ow them three 'ad got on, and just as I was thinking about it there came the worst ringing at the gate-bell I 'ave ever 'eard in my life, and the noise of heavy boots kicking the gate. It was so violent I 'ardly liked to go at fust, thinking it might be bad news; but I opened it at last, and in bust Sam Small, with Ginger and Peter.

For five minutes they all talked at once, with their nasty fists 'eld under my nose. I couldn't make 'ead or tail of it at fust, and then I found as 'ow they 'ad got the dog back with them, and I that the landlord 'ad said 'e wasn't the one.

"But 'e said as he thought the collar was his," ses Sam. "'Ow do you account for that?"

"P'r'aps he made a mistake," I ses; "or p'r'aps he thought you'd turn the dog adrift and he'd get it back for nothing. You know wot landlords are. Try 'im agin."

"I'd pretty well swear he ain't the same dog," ses Peter Russet, looking in a puzzled way at Sam and Ginger.

"You take 'im back tomorrow night," I ses. "It's a nice walk to Bow. And then come back and beg my pardon. I want to 'ave a word with this policeman here. Good night."

38

THE WEAKER VESSEL

Mr. Gribble sat in his small front parlour in a state of angry amazement. It was half-past six and there was no Mrs. Gribble; worse still, there was no tea. It was a state of things that had only happened once before. That was three weeks after marriage, and on that occasion Mr. Gribble had put his foot down with a bang that had echoed down the corridors of thirty years.

The fire in the little kitchen was out, and the untidy remains of Mrs. Gribble's midday meal still disgraced the table. More and more dazed, the indignant husband could only come to the conclusion that she had gone out and been run over. Other things might possibly account for her behaviour; that was the only one that would excuse it.

His meditations were interrupted by the sound of a key in the front door, and a second later a small, anxious figure entered the room and, leaning against the table, strove to get its breath. The process was not helped by the alarming distension of Mr. Gribble's figure.

"I—I got home—quick as I could—Henry," said Mrs. Gribble, panting.

"Where is my tea?" demanded her husband. "What do you mean by it? The fire's out and the kitchen is just as you left it."

"I—I've been to a lawyer's, Henry," said Mrs. Gribble, "and I had to wait."

"Lawyer's?" repeated her husband.

"I got a letter this afternoon telling me to call. Poor Uncle George, that went to America, is gone."

"That is no excuse for neglecting me," said Mr. Gribble. "Of course people die when they are old. Is that the one that got on and made money?"

His wife, apparently struggling to repress a little excitement, nodded. "He—he's left me two hundred pounds a year for life, Henry," she I said, dabbing at her pale blue eyes with a handkerchief. "They're going to pay it monthly; sixteen pounds thirteen shillings and fourpence a month. That's how he left it."

"Two hund—" began Mr. Gribble, forgetting himself. *"Two hun*—Go and get my tea! If you think you're going to give yourself airs because your uncle's left you money, you won't do it in my house."

He took a chair by the window, and, while his wife busied herself in the kitchen, sat gazing in blank delight at the little street. Two hundred a year! It was all he could do to resume his wonted expression as his wife re-entered the room and began to lay the table. His manner, however, when she let a cup and saucer slip from her trembling fingers to smash on the floor left nothing to be desired.

"It's nice to have money come to us in our old age," said Mrs. Gribble timidly, as they sat at tea. "It takes a load off my mind."

"Old age!" said her husband disagreeably. "What d'ye mean by old age? I'm fifty-two, and feel as young as ever I did."

"You look as young as ever you did," said the docile Mrs. Gribble. "I can't see no change in you. At least, not to speak of."

"Not so much talk," said her husband. "When I want your opinion of my looks I'll ask you for it. When do you start getting this money?"

"Tuesday week; first of May," replied his wife. "The lawyers are going to send it by registered letter."

Mr. Gribble grunted.

"I shall be sorry to leave the house for some things," said his wife, looking round. "We've been here a good many years now, Henry."

"Leave the house!" repeated Mr. Gribble, putting down his tea-cup and staring at her. "Leave the house! What are you talking about?"

"But we can't stay here, Henry," faltered Mrs. Gribble. "Not with all that money. They are building some beautiful houses in Charlton Grove now—bathroom, tiled hearths, and beautiful stained glass in the front door; and all for twenty-eight pounds a year."

"Wonderful!" said the other, with a mocking glint in his eye.

"And iron palings to the front garden, painted chocolate-colour picked out with blue," continued his wife, eyeing him wistfully.

Mr. Gribble struck the table a blow with his fist. "This house is good enough for me," he roared; "and what's good enough for me is good enough for you. You want to waste money on show; that's what you want. Stained glass and bow-windows! You want a bow-window to loll about in, do you? Shouldn't wonder if you don't want a servant-gal to do the work."

Mrs. Gribble flushed guiltily, and caught her breath.

"We're going to live as we've always lived," pursued Mr. Gribble. "Money ain't going to spoil me. I ain't going to put on no side just because I've come in for a little bit. If you had your way we should end up in the workhouse."

He filled his pipe and smoked thoughtfully, while Mrs. Gribble cleared away the tea-things and washed up. Pictures, good to look upon, formed in the smoke—pictures of a hale, hearty man walking along the primrose-path arm-in-arm with two hundred a year; of the mahogany and plush of the saloon bar at the "Grafton Arms"; of Sunday jaunts, and the Oval on summer afternoons.

He ate his breakfast slowly on the first of the month, and, the meal finished, took a seat in the window with his pipe and waited for the postman. Mrs. Gribble's timid reminders concerning the flight of time and consequent fines for lateness at work fell on deaf ears. He jumped up suddenly and met the postman at the door.

"Has it come?" inquired Mrs. Gribble, extending her hand.

By way of reply her husband tore open the envelope and, handing her the covering letter, counted the notes and coin and placed them slowly in his pockets. Then, as Mrs. Gribble looked at him, he looked at the clock, and, snatching up his hat, set off down the road.

He was late home that evening, and his manner forbade conversation. Mrs. Gribble, with the bereaved air of one who has sustained an irremediable loss, sighed fitfully, and once applied her handkerchief to her eyes.

"That's no good," said her husband at last; "that won't bring him back."

"Bring who back?" inquired Mrs. Gribble, in genuine surprise.

"Why, your Uncle George," said Mr. Gribble. "That's what you're turning on the water-cart for, ain't it?"

"I wasn't thinking of him," said Mrs. Gribble, trying to speak bravely. "I was thinking of—"

"Well, you ought to be," interrupted her husband. "He wasn't my uncle, poor chap, but I've been thinking of him, off and on, all day. That bloater-paste you are eating now came from his kindness. I brought it home as a treat."

"I was thinking of my clothes," said Mrs. Gribble, clenching her hands together under the table. "When I found I had come in for that money, the first thing I thought was that I should be able to have a decent dress. My old ones are quite worn out, and as for my hat and jacket—"

"Go on," said her husband fiercely. "Go on. That's just what I said: trust you with money, and we should be poorer than ever."

"I'm ashamed to be seen out," said Mrs. Gribble.

"A woman's place is the home," said Mr. Gribble; "and so long as I'm satisfied with your appearance nobody else matters. So long as I am pleased, that's everything. What do you want to go dressing yourself up for? Nothing looks worse than an over-dressed woman."

"What are we going to do with all that money, then?" inquired Mrs. Gribble, in trembling tones.

"That'll do," said Mr. Gribble decidedly. "That'll do. One o' these days you'll go too far. You start throwing that money in my teeth and see what happens. I've done my best for you all these years, and there's no reason to suppose I shan't go on doing so. What did you say? What!"

Mrs. Gribble turned to him a face rendered ghastly by terror. "I—I said—it was my money," she stammered.

Mr. Gribble rose and stood for a full minute regarding her. Then, kicking a chair out of his way, he took his hat from its peg in the passage and, with a bang of the street-door that sent a current of fresh, sweet air circulating through the house, strode off to the "Grafton Arms."

It was past eleven when he returned, but even the spectacle of his wife laboriously darning her old dress failed to reduce his good-humour in the slightest degree. In a frivolous mood he even took a feather from the dismembered hat on the table and stuck it in his hair. He took the stump of a strong cigar from his lips and, exhaling a final cloud of smoke, tossed it into the fireplace.

"Uncle George dead," he said at last, shaking his head. "Hadn't pleasure acquaintance, but good man. Good man."

He shook his head again and gazed mistily at his wife.

"He was a teetotaller," she remarked casually.

"He was tee-toller," repeated Mr. Gribble, regarding her equably. "Good man. Uncle George dead—teetotaller."

Mrs. Gribble gathered up her work and began to put it away.

"Bedtime," said Mr. Gribble, and led the way upstairs, singing.

His good-humour had evaporated by the morning, and, having made a light breakfast of five cups of tea, he went off, with lagging steps, to work. It was a beautiful spring morning, and the idea of a man with two hundred a year and a headache going off to a warehouse instead of a day's outing seemed to border upon the absurd. What use was money without freedom? His toil was sweetened that day by the knowledge that he could drop it any time he liked and walk out, a free man, into the sunlight.

By the end of a week his mind was made up. Each day that passed made his hurried uprising and scrambled breakfast more and more irksome; and on Monday morning, with hands in trouser-pockets and legs stretched out, he leaned back in his chair and received his wife's alarming intimations as to the flight of time with a superior and sphinx-like smile.

"It's too fine to go to work today," he said lazily. "Come to that, any day is too fine to waste at work."

Mrs. Gribble sat gasping at him.

"So on Saturday I gave 'em a week's notice," continued her husband, "and after Potts and Co. had listened while I told 'em what I thought of 'em, they said they'd do without the week's notice."

"You've never given up your job?" said Mrs Gribble.

"I spoke to old Potts as one gentleman of independent means to another," said Mr. Gribble, smiling. "Thirty-five bob a week after twenty years' service! And he had the cheek to tell me I wasn't worth that. When I told him what he was worth he talked about sending for the police. What are you looking like that for? I've worked hard for you for thirty years, and I've had enough of it. Now it's your turn."

"You'd find it hard to get another place at your age," said his wife; "especially if they wouldn't give you a good character."

"Place!" said the other, staring. "Place! I tell you I've done with work. For a man o' my means to go on working for thirty-five bob a week is ridiculous."

"But suppose anything happened to me," said his wife, in a troubled voice.

"That's not very likely," said Mr. Gribble. "You're tough enough. And if it did your money would come to me."

Mrs. Gribble shook her head.

"WHAT?" roared her husband, jumping up.

"I've only got it for life, Henry, as I told you," said Mrs. Gribble in alarm. "I thought you knew it would stop when I died."

"And what's to become of me if anything happens to you, then?" demanded the dismayed Mr. Gribble. "What am I to do?"

Mrs. Gribble put her handkerchief to her eyes.

"And don't start weakening your constitution by crying," shouted the incensed husband. "What are you mumbling?"

"I sa—sa—said, let's hope—you'll go—first," sobbed his wife. "Then it will be all right."

Mr. Gribble opened his mouth, and then, realizing the inadequacy of the English language for moments of stress, closed it again. He broke his silence at last in favour of Uncle George.

"Mind you," he said, concluding a peroration which his wife listened to with her fingers in her ears—"mind you, I reckon I've been absolutely done by you and your precious Uncle George. I've given up a good situation, and now, any time you fancy to go off the hooks, I'm to be turned into the street."

"I'll try and live, for your sake, Henry," said his wife.

"Think of my worry every time you are ill," pursued the indignant Mr. Gribble.

Mrs. Gribble sighed, and her husband, after a few further remarks concerning Uncle George, his past and his future, announced his intention of going to the lawyers and seeing whether anything could be done. He came back in a state of voiceless gloom, and spent the rest of a beautiful day indoors, smoking a pipe which had lost much of its flavour, and regarding with a critical and anxious eye the small, weedy figure of his wife as she went about her work.

The second month's payment went into his pocket as a matter of course, but on this occasion Mrs. Gribble made no requests for new clothes or change of residence. A little nervous cough was her sole comment.

"Got a cold?" inquired her husband, staring.

"I don't think so," replied his wife, and, surprised and touched at this unusual display of interest, coughed again.

"Is it your throat or your chest?" he inquired gruffly.

Mrs. Gribble coughed again to see. After five coughs she said she thought it was her chest.

"You'd better not go out o' doors today, then," said Mr. Gribble. "Don't stand about in draughts; and I'll fetch you in a bottle of cough mixture when I go out. What about a laydown on the sofa?"

His wife thanked him, and, reaching the sofa, watched with half-closed eyes as he cleared the breakfast table. It was the first time he had done such a thing in his life, and a little honest pride in the possession of such a cough would not be denied. Dim possibilities of its vast usefulness suddenly occurred to her.

She took the cough mixture for a week, by which time other symptoms, extremely disquieting to an ease-loving man, had manifested themselves. Going upstairs deprived her of breath; carrying a loaded tea-tray produced a long and alarming stitch in the side. The last time she ever filled the coal-scuttle she was discovered sitting beside it on the floor in a state of collapse.

"You'd better go and see the doctor," said Mr. Gribble.

Mrs. Gribble went. Years before the doctor had told her that she ought to take life easier, and she was now able to tell him that she was prepared to take his advice.

"And, you see, I must take care of myself now for the sake of my husband," she said, after she had explained matters.

"I understand," said the doctor.

"If anything happened to me—" began the patient.

"Nothing shall happen," said the other. "Stay in bed tomorrow morning, and I'll come round and overhaul you."

Mrs. Gribble hesitated. "You might examine me and think I was all right," she objected; "and at the same time you wouldn't know how I feel."

"I know just how you feel," was the reply. "Goodbye."

He came round the following morning and, following the dejected Mr. Gribble upstairs, made a long and thorough investigation of his patient.

"Say 'ninety-nine,'" he said, adjusting his stethoscope.

Mrs. Gribble ticked off "ninety-nines" until her husband's ears ached with them. The doctor finished at last, and, fastening his bag, stood with his beard in his hand, pondering. He looked from the little, white-faced woman on the bed to the bulky figure of Mr. Gribble.

"You had better lie up for a week," he said decidedly. "The rest will do you good."

"Nothing serious, I s'pose?" said Mr. Gribble, as he led the way downstairs to the small parlour.

"She ought to be all right with care," was the reply.

"Care?" repeated the other distastefully. "What's the matter with her?"

"She's not very strong," said the doctor; "and hearts don't improve with age, you know. Under favourable conditions she's good for some years yet. The great thing is never to thwart her. Let her have her own way in everything."

"Own way in everything?" repeated the dumbfounded Mr. Gribble.

The doctor nodded. "Never let her worry about anything," he continued; "and, above all, never find fault with her."

"Not," said Mr. Gribble thickly—"not even for her own good?"

"Unless you want to run the risk of losing her."

Mr. Gribble shivered.

"Let her have an easy time," said the doctor, taking up his hat. "Pamper her a bit if you like; it won't hurt her. Above all, don't let that heart of hers get excited."

He shook hands with the petrified Mr. Gribble and went off, grinning wickedly. He had few favourites, and Mr. Gribble was not one of them.

For two days the devoted husband did the housework and waited on the invalid. Then he wearied, and, at his wife's suggestion, a small girl was engaged as servant. She did most of the nursing as well, and, having a great love for the sensational, took a grave view of her mistress's condition.

It was a relief to Mr. Gribble when his wife came downstairs again, and he was cheered to see that she looked much better. His satisfaction was so marked that it brought on her cough again.

"It's this house, I think," she said, with a resigned smile. "It never did agree with me."

"Well, you've lived in it a good many years," said her husband, controlling himself with difficulty.

"It's rather dark and small," said Mrs. Gribble. "Not but what it is good enough for me. And I dare say it will last my time."

"Nonsense!" said her husband gruffly. "You want to get out a bit more. You've got nothing to do now we are wasting all this money on a servant. Why don't you go out for little walks?"

Mrs. Gribble went, after several promptings, and the fruit of one of them was handed by the postman to Mr. Gribble a few days afterwards. Half-choking with wrath and astonishment, he stood over his trembling wife with the first draper's bill he had ever received.

"One pound two shillings and threepence three-farthings!" he recited. "It must be a mistake. It must be for somebody else."

Mrs. Gribble, with her hand to her heart, tottered to the sofa and lay there with her eyes closed.

"I had to get some dress material," she said, in a quavering voice. "You want me to go out, and I'm so shabby I'm ashamed to be seen."

Mr. Gribble made muffled noises in his throat; then, afraid to trust himself, he went into the backyard and, taking a seat on an upturned bucket, sat with his head in his hands peering into the future.

The dressmaker's bill and a bill for a new hat came after the next monthly payment; and a bill for shoes came a week later. Hoping much from the well-known curative effects of fine feathers, he managed to treat the affair with dignified silence. The only time he allowed full play to his feelings Mrs. Gribble took to her bed for two days, and the doctor had a heart-to-heart talk with him on the doorstep.

It was a matter of great annoyance to him that his wife still continued to attribute her ill-health to the smallness and darkness of the house; and the fact that there were only two of the houses in Charlton Grove left caused a marked depression of spirits. It was clear that she was fretting. The small servant went further, and said that she was fading away.

They moved at the September quarter, and a slight, but temporary, improvement in Mrs. Gribble's health took place. Her cheeks flushed and her eyes sparkled over new curtains and new linoleum. The tiled hearths, and stained glass in the front door, filled her with a deep and solemn thankfulness. The only thing that disturbed her was the fact that Mr. Gribble, to avoid wasting money over necessaries, contrived to spend an unduly large portion on personal luxuries.

"We ought to have some new things for the kitchen," she said one day.

"No money," said Mr. Gribble laconically.

"And a mat for the bathroom."

Mr. Gribble got up and went out.

She had to go to him foreverything. Two hundred a year and not a penny she could call her own! She consulted her heart, and that faithful organ responded with a bound that set her nerves quivering. If she could only screw her courage to the sticking-point the question would be settled for once and all.

White and trembling she sat at breakfast on the first of November, waiting for the postman, while the unconscious Mr. Gribble went on with his meal. The double-knock down the road came nearer and nearer, and Mr. Gribble, wiping his mouth, sat upright with an air of alert and pleased interest. Rapid steps came to the front door and a double bang responded.

"Always punctual," said Mr. Gribble good-humouredly.

His wife made no reply, but, taking a blue-crossed envelope from the maid in her shaking fingers, looked round for a knife. Her gaze encountered Mr. Gribble's outstretched hand.

"After you," he said sharply.

Mrs. Gribble found the knife, and, hacking tremulously at the envelope, peeped inside it and, with her gaze fastened on the window, fumbled for her pocket. She was so pale and shook so much that the words died away on her husband's lips.

"You—you had better let me take care of that," he said at last.

"It is—all right," gasped his wife.

She put her hand to her throat and, hardly able to believe in her victory, sat struggling for breath. Before her, grim and upright, her husband sat, a figure of helpless smouldering wrath.

"You might lose it," he said at last.

"I shan't lose it," said his wife.

To avoid further argument, she arose and went slowly upstairs. Through the doorway Mr. Gribble saw her helping herself up by the banisters, her left hand still at her throat. Then he heard her moving slowly about in the bedroom overhead.

He took out his pipe and filled it mechanically, and was just holding a match to the tobacco when he paused and gazed with a puzzled air at the ceiling. "Blamed if it don't sound like somebody dancing!" he growled.

39

STEPPING BACKWARDS

"Wonderful improvement," said Mr. Jack Mills. "Show 'em to me again."

Mr. Simpson took his pipe from his mouth and, parting his lips, revealed his new teeth.

"And you talk better," said Mr. Mills, taking his glass from the counter and emptying it; "you ain't got that silly lisp you used to have. What does your missis think of 'em?"

"She hasn't seen 'em yet," said the other. "I had 'em put in at dinnertime. I ate my dinner with 'em."

Mr. Mills expressed his admiration. "If it wasn't for your white hair and whiskers you'd look thirty again," he said slowly. "How old are you?"

"Fifty-three," said his friend. "If it wasn't for being laughed at I've often thought of having my whiskers shaved off and my hair dyed black. People think I'm sixty."

"Or seventy," continued Mr. Mills. "What does it matter, people laughing? You've got a splendid head of 'air, and it would dye beautiful."

Mr. Simpson shook his head and, ordering a couple of glasses of bitter, attacked his in silence.

"It might be done gradual," he said, after a long interval. "It don't do anybody good at the warehouse to look old."

"Make a clean job of it," counselled Mr. Mills, who was very fond of a little cheap excitement. "Get it over and done with. You've got good features, and you'd look splendid clean-shaved."

Mr. Simpson smiled faintly.

"Only on Wednesday the barmaid here was asking after you," pursued Mr. Mills.

Mr. Simpson smiled again.

"She says to me, 'Where's Gran'pa?' she says, and when I says, haughty like, 'Who do you mean?' she says, 'Father Christmas!' If you was to tell her that you are only fifty-three, she'd laugh in your face."

"Let her laugh," said the other sourly.

"Come out and get it off," said Mr. Mills earnestly. "There's a barber's in Bird Street; you could go in the little back room, where he charges a penny more, and get it done without anybody being a bit the wiser."

He put his hand on Mr. Simpson's shoulder, and that gentleman, with a glare in the direction of the fair but unconscious offender, rose in a hypnotised fashion and followed him out. Twice on the way to Bird Street Mr. Simpson paused and said he had altered his mind, and twice did the propulsion of Mr. Mills's right hand, and his flattering argument, make him alter it again.

It was a matter of relief to Mr. Simpson that the barber took his instructions without any show of surprise. It appeared, indeed, that an elderly man of seventy-eight had enlisted his services for a similar purpose not two months before, and had got married six weeks afterwards. Age of the bride given as twenty-four, but said to have looked older.

A snip of the scissors, and six inches of white beard fell to the floor. For the first time in thirty years Mr. Simpson felt a razor on his face. Then his hair was cut and shampooed; and an hour later he sat gazing at a dark-haired, clean-shaven man in the glass who gazed back at him with wondering eyes—a lean-jawed, good-looking man, who, in a favourable light, might pass for forty. He turned and met the admiring eyes of Mr. Mills.

"What did I tell you?" inquired the latter. "You look young enough to be your own son."

"Or grandson," said the barber, with professional pride.

Mr. Simpson got up slowly from the chair and, accompanied by the admiring Mr. Mills, passed out into the street. The evening was young, and, at his friend's suggestion, they returned to the "Plume of Feathers."

"You give the order," said Mr. Mills, "and see whether she recognises you."

Mr. Simpson obeyed.

"Don't you know him?" inquired Mr. Mills, as the barmaid turned away.

"I don't think I have that pleasure," said the girl, simpering.

"Gran'pa's eldest boy," said Mr. Mills.

"Oh!" said the girl. "Well, I hope he's a better man than his father, then."

"What do you mean by that?" demanded Mr. Simpson, painfully conscious of his friend's regards.

"Nothing," said the girl, "nothing. Only we can all be better, can't we? He's a nice old gentleman; so simple."

"Don't know you from Adam," said Mr. Mills, as she turned away. "Now, if you ask me, I don't believe as your own missis will recognise you."

"Rubbish," said Mr. Simpson. "My wife would know me anywhere. We've been married over thirty years. Thirty years of sunshine and shadow together. You're a single man, and don't understand these things."

"P'r'aps you're right," said his friend. "But it'll be a bit of a shock to her, anyway. What do you say to me stepping round and breaking the news to her? It's a bit sudden, you know. She's expecting a white-haired old gentleman, not a black-haired boy."

Mr. Simpson looked a bit uneasy. "P'r'aps I ought to have told her first," he murmured, craning his neck to look in the glass at the back of the bar.

"I'll go and put it right for you," said his friend. "You stay here and smoke your pipe."

He stepped out briskly, but his pace slackened as he drew near the house.

"I—I—came—to see you about your husband," he faltered, as Mrs. Simpson opened the door and stood regarding him.

"What's the matter?" she exclaimed, with a faint cry. "What's happened to him?"

"Nothing," said Mr. Mills hastily. "Nothing serious, that is. I just came round to warn you so that you will be able to know it's him."

Mrs. Simpson let off a shriek that set his ears tingling. Then, steadying herself by the wall, she tottered into the front room, followed by the discomfited Mr. Mills, and sank into a chair.

"He's dead!" she sobbed. "He's dead!"

"He is not," said Mr. Mills.

"Is he much hurt? Is he dying?" gasped Mrs. Simpson.

"Only his hair," said Mr. Mills, clutching at the opening. "He is not hurt at all."

Mrs. Simpson dabbed at her eyes and sat regarding him in bewilderment. Her twin chins were still quivering with emotion, but her eyes were beginning to harden. "What are you talking about?" she inquired, in a raspy voice.

"He's been to a hairdresser's," said Mr. Mills. "He's 'ad all his white whiskers cut off, and his hair cut short and dyed black. And, what with that and his new teeth, I thought—he thought—p'r'aps you mightn't know him when he came home."

"Dyed?" cried Mrs. Simpson, starting to her feet.

Mr. Mills nodded. "He looks twenty years younger," he said, with a smile. "He'd pass for his own son anywhere."

Mrs. Simpson's eyes snapped. "Perhaps he'd pass for *my* son," she remarked.

"Yes, easy," said the tactful Mr. Mills. "You can't think what a difference it's made to him. That's why I came to see you—so you shouldn't be startled."

"Thank you," said Mrs. Simpson. "I'm much obliged. But you might have spared yourself the trouble. I should know my husband anywhere."

"Ah, that's what you think," retorted Mr. Mills, with a smile; "but the barmaid at the 'Plume' didn't. That's what made me come to you."

Mrs. Simpson gazed at him.

"I says to myself," continued Mr. Mills, "'If *she* don't know him, I'm certain his missis won't, and I'd better—'"

"You'd better go," interrupted his hostess.

Mr. Mills started, and then, with much dignity, stalked after her to the door.

"As to your story, I don't believe a word of it," said Mrs. Simpson. "Whatever else my husband is, he isn't a fool, and he'd no more think of cutting off his whiskers and dyeing his hair than you would of telling the truth."

"Seeing is believing," said the offended Mr. Mills darkly.

"I'll wait till I do see, and then I shan't believe," was the reply. "It is a put-up job between you and some other precious idiot, I expect. But you can't deceive me. If your black-haired friend comes here, he'll get it, I can tell you."

She slammed the door on his protests and, returning to the parlour, gazed fiercely into the glass on the mantelpiece. It reflected sixteen stone of honest English womanhood, a thin wisp of yellowish-grey hair, and a pair of faded eyes peering through clumsy spectacles.

"Son, indeed!" she said, her lips quivering. "You wait till you come home, my lord!"

Mr. Simpson, with some forebodings, returned home an hour later. To a man who loved peace and quietness the report of the indignant Mr. Mills was not of a reassuring nature. He hesitated on the doorstep for a few seconds while he fumbled for his key, and then, humming unconcernedly, hung his hat in the passage and walked into the parlour.

The astonished scream of his wife warned him that Mr. Mills had by no means exaggerated. She rose from her seat and, crouching by the fireplace, regarded him with a mixture of anger and dismay.

"It—it's all right, Milly," said Mr. Simpson, with a smile that revealed a dazzling set of teeth.

"Who are you?" demanded Mrs. Simpson. "How dare you call me by my Christian name! It's a good job for you my husband is not here."

"He wouldn't hurt me," said Mr. Simpson, with an attempt at facetiousness. "He's the best friend I ever had. Why, we slept in the same cradle."

"I don't want any of your nonsense," said Mrs. Simpson. "You get out of my house before I send for the police. How dare you come into a respectable woman's house in this fashion? Be off with you."

"Now, look here, Milly—" began Mr. Simpson.

His wife drew herself up to her full height of four feet eleven.

"I've had a hair-cut and a shave," pursued her husband; "also I've had my hair restored to its natural colour. But I'm the same man, and you know it."

"I know nothing of the kind," said his wife doggedly. "I don't know you from Adam. I've never seen you before, and I don't want to see you again. You go away."

"I'm your husband, and my place is at home," replied Mr. Simpson. "A man can have a shave if he likes, can't he? Where's my supper?"

"Go on," said his wife. "Keep it up. But be careful my husband don't come in and catch you, that's all."

Mr. Simpson gazed at her fixedly, and then, with an impatient exclamation, walked into the small kitchen and began to set the supper. A joint of cold beef, a jar of pickles, bread, butter, and cheese made an appetising display. Then he took a jug from the dresser and descended to the cellar.

A musical trickling fell on the ear of Mrs. Simpson as she stood at the parlour door, and drew her stealthily to the cellar. The key was in the lock, and, with a sudden movement, she closed the door and locked it. A sharp cry from Mr. Simpson testified to his discomfiture.

"Now I'm off for the police," cried his wife.

"Don't be a fool," shouted Mr. Simpson, tugging wildly at the door-handle. "Open the door."

Mrs. Simpson remained silent, and her husband resumed his efforts until the doorknob, unused to such treatment, came off in his hand. A sudden scrambling noise on the cellar stairs satisfied the listener that he had not pulled it off intentionally.

She stood for a few moments, considering. It was a stout door and opened inwards. She took her bonnet from its nail in the kitchen and, walking softly to the street door, set off to lay the case before a brother who lived a few doors away.

"Poor old Bill," said Mr. Cooper, when she had finished. "Still, it might be worse; he's got the barrel o' beer with him."

"It's not Bill," said Mrs. Simpson.

Mr. Cooper scratched his whiskers and looked at his wife.

"She ought to know," said the latter.

"We'll come and have a look at him," said Mr. Cooper.

Mrs. Simpson pondered, and eyed him dubiously.

"Come in and have a bit of supper," she said at last. "There's a nice piece of beef and pickles."

"And Bill—I mean the stranger—sitting on the beer-barrel," said Mr. Cooper gloomily.

"You can bring your beer with you," said his sister sharply. "Come along."

Mr. Cooper grinned, and, placing a couple of bottles in his coat pockets, followed the two ladies to the house. Seated at the kitchen table, he grinned again, as a persistent drumming took place on the cellar door. His wife smiled, and a faint, sour attempt in the same direction appeared on the face of Mrs. Simpson.

"Open the door!" bellowed an indignant voice. "Open the door!"

Mrs. Simpson, commanding silence with an uplifted finger, proceeded to carve the beef. A rattle of knives and forks succeeded.

"O—pen—the—door!" said the voice again.

"Not so much noise," commanded Mr. Cooper. "I can't hear myself eat."

"Bob!" said the voice, in relieved accents, "Bob! Come and let me out."

Mr. Cooper, putting a huge hand over his mouth, struggled nobly with his feelings.

"Who are you calling 'Bob'?" he demanded, in an unsteady voice. "You keep yourself to yourself. I've heard all about you. You've got to stay there till my brother-in-law comes home."

"It's me, Bob," said Mr. Simpson—"Bill."

"Yes, I dare say," said Mr. Cooper; "but if you're Bill, why haven't you got Bill's voice?"

"Let me out and look at me," said Mr. Simpson.

There was a faint scream from both ladies, followed by protests.

"Don't be alarmed," said Mr. Cooper reassuringly. "I wasn't born yesterday. I don't want to get a crack over the head."

"It's all a mistake, Bob," said the prisoner appealingly. "I just had a shave and a haircut and—and a little hair-dye. If you open the door you'll know me at once."

"How would it be," said Mr. Cooper, turning to his sister, and speaking with unusual distinctness—"how would it be if you opened the door, and just as he put his head out I hit it a crack with the poker?"

"You try it on," said the voice behind the door hotly. "You know who I am well enough, Bob Cooper. I don't want anymore of your nonsense. Milly has put you up to this!"

"If your wife don't know you, how do you think I can?" said Mr. Cooper. "Now, look here; you keep quiet till my brother-in-law comes home. If he don't come home perhaps we shall be more likely to think you're him. If he's not home by tomorrow morning we—*Hsh! Hsh!* Don't you know there's ladies present?"

"That settles it," said Mrs. Cooper, speaking for the first time. "My brother-in-law would never talk like that."

"I should never forgive him if he did," said her husband piously.

He poured himself out another glass of beer and resumed his supper with relish. Conversation turned on the weather, and from that to the price of potatoes. Frantic efforts on the part of the prisoner to join in the conversation and give it a more personal turn were disregarded. Finally he began to kick with monotonous persistency on the door.

"Stop it!" shouted Mr. Cooper.

"I won't," said Mr. Simpson.

The noise became unendurable. Mr. Cooper, who had just lit his pipe, laid it on the table and looked round at his companions.

"He'll have the door down soon," he said, rising. "Halloa, there!"

"Halloa!" said the other.

"You say you're Bill Simpson," said Mr. Cooper, holding up a forefinger at Mrs. Simpson, who was about to interrupt. "If you are, tell us something you know that only you could know;

something we know, so as to identify you. Things about your past."

A strange voice sounded behind the door.

"Sounds as though he is smacking his lips," said Mrs. Cooper to her sister-in-law, who was eyeing Mr. Cooper restlessly.

"Very good," said Mr. Simpson; "I agree. Who is there?"

"Me and my wife and Mrs. Simpson," said Mr. Cooper.

"He *is* smacking his lips," whispered Mrs. Cooper. "Having a go at the beer, perhaps."

"Let's go back fifteen years," said Mr. Simpson in meditative tones. "Do you remember that girl with copper-coloured hair that used to live in John Street?"

"No!" said Mr. Cooper, loudly and suddenly.

"Do you remember coming to me one day—two days after Valentine Day, it was—white as chalk and shaking like a leaf, and—"

"NO!" roared Mr. Cooper.

"Very well, I must try something else, then," said Mr. Simpson philosophically. "Carry your mind back ten years, Bob Cooper—"

"Look here!" said Mr. Cooper, turning round with a ghastly smile. "We'd better get off home, Mary. I don't like interfering in other people's concerns. Never did."

"You stay where you are," said his wife.

"Ten years," repeated the voice behind the door. "There was a new barmaid at the 'Crown,' and one night you—"

"If I listen to anymore of this nonsense I shall burst," remarked Mr. Cooper plaintively.

"Go on," prompted Mrs. Cooper grimly. "One night—"

"Never mind," said Mr. Simpson. "It doesn't matter. But does he identify me? Because if not I've got a lot more things I can try."

The harassed Mr. Cooper looked around appealingly.

"How do you expect me to recognise you—" he began, and stopped suddenly.

"Go back to your courting days, then," said Mr. Simpson, "when Mrs. Cooper wasn't Mrs. Cooper, but only wanted to be."

Mrs. Cooper shivered; so did Mr. Cooper.

"And you came round to me for advice," pursued Mr. Simpson, in reminiscent accents, "because there was another girl you wasn't sure of, and you didn't want to lose them both. Do you remember sitting with the two photographs—one on each knee—and trying to make up your mind?"

"Wonderful imagination," said Mr. Cooper, smiling in a ghastly fashion at his wife. "Hark at him!"

"I am harking," said Mrs. Cooper.

"Am I Bill Simpson or am I not?" demanded Mr. Simpson.

"Bill was always fond of his joke," said Mr. Cooper, with a glance at the company that would have moved an oyster. "He was always fond of making up things. You're like him in that. What do you think, Milly?"

"It's not my husband," said Mrs. Simpson.

"Tell us something about her," said Mr. Cooper hastily.

"I daren't," said Mr. Simpson. "Doesn't that prove I'm her husband? But I'll tell you things about your wife, if you like."

"You dare!" said Mrs. Cooper, turning crimson, as she realised what confidences might have passed between husband and wife. "If you say a word of your lies about me, I don't know what I won't do to you."

"Very well, I must go on about Bob, then—till he recognises me," said Mr. Simpson patiently. "Carry your mind—"

"Open the door and let him out," shouted Mr. Cooper, turning to his sister. "How can I recognise a man through a deal door?"

Mrs. Simpson, after a little hesitation, handed him the key, and the next moment her husband stepped out and stood blinking in the gas-light.

"Do you recognise me?" he asked, turning to Mr. Cooper.

"I do," said that gentleman, with a ferocious growl.

"I'd know you anywhere," said Mrs. Cooper, with emphasis.

"And you?" said Mr. Simpson, turning to his wife.

"You're not my husband," she said obstinately.

"Are you sure?" inquired Mr. Cooper.

"Certain."

"Very good, then," said her brother. "If he's not your husband I'm going to knock his head off for telling them lies about me."

He sprang forward and, catching Mr. Simpson by the collar, shook him violently until his head banged against the dresser. The next moment the hands of Mrs. Simpson were in the hair of Mr. Cooper.

"How dare you knock my husband about!" she screamed, as Mr. Cooper let go and caught her fingers. "You've hurt him."

"Concussion, I think," said Mr. Simpson, with great presence of mind.

His wife helped him to a chair and, wetting her handkerchief at the tap, tenderly bathed the dyed head. Mr. Cooper, breathing hard, stood by watching until his wife touched him on the arm.

"You come off home," she said, in a hard voice. "You ain't wanted. Are you going to stay here all night?"

"I should like to," said Mr. Cooper wistfully.

40

THE THREE SISTERS

Thirty years ago on a wet autumn evening the household of Mallett's Lodge was gathered round the deathbed of Ursula Mallow, the eldest of the three sisters who inhabited it. The dingy moth-eaten curtains of the old wooden bedstead were drawn apart, the light of a smoking oil-lamp falling upon the hopeless countenance of the dying woman as she turned her dull eyes upon her sisters. The room was in silence except for an occasional sob from the youngest sister, Eunice. Outside the rain fell steadily over the streaming marshes.

"Nothing is to be changed, Tabitha," gasped Ursula to the other sister, who bore a striking likeness to her, although her expression was harder and colder; "this room is to be locked up and never opened."

"Very well," said Tabitha brusquely; "though I don't see how it can matter to you then."

"It does matter," said her sister with startling energy. "How do you know, how do I know that I may not sometimes visit it? I have lived in this house so long I am certain that I shall see it again. I *will* come back. Come back to watch over you both and see that no harm befalls you."

"You are talking wildly," said Tabitha, by no means moved at her sister's solicitude for her welfare. "Your mind is wandering; you know that I have no faith in such things."

Ursula sighed, and beckoning to Eunice, who was weeping silently at the bedside, placed her feeble arms around her neck and kissed her.

"Do not weep, dear," she said feebly. "Perhaps it is best so. A lonely woman's life is scarce worth living. We have no hopes, no aspirations; other women have had happy husbands and children, but we in this forgotten place have grown old together. I go first, but you must soon follow."

Tabitha, comfortably conscious of only forty years and an iron frame, shrugged her shoulders and smiled grimly.

"I go first," repeated Ursula in a new and strange voice as her heavy eyes slowly closed, "but I will come for each of you in turn, when your lease of life runs out. At that moment I will be with you to lead your steps whither I now go."

As she spoke the flickering lamp went out suddenly as though extinguished by a rapid hand, and the room was left in utter darkness. A strange suffocating noise issued from the bed, and when the trembling women had relighted the lamp, all that was left of Ursula Mallow was ready for the grave.

That night the survivors passed together. The dead woman had been a firm believer in the existence of that shadowy borderland which is said to form an unhallowed link between the living and the dead, and even stolid Tabitha, slightly unnerved by the events of the night, was not free from certain apprehensions that she might have been right.

With the bright morning their fears disappeared. The sun stole in at the window, and seeing the poor earthworn face on the pillow so touched it and glorified it that only its goodness and weakness were seen, and the beholders came to wonder how they could ever have felt any dread of aught so calm and peaceful. A day or two passed, and the body was transferred to a massive coffin long regarded as the finest piece of work of its kind ever turned out of the village carpenter's workshop. Then a slow and melancholy cortege headed by four bearers wound its solemn way across the marshes to the family vault in the grey old church, and all that was left of Ursula was placed by the father and mother who had taken that self-same journey some thirty years before.

To Eunice as they toiled slowly home the day seemed strange and Sabbath-like, the flat prospect of marsh wilder and more forlorn than usual the roar of the sea more depressing. Tabitha had no such fancies. The bulk of the dead woman's property had been left to Eunice, and her avaricious soul was sorely troubled and her proper sisterly feelings of regret for the deceased sadly interfered with in consequence.

"What are you going to do with all that money, Eunice?" she asked as they sat at their quiet tea.

"I shall leave it as it stands," said Eunice slowly. "We have both got sufficient to live upon, and I shall devote the income from it to supporting some beds in a children's hospital."

"If Ursula had wished it to go to a hospital," said Tabitha in her deep tones, "she would have left the money to it herself. I wonder you do not respect her wishes more."

"What else can I do with it then?" inquired Eunice.

"Save it," said the other with gleaming eyes, "save it."

Eunice shook her head.

"No," said she, "it shall go to the sick children, but the principal I will not touch, and if I die before you it shall become yours and you can do what you like with it."

"Very well," said Tabitha, smothering her anger by a strong effort; "I don't believe that was what Ursula meant you to do with it, and I don't believe she will rest quietly in the grave while you squander the money she stored so carefully."

"What do you mean?" asked Eunice with pale lips. "You are trying to frighten me; I thought that you did not believe in such things."

Tabitha made no answer, and to avoid the anxious inquiring gaze of her sister, drew her chair to the fire, and folding her gaunt arms, composed herself for a nap.

For some time life went on quietly in the old house. The room of the dead woman, in accordance with her last desire, was kept firmly locked, its dirty windows forming a strange contrast to the prim cleanliness of the others. Tabitha, never very talkative, became more taciturn than ever, and stalked about the house and the neglected garden like an unquiet spirit, her brow roughened into the deep wrinkles suggestive of much thought. As the winter came on, bringing with it the long dark evenings, the old house became more lonely than ever, and an air of mystery and dread seemed to hang over it and brood in its empty rooms and dark corridors. The deep silence of night was broken by strange noises for which neither the wind nor the rats could be held accountable. Old Martha, seated in her distant kitchen, heard strange sounds upon the stairs, and once, upon hurrying to them, fancied that she saw a dark figure squatting upon the landing, though a subsequent search with candle and spectacles failed to discover anything. Eunice was disturbed by several vague incidents, and, as she suffered from a complaint of the heart, rendered very ill by them. Even Tabitha admitted a strangeness about the house, but, confident in her piety and virtue, took no heed of it, her mind being fully employed in another direction.

Since the death of her sister all restraint upon her was removed, and she yielded herself up entirely to the stern and hard rules enforced by avarice upon its devotees. Her housekeeping expenses were kept rigidly separate from those of Eunice and her food limited to the coarsest dishes, while in the matter of clothes the old servant was by far the better dressed. Seated alone in her bedroom this uncouth, hard-featured creature revelled in her possessions, grudging even the expense of the candle-end which enabled her to behold them. So completely did this passion change her that both Eunice and Martha became afraid of her, and lay awake in their beds night after night trembling at the chinking of the coins at her unholy vigils.

One day Eunice ventured to remonstrate. "Why don't you bank your money, Tabitha?" she said; "it is surely not safe to keep such large sums in such a lonely house."

"Large sums!" repeated the exasperated Tabitha, "large sums; what nonsense is this? You know well that I have barely sufficient to keep me."

"It's a great temptation to housebreakers," said her sister, not pressing the point. "I made sure last night that I heard somebody in the house."

"Did you?" said Tabitha, grasping her arm, a horrible look on her face. "So did I. I thought they went to Ursula's room, and I got out of bed and went on the stairs to listen."

"Well?" said Eunice faintly, fascinated by the look on her sister's face.

"There was *something* there," said Tabitha slowly. "I'll swear it, for I stood on the landing by her door and listened; something scuffling on the floor round and round the room. At first I thought it was the cat, but when I went up there this morning the door was still locked, and the cat was in the kitchen."

"Oh, let us leave this dreadful house," moaned Eunice.

"What!" said her sister grimly; "afraid of poor Ursula? Why should you be? your own sister who nursed you when you were a babe, and who perhaps even now comes and watches over your slumbers."

"Oh!" said Eunice, pressing her hand to her side, "if I saw her I should die. I should think that she had come for me as she said she would. O God! Have mercy on me, I am dying."

She reeled as she spoke, and before Tabitha could save her, sank senseless to the floor.

"Get some water," cried Tabitha, as old Martha came hurrying up the stairs, "Eunice has fainted."

The old woman, with a timid glance at her, retired, reappearing shortly afterwards with the water, with which she proceeded to restore her much-loved mistress to her senses. Tabitha, as soon as this was accomplished, stalked off to her room, leaving her sister and Martha sitting drearily enough in the small parlour, watching the fire and conversing in whispers.

It was clear to the old servant that this state of things could not last much longer, and she repeatedly urged her mistress to leave a house so lonely and so mysterious. To her great delight Eunice at length consented, despite the fierce opposition of her sister, and at the mere idea of leaving gained greatly in health and spirits. A small but comfortable house was hired in Morville, and arrangements made for a speedy change.

It was the last night in the old house, and all the wild spirits of the marshes, the wind and the sea seemed to have joined forces for one supreme effort. When the wind dropped, as it did at brief intervals, the sea was heard moaning on the distant beach, strangely mingled with the desolate warning of the bell-buoy as it rocked to the waves. Then the wind rose again, and the noise of the sea was lost in the fierce gusts which, finding no obstacle on the open marshes, swept with their full fury upon the house by the creek. The strange voices of the air shrieked in its chimneys, windows rattled, doors slammed, and even the very curtains seemed to live and move.

Eunice was in bed, awake. A small night-light in a saucer of oil shed a sickly glare upon the worm-eaten old furniture, distorting the most innocent articles into ghastly shapes. A wilder gust than usual almost deprived her of the protection afforded by that poor light, and she lay listening fearfully to the creakings and other noises on the stairs, bitterly regretting that she had not asked Martha to sleep with her. But it was not too late even now. She slipped hastily to the floor, crossed to the huge wardrobe, and was in the very act of taking her dressing-gown from its peg when an unmistakable footfall was heard on the stairs. The robe dropped from her shaking fingers, and with a quickly beating heart she regained her bed.

The sounds ceased and a deep silence followed, which she herself was unable to break although she strove hard to do so. A wild gust of wind shook the windows and nearly extinguished the light, and when its flame had regained its accustomed steadiness she saw that the door was slowly opening, while the huge shadow of a hand blotted the papered wall. Still her tongue refused its office. The door flew open with a crash, a cloaked figure entered and, throwing aside its coverings, she saw with a horror past all expression the napkin-bound face of the dead Ursula smiling terribly at her. In her last extremity she raised her faded eyes above for succour, and then as the figure noiselessly advanced and laid its cold hand upon her brow, the soul of Eunice Mallow left its body with a wild shriek and made its way to the Eternal.

Martha, roused by the cry, and shivering with dread, rushed to the door and gazed in terror at the figure which stood leaning over the bedside. As she watched, it slowly removed the cowl and the napkin and exposed the fell face of Tabitha, so strangely contorted between fear and triumph that she hardly recognised it.

"Who's there?" cried Tabitha in a terrible voice as she saw the old woman's shadow on the wall.

"I thought I heard a cry," said Martha, entering. "Did anybody call?"

"Yes, Eunice," said the other, regarding her closely. "I, too, heard the cry, and hurried to her. What makes her so strange? Is she in a trance?"

"Aye," said the old woman, falling on her knees by the bed and sobbing bitterly, "the trance of death. Ah, my dear, my poor lonely girl, that this should be the end of it! She has died of fright," said the old woman, pointing to the eyes, which even yet retained their horror. "She has seen something *devilish.*"

Tabitha's gaze fell. "She has always suffered with her heart," she muttered; "the night has frightened her; it frightened me."

She stood upright by the foot of the bed as Martha drew the sheet over the face of the dead woman.

"First Ursula, then Eunice," said Tabitha, drawing a deep breath. "I can't stay here. I'll dress and wait for the morning."

She left the room as she spoke, and with bent head proceeded to her own. Martha remained by the bedside, and gently closing the staring eyes, fell on her knees and prayed long and earnestly for the departed soul. Overcome with grief and fear, she remained with bowed head until a sudden sharp cry from Tabitha brought her to her feet.

"Well," said the old woman, going to the door.

"Where are you?" cried Tabitha, somewhat reassured by her voice.

"In Miss Eunice's bedroom. Do you want anything?"

"Come down at once. Quick! I am unwell."

Her voice rose suddenly to a scream. "Quick! For God's sake! Quick, or I shall go mad. *There is some strange woman in the house.*"

The old woman stumbled hastily down the dark stairs. "What is the matter?" she cried, entering the room. "Who is it? What do you mean?"

"I saw it," said Tabitha, grasping her convulsively by the shoulder. "I was coming to you when I saw the figure of a woman in front of me going up the stairs. Is it—can it be Ursula come for the soul of Eunice, as she said she would?"

"Or for yours?" said Martha, the words coming from her in some odd fashion, despite herself.

Tabitha, with a ghastly look, fell cowering by her side, clutching tremulously at her clothes. "Light the lamps," she cried hysterically. “Light a fire, make a noise; oh, this dreadful darkness! Will it never be day!”

“Soon, soon,” said Martha, overcoming her repugnance and trying to pacify her. “When the day comes you will laugh at these fears.”

“I murdered her,” screamed the miserable woman, “I killed her with fright. Why did she not give me the money? ’Twas no use to her. Ah! *Look there!*”

Martha, with a horrible fear, followed her glance to the door, but saw nothing.

“It’s Ursula,” said Tabitha, from between her teeth. “Keep her off! Keep her off!”

The old woman, who by some unknown sense seemed to feel the presence of a third person in the room, moved a step forward and stood before her. As she did so Tabitha waved her arms as though to free herself from the touch of a detaining hand, half rose to her feet, and without a word fell dead before her.

At this the old woman’s courage forsook her, and with a great cry she rushed from the room, eager to escape from this house of death and mystery. The bolts of the great door were stiff with age, and strange voices seemed to ring in her ears as she strove wildly to unfasten them. Her brain whirled. She thought that the dead in their distant rooms called to her, and that a devil stood on the step outside laughing and holding the door against her. Then with a supreme effort she flung it open, and heedless of her night-clothes passed into the bitter night. The path across the marshes was lost in the darkness, but she found it; the planks over the ditches slippery and narrow, but she crossed them in safety, until at last, her feet bleeding and her breath coming in great gasps, she entered the village and sank down more dead than alive on a cottage doorstep.

41

THE UNKNOWN

"Handsome is as 'andsome does," said the night-watchman. It's an old saying, but it's true. Give a chap good looks, and it's precious little else that is given to 'im. He's lucky when 'is good looks have gorn—or partly gorn—to get a berth as night-watchman or some other hard and bad-paid job.

One drawback to a good-looking man is that he generally marries young; not because 'e wants to, but because somebody else wants 'im to. And that ain't the worst of it: the handsomest chap I ever knew married five times, and got seven years for it. It wasn't his fault, pore chap; he simply couldn't say No.

One o' the best-looking men I ever knew was Cap'n Bill Smithers, wot used to come up here once a week with a schooner called the *Wild Rose*. Funny thing about 'im was he didn't seem to know about 'is good looks, and he was one o' the quietest, best-behaved men that ever came up the London river. Considering that he was mistook for me more than once, it was just as well.

He didn't marry until 'e was close on forty; and then 'e made the mistake of marrying a widder-woman. She was like all the rest of 'em—only worse. Afore she was married butter wouldn't melt in 'er mouth, but as soon as she 'ad got her "lines" safe she began to make up for it.

For the fust month or two 'e didn't mind it, 'e rather liked being fussed arter, but when he found that he couldn't go out for arf an hour without having 'er with 'im he began to get tired of it. Her idea was that 'e was too handsome to be trusted out alone; and every trip he made 'e had to write up in a book, day by day, wot 'e did with himself. Even then she wasn't satisfied, and, arter saying that a wife's place was by the side of 'er husband, she took to sailing with 'im every v'y'ge.

Wot he could ha' seen in 'er I don't know. I asked 'im one evening—in a roundabout way—and he answered in such a long, roundabout way that I didn't know wot to make of it till I see that she was standing just behind me, listening. Arter that I heard 'er asking questions about me, but I didn't 'ave to listen: I could hear 'er twenty yards away, and singing to myself at the same time.

Arter that she treated me as if I was the dirt beneath 'er feet. She never spoke to me, but used to speak against me to other people. She was always talking to them about the "sleeping sickness" and things 'o that kind. She said night-watchmen always made 'er think of it somehow, but she didn't know why, and she couldn't tell you if you was to ask her. The only thing I was thankful for was that I wasn't 'er husband. She stuck to 'im like his shadow, and I began to think at last it was a pity she 'adn't got something to be jealous about and something to occupy her mind with instead o' me.

"She ought to 'ave a lesson," I ses to the skipper one evening. "Are you going to be follered about like this all your life? If she was made to see the foolishness of 'er ways she might get sick of it."

My idea was to send her on a wild-goose chase, and while the *Wild Rose* was away I thought it out. I wrote a love-letter to the skipper signed with the name of "Dorothy," and asked 'im to meet me at Cleopatra's Needle on the Embankment at eight o'clock on Wednesday. I told 'im to look out for a tall girl (Mrs.

Smithers was as short as they make 'em) with mischievous brown eyes, in a blue 'at with red roses on it.

I read it over careful, and arter marking it "Private," twice in front and once on the back, I stuck it down so that it could be blown open a'most, and waited for the schooner to come back. Then I gave a van-boy twopence to 'and it to Mrs. Smithers, wot was sitting on the deck alone, and tell 'er it was a letter for Captain Smithers.

I was busy with a barge wot happened to be handy at the time, but I 'eard her say that she would take it and give it to 'im. When I peeped round she 'ad got the letter open and was leaning over the side to wind'ard trying to get 'er breath. Every now and then she'd give another look at the letter and open 'er mouth and gasp; but by and by she got calmer, and, arter putting it back in the envelope, she gave it a lick as though she was going to bite it, and stuck it down agin. Then she went off the wharf, and I'm blest if five minutes arterwards, a young fellow didn't come down to the ship with the same letter and ask for the skipper.

"Who gave it you?" ses the skipper, as soon as 'e could speak.

"A lady," ses the young fellow.

The skipper waved 'im away, and then 'e walked up and down the deck like a man in a dream.

"Bad news?" I ses, looking up and catching 'is eye.

"No," he ses, "no. Only a note about a couple o' casks o' soda."

He stuffed the letter in 'is pocket and sat on the side smoking till his wife came back in five minutes' time, smiling all over with good temper.

"It's a nice evening," she ses, "and I think I'll just run over to Dalston and see my Cousin Joe."

The skipper got up like a lamb and said he'd go and clean 'imself.

"You needn't come if you feel tired," she ses, smiling at 'im.

The skipper could 'ardly believe his ears.

"I do feel tired," he ses. "I've had a heavy day, and I feel more like bed than anything else."

"You turn in, then," she ses. "I'll be all right by myself."

She went down and tidied herself up—not that it made much difference to 'er—and, arter patting him on the arm and giving me a stare that would ha' made most men blink, she took herself off.

I was pretty busy that evening. Wot with shifting lighters from under the jetty and sweeping up, it was pretty near ha'-past seven afore I 'ad a minute I could call my own. I put down the broom at last, and was just thinking of stepping round to the "Bull's Head" for a arf-pint when I see Cap'n Smithers come off the ship on to the wharf and walk to the gate.

"I thought you was going to turn in?" I ses.

"I did think of it," he ses; "then I thought p'r'aps I'd better stroll as far as Broad Street and meet my wife."

It was all I could do to keep a straight face. I'd a pretty good idea where she 'ad gorn; and it wasn't Dalston.

"Come in and 'ave 'arf a pint fust," I ses.

"No; I shall be late," he ses, hurrying off.

I went in and 'ad a glass by myself, and stood there so long thinking of Mrs. Smithers walking up and down by Cleopatra's Needle that at last the landlord fust asked me wot I was laughing at, and then offered to make me laugh the other side of my face. And then he wonders why people go to the "Albion."

I locked the gate rather earlier than usual that night. Sometimes if I'm up that end I leave it a bit late, but I didn't want Mrs. Smithers to come along and nip in without me seeing her face.

It was ten o'clock afore I heard the bell go, and when I opened the wicket and looked out I was surprised to see that she 'ad got the skipper with 'er. And of all the miserable-looking objects I ever saw in my life he was the worst. She 'ad him tight by the arm, and there was a look on 'er face that a'most scared me.

"Did you go all the way to Dalston for her?" I ses to 'im.

Mrs. Smithers made a gasping sort o' noise, but the skipper didn't answer a word. She shoved him in in front of her and stood over 'im while 'e climbed aboard. When he held out 'is hand to help 'er she struck it away.

I didn't get word with 'im till five o'clock next morning, when he came up on deck with his 'air all rough and 'is eyes red for want of sleep.

"Haven't 'ad a wink all night," he ses, stepping on to the wharf.

I gave a little cough. "Didn't she 'ave a pleasant time at Dalston?" I ses.

He walked a little further off from the ship. "She didn't go there," he ses, in a whisper.

"You've got something on your mind," I ses. "Wot is it?"

He wouldn't tell me at fust, but at last he told me all about the letter from Dorothy, and 'is wife reading it unbeknown to 'im and going to meet 'er.

"It was an awful meeting!" he ses. "Awful!"

I couldn't think wot to make of it. "Was the gal there, then?" I ses, staring at 'im.

"No," ses the skipper; "but I was."

"*You?*" I ses, starting back. "You! Wot for? I'm surprised at you! I wouldn't ha' believed it of you!"

"I felt a bit curious," he ses, with a silly sort o' smile. "But wot I can't understand is why the gal didn't turn up."

"I'm ashamed of you, Bill," I ses, very severe.

"P'r'aps she did," he ses, 'arf to 'imself, "and then saw my missis standing there waiting. P'r'aps that was it."

"Or p'r'aps it was somebody 'aving a game with you," I ses.

"You're getting old, Bill," he ses, very short. "You don't understand. It's some pore gal that's took a fancy to me, and it's my dooty to meet 'er and tell her 'ow things are."

He walked off with his 'ead in the air, and if 'e took that letter out once and looked at it, he did five times.

"Chuck it away," I ses, going up to him.

"Certainly not," he ses, folding it up careful and stowing it away in 'is breast-pocket. "She's took a fancy to me, and it's my dooty—"

"You said that afore," I ses.

He stared at me nasty for a moment, and then 'e ses: "You ain't seen any young lady hanging about 'ere, I suppose, Bill. A tall young lady with a blue hat trimmed with red roses?"

I shook my 'ead.

"If you should see 'er—" he ses.

"I'll tell your missis," I ses. "It 'ud be much easier for her to do her dooty properly than it would you. She'd enjoy doing it, too."

He went off agin then, and I thought he 'ad done with me, but he 'adn't. He spoke to me that evening as if I was the greatest friend he 'ad in the world. I 'ad two 'arf-pints with 'im at the "Albion"—with his missis walking up and down outside—and arter the second 'arf-pint he said he wanted to meet Dorothy and tell 'er that 'e was married, and that he 'oped she would meet some good man that was worthy of 'er.

I had a week's peace while the ship was away, but she was hardly made fast afore I 'ad it all over agin and agin.

"Are you sure there's been no more letters?" he ses.

"Sartain," I ses.

"That's right," he ses; "that's right. And you 'aven't seen her walking up and down?"

"No," I ses.

"'Ave you been on the lookout?" he ses. "I don't suppose a nice gal like that would come and shove her 'ead in at the gate. Did you look up and down the road?"

"Yes," I ses. "I've fair made my eyes ache watching for her."

"I can't understand it," he ses. "It's a mystery to me, unless p'r'aps she's been taken ill. She must 'ave seen me here in the fust place; and she managed to get hold of my name. Mark my words, I shall 'ear from her agin."

"'Ow do you know?" I ses.

"I feel it 'ere," he ses, very solemn, laying his 'and on his chest.

I didn't know wot to do. Wot with 'is foolishness and his missis's temper, I see I 'ad made a mess of it. He told me she had 'ardly spoke a word to 'im for two days, and when I said—being a married man myself—that it might ha' been I worse, 'e said I didn't know wot I was talking about.

I did a bit o' thinking arter he 'ad gorn aboard agin. I dursn't tell 'im that I 'ad wrote the letter, but I thought if he 'ad one or two more he'd see that someone was 'aving a game with 'im, and that it might do 'im good. Besides which it was a little amusement for me.

Arter everybody was in their beds asleep I sat on a clerk's stool in the office and wrote 'im another letter from Dorothy. I called 'im "Dear Bill," and I said 'ow sorry I was that I 'adn't had even a sight of 'im lately, having been laid up with a sprained ankle and 'ad only just got about agin. I asked 'im to meet me at Cleopatra's Needle at eight o'clock, and said that I should wear the blue 'at with red roses.

It was a very good letter, but I can see now that I done wrong in writing it. I was going to post it to 'im, but, as I couldn't find an envelope without the name of the blessed wharf on it, I put it in my pocket till I got 'ome.

I got 'ome at about a quarter to seven, and slept like a child till pretty near four. Then I went downstairs to 'ave my dinner.

The moment I opened the door I see there was something wrong. Three times my missis licked 'er lips afore she could speak. Her face 'ad gone a dirty white colour, and she was leaning forward with her 'ands on her 'ips, trembling all over with temper.

"Is my dinner ready?" I ses, easy-like. "'Cos I'm ready for *it*."

"I—I wonder I don't tear you limb from limb," she ses, catching her breath.

"Wot's the matter?" I ses.

"And then boil you," she ses, between her teeth. "You in one pot and your precious Dorothy in another."

If anybody 'ad offered me five pounds to speak then, I couldn't ha' done it. I see wot I'd done in a flash, and I couldn't say a word; but I kept my presence o' mind, and as she came round one side o' the table I went round the other.

"Wot 'ave you got to say for yourself?" she ses, with a scream.

"Nothing," I ses, at last. "It's all a mistake."

"Mistake?" she ses. "Yes, you made a mistake leaving it in your pocket; that's all the mistake you've made. That's wot you do, is it, when you're supposed to be at the wharf? Go about with a blue 'at with red roses in it! At your time o' life, and a wife at 'ome working herself to death to make both ends meet and keep you respectable!"

"It's all a mistake," I ses. "The letter wasn't for me."

"Oh, no, o' course not," she ses. "That's why you'd got it in your pocket, I suppose. And I suppose you'll say your name ain't Bill next.

"Don't say things you'll be sorry for," I ses.

"I'll take care o' that," she ses. "I might be sorry for not saying some things, but I don't think I shall."

I don't think she was. I don't think she forgot anything, and she raked up things that I 'ad contradicted years ago and wot I thought was all forgot. And every now and then, when she stopped for breath, she'd try and get round to the same side of the table I was.

She follered me to the street door when I went and called things up the road arter me. I 'ad a snack at a coffee-shop for my dinner, but I 'adn't got much appetite for it; I was too full of trouble and finding fault with myself, and I went off to my work with a 'art as heavy as lead.

I suppose I 'adn't been on the wharf ten minutes afore Cap'n Smithers came sidling up to me, but I got my spoke in fust.

"Look 'ere," I ses, "if you're going to talk about that forward hussy wot's been writing to you, I ain't. I'm sick and tired of 'er."

"Forward hussy!" he ses. "*Forward hussy!*" And afore I could drop my broom he gave me a punch in the jaw that pretty near broke it. "Say another word against her," he ses, "and I'll knock your ugly 'ead off. How dare you insult a lady?"

I thought I should 'ave gone crazy at fust, but I went off into the office without a word. Some men would ha' knocked 'im down for it, but I made allowances for 'is state o' mind, and I stayed inside until I see 'im get aboard agin.

He was sitting on deck when I went out, and his missis too, but neither of 'em spoke a word. I picked up my broom and went on sweeping, when suddenly I 'eard a voice at the gate I thought I knew, and in came my wife.

"Ho!" she ses, calling out. "Ain't you gone to meet that gal at Cleopatra's Needle yet? You ain't going to keep 'er waiting, are you?"

"*H'sh!*" I ses.

"*H'sh!* yourself," she ses, shouting. "*I've* done nothing to be ashamed of. *I* don't go to meet other people's husbands in a blue 'at with red roses. *I* don't write 'em love-letters, and say '*H'sh!*' to my wife when she ventures to make a remark about it. I may work myself to skin and bone for a man's wot old enough to know better, I but I'm not going to be trod on. Dorothy, indeed! I'll Dorothy 'er if I get the chance."

Mrs. Smithers, wot 'ad been listening with all her ears, jumped up, and so did the skipper, and Mrs. Smithers came to the side in two steps.

"Did you say 'Dorothy,' ma'am?" she ses to my missis.

"I did," ses my wife. "She's been writing to my husband."

"It must be the same one," ses Mrs. Smithers. "She's been writing to mine too."

The two of 'em stood there looking at each other for a minute, and then my wife, holding the letter between 'er finger and thumb as if it was pison, passed it to Mrs. Smithers.

"It's the same," ses Mrs. Smithers. "Was the envelope marked 'Private'?"

"I didn't see no envelope," ses my missis. "This is all I found."

Mrs. Smithers stepped on to the wharf and, taking 'old of my missis by the arm, led her away whispering. At the same moment the skipper walked across the deck and whispered to me.

"Wot d'ye mean by it?" he ses. "Wot d'ye mean by 'aving letters from Dorothy and not telling me about it?"

"I can't help 'aving letters anymore than you can," I ses. "Now p'r'aps you'll understand wot I meant by calling 'er a forward hussy."

"Fancy 'er writing to you!" he ses, wrinkling 'is forehead. "*Pph!* She must be crazy."

"P'r'aps it ain't a gal at all," I ses. "My belief is somebody is 'aving a game with us."

"Don't be a fool," he ses. "I'd like to see the party as would make a fool of me like that. Just see 'im and get my 'ands on him. He wouldn't want to play anymore games."

It was no good talking to 'im. He was 'arf crazy with temper. If I'd said the letter was meant for 'im he'd 'ave asked me wot I meant by opening it and getting 'im into more trouble with 'is missis, instead of giving it to 'im on the quiet. I just stood and suffered in silence, and thought wot a lot of 'arm eddication did for people.

"I want some money," ses my missis, coming back at last with Mrs. Smithers.

That was the way she always talked when she'd got me in 'er power. She took two-and-tenpence—all I'd got—and then she ordered me to go and get a cab.

"Me and this lady are going to meet her," she ses, sniffing at me.

"And tell her wot we think of 'er," ses Mrs. Smithers, sniffing too.

"And wot we'll do to 'er," ses my missis.

I left 'em standing side by side, looking at the skipper as if 'e was a waxworks, while I went to find a cab. When I came back they was in the same persition, and 'e was smoking with 'is eyes shut.

They went off side by side in the cab, both of 'em sitting bolt upright, and only turning their 'eads at the last moment to give us looks we didn't want.

"I don't wish her no 'arm," ses the skipper, arter thinking for a long time. "Was that the fust letter you 'ad from 'er, Bill?"

"Fust and last," I ses, grinding my teeth.

"I hope they won't meet 'er, pore thing," he ses.

"I've been married longer than wot you have," I ses, "and I tell you one thing. It won't make I no difference to us whether they do or they don't," I ses.

And it didn't.

42

THE VIGIL

"I'm the happiest man in the world," said Mr. Farrer, in accents of dreamy tenderness.

Miss Ward sighed. "Wait till father comes in," she said.

Mr. Farrer peered through the plants which formed a welcome screen to the window and listened with some uneasiness. He was waiting for the firm, springy step that should herald the approach of ex-Sergeant-Major Ward. A squeeze of Miss Ward's hand renewed his courage.

"Perhaps I had better light the lamp," said the girl, after a long pause. "I wonder where mother's got to?"

"She's on my side, at any rate," said Mr. Farrer.

"Poor mother!" said the girl. "She daren't call her soul her own. I expect she's sitting in her bedroom with the door shut. She hates unpleasantness. And there's sure to be some."

"So do I," said the young man, with a slight shiver. "But why should there be any? He doesn't want you to keep single all your life, does he?"

"He'd like me to marry a soldier," said Miss Ward. "He says that the young men of the present day are too soft. The only thing he thinks about is courage and strength."

She rose and, placing the lamp on the table, removed the chimney, and then sought round the room for the matches. Mr. Farrer, who had two boxes in his pocket, helped her.

They found a box at last on the mantelpiece, and Mr. Farrer steadied her by placing one arm round her waist while she lit the lamp. A sudden exclamation from outside reminded them that the blind was not yet drawn, and they sprang apart in dismay as a grizzled and upright old warrior burst into the room and confronted them.

"Pull that blind down!" he roared. "Not you," he continued, as Mr. Farrer hastened to help. "What do you mean by touching my blind? What do you mean by embracing my daughter? Eh? Why don't you answer?"

"We—we are going to be married," said Mr. Farrer, trying to speak boldly.

The sergeant-major drew himself up, and the young man gazed in dismay at a chest which seemed as though it would never cease expanding.

"Married!" exclaimed the sergeant-major, with a grim laugh. "Married to a little tame bunny-rabbit! Not if I know it. Where's your mother?" he demanded, turning to the girl.

"Upstairs," was the reply.

Her father raised his voice, and a nervous reply came from above. A minute later Mrs. Ward, pale of cheek, entered the room.

"Here's fine goings-on!" said the sergeant-major sharply. "I go for a little walk, and when I come back this—this infernal cockroach has got its arm round my daughter's waist. Why don't you look after her? Do you know anything about it?"

His wife shook her head.

"Five feet four and about thirty round the chest, and wants to marry my daughter!" said the sergeant-major, with a sneer. "Eh? What's that? What did you say? What?"

"I said that's a pretty good size for a cockroach," murmured Mr. Farrer defiantly. "Besides, size isn't everything. If it was, you'd be a general instead of only a sergeant-major."

"You get out of my house," said the other, as soon as he could get his breath. "Go on! Sharp with it."

"I'm going," said the mortified Mr. Farrer. "I'm sorry if I was rude. I came on purpose to see you tonight. Bertha—Miss Ward, I mean—told me your ideas, but I couldn't believe her. I said you'd got more common sense than to object to a man just because he wasn't a soldier."

"I want a *man* for a son-in-law," said the other. "I don't say he's got to be a soldier."

"Just so," said Mr. Farrer. "You're a man, ain't you? Well, I'll do anything that you'll do."

"*Phh!*" said the sergeant-major. "I've done my little lot. I've been in action four times, and wounded in three places. That's my tally."

"The colonel said once' that my husband doesn't know what fear is," said Mrs. Ward timidly, "He's afraid of nothing."

"Except ghosts," remarked her daughter softly.

"Hold your tongue, miss," said her father, twisting his moustache. "No sensible man is afraid of what doesn't exist."

"A lot of people believe they do, though," said Mr. Farrer, breaking in. "I heard the other night that old Smith's ghost has been seen again swinging from the apple tree. Three people have seen it."

"Rubbish!" said the sergeant-major.

"Maybe," said the young man; "but I'll bet you, Mr. Ward, for all your courage, that you won't go up there alone at twelve o'clock one night to see."

"I thought I ordered you out of my house just now," said the sergeant-major, glaring at him.

"Going into action," said Mr. Farrer, pausing at the door, "is one thing—you have to obey orders and you can't help yourself; but going to a lonely cottage two miles off to see the ghost of a man that hanged himself is another."

"Do you mean to say I'm afraid?" blustered the other.

Mr. Farrer shook his head. "I don't say anything," he remarked; "but even a cockroach does a bit of thinking sometimes."

"Perhaps *you'd* like to go," said the sergeant-major.

"I don't mind," said the young man; "and perhaps you'll think a little better of me, Mr. Ward. If I do what you're afraid to do—"

Mrs. Ward and her daughter flung themselves hastily between the sergeant-major and his intended sacrifice. Mr. Farrer, pale but determined stood his ground.

"I'll dare you to go up and spend a night there alone," he said.

"I'll dare you," said the incensed warrior weakly.

"All right; I'll spend Wednesday night there," said Mr. Farrer, "and I'll come round on Thursday and let you know how I got on."

"I dare say," said the other; "but I don't want you here, and, what's more, I won't have you. You can go to Smith's cottage on Wednesday at twelve o'clock if you like, and I'll go up any time between twelve and three and make sure you're there. D'ye understand? I'll show you whether I'm afraid or not."

"There's no reason for you to be afraid," said Mr. Farrer. "I shall be there to protect you. That's very different to being there alone, as I shall be. But, of course, you can go up the next night by yourself, and wait for me, if you like. If you like to prove *your* courage, I mean."

"When I want to be ordered about," said the sergeant-major, in a magnificent voice, "I'll let you know. Now go, before I do anything I might be sorry for afterwards."

He stood at the door, erect as a ramrod, and watched the young man up the road. His con-versation at the supper-table that night related almost entirely to puppy-dogs and the best way of training them.

He kept a close eye upon his daughter for the next day or two, but human nature has its limits. He tried to sleep one afternoon in his easy-chair with one eye open, but the exquisite silence maintained by Miss Ward was too much for it. A hum of perfect content arose from the feature below, and five minutes later Miss Ward was speeding in search of Mr. Farrer.

"I had to come, Ted," she said breathlessly, "because tomorrow's Wednesday. I've got something to tell you, but I don't know whether I ought to."

"Tell me and let me decide," said Mr. Farrer tenderly.

"I—I'm so afraid you might be frightened," said the girl. "I won't tell you, but I'll give you a hint. If you see anything awful, don't be frightened."

Mr. Farrer stroked her hand. "The only thing I'm afraid of is your father," he said softly.

"Oh!" said the girl, clasping her hands together. "You have guessed it."

"Guessed it?" said Mr. Farrer.

Miss Ward nodded. "I happened to pass his door this morning," she said, in a low voice. "It was open a little way, and he was standing up and measuring one of mother's nightgowns against his chest. I couldn't think what he was doing it for at first."

Mr. Farrer whistled and his face hardened.

"That's not fair play," he said at last. "All right; I'll be ready for him."

"He doesn't like to be put in the wrong," said Miss Ward. "He wants to prove that you haven't got any courage. He'd be disappointed if he found you had."

"All right," said Mr. Farrer again. "You're an angel for coming to tell me."

"Father would call me something else, I expect," said Miss Ward, with a smile. "Goodbye. I want to get back before he wakes up."

She was back in her chair, listening to her father's slumbers, half an hour before he awoke.

"I'm making up for tomorrow night," he said, opening his eyes suddenly.

His daughter nodded.

"Shows strength of will," continued the sergeant-major amiably. "Wellington could go to sleep at any time by just willing it. I'm the same way. I can go to sleep at five minutes' notice."

"It's a very useful gift," said Miss Ward piously, "very."

Mr. Ward had two naps the next day. He awoke from the second at 12.30 a.m., and in a somewhat disagreeable frame of mind rose and stretched himself. The house was very still. He took a small brown-paper parcel from behind the sofa and, extinguishing the lamp, put on his cap and opened the front door.

If the house was quiet, the little street seemed dead. He closed the door softly and stepped into the darkness. In terms which would have been understood by "our army in Flanders" he execrated the forefathers, the name, and the upbringing of Mr. Edward Farrer.

Not a soul in the streets; not a light in a window. He left the little town behind, passed the last isolated house on the road, and walked into the greater blackness of a road between tall hedges. He had put on canvas shoes with rubber soles, for the better surprise of Mr. Farrer, and his own progress seemed to partake of a ghostly nature. Every ghost story he had ever heard or read crowded into his memory. For the first time in his experience even the idea of the company of Mr. Farrer seemed better than no company at all.

The night was so dark that he nearly missed the turning that led to the cottage. For the first few yards he had almost to feel his way; then, with a greater yearning than ever for the society of Mr. Farrer, he straightened his back and marched swiftly and noiselessly towards the cottage.

It was a small, tumble-down place, set well back in an overgrown garden. The sergeant-major came to a halt just before reaching the gate, and, hidden by the hedge, unfastened his parcel and shook out his wife's best night-gown.

He got it over his head with some difficulty, and, with his arms in the sleeves, tried in vain to get his big hands through the small, lace-trimmed wrist-bands. Despite his utmost efforts he could only get two or three fingers through, and after a vain search for his cap, which had fallen off in the struggle, he made his way to the gate and stood there waiting. It was at this moment that the thought occurred to him that Mr. Farrer might have failed to keep the appointment.

His knees trembled slightly and he listened anxiously for any sound from the house. He rattled the gate and, standing with white arms outstretched, waited. Nothing happened. He shook it again, and then, pulling himself together, opened it and slipped into the garden. As he did so a large bough which lay in the centre of the footpath thoughtfully drew on one side to let him pass.

Mr. Ward stopped suddenly and, with his gaze fixed on the bough, watched it glide over the grass until it was swallowed up in the darkness. His own ideas of frightening Mr. Farrer were forgotten, and in a dry, choking voice he called loudly upon the name of that gentleman.

He called two or three times, with no response, and then, in a state of panic, backed slowly towards the gate with his eyes fixed on the house. A loud crash sounded from somewhere inside, the door was flung violently open, and a gruesome figure in white hopped out and squatted on the step.

It was evident to Sergeant-Major Ward that Mr. Farrer was not there, and that no useful purpose could be served by remaining. It was clear that the young man's courage had failed him, and, with grey head erect, elbows working like the sails of a windmill, and the ends of the nightgown streaming behind him, the sergeant-major bent his steps towards home.

He dropped into a walk after a time and looked carefully over his shoulder. So far as he could see he was alone, but the silence and loneliness were oppressive. He looked again, and, without stopping to inquire whether his eyes had deceived him, broke into a run again. Alternately walking and running, he got back to the town, and walked swiftly along the streets to his house. Police-Constable Burgess, who was approaching from the other direction, reached it at almost the same moment, and, turning on his lantern, stood gaping with astonishment. "Anything wrong?" he demanded.

"Wrong?" panted the sergeant-major, trying to put a little surprise and dignity into his voice. "No."

"I thought it was a lady walking in her sleep at first," said the constable. "A tall lady."

The sergeant-major suddenly became conscious of the nightgown. "I've been—for a little walk," he said, still breathing hard. "I felt a bit chilly—so I—put this on."

"Suits you, too," said the constable stiffly. "But you Army men always was a bit dressy. Now if *I* put that on I should look ridikerlous."

The door opened before Mr. Ward could reply, and revealed in the light of a bedroom candle, the astonished countenances of his wife and daughter.

"*George!*" exclaimed Mrs. Ward.

"*Father!*" said Miss Ward.

The sergeant-major tottered in and, gaining the front room, flung himself into his armchair. A stiff glass of whisky and water, handed him by his daughter, was swallowed at a gulp.

"Did you go?" inquired Mrs. Ward, clasping her hands.

The sergeant-major, fully conscious of the suspicions aroused by his disordered appearance, rallied his faculties. "Not likely," he said, with a short laugh. "After I got outside I knew it was no good going there to look for that young snippet. He'd no more think of going there than he would of flying. I walked a little way down the road—for exercise—and then strolled back."

"But—my nightgown?" said the wondering Mrs. Ward.

"Put it on to frighten the constable," said her husband.

He stood up and allowed her to help him pull it off. His face was flushed and his hair tousled, but the bright fierceness of his eye was unquenched. In submissive silence she followed him to bed.

He was up late next morning, and made but a poor breakfast. His after-dinner nap was disturbed, and tea was over before he had regained his wonted calm. An hour later the arrival of a dignified and reproachful Mr. Farrer set him blazing again.

"I have come to see you about last night," said Mr. Farrer, before the other could speak. "A joke's a joke, but when you said you would come I naturally expected you would keep your word."

"Keep my word?" repeated the sergeant-major, almost choking with wrath.

"I stayed there in that lonely cottage from twelve to three, as per agreement, waiting for you," said Mr. Farrer.

"You were not there," shouted the sergeant-major.

"How do you know?" inquired the other.

The sergeant-major looked round helplessly at his wife and daughter.

"Prove it," said Mr. Farrer, pushing his advantage. "You questioned my courage, and I stayed there three hours. Where were you?"

"You were not there," said the sergeant-major. "I *know*. You can't bluff me. You were afraid."

"I was there, and I'll swear it," said Mr. Farrer. "Still, there's no harm done. I'll go there again tonight, and I'll dare you to come for me!"

"Dare?" said the sergeant-major, choking. "Dare?"

"Dare," repeated the other; "and if you don't come this time I'll spread it all over Marcham. Tomorrow night you can go there and wait for me. If you see what I saw—"

"Oh, Ted!" said Miss Ward, with a shiver.

"Saw?" said the sergeant-major, starting.

"Nothing harmful," said Mr. Farrer calmly. "As a matter of fact, it was very interesting."

"What was?" demanded the sergeant-major.

"It sounds rather silly, as a matter of fact," said Mr. Farrer slowly. "Still, I did see a broken bough moving about the garden."

Mr. Ward regarded him open-mouthed.

"Anything else?" he inquired, in a husky voice.

"A figure in white," said Mr. Farrer, "with long waving arms, hopping about like a frog. I don't suppose you believe me, but if you come tonight perhaps you'll see it yourself. It's very interesting."

"Wer—weren't you frightened?" inquired the staring Mrs. Ward.

Mr. Farrer shook his head. "It would take more than that to frighten me," he said simply. "I should be ashamed of myself to be afraid of a poor thing like that. It couldn't do me any harm."

"Did you see its face?" inquired Mrs. Ward nervously.

Mr. Farrer shook his head.

"What sort of a body had it got?" said her daughter.

"So far as I could see, very good," said Mr. Farrer. "Very good figure—not tall, but well made."

An incredible suspicion that had been forming in the sergeant-major's mind began to take shape. "Did you see anything else?" he asked sharply.

"One more," said Mr. Farrer, regarding him pleasantly. "One I call the Running Ghost."

"Run—" began the sergeant-major, and stopped suddenly.

"It came in at the front gate," pursued Mr. Farrer. "A tall, well-knit figure of martial bearing—much about your height, Mr. Ward—with a beautiful filmy white robe down to its knees—"

He broke off in mild surprise, and stood gazing at Miss Ward, who, with her handkerchief to her mouth, was rocking helplessly in her chair.

"Knees," he repeated quietly. "It came slowly down the path, and half-way to the house it stopped, and in a frightened sort of voice called out my name. I was surprised, naturally, but before I could get to it—to reassure it—"

"That'll do," said the sergeant-major, rising hastily and drawing himself up to his full height.

"You asked me," said Mr. Farrer, in an aggrieved voice.

"I know I did," said the sergeant-major, breathing heavily. "I know I did; but if I sit here listening to anymore of your lies I shall be ill. The best thing you can do is to take that giggling girl out and give her a breath of fresh air. I have done with her."

43

EASY MONEY

A lad of about twenty stepped ashore from the schooner *Jane*, and joining a girl, who had been avoiding for some ten minutes the ardent gaze of the night-watchman, set off arm-in-arm. The watchman rolled his eyes and shook his head slowly.

Nearly all his money on 'is back, he said, and what little bit 'e's got over he'll spend on 'er. And three months arter they're married he'll wonder wot 'e ever saw in her. If a man marries he wishes he 'adn't, and if he doesn't marry he wishes he 'ad. That's life.

Looking at them two young fools reminds me of a nevy of Sam Small's; a man I think I've spoke to you of afore. As a rule Sam didn't talk much about 'is relations, but there was a sister of 'is in the country wot 'e was rather fond of because 'e 'adn't seen 'er for twenty years. She 'ad got a boy wot 'ad just got a job in London, and when 'e wrote and told 'er he was keeping company with the handsomest and loveliest and best 'arted gal in the whole wide world, she wrote to Sam about it and asked 'im to give 'is nevy some good advice.

Sam 'ad just got back from China and was living with Petter Russet and Ginger Dick as usual, and arter reading the letter about seven times and asking Ginger how 'e spelt "minx,"

’e read the letter out loud to them and asked ’em what they thought about it.

Ginger shook his ’ead, and, arter thinking a bit, Peter shook his too.

“She’s caught ’im rather young,” ses Ginger,

“They get it bad at that age, too,” ses Peter. “When I was twenty, there was a gal as I was fond of, and a regiment couldn’t ha’ parted us.”

“Wot did part you then?” ses Sam.

“Another gal,” ses Peter; “a gal I took a fancy to, that’s wot did it.”

“I was nearly married when I was twenty,” ses Ginger, with a faraway look in his eyes. “She was the most beautiful gal I ever saw in my life; she ’ad one ’undred pounds a year of ’er own and she couldn’t bear me out of her sight. If a thump acrost the chest would do that cough of yours any good, Sam—”

“Don’t take no notice of ’im, Ginger,” ses Peter. “Why didn’t you marry ’er?”

“’Cos I was afraid she might think I was arter ’er money,” ses Ginger, getting a little bit closer to Sam.

Peter ’ad another turn then, and him and Ginger kept on talking about gals whose ’arts they ’ad broke till Sam didn’t know what to do with ’imself.

“I’ll just step round and see my nevy, while you and Peter are amusing each other,” he ses at last. “I’ll ask ’im to come round tomorrow and then you can give ’im good advice.”

The nevy came round next evening. Bright, cheerful young chap ’e was, and he agreed with everything they said. When Peter said as ’ow all gals was deceivers, he said he’d known it for years, but they was born that way and couldn’t ’elp it; and when Ginger said that no man ought to marry afore he was fifty, he corrected ’im and made it fifty-five.

“I’m glad to ’ear you talk like that,” ses Ginger.

“So am I,” ses Peter.

"He's got his 'ead screwed on right," ses Sam, wot thought his sister 'ad made a mistake...

"I'm surprised when I look round at the wimmen men 'ave married," ses the nevy; "wot they could 'ave seen in them I can't think. Me and my young lady often laugh about it."

"Your wot?" ses Sam, pretending to be very surprised.

"My young lady," ses the nevy.

Sam gives a cough. "I didn't know you'd got a young lady," he ses.

"Well, I 'ave," ses his nevy, "and we're going to be married at Christmas."

"But—but you ain't fifty-five," ses Ginger.

"I'm twenty-one," ses the nevy, "but my case is different. There isn't another young lady like mine in the world. She's different to all the others, and it ain't likely I'm going to let 'er be snapped up by somebody else. Fifty-five! Why, 'ow I'm to wait till Christmas I don't know. She's the prettiest and handsomest gal in the world; and she's the cleverest one I ever met. You ought to hear 'er laugh. Like music it is. You'd never forget it."

"Twenty-one is young," ses Ginger, shaking his 'ead. "'Ave you known 'er long?"

"Three months," ses the nevy. "She lives in the same street as I do. 'Ow it is she ain't been snapped up before, I can't think, but she told me that she didn't care for men till she saw me."

"They all say that," ses Ginger.

"If I've 'ad it said to me once, I've 'ad it said twenty times," ses Peter, nodding.

"They do it to flatter," ses old Sam, looking as if he knew all about it. "You wait till you are my age, Joe; then you'll know; why, I should ha' been married dozens o' times if I 'adn't been careful."

"P'r'aps it was a bit on both sides," ses Joe, looking at 'is uncle. "P'r'aps they was careful too. If you only saw my young lady, you wouldn't talk like that. She's got the truthfullest eyes in the world. Large grey eyes like a child's, leastways sometimes they are grey and sometimes they are blue. It seems to depend on the light somehow; I 'ave seen them when they was a brown—brownish-gold. And she smiles with 'er eyes."

"Hasn't she got a mouth?" ses Ginger, wot was getting a bit tired of it.

"You've been crossed in love," ses the nevy, staring at 'im. "That's wot's the matter with you. And looking at you, I don't wonder at it."

Ginger 'arf got up, but Sam gave him a look and 'e sat down agin, and then they all sat quiet while the nevy went on telling them about 'is gal.

"I should like to see 'er," ses his uncle at last.

"Call round for me at seven tomorrow night," ses the young 'un, "and I'll introduce you."

"We might look in on our way," ses Sam, arter Ginger and Peter 'ad both made eyes at 'im. "We're going out to spend the evening."

"The more the merrier," ses his nevy. "Well, so long; I expect she's waiting for me."

He got up and said goodbye, and arter he 'ad gorn, Sam and the other two shook their 'eads together and said what a pity it was to be twenty-one. Ginger said it made 'im sad to think of it, and Peter said 'ow any gal could look at a man under thirty, 'e couldn't think.

They all went round to the nevy's the next evening. They was a little bit early owing to Ginger's watch 'aving been set right by guesswork, and they 'ad to sit in a row on the nevy's bed waiting while 'e cleaned 'imself, and changed his clothes. Although it was only Wednesday 'e changed his collar, and he was so long making up 'is mind about his necktie that 'is uncle tried to make it up for him. By the time he 'ad finished Sam said it made 'im think it was Sunday.

Miss Gill was at 'ome when they got there, and all three of 'em was very much surprised that such a good-looking gal should take up with Sam's nevy. Ginger nearly said so, but Peter gave 'im a dig in the back just in time and 'e called him something under 'is breath instead.

"Why shouldn't we all make an evening of it?" ses Ginger, arter they 'ad been talking for about ten minutes, and the nevy 'ad looked at a the clock three or four times.

"Because two's company," ses Mrs. Gill, "Why, you was young yourself once. Can't you remember?"

"He's young now, mother," ses the gal, giving Ginger a nice smile.

"I tell you wot we might do," ses Mrs. Gill, putting 'er finger to her forehead and considering. "You and Joe go out and 'ave your evening, and me and these gentlemen 'll go off together somewhere. I shall enjoy an outing; I ain't 'ad one for a long time."

Ginger said it would be very nice if she thought it wouldn't make 'er too tired, and afore Sam or Peter could think of anything to say, she was upstairs putting 'er bonnet on. They thought o' plenty to say while they was sitting alone with Ginger waiting for 'er.

"My idea was for the gal and your nevy to come too," ses pore Ginger. "Then I thought we might lose 'im and I would 'ave a little chat with the gal, and show 'er 'ow foolish she was."

"Well, you've done it now," ses Sam. "Spoilt our evening."

"P'r'aps good will come out of it," ses Ginger. "If the old lady takes a fancy to us we shall be able to come agin, and then to please you, Sam, I'll have a go to cut your nevy out."

Sam stared at 'im, and Peter stared too, and then they looked at each other and began to laugh till Ginger forgot where 'e was and offered to put Sam through the winder. They was still quarrelling under their breath and saying wot they'd like to do to each other when Mrs. Gill came downstairs. Dressed up to the nines she was, and they walked down the street with a feeling that everybody was looking at 'em.

One thing that 'elped to spoil the evening was that Mrs. Gill wouldn't go into public-'ouses, but to make up for it she went into sweet-stuff shops three times and 'ad ices while they stood and watched 'er and wondered 'ow she could do it. And arter that she stopped at a place Poplar way, where there was a few swings and roundabouts and things. She was as skittish as a school-gal, and arter taking pore Sam on the roundabout till 'e didn't know whether he was on his 'eels or his 'ead, she got 'im into a boat-swing and swung 'im till he felt like a boy on 'is fust v'y'ge. Arter that she took 'im to the rifle gallery, and afore he had 'ad three shots the man took the gun away from 'im and threatened to send for the police.

It was an expensive evening for all of them, but as Ginger said when they got 'ome they 'ad broken the ice, and he bet Peter Russet 'arf a dollar that afore two days 'ad passed he'd take the nevy's gal for a walk. He stepped round by 'imself the next arternoon and made 'imself agreeable to Mrs. Gill, and the day arter they was both so nice and kind that 'e plucked up 'is courage and offered to take Miss Gill to the Zoo.

She said "No" at fust, of course, but arter Ginger 'ad pointed out that Joe was at work all day and couldn't take 'er 'imself, and that 'e was Joe's uncle's best pal, she began to think better of it.

"Why not?" ses the mother. "Joe wouldn't mind. He wouldn't be so silly as to be jealous o' Mr. Ginger Dick."

"Of course not," ses the gal. "There's! nothing to be jealous of."

She let 'er mother and Ginger persuade 'er arter a time, and then she went upstairs to clean herself and put on a little silver brooch that Ginger said he 'ad picked up coming along.

She took about three-quarters of an hour to get ready, but when she came down, Ginger felt that it was quite worth it. He couldn't take 'is eyes off 'er, as the saying goes, and 'e sat by 'er side on the top of the omnibus like a man in a dream.

"This is better than being at sea," he ses at last.

"Don't you like the sea?" ses the gal. "I should like to go to sea myself."

"I shouldn't mind the sea if you was there, ses Ginger.

Miss Gill turned her 'ead away. "You mustn't talk to me like that," she ses in a soft voice. "Still—"

"Still wot?" ses Ginger, arter waiting a long time.

"I mean, if I did go to sea, it *would* be nice to have a friend on board," she ses. "I suppose I you ain't afraid of storms, are you?"

"I like 'em," ses Ginger.

"You look as if you would," ses the gal, giving 'im a little look under 'er eyelashes. "It must be nice to be a man and be brave. I wish I was a man."

"I don't," ses Ginger.

"Why not?" ses the gal, turning her 'ead away agin.

Ginger didn't answer, he gave 'er elbow a little squeeze instead. She took it away at once, and Ginger was just wishing he 'adn't been so foolish when it came back agin, and they sat for a long time without speaking a word.

"The sea is all right for some things," ses Ginger at last, "but suppose a man married!"

The gal shook her 'ead. "It would be hard on 'is wife," she ses, with another little look at 'im, "but—but—"

Ginger pinched 'er elbow agin.

"But p'r'aps he could get a job ashore," she ses, "and then he could take his wife out for a bus-ride every day."

They 'ad to change buses arter a time, and they got on a wrong bus and went miles out o' their way, but neither of 'em seemed to mind. Ginger said he was thinking of something else, and the gal said she was too. They got to the Zoological Gardens at last, and Ginger said he 'ad never enjoyed himself so much. When the lions roared she squeezed his arm, and when they 'ad an elephant ride she was holding on to 'im with both 'ands.

"I am enjoying myself," she ses, as Ginger 'elped her down and said "*whoa*" to the elephant. "I know it's wicked, but I can't 'elp it, and wot's more, I'm afraid I don't want to 'elp it."

She let Ginger take 'er arm when she nearly tripped up over a peppermint ball some kid 'ad dropped; and, arter a little persuasion, she 'ad a bottle of lemonade and six bath-buns at a refreshment stall for dinner.

She was as nice as she could be to him, but by the time they started for 'ome, she 'ad turned so quiet that Ginger began to think 'e must 'ave offended 'er in some way.

"Are you tired?" he ses.

"No," ses the gal, shaking her 'ead, "I've enjoyed myself very much."

"I thought you seemed a bit tired," ses Ginger, arter waiting a long time.

"I'm not tired," ses the gal, giving 'im a sad sort o' little smile, "but I'm a little bit worried, that's all."

"Worried?" ses Ginger, very tender. "Wot's worrying you?"

"Oh, I can't tell you," ses Miss Gill. "It doesn't matter; I'll try and cheer up. Wot a lovely day it is, isn't it? I shall remember it all my life."

"Wot is it worrying you?" ses Ginger, in a determined voice. "Can't you tell *me*?"

"No," ses the gal, shaking her 'ead, "I can't tell you because you might want to 'elp me, and I couldn't allow that."

"Why shouldn't I 'elp you?" ses Ginger. "It's wot we was put 'ere for: to 'elp one another."

"I couldn't tell you," ses the gal, just dabbing at 'er eyes with a lace pocket-'ankercher about one and a 'arf times the size of 'er nose.

"Not if I ask you to?" ses Ginger.

Miss Gill shook 'er 'ead, and then she tried her 'ardest to turn the conversation. She talked about the weather, and the monkey-'ouse, and a gal in 'er street whose 'air changed from red to black in a single night; but it was all no good, Ginger wouldn't be put off, and at last she ses—

"Well," she ses, "if you must know; I'm in a difficulty; I 'ave got to get three pounds, and where to get it I don't know anymore than the man in the moon. Now let's talk about something else."

"Do you owe it?" ses Ginger.

"I can't tell you anymore," ses Miss Gill, "and I wouldn't 'ave told you that only you asked me, and somehow I feel as though I 'ave to tell you things, when you want me to."

"Three pounds ain't much," ses pore Ginger, wot 'ad just been paid off arter a long v'y'ge. "I can let you 'ave it and welcome."

Miss Gill started away from 'im as though she 'ad been stung, and it took 'im all his time to talk 'er round agin. When he 'ad she begged 'is pardon and said he was the most generous man she 'ad ever met, but it couldn't be.

"I don't know when I could pay it back," she ses, "but I thank you all the same for offering it."

"Pay it back when you like," ses Ginger, "and if you never pay it back, it don't matter."

He offered 'er the money four or five times, but she wouldn't take it; but at last just as they got near her 'ouse he forced it in her 'and, and put his own 'ands in his pockets when she tried to make 'im take it back.

"You are good to me," she ses arter they 'ad gone inside and 'er mother 'ad gone upstairs arter giving Ginger a bottle o' beer to amuse 'imself with; "I shall never forget you. Never."

"I 'ope not," ses Ginger, starting. "Are you coming out agin tomorrow?"

"I'm afraid I can't," ses Miss Gill, shaking her 'ead and looking sorrowful.

"Not with *me*?" ses Ginger, sitting down beside her on the sofa and putting 'is arm so that she could lean against it if she wanted to.

"I don't think I can," ses the gal, leaning back very gentle.

"Think agin," ses Ginger, squeezing 'er waist a little.

Miss Gill shook her 'ead, and then turned and looked at 'im. Her face was so close to his, that, thinking that she had put it there a-purpose, he kissed it, and the next moment 'e got a clout that made his 'ead ring.

"'Ow dare you!" she ses, jumping up with a scream. "'Ow dare you! 'Ow dare—"

"Wot's the matter?" ses her mother, coming downstairs like a runaway barrel of treacle.

"He—he's insulted me," ses Miss Gill, taking out her little 'ankercher and sobbing. "He—k—kissed me!"

"WOT!" ses Mrs. Gill. "Well, I'd never 'ave believed it! Never! Why, 'e ought to be taken up. Wot d'ye mean by it?" she ses, turning on pore Ginger.

Ginger tried to explain, but it was all no good, and two minutes arterwards, 'e was walking back to 'is lodgings like a dog with its tail between its legs. His 'ead was going round and round with astonishment, and 'e was in such a temper that 'e barged into a man twice as big as himself and then offered to knock his 'ead off when 'e objected. And when Sam and Peter asked him 'ow he 'ad got on, he was in such a state of mind it was all 'e could do to answer 'em.

"And I'll trouble you for my 'arf dollar, Peter," he ses; "I've been out with 'er all day, and I've won my bet."

Peter paid it over like a lamb, and then 'e sat thinking 'ard for a bit.

"Are you going out with 'er agin tomorrow, Ginger?" he ses, arter a time.

"I don't know," ses Ginger, careless-like, "I ain't made up my mind yet."

Peter looked at 'im and then 'e looked at Sam and winked. "Let me 'ave a try," he ses; "I'll bet you another 'arf dollar that I take 'er out. P'r'aps I shall come 'ome in a better temper than wot you 'ave."

Old Sam said it wasn't right to play with a gal's 'art in that way, but arter a lot o' talking and telling Sam to shut up, Ginger took the bet. He was quite certain in his own mind that Miss Gill would slam the door in Peter's face, and arter he 'ad started off next morning, Ginger and Sam waited in to 'ave the pleasure of laughing in 'is face.

They got tired of waiting at last, and went out to enjoy themselves, and breathe the fresh air in a pub down Poplar way. They got back at seven o'clock, and ten minutes arterwards Peter came in and sat down on his bed and began to smoke without a word.

"Had a good time?" ses Ginger.

"Rippin'," ses Peter, holding 'is pipe tight between 'is teeth. "You owe me 'arf a dollar, Ginger."

"Where'd you go?" ses Ginger, passing it over.

"Crystal Pallis," ses Peter.

"Are you going to take 'er out tomorrow?" ses Sam.

"I don't think so," ses Peter, taking 'is pipe out of 'is mouth and yawning. "She's rather too young for me; I like talking to gals wot's a bit older. I won't stand in Ginger's way."

"I found 'er a bit young too," ses Ginger. "P'r'aps we'd better let Sam's nevy 'ave 'er. Arter all it's a bit rough on 'im when you come to think of it."

"You're quite right," ses Peter, jumping up. "It's Sam's business, and why we should go out of our way and inconvenience ourselves to do 'im a good turn, I don't know."

"It's Sam all over," ses Ginger; "he's always been like that, and the more you try to oblige 'im, the more you may."

They went on abusing Sam till he got sick and tired of it, and arter telling 'em wot he thought of 'em he slammed the door and went out and spent the evening by 'imself. He would 'ardly speak to them next day, but arter tea he brightened up a bit and they went off together as if nothing 'ad happened, and the fust thing they saw as they turned out of their street was Sam's nevy coming along smiling till it made their faces ache to look at him.

"I was just coming to see you," he ses.

"We're just off—on business," ses Ginger.

"I wasn't going to stop," ses the nevy; "my young lady just told me to step along and show uncle wot she has bought me. A silver watch and chain and a gold ring. Look at it!"

He held his 'and under Ginger's nose, and Ginger stood there looking at it and opening and shutting 'is mouth like a dying fish. Then he took Peter by the arm and led 'im away while the nevy was opening 'is new watch and showing Sam the works.

"'Ow much did she get out of *you*, Peter?" ses Ginger, looking at 'im very hard. "I don't want any lies."

"Three quid," ses Peter, staring at 'im.

"Same 'ere," ses Ginger, grinding his teeth. "Did she give you a smack on the side of your face?"

"Wot—are—you—talking about,' Ginger?" ses Peter.

"Did she smack your face *too?*" ses Ginger.

"Yes," ses Peter.

44

HIS OTHER SELF

"They're as like as two peas, him and 'is brother," said the night-watchman, gazing blandly at the indignant face of the lighterman on the barge below; "and the on'y way I know this one is Sam is because Bill don't use bad langwidge. Twins they are, but the likeness is only outside; Bill's 'art is as white as snow."

He cut off a plug of tobacco, and, placing it in his cheek, waited expectantly.

"White as snow," he repeated.

"That's me," said the lighterman, as he pushed his unwieldy craft from the jetty. "I'll tell Sam your opinion of 'im. So long."

The watchman went a shade redder than usual. That's twins all over, he said, sourly, always deceiving people. It's Bill arter all, and, instead of hurting 'is feelings, I've just been flattering of 'im up.

It ain't the fust time I've 'ad trouble over a likeness. I've been a twin myself in a manner o' speaking. It didn't last long, but it lasted long enough for me to always be sorry for twins, and to make a lot of allowance for them. It must be very 'ard to have another man going about with your face on 'is shoulders, and getting it into trouble.

It was a year or two ago now. I was sitting one evening at the gate, smoking a pipe and looking at a newspaper I 'ad found in the office, when I see a gentleman coming along from the swing-bridge. Well-dressed, clean-shaved chap 'e was, smoking a cigarette. He was walking slow and looking about 'im casual-like, until his eyes fell on me, when he gave a perfect jump of surprise, and, arter looking at me very 'ard, walked on a little way and then turned back. He did it twice, and I was just going to say something to 'im, something that I 'ad been getting ready for 'im, when he spoke to me.

"Good evening," he ses.

"Good evening," I ses, folding the paper over and looking at 'im rather severe.

"I hope you'll excuse me staring," he ses, very perlite; "but I've never seen such a face and figger as yours in all my life—never."

"Ah, you ought to ha' seen me a few years ago," I ses. "I'm like everybody else—I'm getting on."

"Rubbish!" he ses. "You couldn't be better if you tried. It's marvellous! Wonderful! It's the very thing I've been looking for. Why, if you'd been made to order you couldn't ha' been better."

I thought at fust he was by way of trying to get a drink out o' me—I've been played that game afore—but instead o' that he asked me whether I'd do 'im the pleasure of 'aving one with 'im.

We went over to the "Albion," and I believe I could have 'ad it in a pail if I'd on'y liked to say the word. And all the time I was drinking he was looking me up and down, till I didn't know where to look, as the saying is.

"I came down 'ere to look for somebody like you," he ses, "but I never dreamt I should have such luck as this. I'm an actor, and I've got to play the part of a sailor, and I've been worried some time 'ow to make up for the part. D'ye understand?"

"No," I ses, looking at 'im.

"I want to look the real thing," he ses, speaking low so the landlord shouldn't hear. "I want to make myself the living image of you. If that don't fetch 'em I'll give up the stage and grow cabbages."

"Make yourself like me?" I ses. "Why, you're no more like me than I'm like a seasick monkey."

"Not so much," he ses. "That's where the art comes in."

He stood me another drink, and then, taking my arm in a cuddling sort o' way, and calling me "Dear boy," 'e led me back to the wharf and explained. He said 'e would come round next evening with wot 'e called his make-up box, and paint 'is face and make 'imself up till people wouldn't know one from the other.

"And wot about your figger?" I ses, looking at 'im.

"A cushion," he ses, winking, "or maybe a couple. And what about clothes? You'll 'ave to sell me those you've got on. Hat and all. And boots."

I put a price on 'em that I thought would 'ave finished 'im then and there, but it didn't. And at last, arter paying me so manymore compliments that they began to get into my 'ead, he fixed up a meeting for the next night and went off.

"And mind," he ses, coming back, "not a word to a living soul!"

He went off agin, and, arter going to the "Bull's Head" and 'aving a pint to clear my 'ead, I went and sat down in the office and thought it over. It seemed all right to me as far as I could see; but p'r'aps the pint didn't clear my 'ead enough—p'r'aps I ought to 'ave 'ad two pints.

I lay awake best part of next day thinking it over, and when I got up I 'ad made up my mind. I put my clothes in a sack, and then I put on some others as much like 'em as possible, on'y p'r'aps a bit older, in case the missis should get asking questions; and then I sat wondering 'ow to get out with the sack without 'er noticing it. She's got a very inquiring mind, and I wasn't going to tell her any lies about it. Besides which I couldn't think of one.

I got out at last by playing a game on her. I pertended to drop 'arf-a-dollar in the washus, and while she was busy on 'er hands and knees I went off as comfortable as you please.

I got into the office with it all right, and, just as it was getting dark, a cab drove up to the wharf and the actor-chap jumped out with a big leather bag. I took 'im into the private office, and 'e was so ready with 'is money for the clothes that I offered to throw the sack in.

He changed into my clothes fust of all, and then, asking me to sit down in front of 'im, he took a looking-glass and a box out of 'is bag and began to alter 'is face. Wot with sticks of coloured paint, and false eyebrows, and a beard stuck on with gum and trimmed with a pair o' scissors, it was more like a conjuring trick than anything else. Then 'e took a wig out of 'is bag and pressed it on his 'ead, put on the cap, put some black stuff on 'is teeth, and there he was. We both looked into the glass together while 'e gave the finishing touches, and then he clapped me on the back and said I was the handsomest sailorman in England.

"I shall have to make up a bit 'eavier when I'm behind the floats," he ses; "but this is enough for 'ere. Wot do you think of the imitation of your voice? I think I've got it exact."

"If you ask me," I ses, "it sounds like a poll-parrot with a cold in the 'ead."

"And now for your walk," he ses, looking as pleased as if I'd said something else. "Come to the door and see me go up the wharf."

I didn't like to hurt 'is feelings, but I thought I should ha' bust. He walked up that wharf like a dancing-bear in a pair of trousers too tight for it, but 'e was so pleased with 'imself that I didn't like to tell 'im so. He went up and down two or three times, and I never saw anything so ridikerlous in my life.

"That's all very well for us," he ses; "but wot about other people? That's wot I want to know. I'll go and 'ave a drink, and see whether anybody spots me."

Afore I could stop 'im he started off to the "Bull's Head" and went on, while I stood outside and watched 'im.

"'Arf a pint o' four ale," he ses, smacking down a penny.

I see the landlord draw the beer and give it to 'im, but 'e didn't seem to take no notice of 'im. Then, just to open 'is eyes a bit, I walked in and put down a penny and asked for 'arf-pint.

The landlord was just wiping down the counter at the time, and when I gave my order he looked up and stood staring at me with the wet cloth 'eld up in the air. He didn't say a word—not a single word. He stood there for a moment smiling at us foolish-like, and then 'e let go o' the beer-injun, wot 'e was 'olding in 'is left hand, and sat down heavy on the bar floor. We both put our 'eads over the counter to see wot had 'appened to 'im, and 'e started making the most 'orrible noise I 'ave ever heard in my life. I wonder it didn't bring the fire-injuns. The actor-chap bolted out as if he'd been shot, and I was just thinking of follering 'im when the landlord's wife and 'is two daughters came rushing out and asking me wot I 'ad done to him.

"There—there—was two of 'im!" ses the landlord, trembling and holding on to 'is wife's arm, as they helped 'im up and got 'im in the chair. "Two of 'im!"

"Two of wot?" ses his wife.

"Two—two watchmen," ses the landlord; "both exac'ly alike and both asking for 'arf a pint o' four ale."

"Yes, yes," ses 'is wife.

"You come and lay down, pa," ses the gals.

"I tell you there was," ses the landlord, getting 'is colour back, with temper.

"Yes, yes; I know all about it," ses 'is wife. "You come inside for a bit; and, Gertie, you bring your father in a soda—a large soda."

They got 'im in arter a lot o' trouble; but three times 'e came back as far as the door, 'olding on to them, and taking a little peep at me. The last time he shook his 'ead at me, and said if I did it agin I could go and get my 'arf-pints somewhere else.

I finished the beer wot the actor 'ad left, and, arter telling the landlord I 'oped his eyesight 'ud be better in the morning, I went outside, and arter a careful look round walked back to the wharf.

I pushed the wicket open a little way and peeped in. The actor was standing just by the fust crane talking to two of the hands off of the *Saltram*. He'd got 'is back to the light, but 'ow it was they didn't twig his voice I can't think.

They was so busy talking that I crept along by the side of the wall and got to the office without their seeing me. I went into the private office and turned out the gas there, and sat down to wait for 'im. Then I 'eard a noise outside that took me to the door agin and kept me there, 'olding on to the doorpost and gasping for my breath. The cook of the *Saltram* was sitting on a paraffin-cask playing the mouth-organ, and the actor, with 'is arms folded across his stummick, was dancing a horn-pipe as if he'd gorn mad.

I never saw anything so ridikerlous in my life, and when I recollected that they thought it was *me*, I thought I should ha' dropped. A night-watchman can't be too careful, and I knew that it 'ud be all over Wapping next morning that I 'ad been dancing to a tuppenny-ha'penny mouth-orgin played by a ship's cook. A man that does 'is dooty always has a lot of people ready to believe the worst of 'im.

I went back into the dark office and waited, and by and by I 'eard them coming along to the gate and patting 'im on the back and saying he ought to be in a pantermime instead of wasting 'is time night-watching. He left 'em at the gate, and then 'e came into the office smiling as if he'd done something clever.

"Wot d'ye think of me for a understudy?" he ses, laughing. "They all thought it was you. There wasn't one of 'em 'ad the slightest suspicion—not one."

"And wot about my character?" I ses, folding my arms acrost my chest and looking at I him.

"Character?" he ses, staring. "Why, there's no 'arm in dancing; it's a innercent enjoyment."

"It ain't one o' my innercent enjoyments," I ses, "and I don't want to get the credit of it. If they hadn't been sitting in a pub all the evening they'd 'ave spotted you at once."

"Oh!" he ses, very huffy. "How?"

"Your voice," I ses. "You try and mimic a poll-parrot, and think it's like me. And, for another thing, you walk about as though you're a stuffed with sawdust."

"I beg your pardon," he ses; "the voice and the walk are exact. Exact."

"*Wot?*" I ses, looking 'im up and down. "You stand there and 'ave the impudence to tell me that my voice is like that?"

"I do," he ses.

"Then I'm sorry for you," I ses. "I thought you'd got more sense."

He stood looking at me and gnawing 'is finger, and by and by he ses, "Are you married?" he ses.

"I am," I ses, very short.

"Where do you live?" he ses.

I told 'im.

"Very good," he ses; "p'r'aps I'll be able to convince you arter all. By the way, wot do you call your wife? Missis?"

"Yes," I ses, staring at him. "But wot's it got to do with you?"

"Nothing," he ses. "Nothing. Only I'm going to try the poll-parrot voice and the sawdust walk on her, that's all. If I can deceive 'er that'll settle it."

"Deceive *her*?" I ses. "Do you think I'm going to let you go round to my 'ouse and get me into trouble with the missis like that? Why, you must be crazy; that dancing must 'ave got nto your 'ead."

"Where's the 'arm?" he ses, very sulky.

"'*Arm?*" I ses. "I won't 'ave it, that's all; and if you knew my missis you'd know without any telling."

"I'll bet you a pound to a sixpence she wouldn't know me," he ses, very earnest.

"She won't 'ave the chance," I ses, "so that's all about it."

He stood there argufying for about ten minutes; but I was as firm as a rock. I wouldn't move an inch, and at last, arter we was both on the point of losing our tempers, he picked up his bag and said as 'ow he must be getting off 'ome.

"But ain't you going to take those things off fust?" I ses.

"No," he ses, smiling. "I'll wait till I get I 'ome. Ta-ta."

He put 'is bag on 'is shoulder and walked to the gate, with me follering of 'im.

"I expect I shall see a cab soon," he ses "Goodbye."

"Wot are you laughing at?" I ses.

"On'y thoughts," he ses.

"'Ave you got far to go?" I ses.

"No; just about the same distance as you 'ave," he ses, and he went off spluttering like a soda-water bottle.

I took the broom and 'ad a good sweep-up arter he 'ad gone, and I was just in the middle of it when the cook and the other two chaps from the *Saltram* came back, with three other sailormen and a brewer's drayman they 'ad brought to see me DANCE!

"Same as you did a little while ago, Bill," ses the cook, taking out 'is beastly mouth-orgin and wiping it on 'is sleeve. "Wot toon would you like?"

I couldn't get away from 'em, and when I told them I 'ad never danced in my life the cook asked me where I expected to go to. He told the drayman that I'd been dancing like a fairy in sea-boots, and they all got in front of me and wouldn't let me pass. I lost my temper at last, and, arter they 'ad taken the broom away from me and the drayman and one o' the sailormen 'ad said wot they'd do to me if I was on'y fifty years younger, they sheered off.

I locked the gate arter 'em and went back to the office, and I 'adn't been there above 'arf an hour when somebody started ringing the gate-bell as if they was mad. I thought it was the cook's lot come back at fust, so I opened the wicket just a trifle and peeped out. There was a 'ansom-cab standing outside, and I 'ad hardly got my nose to the crack when the actor-chap, still in my clothes pushed the door open and nipped in.

"You've lost," he ses, pushing the door to and smiling all over. "Where's your sixpence?"

"*Lost?*" I ses, hardly able to speak. "D'ye mean to tell me you've been to my wife arter all—arter all I said to you?"

"I do," he ses, nodding, and smiling agin. "They were both deceived as easy as easy."

"*Both?*" I ses, staring at 'im. "Both wot? 'Ow many wives d'ye think I've got? Wot d'ye mean by it?"

"Arter I left you," he ses, giving me a little poke in the ribs, "I picked up a cab and, fust leaving my bag at Aidgate, I drove on to your 'ouse and knocked at the door. I knocked twice, and then an angry-looking woman opened it and asked me wot I wanted.

"'It's all right, missis,' I ses. 'I've got 'arf an hour off, and I've come to take you out for a walk.'

"'*Wot?*' she ses, drawing back with a start.

"'Just a little turn round to see the shops,' I ses; 'and if there's anything particler you'd like and it don't cost too much, you shall 'ave it.'

"I thought at fust, from the way she took it, she wasn't used to you giving 'er things.

"'*'Ow* dare you!' she ses. 'I'll 'ave you locked up. 'Ow dare you insult a respectable married woman! You wait till my 'usband comes 'ome.'

"'But I am your 'usband,' I ses. "Don't you know me, my pretty? Don't you know your pet sailor-boy?'

"She gave a screech like a steam-injin, and then she went next door and began knocking away like mad. Then I see that I 'ad gorn to number twelve instead of number fourteen. Your wife, your real wife, came out of number fourteen—and she was worse than the other. But they both thought it was you—there's no doubt of that. They chased me all the way up the road, and if it 'adn't ha' been for this cab that was just passing I don't know wot would 'ave 'appened to me."

He shook his 'ead and smiled agin, and, arter opening the wicket a trifle and telling the cabman he shouldn't be long, he turned to me and asked me for the sixpence, to wear on his watch-chain.

"*Sixpence!*" I ses. "SIXPENCE! Wot do you think is going to 'appen to me when I go 'ome?"

"Oh, I 'adn't thought o' that," he ses. "Yes, o' course."

"Wot about my wife's jealousy?" I ses. I "Wot about the other, and her 'usband, a cooper as big as a 'ouse?"

"Well, well," he ses, "one can't think of everything. It'll be all the same a hundred years hence."

"Look 'ere," I ses, taking 'is shoulder in a grip of iron. "You come back with me now in that cab and explain. D'ye see? That's wot you've got to do."

"All right," he ses; "certainly. Is—is the husband bad-tempered?"

"You'll see," I ses; "but that's your business. Come along."

"With pleasure," he ses, 'elping me in. "'Arf a mo' while I tell the cabby where to drive to."

He went to the back o' the cab, and afore I knew wot had 'appened the 'orse had got a flick over the head with the whip and was going along at a gallop. I kept putting the little flap up and telling the cabby to stop, but he didn't take the slightest notice. Arter I'd done it three times he kept it down so as I couldn't open it.

There was a crowd round my door when the cab drove up, and in the middle of it was my missis, the woman next door, and 'er husband, wot 'ad just come 'ome. 'Arf-a-dozen of 'em helped me out, and afore I could say a word the cabman drove off and left me there.

I dream of it now sometimes: standing there explaining and explaining, until, just as I feel I can't bear it any longer, two policemen come up and 'elp me indoors. If they had 'elped my missis outside it would be a easier dream to have.

SHIP'S COMPANY

45

FINE FEATHERS

Mr. Jobson awoke with a Sundayish feeling, probably due to the fact that it was Bank Holiday. He had been aware, in a dim fashion, of the rising of Mrs. Jobson some time before, and in a semi-conscious condition had taken over a large slice of unoccupied territory. He stretched himself and yawned, and then, by an effort of will, threw off the clothes and springing out of bed reached for his trousers.

He was an orderly man, and had hung them every night for over twenty years on the brass knob on his side of the bed. He had hung them there the night before, and now they had absconded with a pair of red braces just entering their teens. Instead, on a chair at the foot of the bed was a collection of garments that made him shudder. With trembling fingers he turned over a black tail-coat, a white waistcoat, and a pair of light check trousers. A white shirt, a collar, and tie kept them company, and, greatest outrage of all, a tall silk hat stood on its own band-box beside the chair. Mr. Jobson, fingering his bristly chin, stood regarding the collection with a wan smile.

"So that's their little game, is it?" he muttered. "Want to make a toff of me. Where's my clothes got to, I wonder?"

A hasty search satisfied him that they were not in the room, and, pausing only to drape himself in the counterpane, he made his way into the next. He passed on to the others, and then, with a growing sense of alarm, stole softly downstairs and making his way to the shop continued the search. With the shutters up the place was almost in darkness, and in spite of his utmost care apples and potatoes rolled on to the floor and travelled across it in a succession of bumps Then a sudden turn brought the scales clattering down.

"Good gracious, Alf!" said a voice. "Whatever are you a-doing of?"

Mr. Jobson turned and eyed his wife, who was standing at the door.

"I'm looking for my clothes, mother," he replied briefly.

"Clothes!" said Mrs. Jobson, with an obvious attempt at unconcerned speech. "Clothes! Why, they're on the chair."

"I mean clothes fit for a Christian to wear—fit for a greengrocer to wear," said Mr. Jobson raising his voice.

"It was a little surprise for you, dear," said his wife. "Me and Bert and Gladys and Dorothy 'ave all been saving up for it forever so long."

"It's very kind of you all," said Mr. Jobson, feebly—"very, but—"

"They've all been doing without things themselves to do it," interjected his wife. "As for Gladys, I'm sure nobody knows what she's given up."

"Well, if nobody knows, it don't matter," said Mr. Jobson. "As I was saying, it's very kind of you all, but I can't wear 'em. Where's my others?"

Mrs. Jobson hesitated.

"Where's my others?" repeated her husband.

"They're being took care of," replied his wife, with spirit. "Aunt Emma's minding 'em for you—and you know what she is. *H'sh! Alf!* Alf! *Alf!* I'm surprised at you!"

Mr. Jobson coughed. "It's the collar, mother," he said at last. "I ain't wore a collar for over twenty years; not since we was walking out together. And then I didn't like it."

"More shame for you," said his wife. "I'm sure there's no other respectable tradesman goes about with a handkerchief knotted round his neck."

"P'r'aps their skins ain't as tender as what mine is," urged Mr. Jobson; "and besides, fancy me in a top-'at! Why, I shall be the laughing stock of the place."

"Nonsense!" said his wife. It's only the lower classes what would laugh, and nobody minds what they think."

Mr. Jobson sighed. "Well, I shall 'ave to go back to bed again, then," he said ruefully. "So long, mother. Hope you have a pleasant time at the Palace."

He took a reef in the counterpane and with a fair amount of dignity, considering his appearance, stalked upstairs again and stood gloomily considering affairs in his bedroom. Ever since Gladys and Dorothy had been big enough to be objects of interest to the young men of the neighbourhood the clothes nuisance had been rampant. He peeped through the window-blind at the bright sunshine outside, and then looked back at the tumbled bed. A murmur of voices downstairs apprised him that the conspirators were awaiting the result.

He dressed at last and stood like a lamb—a red-faced, bull-necked lamb—while Mrs. Jobson fastened his collar for him.

"Bert wanted to get a taller one," she remarked, "but I said this would do to begin with."

"Wanted it to come over my mouth, I s'pose," said the unfortunate Mr. Jobson. "Well, 'ave it your own way. Don't mind about me. What with the trousers and the collar, I couldn't pick up a sovereign if I saw one in front of me."

"If you see one I'll pick it up for you," said his wife, taking up the hat and moving towards the door. "Come along!"

Mr. Jobson, with his arms standing out stiffly from his sides and his head painfully erect, followed her downstairs, and a sudden hush as he entered the kitchen testified to the effect produced by his appearance. It was followed by a hum of admiration that sent the blood flying to his head.

"Why he couldn't have done it before I don't know," said the dutiful Gladys. "Why, there ain't a man in the street looks a quarter as smart."

"Fits him like a glove!" said Dorothy, walking round him.

"Just the right length," said Bert, scrutinising the coat.

"And he stands as straight as a soldier," said Gladys, clasping her hands gleefully.

"Collar," said Mr. Jobson briefly. "Can I 'ave it took off while I eat my bloater, mother?"

"Don't be silly, Alf," said his wife. "Gladys, pour your father out a nice, strong, 'ot cup o' tea; and don't forget that the train starts at ha'-past ten."

"It'll start all right when it sees me," observed Mr. Jobson, squinting down at his trousers.

Mother and children, delighted with the success of their scheme, laughed applause, and Mr. Jobson, somewhat gratified at the success of his retort, sat down and attacked his breakfast. A short clay pipe, smoked as a digestive, was impounded by the watchful Mrs. Jobson the moment he had finished it.

"He'd smoke it along the street if I didn't," she declared.

"And why not?" demanded her husband. "I always do."

"Not in a top-'at," said Mrs. Jobson, shaking her head at him.

"Or a tail-coat," said Dorothy.

"One would spoil the other," said Gladys.

"I wish something would spoil the hat," said Mr. Jobson wistfully. "It's no good I must smoke, mother."

Mrs. Jobson smiled, and, going to the cupboard, produced, with a smile of triumph, an envelope containing seven dangerous-looking cigars. Mr. Jobson whistled, and taking one up examined it carefully.

"What do they call 'em, mother?" he inquired. "The 'Cut and Try Again Smokes'?"

Mrs. Jobson smiled vaguely. "Me and the girls are going upstairs to get ready now," she said. "Keep your eye on him, Bert!"

Father and son grinned at each other, and, to pass the time, took a cigar apiece. They had just finished them when a swish and rustle of skirts sounded from the stairs, and Mrs. Jobson and the girls, beautifully attired, entered the room and stood buttoning their gloves. A strong smell of scent fought with the aroma of the cigars.

"You get round me like, so as to hide me a bit," entreated Mr. Jobson, as they quitted the house. "I don't mind so much when we get out of our street."

Mrs. Jobson laughed his fears to scorn.

"Well, cross the road, then," said Mr. Jobson urgently. "There's Bill Foley standing at his door."

His wife sniffed. "Let him stand," she said haughtily.

Mr. Foley failed to avail himself of the permission. He regarded Mr. Jobson with dilated eyeballs, and, as the party approached, sank slowly into a sitting position on his doorstep, and as the door opened behind him rolled slowly over on to his back and presented an enormous pair of hob-nailed soles to the gaze of an interested world.

"I told you 'ow it would be," said the blushing Mr. Jobson. "You know what Bill's like as well as I do."

His wife tossed her head and they all quickened their pace. The voice of the ingenious Mr. Foley he calling piteously for his mother pursued them to the end of the road.

"I knew what it 'ud be," said Mr. Jobson, wiping his hot face. "Bill will never let me 'ear the end of this."

"Nonsense!" said his wife, bridling. "Do you mean to tell me you've got to ask Bill Foley 'ow you're to dress? He'll soon get tired of it; and, besides, it's just as well to let him see who you are. There's not many tradesmen as would lower themselves by mixing with a plasterer."

Mr. Jobson scratched his ear, but wisely refrained from speech. Once clear of his own district mental agitation subsided, but bodily discomfort increased at every step. The hat and the collar bothered him most, but every article of attire contributed its share. His uneasiness was so manifest that Mrs. Jobson, after a little womanly sympathy, suggested that, besides Sundays, it might be as well to wear them occasionally of an evening in order to get used to them.

"What, 'ave I got to wear them every Sunday?" demanded the unfortunate blankly; "why, I thought they was only for Bank Holidays."

Mrs. Jobson told him not to be silly.

"Straight, I did," said her husband earnestly. "You've no idea 'ow I'm suffering; I've got a headache, I'm arf choked, and there's a feeling about my waist as though I'm being cuddled by somebody I don't like."

Mrs. Jobson said it would soon wear off, and, seated in the train that bore them to the Crystal Palace, put the hat on the rack. Her husband's attempt to leave it in the train was easily frustrated and his explanation that he had forgotten all about it received in silence. It was evident that he would require watching, and under the clear gaze of his children he seldom had a button undone for more than three minutes at a time.

The day was hot and he perspired profusely. His collar lost its starch—a thing to be grateful for—and for the greater part of the day he wore his tie under the left ear. By the time they had arrived home again he was in a state of open mutiny.

"Never again," he said loudly, as he tore the collar off and hung his coat on a chair.

There was a chorus of lamentation; but he remained firm. Dorothy began to sniff ominously, and Gladys spoke longingly of the fathers possessed by other girls. It was not until Mrs. Jobson sat eyeing her supper, instead of eating it, that he began to temporise. He gave way bit by bit, garment by garment.

When he gave way at last on the great hat question, his wife took up her knife and fork.

His workaday clothes appeared in his bedroom next morning, but the others still remained in the clutches of Aunt Emma. The suit provided was of considerable antiquity, and at closing time, Mr. Jobson, after some hesitation, donned; his new clothes and with a sheepish glance at his wife went out. Mrs. Jobson nodded delight at her daughters.

"He's coming round," she whispered. "He liked that ticket-collector calling him 'sir' yesterday. I noticed it. He's put on everything but the topper. Don't say nothing about it; take it as a matter of course."

It became evident as the days wore on that she was right. Bit by bit she obtained the other clothes—with some difficulty—from Aunt Emma, but her husband still wore his best on Sundays and sometimes of an evening; and twice, on going into the bedroom suddenly, she had caught him surveying himself at different angles in the glass. And, moreover, he had spoken with some heat—for such a good-tempered man—on the shortcomings of Dorothy's laundry work.

"We'd better put your collars out," said his wife.

"And the shirts," said Mr. Jobson. "Nothing looks worse than a bad got-up cuff."

"You're getting quite dressy," said his wife, with a laugh.

Mr. Jobson eyed her seriously.

"No, mother, no," he replied. "All I've done is to find out that you're right, as you always 'ave been. A man in my persition has got no right to dress as if he kept a stall on the kerb. It ain't fair to the gals, or to young Bert. I don't want 'em to be ashamed of their father."

"They wouldn't be that," said Mrs. Jobson.

"I'm trying to improve," said her husband. "O' course, it's no use dressing up and behaving wrong, and yesterday I bought a book what tells you all about behaviour."

"Well done!" said the delighted Mrs. Jobson.

Mr. Jobson was glad to find that her opinion on his purchase was shared by the rest of the family. Encouraged by their approval, he told them of the benefit he was deriving from it; and at tea-time that day, after a little hesitation, ventured to affirm that it was a book that might do them all good.

"Hear, hear!" said Gladys.

"For one thing," said Mr. Jobson slowly, "I didn't know before that it was wrong to blow your tea; and as for drinking it out of a saucer, the book says it's a thing that is only done by the lower orders."

"If you're in a hurry?" demanded Mr. Bert Jobson, pausing with his saucer half-way to his mouth.

"If you're in anything," responded his father. "A gentleman would rather go without his tea than drink it out of a saucer. That's the sort o' thing Bill Foley would do."

Mr. Bert Jobson drained his saucer thoughtfully. "Picking your teeth with your finger is wrong, too," said Mr. Jobson, taking a breath. "Food should be removed in a—a—un—undemonstrative fashion with the tip of the tongue."

"I wasn't," said Gladys.

"A knife," pursued her father—"a knife should never in any circumstances be allowed near the mouth."

"You've made mother cut herself," said Gladys sharply; "that's what you've done."

"I thought it was my fork," said Mrs. Jobson. "I was so busy listening I wasn't thinking what I was doing. Silly of me."

"We shall all do better in time," said Mr. Jobson. "But what I want to know is, what about the gravy? You can't eat it with a fork, and it don't say nothing about a spoon. Oh, and what about our cold tubs, mother?"

"Cold *tubs*?" repeated his wife, staring at him. "What cold tubs?"

"The cold tubs me and Bert ought to 'ave," said Mr. Jobson. "It says in the book that an Englishman would just as soon think of going without his breakfus' as his cold tub; and you know how fond I am of my breakfus'."

"And what about me and the gals?" said the amazed Mrs. Jobson.

"Don't you worry about me, ma," said Gladys hastily.

"The book don't say nothing about gals; it says Englishmen," said Mr. Jobson.

"But we ain't got a bathroom," said his son.

"It don't signify," said Mr. Jobson. "A washtub'll do. Me and Bert'll 'ave a washtub each brought up overnight; and it'll be exercise for the gals bringing the water up of a morning to us."

"Well, I don't know, I'm sure," said the bewildered Mrs. Jobson. "Anyway, you and Bert'll 'ave to carry the tubs up and down. Messy, *I* call it."

"It's got to be done, mother," said Mr. Jobson cheerfully. "It's only the lower orders what don't 'ave their cold tub reg'lar. The book says so."

He trundled the tub upstairs the same night and, after his wife had gone downstairs next morning, opened the door and took in the can and pail that stood outside. He poured the contents into the tub, and, after eyeing it thoughtfully for some time, agitated the surface with his right foot. He dipped and dried that much enduring member some ten times, and after regarding the damp condition of the towels with great satisfaction, dressed himself and went downstairs.

"I'm all of a glow," he said, seating himself at the table. "I believe I could eat a elephant. I feel as fresh as a daisy: don't you, Bert?"

Mr. Jobson, junior, who had just come in from the shop, remarked, shortly, that he felt more like a blooming snowdrop.

"And somebody slopped a lot of water over the stairs carrying it up," said Mrs. Jobson. "I don't believe as everybody has cold baths of a morning. It don't seem wholesome to me."

Mr. Jobson took a book from his pocket, and opening it at a certain page, handed it over to her.

"If I'm going to do the thing at all I must do it properly," he said gravely. "I don't suppose Bill Foley ever 'ad a cold tub in his life; he don't know no better. *Gladys!*"

"Hallo!" said that young lady, with a start.

"Are you—are you eating that kipper with a your fingers?"

Gladys turned and eyed her mother appealingly.

"Page—page one hundred and something, I think it is," said her father, with his mouth full. "'Manners at the Dinner Table.' It's near the end of the book, I know."

"If I never do no worse than that I shan't come to no harm," said his daughter.

Mr. Jobson shook his head at her, and after eating his breakfast with great care, wiped his mouth on his handkerchief and went into the shop.

"I suppose it's all right," said Mrs. Jobson, looking after him, "but he's taking it very serious—very."

"He washed his hands five times yesterday morning," said Dorothy, who had just come in from the shop to her breakfast; "and kept customers waiting while he did it, too."

"It's the cold-tub business I can't get over," said her mother. "I'm sure it's more trouble to empty them than what it is to fill them. There's quite enough work in the 'ouse as it is."

"Too much," said Bert, with unwonted consideration.

"I wish he'd leave me alone," said Gladys. "My food don't do me no good when he's watching every mouthful I eat."

Of murmurings such as these Mr. Jobson heard nothing, and in view of the great improvement in his dress and manners, a strong resolution was passed to avoid the faintest appearance of discontent. Even when, satisfied with his own appearance, he set to work to improve that of Mrs. Jobson, that admirable woman made no complaint. Hitherto the brightness of her attire and the size of her hats had been held to atone for her lack of figure and the roomy comfort of her boots, but Mr. Jobson, infected with new ideas, refused to listen to such sophistry. He went shopping with Dorothy; and the Sunday after, when Mrs. Jobson went for an airing with him, she walked in boots with heels two inches high and toes that ended in a point. A waist that had disappeared some years before was recaptured and placed in durance vile; and a hat which called for a new style of hair-dressing completed the effect.

"You look splendid, ma!" said Gladys, as she watched their departure. "Splendid!"

"I don't feel splendid," sighed Mrs. Jobson to her husband. "These 'ere boots feel red-'ot."

"Your usual size," said Mr. Jobson, looking across the road.

"And the clothes seem just a teeny-weeny bit tight, p'r'aps," continued his wife.

Mr. Jobson regarded her critically. "P'r'aps I they might have been let out a quarter of an inch," he said thoughtfully. "They're the best fit you've 'ad for a long time, mother. I only 'ope the gals'll 'ave such good figgers."

His wife smiled faintly, but, with little breath for conversation walked on for some time in silence. A growing redness of face testified to her distress.

"I—I feel awful," she said at last, pressing her hand to her side. "*Awful.*"

"You'll soon get used to it," said Mr. Jobson gently. "Look at me! I felt like you do at first, and now I wouldn't go back to old clothes—and comfort—for anything. You'll get to love them boots."

"If I could only take 'em off I should love 'em better," said his wife, panting; "and I can't breathe properly—I can't breathe."

"You look ripping, mother," said her husband simply.

His wife essayed another smile, but failed. She set her lips together and plodded on, Mr. Jobson chatting cheerily and taking no notice of the fact that she kept lurching against him. Two miles from home she stopped and eyed him fixedly.

"If I don't get these boots off, Alf, I shall be a 'elpless cripple for the rest of my days," she murmured. "My ankle's gone over three times."

"But you can't take 'em off here," said Mr. Jobson hastily. "Think 'ow it would look."

"I must 'ave a cab or something," said his wife hysterically. "If I don't get 'em off soon I shall scream."

She leaned against the iron palings of a house for support, while Mr. Jobson, standing on the kerb, looked up and down the road for a cab. A four-wheeler appeared just in time to prevent the scandal of Mrs. Jobson removing her boots in the street.

"Thank goodness," she gasped, as she climbed in. "Never mind about untying 'em, Alf; cut the laces and get 'em off quick."

They drove home with the boots standing side by side on the seat in front of them. Mr. Jobson got out first and knocked at the door, and as soon as it opened Mrs. Jobson pattered across the intervening space with the boots dangling from her hand. She had nearly reached the door when Mr. Foley, who had a diabolical habit of always being on hand when he was least wanted, appeared suddenly from the off-side of the cab.

"Been paddlin'?" he inquired.

Mrs. Jobson, safe in her doorway, drew herself up and, holding the boots behind her, surveyed him with a stare of high-bred disdain.

"I see you going down the road in 'em," said the unabashed Mr. Foley, "and I says to myself, I says, 'Pride 'll bear a pinch, but she's going too far. If she thinks that she can squeedge those little tootsy-wootsies of 'ers into them boo—'"

The door slammed violently and left him exchanging grins with Mr. Jobson.

"How's the 'at?" he inquired.

Mr. Jobson winked. "Bet you a level 'arf-dollar I ain't wearing it next Sunday," he said, in a hoarse whisper.

Mr. Foley edged away.

"Not good enough," he said, shaking his head. "I've had a good many bets with you first and last, Alf, but I can't remember as I ever won one yet. So long."

46

FRIENDS IN NEED

Mr. Joseph Gibbs finished his half-pint in the private bar of the "Red Lion" with the slowness of a man unable to see where the next was coming from, and, placing the mug on the counter, filled his pipe from a small paper of tobacco and shook his head slowly at his companions.

"First I've 'ad since ten o'clock this morning," he said, in a hard voice.

"Cheer up," said Mr. George Brown.

"It can't go on forever," said Bob Kidd encouragingly.

"All I ask for—is work," said Mr. Gibbs impressively. "Not slavery, mind yer, but work."

"It's rather difficult to distinguish," said Mr. Brown.

"'Specially for some people," added Mr. Kidd.

"Go on," said Mr. Gibbs gloomily. "Go on. Stand a man 'arf a pint and then go and hurt 'is feelings. Twice yesterday I wondered to myself what it would feel like to make a hole in the water."

"Lots o' chaps *do* do it," said Mr. Brown musingly.

"And leave their wives and families to starve," said Mr. Gibbs icily.

"Very often the wife is better off," said his friend. "It's one mouth less for her to feed. Besides, she gen'rally gets something.

When pore old Bill went they 'ad a Friendly Lead at the 'King's Head' and got his missis pretty? Nearly seventeen pounds."

"And I believe we'd get more than that for your old woman," said Mr. Kidd. "There's no kids, and she could keep 'erself easy. Not that I want to encourage you to make away with youself."

Mr. Gibbs scowled and, tilting his mug, peered gloomily into the interior.

"Joe won't make no 'ole in the water," said Mr. Brown, wagging his head.' "If it was beer now—"

Mr. Gibbs turned and, drawing himself up to five feet three, surveyed the speaker with an offensive stare.

"I don't see why he need make a 'ole in anything," said Mr. Kidd slowly. "It 'ud do just as well if we said he 'ad. Then we could pass the hat round and share it."

"Divide it into three halves and each 'ave one," said Mr. Brown, nodding; "but 'ow is it I to be done?"

"'Ave some more beer and think it over," said Mr. Kidd, pale with excitement. "Three pints, please."

He and Mr. Brown took up their pints, and nodded at each other. Mr. Gibbs, toying idly with the handle of his, eyed them carefully. "Mind, I'm not promising anything," he said I slowly. "Understand, I ain't a-committing of myself by drinking this 'ere pint."

"You leave it to me, Joe," said Mr. Kidd.

Mr. Gibbs left it to him after a discussion in which pints played a persuasive part; with the result that Mr. Brown, sitting in the same bar the next evening with two or three friends, was rudely disturbed by the cyclonic entrance of Mr. Kidd, who, dripping with water, sank on a bench and breathed heavily.

"What's up? What's the matter?" demanded several voices.

"It's Joe—poor Joe Gibbs," said Mr. Kidd. "I was on Smith's wharf shifting that lighter to the next berth, and, o' course Joe must come aboard to help. He was shoving her off with 'is foot when—"

He broke off and shuddered and, accepting a mug of beer, pending the arrival of some brandy that a sympathiser had ordered, drank it slowly.

"It all 'appened in a flash," he said, looking round. "By the time I 'ad run round to his end he was just going down for the third time. I hung over the side and grabbed at 'im, and his collar and tie came off in my hand. Nearly went in, I did."

He held out the collar and tie; and approving notice was taken of the fact that he was soaking wet from the top of his head to the middle button of his waistcoat.

"Pore chap!" said the landlord, leaning over the bar. "He was in 'ere only 'arf an hour ago, standing in this very bar."

"Well, he's 'ad *his* last drop o' beer," said a carman in a chastened voice.

"That's more than anybody can say," said the landlord sharply. "I never heard anything against the man; he's led a good life so far as I know, and 'ow can we tell that he won't 'ave beer?"

He made Mr. Kidd a present of another small glass of brandy.

"He didn't leave any family, did he?" he inquired, as he passed it over.

"Only a wife," said Mr. Kidd; "and who's to tell that pore soul I don't know. She fair doated on 'im. 'Ow she's to live I don't know. I shall do what I can for 'er."

"Same 'ere," said Mr. Brown, in a deep voice.

"Something ought to be done for 'er," said the carman, as he went out.

"First thing is to tell the police," said the landlord. "They ought to know; then p'r'aps one of them'll tell her. It's what they're paid for."

"It's so awfully sudden. I don't know where I am 'ardly," said Mr. Kidd. "I don't believe she's got a penny-piece in the 'ouse. Pore Joe 'ad a lot o' pals. I wonder whether we couldn't get up something for her."

"Go round and tell the police first," said the landlord, pursing his lips up thoughtfully. "We can talk about that later on."

Mr. Kidd thanked him warmly and withdrew, accompanied by Mr. Brown. Twenty minutes later they left the station, considerably relieved at the matter-of-fact way in which the police had received the tidings, and, hurrying across London Bridge, made their way towards a small figure supporting its back against a post in the Borough market.

"Well?" said Mr. Gibbs snappishly, as he turned at the sound of their footsteps.

"It'll be all right, Joe," said Mr. Kidd. "We've sowed the seed."

"Sowed the wot?" demanded the other.

Mr. Kidd explained.

"Ho!" said Mr. Gibbs. "An' while your precious seed is a-coming up, wot am I to do? Wot about my comfortable 'ome? Wot about my bed—*and* grub?"

His two friends looked at each other uneasily. In the excitement of the arrangements they had forgotten these things, and a long and sometimes painful experience of Mr. Gibbs showed them only too plainly where they were drifting.

"You'll 'ave to get a bed this side o' the river somewhere," said Mr. Brown slowly. "Coffee-shop or something; and a smart, active man wot keeps his eyes open can always pick up a little money."

Mr. Gibbs laughed.

"And mind," said Mr. Kidd furiously, in reply to the laugh, "anything we lend you is to be paid back out of your half when you get it. And, wot's more, you don't get a ha'penny till you've come into a barber's shop and 'ad them whiskers off. We don't want no accidents."

Mr. Gibbs, with his back against the post, fought for his whiskers for nearly half an hour, and at the end of that time was led into a barber's, and in a state of sullen indignation proffered his request for a "clean" shave. He gazed at the barefaced creature that confronted him in the glass after the operation in open-eyed consternation, and Messrs. Kidd and Brown's politeness easily gave way before their astonishment.

"Well, I may as well have a 'air-cut while I'm here," said Mr. Gibbs, after a lengthy survey.

"And a shampoo, sir?" said the assistant.

"Just as you like," said Mr. Gibbs, turning a deaf ear to the frenzied expostulations of his financial backers. "Wot is it?"

He sat in amazed discomfort during the operation, and emerging with his friends remarked that he felt half a stone lighter. The information was received in stony silence, and, having spent some time in the selection, they found a quiet public-house, and in a retired corner formed themselves into a Committee of Ways and Means.

"That'll do for you to go on with," said Mr. Kidd, after he and Mr. Brown had each made a contribution; "and, mind, it's coming off of your share."

Mr. Gibbs nodded. "And any evening you want to see me you'll find me in here," he remarked. "Beer's ripping. Now you'd better go and see my old woman."

The two friends departed, and, to their great relief, found a little knot of people outside the abode of Mrs. Gibbs. It was clear that the news had already been broken, and, pushing their way upstairs, they found the widow with a damp handkerchief in her hand surrounded by attentive friends. In feeble accents she thanked Mr. Kidd for his noble attempts at rescue.

"He ain't dry yet," said Mr. Brown.

"I done wot I could," said Mr. Kidd simply. "Pore Joe! Nobody could ha' had a better pal. Nobody!"

"Always ready to lend a helping 'and to them as was in trouble, he was," said Mr. Brown, looking round.

"'Ear, 'ear!" said a voice.

"And we'll lend 'zm a helping 'and," said Mr. Kidd energetically. "We can't do *'im* no good, pore chap, but we can try and do something for 'er as is left behind."

He moved slowly to the door, accompanied by Mr. Brown, and catching the eye of one or two of the men beckoned them to follow. Under his able guidance a small but gradually increasing crowd made its way to the "Red Lion."

For the next three or four days the friends worked unceasingly. Cards stating that a Friendly Lead would be held at the "Red Lion," for the benefit of the widow of the late Mr. Joseph Gibbs, were distributed broadcast; and anecdotes portraying a singularly rare and beautiful character obtained an even wider circulation. Too late Wapping realised the benevolent disposition and the kindly but unobtrusive nature that had departed from it forever.

Mr. Gibbs, from his retreat across the water, fully shared his friends' enthusiasm, but an insane desire—engendered by vanity—to be present at the function was a source of considerable trouble and annoyance to them. When he offered to black his face and take part in the entertainment, Mr. Kidd had to be led outside and kept there until such time as he could converse in English pure and undefiled.

"Getting above 'imself, that's wot it is," said Mr. Brown, as they wended their way home. "He's having too much money out of us to spend; but it won't be for long now."

"He's having a lord's life of it, while we're slaving ourselves to death," grumbled Mr. Kidd. "I never see 'im looking so fat and well. By rights he oughtn't to 'ave the same share as wot we're going to 'ave; he ain't doing none of the work."

His ill-humour lasted until the night of the "Lead," which, largely owing to the presence of a sporting fishmonger who had done well at the races that day, and some of his friends, realised a sum far beyond the expectations of the hardworking promoters. The fishmonger led off by placing a five-pound note in the plate, and the packed audience breathed so hard that the plate-holder's responsibility began to weigh upon his spirits. In all, a financial tribute of thirty-seven pounds three and fourpence was paid to the memory of the late Mr. Gibbs.

"Over twelve quid apiece," said the delighted Mr. Kidd as he bade his co-worker good night. "Sounds too good to be true."

The next day passed all too slowly, but work was over at last, and Mr. Kidd led the way over London Bridge a yard or two ahead of the more phlegmatic Mr. Brown. Mr. Gibbs was in his old corner at the "Wheelwright's Arms," and, instead of going into ecstasies over the sum realised, hinted darkly that it would have been larger if he had been allowed to have had a hand in it.

"It'll 'ardly pay me for my trouble," he said, shaking his head. "It's very dull over 'ere all alone by myself. By the time you two have 'ad your share, besides taking wot I owe you, there'll be 'ardly anything left."

I'll talk to you another time," said Mr. Kidd, regarding him fixedly. "Wot you've got to do now is to come acrost the river with us."

"Whaffor?" demanded Mr. Gibbs.

"We're going to break the joyful news to your old woman that you're alive afore she starts spending money wot isn't hers," said Mr. Kidd. "And we want you to be close by in case she don't believe us."

"Well, do it gentle, mind," said the fond husband. "We don't want 'er screaming, or anything o' that sort. I know 'er better than wot you do, and my advice to you is to go easy."

He walked along by the side of them, and, after some demur, consented, as a further disguise, to put on a pair of spectacles, for which Mr. Kidd's wife's mother had been hunting high and low since eight o'clock that morning.

"You doddle about 'ere for ten minutes," said Mr. Kidd, as they reached the Monument, "and then foller on. When you pass a lamp-post 'old your handkerchief up to your face. And wait for us at the corner of your road till we come for you."

He went off at a brisk pace with Mr. Brown, a pace moderated to one of almost funereal solemnity as they approached the residence of Mrs. Gibbs. To their relief she was alone, and after the usual amenities thanked them warmly for all they had done for her.

"I'd do more than that for pore Joe," said Mr. Brown.

"They—they 'aven't found 'im yet?" said the widow.

Mr. Kidd shook his head. "My idea is they won't find 'im," he said slowly.

"Went down on the ebb tide," explained Mr. Brown; and spoilt Mr. Kidd's opening.

"Wherever he is 'e's better off," said Mrs. Gibbs. "No more trouble about being out o' work; no more worry, no more pain. We've all got to go some day."

"Yes," began Mr. Kidd; "but—"

"I'm sure I don't wish 'im back," said Mrs. Gibbs; "that would be sinful."

"But 'ow if he wanted to come back?" said Mr. Kidd, playing for an opening.

"And 'elp you spend that money," said Mr. Brown, ignoring the scowls of his friend.

Mrs. Gibbs looked bewildered. "Spend the money?" she began.

"Suppose," said Mr. Kidd, "suppose he wasn't drowned after all? Only last night I dreamt he was alive."

"So did I," said Mr. Brown.

"He was smiling at me," said Mr. Kidd, in a tender voice. "'Bob,' he ses, 'go and tell my pore missis that I'm alive,' he ses; 'break it to 'er gentle.'"

"It's the very words he said to me in my dream," said Mr. Brown. "Bit strange, ain't it?"

"Very," said Mrs. Gibbs.

"I suppose," said Mr. Kidd, after a pause, "I suppose you haven't been dreaming about 'im?"

"No; I'm a teetotaller," said the widow.

The two gentlemen exchanged glances, and Mr. Kidd, ever of an impulsive nature, resolved to bring matters to a head.

"Wot would you do if Joe was to come in 'ere at this door?" he asked.

"Scream the house down," said the widow promptly.

"Scream—scream the 'ouse down?" said the distressed Mr. Kidd.

Mrs. Gibbs nodded. "I should go screaming, raving mad," she said, with conviction.

"But—but not if 'e was *alive*!" said Mr. Kidd.

"I don't know what you're driving at," said Mrs. Gibbs. "Why don't you speak out plain? Poor Joe is drownded, you know that; you saw it all, and yet you come talking to me about dreams and things."

Mr. Kidd bent over her and put his hand affectionately on her shoulder. "He escaped," he said, in a thrilling whisper. "He's alive and well."

"WHAT?" said Mrs. Gibbs, starting back.

"True as I stand 'ere," said Mr. Kidd; "ain't it, George?"

"Truer," said Mr. Brown loyally.

Mrs. Gibbs leaned back, gasping. "Alive!" she said. "But 'ow? 'Ow can he be?"

"Don't make such a noise," said Mr. Kidd earnestly. "Mind, if anybody else gets to 'ear of it you'll 'ave to give that money back."

"I'd give more than that to get *'im* back," said Mrs. Gibbs wildly. "I believe you're deceiving me."

"True as I stand 'ere," asseverated the other. "He's only a minute or two off, and if it wasn't for you screaming I'd go out and fetch 'im in."

"I won't scream," said Mrs. Gibbs, "not if I know it's flesh and blood. Oh, where is he? Why don't you bring 'im in? Let me go to 'im."

"All right," said Mr. Kidd, with a satisfied smile at Mr. Brown; "all in good time. I'll go and fetch 'im now; but, mind, if you scream you'll spoil everything."

He bustled cheerfully out of the room and downstairs, and Mrs. Gibbs, motioning Mr. Brown to silence, stood by the door with parted lips, waiting. Three or four minutes elapsed.

"'Ere they come," said Mr. Brown, as footsteps sounded on the stairs. "Now, no screaming, mind!"

Mrs. Gibbs drew back, and, to the gratification of all concerned, did not utter a sound as Mr. Kidd, followed by her husband, entered the room. She stood looking expectantly towards the doorway.

"Where is he?" she gasped.

"Eh?" said Mr. Kidd, in a startled voice. "Why, here. Don't you know 'im?"

"It's me, Susan," said Mr. Gibbs, in a low voice.

"Oh, I might 'ave known it was a joke," cried Mrs. Gibbs, in a faint voice, as she tottered to a chair. "Oh, 'ow cruel of you to tell me my pore Joe was alive! Oh, 'ow could you?"

"Lor' lumme," said the incensed Mr. Kidd, pushing Mr. Gibbs forward. "Here he is. Same as you saw 'im last, except for 'is whiskers. Don't make that sobbing noise; people'll be coming in."

"Oh! Oh! *Oh!* Take 'im away," cried Mrs. Gibbs. "Go and play your tricks with somebody else's broken 'art."

"But it's your husband," said Mr. Brown.

"Take 'im away," wailed Mrs. Gibbs.

Mr. Kidd, grinding his teeth, tried to think. "'Ave you got any marks on your body, Joe?" he inquired.

"I ain't got a mark on me," said Mr. Gibbs, with a satisfied air, "or a blemish. My skin is as whi—"

"That's enough about your skin," interrupted Mr. Kidd rudely.

"If you ain't all of you gone before I count ten," said Mrs. Gibbs, in a suppressed voice, "I'll scream. 'Ow dare you come into a respectable woman's place and talk about your skins? Are you going? One! Two! Three! Four! Five!"

Her voice rose with each numeral; and Mr. Gibbs himself led the way downstairs, and, followed by his friends, slipped nimbly round the corner.

"It's a wonder she didn't rouse the whole 'ouse," he said, wiping his brow on his sleeve; and where should we ha' been then? I thought at the time it was a mistake you making me 'ave my whiskers off, but I let you know best. She's never seen me without 'em. I 'ad a remarkable strong growth when I was quite a boy. While other boys was—"

"Shut—up!" vociferated Mr. Kidd.

"Shan't!" said Mr. Gibbs defiantly. "I've 'ad enough of being away from my comfortable little 'ome and my wife; and I'm going to let 'em start growing agin this very night. She'll never reckernise me without 'em, that's certain."

"He's right, Bob," said Mr. Brown, with conviction.

"D'ye mean to tell me we've got to wait till 'is blasted whiskers grow?" cried Mr. Kidd, almost dancing with fury. "And go on keeping 'im in idleness till they do?"

"You'll get it all back out o' my share," said Mr. Gibbs, with dignity. "But you can please yourself. If you like to call it quits now, I don't mind."

Mr. Brown took his seething friend aside, and conferred with him in low but earnest tones. Mr. Gibbs, with an indifferent air, stood by whistling softly.

"'Ow long will they take to grow?" inquired Mr. Kidd, turning to him with a growl.

Mr. Gibbs shrugged his shoulders. "Can't say," he replied; "but I should think two or three weeks would be enough for 'er to reckernise me by. If she don't, we must wait another week or So, that's all."

"Well, there won't be much o' your share left, mind that," said Mr. Kidd, glowering at him.

"I can't help it," said Mr. Gibbs. "You needn't keep reminding me of it."

They walked the rest of the way in silence; and for the next fortnight Mr. Gibbs's friends paid nightly visits to note the change in his appearance, and grumble at its slowness.

"We'll try and pull it off tomorrow night," said Mr. Kidd, at the end of that period. "I'm fair sick o' lending you money."

Mr. Gibbs shook his head and spoke sagely about not spoiling the ship for a ha'porth o' tar; but Mr. Kidd was obdurate.

"There's enough for 'er to reckernise you by," he said sternly, "and we don't want other people to. Meet us at the Monument at eight o'clock tomorrow night, and we'll get it over."

"Give your orders," said Mr. Gibbs, in a nasty voice.

"Keep your 'at well over your eyes," commanded Mr. Kidd sternly. "Put them spectacles on wot I lent you, and it wouldn't be a bad idea if you tied your face up in a piece o' red flannel."

"I know wot I'm going to do without you telling me," said Mr. Gibbs, nodding. "I'll bet you pots round that you don't either of you reckernise me tomorrow night."

The bet was taken at once, and from eight o'clock until ten minutes to nine the following night Messrs. Kidd and Brown did their best to win it. Then did Mr. Kidd, turning to Mr. Brown in perplexity, inquire with many redundant words what it all meant.

"He must 'ave gone on by 'imself," said Mr. Brown. "We'd better go and see."

In a state of some disorder they hurried back to Wapping, and, mounting the stairs to Mrs. Gibbs's room, found the door fast. To their fervent and repeated knocking there was no answer.

"Ah, you won't make *her* 'ear," said a woman, thrusting an untidy head over the balusters on the next landing. "She's gone."

"*Gone!*" exclaimed both gentlemen. "Where?"

"Canada," said the woman. "She went off this morning."

Mr. Kidd leaned up against the wall for support; Mr. Brown stood open-mouthed and voiceless.

"It was a surprise to me," said the woman, "but she told me this morning she's been getting ready on the quiet for the last fortnight. Good spirits she was in, too; laughing like anything."

"*Laughing!*" repeated Mr. Kidd, in a terrible voice.

The woman nodded. "And when I spoke about it and reminded 'er that she 'ad only just lost 'er pore husband, I thought she would ha' burst," she said severely. "She sat down on that stair and laughed till the tears ran down 'er face like water."

Mr. Brown turned a bewildered face upon his partner. "Laughing!" he said slowly. "Wot 'ad she got to laugh at?"

"Two—born—fools," replied Mr. Kidd.

47

GOOD INTENTIONS

"Jealousy; that's wot it is," said the night-watchman, trying to sneer—"pure jealousy."

He had left his broom for a hurried half-pint at the "Bull's Head"—left it leaning in a negligent attitude against the warehouse wall; now, lashed to the top of the crane at the jetty end, it pointed its soiled bristles towards the evening sky and defied capture.

"And I know who it is, and why 'e's done it," he continued. "Fust and last, I don't suppose I was talking to the gal for more than ten minutes, and arf of that was about the weather.

"I don't suppose anybody 'as suffered more from jealousy than wot I 'ave. Other people's I jealousy, I mean. Ever since I was married the missis has been setting traps for me, and asking people to keep an eye on me. I blacked one of the eyes once—like a fool—and the chap it belonged to made up a tale about me that I ain't lived down yet.

"Years ago, when I was out with the missis one evening, I saved a gal's life for her. She slipped as she was getting off a 'bus, and I caught 'er just in time. Fine strapping gal she was, and afore I could get my balance we 'ad danced round and round 'arf-way acrost the road with our arms round each other's necks, and my missis watching us from the pavement. When we were safe, she said the gal 'adn't slipped at all; and, as soon as the gal 'ad got 'er breath, I'm blest if she didn't say so too.

"You can't argufy with jealous people, and you can't shame 'em. When I told my missis once that I should never dream of being jealous of *her*, instead of up and thanking me for it, she spoilt the best frying-pan we ever had. When the widder-woman next door but two and me 'ad rheumatics at the same time, she went and asked the doctor whether it was catching.

"The worst trouble o' that kind I ever got into was all through trying to do somebody else a kindness. I went out o' my way to do it; I wasted the whole evening for the sake of other people, and got into such trouble over it that even now it gives me the cold shivers to think of.

"Cap'n Tarbell was the man I tried to do a good turn to; a man that used to be master of a ketch called the *Lizzie and Annie*, trading between 'ere and Shoremouth. 'Artful Jack' he used to be called, and if ever a man deserved the name, he did. A widder-man of about fifty, and as silly as a boy of fifteen. He 'ad been talking of getting married agin for over ten years, and, thinking it was only talk, I didn't give 'im any good advice. Then he told me one night that 'e was keeping company with a woman named Lamb, who lived at a place near Shoremouth. When I asked 'im what she looked like, he said that she had a good 'art, and, knowing wot that meant, I wasn't at all surprised when he told me some time arter that 'e had been a silly fool.

"'Well, if she's got a good 'art,' I ses, 'p'r'aps she'll let you go.'

"'Talk sense,' he ses. 'It ain't good enough for that. Why, she worships the ground I tread on. She thinks there is nobody like me in the whole wide world.'

"'Let's 'ope she'll think so arter you're married,' I ses, trying to cheer him up.

"'I'm not going to get married,' he ses. 'Leastways, not to 'er. But 'ow to get out of it without breaking her 'art and being had up for breach o' promise I can't think. And if the other one got to 'ear of it, I should lose her too.'

"'Other one?' I ses, 'wot other one?'

"Cap'n Tarbell shook 'is head and smiled like a silly gal.

"She fell in love with me on top of a bus in the Mile End Road,' he ses. 'Love at fust sight it was. She's a widder lady with a nice little 'ouse at Bow, and plenty to live on—her 'usband having been a builder. I don't know what to do. You see, if I married both of 'em it's sure to be found out sooner or later.'

"'You'll be found out as it is,' I ses, 'if you ain't careful. I'm surprised at you.'

"'Yes,' he ses, getting up and walking backwards and forwards; 'especially as Mrs. Plimmer is always talking about coming down to see the ship. One thing is, the crew won't give me away; they've been with me too long for that. P'r'aps you could give me a little advice, Bill.'

"I did. I talked to that man for an hour and a 'arf, and when I 'ad finished he said he didn't want that kind of advice at all. Wot 'e wanted was for me to tell 'im 'ow to get rid of Miss Lamb and marry Mrs. Plimmer without anybody being offended or having their feelings hurt.

"Mrs. Plimmer came down to the ship the very next evening. Fine-looking woman she was, and wot with 'er watch and chain and di'mond rings and brooches and such-like, I should think she must 'ave 'ad five or six pounds' worth of jewell'ry on 'er. She gave me a very pleasant smile, and I gave 'er one back, and we stood chatting there like old friends till at last she tore 'erself away and went on board the ship.

"She came off by and by hanging on Cap'n Tarbell's arm. The cap'n was dressed up in 'is Sunday clothes, with one of the cleanest collars on I 'ave ever seen in my life, and smoking a cigar that smelt like an escape of gas. He came back alone at ha'past eleven that night, and 'e told me that if it wasn't for the other one down Shoremouth way he should be the 'appiest man on earth.

"'Mrs. Plimmer's only got one fault,' he ses, shaking his 'ead, 'and that's jealousy. If she got to know of Laura Lamb, it would be all U.P. It makes me go cold all over when I think of it. The only thing is to get married as quick as I can; then she can't help 'erself.'

"'It wouldn't prevent the other one making a fuss, though,' I ses.

"'No,' he ses, very thoughtfully, 'it wouldn't. I shall 'ave to do something there, but wot, I don't know.'

"He climbed on board like a man with a load on his mind, and arter a look at the sky went below and forgot both 'is troubles in sleep.

"Mrs. Plimmer came down to the wharf every time the ship was up arter that. Sometimes she'd spend the evening aboard, and sometimes they'd go off and spend it somewhere else. She 'ad a fancy for the cabin, I think, and the cap'n told me that she 'ad said when they were married she was going to sail with 'im sometimes.

"'But it ain't for six months yet,' he ses, 'and a lot o' things might 'appen to the other one in that time, with luck.'

"It was just about a month arter that that 'e came to me one evening trembling all over. I ad just come on dooty, and afore I could ask 'im wot was the matter he 'ad got me in the 'Bull's Head' and stood me three 'arf-pints, one arter the other.

"'I'm ruined,' he ses, in a 'usky whisper; 'I'm done for. Why was wimmen made? Wot good are they? Fancy 'ow bright and 'appy we should all be without 'em.'

"I started to p'int out one or two things to 'im that he seemed to 'ave forgot, but 'e wouldn't listen. He was so excited that he didn't seem to know wot 'e was doing, and arter he 'ad got three more 'arf-pints waiting for me, all in a row on the counter,

I 'ad to ask 'im whether he thought I was there to do conjuring tricks, or wot?

"'There was a letter waiting for me in the office,' he ses. 'From Miss Lamb—she's in London. She's coming to pay me a surprise visit this evening—I know who'll get the surprise. Mrs. Plimmer's coming too.'

"I gave 'im one of my 'arf-pints and made 'im drink it. He chucked the pot on the floor when he 'ad done, in a desprit sort o' way, and 'im and the landlord 'ad a little breeze then that did 'im more good than wot the beer 'ad. When we came outside 'e seemed more contented with 'imself, but he shook his 'ead and got miserable as soon as we got to the wharf agin.

"'S'pose they both come along at the same time,' he ses. 'Wot's to be done? '

"I shut the gate with a bang and fastened the wicket. Then I turned to 'im with a smile.

"'I'm watchman 'ere,' I ses, 'and I lets in who I thinks I will. This ain't a public 'ighway,' I ses; 'it's a wharf.'

"'Bill,' he ses, 'you're a genius.'

"'If Miss Lamb comes 'ere asking arter you,' I ses, 'I shall say you've gone out for the evening.'

"'Wot about her letter?' he ses.

"'You didn't 'ave it,' I ses, winking at 'im.

"'And suppose she waits about outside for me, and Mrs. Plimmer wants me to take 'er out?' he ses, shivering. 'She's a fearful obstinate woman; and she'd wait a week for me.'

"He kept peeping up the road while we, talked it over, and then we both see Mrs. Plimmer coming along. He backed on to the wharf and pulled out 'is purse.

"'Bill,' he ses, gabbling as fast as 'e could gabble, 'here's five or six shillings. If the other one comes and won't go away tell 'er I've gone to the Pagoda Music-'all and you'll take 'er to me; keep 'er out all the evening some'ow, if you can; if she comes back too soon keep 'er in the office.'

"'And wot about leaving the wharf and my dooty?' I ses, staring.

"'I'll put Joe on to keep watch for you,' he ses, pressing the money in my 'and. 'I rely on you, Bill, and I'll never forget you. You won't lose by it, trust me.'

"He nipped off and tumbled aboard the ship afore I could say a word. I just stood there staring arter 'im and feeling the money, and afore I could make up my mind Mrs. Plimmer came up.

"I thought I should never ha' got rid of her. She stood there chatting and smiling, and seemed to forget all about the cap'n, and every moment I was afraid that the other one might come up. At last she went off, looking behind 'er, to the ship, and then I went outside and put my back up agin the gate and waited.

"I 'ad hardly been there ten minutes afore the other one came along. I saw 'er stop and speak to a policeman, and then she came straight over to me.

"'I want to see Cap'n Tarbell,' she ses.

"'Cap'n Tarbell?' I ses, very slow; 'Cap'n Tarbell 'as gone off for the evening.'

"'Gone off!' she ses, staring. 'But he can't 'ave. Are you sure?'

"'Sartain,' I ses. Then I 'ad a bright idea. 'And there's a letter come for 'im,' I ses.

"'Oh, dear!' she ses. 'And I thought it would be in plenty of time. Well, I must go on the ship and wait for 'im, I suppose.'

"If I had only let 'er go I should ha' saved myself a lot o' trouble, and the man wot deserved it would ha' got it. Instead o' that I told 'er about the music-'all, and arter carrying on like a silly gal o' seventeen and saying she couldn't think of it, she gave way and said she'd go with me to find 'im. I was all right so far as clothes went as it happened. Mrs. Plimmer said once that I got more and more dressy every time she saw me, and my missis 'ad said the same thing only in a different way. I just took a peep through the wicket and saw that Joe 'ad taken up my dooty, and then we set off.

"I said I wasn't quite sure which one he'd gone to, but we'd try the Pagoda Music-'all fust, and we went there on a bus from Aidgate. It was the fust evening out I 'ad 'ad for years, and I should 'ave enjoyed it if it 'adn't been for Miss Lamb. Wotever Cap'n Tarbell could ha' seen in 'er, I can't think. She was quiet, and stupid, and bad-tempered. When the bus-conductor came round for the fares she 'adn't got any change; and when we got to the hall she did such eggsterrordinary things trying to find 'er pocket that I tried to look as if she didn't belong to me. When she left off she smiled and said she was farther off than ever, and arter three or four wot was standing there 'ad begged 'er to have another try, I 'ad to pay for the two.

"The 'ouse was pretty full when we got in, but she didn't take no notice of that. Her idea was that she could walk about all over the place looking for Cap'n Tarbell, and it took three men in buttons and a policeman to persuade 'er different. We were pushed into a couple o' seats at last, and then she started finding fault with me.

"'Where is Cap'n Tarbell?' she ses. 'Why don't you find him?'

"'I'll go and look for 'im in the bar presently,' I ses. 'He's sure to be there, arter a turn or two.'

"I managed to keep 'er quiet for 'arf an hour—with the 'elp of the people wot sat near us—and then I 'ad to go. I 'ad a glass o' beer to pass the time away, and, while I was drinking it, who should come up but the cook and one of the hands from the *Lizzie and Annie*.

"'We saw you,' ses the cook, winking; 'didn't we, Bob?'

"'Yes,' ses Bob, shaking his silly 'ead; 'but it wasn't no surprise to me. I've 'ad my eye on 'im for a long time past.'

"'I thought 'e was married,' ses the cook.

"'So he is,' ses Bob, 'and to the best wife in London. I know where she lives. Mine's a bottle o' Bass,' he ses, turning to me.

"'So's mine,' ses the cook.

"I paid for two bottles for 'em, and arter that they said that they'd 'ave a whisky-and-soda apiece just to show as there was no ill-feeling.

"'It's very good,' ses Bob, sipping his, 'but it wants a sixpenny cigar to go with it. It's been the dream o' my life to smoke a sixpenny cigar.'

"So it 'as mine,' ses the cook, 'but I don't suppose I ever shall.'

"They both coughed arter that, and like a good-natured fool I stood 'em a sixpenny cigar apiece, and I 'ad just turned to go back to my seat when up come two more hands from the *Lizzie and Annie.*

"'Hallo, watchman!' ses one of 'em. 'Why, I thought you was a-taking care of the wharf.'

"'He's got something better than the wharf to take care of,' ses Bob, grinning.

"'I know; we see 'im,' ses the other chap. 'We've been watching 'is goings-on for the last 'arf-hour; better than a play it was.'

"I stopped *their* mouths with a glass o' bitter each, and went back to my seat while they was drinking it. I told Miss Lamb in whispers that 'e wasn't there, but I'd 'ave another look for him by and by. If she'd ha' whispered back it would ha' been all right, but she wouldn't, and, arter a most unpleasant scene, she walked out with her 'ead in the air follered by me with two men in buttons and a policeman.

"O' course, nothing would do but she must go back to the wharf and wait for Cap'n Tarbell, and all the way there I was wondering wot would 'appen if she went on board and found 'im there with Mrs. Plimmer. However, when we got there I persuaded 'er to go into the office while I went aboard to see if I could find out where he was, and three minutes arterwards he was standing with me behind the galley, trembling all over and patting me on the back.

"'Keep 'er in the office a little longer,' he ses, in a whisper. 'The other's going soon. Keep 'er there as long as you can.'

"'And suppose she sees you and Mrs. Plimmer passing the window?' I ses.

"'That'll be all right; I'm going to take 'er to the stairs in the ship's boat,' he ses. 'It's more romantic.'

"He gave me a little punch in the ribs, playful-like, and, arter telling me I was worth my weight in gold-dust, went back to the cabin agin.

"I told Miss Lamb that the cabin was locked up, but that Cap'n Tarbell was expected back in about 'arf-an-hour's time. Then I found 'er an old newspaper and a comfortable chair and sat down to wait. I couldn't go on the wharf for fear she'd want to come with me, and I sat there as patient as I could, till a little clicking noise made us both start up and look at each other.

"'Wot's that?' she ses, listening.

"'It sounded,' I ses—'it sounded like somebody locking the door.'

"I went to the door to try it just as somebody dashed past the window with their 'ead down. It was locked fast, and arter I had 'ad a try at it and Miss Lamb had 'ad a try at it, we stood and looked at each other in surprise.

"'Somebody's playing a joke on us,' I ses.

"'Joke!' ses Miss Lamb. 'Open that door at once. If you don't open it I'll call for the police.'

"She looked at the windows, but the iron bars wot was strong enough to keep the vans outside was strong enough to keep 'er in, and then she gave way to such a fit o' temper that I couldn't do nothing with 'er.

"'Cap'n Tarbell can't be long now,' I ses, as soon as I could get a word in. 'We shall get out as soon as 'e comes.'

"She flung 'erself down in the chair agin with 'er back to me, and for nearly three-quarters of an hour we sat there without a word. Then, to our joy, we 'eard footsteps turn in at the gate. Quick footsteps they was. Somebody turned the handle of the door, and then a face looked in at the window that made me nearly jump out of my boots in surprise. A face that was as white as chalk with temper, and a bonnet cocked over one eye with walking fast. She shook 'er fist at me, and then she shook it at Miss Lamb.

"'Who's that?' ses Miss Lamb.

"'My missis,' I ses in a loud voice. 'Thank goodness she's come.'

"'*Open the door!*" ses my missis, with a screech. 'OPEN THE DOOR!'

"'I can't,' I ses. 'Somebody's locked it. This is Cap'n Tarbell's young lady.'

"'I'll Cap'n Tarbell 'er when I get in!' ses my wife. 'You too. I'll music-'all you! I'll learn you to go gallivanting about! *Open the door!*'

"She walked up and down the alley-way in front of the window waiting for me just like a lion walking up and down its cage waiting for its dinner, and I made up my mind then and there that I should 'ave to make a clean breast of it and let Cap'n Tarbell get out of it the best way he could. I wasn't going to suffer for him.

"'Ow long my missis walked up and down there I don't know. It seemed ages to me; but at last I 'eard footsteps and voices, and Bob and the cook and the other two chaps wot we 'ad met at the music-'all came along and stood grinning in at the window.

"'Somebody's locked us in,' I ses. 'Go and fetch Cap'n Tarbell.'

"'Cap'n Tarbell?' ses the cook. "You don't want to see 'im. Why, he's the last man in the world you ought to want to see! You don't know 'ow jealous he is.'

"'You go and fetch 'im,' I ses. ''Ow dare you talk like that afore my wife!'

"'I dursen't take the responserbility,' ses the cook. 'It might mean bloodshed.'

"'You go and fetch 'im,' ses my missis. 'Never mind about the bloodshed. I don't. *Open the door!*'

"She started banging on the door agin, and arter talking among themselves for a time they moved off to the ship. They came back in three or four minutes, and the cook 'eld up something in front of the window.

"'The boy 'ad got it,' he ses. 'Now shall I open the door and let your missis in, or would you rather stay where you are in peace and quietness?'

"I saw my missis jump at the key, and Bob and the others, laughing fit to split their sides, 'olding her back. Then I heard a shout, and the next moment Cap'n Tarbell came up and asked 'em wot the trouble was about.

"They all started talking at once, and then the cap'n, arter one look in at the window, threw up his 'ands and staggered back as if 'e couldn't believe his eyesight. He stood dazed-like for a second or two, and then 'e took the key out of the cook's 'and, opened the door, and walked in. The four men was close be'ind 'im, and, do all she could, my missis couldn't get in front of 'em.

"'Watchman!' he ses, in a stuck-up voice, 'wot does this mean? Laura Lamb! Wot 'ave! you got to say for yourself? Where 'ave you been all the evening?'

"'She's been to a music-'all with Bill,' ses the cook. 'We saw 'em.'

"'WOT?' ses the cap'n, falling back again, a 'It can't be!'

"'It was them,' ses my wife. 'A little boy brought me a note telling me. You let me go; it's my husband, and I want to talk to 'im.'

"'It's all right,' I ses, waving my 'and at Miss Lamb, wot was going to speak, and smiling at my missis, wot was trying to get at me.

"'We went to look for you,' ses Miss Lamb, very quick. 'He said you were at the music-'all, and as you 'adn't got my letter I thought it was very likely.'

"'But I did get your letter,' ses the cap'n.

"'He said you didn't,' ses Miss Lamb.

"'Look 'ere,' I ses. 'Why don't you keep quiet and let me explain? I can explain everything.'

"'I'm glad o' that, for your sake, my man,' ses the cap'n, looking at me very hard. 'I 'ope you will be able to explain 'ow it was you *came to leave the wharf for three hours.*'

"I saw it all then. If I split about Mrs. Plimmer, he'd split to the guv'nor about my leaving my dooty, and I should get the sack. I thought I should ha' choked, and, judging by the way they banged me on the back, Bob and the cook thought so too. They 'elped me to a chair when I got better, and I sat there 'elpless while the cap'n went on talking.

"'I'm no mischief-maker,' he ses; 'and, besides, p'r'aps he's been punished enough. And as far as I'm concerned he can take this lady to a music-'all every night of the week if 'e likes. I've done with her.'

"There was an eggsterrordinary noise from where my missis was standing; like the gurgling water makes sometimes running down the kitchen sink at 'ome only worse. Then they all started talking together, and arf-a-dozen times or more Miss Lamb called me to back 'er up in wot she was saying, but I only shook my 'ead, and at last, arter tossing her 'ead at Cap'n Tarbell and telling 'im she wouldn't 'ave 'im if he'd got fifty million a year, the five of 'em 'eld my missis while she went off.

"They gave 'er ten minutes' start, and then Cap'n Tarbell, arter looking at me and shaking his 'ead, said he was afraid they must be going.

"'And I 'ope this night'll be a lesson to you,' he ses. 'Don't neglect your dooty agin. I shall keep my eye on you, and if you be'ave yourself I shan't say anything. Why, for all you know or could ha' done the wharf might ha' been burnt to the ground while you was away!'

"He nodded to his crew, and they all walked out laughing and left me alone—with the missis."

48

FAIRY GOLD

"Come and have a pint and talk it over," said Mr. Augustus Teak. "I've got reasons in my 'ead that you don't dream of, Alf."

Mr. Chase grunted and stole a side-glance at the small figure of his companion. "All brains, you are, Gussie," he remarked. "That's why it is you're so well off."

"Come and have a pint," repeated the other, and with surprising ease pushed his bulky friend into the bar of the "Ship and Anchor." Mr. Chase, mellowed by a long draught, placed his mug on the counter and eyeing him kindly, said—

"I've been in my lodgings thirteen years."

"I know," said Mr. Teak; "but I've got a partikier reason for wanting you. Our lodger, Mr. Dunn, left last week, and I only thought of you yesterday. I mentioned you to my missis, and she was quite pleased. You see, she knows I've known you for over twenty years, and she wants to make sure of only 'aving honest people in the 'ouse. She has got a reason for it."

He closed one eye and nodded with great significance at his friend.

"Oh!" said Mr. Chase, waiting.

"She's a rich woman," said Mr. Teak, pulling the other's ear down to his mouth. "She—"

"When you've done tickling me with your whiskers," said Mr. Chase, withdrawing his head and rubbing his ear vigorously, "I shall be glad"

Mr. Teak apologised. "A rich woman," he repeated. "She's been stinting me for twenty-nine years and saving the money—my money!—Money that I 'ave earned with the sweat of my brow. She 'as got over three 'undred pounds!"

"'*Ow* much?" demanded Mr. Chase.

"Three 'undred pounds and more," repeated the other; "and if she had 'ad the sense to put it in a bank it would ha' been over four 'undred by this time. Instead o' that she keeps it hid in the 'ouse."

"Where?" inquired the greatly interested Mr. Chase.

Mr. Teak shook his head. "That's just what I want to find out," he answered. "She don't know I know it; and she mustn't know, either. That's important."

"How did you find out about it, then?" inquired his friend.

"My wife's sister's husband, Bert Adams, told me. His wife told 'im in strict confidence; and I might 'ave gone to my grave without knowing about it, only she smacked his face for 'im the other night."

"If it's in the house you ought to be able to find it easy enough," said Mr. Chase.

"Yes, it's all very well to talk," retorted Mr. Teak. "My missis never leaves the 'ouse unless I'm with her, except when I'm at work; and if she thought I knew of it she'd take and put it in some bank or somewhere unbeknown to me, and I should be farther off it than ever."

"Haven't you got no idea?" said Mr. Chase.

"Not the leastest bit," said the other. "I never thought for a moment she was saving money. She's always asking me for more, for one thing; but, then, women always do. And look 'ow bad it is for her—saving money like that on the sly. She might grow into a miser, pore thing. For 'er own sake I ought to get hold of it, if it's only to save her from 'erself."

Mr. Chase's face reflected the gravity of his own.

"You're the only man I can trust," continued Mr. Teak, "and I thought if you came as lodger you might be able to find out where it is hid, and get hold of it for me."

"Me steal it, d'ye mean?" demanded the gaping Mr. Chase. "And suppose she got me locked up for it? I should look pretty, shouldn't I?"

"No; you find out where it is hid," said the other; "that's all you need do. I'll find some way of getting hold of it then."

"But if you can't find it, how should I be able to?" inquired Mr. Chase.

"'Cos you'll 'ave opportunities," said the other. "I take her out some time when you're supposed to be out late; you come 'ome, let yourself in with your key, and spot the hiding-place. I get the cash, and give you ten—golden—sovereigns—all to your little self. It only occurred to me after Bert told me about it, that I ain't been in the house alone for years."

He ordered some more beer, and, drawing Mr. Chase to a bench, sat down to a long and steady argument. It shook his faith in human nature to find that his friend estimated the affair as a twenty-pound job, but he was in no position to bargain. They came out smoking twopenny cigars whose strength was remarkable for their age, and before they parted Mr. Chase was pledged to the hilt to do all that he could to save Mrs. Teak from the vice of avarice.

It was a more difficult undertaking than he had supposed. The house, small and compact, seemed to offer few opportunities for the concealment of large sums of money, and after a fortnight's residence he came to the conclusion that the treasure must have been hidden in the garden. The unalloyed pleasure, however, with which Mrs. Teak regarded the efforts of her husband to put under cultivation land that had lain fallow for twenty years convinced both men that they were on a wrong scent. Mr. Teak, who did the digging, was the first to realise it, but his friend, pointing out the suspicions that might be engendered by a sudden cessation of labour, induced him to persevere.

"And try and look as if you liked it," he said severely. "Why, from the window even the back view of you looks disagreeable."

"I'm fair sick of it," declared Mr. Teak. "Anybody might ha' known she wouldn't have buried it in the garden. She must 'ave been saving for pretty near thirty years, week by week, and she couldn't keep coming out here to hide it. 'Tain't likely."

Mr Chase pondered. "Let her know, casual like, that I shan't be 'ome till late on Saturday," he said slowly. "Then you come 'ome in the afternoon and take her out. As soon as you're gone I'll pop in and have a thorough good hunt round. Is she fond of animals?"

"I b'lieve so," said the other, staring. "Why?"

"Take 'er to the Zoo," said Mr. Chase impressively. "Take two-penn'orth o' nuts with you for the monkeys, and some stale buns for—for—for animals as likes 'em. Give 'er a ride on the elephant and a ride on the camel."

"Anything else?" inquired Mr. Teak disagreeably. "Anymore ways you can think of for me to spend my money?"

"You do as I tell you," said his friend. "I've got an idea now where it is. If I'm able to show you where to put your finger on three 'undred pounds when you come 'ome it'll be the cheapest outing you have ever 'ad. Won't it?"

Mr. Teak made no reply, but, after spending the evening in deliberation, issued the invitation at the supper-table. His wife's eyes sparkled at first; then the light slowly faded from them and her face fell.

"I *can't* go," she said, at last. "I've got nothing to go in."

"Rubbish!" said her husband, starting uneasily.

"It's a fact," said Mrs. Teak. "I should like to go, too—it's years since I was at the Zoo. I might make my jacket do; it's my hat I'm thinking about."

Mr. Chase, meeting Mr. Teak's eye, winked an obvious suggestion.

"So, thanking you all the same," continued Mrs. Teak, with amiable cheerfulness, "I'll stay at home."

"'Ow—'ow much are they?" growled her husband, scowling at Mr. Chase.

"All prices," replied his wife.

"Yes, I know," said Mr. Teak, in a grating voice. "You go in to buy a hat at one and elevenpence; you get talked over and flattered by a man like a barber's block, and you come out with a four-and-sixpenny one. The only real difference in hats is the price, but women can never see it."

Mrs. Teak smiled faintly, and again expressed her willingness to stay at home. They could spend the afternoon working in the garden, she said. Her husband, with another indignant glance at the right eye of Mr. Chase, which was still enacting the part of a camera-shutter, said that she could have a hat, but asked her to remember when buying it that nothing suited her so well as a plain one.

The remainder of the week passed away slowly; and Mr. Teak, despite his utmost efforts, was unable to glean any information from Mr. Chase as to that gentleman's ideas concerning the hiding-place. At every suggestion Mr. Chase's smile only got broader and more indulgent.

"You leave it to me," he said. "You leave it to me, and when you come home from a happy outing I 'ope to be able to cross your little hand with three 'undred golden quids."

"But why not tell me?" urged Mr. Teak.

"'Cos I want to surprise you," was the reply. "But mind, whatever you do, don't let your wife run away with the idea that

I've been mixed up in it at all. Now, if you worry me anymore I shall ask you to make it thirty pounds for me instead of twenty."

The two friends parted at the corner of the road on Saturday afternoon, and Mr. Teak, conscious of his friend's impatience, sought to hurry his wife by occasionally calling the wrong time up the stairs. She came down at last, smiling, in a plain hat with three roses, two bows, and a feather.

"I've had the feather for years," she remarked. "This is the fourth hat it has been on—but, then, I've taken care of it."

Mr. Teak grunted, and, opening the door, ushered her into the street. A sense of adventure and the hope of a profitable afternoon made his spirits rise. He paid a compliment to the hat, and then, to the surprise of both, followed it up with another—a very little one—to his wife.

They took a tram at the end of the street, and for the sake of the air mounted to the top. Mrs. Teak leaned back in her seat with placid enjoyment, and for the first ten minutes amused herself with the life in the streets. Then she turned suddenly to her husband and declared that she had felt a spot of rain.

"'Magination," he said shortly.

Something cold touched him lightly on the eyelid, a tiny pattering sounded from the seats, and then—swish, down came the rain. With an angry exclamation he sprang up and followed his wife below.

"Just our luck," she said mournfully. "Best thing we can do is to stay in the car and go back with it."

"Nonsense!" said her husband, in a startled voice; "it'll be over in a minute."

Events proved the contrary. By the time the car reached the terminus it was coming down heavily. Mrs. Teak settled herself squarely in her seat, and patches of blue sky, visible only to the eye of faith and her husband, failed to move her. Even his reckless reference to a cab failed.

"It's no good," she said tartly. "We can't go about the grounds in a cab, and I'm not going to slop about in the wet to please anybody. We must go another time. It's hard luck, but there's worse things in life."

Mr. Teak, wondering as to the operations of Mr. Chase, agreed dumbly. He stopped the car at the corner of their road, and, holding his head down against the rain, sprinted towards home. Mrs. Teak, anxious for her hat, passed him.

"What on earth's the matter?" she inquired, fumbling in her pocket for the key as her husband executed a clumsy and noisy breakdown on the front step.

"Chill," replied Mr. Teak. "I've got wet."

He resumed his lumberings and, the door being opened, gave vent to his relief at being home again in the dry, in a voice that made the windows rattle. Then with anxious eyes he watched his wife pass upstairs.

"Wonder what excuse old Alf 'll make for being in?" he thought.

He stood with one foot on the bottom stair listening acutely. He heard a door open above, and then a wild, ear-splitting shriek ran through the house. Instinctively he dashed upstairs and, following his wife into their bedroom, stood by her side gaping stupidly at a pair of legs standing on the hearthstone. As he watched they came backwards into the room, the upper part of a body materialised from the chimney, and turning round revealed the soot-stained face of Mr. Alfred Chase. Another wild shriek from Mrs. Teak greeted its appearance.

"Hul-lo!" exclaimed Mr. Teak, groping for the right thing to say. "Hul-lo! What—what are you doing, Alf?"

Mr. Chase blew the soot from his lips. "I—I—I come 'ome unexpected," he stammered.

"But—what are—you *doing*?" panted Mrs. Teak, in a rising voice.

"I—I was passing your door," said Mr. Chase, "passing your door—to go to my room to—to 'ave a bit of a rinse, when—"

"Yes?" said Mrs. Teak.

Mr. Chase gave Mr. Teak a glance the pathos of which even the soot could not conceal. "When I—I heard a pore little bird struggling in your chimbley," he continued, with a sigh of relief. "Being fond of animals, I took the liberty of comin' into your room and saving its life."

Mr. Teak drew a breath, which he endeavoured in vain to render noiseless.

"It got its pore little foot caught in the brick-work," continued the veracious Mr. Chase tenderly. "I released it, and it flowed—I mean flew—up the chimbley."

With the shamefaced air of a man detected in the performance of a noble action, he passed out of the room. Husband and wife eyed each other.

"That's Alf—that's Alf all over," said Mr. Teak, with enthusiasm. "He's been like it from a child. He's the sort of man that 'ud dive off Waterloo Bridge to save the life of a drownding sparrow."

"He's made an awful mess," said his wife, frowning; "it'll take me the rest of the day to clean up. There's soot everywhere. The rug is quite spoilt."

She took off her hat and jacket and prepared for the fray. Down below Messrs. Teak and Chase, comparing notes, sought, with much warmth, to put the blame on the right shoulders.

"Well, it ain't there," said Mr. Chase finally. "I've made sure of that. That's something towards it. I shan't 'ave to look there again, thank goodness."

Mr. Teak sniffed. "Got anymore ideas?" he queried.

"I have," said the other sternly. "There's plenty of places to search yet. I've only just begun. Get her out as much as you can and I'll 'ave my hands on it afore you can say—"

"Soot?" suggested Mr. Teak sourly.

"Anymore of your nasty snacks and I chuck it up altogether," said Mr. Chase heatedly. "If I wasn't hard up I'd drop it now."

He went up to his room in dudgeon, and for the next few days Mr. Teak saw but little of him. To lure Mrs. Teak out was almost as difficult as to persuade a snail to leave its shell, but he succeeded on two or three occasions, and each time she added something to her wardrobe.

The assistant fortune-hunter had been in residence just a month when Mr. Teak, returning home one afternoon, stood in the small passage listening to a suppressed wailing noise proceeding from upstairs. It was so creepy that halfway up he hesitated, and, in a stern but trembling voice, demanded to know what his wife meant by it. A louder wail than before was the only reply, and, summoning up his courage, he pushed open the door of the bedroom and peeped in. His gaze fell on Mrs. Teak, who was sitting on the hearth-rug, rocking to and fro in front of a dismantled fireplace.

"What—what's the matter?" he said hastily.

Mrs. Teak raised her voice to a pitch that set his teeth on edge. "My money I" she wailed. "It's all gone! All gone!"

"*Money*?" repeated Mr. Teak, hardly able to contain himself. "What money?"

"All—all my savings!" moaned his wife.

"Savings!" said the delighted Mr. Teak. "What savings?"

"Money I have been putting by for our old age," said his wife. "Three-hundred and twenty-two pounds. All gone!"

In a fit of sudden generosity Mr. Teak decided then and there that Mr. Chase should have the odd twenty-two pounds.

"You're dreaming!" he said sternly.

"I wish I was," said his wife, wiping her eyes. "Three hundred and twenty-two pounds, in empty mustard-tins. Every ha'penny's gone!

Mr. Teak's eye fell on the stove. He stepped forward and examined it. The back was out, and Mrs. Teak, calling his attention to a tunnel at the side, implored him to put his arm in and satisfy himself that it was empty.

"But where could you get all that money from?" he demanded, after a prolonged groping.

"Sa—sa—saved it," sobbed his wife, "for our old age."

"Our old age?" repeated Mr. Teak, in lofty tones. "And suppose I had died first? Or suppose you had died sudden? This is what comes of deceitfulness and keeping things from your husband. Now somebody has stole it."

Mrs. Teak bent her head and sobbed again. "I—I had just been out for—for an hour," she gasped. "When I came back I fou—fou—found the wash-house window smashed, and—"

Sobs choked her utterance. Mr. Teak, lost in admiration of Mr. Chase's cleverness, stood regarding her in silence.

"What—what about the police?" said his wife at last.

"Police! repeated Mr. Teak, with extraordinary vehemence. "Police! Certainly not. D'ye think I'm going to let it be known all round that I'm the husband of a miser? I'd sooner lose ten times the money."

He stalked solemnly out of the room and downstairs, and, safe in the parlour, gave vent to his feelings in a wild but silent hornpipe. He cannoned against the table at last, and, subsiding into an easy chair, crammed his handkerchief to his mouth and gave way to suppressed mirth.

In his excitement he forgot all about tea, and the bereaved Mrs. Teak made no attempt to come downstairs to prepare it. With his eye on the clock he waited with what patience he might for the arrival of Mr. Chase. The usual hour for his return came and went. Another hour passed; and another. A horrible idea that Mr. Chase had been robbed gave way to one more horrible still. He paced the room in dismay, until at nine o'clock his wife came down, and in a languid fashion began to set the supper-table.

"Alf's very late," said Mr. Teak thickly.

"Is he?" said his wife dully.

"Very late," said Mr. Teak. "I can't think—Ah, there he is!"

He took a deep breath and clenched his hands together. By the time Mr. Chase came into the room he was able to greet him with a stealthy wink. Mr. Chase, with a humorous twist of his mouth, winked back.

"We've 'ad a upset," said Mr. Teak, in warning tones.

"Eh?" said the other, as Mrs. Teak threw her apron over her head and sank into a chair. "What about?"

In bated accents, interrupted at times by broken murmurs from his wife, Mr. Teak informed him of the robbery. Mr. Chase, leaning against the doorpost, listened with open mouth and distended eyeballs. Occasional interjections of pity and surprise attested his interest. The tale finished, the gentlemen exchanged a significant wink and sighed in unison.

"And now," said Mr. Teak an hour later, after his wife had retired, "where is it?"

"Ah, that's the question," said Mr. Chase roguishly. "I wonder where it can be?"

"I—I hope it's in a safe place," said Mr. Teak anxiously. "Where 'ave you put it?"

"*Me?*" said Mr. Chase. "Who are you getting at? I ain't put it anywhere. You know that."

"Don't play the giddy goat," said the other testily. "Where've you hid it? Is it safe?"

Mr. Chase leaned back in his chair, and, shaking his head at him, smiled approvingly. "You're a little wonder, that's what you are, Gussie," he remarked. "No wonder your pore wife is took in so easy."

Mr. Teak sprang up in a fury. "Don't play the fool," he said hoarsely. "Where's the money? I want it. Now, where've you put it?"

"Go on," said Mr. Chase, with a chuckle. "Go on. Don't mind me. You ought to be on the stage, Gussie, that's where you ought to be."

"I'm not joking," said Mr. Teak, in a trembling voice, "and I don't want you to joke with me. If you think you are going off with my money, you're mistook. If you don't tell me in two minutes where it is, I shall give you in charge for theft."

"Oh!" said Mr. Chase. He took a deep breath. "Oh, really!" he said. "I wouldn't 'ave thought it of you, Gussie. I wouldn't 'ave thought you'd have played it so low down. I'm surprised at you."

"You thought wrong, then," said the other.

"Trying to do me out o' my twenty pounds, that's what you are," said Mr. Chase, knitting his brows. "But it won't do, my boy. I wasn't born yesterday. Hand it over, afore I lose my temper. Twenty pounds I want of you, and I don't leave this room till I get it."

Speechless with fury, Mr. Teak struck at him. The next moment the supper-table was overturned with a crash, and Mr. Chase, with his friend in his powerful grasp, was doing his best, as he expressed it, to shake the life out of him. A faint scream sounded from above, steps pattered on the stairs, and Mrs. Teak, with a red shawl round her shoulders, burst hurriedly into the room. Mr. Chase released Mr. Teak, opened his mouth to speak, and then, thinking better of it, dashed into the passage, took his hat from the peg, and, slamming the front door with extraordinary violence, departed.

* * *

He sent round for his clothes next day, but he did not see Mr. Teak until a month afterwards. His fists clenched and his mouth hardened, but Mr. Teak, with a pathetic smile, held out his hand, and Mr. Chase, after a moment's hesitation, took it. Mr. Teak, still holding his friend's hand, piloted him to a neighbouring hostelry.

"It was my mistake, Alf," he said, shaking his head, "but it wasn't my fault. It's a mistake anybody might ha' made."

"Have you found out who took it?" inquired Mr. Chase, regarding him suspiciously.

Mr. Teak gulped and nodded. "I met Bert Adams yesterday," he said slowly. "It took three pints afore he told me, but I got it out of 'im at last. My missis took it herself."

Mr. Chase put his mug down with a bang. "*What?*" he gasped.

"The day after she found you with your head up the chimbley," added Mr. Teak mournfully. "She's shoved it away in some bank now, and I shall never see a ha'penny of it. If you was a married man, Alf, you'd understand it better. You wouldn't be surprised at anything."

49

WATCH-DOGS

"It's a'most the only enj'yment I've got left," said the oldest inhabitant, taking a long, slow draught of beer, "that and a pipe o' baccy. Neither of 'em wants chewing, and that's a great thing when you ain't got anything worth speaking about left to chew with."

He put his mug on the table and, ignoring the stillness of the summer air, sheltered the flame of a match between his cupped hands and conveyed it with infinite care to the bowl of his pipe. A dull but crafty old eye squinting down the stem assured itself that the tobacco was well alight before the match was thrown away.

"As I was a-saying, kindness to animals is all very well," he said to the wayfarer who sat opposite him in the shade of the "Cauliflower" elms; "but kindness to your feller-creeturs is more. The pint wot you give me is gone, but I'm just as thankful to you as if it wasn't."

He half closed his eyes and, gazing on to the fields beyond, fell into a reverie so deep that he failed to observe the landlord come for his mug and return with it filled. A little start attested his surprise, and, to his great annoyance, upset a couple of tablespoonfuls of the precious liquid.

"Some people waste all their kindness on dumb animals," he remarked, after the landlord had withdrawn from his offended vision, "but I was never a believer in it. I mind some time ago when a gen'leman from Lunnon wot 'ad more money than sense offered a prize for kindness to animals. I was the only one that didn't try for to win it.

"Mr. Bunnett 'is name was, and 'e come down and took Farmer Hall's 'ouse for the summer. Over sixty 'e was, and old enough to know better. He used to put saucers of milk all round the 'ouse for cats to drink, and, by the time pore Farmer Hall got back, every cat for three miles round 'ad got in the habit of coming round to the backdoor and asking for milk as if it was their right. Farmer Hall poisoned a saucer o' milk at last, and then 'ad to pay five shillings for a thin black cat with a mangy tail and one eye that Bob Pretty said belonged to 'is children. Farmer Hall said he'd go to jail afore he'd pay, at fust, but arter five men 'ad spoke the truth and said they 'ad seen Bob's youngsters tying a empty mustard-tin to its tail on'y the day afore, he gave way.

"That was Bob Pretty all over, that was; the biggest raskel Claybury 'as ever had; and it wasn't the fust bit o' money 'e made out o' Mr. Bunnett coming to the place.

"It all come through Mr. Bunnett's love for animals. I never see a man so fond of animals as 'e was, and if he had 'ad 'is way Claybury would 'ave been overrun by 'em by this time. The day arter 'e got to the farm he couldn't eat 'is breakfuss because of a pig that was being killed in the yard, and it was no good pointing out to 'im that the pig was on'y making a fuss about it because it was its nature so to do. He lived on wegetables and such like, and the way 'e carried on one day over 'arf a biled caterpillar 'e found in his cabbage, wouldn't be believed. He wouldn't eat another mossel, but sat hunting 'igh and low for the other 'arf.

"He 'adn't been in Claybury more than a week afore he said 'ow surprised 'e was to see 'ow pore dumb animals was treated. He made a little speech about it one evening up at the schoolroom, and, arter he 'ad finished, he up and offered to give a prize of a gold watch that used to belong to 'is dear sister wot loved animals, to the one wot was the kindest to 'em afore he left the place.

"If he'd ha' known Claybury better 'e wouldn't ha' done it. The very next morning Bill Chambers took 'is baby's milk for the cat, and smacked 'is wife's 'ead for talking arter he'd told 'er to stop. Henery Walker got into trouble for leaning over Charlie Stubbs's fence and feeding his chickens for 'im, and Sam Jones's wife had to run off 'ome to 'er mother 'arf-dressed because she had 'appened to overlay a sick rabbit wot Sam 'ad taken to bed with 'im to keep warm.

"People used to stop animals in the road and try to do 'em a kindness—especially when Mr. Bunnett was passing—and Peter Gubbins walked past 'is house one day with ole Mrs. Broad's cat in 'is arms. A bad-tempered old cat it was, and, wot with Peter kissing the top of its 'ead and calling of it Tiddleums, it nearly went out of its mind.

"The fust time Mr. Bunnett see Bob Pretty was about a week arter he'd offered that gold watch. Bob was stooping down very careful over something in the hedge, and Mr. Bunnett, going up quiet-like behind 'im, see 'im messing about with a pore old toad he 'ad found, with a smashed leg.

"'Wot's the matter with it?' ses Mr. Bunnett.

"Bob didn't seem to hear 'im. He was a-kneeling on the ground with 'is 'ead on one side looking at the toad; and by and by he pulled out 'is pocket-'an'kercher and put the toad in it, as if it was made of eggshells, and walked away.

"'Wot's the matter with it?' ses Mr. Bunnett, a'most trotting to keep up with 'im.

"'Got its leg 'urt in some way, pore thing,' ses Bob. 'I want to get it 'ome as soon as I can and wash it and put it on a piece o' damp moss. But I'm afraid it's not long for this world.'

"Mr. Bunnett said it did 'im credit, and walked home alongside of 'im talking. He was surprised to find that Bob hadn't 'eard anything of the gold watch 'e was offering, but Bob said he was a busy, 'ard-working man and didn't 'ave no time to go to hear speeches or listen to tittle-tattle.

"'When I've done my day's work,' he ses, 'I can always find a job in the garden, and arter that I go in and 'elp my missis put the children to bed. She ain't strong, pore thing, and it's better than wasting time and money up at the "Cauliflower."'

"He 'ad a lot o' talk with Mr. Bunnett for the next day or two, and when 'e went round with the toad on the third day as lively and well as possible the old gen'leman said it was a miracle. And so it would ha' been if it had been the same toad.

"He took a great fancy to Bob Pretty, and somehow or other they was always dropping acrost each other. He met Bob with 'is dog one day—a large, ugly brute, but a'most as clever as wot Bob was 'imself. It stood there with its tongue 'anging out and looking at Bob uneasy-like out of the corner of its eye as Bob stood a-patting of it and calling it pet names.

"'Wunnerful affectionate old dog, ain't you, Joseph?' ses Bob.

"'He's got a kind eye,' ses Mr. Bunnett.

"'He's like another child to me, ain't you, my pretty?' ses Bob, smiling at 'im and feeling in 'is pocket. 'Here you are, old chap.'

"He threw down a biskit so sudden that Joseph, thinking it was a stone, went off like a streak o' lightning with 'is tail between 'is legs and yelping his 'ardest. Most men would ha' looked a bit foolish, but Bob Pretty didn't turn a hair.

"'Ain't it wunnerful the sense they've got,' he ses to Mr. Bunnett, wot was still staring arter the dog.

"'Sense?' ses the old gen'leman.

"'Yes," ses Bob, smiling. 'His food ain't been agreeing with 'im lately and he's starving hisself for a bit to get round agin, and 'e knew that 'e couldn't trust hisself alongside o' this biskit. Wot a pity men ain't like that with beer. I wish as 'ow Bill Chambers and Henery Walker and a few more 'ad been 'ere just now.'

"Mr. Bunnett agreed with 'im, and said wot a pity it was everybody 'adn't got Bob Pretty's common-sense and good feeling.

"'It ain't that,' ses Bob, shaking his 'ead at him; 'it ain't to my credit. I dessay if Sam Jones and Peter Gubbins, and Charlie Stubbs and Dicky Weed 'ad been brought up the same as I was they'd 'ave been a lot better than wot I am.'

"He bid Mr. Bunnett goodbye becos 'e said he'd got to get back to 'is work, and Mr. Bunnett had 'ardly got 'ome afore Henery Walker turned up full of anxiousness to ask his advice about five little baby kittens wot 'is old cat had found in the wash-place the night afore.

"'Drownd them little innercent things, same as most would do, I can't,' he ses, shaking his 'ead; 'but wot to do with 'em I don't know.'

"Couldn't you find 'omes for 'em?' ses Mr. Bunnett.

"Henery Walker shook Jais 'ead agin. "Tain't no use thinking o' that,' he ses. 'There's more cats than 'omes about 'ere. Why, Bill Chambers drownded six on'y last week right afore the eyes of my pore little boy. Upset 'im dreadful it did.'

"Mr. Bunnett walked up and down the room thinking. 'We must try and find 'omes for 'em when they are old enough,' he says at last; 'I'll go round myself and see wot *I* can do for you.'

"Henery Walker thanked 'im and went off 'ome doing a bit o' thinking; and well he 'ad reason to. Everybody wanted one o' them kittens. Peter Gubbins offered for to take two, and Mr. Bunnett told Henery Walker next day that 'e could ha' found 'omes for 'em ten times over.

"'You've no idea wot fine, kind-'arted people they are in this village when their 'arts are touched,' he ses, smiling at Henery. 'You ought to 'ave seen Mr. Jones's smile when I asked 'im to take one. It did me good to see it. And I spoke to Mr. Chambers about drowning 'is kittens, and he told me 'e hadn't slept a wink ever since. And he offered to take your old cat to make up for it, if you was tired of keeping it.'

"It was very 'ard on Henery Walker, I must say that. Other people was getting the credit of bringing up 'is kittens, and more than that, they used to ask Mr. Bunnett into their places to see 'ow the little dears was a-getting on.

"Kindness to animals caused more unpleasantness in Claybury than anything 'ad ever done afore. There was hardly a man as 'ud speak civil to each other, and the wimmen was a'most as bad. Cats and dogs and such-like began to act as if the place belonged to 'em, and seven people stopped Mr. Bunnett one day to tell 'im that Joe Parsons 'ad been putting down rat-poison and killed five little baby rats and their mother.

"It was some time afore anybody knew that Bob Pretty 'ad got 'is eye on that gold watch, and when they did they could 'ardly believe it. They give Bob credit for too much sense to waste time over wot they knew 'e couldn't get, but arter they 'ad heard one or two things they got alarmed, and pretty near the whole village went up to see Mr. Bunnett and tell 'im about Bob's true character. Mr. Bunnett couldn't believe 'em at fust, but arter they 'ad told 'im of Bob's poaching and the artful ways and tricks he 'ad of getting money as didn't belong to 'im, 'e began to think different. He spoke to parson about 'im, and arter that 'e said he never wanted for to see Bob Pretty's face again.

"There was a fine to-do about it up at this 'ere 'Cauliflower' public-'ouse that night, and the quietest man o' the whole lot was Bob Pretty. He sat still all the time drinking 'is beer and smiling at 'em and giving 'em good advice 'ow to get that gold watch.

"'It's no good to me,' he ses, shaking his 'ead. 'I'm a pore labourin' man, and I know my place.'

"''Ow you could ever 'ave thought you 'ad a chance, Bob, *I* don't know,' ses Henery Walker.

"''Ow's the toad, Bob?' ses Bill Chambers; and then they all laughed.

"'Laugh away, mates,' ses Bob; 'I know you don't mean it. The on'y thing I'm sorry for is you can't all 'ave the gold watch, and I'm sure you've worked 'ard enough for it; keeping Henery Walker's kittens for 'im and hanging round Mr. Bunnett's.'

"'We've all got a better chance than wot you 'ave, Bob,' ses little Dicky Weed the tailor.

"'Ah, that's your iggernerance, Dicky,' ses Bob. 'Come to think it over quiet like, I'm afraid I shall win it arter all. Cos why? Cos I deserves it.'

"They all laughed agin, and Bill Chambers laughed so 'arty that 'e joggled Peter Gubbins's arm and upset 'is beer.

"'Laugh away,' ses Bob, pretending to get savage. 'Them that laughs best laughs last, mind. I'll 'ave that watch now, just to spite you all.'

"''Ow are you going to get it, Bob?' ses Sam Jones, jeering.

"'Never you mind, mate,' ses Bob, stamping 'is foot; 'I'm going to win it fair. I'm going to 'ave it for kindness to pore dumb animals.'

"''Ear! 'Ear!' ses Dicky Weed, winking at the others. 'Will you 'ave a bet on it, Bob?'

"'No,' ses Bob Pretty : 'I don't want to win no man's money. I like to earn my money in the sweat o' my brow.'

"'But you won't win it, Bob,' ses' Dicky, grinning. 'Look 'ere! I'll lay you a level bob you don't get it.'

"Bob shook his 'ead, and started talking to Bill Chambers about something else.

"'I'll bet you two bob to one, Bob,' ses Dicky. 'Well, three to one, then.'

"Bob sat up and looked at 'im for a long time, considering, and at last he ses, 'All right,' he ses, 'if Smith the landlord will mind the money I win.'

"He 'anded over his shillin', but very slow-like, and Dicky Weed 'anded over 'is money. Arter that Bob sat looking disagreeable like, especially when Dicky said wot 'e was goin' to do with the money, and by an' by Sam Jones dared 'im to 'ave the same bet with 'im in sixpences.

"Bob Pretty 'ad a pint more beer to think it over, and arter Bill Chambers 'ad stood 'im another, he said 'e would. He seemed a bit dazed like, and by the time he went home he 'ad made bets with thirteen of 'em. Being Saturday night they 'ad all got money on 'em, and, as for Bob, he always 'ad some. Smith took care of the money and wrote it all up on a slate.

"'Why don't you 'ave a bit on, Mr. Smith?' says Dicky.

"'Oh, I dunno,' ses Smith, wiping down the bar with a wet cloth.

"'It's the chance of a lifetime,' ses Dicky.

"'Looks like it,' ses Smith, coughing.

"'But 'e can't win,' ses Sam Jones, looking a bit upset. 'Why, Mr. Bunnett said 'e ought to be locked up.'

"'He's been led away,' ses Bob Pretty, shaking 'is head. 'He's a kind-'arted old gen'leman when 'e's left alone, and he'll soon see wot a mistake 'e's made about me. I'll show 'im. But I wish it was something more useful than a gold watch.'

"You ain't got it yet,' ses Bill Chambers.

"'No, mate,' ses Bob.

"'And you stand to lose a sight o' money,' ses Sam Jones. 'If you like, Bob Pretty, you can 'ave your bet back with me.'

"'Never mind, Sam,' ses Bob; 'I won't take no advantage of you. If I lose you'll 'ave sixpence to buy a rabbit-hutch with. Goodnight, mates all."

"He rumpled Bill Chambers's'air for'im as he passed—a thing Bill never can abear—and gave Henery Walker, wot was drinking beer, a smack on the back wot nearly ruined 'im for life.

"Some of 'em went and told Mr. Bunnett some more things about Bob next day, but they night as well ha' saved their breath. The old gentleman said he knew all about 'im and he never wanted to 'ear his name mentioned agin. Arter which they began to 'ave a more cheerful way of looking at things; and Sam Jones said 'e was going to 'ave a hole bored through 'is sixpence and wear it round 'is neck to aggravate Bob Pretty with.

"For the next three or four weeks Bob Pretty seemed to keep very quiet, and we all began to think as 'ow he 'ad made a mistake for once. Everybody else was trying their 'ardest for the watch, and all Bob done was to make a laugh of 'em and to say he believed it was on'y made of brass arter all. Then one arternoon, just a few' days afore Mr. Bunnett's time was up at the farm, Bob took his dog out for a walk, and arter watching the farm for some time met the old gen'leman by accident up at Coe's plantation.

"'Good arternoon, sir,' he ses, smiling at 'im. 'Wot wunnerful fine weather we're a-having for the time o' year. I've just brought Joseph out for a bit of a walk. He ain't been wot I might call hisself for the last day or two, and I thought a. little fresh air might do 'im good.'

"Mr. Bunnett just looked at him, and then 'e passed 'im by without a word.

"'I wanted to ask your advice about 'im,' ses Bob, turning round and follering of 'im. 'He's a delikit animal, and sometimes I wonder whether I 'aven't been a-pampering of 'im too much.'

"'Go away,' ses Mr. Bunnett; 'I've heard all about you. Go away at once.'

"'Heard all about me?' ses Bob Pretty, looking puzzled. 'Well, you can't 'ave heard no 'arm, that's one comfort.'

"'I've been told your true character,' ses the old gen'leman, very firm. 'And I'm ashamed that I should have let myself be deceived by you. I hope you'll try and do better while there is still time.'

"'If anybody 'as got anything to say agin my character,' says Bob, 'I wish as they'd say it to my face. I'm a pore, hard-working man, and my character's all I've got.'

"'You're poorer than you thought you was, then,' says Mr. Bunnett. 'I wish you good arter-noon.'

"'Good arternoon, sir,' ses Bob, very humble. 'I'm afraid some of 'em 'ave been telling lies about me, and I didn't think I'd got a enemy in the world. Come on, Joseph. Come on, old pal. We ain't wanted here.'

"He shook 'is 'ead with sorrow, and made a little sucking noise between 'is teeth, and afore you could wink, his dog 'ad laid hold of the old gen'leman's leg and kep' quiet waiting orders.

"'*Help!*' screams Mr. Bunnett. 'Call 'im off! Call 'im off!"

"Bob said ar terwards that 'e was foolish enough to lose 'is presence o' mind for a moment, and instead o' doing anything he stood there gaping with 'is mouth open.

"'Call 'im off!' screams Mr. Bunnett, trying to push the dog away. 'Why don't you call him off?'

"'Don't move,' ses Bob Pretty in a frightened voice. 'Don't move, wotever you do.'

"'Call him off! Take 'im away!' ses Mr. Bunnett.

"'Why, Joseph! Joseph! Wotever are you a-thinking of?' ses Bob, shaking 'is 'ead at the dog. 'I'm surprised at you! Don't you know Mr. Bunnett wot is so fond of animals?'

"'If you don't call 'im off,' ses Mr. Bunnett, trembling all over, 'I'll have you locked up.'

"'I *am* a-calling 'im off,' ses Bob, looking very puzzled. 'Didn't you 'ear me? It's you making that noise that excites 'im, I think. P'r'aps if you keep quiet he'll leave go. Come off, Joseph, old boy, there's a good doggie. That ain't a bone.'

"'It's no good talking to 'im like that,' ses Mr. Bunnett, keeping quiet but trembling worse than ever. 'Make him let go.'

"'I don't want to 'urt his feelings,' ses Bob; 'they've got their feelings the same as wot we 'ave. Besides, p'r'aps it ain't 'is fault—p'r'aps he's gone mad.'

"'HELP!' ses the old gen'leman, in a voice that might ha' been heard a mile away. 'HELP!'

"'Why don't you keep quiet?' ses Bob. 'You're on'y frightening the pore animal and making things worse. Joseph, leave go and I'll see whether there's a biskit in my pocket. Why don't you leave go?'

"'Pull him off. Hit 'im,' ses Mr. Bunnett, shouting.

"'*Wot?*' ses Bob Pretty, with a start. 'Hit a pore, dumb animal wot don't know no better! Why, you'd never forgive me, sir, and I should lose the gold watch besides.'

"'No, you won't,' ses Mr. Bunnett, speaking very fast. 'You'll 'ave as much chance of it as ever you had. Hit 'im! Quick!'

"'It 'ud break my 'art,' ses Bob. 'He'd never forgive me; but if you'll take the respon-serbility, and then go straight 'ome and give me the gold watch now for kindness to animals, I will."

"He shook his 'ead with sorrow and made that sucking noise agin.

"'All right, you shall 'ave it,' ses Mr. Bunnett, shouting. 'You shall 'ave it.'

"'For kindness to animals?' ses Bob. 'Honour bright?'

"'Yes,' ses Mr. Bunnett.

"Bob Pretty lifted 'is foot and caught Joseph one behind that surprised 'im. Then he 'elped Mr. Bunnett look at 'is leg, and arter pointing out that the skin wasn't hardly broken, and saying that Joseph 'ad got the best mouth of any dog in Claybury, 'e walked 'ome with the old gen'leman and got the watch. He said Mr. Bunnett made a little speech when 'e gave it to 'im wot he couldn't remember, and wot he wouldn't repeat if 'e could.

"He came up to this 'ere 'Cauliflower' public-'ouse the same night for the money 'e had won, and Bill Chambers made another speech, but, as Smith the landlord put 'im outside for it, it didn't do Bob Pretty the good it ought to ha' done."

50

THE BEQUEST

Mr. Robert Clarkson sat by his fire, smoking thoughtfully. His lifelong neighbour and successful rival in love had passed away a few days before, and Mr. Clarkson, fresh from the obsequies, sat musing on the fragility of man and the inconvenience that sometimes attended his departure.

His meditations were disturbed by a low knocking on the front door, which opened on to the street. In response to his invitation it. opened slowly, and a small middle-aged man of doleful aspect entered softly and closed it behind him.

"Evening, Bob," he said, in stricken accents. "I thought I'd just step round to see how you was bearing up. Fancy pore old Phipps! Why, I'd a'most as soon it had been me. A'most."

Mr. Clarkson nodded.

"Here today and gone tomorrow," continued Mr. Smithson, taking a seat. "Well, well! So you'll have her at last—pore thing."

"That was his wish," said Mr. Clarkson, in a dull voice.

"And very generous of him too," said Mr. Smithson. "Everybody is saying so. Certainly he couldn't take her away with him. How long is it since you was both of you courting her?"

"Thirty years come June," replied the other.

"Shows what waiting does, and patience," commented Mr. Smithson. "If you'd been like some chaps and gone abroad, where would you have been now? Where would have been the reward of your faithful heart?"

Mr. Clarkson, whose pipe had gone out, took a coal from the fire and lit it again.

"I can't understand him dying at his age," he said darkly. "He ought to have lived to ninety if he'd been taken care of."

"Well, he's gone, pore chap," said his friend. "What a blessing it must ha' been to him in his I last moments to think that he had made provision for his wife."

"Provision!" exclaimed Mr. Clarkson. "Why, he's left her nothing but the furniture and fifty pounds insurance money—nothing in the world."

Mr. Smithson fidgeted. "I mean you," he said, staring.

"Oh!" said the other. "Oh, yes—yes, of course."

"And he doesn't want you to eat your heart out in waiting," said Mr. Smithson. "'Never mind about me,' he said to her; 'you go and make Bob happy.' Wonderful pretty girl she used to be, didn't she?"

Mr. Clarkson assented.

"And I've no doubt she looks the same to you as ever she did," pursued the sentimental Mr. Smithson. "That's the extraordinary part of it."

Mr. Clarkson turned and eyed him; removed the pipe from his mouth, and, after hesitating a moment, replaced it with a jerk.

"She says she'd rather be faithful to his memory," continued the persevering Mr. Smithson, "but his wishes are her law. She said so to my missis only yesterday."

"Still, she ought to be considered," said Mr. Clarkson, shaking his head. "I think that somebody ought to put it to her. She has got her feelings, poor thing, and, if she would rather *not* marry again, she oughtn't to be compelled to."

"Just what my missis did say to her," said the other; "but she didn't pay much attention. She said it was Henry's wish and she didn't care what happened to her now he's gone. Besides, if you come to think of it, what else *is* she to do? Don't you worry, Bob; you won't lose her again."

Mr. Clarkson, staring at the fire, mused darkly. For thirty years he had played the congenial part of the disappointed admirer but faithful friend. He had intended to play it for at least fifty or sixty. He wished that he had had the strength of mind to refuse the bequest when the late Mr. Phipps first mentioned it, or taken a firmer line over the congratulations of his friends. As it was, Little Molton quite understood that after thirty years' waiting the faithful heart was to be rewarded at last. Public opinion seemed to be that the late Mr. Phipps had behaved with extraordinary generosity.

"It's rather late in life for me to begin," said Mr. Clarkson at last.

"Better late than never," said the cheerful Mr. Smithson.

"And something seems to tell me that I ain't long for this world," continued Mr. Clarkson, eyeing him with some disfavour.

"Stuff and nonsense," said Mr. Smithson, "You'll lose all them ideas as soon as you're married. You'll have somebody to look after you and help you spend your money."

Mr. Clarkson emitted a dismal groan, and clapping his hand over his mouth strove to make it pass muster as a yawn. It was evident that the malicious Mr. Smithson was deriving considerable pleasure from his discomfiture—the pleasure natural to the father of seven over the troubles of a comfortable bachelor. Mr. Clarkson, anxious to share his troubles with somebody, came to a sudden and malicious determination to share them with Mr. Smithson.

"I don't want anybody to help me spend my money," he said slowly. "First and last I've saved a tidy bit. I've got this house, those three cottages in Turner's Lane, and pretty near six hundred pounds in the bank."

Mr. Smithson's eyes glistened.

"I had thought—it had occurred to me," said Mr. Clarkson, trying to keep as near the truth as possible, "to leave my property to a friend o' mine—a hard-working man with a large family. However, it's no use talking about that now. It's too late."

"Who—who was it?" inquired his friend, trying to keep his voice steady.

Mr. Clarkson shook his head. "It's no good talking about that now, George," he said, eyeing him with sly enjoyment. "I shall have to leave everything to my wife now. After all, perhaps it does more harm than good to leave money to people."

"Rubbish!" said Mr. Smithson sharply. "Who was it?"

"You, George," said Mr. Clarkson softly.

"Me?" said the other, with a gasp. "*Me?*" He jumped up from his chair, and, seizing the other's hand, shook it fervently.

"I oughtn't to have told you, George," said Mr. Clarkson, with great satisfaction. "It'll only make you miserable. It's just one o' the might ha' beens."

Mr. Smithson, with his back to the fire and his hands twisted behind him, stood with his eyes fixed in thought.

"It's rather cool of Phipps," he said, after a long silence; "rather cool, I think, to go out of the world and just leave his wife to you to look after. Some men wouldn't stand it. You're too easygoing, Bob; that's what's the matter with you."

Mr. Clarkson sighed.

"And get took advantage of," added his friend.

"It's all very well to talk," said Mr. Clarkson, "but what can I do? I ought to have spoke up at the time. It's too late now."

"If I was you," said his friend very earnestly, "and didn't want to marry her, I should tell her so. Say what you like, it ain't fair to her, you know. It ain't fair to the pore woman. She'd never forgive you if she found it out."

"Everybody's taking it for granted," said the other.

"Let everybody look after their own business," said Mr. Smithson tartly. "Now, look here, Bob; suppose I get you out of this business, how am I to be sure you'll leave your property to me?—Not that I want it. Suppose you altered your will?"

"If you get me out of it every penny I leave will go to you," said Mr. Clarkson fervently. "I haven't got any relations, and it don't matter in the slightest to me who has it after I'm gone."

"As true as you stand there?" demanded the other, eyeing him fixedly.

"As true as I stand here," said Mr. Clarkson, smiting his chest, and shook hands again.

Long after his visitor had gone he sat gazing in a brooding fashion at the fire. As a single man his wants were few, and he could live on his savings; as the husband of Mrs. Phipps he would be compelled to resume the work he thought he had dropped for good three years before. Moreover, Mrs Phipps possessed a strength of character that had many times caused him to congratulate himself upon her choice of a husband.

Slowly but surely his fetters were made secure. Two days later the widow departed to spend six weeks with a sister; but any joy that he might have felt over the circumstance was marred by the fact that he had to carry her bags down to the railway station and see her off. The key of her house was left with him, with strict injunctions to go in and water her geraniums every day, while two canaries and a bullfinch had to be removed to his own house in order that they might have constant attention and company.

"She's doing it on purpose," said Mr. Smithson fiercely; "she's binding you hand and foot."

Mr. Clarkson assented gloomily. "I'm trusting to you, George," he remarked.

"How'd it be to forget to water the geraniums and let the birds die because they missed her so much?" suggested Mr. Smithson, after prolonged thought.

Mr. Clarkson shivered.

"It would be a hint," said his friend.

Mr. Clarkson took some letters from the mantelpiece and held them up. "She writes about them every day," he said briefly, "and I have to answer them."

"She—she don't refer to your getting married, I suppose?" said his friend anxiously.

Mr. Clarkson said, "No. But her sister does," he added. "I've had two letters from her."

Mr. Smithson got up and paced restlessly up and down the room. "That's women all over," he said bitterly. "They never ask for things straight out; but they always get 'em in roundabout ways. She can't do it herself, so she gets her sister to do it."

Mr. Clarkson groaned. "And her sister is hinting that she can't leave the house where she spent so many happy years," he says, "and says what a pleasant surprise it would be for Mrs. Phipps if she was to come home and find it done up."

"That means you've got to live there when you're married," said his friend solemnly.

Mr. Clarkson glanced round his comfortable room and groaned again. "She asked me to get an estimate from Digson," he said dully. "She knows as well as I do her sister hasn't got any money. I wrote to say that it had better be left till she comes home, as I might not know what was wanted."

Mr. Smithson nodded approval.

"And Mrs. Phipps wrote herself and thanked me for being so considerate," continued his friend grimly, "and says that when she comes back we must go over the house together and see what wants doing."

Mr. Smithson got up and walked round the room again.

"You never promised to marry her?" he said, stopping suddenly.

"No," said the other. "It's all been arranged for me. I never said a word. I couldn't tell Phipps I wouldn't have her with them all standing round, and him thinking he was doing me the greatest favour in the world."

"Well, she can't name the day unless you ask her," said the other. "All you've got to do is to keep quiet and not commit yourself. Be as cool as you can, and, just before she comes home, you go off to London on business and stay there as long as possible."

Mr. Clarkson carried out his instructions to the letter, and Mrs. Phipps, returning home at the end of her visit, learned that he had left for London three days before, leaving the geraniums and birds to the care of Mr. Smithson. From the hands of that unjust steward she received two empty birdcages, together with a detailed account of the manner in which the occupants had effected their escape, and a bullfinch that seemed to be suffering from torpid liver. The condition of the geraniums was ascribed to worms in the pots, frost, and premature decay.

"They go like it sometimes," said Mr. Smithson, "and when they do nothing will save 'em.

Mrs. Phipps thanked him. "It's very kind of you to take so much trouble," she said quietly; "some people would have lost the cages too while they were about it."

"I did my best," said Mr. Smithson, in a surly voice.

"I know you did," said Mrs. Phipps thoughtfully, "and I am sure I am much obliged to you. If there is anything of yours I can look after at any time I shall be only too pleased. When did you say Mr. Clarkson was coming back?"

"He don't know," said Mr. Smithson promptly. "He might be away a month; and then, again, he might be away six. It all depends. You know what business is."

"It's very thoughtful of him," said Mrs. Phipps. "Very."

"Thoughtful!" repeated Mr. Smithson.

"He has gone away for a time out of consideration for me," said the widow. "As things are, it is a little bit awkward for us to meet much at present."

"I don't think he's gone away for that at all," said the other bluntly.

Mrs. Phipps shook her head. "Ah, you don't know him as well as I do," she said fondly. "He has gone away on my account, I feel sure."

Mr. Smithson screwed his lips together and remained silent.

"When he feels that it is right and proper for him to come back," pursued Mrs. Phipps, turning her eyes upwards, "he will come. He has left his comfortable home just for my sake, and I shall not forget it."

Mr. Smithson coughed—a short, dry cough, meant to convey incredulity.

"I shall not do anything to this house till he comes back," said Mrs. Phipps. "I expect he would like to have a voice in it. He always used to admire it and say how comfortable it was. Well, well, we never know what is before us."

Mr. Smithson repeated the substance of the interview to Mr. Clarkson by letter, and in the lengthy correspondence that followed kept him posted as to the movements of Mrs. Phipps. By dint of warnings and entreaties he kept the bridegroom-elect in London for three months. By that time Little Molton was beginning to talk.

"They're beginning to see how the land lays," said Mr. Smithson, on the evening of his friend's return, "and if you keep quiet and do as I tell you she'll begin to see it too. As I said before, she can't name the day till you ask her."

Mr. Clarkson agreed, and the following morning, when he called upon Mrs. Phipps at her request, his manner was so distant that she attributed it to ill-health following business worries and the atmosphere of London. In the front parlour Mr. Digson, a small builder and contractor, was busy whitewashing.

"I thought we might as well get on with that," said Mrs. Phipps; "there is only one way of doing whitewashing, and the room has got to be done. Tomorrow Mr. Digson will bring up some papers, and, if you'll come round, you can help me choose."

Mr. Clarkson hesitated. "Why not choose 'em yourself?" he said at last.

"Just what I told her," said Mr. Digson, stroking his black beard. "'What'll please you will be sure to please him,' I says; and if it don't it ought to."

Mr. Clarkson started. "Perhaps you could help her choose," he said sharply.

Mr. Digson came down from his perch. "Just what I said," he replied. "If Mrs. Phipps will let me advise her, I'll make this house so she won't know it before I've done with it."

"Mr. Digson has been very kind," said Mrs. Phipps reproachfully.

"Not at all, ma'am," said the builder softly. "Anything I can do to make you happy or comfortable will be a pleasure to me."

Mr. Clarkson started again, and an odd idea sent his blood dancing. Digson was a widower; Mrs. Phipps was a widow. Could anything be more suitable or desirable?

"Better let him choose," he said. "After all, he ought to be a good judge."

Mrs. Phipps, after a faint protest, gave way, and Mr. Digson, smiling broadly, mounted his perch again.

Mr. Clarkson's first idea was to consult Mr. Smithson; then he resolved to wait upon events. The idea was fantastic to begin with, but, if things did take such a satisfactory turn, he could not help reflecting that it would not be due to any efforts on the part of Mr. Smithson, and he would no longer be under any testamentary obligations to that enterprising gentleman.

By the end of a week he was jubilant. A child could have told Mr. Digson's intentions—I and Mrs. Phipps was anything but a child. Mr. Clarkson admitted cheerfully that Mr. Digson was a younger and better-looking man than himself—a more suitable match in every way. And, so far as he could judge, Mrs. Phipps seemed to think so. At any rate, she had ceased to make the faintest allusion to any tie between them. He left her one day painting a door, while the attentive Digson guided the brush, and walked homewards smiling.

"Morning!" said a voice behind him.

"Morning, Bignell," said Mr. Clarkson.

"When—when is it to be?" inquired his friend, walking beside him.

Mr. Clarkson frowned. "When is what to be?" he demanded disagreeably.

Mr. Bignell lowered his voice. "You'll lose her if you ain't careful," he said. "Mark my words. Can't you see Digson's little game?"

Mr. Clarkson shrugged his shoulders.

"He's after her money," said the other, with a cautious glance around.

"*Money?*" said the other, with an astonished laugh. "Why, she hasn't got any."

"Oh, all right," said Mr. Bignell. "You know best, of course. I was just giving you the tip, but if you know better—why, there's nothing more to be said. She'll be riding in her carriage and pair in six months, anyhow; the richest woman in Little Molton."

Mr. Clarkson stopped short and eyed him in perplexity.

"Digson got a bit sprung one night and told me," said Mr. Bignell. "She don't know it herself yet—uncle on her mother's side in America. She might know at any moment."

"But—but how did Digson know?" inquired the astonished Mr. Clarkson.

"He wouldn't tell me," was the reply. "But it's good enough for him. What do you *think* he's after? Her? And mind, don't let on to a soul that I told you."

He walked on, leaving Mr. Clarkson standing in a dazed condition in the centre of the footpath. Recovering himself by an effort, he walked slowly away, and, after prowling about for some time in an aimless fashion, made his way back to Mrs. Phipps's house.

He emerged an hour later an engaged man, with the date of the wedding fixed. With jaunty steps he walked round and put up the banns, and then, with the air of a man who has completed a successful stroke of business, walked homewards.

Little Molton is a small town, and news travels fast, but it did not travel faster than Mr. Smithson as soon as he had heard it. He burst into Mr. Clarkson's room like the proverbial hurricane, and, gasping for breath, leaned against the table and pointed at him an incriminating finger.

"You—you've been running," said Mr. Clarkson uneasily.

"What—what—what do you—mean by it?" gasped Mr. Smithson. "After all my trouble. After our—bargain."

"I altered my mind," said Mr. Clarkson, with dignity.

"*Pah!*" said the other.

"Just in time," said Mr. Clarkson, speaking rapidly. "Another day and I believe I should ha' been too late. It took me pretty near an hour to talk her over. Said I'd been neglecting her, and all that sort of thing; said that she was beginning to think I didn't want her. As hard a job as ever I had in my life."

"But you didn't want her," said the amazed Mr. Smithson. "You told me so."

"You misunderstood me," said Mr. Clarkson, coughing. "You jump at conclusions."

Mr. Smithson sat staring at him. "I heard," he said at last, with an effort—"I heard that Digson was paying her attentions."

Mr. Clarkson spoke without thought. "Ha, he was only after her money," he said severely. "Good heavens! *What's the matter?*"

Mr. Smithson, who had sprung to his feet, made no reply, but stood for some time incapable of speech.

"What—is—the—matter?" repeated Mr. Clarkson. "Ain't you well?"

Mr. Smithson swayed a little, and sank slowly back into his chair again.

"Room's too hot," said his astonished host.

Mr. Smithson, staring straight before him, nodded.

"As I was saying," resumed Mr. Clarkson, in the low tones of confidence, "Digson was after her money. Of course her money don't make any difference to me, although, perhaps, I may be able to do something for friends like you. It's from an uncle in America on her mother's—"

Mr. Smithson made a strange moaning noise, and, snatching his hat from the table, clapped it on his head and made for the door. Mr. Clarkson flung his arms around him and dragged him back by main force.

"What are you carrying on like that for?" he demanded. "What do you mean by it?"

"Fancy!" returned Mr. Smithson, with intense bitterness. "I thought Digson was the biggest fool in the place, and I find I've made a mistake. So have you. Good night."

He opened the door and dashed out. Mr. Clarkson, with a strange sinking at his heart, watched him up the road.

51

THE GUARDIAN ANGEL

The night-watchman shook his head. "*I* never met any of these phil—philantherpists, as you call 'em," he said decidedly. "If I 'ad they wouldn't 'ave got away from me in a hurry, I can tell you. I don't say I don't believe in 'em; I only say I never met any of 'em. If people do you a kindness it's generally because they warn to get something out of you; same as a man once—a perfick stranger—wot stood me eight 'arf-pints becos I reminded 'im of his dead brother, and then borrered five bob off of me.

"O' course, there must be some kind-'arted people in the world—all men who get married must 'ave a soft spot somewhere, if it's only in the 'ead—but they don't often give things away. Kind-'artedness is often only another name for artfulness, same as Sam Small's kindness to Ginger Dick and Peter Russet.

"It started with a row. They was just back from a v'y'ge and 'ad taken a nice room together in Wapping, and for the fust day or two, wot with 'aving plenty o' money to spend and nothing to do, they was like three brothers. Then, in a little, old-fashioned public-'ouse down Poplar way, one night they fell out over a little joke Ginger played on Sam.

"It was the fust drink that evening, and Sam 'ad just ordered a pot o' beer and three glasses, when Ginger winked at the landlord and offered to bet Sam a level 'arf-dollar that 'e wouldn't drink off that pot o' beer without taking breath. The landlord held the money, and old Sam, with a 'appy smile on 'is face, 'ad just taken up the mug, when he noticed the odd way in which they was all watching him. Twice he took the mug up and put it down agin without starting and asked 'em wot the little game was, but they on'y laughed. He took it up the third time and started, and he 'ad just got about 'arf-way through when Ginger turns to the landlord and ses—

"'Did you catch it in the mouse-trap,' he ses, 'or did it die of poison?'

"Pore Sam started as though he 'ad been shot, and, arter getting rid of the beer in 'is mouth, stood there 'olding the mug away from 'im and making such 'orrible faces that they was a'most frightened.

"'Wot's the matter with him? I've never seen 'im carry on like that over a drop of beer before,' ses Ginger, staring.

"'He usually likes it,' ses Peter Russet.

"'Not with a dead mouse in it,' ses Sam, trembling with passion.

"'Mouse?' ses Ginger, innercent - like, '*Mouse?* Why, I didn't say it was in your beer, Sam. Wotever put that into your 'ead?'

"'And made you lose your bet,' ses Peter.

"Then old Sam see 'ow he'd been done, and the way he carried on when the landlord gave Ginger the 'arf-dollar, and said it was won fair and honest, was a disgrace. He 'opped about that bar 'arf crazy, until at last the landlord and 'is brother, and a couple o' soldiers, and a helpless cripple wot wos selling matches, put 'im outside and told 'im to stop there.

"He stopped there till Ginger and Peter came out, and then, drawing 'imself up in a proud way, he told 'em their characters and wot he thought about 'em. And he said 'e never wanted to see wot they called their faces agin as long as he lived.

"'I've done with you,' he ses, 'both of you, forever.'

"'All right,' ses Ginger, moving off. 'Ta-ta for the present. Let's 'ope he'll come 'ome in a better temper, Peter.'

"''Ome?' ses Sam, with a nasty laugh, ''*ome?* D'ye think I'm coming back to breathe the same air as you, Ginger. D'ye think I want to be suffocated?'

"He held his 'ead up very 'igh, and, arter looking at them as if they was dirt, he turned round and walked off with his nose in the air to spend the evening by 'imself.

"His temper kept him up for a time, but arter a while he 'ad to own up to 'imself that it was very dull, and the later it got the more he thought of 'is nice warm bed. The more 'e thought of it the nicer and warmer it seemed, and, arter a struggle between his pride and a few 'arf-pints, he got 'is good temper back agin and went off 'ome smiling.

"The room was dark when 'e got there, and, arter standing listening a moment to Ginger and Peter snoring, he took off 'is coat and sat down on 'is bed to take 'is boots off. He only sat down for a flash, and then he bent down and hit his 'ead an awful smack against another 'ead wot 'ad just started up to see wot it was sitting on its legs.

"He thought it was Peter or Ginger in the wrong bed at fust, but afore he could make it out Ginger 'ad got out of 'is own bed and lit the candle. Then 'e saw it was a stranger in 'is bed, and without saying a word he laid 'old of him by the 'air and began dragging him out.

"'Here, stop that!' ses Ginger, catching hold of 'im. 'Lend a hand 'ere, Peter.'

"Peter lent a hand and screwed it into the back o' Sam's neck till he made 'im leave go, and then the stranger, a nasty-looking little chap with and a little dark moustache, told Sam wot he'd like to do to him.

"'Who are you?' ses Sam, 'and wot are you a-doing of in my bed?'

"'It's our lodger,' ses Ginger.

"'Your—*wot?*' ses Sam, 'ardly able to believe his ears.

"'Our lodger,' ses Peter Russet. 'We've let 'im the bed you said you didn't want for sixpence a night. Now you take yourself off.'

"Old Sam couldn't speak for a minute; there was no words that he knew bad enough, but at last he licks 'is lips and ses, 'I've paid for that bed up to Saturday, and I'm going to have it.'

"He rushed at the lodger, but Peter and Ginger got hold of 'im agin and put 'im down on the floor and sat on 'im till he promised to be'ave himself. They let 'im get up at last, and then, arter calling themselves names for their kind-'artedness, they said if he was very good he might sleep on the floor.

"Sam looked at 'em for a moment, and then, without a word, he took off 'is boots and put on 'is coat and went up in a corner to be out of the draught, but, wot with the cold and 'is temper, and the hardness of the floor, it was a long time afore 'e could get to sleep. He dropped off at last, and it seemed to 'im that he 'ad only just closed 'is eyes when it was daylight. He opened one eye and was just going to open the other when he saw something as made 'im screw 'em both up sharp and peep through 'is eyelashes. The lodger was standing at the foot of Ginger's bed, going through 'is pockets, and then, arter waiting a moment and 'aving a look round, he went through Peter Russet's. Sam lay still as a mouse while the lodger tiptoed out o' the room with 'is boots in his 'and, and then, springing up, follered him downstairs.

"He caught 'im up just as he 'ad undone the front door, and, catching hold of 'im by the back o' the neck, shook 'im till 'e was tired. Then he let go of 'im and, holding his fist under 'is nose, told 'im to hand over the money, and look sharp about it.

"'Ye—ye—yes, sir,' ses the lodger, who was 'arf choked.

"Sam held out his 'and, and the lodger, arter saying it was only a little bit o' fun on 'is part, and telling 'im wot a fancy he 'ad taken to 'im from the fust, put Ginger's watch and chain into his 'ands and eighteen pounds four shillings and sevenpence. Sam put it into his pocket, and, arter going through the lodger's pockets to make sure he 'adn't forgot anything, opened the door and flung 'im into the street. He stopped on the landing to put the money in a belt he was wearing under 'is clothes, and then 'e went back on tiptoe to 'is corner and went to sleep with one eye open and the 'appiest smile that had been on his face for years.

"He shut both eyes when he 'eard Ginger wake up, and he slept like a child through the 'orrible noise that Peter and Ginger see fit to make when they started to put their clothes on. He got tired of it afore they did, and, arter opening 'is eyes slowly and yawning, he asked Ginger wot he meant by it.

"You'll wake your lodger up if you ain't careful, making that noise,' he ses. 'Wot's the matter?'

"'Sam,' ses Ginger in a very different voice to wot he 'ad used the night before, 'Sam, old pal, he's taken all our money and bolted.'

"'Wot?' ses Sam, sitting up on the floor and blinking. 'Nonsense!'

"'Robbed me and Peter,' ses Ginger, in a trembling voice; 'taken every penny we've got, and my watch and chain.'

"'You're dreaming,' ses Sam.

"'I wish I was,' ses Ginger.

"'But surely, Ginger,' ses Sam, standing up, 'surely you didn't take a lodger without a character?'

"'He seemed such a nice chap,' ses Peter. 'We was only saying wot a much nicer chap he was than—than—'

"'Go on, Peter,' ses Sam, very perlite.

"'Than he might ha' been,' ses Ginger, very quick.

"'Well, I've 'ad a wonderful escape,' ses Sam. 'If it hadn't ha' been for sleeping in my clothes I suppose he'd ha' 'ad my money as well.'

"He felt in 'is pockets anxious-like, then he smiled, and stood there letting 'is money fall through 'is fingers into his pocket over and over agin.

"'Pore chap,' he ses; 'pore chap; p'r'aps he'd got a starving wife and family. Who knows? It ain't for us to judge 'im, Ginger.'

"He stood a little while longer chinking 'is money, and when he took off his coat to wash Ginger Dick poured the water out for 'im and Peter Russet picked up the soap, which 'ad fallen on the floor. Then they started pitying themselves, looking very 'ard at the back of old Sam while they did it.

"'I s'pose we've got to starve, Peter,' ses Ginger, in a sad voice.

"'Looks like it,' ses Peter, dressing hisselt very slowly.

"'There's nobody'll mourn for me, that's one comfort,' ses Ginger.

"'Or me,' ses Peter.

"'P'r'aps Sam'll miss us a bit,' ses Ginger, grinding 'is teeth as old Sam went on washing as if he was deaf. 'He's the only real pal we ever 'ad.'

"'Wot are you talking about?' ses Sam, turning round with the soap in his eyes, and feeling for the towel. 'Wo't d'ye want to starve for? Why don't you get a ship?'

"'I thought we was all going to sign on in the *Chesapeake* agin, Sam,' ses Ginger, very mild.

"'She won't be ready for sea for pretty near three weeks,' ses Sam. 'You know that.'

"'P'r'aps Sam would lend us a trifle to go on with, Ginger,' ses Peter Russet. 'Just enough to keep body and soul together, so as we can hold out and 'ave the pleasure of sailing with 'im agin.'

"'P'r'aps he wouldn't,' ses Sam, afore Ginger could open his mouth. 'I've just got about enough to last myself; I 'aven't got any to lend. Sailormen wot turns on their best friends and makes them sleep on the cold 'ard floor while their new pal is in his bed don't get money lent to 'em. My neck is so stiff it creaks every time I move it, and I've got the rheumatics in my legs something cruel.'

"He began to 'um a song, and putting on 'is cap went out to get some brekfuss. He went to a little eating-'ouse near by, where they was in the 'abit of going, and 'adjust started on a plate of eggs and bacon when Ginger Dick and Peter came into the place with a pocket-'ankercher of 'is wot they 'ad found in the fender.

"'We thought you might want it, Sam,' ses Peter.

"'So we brought it along,' ses Ginger. 'I'ope you're enjoying of your brekfuss, Sam.'

"Sam took the 'ankercher and thanked 'em very perlite, and arter standing there for a minute or two as if they wanted to say something they couldn't remember, they sheered off. When Sam left the place 'arf-an-hour arterwards they was still hanging about, and as Sam passed Ginger asked 'im if he was going for a walk.

"'Walk!' ses Sam. 'Cert'nly not. I'm going to bed; *I* didn't 'ave a good night's rest like you and your lodger.'

"He went back 'ome, and arter taking off 'is coat and boots got into bed and slept like a top till one o'clock, when he woke up to find Ginger shaking 'im by the shoulders.

"'Wot's the matter?' he ses. 'Wot are you up to?'

"'It's dinnertime,' ses Ginger. 'I thought p'r'aps you'd like to know, in case you missed it.'

"'You leave me alone,' ses Sam, cuddling into the clothes agin. 'I don't want no dinner. You go and look arter your own dinners.'

"He stayed in bed for another 'arf-hour, listening to Peter and Ginger telling each other in loud whispers 'ow hungry they was, and then he got up and put 'is things on and went to the door.

"'I'm going to get a bit o' dinner,' he ses. 'And mind, I've got my pocket-'ankercher.'

"He went out and 'ad a steak and onions and a pint o' beer, but, although he kept looking up sudden from 'is plate, he didn't see Peter or Ginger. It spoilt 'is dinner a bit, but arter he got outside 'e saw them standing at the corner, and, pretending not to see them, he went off for a walk down the Mile End Road.

"He walked as far as Bow with them follering 'im, and then he jumped on a bus and rode back as far as Whitechapel. There was no sign of 'em when he got off, and, feeling a bit lonesome, he stood about looking in shop windows until 'e see them coming along as hard as they could come.

"'Why, halloa!' he ses. 'Where did you spring from?'

"'We—we—we've been—for a bit of a walk,' ses Ginger Dick, puffing and blowing like a grampus.

"'To—keep down the 'unger,' ses Peter Russet.

"Old Sam looked at 'em very stern for a moment, then he beckoned 'em to foller 'im, and, stopping at a little public-'ouse, he went in and ordered a pint o' bitter.

"'And give them two pore fellers a crust o' bread and cheese and 'arf-a-pint of four ale each,' he ses to the barmaid.

"Ginger and Peter looked at each other, but they was so hungry they didn't say a word; they just stood waiting.

"'Put that inside you, my pore fellers,' ses Sam, with an oily smile. 'I can't bear to see people suffering for want o' food,' he ses to the barmaid, as he chucked down a sovereign on the counter.

"The barmaid, a very nice gal with black 'air and her fingers covered all over with rings, said that it did 'im credit, and they stood there talking about tramps and beggars and such-like till Peter and Ginger nearly choked. He stood there watching 'em and smoking a threepenny cigar, and when they 'ad finished he told the barmaid to give 'em a sausage-roll each, and went off.

"Peter and Ginger snatched up their sausage-rolls and follered 'im, and at last Ginger swallowed his pride and walked up to 'im and asked 'im to lend them some money.

"'You'll get it back agin,' he ses. 'You know that well enough.'

"'Cert'nly not,' ses Sam; 'and I'm surprised at you asking. Why, a child could rob you. It's 'ard enough as it is for a pore man like me to 'ave to keep a couple o' hulking sailormen, but I'm not going to give you money to chuck away on lodgers. No more sleeping on the floor for me! Now, I don't want none o' your langwidge, and I don't want you follering me like a couple o' cats arter a meat-barrer. I shall be 'aving a cup o' tea at Brown's coffee-shop by and by, and if you're there at five sharp I'll see wot I can do for you. *Wot* did you call me?'

"Ginger told 'im three times, and then Peter Russet dragged 'im away. They turned up outside Brown's at a quarter to five, and at ten past six Sam Small strolled up smoking a cigar, and, arter telling them that he 'ad forgot all about 'em, took 'em inside and paid for their teas. He told Mr. Brown 'e was paying for 'em, and 'e told the gal wot served 'em 'e was paying for 'em, and it was all pore Ginger could do to stop 'imself from throwing his plate in 'is face.

"Sam went off by 'imself, and arter walking about all the evening without a ha'penny in their pockets, Ginger Dick and Peter went off 'ome to bed and went to sleep till twelve o'clock, when Sam came in and woke 'em up to tell 'em about a music-'all he 'ad been to, and 'ow many pints he had 'ad. He sat up in bed till past one o'clock talking about 'imself, and twice Peter Russet woke Ginger up to listen and got punched for 'is trouble.

"They both said they'd get a ship next morning, and then old Sam turned round and wouldn't 'ear of it. The airs he gave 'imself was awful. He said *he'd* tell 'em when they was to get a ship, and if they went and did things without asking 'im he'd let 'em starve.

"He kept 'em with 'im all that day for fear of losing 'em and having to give 'em their money when 'e met 'em agin instead of spending it on 'em and getting praised for it. They 'ad their dinner with 'im at Brown's, and nothing they could do pleased him. He spoke to Peter Russet out loud about making a noise while he was eating, and directly arterwards he told Ginger to use his pocket-'ankercher. Pore Ginger sat there looking at 'im and swelling and swelling until he nearly bust, and Sam told 'im if he couldn't keep 'is temper when people was trying to do 'im a kindness he'd better go and get somebody else to keep him.

"He took 'em to a music-'all that night, but he spoilt it all for 'em by taking 'em into the little public-'ouse in Whitechapel Road fust and standing 'em a drink. He told the barmaid 'e was keeping 'em till they could find a job, and arter she 'ad told him he was too soft-'arted and would only be took advantage of, she brought another barmaid up to look at 'em and ask 'em wot they could do, and why they didn't do it.

"Sam served 'em like that for over a week, and he 'ad so much praise from Mr. Brown and other people that it nearly turned his 'ead. For once in his life he 'ad it pretty near all 'is own way. Twice Ginger Dick slipped off and tried to get a ship and came back sulky and hungry, and once Peter Russet sprained his thumb trying to get a job at the docks.

"They gave it up then, and kept to Sam like a couple o' shadders, only giving 'im back-answers when they felt as if something 'ud give way inside if they didn't. For the fust time in their lives they began to count the days till their boat was ready for sea. Then something happened.

"They was all coming 'ome late one night along the Minories, when Ginger Dick gave a shout, and, suddenly bolting up a little street arter a man that 'ad turned up there, fust of all sent 'im flying with a heavy punch of 'is fist, and then knelt on 'im.

"'Now then, Ginger,' ses Sam, bustling up with Peter Russet, 'wot's all this? Wot yer doing?'

"'It's the thief,' ses Ginger. 'It's our lodger. You keep still!' he ses, shaking the man. 'D'ye hear?'

"Peter gave a shout of joy, and stood by to help.

"'Nonsense!' ses old Sam, turning pale. 'You've been drinking, Ginger. This comes of standing you 'arf-pints.'

"'It's him right enough,' ses Ginger. 'I'd know 'is ugly face anywhere.'

"'You come off 'ome at once,' ses Sam, very sharp, but his voice trembling. 'At *once*. D'ye hear me?'

"'Fetch a policeman, Peter,' ses Ginger.

"'Let the pore feller go, I tell you,' ses Sam, stamping his foot. ''Ow would you like to be locked up? 'Ow would you like to be torn away from your wife and little ones? 'Ow would you—'

"'Fetch a policeman, Peter,' ses Ginger again. 'D'ye hear?'

"'Don't do that, guv'nor,' ses the lodger. 'You got your money back. Wot's the good o' putting me away?'

"'Got our *wot* back?' ses Ginger, shaking 'im agin. 'Don't you try and be funny with me, else I'll tear you into little pieces.'

"'But he took it back,' ses the man, trying to sit up and pointing at Sam. 'He follered me downstairs and took it all away from me. Your ticker as well.'

"'WOT?' ses Ginger and Peter both together.

"''Strue as I'm 'ere,' ses the lodger. 'You turn 'is pockets out and see. Look out! He's going off!'

"Ginger turned his 'ead just in time to see old Sam nipping round the corner. He pulled the lodger up like a flash, and, telling Peter to take hold of the other side of him, they Jet off arter Sam.

"'Little—joke—o' mine—Ginger,' ses Sam, when they caught 'im. 'I was going to tell you about it tonight. It ain't often I get the chance of a joke agin you, Ginger; you're too sharp for a old man like me.'

"Ginger Dick didn't say anything. He kept 'old o' Sam's arm with one hand and the lodger's neck with the other, and marched 'em off to his lodgings. He shut the door when 'e got in, and arter Peter 'ad lit the candle they took hold o' Sam and went through 'im, and arter trying to find pockets where he 'adn't got any, they took off 'is belt and found Ginger's watch, seventeen pounds five shillings, and a few coppers.

"'We 'ad over nine quid each, me and Peter,' ses Ginger. 'Where's the rest?'

"'It's all I've got left,' ses Sam; 'every ha'penny.'

"He 'ad to undress and even take 'is boots off afore they'd believe 'im, and then Ginger took 'is watch and he ses to Peter, 'Lemme see; 'arf of seventeen pounds is eight pounds ten; 'arf of five shillings is 'arf-a-crown; and arf of fourpence is twopence.'

"'What about me, Ginger, old pal,' ses Sam, in a kind voice. 'We must divide it into threes.'

"'*Threes?*' ses Ginger, staring at 'im. 'Whaffor?'

"''Cos part of it's mine,' ses Sam, struggling 'ard to be perlite. 'I've paid foreverything for the last ten days, ain't I?'

"'Yes,' ses Ginger. 'You 'ave, and I thank you for it.'

"'So do I,' ses Peter Russet. 'Hearty I do.'

"'It was your kind-'artedness,' ses Ginger, grinning like mad. 'You gave it to us, and we wouldn't dream of giving it to you back.'

"'Nothin' o' the kind,' ses Sam, choking.

"'Oh yes, you did,' ses Ginger, 'and you lidn't forget to tell people neither. You told everybody. Now it's our turn.'

"He opened the door and kicked the lodger out. Leastways, he would 'ave kicked 'im, but the chap was too quick for 'im. And then 'e came back, and putting his arm round Peter's waist, danced a waltz round the room with 'im, while pore old Sam got on to his bed to be out of the way. They danced for nearly 'arf-an-hour, and then they undressed and sat on Peter's bed and talked. They talked in whispers at fust, but at last Sam 'eard Peter say—

"'Threepence for 'is brekfuss; sevenpence for 'is dinner; threepence for 'is tea; penny for beer and a penny for bacca. 'Ow much is that, Ginger?'

"'One bob,' ses Ginger.

"Peter counted up to 'imself. 'I make it more than that, old pal,' he ses, when he 'ad finished.

"'Do you?' ses Ginger, getting up. 'Well, *he* won't; not if he counts it twenty times over he won't. Good night, Peter. 'Appy dreams.'"

52

DUAL CONTROL

"Never say 'die,' Bert," said Mr. Culpepper kindly; "I like you, and so do most other people who knows what's good for 'em; and if Florrie don't like you she can keep single till she does."

Mr. Albert Sharp thanked him.

"Come in more oftener," said Mr. Culpepper. "If she don't know a steady young man when she sees him, it's her mistake."

"Nobody could be steadier than what I am," sighed Mr. Sharp.

Mr. Culpepper nodded. "The worst of it is, girls don't like steady young men," he said, rumpling his thin grey hair; "that's the silly part of it."

"But you was always steady, and Mrs. Culpepper married you," said the young man.

Mr. Culpepper nodded again. "She thought was, and that came to the same thing," he said composedly. "And it ain't for me to say, but she had an idea that I was very good-looking in them days. I had chestnutty hair. She burnt a piece of it only the other day she'd kept for thirty years."

"Burnt it? What for?" inquired Mr. Sharp.

"Words," said the other, lowering his voice. "When I want one thing nowadays she generally wants another; and the things she wants ain't the things I want."

Mr. Sharp shook his head and sighed again.

"You ain't talkative enough for Florrie, you know," said Mr. Culpepper, regarding him.

"I can talk all right as a rule," retorted Mr. Sharp. "You ought to hear me at the debating society; but you can't talk to a girl who doesn't talk back."

"You're far too humble," continued the other. "You should cheek her a bit now and then. Let 'er see you've got some spirit. Chaff 'er."

"That's no good," said the young man restlessly. "I've tried it. Only the other day I called her 'a saucy little kipper,' and the way she went on, anybody would have thought I'd insulted her. Can't see a joke, I s'pose. Where is she now?"

"Upstairs," was the reply.

"That's because I'm here," said Mr. Sharp, "If it had been Jack Butler she'd have been down fast enough."

"It couldn't be him," said Mr. Culpepper, "because I won't have 'im in the house. I've told him so; I've told her so, and I've told her aunt so. And if she marries without my leave afore she's thirty she loses the seven hundred pounds 'er father left her. You've got plenty of time—ten years."

Mr. Sharp, sitting with his hands between his knees, gazed despondently at the floor. "There's a lot o' girls would jump at me," he remarked. "I've only got to hold up my little finger and they'd jump."

"That's because they've got sense," said Mr. Culpepper. "They've got the sense to prefer steadiness and humdrumness to good looks and dash. A young fellow like you earning thirty-two-and-six a week can do without good looks, and if I've told Florrie so once I have told her fifty times."

"Looks are a matter of taste," said Mr. Sharp morosely. "Some of them girls I was speaking about just now—"

"Yes, yes," said Mr. Culpepper hastily. "Now, look here; you go on a different tack. Take a glass of ale like a man or a couple o' glasses; smoke a cigarette or a pipe. Be like other young men. Cut a dash, and don't be a namby-pamby. After you're married you can be as miserable as you like."

Mr. Sharp, after a somewhat lengthy interval, thanked him.

"It's my birthday next Wednesday," continued Mr. Culpepper, regarding him benevolently; "come round about seven, and I'll ask you to stay to supper. That'll give you a chance. Anybody's allowed to step a bit over the mark on birthdays, and you might take a glass or two and make a speech, and be so happy and bright that they'd 'ardly know you. If you want an excuse for calling, you could bring me a box of cigars for my birthday."

"Or come in to wish you 'Many Happy Returns of the Day,'" said the thrifty Mr. Sharp.

"And don't forget to get above yourself," said Mr. Culpepper, regarding him sternly; "in a gentlemanly way, of course. Have as many glasses as you like—there's no stint about me."

"If it ever comes off," said Mr. Sharp, rising—"if I get her through you, you shan't have reason to repent it. I'll look after that."

Mr. Culpepper, whose feelings were a trifle ruffled, said that he would "look after it too." He had a faint idea that, even from his own point of view, he might have made a better selection for his niece's hand.

Mr. Sharp smoked his first cigarette the following morning, and, encouraged by the entire absence of any after-effects, purchased a pipe, which was taken up by a policeman the same evening for obstructing the public footpath in company with a metal tobacco-box three parts full.

In the matter of ale he found less difficulty. Certainly the taste was unpleasant, but, treated as medicine and gulped down quickly, it was endurable. After a day or two he even began to be critical, and on Monday evening went so far as to complain of its flatness to the wide-eyed landlord of the "Royal George."

"Too much cellar-work," he said, as he finished his glass and made for the door.

"Too much—! 'Ere, come 'ere," said the landlord thickly. "I want to speak to you."

The expert shook his head, and, passing out into the street, changed colour as he saw Miss Garland approaching. In a blundering fashion he clutched at his hat and stammered out a "Good evening."

Miss Garland returned the greeting and, instead of passing on, stopped and, with a friendly smile, held out her hand. Mr. Sharp shook it convulsively.

"You are just the man I want to see," she exclaimed. "Aunt and I have been talking about you all the afternoon."

Mr. Sharp said "Really!"

"But I don't want uncle to see us," pursued Miss Garland, in the low tones of confidence. "Which way shall we go?"

Mr. Sharp's brain reeled. All ways were alike to him in such company. He walked beside her like a man in a dream.

"We want to give him a lesson," said the girl presently. "A lesson that he will remember."

"Him?" said the young man.

"Uncle," explained the girl. "It's a shocking thing, a wicked thing, to try and upset a steady young man like you. Aunt is quite put out about it, and I feel the same as she does."

"But," gasped the astonished Mr. Sharp, "how did you—?"

"Aunt heard him," said Miss Garland. "She was just going into the room when she caught a word or two, and she stayed outside and listened. You don't know what a lot she thinks of you."

Mr. Sharp's eyes opened wider than ever. "I—I thought she didn't like me," he said slowly.

"Good gracious!" said Miss Garland. "Whatever could have put such an idea as that into your head? Of course, aunt isn't always going to let uncle see that she agrees with him. Still, as if anybody could help—" she murmured to herself.

"Eh?" said the young man, in a trembling voice.

"Nothing."

Miss Garland walked along with averted face; Mr. Sharp, his pulses bounding, trod on air beside her.

"I thought," he said at last—"I thought that Jack Butler was a favourite of hers?"

"Jack Butler!" said the girl, in tones of scornful surprise. "The idea! How blind men are; you're all alike, I think. You can't see two inches in front of you. She's as pleased as possible that you are coming on Wednesday; and so am—"

Mr. Sharp caught his breath. "Yes?" he murmured.

"Let's go down here," said Miss Garland quickly; "down by the river. And I'll tell you what we want you to do."

She placed her hand lightly on his arm, and Mr. Sharp, with a tremulous smile, obeyed. The smile gradually faded as he listened, and an expression of anxious astonishment took its place. He shook his head as she proceeded, and twice ventured a faint suggestion that she was only speaking in jest. Convinced at last, against his will, he walked on in silent consternation.

"But," he said at last, as Miss Garland paused for breath, "your uncle would never forgive me. He'd never let me come near the house again."

"Aunt will see to that," said the girl confidently. "But, of course, if you don't wish to please me—"

She turned away, and Mr. Sharp, plucking up spirit, ventured to take her hand and squeeze it. A faint, a very faint, squeeze in return decided him.

"It will come all right afterwards," said Miss Garland, "especially with the hold it will give aunt over him."

"I hope so," said the young man. "If not, I shall be far—farther off than ever."

Miss Garland blushed and, turning her head, gazed steadily at the river.

"Trust me," she said at last. "Me and auntie."

Mr. Sharp said that so long as he pleased her nothing else mattered, and, in the seventh heaven of delight, paced slowly along the towpath by her side.

"And you mustn't mind what auntie and I say to you," said the girl, continuing her instructions. "We must keep up appearances, you know; and if we seem to be angry, you s must remember we are only pretending."

Mr. Sharp, with a tender smile, said that he understood perfectly.

"And now I had better go," said Florrie, returning the smile. "Uncle might see us together, or somebody else might see us and tell aim. Goodbye."

She shook hands and went off, stopping three times to turn and wave her hand. In a state of bewildered delight Mr. Sharp continued his stroll, rehearsing, as he went, the somewhat complicated and voluminous instructions she had given him.

By Wednesday evening he was part-perfect, and, in a state of mind divided between nervousness and exaltation, set out for Mr. Culpepper's. He found that gentleman, dressed in his best, sitting in an easy chair with his hands folded over a fancy waistcoat of startling design, and, placing a small box of small cigars on his knees, wished him the usual "Happy Returns." The entrance of the ladies, who seemed as though they had just come off the ice, interrupted Mr. Cidpepper's thanks.

"Getting spoiled, that's what I am," he remarked playfully. "See this waistcoat? My old Aunt Elizabeth sent it this morning."

He leaned back in his chair and glanced down in warm approval. "The missis gave me a pipe, and Florrie gave me half a pound of tobacco. And I bought a bottle of port wine myself, for all of us."

He pointed to a bottle that stood on the supper-table, and, the ladies retiring to the kitchen to bring in the supper, rose and placed chairs. A piece of roast beef was placed before him, and, motioning Mr. Sharp to a seat opposite Florrie, he began to carve.

"Just a nice comfortable party," he said, genially, as he finished. "Help yourself to the ale, Bert."

Mr, Sharp, ignoring the surprise on the faces of the ladies, complied, and passed the bottle to Mr. Culpepper. They drank to each other, and again a flicker of surprise appeared on the faces of Mrs. Culpepper and her niece. Mr. Culpepper, noticing it, shook his head waggishly at Mr. Sharp.

"He drinks it as if he likes it," he remarked.

"I do," asserted Mr. Sharp, and, raising his glass, emptied it, and resumed the attack on his plate. Mr. Culpepper unscrewed the top of another bottle, and the reckless Mr. Sharp, after helping himself, made a short and feeling speech, in which he wished Mr. Culpepper long life and happiness. "If you ain't happy with Mrs. Culpepper," he concluded gallantly, "you ought to be."

Mr. Culpepper nodded and went on eating in silence until, the keen edge of his appetite having been taken off, he put down his knife and fork and waxed sentimental.

"Been married over thirty years," he said, slowly, with a glance at his wife, "and never regretted it."

"Who hasn't?" inquired Mr. Sharp.

"Why, me," returned the surprised Mr. Culpepper.

Mr. Sharp, who had just raised his glass, put it down again and smiled. It was a faint smile, but it seemed to affect his host unfavourably.

"What are you smiling at?" he demanded.

"Thoughts," said Mr. Sharp, exchanging a covert glance with Florrie. "Something you told me the other day."

Mr. Culpepper looked bewildered. "I'll give you a penny for them thoughts," he said, with an air of jocosity.

Mr. Sharp shook his head. "Money couldn't buy 'em," he said, with owlish solemnity, "espec-especially after the good supper you're giving me."

"Bert," said Mr. Culpepper, uneasily, as his wife sat somewhat erect—"Bert, it's my birthday, and I don't grudge nothing to nobody; but go easy with the beer. You ain't used to it, you know."

"What's the matter with the beer?" inquired Mr. Sharp. "It tastes all right—what there is of it."

"It ain't the beer; it's you," explained Mr. Culpepper.

Mr. Sharp stared at him. "Have I said anything I oughtn't to?" he inquired.

Mr. Culpepper shook his head, and, taking up a fork and spoon, began to serve a plum-pudding that Miss Garland had just placed on the table.

"What was it you said I was to be sure and not tell Mrs. Culpepper?" inquired Mr. Sharp dreamily. "I haven't said that, have I?"

"No!" snapped the harassed Mr. Culpepper, laying down the fork and spoon and regarding him ferociously. "I mean, there wasn't anything. I mean, I didn't say so. You're raving."

"If I did say it, I'm sorry," persisted Mr. Sharp. "I can't say fairer than that, can I?"

"You're all right," said Mr. Culpepper, trying, but in vain, to exchange a waggish glance with his wife.

"I didn't say it?" inquired Mr. Sharp.

"No," said Mr. Culpepper, still smiling in a wooden fashion.

"I mean the *other* thing?" said Mr. Sharp, in a thrilling whisper.

"Look here!" exclaimed the overwrought Mr. Culpepper; "why not eat your pudding, and leave off talking nonsense? Nobody's listening to you."

"Speak for yourself," said his wife tartly. "I like to hear Mr. Sharp talk. What was it he told you not to tell me?"

Mr. Sharp eyed her mistily. "I—I can't tell you," he said slowly.

"Why not?" asked Mrs. Culpepper coaxingly.

"Because it—it would make your hair stand on end," said the industrious Mr. Sharp.

"Nonsense," said Mrs. Culpepper, sharply.

"He said it would," said Mr. Sharp, indicating his host with his spoon, "and he ought—to know—who's that kicking me under the table?"

Mr. Culpepper, shivering with wrath and dread, struggled for speech. "You'd better get home, Bert," he said at last. "You're not yourself. There's nobody kicking you under the table. You don't know what you are saying. You've been dreaming things. I never said anything of the kind."

"Memory's gone," said Mr. Sharp, shaking his head at him. "Clean gone. Don't you remember—"

"NO!" roared Mr. Culpepper.

Mr. Sharp sat blinking at him, but his misgivings vanished before the glances of admiring devotion which Miss Garland was sending in his direction. He construed them rightly not only as a reward, but as an incentive to further efforts. In the midst of an impressive silence Mrs. Culpepper collected the plates and, producing a dish of fruit from the sideboard, placed it upon the table.

"Help yourself, Mr. Sharp," she said, pushing the bottle of port towards him.

Mr. Sharp complied, having first, after several refusals, put a little into the ladies' glasses, and a lot on the tablecloth near Mr. Culpepper. Then, after a satisfying sip or two, he rose with a bland smile and announced his intention of making a speech.

"But you've made one," said his host, in tones of fierce expostulation.

"That—that was *las'* night," said Mr. Sharp. "This is tonight—your birthday."

"Well, we don't want anymore," said Mr. Culpepper.

Mr. Sharp hesitated. "It's only his fun," he said, looking round and raising his glass. "He's afraid I'm going to praise him up—praise him up. Here's to my old friend, Mr. Culpepper: one of the best. We all have our—faults, and he has his—has his. Where was I?"

"Sit down," growled Mr. Culpepper.

"Talking about my husband's faults," said his wife.

"So I was," said Mr. Sharp, putting his hand to his brow. "Don't be alarm'," he continued, turning to his host; "nothing to be alarm' about. I'm not going to talk about 'em. Not so silly as that, I hope. I don't want spoil your life."

"Sit down," repeated Mr. Culpepper.

"You're very anxious he should sit down," said his wife sharply.

"No, I'm not," said Mr. Culpepper; "only he's talking nonsense."

Mr. Sharp, still on his legs, took another sip of port and, avoiding the eye of Mr. Culpepper, which was showing signs of incipient inflammation, looked for encouragement to Miss Garland.

"He's a man we all look up to and respect," he continued. "If he does go off to London every now and then on business, that's his lookout. My idea is he always ought to take Mrs. Culpepper with him. He'd have pleasure of her company and, same time, he'd be money in pocket by it. And why shouldn't *she* go to music-halls sometimes? Why shouldn't she—"

"You get off home," said the purple Mr. Culpepper, rising and hammering the table with his fist. "Get off home; and if you so much as show your face inside this 'ouse again there'll be trouble. Go on. Out you go!"

"Home?" repeated Mr. Sharp, sitting down suddenly. "Won't go home till morning."

"Oh, we'll soon see about that," said Mr. Culpepper, taking him by the shoulders. "Gome on, now."

Mr. Sharp subsided lumpishly into his chair, and Mr. Culpepper, despite his utmost efforts, failed to move him. The two ladies exchanged a glance, and then, with their heads in the air, sailed out of the room, the younger pausing at the door to bestow a mirthful glance upon Mr. Sharp ere she disappeared.

"Come—out," said Mr. Culpepper, panting.

"You trying tickle me?" inquired Mr. Sharp.

"You get off home," said the other. "You've been doing nothing but make mischief ever since you came in. What put such things into your silly head, I don't know. I shall never hear the end of 'em as long as I live."

"Silly head?" repeated Mr. Sharp, with an alarming change of manner. "Say it again."

Mr. Culpepper repeated it with gusto.

"Very good," said Mr. Sharp. He seized him suddenly, and pushing him backwards into his easy chair, stood over him with such hideous contortions of visage that Mr. Culpepper was horrified. "Now you sit there and keep quite still," he said, with smouldering ferocity. "Where did you put carving-knife? Eh? Where's carving-knife?"

"No, no, Bert," said Mr. Culpepper, clutching at his sleeve. "I—I was only joking. You—you ain't quite yourself, Bert."

"*What?*" demanded the other, rolling his eyes and clenching his fists.

"I—I mean you've improved," said Mr. Culpepper hurriedly. "Wonderful, you have."

Mr. Sharp's countenance cleared a little. "Let's make a night of it," he said. "Don't move, whatever you do."

He closed the door and, putting the wine and a couple of glasses on the mantelpiece, took a chair by Mr. Culpepper and prepared to spend the evening. His instructions were too specific to be disregarded, and three times he placed his arm about the waist of the frenzied Mr. Culpepper and took him for a lumbering dance up and down the room. In the intervals I between dances he regaled him with interminable extracts from speeches made at the debating society and recitations learned at school. Suggestions relating to bed, thrown out by Mr. Culpepper from time to time, were repelled with scorn. And twice, in deference to Mr. Sharp's desires, he had to join in the chorus of a song.

Ten o'clock passed, and the hands of the clock crawled round to eleven. The hour struck, and, as though in answer, the door opened and the agreeable face of Florrie Garland appeared. Behind her, to the intense surprise of both gentlemen, loomed the stalwart figure of Mr. Jack Butler.

"I thought he might be useful, uncle," said Miss Garland, coming into the room. "Auntie wouldn't let me come down before."

Mr. Sharp rose in a dazed fashion and saw Mr. Culpepper grasp Mr. Butler by the hand. More dazed still, he felt the large and clumsy hand of Mr. Butler take him by the collar and propel him with some violence along the small passage, while another hand, which he dimly recognised as belonging to Mr. Culpepper, was inserted in the small of his back. Then the front door opened and he was thrust out into the night. The door closed, and a low feminine laugh sounded from a window above.

53

SKILLED ASSISTANCE

The night-watchman, who had left his seat on the jetty to answer the gate-bell, came back with disgust written on a countenance only too well designed to express it.

"If she's been up 'ere once in the last week to know whether the *Silvia* is up she's been four or five times," he growled. "He's forty-seven if he's a day; 'is left leg is shorter than 'is right, and he talks with a stutter. When she's with g 'im you'd think as butter wouldn't melt in 'er mouth; but the way she talked to me just now you'd think I was paid a-purpose to wait on her. I asked 'er at last wot she thought I was here for, and she said she didn't know, and nobody else neither. And afore she went off she told the potman from the 'Albion,' wot was listening, that I was known all over Wapping as the Sleeping Beauty.

"She ain't the fust I've 'ad words with, not by a lot. They're all the same; they all start in a nice, kind, soapy sort o' way, and, as soon as they don't get wot they want, fly into a temper and ask me who I think I am. I told one woman once not to be silly, and I shall never forget it as long as I live—never. For all I know, I she's wearing a bit o' my 'air in a locket to this day, and very likely boasting that I gave it to her.

"Talking of her reminds me of another woman. There was a Cap'n Pinner, used to trade between 'ere and Hull on a schooner named the *Snipe*. Nice little craft she was, and 'e was a very nice feller. Many and many's the pint we've 'ad together, turn and turnabout, and the on'y time we ever 'ad a cross word was when somebody hid his clay pipe in my beer and 'e was foolish enough to think I'd done it.

"He 'ad a nice little cottage, 'e told me about, near Hull, and 'is wife's father, a man of pretty near seventy, lived with 'em. Well off, the old man was, and, as she was his only daughter, they looked to 'ave all his money when he'd gorn. Their only fear was that 'e might marry agin, and, judging from what 'e used to tell me about the old man, I thought it more than likely.

"'If it wasn't for my missis he'd ha' been married over and over agin,' he ses one day. 'He's like a child playing with gunpowder.'

"'Ow would it be to let 'im burn hisself a bit?' I ses.

"'If you was to see some o' the gunpowder he wants to play with, you wouldn't talk like that,' ses the cap'n. 'You'd know better. The on'y thing is to keep 'em apart, and my pore missis is wore to a shadder a-doing of it.'

"It was just about a month arter that that he brought the old man up to London with 'im. They 'ad some stuff to put out at Smith's Wharf, t'other side of the river, afore they came to us, and though they was on'y there four or five days, it was long enough for that old man to get into trouble.

"The skipper told me about it ten minutes arter they was made snug in the inner berth 'ere. He walked up and down like a man with a raging toothache, and arter follering 'im up and down the wharf till I was tired out, I discovered that 'is father-in-law 'ad got 'imself mixed up with a widder-woman ninety years old and weighing twenty stun. Arter he 'ad cooled down a bit, and I 'ad given 'im a few little pats on the shoulder, 'e made it forty-eight years old and fourteen stone.

"'He's getting ready to go and meet her now,' he ses, 'and wot my missis'll say to me I don't know.'

"His father-in-law came up on deck as 'e spoke, and began to brush 'imself all over with a clothes-brush. Nice-looking little man 'e was, with blue eyes, and a little white beard, cut to a point, and dressed up in a serge suit with brass buttons, and a white yachting cap. His real name was Mr. Finch, but the skipper called 'im Uncle Dick, and he took such a fancy to me that in five minutes I was calling 'im Uncle Dick too.

"'Time I was moving,' he ses, by and by. 'I've got an app'intment.'

"'Oh! Who with?' ses the skipper, pretending not to know.

"'Friend o' mine, in the army,' ses the old man, with a wink at me. 'So long.'

"He went off as spry as a boy, and as soon as he'd gorn the skipper started walking back'ards and for'ards agin, and raving.

"Let's 'ope as he's on'y amusing 'imself," I ses.

"'Wait till you see 'er,' ses the skipper; 'then you won't talk foolishness.'

"As it 'appened she came back with Uncle Dick that evening, to see 'im safe, and I see at once wot sort of a woman it was. She 'adn't been on the wharf five minutes afore you'd ha' thought it belonged to 'er, and when she went and sat on the schooner it seemed to be about 'arf its size. She called the skipper Tom, and sat there as cool as you please holding Uncle Dick's 'and, and patting it.

"I took the skipper round to the 'Bull's Head' arter she 'ad gorn, and I wouldn't let 'im say a word until he had 'ad two pints. He felt better then, and some o' the words 'e used surprised me.

"'Wot's to be done?' he ses at last. 'You see 'ow it is, Bill.'

"'Can't you get 'im away?' I ses. 'Who is she, and wot's 'er name?"

"'Her name,' ses the skipper, 'her name is Jane Maria Elizabeth Muffit, and she lives over at Rotherhithe.'

"'She's very likely married already,' I ses.

"'Her 'usband died ten years ago,' ses the skipper; 'passed away in 'is sleep. Overlaid, I should say.'

"He sat there smoking, and I sat there thinking. Twice 'e spoke to me, and I held my 'and up and said '*H'sh.* Then I turned to 'im all of a sudden and pinched his arm so hard he nearly dropped 'is beer.

"'Is Uncle Dick a nervous man?' I ses.

"'Nervous is no name for it,' he ses, staring.

"'Very good, then,' I ses. 'I'll send 'er husband to frighten 'im."

"The skipper looked at me very strange. 'Yes,' he ses. 'Yes, yes.'

"'Frighten 'im out of 'is boots, and make him give 'er up,' I ses. 'Or, better still, get 'im to run away and go into hiding for a time. That'ud be best, in case 'e found out.'

"Found out *wot?*' ses the skipper.

"'Found out it wasn't 'er husband,' I ses.

"'Bill,' ses the skipper, very earnest, 'this is the fust beer I've 'ad today, and I wish I could say the same for you.'

"I didn't take 'im at fust, but when I did I gave a laugh that brought in two more customers to see wot was the matter. Then I took 'im by the arm—arter a little trouble—and, taking 'im back to the wharf, explained my meaning to 'im.

"'I know the very man,' I ses. 'He comes into a public-'ouse down my way sometimes. Artful 'Arry, he's called, and, for 'arf a quid, say, he'd frighten Uncle Dick 'arf to death. He's big and ugly, and picks up a living by selling meerschaum pipes he's found to small men wot don't want' em. Wonderful gift o' the gab he's got.'

"We went acrosr to the 'Albion' to talk it over. There's several bars there, and the landlady always keeps cotton-wool in 'er ears, not 'aving been brought up to the public line. The skipper told me all 'e knew about Mrs. Muffit, and we arranged that

Artful 'Arry should come down at seven o'clock next night, if so be as I could find 'im in time.

"I got up early the next arternoon, and as it 'appened, he came into the 'Duke of Edinburgh' five minutes arter I got there. Nasty temper 'e was in, too. He'd just found a meerschaum pipe, as usual, and the very fust man 'e tried to sell it to said that it was the one 'e lost last Christmas, and gave 'im a punch in the jaw for it.

"'He's a thief, that's wot he is,' ses 'Arry; 'and I 'ate thiefs. 'Ow's a honest tradesman to make a living when there's people like that about?'

"I stood 'im 'arf a pint, and though it hurt 'im awful to drink it, he said 'e'd 'ave another just to see if he could bear the pain. Arter he had 'ad three 'e began for to take a more cheerful view o' life, and told me about a chap that spent three weeks in the London 'Orsepittle for calling 'im a liar.

"'Treat me fair,' he ses, 'and I'll treat other people fair. I never broke my word without a good reason for it, and that's more than everybody can say. If I told you the praise I've 'ad from some people you wouldn't believe it.'

"I let 'im go on till he 'ad talked 'imself into a good temper, and then I told 'im of the little job I 'ad got for 'im. He listened quiet till I 'ad finished, and then he shook 'is 'ead.

"'It ain't in my line,' he ses.

"'There's 'arf a quid 'anging to it,' I ses.

" 'Arry shook his 'ead agin. ''Tain't enough, mate,' he ses. 'If you was to make it a quid I won't say as I mightn't think of it.'

"I 'ad told the skipper that it might cost 'im a quid, so I knew 'ow far I could go; and at last, arter 'Arry 'ad got as far as the door three times, I gave way.

"'And I'll 'ave it now,' he ses, 'to prevent mistakes.'

"'No, 'Arry,' I ses, very firm. 'Besides, it ain't my money, you see.'

"'You mean to say you don't trust me,' 'e ses, firing up.

"'I'd trust you with untold gold,' I ses, 'but not with a real quid; you're too fond of a joke, 'Arry.'

"We 'ad another long argyment about it, and I had to tell 'im plain at last that when I wanted to smell 'is fist, I'd say so.

"'You turn up at the wharf at five minutes to seven,' I ses, 'and I'll give you ten bob of it; arter you've done your business I'll give you the other. Come along quiet, and you'll see me waiting at the gate for you.'

"He gave way arter a time, and, fust going 'ome for a cup o' tea, I went on to the wharf to tell the skipper 'ow things stood.

"'It couldn't 'ave 'appened better,' he ses. 'Uncle Dick is sure to be aboard at that time, 'cos 'e's going acrost the water at eight o'clock to pay 'er a visit. And all the hands'll be away. I've made sure of that.'

"He gave me the money for Artful 'Arry in two 'arf-suverins, and then we went over to the 'Albion' for a quiet glass and a pipe, and to wait for seven o'clock.

"I left 'im there at ten minutes to, and at five minutes to, punctual to the minute, I see 'Arry coming along swinging a thick stick with a knob on the end of it.

"'Where's the 'arf thick un?' he ses, looking round to see that the coast was clear.

"I gave it to 'im, and arter biting it in three places and saying it was a bit short in weight he dropped it in 'is weskit pocket and said 'e was ready.

"I left 'im there for a minute while I went and 'ad a look round. The deck of the *Snipe* was empty, but I could 'ear Uncle Dick down in the cabin singing; and, arter listening for a few seconds to make sure that it was singing, I went back and beckoned to 'Arry.

"'He's down in the cabin,' I ses, pointing. 'Don't overdo it, 'Arry, and at the same time don't underdo it, as you might say.'

"'I know just wot you want,' ses 'Arry, 'and if you'd got the 'art of a man in you, you'd make it *two* quids.'

"He climbed on board and stood listening for a moment at the companion, and then 'e went down, while I went off outside the gate, so as to be out of earshot in case Uncle Dick called for me. I knew that I should 'ear all about wot went on arterwards—and I did.

"Artful 'Arry went down the companion-ladder very quiet, and then stood at the foot of it looking at Uncle Dick. He looked 'im up and down and all over, and then 'e gave a fierce, loud cough.

"'Good evening,' he ses.

"'Good evening,' ses Uncle Dick, staring at 'im. 'Did you want to see anybody? '

"'I did,' ses 'Arry. 'I do. And when I see 'im I'm going to put my arms round 'im and twist 'is neck; then I'm going to break every bone in 'is body, and arter that I'm going to shy 'im overboard to pison the fishes with.'

"'Dear me!' ses Uncle Dick, shifting away as far as 'e could.

"'I ain't 'ad a wink o' sleep for two nights,' ses 'Arry—'not ever since I 'eard of it. When I think of all I've done for that woman—working for 'er, and such-like-my blood boils. When I think of her passing 'erself off as a widder—my widder—and going out with another man, I don't know wot to do with myself.'

"Uncle Dick started and turned pale. Fust 'e seemed as if 'e was going to speak, and then 'e thought better of it. He sat staring at 'Arry as if 'e couldn't believe his eyes.

"'Wot would you do with a man like that?' ses 'Arry. 'I ask you, as man to man, wot would you do to 'im?'

"'P'r'aps—p'r'aps 'e didn't know,' ses Uncle Dick, stammering.

"'Didn't know!' ses 'Arry. 'Don't care, you mean. We've got a nice little 'ome, and, just because I've 'ad to leave it for a bit and lay low for knifing a man, she takes advantage of it. And it ain't the fust time, neither. Wot's the matter?'

"'Touch—touch of ague; I get it sometimes,' ses Uncle Dick.

"'I want to see this man Finch,' ses 'Arry, shaking 'is knobby stick. 'Muffit, my name is, and I want to tell 'im so.'

"Uncle Dick nearly shook 'imself on to the floor.

"'I—I'll go and see if'e's in the fo'c'sle,' he ses at last.

"'He ain't there, 'cos I've looked,' ses 'Arry, 'arf shutting 'is eyes and looking at 'im hard. 'Wot might your name be? '

"'My name's Finch,' ses Uncle Dick, putting out his 'ands to keep him off, 'but I thought she was a widder. She told me her 'usband died ten years ago; she's deceived me as well as you. I wouldn't ha' dreamt of taking any notice of 'er if I'd known. Truth, I wouldn't. I shouldn't ha' dreamt of such a thing.'

"Artful 'Arry played with 'is stick a little, and stood looking at 'im with a horrible look on 'is face.

"''Ow am I to know you're speaking the truth?' he ses, very slow. '*Eh?* 'Ow can you prove it?'

"'If it was the last word I was to speak I'd say the same,' ses Uncle Dick. 'I tell you, I am as innercent as a newborn babe.'

"'If that's true,' ses 'Arry, "she's deceived both of us. Now, if I let you go will you go straight off and bring her 'ere to me?'

"'I will,' ses Uncle Dick, jumping up.

"''Arf a mo,' ses 'Arry, holding up 'is stick very quick. 'One thing is, if you don't come back, I'll 'ave you another day. I can't make up my mind wot to do. I can't think—I ain't tasted food for two days. If I 'ad any money in my pocket I'd 'ave a bite while you're gone.'

"Why not get something?' ses Uncle Dick, putting his 'and in his pocket, in a great 'urry to please him, and pulling out some silver.

" 'Arry said 'e would, and then he stood on one side to let 'im pass, and even put the knobby stick under 'im to help 'im up the companion-ladder.

"Uncle Dick passed me two minutes arter-wards without a word, and set off down the road as fast as 'is little legs 'ud carry 'im. I watched 'im out o' sight, and then I went on board the schooner to see how 'Arry 'ad got on.

"''Arry,' I ses, when he 'ad finished, 'you're a masterpiece!'

"'I know I am,' he ses. 'Wot about that other 'arf-quid?'

"'Here it is,' I ses, giving it to 'im. 'Fair masterpiece, that's wot you are. They may well call you Artful. Shake 'ands.'

"I patted 'im on the shoulder arter we 'ad shook 'ands, and we stood there smiling at each other and paying each other compliments.

"'Fancy 'em sitting 'ere and waiting for you to come back from that bite,' I ses.

"'I ought to 'ave 'ad more off of him,' ses 'Arry. ''Owever, it can't be helped. I think I'll 'ave a lay down for a bit; I'm tired.'

"'Better be off,' I ses, shaking my 'ead. 'Time passes, and they might come back afore you think.'

"'Well, wot of it?' ses 'Arry.

"'*Wot of it?*' I ses. 'Why, it 'ud spoil everything. It 'ud be blue ruin.'

"'Are you sure?' ses 'Arry.

"'Sartain,' I ses.

"'Well, make it five quid, and I'll go, then,' he ses, sitting down agin.

"I couldn't believe my ears at fust, but when I could I drew myself up and told 'im wot I thought of 'im; and he sat there and laughed at me.

"'Why, you called me a masterpiece just now,' he ses. 'I shouldn't be much of a masterpiece if I let a chance like this slip. Why, I shouldn't; be able to look myself in the face. Where's the skipper?'

"'Sitting in the "Albion," ' *I ses*, 'arf choking.

"'Go and tell 'im it's five quid,' ses 'Arry. 'I don't mean five more, on'y four. Some people would ha' made it five, but I like to deal square and honest.'

"I run over for the skipper in a state of mind that don't bear thinking of, and he came back with me, 'arf crazy. When we got to the cabin we found the door was locked, and, arter the skipper 'ad told Artful wot he'd do to 'im if he didn't open it, he 'ad to go on deck and talk to 'im through the skylight.

"'If you ain't off of my ship in two twos,' he ses, 'I'll fetch a policeman.'

"'You go and fetch four pounds,' ses 'Arry; 'that's wot I'm waiting for, not a policemans Didn't the watchman tell you? '

"'The bargain was for one pound,' ses the skipper, 'ardly able to speak.

"'Well, you tell that to the policeman,' ses Artful 'Arry.

"It was no use, he'd got us every way; and at last the skipper turns out 'is pockets, and he ses, 'Look 'ere,' he ses, 'I've got seventeen and tenpence ha'penny. Will you go if I give you that?'

"''Ow much has the watchman got?' ses 'Arry. 'His lodger lost 'is purse the other day.'

"I'd got two and ninepence, as it 'appened, and then there was more trouble because the skipper wouldn't give 'im the money till he 'ad gone, and 'e wouldn't go till he 'ad got it. The skipper gave way at last, and as soon as he 'ad got it 'Arry ses, 'Now 'op off and borrer the rest, and look slippy about it.'

"I put one hand over the skipper's mouth fust, and then, finding that was no good, I put the other. It was no good wasting bad lang-widge on 'Arry.

"I pacified the skipper at last, and arter 'Arry 'ad swore true 'e'd go when 'e'd got the money, the skipper rushed round to try and raise it. It's a difficult job at the best o' times, and I sat there on the skylight shivering and wondering whether the skipper or Mrs. Muffit would turn up fust.

"Hours seemed to pass away, and then I see the wicket in the gate open, and the skipper come through. He jumped on deck without a word, and then, going over to the skylight, 'anded down the money to 'Arry.

"'Right-o,' ses 'Arry. 'It on'y shows you wot you can do by trying.'

"He unlocked the door and came up on deck, looking at us very careful, and playing with 'is stick.

"'You've got your money,' ses the skipper; 'now go as quick as you can.'

" 'Arry smiled and nodded at him. Then he stepped on to the wharf, and was just moving to the gate, with us follering, when the wicket opened and in came Mrs. Muffit and Uncle Dick.

"'There he is,' ses Uncle Dick. "That's the man!"

"Mrs. Muffit walked up to 'im, and my 'art a'most stopped beating. Her face was the colour of beet-root with temper, and you could 'ave heard her breath fifty yards away.

"'Ho!' she says, planting 'erself in front of Artful 'Arry, 'so you're the man that ses you're my 'usband, are you?"

"'That's all right,' ses 'Arry, 'it's all a mistake.'

"'MISTAKE?' ses Mrs. Muffit.

"'Mistake o' Bill's,' ses 'Arry, pointing to me. 'I told 'im I thought 'e was wrong, but 'e would 'ave it. I've got a bad memory, so I left it to 'im.'

"'Ho!' ses Mrs. Muffit, taking a deep breath. 'Ho! I thought as much. Wot 'ave you got to say for yourself—eh? '

"She turned on me like a wild cat, with her 'ands in front of her. I've been scratched once in my life, and I wasn't going to be agin, so, fixing my eyes on 'er, I just stepped back a bit, ready for 'er. So long as I kept my eye fixed on 'ers she couldn't do anything. I knew that. Unfortunately I stepped back just an inch too far, and next moment I went over back'ards in twelve foot of water.

"Arter all, p'r'aps it was the best thing that could have 'appened to me; it stopped her talking. It ain't the fust time I've 'ad a wet jacket; but as for the skipper, and pore Uncle Dick—wot married her—they've been in hot water ever since."

54

FOR BETTER OR WORSE

Mr. George Wotton, gently pushing the swing doors of the public bar of the "King's Head" an inch apart, applied an eye to the aperture, in the hope of discovering a moneyed friend. His gaze fell on the only man in the bar, a greybeard of sixty, whose weather-beaten face and rough clothing spoke of the sea. With a faint sigh he widened the opening and passed through.

"Mornin', Ben," he said, with an attempt at cheerfulness.

"Have a drop with me," said the other heartily. "Got any money about you?"

Mr. Wotton shook his head and his face fell, clearing somewhat as the other handed him his mug. "Drink it all up, George," he said.

His friend complied. A more tactful man might have taken longer over the job, but Mr. Benjamin Davis, who appeared to be labouring under some strong excitement, took no notice.

"I've had a shock, George," he said, regarding the other steadily. "I've heard news of my old woman."

"Didn't know you had one," said Mr. Wotton calmly. "Wot's she done?"

"She left me," said Mr. Davis solemnly—"she left me thirty-five years ago. I went off to sea one fine morning, and that was the last I ever see of 'er."

"Why, did she bolt?" inquired Mr. Wotton, with mild interest.

"No," said his friend, "but I did. We'd been married three years—three long years—and I had 'ad enough of it. Awful temper she had. The last words I ever heard 'er say was: 'Take that!'"

Mr. Wotton took up the mug and, after satisfying himself as to the absence of contents, put it down again and yawned.

"I shouldn't worry about it if I was you," he remarked. "She's hardly likely to find you now. And if she does she won't get much."

Mr. Davis gave vent to a contemptuous laugh. "Get much!" he repeated. "It's her what's got it. I met a old shipmate of mine this morning what I 'adn't seen for ten years, and he told me he run acrost 'er only a month ago. After she left me—"

"But you said you left her!" exclaimed his listening friend.

"Same thing," said Mr. Davis impatiently. "After she left me to work myself to death at sea, running here and there at the orders of a pack o' lazy scuts aft, she went into service and stayed in one place for fifteen years. Then 'er missis died and left her all 'er money. For twenty years, while I've been working myself to skin and bone, she's been living in comfort and idleness."

"'Ard lines," said Mr. Wotton, shaking his head. "It don't bear thinking of."

"Why didn't she advertise for me?" said Mr. Davis, raising his voice. "That's what I want to know. Advertisements is cheap enough; why didn't she advertise? I should 'ave come at once if she'd said anything about money."

Mr. Wotton shook his head again. "P'r'aps she didn't want you," he said slowly.

"What's that got to do with it?" demanded the other. "It was 'er dooty. She'd got money, and I ought to have 'ad my 'arf of it. Nothing can make up for that wasted twenty years—nothing."

"P'r'aps she'll take you back," said Mr. Wotton.

"Take me back?" repeated Mr. Davis. "O' course she'll take me back. She'll have to. There's a law in the land, ain't there? What I'm thinking of is: Can I get back my share what I ought to have 'ad for the last twenty years?"

"Get 'er to take you back first," counselled his friend. "Thirty-five years is a long time, and p'r'aps she has lost 'er love for you. Was you good-looking in those days?"

"Yes," snapped Mr. Davis; "I ain't altered much. 'Sides, what about her?"

"That ain't the question," said the other. "She's got a home and money. It don't matter about *'er* looks; and, wot's more, she ain't bound to keep you. If you take my advice you won't dream of letting her know you run away from her. Say you was cast away at sea, and when you came back years afterwards you couldn't find her."

Mr. Davis pondered for some time in sulky silence.

"P'r'aps it would be as well," he said at last; "but I shan't stand no nonsense, mind."

"If you like I'll come with you," said Mr. Wotton. "I ain't got nothing to do. I could tell 'er I was cast away with you, if you liked. Anything to help a pal."

Mr. Davis took two inches of soiled clay pipe from his pocket and puffed thoughtfully.

"You can come," he said at last. "If you'd only got a copper or two we could ride; it's down Clapham way."

Mr. Wotton smiled feebly, and after going carefully through his pockets shook his head and followed his friend outside.

"I wonder whether she'll be pleased?" he remarked, as they walked slowly along. "She might be—women are funny creatures—so faithful. I knew one whose husband used to knock 'er about dreadful, and after he died she was so true to his memory she wouldn't marry again."

Mr. Davis grunted, and, with a longing eye at the omnibuses passing over London Bridge, asked a policeman the distance to Clapham.

"Never mind," said Mr. Wotton, as his friend uttered an exclamation. "You'll have money in your pocket soon."

Mr. Davis's face brightened. "And a watch and chain, too," he said.

"And smoke your cigar of a Sunday," said Mr. Wotton, "and have a easy chair and a glass for a friend."

Mr. Davis almost smiled, and then, suddenly remembering his wasted twenty years, shook his head grimly over the friendship that attached itself to easy chairs and glasses of ale, and said that there was plenty of it about. More friendship than glasses of ale and easy chairs, perhaps.

At Clapham they inquired the way of a small boy, and, after following the road indicated, retraced their steps, cheered by a faint but bloodthirsty hope of meeting him again.

A friendly baker put them on the right track at last, both gentlemen eyeing the road with a mixture of concern and delight. It was a road of trim semi-detached villas, each with a well-kept front garden and neatly-curtained windows. At the gate of a house with the word "Blair-gowrie" inscribed in huge gilt letters on the fanlight Mr. Davis paused for a moment uneasily, and then, walking up the path, followed by Mr. Wotton, knocked at the door.

He retired a step in disorder before the apparition of a maid in cap and apron. A sharp "Not today!" sounded in his ears and the door closed again. He faced his friend gasping.

"I should give her the sack first thing," said Mr. Wotton.

Mr. Davis knocked again, and again. The maid reappeared, and after surveying them through the glass opened the door a little way and parleyed.

"I want to see your missis," said Mr. Davis fiercely.

"What for?" demanded the girl.

"You tell 'er," said Mr. Davis, inserting his foot just in time, "you tell 'er that there's two gentlemen here what have brought 'er news of her husband, and look sharp about it."

"They was cast away with 'im," said Mr. Wotton.

"On a desert island," said Mr. Davis. He pushed his way in, followed by his friend, and a head that had been leaning over the banisters was suddenly withdrawn. For a moment he stood irresolute in the tiny passage, and then, with a husband's boldness, he entered the front room and threw himself into an easy chair. Mr. Wotton, after a scared glance around the well-furnished room, seated himself on the extreme edge of the most uncomfortable chair he could find and coughed nervously.

"Better not be too sudden with her," he whispered. "You don't want her to faint, or anything of that sort. Don't let her know who you are at first; let her find it out for herself."

Mr. Davis, who was also suffering from the stiff grandeur of his surroundings, nodded.

"P'r'aps you'd better start, in case she reckernises my voice," he said slowly. "Pitch it in strong about me and 'ow I was always wondering what had 'appened to her."

"You're in luck, that's wot you are," said his friend enviously. "I've only seen furniture like this in shop windows before. *H'sh!* Here she comes."

He started, and both men tried to look at their ease as a stiff rustling sounded from the stairs. Then the door opened and a tall, stoutly-built old lady with white hair swept into the room and stood regarding them.

Mr. Davis, unprepared for the changes wrought by thirty-five years, stared at her aghast. The black silk dress, the gold watch-chain, and huge cameo brooch did not help to reassure him.

"Good—good afternoon, ma'am," said Mr. Wotton in a thin voice.

The old lady returned the greeting, and, crossing to a chair and seating herself in a very upright fashion, regarded him calmly.

"We—we called to see you about a dear old pal—friend, I mean," continued Mr. Wotton; "one o' the best. The best."

"Yes?" said the old lady.

"He's been missing," said Mr. Wotton, watching closely for any symptoms of fainting, "for thirty-five years. Thirty-five years ago—very much against his wish—he left 'is young and handsome wife to go for a sea v'y'ge, and was shipwrecked and cast away on a desert island."

"Yes?" said the old lady again.

"I was cast away with 'im," said Mr. Wotton. "Both of us was cast away with him."

He indicated Mr. Davis with his hand, and the old lady, after a glance at that gentleman, turned to Mr. Wotton again.

"We was on that island for longer than I like to think of," continued Mr. Wotton, who had a wholesome dread of dates. "But we was rescued at last, and ever since then he has been hunting high and low for his wife."

"It's very interesting," murmured the old lady; "but what has it got to do with me?"

Mr. Wotton gasped, and cast a helpless glance at his friend.

"You ain't heard his name yet," he said impressively. "Wot would you say if I said it I was—Ben Davis?"

"I should say it wasn't true, said the old lady promptly.

"Not—true?" said Mr. Wotton, catching his breath painfully. "Wish I may die—"

"About the desert island," continued the old lady calmly. "The story that I heard was that he went off like a cur and left his young wife to do the best she could for herself. I suppose he's heard since that she has come in for a bit of money."

"*Money!*" repeated Mr. Wotton, in a voice that he fondly hoped expressed artless surprise.

"Money!"

"Money," said the old lady; "and I suppose he sent you two gentlemen round to see how the land lay."

She was looking full at Mr. Davis as she spoke, and both men began to take a somewhat sombre view of the situation.

"You didn't know him, else you wouldn't talk like that," said Mr. Wotton. "I don't suppose you'd know 'im if you was to see him now."

"I don't suppose I should," said the other.

"P'r'aps you'd reckernise his voice?" said Mr. Davis, breaking silence at last.

Mr. Wotton held his breath, but the old lady merely shook her head thoughtfully. "It was a disagreeable voice when his wife used to hear it," she said at last. "Always fault-finding, when it wasn't swearing."

Mr. Wotton glanced at his friend, and, raising his eyebrows slightly, gave up his task.

"Might ha' been faults on both sides," said Mr. Davis gruffly. "You weren't all that you should ha' been, you know."

"*Me*?" said his hostess, raising her voice.

"Yes, you," said Mr. Davis, rising. "Don't you know me, Mary? Why, I knew you the moment you come into the room."

He moved towards her awkwardly, but she rose in her turn and drew back.

"If you touch me I'll scream," she said firmly. "How dare you! Why, I've never seen you before in my life."

"It's Ben Davis, ma'am; it's 'im, right enough," said Mr. Wotton meekly.

"Hold your tongue," said the old lady.

"Look at me!" commanded Mr. Davis sternly. "Look at me straight in the eye."

"Don't talk nonsense," said the other sharply. "Look you in the eye, indeed! I don't want to look in your eye. What would people think?"

"Let 'em think wot they like," said Mr. Davis recklessly. "This is a nice home-coming after being away thirty-five years."

"Most of it on a desert island," put in Mr. Wotton pathetically.

"And now I've come back," resumed Mr. Davis; "come back to stop."

He hung his cap on a vase on the mantelpiece that reeled under the shock, and, dropping into his chair again, crossed his legs and eyed her sternly. Her gaze was riveted on his dilapidated boots. She looked up and spoke mildly.

"You're not my husband," she said. "You've made a mistake—I think you had better go."

"Ho!" said Mr. Davis, with a hard laugh. "Indeed! And how do you know I'm not?"

"For the best of reasons," was the reply. "Besides, how can you prove that you are? Thirty-five years is a long time."

"'Specially on a desert island," said Mr. Wotton rapidly. "You'd be surprised 'ow slow; the time passes. I was there with 'im, and I can lay my hand on my 'art and assure you that that is your husband."

"Nonsense!" said the old lady vigorously. "Rubbish!"

"I can prove it," said Mr. Davis, fixing her with a glittering eye. "Do you remember the serpent I 'ad tattooed on my leg for a garter?

"If you don't go at once," said the old lady, hastily, "I'll send for the police."

"You used to admire it," said Mr. Davis reproachfully. "I remember once—"

"If you say another word," said the other in a fierce voice, "I'll send straight off for the police. You and your serpents! I'll tell my husband of you, that's what I'll do."

"Your WHAT?" roared Mr. Davis, springing; to his feet.

"My husband. He won't stand any of your nonsense, I can tell you. You'd better go before he comes in."

"O-oh," said Mr. Davis, taking a long breath. "Oh, so you been and got married again, 'ave you? That's your love for your husband as was cast away while trying to earn a living for you. That's why you don't want me, is it? We'll see. I'll wait for him."

"You don't know what you're talking about," said the other, with great dignity. "I've only been married once."

Mr. Davis passed the back of his hand across his eyes in a dazed fashion and stared at her.

"Is—is somebody passing himself off as me?" he demanded. "'Cos if he is I'll 'ave you both up for bigamy."

"Certainly not."

"But—but—"

Mr. Davis turned and looked blankly at his friend. Mr. Wotton met his gaze with dilated eyes.

"You say you recognise me as your wife?" said the old lady.

"Certainly," said Mr. Davis hotly.

"It's very curious," said the other—"very. But are you sure? Look again."

Mr. Davis thrust his face close to hers and stared hard. She bore his scrutiny without flinching.

"I'm positive certain," said Mr. Davis, taking a breath.

"That's very curious," said the old lady; "but, then, I suppose we are a bit alike. You see, Mrs. Davis being away, I'm looking after her house for a bit. My name happens to be Smith."

Mr. Davis uttered a sharp exclamation, and, falling back a step, stared at her open-mouthed.

"We all make mistakes," urged Mr. Wotton, after a long silence, "and Ben's sight ain't wot it used to be. He strained it looking out for a sail when we was on that desert—"

"When—when'll she be back?" inquired Mr. Davis, finding his voice at last.

The old lady affected to look puzzled. "But I thought you were certain that I was your wife?" she said smoothly.

"My mistake," said Mr. Davis ruefully. "Thirty-five years is a long time, and people change a bit; I have myself. For one thing, I must say I didn't expect to find 'er so stout."

"*Stout!*" repeated the other quickly.

"Not that I mean you're too stout," said Mr. Davis hurriedly—"for people that like stoutness, that is. My wife used to 'ave a very good figger."

Mr. Wotton nodded. "He used to rave about it on that des—"

"When will she be back?" inquired Mr. Davis, interrupting him.

Mrs. Smith shook her head. "I can't say," she replied, moving towards the door. "When she's off holidaying I never know when she'll return. Shall I tell her you called?"

"Tell her I—*certainly*," said Mr. Davis, with great vehemence. "I'll come in a week's time and see if she's back."

"She might be away for months," said the old lady, moving slowly to the passage and opening the street door. "Good—afternoon,"

She closed the door behind them and stood watching them through the glass as they passed disconsolately into the street. Then she went back into the parlour and, standing before the mantelpiece, looked long and earnestly into the mirror.

Mr. Davis returned a week later—alone, and, pausing at the gate, glanced in dismay at a bill in the window announcing that the house was to be sold. He walked up the path still looking at it, and being admitted by the trim servant, was shown into the parlour, and stood in a dispirited fashion before Mrs. Smith.

"Not back yet?" he inquired gruffly.

The old lady shook her head.

"What—what—is that bill for?" demanded Mr. Davis, jerking his thumb towards it.

"She is thinking of selling the house," said Mrs. Smith. "I let her know you had been, and that is the result. She won't come back. You won't see her again."

"Where is she?" inquired Mr. Davis, frowning.

Mrs. Smith shook her head again. "And it would be no use my telling you," she said. "What she has got is her own, and the law won't let you touch a penny of it without her consent. You must have treated her badly; why did you leave her?"

"Why?" repeated Mr. Davis. "Why? Why, because she hit me over the 'ead with a broom-handle."

Mrs. Smith tossed her head.

"Fancy you remembering that for thirty-five years!" she said.

"Fancy forgetting it!" retorted Mr. Davis.

"I suppose she had a hot temper," said the old lady.

"'Ot temper?" said the other. "Yes." He leaned forward, and holding his chilled hands over the fire stood for some time deep in thought.

"I don't know what it is," he said at last, "but there's a something about you that reminds me of her. It ain't your voice, 'cos she had a very nice voice—when she wasn't in a temper—and it ain't your face, because—"

"Yes?" said Mrs. Smith sharply.

"Because it don't remind me of her."

"And yet the other day you said you recognised me at once," said the old lady.

"I thought I did," said Mr. Davis. "One thing is, I was expecting to see her, I s'pose."

There was a long silence.

"Well, I won't keep you," said Mrs. Smith at last, "and it's no good for you to keep coming here to see her. She will never come here again. I don't want to hurt your feelings, but you don't look over and above respectable. Your coat is torn, your trousers are patched in a dozen places, and your boots are half off your feet—I don't know what the servant must think."

"I—I only came to look for my wife," said Mr. Davis in a startled voice. "I won't come again."

"That's right," said the old lady. "That'll please her, I know. And if she should happen to ask what sort of a living you are making, what shall I tell her?"

"Tell her what you said about my clothes, ma'am," said Mr. Davis, with his hand on the doorknob. "She'll understand then. She's known wot it is to be poor herself. She's got a bad temper, but she'd have cut her tongue out afore she'd 'ave thrown a poor devil's rags in his face. Good afternoon."

"Good afternoon, Ben," said the old woman in a changed voice.

Mr. Davis, half-way through the door, started as though he had been shot, and, facing about, stood eyeing her in dumb bewilderment.

"It isn't the same voice and it isn't the same face," said the old woman; "but if I'd only got a broom-handle handy—"

Mr. Davis made an odd noise in his throat.

"If you hadn't been so down on your luck," said his wife, blinking her eyes rapidly, "I'd have let you go. If you hadn't looked so miserable I could have stood it. If I take you back, are you going to behave yourself?"

Mr. Davis stood gaping at her.

"If I take you back again," repeated his wife, speaking very slowly, "are you going to behave yourself?"

"Yes," said Mr. Davis, finding his voice at last. "Yes, if you are."

55

THE OLD MAN OF THE SEA

"What I want you to do," said Mr. George Wright, as he leaned towards the old sailor, "is to be an uncle to me."

"Aye, aye," said the mystified Mr. Kemp, pausing with a mug of beer midway to his lips.

"A *rich* uncle," continued the young man, lowering his voice to prevent any keen ears in the next bar from acquiring useless knowledge. "An uncle from New Zealand, who is going to leave me all 'is money."

"Where's it coming from?" demanded Mr. Kemp, with a little excitement.

"It ain't coming," was the reply. "You've only got to say you've got it. Fact of the matter is, I've got my eye on a young lady; there's another chap after 'er too, and if she thought I'd got a rich uncle it might make all the difference. She knows I 'ad an uncle that went to New Zealand and was never heard of since. That's what made me think of it."

Mr. Kemp drank his beer in thoughtful silence. How can I be a rich uncle without any brass?" he inquired at length.

"I should 'ave to lend you some—a little," said Mr. Wright.

The old man pondered. "I've had money lent me before," he said candidly, "but I can't call to mind ever paying it back. I always meant to, but that's as far as it got."

"It don't matter," said the other. "It'll only be for a little while, and then you'll 'ave a letter calling you back to New Zealand. See? And you'll go back, promising to come home in a year's time, after you've wound up your business, and leave us all your money. See?"

Mr. Kemp scratched the back of his neck. "But she's sure to find it out in time," he objected.

"P'raps," said Mr. Wright. "And p'r'aps not. There'll be plenty of time for me to get married before she does, and you could write back and say you had got married yourself, or given your money to a hospital."

He ordered some more beer for Mr. Kemp, and in a low voice gave him as much of the family history as he considered necessary.

"I've only known you for about ten days," he concluded, "but I'd sooner trust you than people I've known for years."

"I took a fancy to you the moment I set eyes on you," rejoined Mr. Kemp. "You're the living image of a young feller that lent me five pounds once, and was drowned afore my eyes the week after. *He* 'ad a bit of a squint, and I s'pose that's how he came to fall overboard."

He emptied his mug, and then, accompanied by Mr. Wright, fetched his sea-chest from the boarding-house where he was staying, and took it to the young man's lodgings. Fortunately for the latter's pocket the chest contained a good best suit and boots, and the only expenses incurred were for a large, soft felt hat and a gilded watch and chain. Dressed in his best, with a bulging pocketbook in his breast pocket, he set out with Mr. Wright on the following evening to make his first call.

Mr. Wright, who was also in his best clothes, led the way to a small tobacconist's in a side street off the Mile End Road, and, raising his hat with ceremony, shook hands with a good-looking young woman who stood behind the counter; Mr.

Kemp, adopting an air of scornful dignity intended to indicate the possession of great wealth, waited.

"This is my uncle," said Mr. Wright, speaking rapidly, "from New Zealand, the one I spoke to you about. He turned up last night, and you might have knocked me down with a feather. The last person in the world I expected to see."

Mr. Kemp, in a good rolling voice, said, "Good evening, miss; I hope you are well," and, subsiding into a chair, asked for a cigar. His surprise when he found that the best cigar they stocked cost only sixpence almost assumed the dimensions of a grievance.

"It'll do to go on with," he said, smelling it suspiciously. "Have you got change for a fifty-pound note?"

Miss Bradshaw, concealing her surprise by an effort, said that she would see, and was scanning the contents of a drawer, when Mr. Kemp in some haste discovered a few odd sovereigns in his waistcoat pocket. Five minutes later he was sitting in the little room behind the shop, holding forth to an admiring audience.

"So far as I know," he said, in reply to a question of Mrs. Bradshaw's, "George is the only relation I've got. Him and me are quite alone, and I can tell you I was glad to find him."

Mrs. Bradshaw sighed. "It's a pity you are so far apart," she said.

"It's not for long," said Mr. Kemp. "I'm just going back for about a year to wind up things out there, and then I'm coming back to leave my old bones over here. George has very kindly offered to let me live with him."

"He won't suffer for it, I'll be bound," said Mrs. Bradshaw archly.

"So far as money goes he won't," said the old man. "Not that that would make any difference to George."

"It would be the same to me if you hadn't got a farthing," said Mr. Wright promptly.

Mr. Kemp, somewhat affected, shook hands with him, and leaning back in the most comfortable chair in the room, described his life and struggles in New Zealand. Hard work, tee-totalism, and the simple life combined appeared to be responsible for a fortune which he affected to be too old to enjoy. Misunderstandings of a painful nature were avoided by a timely admission that under medical advice he was now taking a fair amount of stimulant.

"Mind," he said as he walked home with the elated George, "it's your game, not mine, and it's sure to come a bit expensive. I can't be a rich uncle without spending a bit. 'Ow much did you say you'd got in the bank?"

"We must be as careful as we can," said Mr. Wright hastily. "One thing is they can't leave the shop to go out much. It's a very good little business, and it ought to be all right for me and Bella one of these days, eh?"

Mr. Kemp, prompted by a nudge in the ribs, assented. "It's wonderful how they took it all in about me," he said; "but I feel certain in my own mind that I ought to chuck some money about."

"Tell 'em of the money you *have* chucked about," said Mr. Wright. "It'll do just as well, and come a good deal cheaper. And you had better go round alone tomorrow evening. It'll look better. Just go in for another one of their sixpenny cigars."

Mr. Kemp obeyed, and the following evening, after sitting a little while chatting in the shop, was invited into the parlour, where, mindful of Mr. Wright's instructions, he held his listeners enthralled by tales of past expenditure. A tip of fifty pounds to his bedroom steward coming over was characterised by Mrs. Bradshaw as extravagant.

"Seems to be going all right," said Mr. Wright, as the old man made his report; "but be careful; don't go overdoing it."

Mr. Kemp nodded. "I can turn 'em round my little finger," he said. "You'll have Bella all to yourself tomorrow evening."

Mr. Wright flushed. "How did you manage that?" he inquired. "It's the first time she has ever been out with me alone."

"She ain't coming out," said Mr. Kemp. "She's going to stay at home and mind the shop; it's the mother what's coming out. Going to spend the evening with me!"

Mr. Wright frowned. "What did you do that for?" he demanded hotly.

"I didn't do it," said Mr. Kemp equably; "they done it. The old lady says that, just for once in her life, she wants to see how it feels to spend money like water."

"*Money like water!*" repeated the horrified Mr. Wright. "Money like—I'll 'money' her—I'll—"

"It don't matter to me," said Mr. Kemp. "I can have a headache or a chill, or something of that sort, if you like. I don't want to go. It's no pleasure to me."

"What will it cost?" demanded Mr. Wright, pacing up and down the room.

The rich uncle made a calculation. "She wants to go to a place called the Empire," he said slowly, "and have something for supper, and there'd be cabs and things. I dessay it would cost a couple o' pounds, and it might be more. But I'd just as soon 'ave a chill—just."

Mr. Wright groaned, and after talking of Mrs. Bradshaw as though she were already his mother-in-law, produced the money. His instructions as to economy lasted almost up to the moment when he stood with Bella outside the shop on the following evening and watched the couple go off.

"It's wonderful how well they get on together," said Bella as they re-entered the shop and passed into the parlour. "I've never seen mother take to anybody so quick as she has to him."

"I hope you like him, too," said Mr. Wright.

"He's a dear," said Bella. "Fancy having all that money. I wonder what it feels like?"

"I suppose I shall know some day," said the young man slowly; "but it won't be much good to me unless—"

"Unless?" said Bella after a pause.

"Unless it gives me what I want," replied the other. "I'd sooner be a poor man and married to the girl I love, than a millionaire."

Miss Bradshaw stole an uneasy glance at his somewhat sallow features, and became thoughtful.

"It's no good having diamonds and motorcars and that sort of thing unless you have somebody to share them with," pursued Mr. Wright.

Miss Bradshaw's eyes sparkled, and at that moment the shop bell tinkled and a lively whistle sounded. She rose and went into the shop, and Mr. Wright settled back in his chair and scowled darkly as he saw the intruder.

"Good evening," said the latter. "I want a sixpenny smoke for twopence, please. How are we this evening? Sitting up and taking nourishment?"

Miss Bradshaw told him to behave himself.

"Always do," said the young man. "That's why I can never get anybody to play with. I had such an awful dream about you last night that I couldn't rest till I saw you. Awful, it was."

"What was it?" inquired Miss Bradshaw.

"Dreamt you were married," said Mr. Hills, smiling at her.

Miss Bradshaw tossed her head. "Who to, pray?" she inquired.

"Me," said Mr. Hills simply. "I woke up in a cold perspiration. Halloa! Is that Georgie in there? How are you, George? Better?"

"I'm all right," said Mr. Wright, with dignity, as the other hooked the door open with his stick and nodded at him.

"Well, why don't you look it?" demanded the lively Mr. Hills. "Have you got your feet wet, or what?"

"Oh, be quiet," said Miss Bradshaw, smiling at him.

"Right-o," said Mr. Hills, dropping into a chair by the counter and caressing his moustache. "But you wouldn't speak to me like that if you knew what a terrible day I've had."

"What have you been doing?" asked the girl.

"Working," said the other, with a huge sigh. "Where's the millionaire? I came round on purpose to have a look at him."

"Him and mother have gone to the Empire," said Miss Bradshaw.

Mr. Hills gave three long, penetrating whistles, and then, placing his cigar with great care on the counter, hid his face in a huge handkerchief. Miss Bradshaw glanced from him to the frowning Mr. Wright, and then, entering the parlour, closed the door with a bang. Mr. Hills took the hint, and with a somewhat thoughtful grin departed.

He came in next evening for another cigar, and heard all that there was to hear about the Empire. Mrs. Bradshaw would have treated him but coldly, but the innocent Mr. Kemp, charmed by his manner, paid him great attention.

"He's just like what I was at his age," he said. "Lively."

"I'm not a patch on you," said Mr. Hills, edging his way by slow degrees into the parlour. "*I* don't take young ladies to the Empire. Were you telling me you came over here to get married, or did I dream it?"

"'Ark at him," said the blushing Mr. Kemp, as Mrs. Bradshaw shook her head at the offender and told him to behave himself.

"He's a man any woman might be happy with," said Mr. Hills. "He never knows how much there is in his trousers pocket. Fancy sewing on buttons for a man like that. Gold-mining ain't in it."

Mrs. Bradshaw shook her head at him again, and Mr. Hills, after apologising to her for revealing her innermost thoughts before the most guileless of men, began to question Mr. Kemp as to the prospects of a bright and energetic young man, with a distaste for work, in New Zealand. The audience listened with keen attention to the replies, the only disturbing factor being a cough of Mr. Wright's, which became more and more troublesome as the evening wore on. By the time uncle and nephew rose to depart the latter was so hoarse that he could scarcely speak.

"Why didn't you tell 'em you had got a letter calling you home, as I told you?" he vociferated, as soon as they were clear of the shop.

"I—I forgot it," said the old man.

"Forgot it!" repeated the incensed Mr. Wright. "What did you think I was coughing like that for—fun?"

"I forgot it," said the old man doggedly. "Besides, if you take my advice, you'd better let me stay a little longer to make sure of things."

Mr. Wright laughed disagreeably. "I dare say," he said: "but I am managing this affair, not you. Now, you go round tomorrow afternoon and tell them you're off. D'ye hear? D'ye think I'm made of money? And what do you mean by making such a fuss of that fool, Charlie Hills? You know he is after Bella."

He walked the rest of the way home in indignant silence, and, after giving minute instructions to Mr. Kemp next morning at breakfast, went off to work in a more cheerful frame of mind. Mr. Kemp was out when he returned, and after making his toilet he followed him to Mrs. Bradshaw's.

To his annoyance, he found Mr. Hills there again; and, moreover, it soon became clear to him that Mr. Kemp had said nothing about his approaching departure. Coughs and scowls passed unheeded, and at last in a hesitating voice, he broached the subject himself. There was a general chorus of lamentation.

"I hadn't got the heart to tell you," said Mr. Kemp. "I don't know when I've been so happy"

"But you haven't got to go back immediate, said Mrs. Bradshaw.

"Tomorrow," said Mr. Wright, before the old man could reply. "Business."

"Must you go?" said Mrs. Bradshaw.

Mr. Kemp smiled feebly. "I suppose I ought to," he replied in a hesitating voice.

"Take my tip and give yourself a bit of a holiday before you go back," urged Mr. Hills.

"Just for a few days," pleaded Bella.

"To please us," said Mrs. Bradshaw. "Think 'ow George'll miss you."

"Lay hold of him and don't let him go," said Mr. Hills.

He took Mr. Kemp round the waist, and the laughing Bella and her mother each secured an arm. An appeal to Mr. Wright to secure his legs passed unheeded.

"We don't let you go till you promise," said Mrs. Bradshaw.

Mr. Kemp smiled and shook his head.

"Promise?" said Bella.

"Well, well," said Mr. Kemp; "p'r'aps—"

"He *must* go back," shouted the alarmed Mr. Wright.

"Let him speak for himself," exclaimed Bella indignantly.

"Just another week, then," said Mr. Kemp. "It's no good having money if I can't please myself."

"A *week!*" shouted Mr. Wright, almost beside himself with rage and dismay. "A week! Another *week!* Why, you told me—"

"Oh, don't listen to him," said Mrs. Bradshaw. "Croaker! It's his own business, ain't it? And he knows best, don't he? What's it got to do with you?"

She patted Mr. Kemp's hand; Mr. Kemp patted back, and with his disengaged hand helped himself to a glass of beer—the fourth—and beamed in a friendly fashion upon the company.

"George!" he said suddenly.

"Yes," said Mr. Wright in a harsh voice.

"Did you think to bring my pocketbook along with you?"

"No," said Mr. Wright sharply, "I didn't."

"*Tt—tt*," said the old man, with a gesture of annoyance. "Well, lend me a couple of pounds, then—or else run back and fetch my pocketbook," he added, with a sly grin.

Mr. Wright's face worked with impotent fury. "What—what—do you—want it for?" he gasped.

Mrs. Bradshaw's "Well! Well!" seemed to sum up the general feeling; Mr. Kemp, shaking his head, eyed him with gentle reproach.

"Me and Mrs. Bradshaw are going to 'ave another evening out," he said quietly. "I've only got a few more days, and I must make hay while the sun shines."

To Mr. Wright the room seemed to revolve slowly on its axis, but, regaining his self-possession by a supreme effort, he took out his purse and produced the amount. Mrs. Bradshaw, after a few feminine protestations, went upstairs to put her bonnet on.

"And you can go and fetch a hansom-cab, George, while she's a-doing it," said Mr. Kemp. "Pick out a good 'orse—spotted grey, if you can."

Mr. Wright arose and, departing with a suddenness that was almost startling, exploded harmlessly in front of the barber's, next door but one. Then with lagging steps he went in search of the shabbiest cab and oldest horse he could find.

"Thankee, my boy," said Mr. Kemp bluffly, as he helped Mrs. Bradshaw in and stood with his foot on the step. "By the way, you had better go back and lock my pocketbook up. I left it on the washstand, and there's best part of a thousand pounds in it. You can take fifty for yourself to buy smokes with."

There was a murmur of admiration, and Mr. Wright, with a frantic attempt to keep up appearances, tried to thank him, but in vain. Long after the cab had rolled away he stood on the pavement trying to think out a position which was rapidly becoming unendurable. Still keeping up appearances, he had to pretend to go home to look after the pocketbook, leaving the jubilant Mr. Hills to improve the shining hour with Miss Bradshaw.

Mr. Kemp, returning home at midnight—in a cab—found the young man waiting up for him, and, taking a seat on the edge of the table, listened unmoved to a word-picture of himself which seemed interminable. He was only moved to speech when Mr. Wright described him as a white-whiskered Jezebel who was a disgrace to his sex, and then merely in the interests of natural science.

"Don't you worry," he said as the other paused from exhaustion. "It won't be for long now."

"*Long?*" said Mr. Wright, panting. "First thing tomorrow morning you have a telegram calling you back—a telegram that must be minded. D'ye see?"

"No, I don't," said Mr. Kemp plainly. "I'm not going back, never no more—never! I'm going to stop here and court Mrs. Bradshaw."

Mr. Wright fought for breath. "You—you can't!" he gasped.

"I'm going to have a try," said the old man. "I'm sick of going to sea, and it'll be a nice comfortable home for my old age. You marry Bella, and I'll marry her mother. Happy family!"

Mr. Wright, trembling with rage, sat down to recover, and, regaining his composure after a time, pointed out almost calmly the various difficulties in the way.

"I've thought it all out," said Mr. Kemp, nodding. "She mustn't know I'm not rich till after we're married; then I 'ave a letter from New Zealand saying I've lost all my money. It's just as easy to have that letter as the one you spoke of."

"And I'm to find you money to play the rich uncle with till you're married, I suppose," said Mr. Wright in a grating voice, "and then lose Bella when Mrs. Bradshaw finds you've lost your money?"

Mr. Kemp scratched his ear. "That's your lookout," he said at last.

"Now, look here," said Mr. Wright, with great determination. "Either you go and tell them that you've been telegraphed for—cabled is the proper word—or I tell them the truth."

"That'll settle you then," said Mr. Kemp.

"No more than the other would," retorted the young man, "and it'll come cheaper. One thing I'll take my oath of, and that is I won't give you another farthing; but if you do as I tell you I'll give you a quid for luck. Now, think it over."

Mr. Kemp thought it over, and after a vain attempt to raise the promised reward to five pounds, finally compounded for two, and went off to bed after a few stormy words on selfishness and ingratitude. He declined to speak to his host at breakfast next morning, and accompanied him in the evening with the air of a martyr going to the stake. He listened in stony silence to the young man's instructions, and only spoke when the latter refused to pay the two pounds in advance.

The news, communicated in halting accents by Mr. Kemp, was received with flattering dismay. Mrs. Bradshaw refused to believe her ears, and it was only after the information had been repeated and confirmed by Mr. Wright that she understood.

"I must go," said Mr. Kemp. "I've spent over eleven pounds cabling today; but it's all no good."

"But you're coming back?" said Mr. Hills.

"O' course I am," was the reply. "George is the only relation I've got, and I've got to look after him, I suppose. After all, blood is thicker than water."

"Hear, hear!" said Mrs. Bradshaw piously.

"And there's you and Bella," continued Mr. Kemp; "two of the best that ever breathed."

The ladies looked down.

"And Charlie Hills; I don't know—I don't know *when* I've took such a fancy to anybody as I have to 'im. If I was a young gal—a single young gal—he's just the one I should fancy. He's a good-'arted, good-looking—"

"Draw it mild," interrupted the blushing Mr. Hills, as Mr. Wright bestowed a ferocious glance upon the speaker.

"Clever, lively young fellow," concluded Mr. Kemp. "George!"

"Yes," said Mr. Wright.

"I'm going now. I've got to catch the train for Southampton, but I don't want you to come with me. I prefer to be alone. You stay here and cheer them up. Oh, and before I forget it, lend me a couple o' pounds out o' that fifty I gave you last night. I've given all my small change away."

He looked up and met Mr. Wright's eye; the latter, too affected to speak, took out the money and passed it over.

"We never know what may happen to us," said the old man solemnly as he rose and buttoned his coat. "I'm an old man, and I like to have things ship-shape. I've spent nearly the whole day with my lawyer, and if anything 'appens to my old carcass it won't make any difference. I have left half my money to George; half of all I have is to be his."

In the midst of an awed silence he went round and shook hands.

"The other half," he said slowly, as he paused with his hand on the door—"the other half and my best gold watch and chain I have left to my dear young pal, Charlie Hills. Goodbye, George!"

56

"MANNERS MAKYTH MAN"

The night-watchman appeared to be out of sorts. His movements were even slower than usual, and, when he sat, the soap-box seemed to be unable to give satisfaction. His face bore an expression of deep melancholy, but a smouldering gleam in his eye betokened feelings deeply moved.

"Play-acting I don't hold with," he burst out, with sudden ferocity. "Never did. I don't say I ain't been to a theayter once or twice in my life, but I always come away with the idea that anybody could act if they liked to try. It's a kid's game, a silly kid's game, dressing up and pretending to be somebody else."

He cut off a piece of tobacco and, stowing it in his left cheek, sat chewing, with his lacklustre eyes fixed on the wharves across the river. The offensive antics of a lighterman in midstream, who nearly fell overboard in his efforts to attract his attention, he ignored.

"I might ha' known it, too," he said, after a long silence. "If I'd only stopped to think, instead o' being in such a hurry to do good to others, I should ha' been all right, and the pack o' monkey-faced swabs on the *Lizzie and Annie* wot calls themselves sailormen would 'ave had to 'ave got something else to laugh about. They've told it in every pub for 'arf a mile round, and last night, when I went into the 'Town of Margate' to get a drink, three chaps climbed over the partition to 'ave a look at me.

"It all began with young Ted Sawyer, the mate o' the *Lizzie and Annie*. He calls himself a mate, but if it wasn't for 'aving the skipper for a brother-in-law 'e'd be called something else, very quick. Two or three times we've 'ad words over one thing and another, and the last time I called 'im something that I can see now was a mistake. It was one o' these 'ere clever things that a man don't forget, let alone a lop-sided monkey like 'im.

"That was when they was up time afore last, and when they made fast 'ere last week I could see as he 'adn't forgotten it. For one thing he pretended not to see me, and, arter I 'ad told him wot I'd do to him if 'e ran into me agin, he said 'e thought I was a sack o' potatoes taking a airing on a pair of legs wot somebody 'ad throwed away. Nasty tongue 'e's got; not clever, but nasty.

"Arter that I took no notice of 'im, and, o' course, that annoyed 'im more than anything. All I could do I done, and 'e was ringing the gate-bell that night from five minutes to twelve till ha'-past afore I heard it. Many a night-watchman gets a name for going to sleep when 'e's only getting a bit of 'is own back.

"We stood there talking for over 'arf an hour arter I 'ad let 'im in. Leastways, he did. And whenever I see as he was getting tired I just said, '*H'sh!*' and 'e'd start agin as fresh as ever. He tumbled to it at last, and went aboard shaking 'is little fist at me and telling me wot he'd do to me if it wasn't for the lor.

"I kept by the gate as soon as I came on dooty next evening, just to give 'im a little smile as 'e went out. There is nothing more aggravating than a smile when it is properly done; but there was no signs o' my lord, and, arter practising it on a carman by mistake, I 'ad to go inside for a bit and wait till he 'ad gorn.

"The coast was clear by the time I went back, and I 'ad just stepped outside with my back up agin the gate-post to 'ave a pipe, when I see a boy coming along with a bag. Good-looking lad of about fifteen 'e was, nicely dressed in a serge suit, and he no sooner gets up to me than 'e puts down the bag and looks up at me with a timid sort o' little smile.

"'Good evening, cap'n,' he ses.

"He wasn't the fust that has made that mistake; older people than 'im have done it.

"'Good evening, my lad,' I ses.

"'I s'pose,' he ses in a trembling voice, 'I suppose you ain't looking out for a cabin-boy, sir?'

"'Cabin-boy?' I ses. 'No, I ain't.'

"'I've run away from 'ome to go to sea,' he ses, 'and I'm afraid of being pursued. Can I come inside?'

"Afore I could say 'No' he 'ad come, bag and all; and afore I could say anything else he 'ad nipped into the office and stood there with his 'and on his chest, panting.

"'I know I can trust you,' he ses; 'I can see it by your face.'

"'Wot 'ave you run away from 'ome for?' I ses. 'Have they been ill-treating of you?'

"'Ill-treating me?' he ses, with a laugh. 'Not much. Why, I expect my father is running about all over the place offering rewards for me. He wouldn't lose me for a thousand pounds.'

"I pricked up my ears at that; I don't deny it. Anybody would. Besides, I knew it would be doing him a kindness to hand 'im back to 'is father. And then I did a bit o' thinking to see 'ow it was to be done.

"'Sit down,' I ses, putting three or four ledgers on the floor behind one of the desks. 'Sit down, and let's talk it over.'

"We talked away forever so long, but, do all I would, I couldn't persuade 'im. His 'ead was stuffed full of coral islands and smugglers and pirates and foreign ports. He said 'e wanted to see the world, and flying-fish.

"'I love the blue billers,' he ses; 'the heaving blue billers is wot I want.'

"I tried to explain to 'im who would be doing the heaving, but 'e wouldn't listen to me. He sat on them ledgers like a little wooden image, looking up at me and shaking his 'ead, and when I told 'im of storms and shipwrecks he just smacked 'is lips and his blue eyes shone with joy. Arter a time I saw it was no good trying I to persuade 'im, and I pretended to give way.

"'I think I can get you a ship with a friend o' mine,' I ses; 'but, mind, I've got to relieve your pore father's mind—I must let 'im know wot's become of you.'

"'Not before I've sailed,' he ses, very quick.

"'Certainly not,' I ses. 'But you must give me 'is name and address, and, arter the *Blue Shark*—that's the name of your ship—is clear of the land, I'll send 'im a letter with no name to it, saying where you 'ave gorn.'

"He didn't seem to like it at fust, and said 'e would write 'imself, but arter I 'ad pointed out that 'e might forget and that I was responsible, 'e gave way and told me that 'is father was named Mr. Watson, and he kept a big draper's shop in the Commercial Road.

"We talked a bit arter that, just to stop 'is suspicions, and then I told 'im to stay where 'e was on the floor, out of sight of the window, while I went to see my friend the captin.

"I stood outside for a moment trying to make up my mind wot to do. O' course, I 'ad no business, strictly speaking, to leave the wharf, but, on the other 'and there was a father's 'art to relieve. I edged along bit by bit while I was thinking, and then, arter looking back once or twice to make sure that the boy wasn't watching me, I set off for the Commercial Road as hard as I could go.

"I'm not so young as I was. It was a warm evening, and I 'adn't got even a bus fare on me. I 'ad to walk all the way, and by the time I got there I was 'arf melted. It was a tidy-sized shop, with three or four nice-looking gals behind the counter, and things like babies' high chairs for the customers to sit on—long in the leg and ridikerlously small in the seat. I went up to one of the gals and told 'er I wanted to see Mr. Watson.

"'On private business,' I ses. 'Very important.'

"She looked at me for a moment, and then she went away and fetched a tall, bald-headed man with grey side-whiskers and a large nose.

"'Wot d'you want?' he ses, coming up to me.

"'I want a word with you in private,' I ses.

"'This is private enough for me,' he ses. 'Say wot you 'ave to say, and be quick about it,'

"I drawed myself up a bit and looked at him. 'P'r'aps you ain't missed 'im yet,' I ses.

"'Missed 'im?' he ses, with a growl. 'Missed who?'

"'Your—son. Your blue-eyed son,' I ses, looking 'im straight in the eye.

"'Look here!' he ses, spluttering. 'You be off. 'Ow dare you come here with your games? Wot d'ye mean by it?'

"'I mean,' I ses, getting a bit out o' temper, 'that your boy has run away to go to sea, and I've come to take you to 'im.'

"He seemed so upset that I thought 'e was going to 'ave a fit at fust, and it seemed only natural, too. Then I see that the best-looking girl and another *was* 'aving a fit, although trying 'ard not to.

"'If you don't get out o' my shop,' he ses at last, 'I'll 'ave you locked up.'

"'Very good!' I ses in a quiet way. 'Very good; but, mark my words, if he's drownded you'll never forgive yourself as long as you live for letting your temper get the better of you—you'll never know a good night's rest agin. Besides, wot about 'is mother?"

"One o' them silly gals went off agin just like a damp firework, and Mr. Watson, arter nearly choking 'imself with temper, shoved me out o' the way and marched out o' the shop. I didn't know wot to make of 'im at fust, and then one o' the gals told me that 'e was a bachelor and 'adn't got no son, and that somebody 'ad been taking advantage of what she called my inner-cence to pull my leg.

"'You toddle off 'ome,' she ses, 'before Mr. Watson comes back.'

"'It's a shame to let 'im come out alone,' ses one o' the other gals. 'Where do you live, gran'pa?'

"I see then that I 'ad been done, and I was just walking out o' the shop, pretending to be deaf, when Mr. Watson come back with a silly young policeman wot asked me wot I meant by it. He told me to get off 'ome quick, and actooally put his 'and on my shoulder, but it'ud take more than a thing like that to push me, and, arter trying his 'ardest, he could only rock me a bit.

"I went at last because I wanted to see that boy agin, and the young policeman follered me quite a long way, shaking his silly 'ead at me and telling me to be careful.

"I got a ride part o' the way from Commercial Road to Aldgate by getting on the wrong bus, but it wasn't much good, and I was quite tired by the time I got back to the wharf. I waited outside for a minute or two to get my wind back agin, and then I went in—boiling.

"You might ha' knocked me down with a feather, as the saying is, and I just stood inside the office speechless. The boy 'ad disappeared, and sitting on the floor where I 'ad left 'im was a very nice-looking gal of about eighteen, with short 'air and a white blouse.

"'Good evening, sir,' she ses, jumping up and giving me a pretty little frightened look. 'I'm so sorry that my brother has been deceiving you. He's a bad, wicked, ungrateful boy. The idea of telling you that Mr. Watson was 'is father! Have you been there? I do 'ope you're not tired.'

"'Where is he?' I ses.

"'He's gorn,' she ses, shaking her 'ead. 'I begged and prayed of 'im to stop, but 'e wouldn't. He said 'e thought you might be offended with 'im. "Give my love to old Roley-Poley, and tell him I don't trust 'im," he ses.'

"She stood there looking so scared that I didn't know wot to say. By and by she took out 'er little pocket-'ankercher and began to cry.

"'Oh, get 'im back,' she ses. 'Don't let it be said I follered 'im 'ere all the way for nothing. Have another try. For my sake!'

"''Ow can I get 'im back when I don't know where he's gorn?' I ses.

"'He—he's gorn to 'is godfather,' she ses, dabbing her eyes. 'I promised 'im not to tell anybody; but I don't know wot to do for the best.'

"'Well, p'r'aps his godfather will 'old on to 'im,' I ses.

"'He won't tell 'im anything about going to sea,' she ses, shaking 'er little head. 'He's just gorn to try and bo-bo-borrow some money to go away with.'

"She bust out sobbing, and it was all I could do to get the godfather's address out of 'er. When I think of the trouble I took to get it I come over quite faint. At last she told me, between 'er sobs, that 'is name was Mr. Kiddem, and that he lived at 27, Bridge Street.

"'He's one o' the kindest-'arted and most generous men that ever lived,' she ses; 'that's why my brother Harry 'as gone to 'im. And you needn't mind taking anything 'e likes to give you; he's rolling in money."

"I took it a bit easier going to Bridge Street, but the evening seemed 'otter than ever, and by the time I got to the 'ouse I was pretty near done up. A nice, tidy-looking woman opened the door, but she was a'most stone deaf, and I 'ad to shout the name pretty near a dozen times afore she 'eard it.

"'He don't live 'ere,' she ses.

"''As he moved?' I ses. 'Or wot?'

"She shook her 'ead, and, arter telling me to wait, went in and fetched her 'usband.

"'Never 'eard of him,' he ses, 'and we've been 'ere seventeen years. Are you sure it was twenty-seven?'

"'Sartain,' I ses.

"'Well, he don't live 'ere,' he ses. 'Why not try thirty-seven and forty-seven?'

"I tried 'em: thirty-seven was empty, and a pasty-faced chap at forty-seven nearly made 'im-self ill over the name of 'Kiddem.' It 'adn't struck me before, but it's a hard matter to deceive me, and all in a flash it came over me that I 'ad been done agin, and that the gal was as bad as 'er brother.

"I was so done up I could 'ardly crawl back, and my 'ead was all in a maze. Three or four times I stopped and tried to think, but couldn't, but at last I got back and dragged myself into the office.

"As I 'arf expected, it was empty. There was no sign of either the gal or the boy; and I dropped into a chair and tried to think wot it all meant. Then, 'appening to look out of the winder, I see somebody running up and down the jetty.

"I couldn't see plain owing to the things in the way, but as soon as I got outside and saw who it was I nearly dropped. It was the boy, and he was running up and down wringing his 'ands and crying like a wild thing, and, instead o' running away as soon as 'e saw me, he rushed right up to me and threw 'is grubby little paws round my neck.

"'Save her!' 'eses. 'Save'er! *Help! Help!*'

"'Look 'ere,' I ses, shoving 'im off.

"'She fell overboard,' he ses, dancing about. 'Oh, my pore sister! Quick! Quick! I can't swim!'

"He ran to the side and pointed at the water, which was just about at 'arf-tide. Then 'e caught 'old of me agin.

"'Make 'aste,' he ses, giving me a shove behind. 'Jump in. Wot are you waiting for?'

"I stood there for a moment 'arf dazed, looking down at the water. Then I pulled down a lifebelt from the wall 'ere and threw it in, and, arter another moment's thought, ran back to the *Lizzie and Annie*, wot was in the inside berth, and gave them a hail. I've always 'ad a good voice, and in a flash the skipper and Ted Sawyer came tumbling up out of the cabin and the 'ands out of the fo'c'sle.

"'Gal overboard!' I ses, shouting.

"The skipper just asked where, and then 'im and the mate and a couple of 'ands tumbled into their boat and pulled under the jetty for all they was worth. Me and the boy ran back and stood with the others, watching.

"'Point out the exact spot,' ses the skipper.

"The boy pointed, and the skipper stood up in the boat and felt round with a boat-hook. Twice 'e said he thought 'e touched something, but it turned out as 'e was mistaken. His face got longer and longer and 'e shook his 'ead, and said he was afraid it was no good.

"'Don't stand cryin' 'ere,' he ses to the boy kindly. "Jem, run round for the Thames police, and get them and the drags. Take the boy with you. It'll occupy 'is mind.'

"He 'ad another go with the boat-hook arter they 'ad gone; then 'e gave it up, and sat in the boat waiting.

"'This'll be a bad job for you, watchman,' he ses, shaking his 'ead. 'Where was you when it 'appened?"

"'He's been missing all the evening,' ses the cook, wot was standing beside me. 'If he'd been doing 'is dooty, the pore gal wouldn't 'ave been drownded. Wot was she doing on the wharf?

"'Skylarkin', I s'pose,' ses the mate. 'It's a wonder there ain't more drownded. Wot can you expect when the watchman is sitting in a pub all the evening?"

"The cook said I ought to be 'ung, and a young ordinary seaman wot was standing beside 'im said he would sooner I was boiled. I believe they 'ad words about it, but I was feeling too upset to take much notice.

"'Looking miserable won't bring 'er back to life agin,' ses the skipper, looking up at me and shaking his 'ead. 'You'd better go down to my cabin and get yourself a drop o' whisky; there's a bottle on the table. You'll want all your wits about you when the police come. And wotever you do don't say nothing to criminate yourself.'

"'We'll do the criminating for 'im all right,' ses the cook.

"'If I was the pore gal I'd haunt 'im,' ses the ordinary seaman; 'every night of 'is life I'd stand afore 'im dripping with water and moaning.'

"'P'r'aps she will,' ses the cook; 'let's 'ope so, at any rate.'

"I didn't answer 'em; I was too dead-beat. Besides which I've got a 'orror of ghosts, and the idea of being on the wharf alone of a night arter such a thing was a'most too much for me. I went on board the *Lizzie and Annie*, and down in the cabin I found a bottle o' whisky, as the skipper 'ad said. I sat down on the locker and 'ad a glass, and then I sat worrying and wondering wot was to be the end of it all.

"The whisky warmed me up a bit, and I 'ad just taken up the bottle to 'elp myself agin when I 'eard a faint sort o' sound in the skipper's stateroom. I put the bottle down and listened, but everything seemed deathly still. I took it up agin, and 'ad just poured out a drop o' whisky when I distinctly 'eard a hissing noise and then a little moan.

"For a moment I sat turned to stone. Then I put the bottle down quiet, and 'ad just got up to go when the door of the state-room opened, and I saw the drownded gal, with 'er little face and hair all wet and dripping, standing before me.

"Ted Sawyer 'as been telling everybody that I came up the companion-way like a fog-horn that 'ad lost its ma; I wonder how he'd 'ave come up if he'd 'ad the evening I had 'ad?

"They were all on the jetty as I got there and tumbled into the skipper's arms, and all asking at once wot was the matter. When I got my breath back a bit and told 'em, they laughed. All except the cook, and 'e said it was only wot I might expect. Then, like a man in a dream, I see the gal come out of the companion and walk slowly to the side.

"'Look!' I ses. 'Look! *There she is!*'

"'You're dreaming,' ses the skipper; 'there's nothing there.'

"They all said the same, even when the gal stepped on to the side and climbed on to the wharf. She came along towards me with 'er arms held close to 'er sides, and making the most 'orrible faces at me, and it took five of 'em all their time to 'old me. The wharf and everything seemed to me to spin round and round. Then she came straight up to me and patted me on the cheek.

"'Pore old gentleman,' she ses. 'Wot a shame it is, Ted! It's too bad.'

"They let go o' me then, and stamped up and down the jetty laughing fit to kill themselves. If they 'ad only known wot a exhibition they was making of themselves, and 'ow I pitied them, they wouldn't ha' done it. And by and by Ted wiped his eyes and put his arm round the gal's waist and ses—

"'This is my intended, Miss Florrie Price,' he ses. 'Ain't she a little wonder? Wot d'ye think of 'er?'

"'I'll keep my own opinion,' I ses. 'I ain't got nothing to say against gals, but if I only lay my hands on that young brother of 'ers—'

"They went off agin then, worse than ever; and at last the cook came and put 'is skinny arm round my neck and started spluttering in my ear. I shoved 'im off hard, because I see it all then; and I should ha' seen it afore only I didn't 'ave time to think. I don't bear no malice, and all I can say is that I don't wish 'er any harder punishment than to be married to Ted Sawyer."

LOVE-LETTERS

LOVE-LETTERS

The summer evening was giving way to night and the craft on the river were already putting out their lights. The master of the barge which was sitting on the mud at the end of the jetty stood, a forlorn figure in the gloom, listening to an oration proceeding from the cabin. It was in a female voice pitched in a high key, and of such a personal nature that the night-watchman, gazing on the deck from above, sent down a little message of brotherly sympathy.

"She can't keep on all night," he said.

The man below spat over the side, hitched up his trousers, glanced at the sky, and finally looked up at the night-watchman.

"*Can't* she!" he said dispassionately.

"P'r'aps she'll break a blood-vessel," said the night-watchman thoughtfully.

He spoke in a low voice, but not low enough. The voice from the cabin joined in the conversation and monopolised it. Beginning by speculations as to the night-watchman's origin, it passed swiftly to a description of his age, his figure, his morals, his treatment of his wife, and his future destination. In a passage of real eloquence it paid admiring tribute to the way in which he had eluded the police for so many years, but foretold a speedy downfall. Charges of bigamy completed the discomfiture of the leading misogamist in Wapping, and gasping for breath he turned and stumped up the jetty.

"Wimmin," he said, as he lowered himself carefully to his favourite box, "wimmin are all alike. When they are young and good-looking and trying to catch a husband, nothing could be nicer. As soon as they 'ave caught 'im they begin to put on airs and their true nature comes out. Nothing he does is right. Nothing. If 'e does 'em a kindness they get suspicious at once and try and find out wot he 'as been up to. If 'e takes no notice of 'em they tell 'im they wish they was dead, but he needn't think they're going to die just to please 'im and the cat with yeller 'air acrost the road, 'cos they're not."

He rose impatiently and took a turn or two farther up the jetty.

And no woman minds whether wot she ses is true or not (he said, resuming his seat). Catch a man out in a lie and he looks a bit ashamed of himself; catch a woman out in a lie and she smacks your face for you.

I felt sorry for that chap below, 'cos I know wot it is. I've known my missis talk, off and on, for three weeks about something I 'adn't done; 'ow long she'd 'ave talked about some of the things I *'ave* done—if she only got to know of 'em—I can't imagine. I've often wondered, but I'd sooner wonder than know.

I 'ad a nasty turn two or three years ago. I was as innercent as a newborn babe, but that didn't make a bit o' difference. A woman don't mind if a man is innercent or not so long as 'e can't prove it. If a man could get 'arf-a-dozen angels, 'arps and all, swearin' as he was telling the truth, she wouldn't believe 'em. She'd on'y say he 'ad been standing 'em 'arf-pints.

It all come about through a chap called Slinker, a man as disgraces my street by living in it. I don't suppose anybody knows 'is real name, Slinker being such a proper one for 'im that you couldn't call 'im anything else. Little shrimp of a man he is, with a face like a rat and a nasty way of getting even with people 'e don't like. And the people 'e don't like are them as won't pay for beer for 'im.

We both 'ave the same 'ouse of call, the "Carpenters' Arms"; a nice quiet little pub close to where I live. Arternoon is my on'y time there, o' course, and I generally 'ave 'arf a pint to 'elp me on my way to the wharf.

I don't like Slinker, and one day in the "Carpenters' Arms" I told 'im so. There was three or four there, and one o' them gave me the tip to look round, just in time to see Slinker drinking up my beer. He said it was a mistake, and arter I 'ad taken it from 'im and drunk it up—to prevent anymore mistakes—I told 'im just wot I thought of 'im. And I told 'im wot other people thought about 'im and 'is nasty artful ways.

"You ain't a man," I ses; "you're a shadder, a shadder wot is always follering behind people to find anything they lose; you ain't got the pluck to steal. You're a nasty crawling shadder wot gives a honest man the creeps to look at you."

"'Ear, 'ear," ses a brewer's drayman, wot was big enough to say anything he liked to anybody.

"You've got a nasty mind, Bill," ses Slinker, shaking his 'ead. "If I 'ad a mind like yours I should join the Salvation Army and see wot they could do for me. You'd look a fair treat playing the tambourine; your stummick's just made for it."

"And dancing backwards," ses that fool of a drayman, spluttering 'is beer all over the floor.

I watched 'em for a moment, grinning all over their pore silly faces, and then I sat down and told 'em a few things about Slinker wot 'e didn't know I knew about. Some of 'em was reely about another man, but Slinker would 'ave done 'em if he 'ad thought of 'em. Afore I 'ad finished he was shaking all over with temper, and the big drayman was asking 'im why he didn't poison 'imself. He gave me one look afore 'e went out, and then 'e come back and put his 'ead in at the door and gave me another.

"Get off," I ses, "get off 'ome, and mind you don't eat the cat's supper this time."

I 'ad a pint or two with the drayman—a very nice feller when you come to know 'im—and by the time I 'ad left I 'ad forgot all about Slinker. If he 'ad only forgot about me too it would ha' been better for me.

I didn't think anything of 'im for two or three days, and then one arternoon as I was standing at the front door with my missis, having a little talk about dirty boots and slopping tea on the kitchen table, I saw 'im on the other side of the road. He came across smiling all over 'is face, and at fust I thought 'e was going to try and shake 'ands with me.

"Arternoon, Bill," he ses. "This is a bit o' luck; I thought I might catch you afore you went to the pub, and 'ere you are."

I just looked at 'im.

"I've got a letter for you," he ses, smiling again.

"Letter!" says my missis. "Letter!"

"Yes," ses Slinker, nodding. "A lady friend o' Bill's gave it to me to give 'im, with 'er love."

"Ho!" ses my missis. "Indeed!"

She held out her 'and for the letter, and Slinker gave a little cough and looked at me as if 'e was asking me wot he was to do.

"I was told to put it into Bill's 'ands," he ses at last.

"You'll put it into mine instead," ses my missis, trembling all over with passion.

I didn't know wot to do. I knew that wotever I done would be wrong.

"Give it to my missis," I ses; "I 'ave no secrets from 'er."

My missis looked at me; then she made such a funny noise I thought she was going to 'ave a fit. I was just going to give Slinker the tip to 'old on for a minute in case she did, when she laughed. At least, it was a kind of laugh.

"Come on," she ses, "I want that letter."

Slinker put his 'and in his pocket, then 'e took it out and put it in another. He tried pocket arter pocket while we stood watching 'im. Then 'e tried 'em all over agin.

"Funny," he ses. "Wot could I 'ave done with it?"

He went through 'is pockets once more and then 'e turned to me and winked—right in front of my missis.

"I must 'ave lost it," he ses, grinning like a monkey.

"I don't want none o' your lies," ses my missis. "I saw you wink at 'im. You give me that letter."

"It's gorn," ses Slinker, looking round on the pavement. "It was a long letter, too; on pink notepaper with a lovely smell. You could smell it a mile off. Well, so long."

My missis made a grab at 'is jacket, but he dodged to one side and then twisted out of the way agin as she rushed at 'im.

"See you later, Bill," he ses, and then 'e turned and run up the road with my missis full pelt arter 'im.

She gave up in about twenty yards and then come back very slow and careful with 'er eyes fixed on me and walked straight into the kitchen and sat down without saying a word. Anybody might ha' thought she'd been struck dumb for life—but I knew better. Things like that only happen in books.

I was about 'arf way to the wharf when I see Slinker's little game. Nobody 'ad given 'im a letter and 'e was just trying to get me into trouble. That was Slinker all over; but I knew my missis wouldn't believe it.

As I expected, when I got 'ome next morning there was no breakfuss and I 'ad to go and waste money in a coffee-shop. When I got back I found the bed wasn't made for me, and not only that, the bedclothes was being washed. Even the mattress was 'aving an airing in the backyard, and when I asked where I was to sleep, my missis sniffed three times and went on with 'er washing.

I 'ad to sleep on a chair, and I 'ad just got to sleep when she came in with a bucket o' water and went down on 'er 'ands and knees and began to scrub the floor. I 'ad taken off my boots so as I could sleep more easy, and the fust thing I knew of it my feet was in a puddle of very cold water.

She cleaned that 'ouse for three days. There was a smell of soap all over the place; and when one part of the floor was drying another part was getting wet; especially chairs that I wanted to set in and such like. And then, without putting anything back in its place, she went off to stay with 'er married niece at Clerkenwell.

She was away for a week, and any good the change might ha' done me was upset by 'aving to get my own food ready and make my own bed. The fust bit o' steak I cooked I gave to the cat, and the second—which was all right—she took 'erself while I was dishing up the taters. Everything seemed to go wrong. If I remembered the bread and bloaters I forgot the butter, and even when I forgot the bread and remembered the butter I didn't remember that I 'ad put it on a chair. Looking arter a house isn't a man's work. It's a easy job, mind you, but it's a job for little minds. A man can make a bed; the thing is, can he sleep in it when he 'as made it?

Then, o'course, I 'ad trouble from people as couldn't mind their own business. I came 'ome one morning, dead beat arter a night's watching, and, arter cooking myself a rasher or two of bacon, went upstairs to bed, and I 'ad just got to sleep when somebody started knocking at the street door. I laid awake listening for a time, and then, finding they was knocking louder and louder, I got on some of my clothes and went down.

It was a party from next door but two. A dirty little woman with red 'air screwed up in bits of old newspaper, and a nose that wouldn't know a pocket-'ankerchif if it saw one.

"I just come to see 'ow your pore wife is," she ses. "Is she very bad?"

"Bad?" I ses. "She ain't bad; she 'as gorn away for a day or two to see 'er niece."

"When'll she be back?" she ses, sticking her 'ead into the passage like a tortoise.

"I dunno," I ses, "and wot's more, I don't care."

"Don't know?" she ses. "Why not?"

I slammed the door 'ard and went off up to bed agin, and I 'ad scarcely taken my things off and snuggled down than there was another knock. I could 'ardly believe my ears at fust, but arter a couple o' minutes there was no doubt about it. It was the woman from opposite this time, and she came up as bold as brass and said she wanted to see my wife.

"She drownded 'erself last night," I ses, slamming the door.

I went back to bed, but something seemed to tell me not to take my trousers off, 'cos I should be sure to want them agin. And I 'ad just got to sleep once more when I did.

There was some wirnmin outside when I got down and more hurrying up. I just 'ad time to see that when I was swept up the passage like a dead leaf and jammed up agin the kitchen door.

"You clear out," I ses, "or else I'll put you out."

They all screamed at me at once then, and the things they said you might 'ave thought they was talking to their own 'usbands. The noise was awful. Some of 'em stood there calling me names and some of 'em went upstairs to look for my missis.

I believe they looked everywhere, and they was so angry at not finding anything that they went 'arf crazy with disappointment. Some of 'em told me wot I ought to be done to, and some of 'em said they would do it. And they talked of my missis as if she'd bin a angel without wings.

It took four policemen to get 'em outside, all screaming and pushing and taking away my character. Besides saying I 'ad murdered my wife, they said I 'ad done bigamy and picked pockets, set houses on fire, and owed for the milk. And while a woman was 'olding me by the coat-collar and kicking me on the legs one of them silly policemen gave me a little pat on the shoulder and told me not to take no notice of 'em.

By the time they got 'em out the street was 'arf full of people, all trying to mind my business instead of their own. It took the police 'arf an hour to clear the road, and when I went back to bed agin the people opposite was still standing at their doors looking up at my winders.

'Ow I got through the next day or two I don't know. Twice I 'ad to run for my life; and three times men, egged on by their wives, offered to fight me and wouldn't take "no" for an answer. And I was just thinking of going back to sea agin when my missis come back.

I found 'er there when I got 'ome one morning. She was sitting in the kitchen having 'er breakfuss, and when I went in she just sat straight up and looked at me as if I was something wot 'ad been kept too long. Some men would 'ave pointed out to her that she was eating the bacon and egg wot they 'ad got in for theirselves the day before, but I didn't, I know 'er too well.

For two days she didn't say a word; on'y sniffed; but when she did start I thought she'd never stop. It turned out that 'er niece's 'usband—a feller I always liked—'ad pushed 'er out of the 'ouse and chucked 'er box arter 'er. Then the red-'aired woman and the woman opposite 'ad both asked 'er where she'd been and wouldn't believe 'er when she told 'em; and they both said I was too good for 'er, and they wondered at me for taking 'er back. That's wimmin all over.

I slept through most of it—it takes a lot to keep me awake—but she was talking when I went to bed and she was still at it at three o'clock in the arternoon when I got up. And when I started off to work she walked a little way up the street with me to tell me some more things about myself that I didn't want to know, or the fools that was follerin' us to 'ear.

She was pretty quiet next day—gumboil or something—but the day arter it was worse than ever.

I came 'ome tired out. I had 'ad a very bad night of it. Wot with a lighterman as was drunk and thought I owed 'im five bob, and a couple o' Scotch sailormen that rang the bell and pushed their way on to the wharf to go aboard a craft that wasn't there, and then asked me wot I 'ad done with it, I was wore out.

I just crawled into the kitchen and tumbled into a chair and sat wondering whether my missis was going to get my breakfuss ready.

I didn't 'ave to wonder long, and I could see at once that I was in for more trouble. White as chalk she was, and her 'ands trembling. Then she stood bolt upright and tried to stare me down.

"There's another letter for you," she ses, arter she found she couldn't.

"If I get my 'ands on that man Slinker," I ses, "I'll—"

"It wasn't Mr. Slinker," she ses, screwing up 'er mouth and looking down 'er nose. "It come by post, soon arter you 'ad gorn last night."

She looked at the letter, wot I 'adn't noticed afore, sticking up on the mantelpiece, and I got up, very slow and careless, and looked at it too.

"It's from the mate of the *Priscilla*," I ses; "I'd know 'is 'andwriting anywhere."

"And the kisses on the back of the envelope, too, I suppose," she ses.

"He—he's a man as will 'ave 'is joke," I ses, arter she 'ad tried to glare me down agin. "Often and often I've said to 'im, 'Bob,' I ses—"

"I don't want none o' your lies," she ses, grabbing the letter afore I could stop 'er. "Are you sure it's 'is 'andwriting?"

"A'most," I ses.

She tore the letter open and looked at it, and then she let off the most awful screech I've ever heard and fell into a chair kicking her 'eels on to the floor and carrying on like a madman. When I tell you that the cat jumped on to the top shelf and got into a saucepan, you'll 'ave some idea wot she was like.

I couldn't do anything with 'er. As for breakfuss, if you'd brought me the best one in the world and held my 'ead down in the plate I couldn't 'ave looked at it.

"Read it," she ses, choking and 'olding out the letter; "read it."

I took hold of it and looked at it. It was on pink notepaper with pie-crust edges and a smell like scented soap. I smelt it two or three times, 'ardly knowing wot I was doing, and then I read it. Short and sweet it was, and I read it over and over agin, wondering wot I was going to say. It said:—

Darling Billy—
It seems ages since I saw you. Wot about a music-'all on Toosday if you can get someone to look arter the wharf for you? And wot about the hat and jacket you promised me? I'm so shabby I ain't fit to be seen with you.
"From your loving Popsy."

There was kisses arter the name and kisses on the top and kisses on each side. I 'ad never 'ad so many afore in my life.

"Wot 'ave you got to say for yourself?" ses my wife, beginning to rave agin.

"I don't know nothing about it," I ses, "and wot's more I don't want to."

"Who is Popsy?" she ses. "Who is she?"

"I don't know 'er from Adam," I ses.

"Wot's 'er other name?" she ses.

"I don't know," I ses. "Wot's it got to do with me? If a young woman takes a fancy to me and sends me letters I can't help it, can I?"

"I thought you said you didn't know 'er," she ses.

"I don't," I ses.

"'Ow do you know she's *young*, then?" ses my wife, pointing 'er finger at me. "'Ow dare she write letters to my 'usband and ask 'im to take 'er to music-'alls and give 'er hats and jackets 1 No wonder I 'aven't got a rag to my back. No wonder nothing I do is right. No wonder when I was 'aving a few words with

Mrs. O'Brien the other day she asked me wot dustbin I went to for my hats. I often wondered wot you did with all your money. Now I know."

I couldn't get a word in edgeways. Every time I opened my mouth she shoved that 'at and jacket in it, in a manner o' speaking. Then she went upstairs and brought 'er own down and shoved 'em in my face for me to look at.

"You're going to buy me a hat and a jacket," she ses, throwing the old ones on the floor, "*and* a pair o' boots. If *I* 'ave 'em p'r'aps you won't 'ave the money to buy any for that hussy."

"I 'aven't got money to buy 'em for anybody," I ses.

"I'll get 'em on tick and pay so much a week," she ses. "If you could buy 'em for 'er you can buy 'em for me, and you will, too."

I tried to make 'er listen to reason, but it was no good. She kept on throwing Popsy into my face until I didn't know where I was, and at' last I gave way. Married men'll understand, if others don't.

And she didn't lose no time about it, neither. When I got up, at four o'clock, and came downstairs to tell 'er that I 'ad altered my mind, she 'ad got 'em, and was just going out for a walk in 'em, to be looked at. I watched 'er go up the street very slow, and looking like a real lady at the back.

'Ow I got through the next few weeks I don't know. If it 'adn't ha' been for a few real pals standing me a 'arf pint now and then 1 don't know wot I should ha' done. Casting 'is beer on the waters, one of 'em called it. I didn't know wot 'e meant, and when I told 'im so 'e called me a lot o' nasty names and offered to fight me. I didn't 'ave two ha'pennies to rub together, and when I passed the landlord of the "Bull's Head" I was afraid to look at 'im.

I 'ad just paid up all but the last two weeks when I found out something. My missis was out and I was just looking round to see whether I could find a few odd coppers anywhere.

I 'appened to look in a box in the bedroom cupboard, among other things, and hid away under a pile of odds and ends I found some notepaper and envelopes. *Pink, with pie-crust edges and a strong smell o' scented soap!*

At fust I couldn't believe my eyes, *or* my nose. Then I see 'ow I'd been done, and, 'ardly able to speak, I went downstairs. My missis 'ad just come in. I marched into the kitchen like a lion and held the paper out to 'er.

"Well?" she ses, very cool.

"You—wrote—that—letter," I ses, fixing 'er with my eye.

"Wot about it?" she ses.

"Wot about it?" I ses. "*Wot about it?* Do you remember the way you carried on and the things you said about me?"

"Wot about Slinker's letter, that 'e didn't give you?" she ses. "If other wimmin can write to my 'usband I suppose I can. Though not so welcome, perhaps."

"And wot about the 'at and jacket and boots?" I ses.

"Surely a woman can ask 'er own 'usband for clothes," she ses.

"And wot about the deceitfulness of it?" I ses. "Pretending to be another woman and taking away my character about it. Wot about putting a wrong name to the letter?"

"It wasn't a wrong name," she ses. "Popsy is my pet name."

"First time I've 'eard of it," I ses. "Who gave it to you? Who calls you by it?"

"You did," she ses.

"*Me!*" I ses. "*Me!* Why, you must be mad. When did I ever call you Popsy?"

"When we was keeping company," she ses, blowing 'er nose.

That's the worst o' wimmin; always remembering something that ought to be forgot just to get their own way. And then snivelling about it. If I did call 'er that name, it was when I was young and foolish; and if young men I were not foolish they would go on keeping company instead of getting married.

I went out of the 'ouse in a daze, and I was so upset that when I ran into Slinker just outside the "Carpenters' Arms" and got 'old of him by the throat, instead of wringing 'is neck I let 'im stand me a couple o' pints.

THE END